l Laymon wrote over thirty novels and seventy short stories. In May
he Travelling Vampire Show won the Bram Stoker Award for Best Horror
a prize for which Laymon had previously been shortlisted with *Flesh*,
l, *A Good, Secret Place* (Best Anthology) and *A Writer's Tale* (Best Non-
Laymon's works include the books of the Beast House Chronicles:
lar, *The Beast House* and *The Midnight Tour*. Some of his recent novels
:n Night in the Lonesome October, *No Sanctuary*, and *Amara*.

e of Chicago, Laymon attended Willamette University in Salem,
n, and took an MA in English Literature from Loyola University, Los
:s. In 2000, he was elected President of the Horror Writers Association.
:d in February 2001.

>n's fiction is published in the United Kingdom by Headline, and in the
l States by Leisure Books and Cemetery Dance Publications. To learn
visit the Laymon website at: http://rlk.cjb.net

u're not already well aquainted with Richard Laymon, get to know him
Manchester Evening News

t-crunching writer' *Time Out*

aymon's books, blood doesn't so much as drip as explode, splatter and
ate' *Independent*

author knows how to sock it to the reader' *The Times*

e writes like Laymon and you're going to have a good time with anything
es' Dean Koontz

iant writer' *Sunday Express*

n King without a conscienc

an author that does not pul   imes
ly shocking, read' *SFX Ma*

'In_ ble of writing a disappointing book' *New York Review of Science Fiction*

'One of the best, and most underrated, writers working in the genre today'
Cemetery Dance

* Previously published under the pseudonym of Richard Kelly
Dark Mountain was first published as Tread Softly

Night In The Lonesome October

and

No Sanctuary

Richard Laymon

headline

NIGHT IN THE LONESOME OCTOBER first published in Great Britain in
2001 by HEADLINE PUBLISHING GROUP

NO SANCTUARY first published in Great Britain in 2001 by
HEADLINE PUBLISHING GROUP

First published in this omnibus edition in 2007 by
HEADLINE PUBLISHING GROUP

A HEADLINE paperback

2

ISBN 978 0 7553 3183 3

Typeset in Janson by Palimpsest Book Production Limited,
Grangemouth, Stirlingshire

Printed and bound in Great Britain by
CPI Group (UK) Ltd, Croydon, CR0 4YY

Headline's policy is to use papers that are natural, renewable and recyclable products and
made from wood grown in sustainable forests. The logging and manufacturing processes
are expected to conform to the environmental regulations of the country of origin.

HEADLINE PUBLISHING GROUP
A division of Hachette Livre UK Ltd
338 Euston Road
London NW1 3BH

www.headline.co.uk
www.hodderheadline.com

Night In The Lonesome October

'Casey at the Bat', a poem by Ernest Lawrence Thayer, was first published under the pen name 'Phin' in the *San Francisco Examiner* on 3 June 1888. The classic poem, known to most Americans, contains the famous final stanza:

Oh, somewhere in this favored land the sun is shining bright,
The Band is playing somewhere, and somewhere hearts are
   light;
And somewhere men are laughing, and somewhere children
   shout,
But there is no joy in Mudville: Mighty Casey has struck out.

This book is dedicated to
Jerry and Jackie Lentz,
our fine friends
who always seem to know
what we're laughing about.

The skies they were ashen and sober;
The leaves they were crisped and sere—
The leaves they were withering and sere;
It was night in the lonesome October
Of my most immemorial year . . .

'Ulalume'
Edgar Allan Poe

Chapter One

I was twenty years old and heartbroken the night it started.

My name is Ed Logan.

Yes, guys can be heartbroken, too. It isn't an affliction reserved for women only.

Except I think it feels more like an empty stomach than a broken heart. An aching hollowness that food can't cure. You know. You've felt it yourself, I bet. You hurt all the time, you're restless, you can't think straight, you sort of wish you were dead but what you *really* want is for everything to be the same as it was when you were still *with* her . . . or him.

In my case, her name was Holly Johnson.

Holly Johnson.

God. I'd better not get started on her. Suffice it to say, I fell in love with Holly with all my stupid heart and soul last spring when we were both sophomores at Willmington University. And she seemed to be in love with me. But then the semester ended. I went home to Mill Valley and she went home to Seattle where she worked as a guidance counselor at some sort of fucking summer camp and got involved with some *other* counselor. Only I didn't hear about that until two weeks into the fall semester. I knew she wasn't on campus, but didn't know why. Her sorority sisters pleaded ignorance. On the phone, her mother was evasive: 'Holly isn't home just now, but I'll tell her you called.'

Then, on October first, a letter came: 'Dear Ed, I will always cherish the times we had . . .' And so on. It might as well have been a letter

1

bomb . . . a letter carrying a voodoo bomb that first killed me, then resurrected me as a zombie.

The night after receiving the letter, I stayed in my apartment all by myself, drinking vodka (bought by a friend of legal age) and orange juice until I passed out. In the morning, I cleaned up the vomit. Then I had to live through the worst hangover of my life. Luckily, the letter had arrived on Friday. By Monday, I'd mostly recovered from my hangover. But not from my loss.

I attended my classes, going through the motions, pretending to care, trying to act like the guy people knew as Ed Logan.

That night, I studied until about eleven o'clock. *Tried* to study is more like it. Though my eyes traveled over the lines of my book, my thoughts dwelled on Holly. I lingered on memories of her. And ached to have her back. And agonized over vivid images of her making love with my replacement, Jay. *He's so special and sensitive*, her letter had said.

How could she fall in love with a guy named Jay?

I'd known three or four Jays, and every last one of them was an asshole.

He's so special and sensitive.

I wanted to kill him.

I wanted to kill her.

I hated her, but I wanted her back. I pictured her return, myself weeping as we hugged and kissed. She was weeping, too, and gasping, 'I love you so much, Ed. I'm so sorry I hurt you. I'll never leave you again.'

Yeah, right.

Anyway, that's how it was going Monday night. Around eleven, I gave up trying to study. I turned on the television, but just stared at the screen without really seeing what was there. I thought about going to bed, but knew I would end up wide awake, tormented by Holly and Jay.

At last, I decided to take a walk. Just to get out of my apartment. Just to be doing something. Just to kill time.

Thoreau wrote, 'You can't kill time without injuring eternity.'

Screw it, I thought. Screw Thoreau. Screw eternity. Screw everything.

I wanted to go out walking in the night and get *lost* in the night and never come back.

Maybe I would get hit by a car. Maybe someone would attack and murder me. Maybe I would hike on over to the train tracks and look for a train with my number on it. Or maybe I would just keep walking forever, out of town, out of the state, just *out*.

Out was where I wanted most to be.

Outside, the darkness smelled sweet and moist and a soft wind was blowing. The October night felt more like summer than fall. Soon, with the exertion of fast walking, I was sweating inside my chamois shirt and jeans. So I slowed down. I was in no hurry, after all.

Though I'd started out with no destination in mind, I found myself heading east.

No destination in mind?

Maybe, maybe not.

I hadn't set off on my walk with any plan to make a pilgrimage to Holly's sorority house, but that's where I went. My feet seemed to take me there all on their own. Of course, that's nonsense. *I* guided them there. We walked a route we had walked so many times before. Instead of hurrying eagerly to the front door, however, we crossed to the opposite side of the street. We didn't stop, but walked very slowly.

There was the veranda where Holly and I had so often kissed goodnight – sometimes for an hour or longer.

There, one story up and three windows from the south corner, was the large picture window of Holly's room. Her *former* room. The window was dark, now. Some other girl was probably asleep in the room behind it . . . in the same bed where Holly used to sleep.

And where was Holly now? In her own bed in her parents' house near Seattle? Or in *Jay's* bed?

He's probably fucking her right this second.

I could picture it. I could feel it. I could feel Holly's soft, warm body under me, her eager mouth on my lips, her tongue in my mouth, one of her breasts in my hand, her slippery wet tightness hugging me.

3

Except it wasn't me, it was Jay.

He's so special and sensitive.

'Ed?'

Shit!

Managing a smile, I turned my head. 'Oh, hi, Eileen.'

Eileen Danforth, one of Holly's sorority sisters and best friends. She held some books and binders clutched against her chest. She was probably on her way back from studying in the library or the student union. The wind was blowing her long, dark hair.

'How's it going?' she asked.

I shrugged.

'Guess you must've gotten Holly's letter.'

Naturally, Eileen knew all about the letter.

'Yeah,' I said.

'Rough.'

I nodded. I didn't trust myself to speak.

'Just between you and me, I think Holly blew it.'

'Thanks.'

'Can't imagine what got into her.'

'I can,' I muttered.

Eileen's face twitched slightly as if she felt a small, sharp pain. 'Yeah,' she said. 'Me, too. I'm really sorry.'

'Thanks.'

She sighed and shook her head. 'It's really a shame. Who knows, though? Maybe you're better off.'

'Doesn't feel that way.'

Eileen pressed her lips together. She almost looked ready to cry. 'I know how it feels,' she said. 'God, do I ever.' She lifted her eyebrows. 'So, did you just come over here to stare at the house?'

I shook my head. 'I'm on my way to the donut shop.'

'Dandi?'

'Yeah.'

'At this hour?'

'It's open all night.'

'I know, but . . . it's really *out* there.'

4

'Seven miles.'

She grimaced. 'That's a *long* way.'

'I've got nothing better to do.'

She looked into my eyes for a while. Then she said, 'Could you use some company? Just give me a couple of minutes to drop off my books, and . . .'

I was shaking my head. 'I think I'd rather be alone.'

'You shouldn't walk all that way by yourself.'

'I'll be fine.'

'It's the middle of the night.'

'I know, but . . .'

'Let me come with you, okay?'

I shook my head again. 'Maybe some other night.'

'Well, it's up to you. I don't want to . . . you know, make a nuisance out of myself.'

'It's not that.'

'I know. I understand. You just want to be alone.'

'Yeah.'

'But be careful, okay?'

'I will be.'

'And don't do anything . . . crazy.'

'I'll try not to.'

'It isn't the end of the world, you know.'

I figured my mother would say exactly the same thing if and when I phoned home and explained about Holly.

'Just seems that way,' Eileen added.

I don't think Mom would've added that.

'Yeah,' I said.

'But things'll get better. They really will. You'll meet someone else . . .'

That would probably be my father's commentary.

'You'll fall in love again.'

'God, I hope not.'

'Don't say that.'

'Sorry.'

'Do me a favor, okay? Bring me back a couple of donuts?' This was Eileen to the hilt. I knew she wasn't making the request simply due to a fondness for donuts – though Dandi's were spectacular. For one thing, she had a car; she could drive out to Dandi Donuts whenever the mood struck her. For another, she was slender and very pretty and tried to stay that way by avoiding such delicacies as donuts.

Which is not to say she never ate them. She did. But rarely.

And I knew that tonight her real intent was to give me a task . . . to divert at least a fraction of my attention away from Holly.

'Sure,' I said. 'What kind do you want?'

'Glazed old-fashioneds.'

'The specialty of the house.'

'Yeah.' Eileen smiled a little sadly and licked her lips. 'I can taste them now.'

'Only thing is, I'm not sure what time I'll be back.'

'Before I have to go to my ten o'clock, I hope.'

'I'll try.'

'I'll be in the student union, drooling with anticipation.'

'I'll make sure you don't go hungry.'

'Thanks.' Keeping the books clamped against her chest with her left arm, she reached out with her right hand and gave my shoulder a gentle squeeze. I expected her to say something more, but she didn't. After squeezing my shoulder, she let go and turned away and went trotting across the street toward the front of the sorority house, her dark hair blowing behind her head, her pleated skirt dancing around her thighs.

If she'd been Holly, I would've been enthralled by how she looked.

But she wasn't.

Watching Eileen, I felt nothing.

That's not quite true. What I actually felt was a vague wish that she would somehow *turn into* Holly.

Not Holly the faithless slut who'd dumped me for her summer-camp flame, but the Holly I'd known last spring, the one I'd loved. *That* Holly.

God, how I wanted her to be with me again!

Night In The Lonesome October

On the veranda, Eileen looked back at me and waved. Then she pulled open the door. As she entered the sorority house, I caught a glimpse of the reception area.

I used to wait in there for Holly to come down from her room. Last spring, I spent so many hours in that reception area that it seemed like a second home. There were easy chairs, a couple of sofas, several lamps and tables. There was reading material, too, to help visitors while away the time as they waited for their girlfriends . . . or daughters.

Old magazines, crossword-puzzle books, a few well-worn paperbacks. And an old, hardbound copy of *Look Homeward, Angel*. I used to pick up the Wolfe book and read it and look at the wonderful Douglas W. Gorsline illustrations while I waited for Holly. The waiting always seemed to last forever. But finally she would come walking through the entryway, smiling and so beautiful that it hurt me to look at her.

O lost, and by the wind grieved, ghost, come back again!

Chapter Two

Setting out from my apartment Monday night, I'd had no intention of hiking seven miles to Dandi Donuts and seven miles back. I'd just wanted *out*, just wanted *away*.

Now, thanks to Eileen, I had a reason to go there.

A purpose for my walk.

If anybody asks, I thought, I can explain I'm on my way to Dandi Donuts to pick up a couple of glazed old-fashioneds for a friend.

Better than saying, 'Just out for a stroll.'

Not that anyone was likely to ask.

Away from the campus, few people were wandering about. Only rarely did a car pass by. Most students were in their rooms, studying or messing around on their computers or indulging in deep, philosophical bullshit sessions with friends or having sex or sleeping. Non-students were mostly in *their* rooms, too, I supposed. Reading, watching television, having sex, or sleeping.

As I walked along Division Street, some of the houses had one or two lighted windows. Others had no lights on, but a window glowed with the trembling light from a television. Most of the houses, however, were dark except for porch lights. Some didn't even have porch lights on.

Sometimes, I heard voices, thuds, laughter and other quiet sounds coming from the houses I passed. Many of them, though, were silent. A few birds were awake in the trees or air. I heard them twitter and warble. Mostly, though, I heard my footsteps on the concrete of the sidewalk. Each step came regularly. They all sounded just the same except when I stood on something: a leaf, a stone, a twig.

8

I noticed how quickly one step followed another, so I slowed down. What was the hurry? My only destination was a donut shop that never closed.

And it was only a random destination, anyway. I had no real need to get there at all.

What about the donuts I'd promised Eileen?

Not exactly a promise.

But I'd told her I would get them and I intended to keep my word.

More than likely, I would've headed for Dandi Donuts even if she hadn't entered the picture. So it was no big deal. Not really. Except that now I had an obligation to go there.

And to get back with the donuts before her ten o'clock class.

I don't *have* to, I told myself. I don't *have* to go back to campus at all, or back to my apartment, or anywhere. If I want, I can just keep walking.

It struck me then that I was walking north. If I kept on going north, I would eventually end up in Seattle . . . the land of Holly and Jay.

Desire, rage and sorrow slammed into me.

But I kept on walking.

I'm *not* going to walk to Seattle, I told myself.

Actually, I'd thought seriously about *flying* there after I got Holly's letter on Friday. Decided against it, though. If she wanted to dump me for some asshole she met at summer camp, far be it from me to interfere . . . or to go pleading for her love like some sort of total loser. She could keep her Jay and I could keep my dignity. I got drunk.

There would be no visits to Seattle by me.

With any luck, I would never again set eyes on Holly Johnson.

I only wished I could take my *mind* off her. And that happened a few minutes later when a man and his dog came down the sidewalk toward me. The man, stout, swarthy and bearded, wore a dark turban. The dog on his leash looked like a Rottweiler.

A Rottweiler on one of those endless leashes that would allow him several minutes of mauling time while his owner tried to reel him in.

I almost crossed the street, but it would've been so *obvious*. The man might be offended or take me for a coward . . . or even assume

9

I'm some sort of anti-turban bigot. So I stayed on my side of the street.

As they approached, I smiled and nodded and politely stepped off the sidewalk to let them by.

The dog, well ahead of the man, came trotting over to me and began to sniff the crotch of my jeans.

One good chomp . . .

The man at the other end of the leash seemed uninterested in his dog's activities.

'Nice doggie,' I said in a soft voice.

Its muzzle nudged me. I took a step backward, and it growled.

The man finally came along. Keeping his head straight forward, he walked past us without even giving us a glance. After he'd gone by, his dog licked the fly of my jeans.

'Get outa here,' I muttered.

Though at least fifteen feet away, the man turned his head and glowered at me. 'Speaking to my dog is not permitted.'

'Sorry.'

He continued on his way, reeling in. The dog gave me one last prod with his muzzle, then wheeled around and went trotting after its master.

I scowled in their direction, but neither noticed.

I guess the fellow figured he owned the sidewalk and his dog owned my crotch.

'Assholes,' I muttered.

Neither of them noticed that, either. Which was maybe a good thing; the bastard might've sicced his dog on me . . . or chased me with a scimitar. (If he had one on him, I couldn't see it . . . but no telling *what* he might've had hidden inside his flowing robe.)

Anyway, I resumed walking and kept a sharp eye out for dogs. Though none seemed to be coming, several times my passing triggered fits of wild barking from hounds behind fences or gates. They couldn't get to me, but their mindless uproar announced my presence to everyone in the neighborhood. All I wanted to do was go by, silent and invisible, nobody even knowing I was there.

Soon, the barking grew less frequent. Maybe I was walking more quietly, or maybe I'd simply entered a neighborhood with fewer dogs. Whatever the reason, I began to feel more calm.

The night was very peaceful.

I saw a white cat scurry across the street and take shelter underneath a parked car. I heard a hooting owl. Sometimes, things were so quiet that I could hear the soft buzz of the streetlights.

As I stepped off a curb, a loud *bring-bring-bringgg!* made my throat catch. I leaped back just as a bike whished by.

I blurted, 'Shit!'

'*Wheeee!*' squealed the bike's rider – a skinny old woman in black spandex, wearing her ballcap backward.

A *happenin'* crone.

Looking back over her shoulder, she smiled at me. I couldn't see her face very well, but it was pale and thin and I got the impression she was missing most of her front teeth. For some reason, I got goosebumps. They stayed with me as she faced forward and pedaled off.

At the end of the block, she turned a corner. I was glad to have her out of sight, but I started to worry that she might be circling around for another pass at me.

Maybe I'd offended her. Maybe she wanted retribution. Maybe she planned to reach out on her next pass and touch me with a gnarled finger and whisper, 'thinner', or 'toad', or 'rectum', or something.

I didn't *really* think it would happen, but it sure did cross my mind.

So I *did* cross Division Street.

For a while, I walked slowly and kept looking back. I had a funny tickle in my chest that felt like a giggle or a scream might be crouched inside me, just waiting for the hag to come wheeling around the corner.

Finally, to play it safe and give myself a chance to calm down, I headed down a sidestreet. I walked two short blocks, then came to Franklin Street and resumed my journey northward.

She won't find me over here, I thought.

For more than half an hour, not much happened. I just kept walking up Franklin. The houses seemed a little older here than those I'd passed on Division Street. Now and then, dogs barked. Fewer of the houses had lights on. Only one or two cars went by. I saw nobody out walking . . . or riding bikes.

But then from the east a girl came walking.

She moved in from the right, some thirty feet ahead of me, following the sidewalk along the end of the block. She happened to be facing forward. I happened to be standing in the shadow of a tree.

I stopped and held my breath.

At the corner, she turned her back to me, stepped off the curb and started crossing the street.

Standing motionless, I watched her.

I didn't begin to walk until she was about halfway up the next block. Then I moved out of the tree's shadows, went to the corner and stepped off the curb.

Chapter Three

I wasn't following her. I was simply continuing on my course toward Dandi Donuts.

Not following her.

If she'd gone a different way at the corner and I'd abandoned my previous route to pursue her, *then* I would have been following her. But that wasn't the case. She had simply positioned herself ahead of me on the sidewalk I was already using.

She had every right to do so, and I had every right to proceed without changing my route.

That's what I told myself when I started to follow her.

I walked at my normal pace for a while, closing the gap that separated us. Then I slowed down. I didn't want to overtake her.

Overtaking a woman on a sidewalk, especially at night and when no one else is nearby, *always* makes me uncomfortable. As I come up behind one, she obviously worries she's about to be robbed, raped or killed. Such women almost always cast a nervous glance back at me while I'm closing in. And then they stiffen as I hurry past them.

It's not that I'm a monster, either. I look pleasant, cheerful and harmless. But I'm a guy. That's apparently enough to make some women fear my approach.

To avoid tormenting them, I've learned not to overtake them on sidewalks. I cross the street or turn a corner to get off their tails, or I drastically slow my pace.

What usually happens, I cut my speed to a dawdle and sometimes stop entirely for short periods of time, hoping the woman will turn a corner, reach her destination, or otherwise get out of my way. When it becomes obvious that she'll be continuing in front of me, I resign myself to passing her or I change my own course.

Being in no hurry to reach Dandi Donuts . . . or anywhere else . . . I saw no reason to cross the street or turn a corner.

Just don't spook her, I told myself. Keep a nice, slow pace and a good distance between us.

She'll never even know I'm here.

So far, the young woman in front of me seemed completely unaware of my presence. She just kept walking along with a bouncy, carefree stride, swinging her arms, turning her head to look this way and that (but never behind her). Her pale hair was in a ponytail that bobbed and swayed as she walked. She wore a dark sweatshirt, dark trousers and sneakers. She carried nothing at all, not even a purse. I thought this strange. Women almost never go anywhere without a purse.

Where is *this* one going? I wondered.

Maybe to Dandi Donuts?

That was too much to hope for. More than likely, she was on her way home from somewhere. I wondered if her parents knew she was out on the streets at such an hour.

Who says she lives with her parents?

For all I knew, she might've been in her mid-twenties, living on her own, even married.

But I doubted it.

Though I'd only seen her at a distance and never in very good light, I'd formed an impression that she was somewhat younger than me – perhaps sixteen to eighteen years old. If that was the case, she most likely lived at home with her parents.

I'd also formed an impression that she was extremely attractive.

In the glow of the streetlights, her face had looked as if it *might* be beautiful. Distance and poor lights can be misleading, though. Seen clearly, she might have flaws. Or she might be twice the age I suspected.

There was, however, more than enough light to reveal the fine shape of her body underneath her sweatshirt and trousers.

Not that I felt any desire for her. Thanks to Holly, women had lost their appeal for me.

I did, however, feel a certain connection to her. We were two strangers sharing the same route. We had that in common. She was walking past the same parked cars, same trees, same lawns, same houses as me . . . seconds sooner, that's all. She and I were seeing similar sights, hearing very much the same sounds, smelling and breathing nearly the same air, feeling the same concrete under our shoes. In all eternity and infinity, we were existing together in the same time and place . . . almost.

I couldn't help feeling connected to her.

Connected and protective.

She seemed much too young to be roaming the streets alone at such an hour of the night, so I intended to make sure she got home safely.

I now had *two* missions: pick up donuts for Eileen and guard my new companion.

I *was* her companion, though she didn't know it.

I won't let anything happen to you, I told her in my mind.

Suddenly, she stopped walking. As I halted, her head began turning to the left.

She's going to look back!

Though standing in the brightness of a streetlight, I made no attempt to find cover; movement might catch her eye. Total stillness was my best defense.

Watching her, I didn't dare breathe.

After a few moments, I realized her eyes were on a lean white cat sauntering in her direction from the other side of Franklin Street.

She turned toward the cat and I saw her in profile for the second time that night. Her outline . . . her high ponytail, the tilt of her head, the shape of her face, her slender neck, her high breasts in front and her rear end pushing out at the seat of her trousers . . . I don't want to say she looked athletic because that suggests *power*. That would give the wrong impression. More than anything else, she seemed confident, springy and pert.

She squatted down. With her rear end a few inches above the sidewalk, she lowered her head and spoke to the cat. 'Come here, kitty,' I heard. A hand reached out past her right knee and beckoned to it.

The cat opened its mouth wide and let out a loud '*Reeoww!*' as if to say, 'I see you. Hold your horses. I'm on my way.' Full of disdain and coyness until it finally got to her hands.

Moments later, it seemed to slump and melt with pleasure. She spoke softly as she caressed it, but I couldn't hear what she was saying. She must've spent three or four minutes petting it. When she stood up to leave, the cat rubbed itself against her shins and calves, slithered between her legs, acted as if it wanted to wrap itself around her and stop her from going away.

Almost tripping on it, she let out a quiet laugh and leaped clear. The moment she began walking away, I ducked behind a nearby tree. I peered around its trunk and saw the cat prancing after her, tail high.

'*Rowww!*'

She looked back at it and said, 'Okay, but just for a minute.'

Then she turned all the way around, facing the cat and me.

I pulled back my head. Staring at the bark of the tree an inch in front of my nose, I waited.

'Yes,' I heard her say. 'You're a needy little fellow, aren't you? Yes, you are.'

I couldn't look at her. I could only listen. She had a wonderful, strange voice. There was nothing girlish about it. I would almost say it sounded masculine, but it was too smooth and lilting for that. It even had a hint of a purr in it as she talked to the cat.

'Oh, yes, you like that, don't you? Mmm, yes. That feels *real* good.'

When I risked a peek around the trunk, I found that she was squatting over the cat, reaching down between her spread knees to caress it with both hands. The cat was stretched out on its side.

'Think you've had enough?' she asked it. 'No such thing as enough, is there?' After giving it a final pat, she started to rise so I had to quit watching.

A few seconds passed. Then the girl said, 'Bye-bye, kitty,' in that rich, low voice of hers.

I stayed hidden, listening. No more sounds came from the direction of the girl or the cat. Finally, I dared to take another peek. The cat was still sprawled on the sidewalk, apparently too languid to move on. The girl had already crossed the next street.

She wasn't looking back.

I left the shelter of my tree and hurried up the sidewalk. As I stepped over the cat, I heard the rumble of its purr. It raised its head and squawked at me as if annoyed by the intrusion.

I kept on walking.

When I glanced back, the cat was still there, stretched out long and slim on the pale concrete . . . luxuriating in memories of the girl's hands, more than likely, and hoping for her return.

By the time I reached the other side of the street, she was halfway up the next block. I quickened my pace, hoping to close the distance between us.

I felt as if my eyes were locked on her back.

But I must've glanced away for an instant. I'm not sure what distracted me.

When I looked forward again, the sidewalk ahead of me was empty.

My heart sickened.

Where'd she go?

My first thought was that she had been snatched away by an assailant. Just where I'd last seen her, the yard to the right was partly enclosed by thick hedges. He might've dragged her out of sight . . . I started to run.

But what if she'd wandered into the yard for a reason of her own . . . maybe to visit a stray dog or another cat?

I quit running.

Still moving too fast, I told myself. *Slow down. I'm just a guy walking by.*

Though I tried to walk slowly, my heart raced.

What if she's down? What if some bastard's raping her?

She'd be yelling, I thought.

Not if he knocked her out. Or killed her.

Aching to run, but holding back, I walked past the row of hedges.

17

The house was dark, its front lawn shrouded by shadows. I kept walking, but slowly. Very slowly. Watching and listening.

Nobody seemed to be down on the ground.

I heard no sounds of struggle.

Did he take her behind the house?

On the dark porch, something moved.

Chapter Four

Looking straight forward, I walked on. I even took a few additional steps after passing the hedge at the border of the lawn. Then, crouching low, I crept back to the bushes. I peered around them and squinted toward the porch.

Several steps above the walkway leading to it, the porch was enclosed by a low wooden railing. Its roof sheltered it from most of the night's vague light. Staring into that darkness, I wondered how I'd managed to notice any movement at all. Perhaps I'd only imagined it.

Then a thin, horizontal strip of grayness six or seven feet high appeared in the blackness of the porch. I didn't know what it was. As it slowly thickened, however, I realized the gray strip was made of vague light from inside the house . . . growing wider because the front door was being opened.

But opened with such slowness, such stealth, that it seemed to be some sort of forbidden act.

Chills tingled their way up my spine.

What's going on?

When the area of grayness was wide enough, a black shape slipped through it. The shape seemed to have a ponytail.

A moment later, the grayness began to narrow. Then it was gone.

Suddenly, I smiled.

Of course!

The girl had been away from the house without her parents' knowledge. She'd probably crept out after their bedtime, maybe for a tryst with a boyfriend, and I had just witnessed her return.

19

The little sneak!

I almost laughed. Not only was I giddy with relief, but impressed by her daring.

From my place beside the bush, I continued to watch her house. All the windows remained dark. This made sense. After sneaking in so smoothly, she would hardly start running around flicking on lights. No, she would make her way through the darkness.

She had probably taken off her shoes in the foyer. Carrying them in one hand, gliding her other hand along the banister, she'd silently climbed the stairs.

I knew the routine; I'd done it myself a few times during my teenaged years. I knew how she must be moving very slowly, fearful that a board might squeak underfoot. And I knew the excitement that she probably felt.

I also knew she might eventually turn on a light.

Upstairs, if she played it smart, she would sneak into her bedroom and take off her clothes in the darkness. Once you've made an undiscovered entry, your clothes are the only giveaway. Get them off, put on your pajamas or nightgown or whatever you wear at bedtime, and you've made it home free. You can turn on your bedroom light if you wish, go to the bathroom and turn on its light . . . Even if you're seen, nobody will know you'd been outside.

Waiting for a light to come on, I found myself staring at the third upstairs window from the corner.

Stupid.

This wasn't Holly's sorority house, it was the home of a stranger. Any of the windows might belong to the girl's bedroom. Or none of them; her windows *might* face the rear of the house. Her room might even be downstairs, though that didn't seem likely; in old, two-story houses, the bedrooms were nearly always upstairs.

Though several minutes went by, no light appeared in any of the windows.

She'd had plenty of time to reach her bedroom. She was probably in her room now, undressing in the dark. In my mind, it wasn't *complete* darkness. A dim glow of moonlight entered through the window, illuminating her as she pulled off her dark sweatshirt.

But in which room? I wondered. Behind which window?

I suddenly realized that her bedroom was most likely one with windows directly over the porch. Three windows overlooked its roof. A simple matter to climb out any of them, walk to the edge of the porch roof, then slip down a support post to the railing and hop to the ground.

Was that how the girl had escaped from her house earlier that night?

I gazed at the windows above the porch. A couple of them – maybe all three – were likely to be the windows of her bedroom. She was probably standing just beyond one of them . . . near enough to take advantage of the faint light coming in.

But I couldn't see her.

Each window looked like a mirror reflecting black night and moon-light. Only a person standing on the porch roof, face pressed to the glass, would be able to see in.

I pictured myself up there.

It excited and appalled me.

You've gotta be kidding.

Then I suddenly realized I'd been squatting by the hedge, gazing at the house for a *long* time . . . five minutes? Ten? What if someone had noticed me lurking there and called the cops?

I want to report a prowler.

A Peeping Tom.

Scared, I scooted around to the other side of the bushes, got to my feet and walked away. I walked fast. At any moment, a neighbor might shout at me or confront me with a weapon. Or a squad car might swing around one of the corners and roar down the street to hunt me down.

I ached to break into a run and put some real distance between me and the girl's house.

If I'd been dressed like a fellow out for a jog, I might've tried running. But I was in my chamois shirt and jeans. Such clothes would draw suspicion from anyone seeing me race through the night. So I held back. I even slowed the pace of my walking and tried very hard to look carefree.

I actually pursed my lips and prepared to whistle a tune, but good sense put a stop to that.

I walked in silence, my heart hammering, my mouth parched, my body spilling sweat from every pore.

Nobody shouted. Nobody chased me. No cars came toward me from either direction.

At last, I reached the end of the block. I crossed to the other side of Franklin and continued westward on the sidestreet until I found my way back to Division. Vastly relieved by my escape, I walked two or three blocks north on Division before I even remembered about the bike hag.

A chill scampered up my hot, sweaty back and raised goosebumps on the nape of my neck.

I whirled around and looked behind me.

No sign of her. Of course not.

Continuing on my way, I felt a little silly for letting her scare me at all.

But I was glad she *had* scared me. I'd detoured over to Franklin Street for no other reason than to get away from her. If I hadn't done that, the girl and I would have passed each other in the night, two blocks apart, never converging.

For a while, I toyed with the idea that I'd been *meant* to flee from the bike hag and find the girl. (I often think strange thoughts in the dead of night.) Forces of good or evil had perhaps given the hag a mission: scare the hell out of Ed Logan so he'll run over to Franklin Street . . .

Not likely.

But I'd been afraid she might reach out as she pedaled by, touch me with a crooked finger and mark me with a curse. So I'd fled. And maybe in fleeing from a harmless, somewhat daffy old crone, I'd run into the sort of curse I'd never expected.

Curse or blessing.

As I walked up Division Street on my way to Dandi Donuts, I felt

22

cursed *and* blessed . . . and bewitched. Not by the bike hag, but by a certain mysterious girl who'd shared the sidewalk and some of her secret life with me, watching unseen in the night.

Chapter Five

Still more than a block away from Dandi Donuts, I could see the hazy glow from its picture windows hovering over the sidewalk.

The houses had already been left behind. Businesses lined both sides of the street: a deli, a barber shop, a gas station, an Italian restaurant called Louie's, a flower shop, a thrift shop. All were shut for the night. Most were dark inside, but some were dimly lighted.

The display window of the thrift shop, for instance. There, gloomy lights illuminated a pair of sorry mannequins with fading, chipped paint on their faces. They stood frozen in odd stances, looking cheerful for no good reason.

A slender, debonair man in a dusty top hat and tails wanted to look like Clark Gable but one side of his mustache was gone. His lady friend, her red wig slightly askew, wore a red-sequined dress like a 'flapper' from the Roaring Twenties. The original owner of the gown was probably as gone as the missing half of Clark's mustache.

A fairly regular patron of Dandi Donuts, I'd noticed the thrift-shop window early during my first year at the university. In the beginning, I'd been amused by the battered mannequins and their outdated costumes. I'd also enjoyed looking at other items displayed in the window: old tableware, vases, phonograph records, and even a few framed paintings. But then, on my way to Dandi Donuts alone one night, I'd paused at the window longer than usual. That's when I realized that the mannequins, clothes, and just about everything else displayed behind the window were relics of the dead.

They made me uneasy and depressed.

The next time I went to Dandi Donuts, I walked on the other side of the street and didn't look at the thrift-shop window as I passed by. But I still knew it was there.

After that, I stayed away from the donut shop. I pretty much intended to avoid it forever, but on a warm night in the late spring of last year, Holly and I were out walking. I knew that we'd walked a very long distance, but I'd been paying attention to Holly, not to our location. We were holding hands. Suddenly, she stopped. I stopped, too. In front of the thrift-shop window.

'Oh, wow,' she'd said. 'Look at this stuff.'

I looked. Having Holly at my side, however, I felt untouched by the gloom. 'Clark Gable,' I said.

'Looks like half his mustache is *gone with the wind*!'

I laughed.

'Is this supposed to be Scarlet?' she asked.

'More likely Zelda, I think.'

'But she's *got* to be Scarlet. The red hair.'

'Well, maybe.'

'If you want her to be Zelda . . .'

'No, that's all right.'

'He put her in his books, didn't he?'

'I guess so. I guess she's in *Tender is the Night*. But he didn't call her Zelda.'

Holly turned to me and put her arms around me the way she often did, not hugging me exactly but holding herself just slightly against me so I could feel her breasts as she tilted back her head and stared up into my eyes. 'Will you put *me* in a book someday?' she asked.

'Sure I will.' It always embarrassed and thrilled me when she spoke of my being a writer – as if she actually believed it could happen.

'But use my real name, okay? Holly would be a good name for my character, don't you think?'

I nodded. I couldn't actually imagine her with any name other than Holly.

'When you're big and famous,' she said, 'I'll show the book to my kids and tell them how I knew you back in the early days.'

'You mean *our* kids?' I knew she hadn't meant *our* kids, but I'd felt compelled to ask, anyway.

Soft eyes looking up at me, her face solemn, she said, 'You deserve someone better than me.'

'What?' I'd heard her just fine.

'You'll find someone else, someone prettier than I am, and smarter . . .'

'I don't *want* anyone else.'

'You only *think* you don't.'

'I love you, Holly.'

'You love your *idea* of me.'

'What's that supposed to mean?'

'Maybe I'm not who you think I am.'

'Then who are you?'

Smiling gently, she rubbed herself against me and said, '"I'm nobody, who are you?"' Throwing Emily Dickinson at me.

'You're not nobody. You're Holly Johnson and I love everything about you.'

'Just remember my name, darling, when it comes time to put me in that book.'

I had a tightness in my throat, but I managed to say, 'I'll never forget your name. But if you go away and leave me, how will I know where to send a copy?'

'I won't leave you. You'll leave me. But don't worry about sending me a copy. I'll read all your books. I'll be your biggest fan.'

Then we'd kissed, standing in front of the thrift-shop window with Rhett and Scarlet (or Zelda) staring out at us. I'd felt broken inside. But afterwards, we'd gone on into the donut shop and Holly acted as if nothing horrible had happened. After the donuts, we went to a large wooded park and made love under the trees and everything seemed sweeter, more urgent and intense than ever before.

I remembered all that as I stood in front of the window, staring in at the dummies for the first time after being dumped by Holly.

I'll never leave you, she'd said. *You'll leave me.*

Yeah, right.

26

Bitch, I thought.

And then I thought worse.

The tattered mannequins smiled out at me through the glass. They looked exactly the same as they'd looked the night I stood out here with Holly. For them, nothing had changed. Lucky them.

I never should've come out here, I thought. North had been a big mistake.

But then, *any* direction would've been a mistake of nearly the same magnitude. There was almost no place to go where I hadn't been with Holly when we were in love. One place, I supposed, was just as bad as any other.

And north, at least, had the advantage of donuts.

As I walked through the hazy glow of light from Dandi Donuts, I glanced inside. Someone at the counter was making a purchase. The display racks had a meager selection, but I spotted several old-fashioneds. Some were chocolate covered. As for the others, I couldn't be sure whether they were plain or glazed. I pushed open the door and stepped into the warm, sweet aromas I knew so well.

The clerk – someone new since last year – was busy giving change to a customer.

I walked up to the counter and bent over.

Three of the old-fashioneds were glazed. They looked crusty and mouthwatering. I decided to buy all three, save two for Eileen and eat one here myself while I enjoyed a hot cup of coffee.

A long walk like this, I deserved two donuts.

What should the second one be? A chocolate-covered old-fashioned? Maybe a maple bar? Or one of those fat, sugar-sprinkled donuts that was loaded with jelly?

So many possibilities.

Most of them looked luscious.

From behind me came a familiar voice. 'Hey, Eddie. Fancy meeting you here.'

Chapter Six

I straightened up, turned around, and spotted Eileen waving at me from a corner table. She was alone. In front of her was a white Styrofoam coffee cup and a napkin with about half a donut sitting on it.

She'd come!

Smiling and shaking my head, I walked toward her.

'Go ahead and get something,' she said. 'I'm not going anywhere.'

'I was supposed to *bring* you some donuts,' I said.

'I decided to bring myself to them.'

'So . . . you want to cancel your order?'

'Guess so. I've already got one and a half inside me.'

'Can I get you anything?'

She shook her head. 'Just go ahead and buy what you want for yourself.'

So I returned to the counter. I bought a coffee and two glazed old-fashioneds, paid for them, and carried them toward Eileen's table.

She looked very fresh and pretty sitting there and watching me. Her dark-brown hair flowed down and draped the tops of her shoulders. Since I'd last seen her, she had changed out of her sweater and pleated skirt. She now wore blue jeans and a bright plaid chamois shirt. Below her throat was a wedge of bare skin. Her shirt wasn't buttoned until almost halfway down. Slightly crooked, it was open wide enough to show an edge of her black bra.

As I sat down across from her, she said, 'I changed my mind about being a nuisance.'

'You're not a nuisance.'

'You wanted to be alone.'

'That's all right. I'm glad you're here.' It wasn't quite a lie.

She beamed. 'Really?'

'Sure.'

'I just . . . it's an awfully long hike out here, you know? So I figured, well, I'd give you a good headstart then drive on out and at least *offer* you a ride home. I mean, in case seven miles was enough for one night.'

'How long did you wait?' I asked.

'Before leaving the house?' She shrugged. 'About an hour and a half. I set the alarm and took a little nap. Thought maybe I'd pass you along the way. Then I didn't, so I figured you must've gotten here ahead of me. Only *that* sure didn't happen. Not that it matters. I didn't mind waiting.'

'I took sort of an indirect route.'

'So I gathered.'

She didn't look as if she minded. She just seemed glad that I was with her now.

'You sure went to a lot of trouble,' I said.

'Nah. It was nothing.'

'It was a lot.'

'Well . . . That's okay. I'll be fine for my ten o'clock. What about you?'

'Nothing till one.'

'Oh, aren't *you* the lucky one?'

I smiled at that and tried one of the donuts. My teeth crunched through its crust and sank into soft, moist cake inside. The sweetness seemed to flood my mouth.

'What do you have at one?' Eileen asked.

I swallowed some donut. 'Shakespeare seminar.'

'Ah. With Horrible Hillary Hatchens.'

I laughed. 'Oh, yeah.'

'I had her last year. Yug.'

Eileen, by the way, was a year older than me. A year older than Holly, too. She'd been Holly's roommate at the sorority house last

29

year. Now she was a senior and, like me, an English major.

Holly had been a psych major. That should come as no surprise. As everybody knows, the field of psychology mostly attracts people who are fucked up.

'In case you haven't noticed,' Eileen said, 'Hatchens hates guys.'

'I've noticed, all right.'

'Must've gotten dumped big time somewhere along the line.'

'I can't imagine anyone *not* dumping her,' I said.

'She's pretty cute, though, don't you think?'

'I guess so. Cute but scary.'

Nodding and grinning, Eileen said, 'It's hard to imagine any guy having the nerve to ask her out in the first place. She *likes* me and *I'm* scared of her.'

I sipped coffee, ate some more donut and nodded now and then as Eileen continued.

'Anyway, I took pretty good notes last year. I also have copies of all her exams. You're welcome to borrow them. I'd let you use my term paper, too, but she'd probably catch on. She's a bitch, but she's not stupid.' Grinning, Eileen added, 'Though I'm sure she's not as smart as she *thinks* she is. I mean, how *could* she be? Nobody's *that* smart.'

With that, she had me laughing. It felt good.

But even as I laughed at her attack on Dr Hatchens, I wondered what was going on with Eileen. Had she come all the way out here in the middle of the night simply to cheer me up? Or was she trying to start something?

Last year, she'd seemed like an older sister to Holly. (Indeed, she *was* Holly's sorority sister.) She'd always treated me very well, but only because she considered me to be a good boyfriend/lover for Holly.

That's what I'd thought, anyway.

Maybe I'd had it wrong.

Or maybe that's how it *had* been last year. Now, however, Holly was out of the picture. Maybe Eileen had hopes of stepping in to take her place.

Hard to imagine why she would *want* to. I wasn't exactly a prize.

She was much too pretty to be interested in a guy like me.

After giving me a little while to work on my coffee and donuts, Eileen said, 'So how did your walk go?'

'Not bad. It was nice to get out of my apartment. And I think it helped take my mind off . . .' I couldn't force myself to speak the name.

'*La belle dame sans merci?*' Eileen suggested.

'I guess you could call her that. I'd probably call her something else. Short with four letters.'

Eileen laughed a bit sadly.

'Sod her,' I said.

'Keeping it literary.'

'Right. Sod her and the steed she rode in on.'

Eileen laughed a bit more, then shook her head. 'It's so awful. I'm so sorry.'

'That's the way it goes.'

'Don't I know it.'

I nodded. I knew that she knew it. My freshman year at Willmington, I'd seen Eileen around campus quite a lot. I'd known who she was, that she was an English major a year ahead of me, and that she was supposedly engaged to her high-school sweetheart. Her fiancé wasn't on campus, though. He was attending the University of California at Berkeley . . . about a two-day drive from Willmington. At some point before Holly and I started going together last spring, the guy dumped Eileen. After that, she went around with a lot of guys, but none for very long.

'Maybe we're both better off,' she said.

'I don't know.'

'It's just too bad these things always have to end so badly.'

'I'm not sure anything doesn't,' I said.

'Oh, I don't know.' A smile drifted across her face. 'I was always very glad to see the end of the Shakespeare seminar. I mean, I love Shakespeare, but Horrible Hillary Hatchens . . .'

'That's a little different.'

'I know. You meant good things. Relationships and stuff.'

31

'Yeah.'

'I've heard of people staying friends afterwards.'

'I think that's a crock,' I said. 'How can they stay friends? If they love each other and one of them stabs the other in the back . . . I don't think so. The stab*ber* might want to stay friends, but not the stab*bee*.'

Eileen laughed softly. 'Being a stab*bee* myself, I guess I'd have to agree with you. I pretty much just hate Warren. But I don't like feeling that way. I wish it were different. And I hate to think that you might end up hating Holly.'

'Yeah, well.'

I went ahead and ate my last donut. I didn't enjoy it much, though.

Just like I didn't much enjoy talking about Holly and busted relationships.

As I polished off my coffee, Eileen said, 'So, what's the verdict? Do you want to ride back with me? Or would you rather hike those seven long, lonely miles back to your apartment?'

The question didn't exactly take me by surprise.

Until encountering Eileen in Dandi Donuts, I'd expected to walk back . . . with a detour over to Franklin Street for another look at the house of the mystery girl.

I'd wanted very much to take another look at her house. With the possibility, I guess, of seeing her again.

I wanted badly to see her again.

But I couldn't refuse Eileen. Her offer to drive me home was an unwanted gift, but I didn't have the heart to turn it down.

'I'd rather ride back with you,' I said.

The look on her face made me glad I'd accepted.

We got up to leave. 'Want any donuts for the road?' I asked.

'No no no. I'll turn into a tub.'

Outside, we walked around the corner. Nobody else was around. The air had the strange damp smell that it only seemed to get in the hours after midnight. I heard a shopping cart, but it sounded far away.

Eileen's car was parked off Division Street. That's why I hadn't seen it during my approach to the donut shop.

She'd left it unlocked.

We put on our seatbelts and she started the car. As she pulled away from the curb, I said, 'This sure beats walking.'

'Glad to be of service, sir.'

It's for the best, I told myself. Going back for another look at the girl's house would've been a very bad idea.

Do yourself a favor and forget about her.

Eileen drove around the block, returned to Division, and turned left.

'Is this the way you came?' she asked.

'I went on over to Franklin. Too many people walking dogs and stuff along here.'

'Maybe that's why it took you so long.'

'Oh, I took a lot of detours.'

'See any interesting sights?'

'Not really. Just a lot of dark houses.'

'It's strange to be out this time of night,' Eileen said. 'Everything's so quiet and still. It's almost as if we're the only people on the face of the earth.'

'Yeah,' I said.

And then I saw someone striding along the sidewalk on the right side of the street. A girl in a dark sweatshirt and trousers. She moved with a brisk and bouncy stride, arms swinging, ponytail bobbing and swaying behind her head.

My mystery girl.

She's out?

She was out, all right.

As we drove by her, I turned my head to see her from the front.

'What is it?' Eileen asked.

I faced forward nonchalantly and said, 'Just someone walking by.'

'Maybe another donut hound,' Eileen said.

'Maybe so.'

Chapter Seven

'You're still in the place on Church Steet?' she asked.

'Yep.'

Last year, Eileen had been there fairly often for one reason or another . . . always involving Holly. She often dropped Holly off or picked her up at my place. Sometimes, she came over for small get-togethers of one sort or another.

Eileen and I had even been alone with each other in my apartment now and then. It might be just the three of us, for instance, and Holly would disappear into the bathroom or run off on an errand. Nothing had ever happened while Holly was gone. If Eileen felt any attraction for me, she'd kept it to herself.

And though she was very beautiful and I liked her as a person, I'd never felt any *desire* for her. My primary desire in regard to Eileen had been for her to *leave* so Holly and I could start fooling around.

'Are you in the same rooms and everything?' Eileen asked.

'Yeah.'

'Doesn't it bother you?

'Doesn't what?'

'There must be a lot of memories.'

'I guess.'

Guess? The final weeks of school last year, Holly had almost lived there. Now, every corner of every room, every piece of furniture, gave me sweet, sad memories of her. Though alive somewhere else (in Jay's bed?), she haunted my apartment.

'She was planning to move *in* this semester,' I said.

'I know. Have you thought about finding yourself a different place?'

'It'd be a lot of trouble. Anyway, it's no big deal.'

'All those reminders . . .'

'Yeah, well. Life goes on.'

I can be full of clichés when I've got nothing to say.

That pretty much killed the conversation until we reached Church Street. The road had several churches on it. One of them was next door to the old, two-story brick apartment house where I lived.

'*That'd* be enough to make *me* move out,' Eileen said.

'It doesn't bother me much.'

'I know. But it creeps *me* out.'

'Maybe because you're a heathen.'

She laughed. 'Maybe because I'm not.' She stopped at the curb in front of my building. Hand on the ignition key, she asked, 'Mind if I come up for a minute?'

'I . . . uh . . .' Before I could decide where to go from there, Eileen spoke again.

'I *really* need to use your bathroom. I'm sorry. I should've gone at the donut shop, I guess, but . . .'

'No, that's all right. Come on up.'

'Thanks.' She killed the headlights, shut off the engine and plucked out her ignition key. 'I'll make it quick,' she said. 'I promise.'

'No problem,' I said.

We hurried to the front door of the apartment building. I unlocked it and let us in. Then I eased the door shut. The interior was silent and smelled of stale cigarette smoke.

We stepped through the vestibule, turned to the right and walked softly, speaking not a word as we approached the landlords' door.

Usually, it stood open.

The landlords, Mr and Mrs Fisher, would be inside with their television on. But they only pretended to be watching it. They were *actually* watching the corridor outside their door, which led to the only stairway. They seemed to have an abiding curiosity about the comings and goings of their tenants. I knew they would *love* to catch me going by with Eileen at this hour.

But this hour was apparently too late for them. Their door was shut. As we crept past it, I couldn't even hear their television.

I half expected their door to fly open as we started to climb the stairs, but it didn't. Finally, we reached the landing, made the turn and resumed climbing.

'Safe,' I whispered.

Eileen grinned.

Even though we didn't have much to fear from the Fishers anymore, the late hour and the silence of the building made me reluctant to speak. Quietly, we reached the top of the stairs and followed the hallway to the door of my rooms. As I eased my key into the lock, I felt Eileen standing close behind me, not quite touching me.

She followed me in.

A couple of lamps were on. I'd left them that way before embarking on my walk.

I shut the door. Eileen put a hand on my shoulder and whispered, 'I'll just be a minute.'

'You don't need to whisper anymore.'

'Okay,' she said, a trifle more loudly.

Then she took her hand off my shoulder and hurried away. The bathroom was located off a narrow hall on the way to my bedroom. She vanished into the hall. A couple of seconds later, the door bumped shut.

While I waited for her, I took a quick look around. I hadn't expected company. The living room was cluttered with books and magazines, notebooks and pens and so on. It wasn't filthy, though. I've got no problem with clutter, but I like to keep things reasonably clean. For the quarters of a lone male student who'd spent the past weekend wallowing in despair, things didn't look too bad.

I could hear Eileen peeing.

She hadn't lied about needing to go.

I went over to the coffee table, found the remote, and turned my TV on.

A condom commercial. '. . . puts the pleasure back into safety.'

I changed channels. An ancient black-and-white movie showed Lon

Chaney Jr running through a forest. From his scared and guilty look, I figured this must be *The Wolfman*.

The toilet flushed.

I put down the remote and stared at poor, doomed Lawrence Talbot.

'Anything good on?' Eileen asked as she came into the living room.

'*All* the good stuff's on now – in the dead waste and middle of the night . . .'

'When churchyards yawn,' she added. Then she yawned herself.

I yawned, too.

They're contagious.

'Well,' she said. 'I'd better get going. Thanks for the use of your facilities.'

'Thanks for the ride.'

'My pleasure.' She reached the door ahead of me. Instead of opening it, however, she leaned her back against it, put out one of her hands and caressed my face. 'Are you going to be all right?'

'Sure.'

'*Are* you sure?'

I shrugged.

'*I'm* not so sure,' she said. She took her hand away from my face, but kept on gazing into my eyes. She looked very intense and solemn. 'That's why I drove out there. You seemed so . . . I don't know, *lost*.'

'Good word for it.'

'I want you to be all right, Ed.'

I muttered, 'Thanks.'

''Cause I know what it's like.'

'Yeah.'

'To lose someone you love.'

I nodded.

'It's hard. It feels like the end of the world.'

'Sort of.'

'But it isn't. It isn't the end of the world. You go on. Even though you hurt, you go on. And good stuff does happen to you again. You still have the hurt, but there's also the good stuff. And sometimes you even forget about the hurt.'

'If you say so,' I said.

'I do. And I mean it.'

And then she glided forward away from the door and put her arms around me and kissed me. Her mouth tasted of lipstick and coffee and donuts. Her hands moved up and down my back. I felt her breasts pushing against me through our clothes. Then her hands went under the back of my shirt, so I put my hands under the back of *her* shirt. Her skin was warm and smooth all the way up from her waist to her shoulders.

What happened to her bra?

She must've taken it off in the bathroom.

She plotted this!

I wondered vaguely how much she'd plotted and how much had been spontaneous. I vaguely resented being tricked and manipulated. I vaguely knew I should stop this nonsense and politely ask her to leave.

But the smooth soft bareness of her back indicated a bare front.

She wouldn't have taken off her bra unless she wanted me to go there. So I did. Soon, my hands were savoring the heft and smoothness of her breasts. She had bigger ones than Holly. When I fingered their nipples, she moaned into my mouth and writhed.

Then she unbuckled my belt. She unbuttoned my jeans and lowered my zipper and slipped her hand inside my underwear. Her fingers wrapped around me, smooth and cool.

Following her lead, I opened her jeans.

She had no underwear on.

I must've hesitated too long.

'Touch me,' she whispered.

So I put my hand inside the front of her jeans. The denim was damp against the backs of my fingers.

'In,' she whispered.

I did. She was all wet and slippery around my fingers.

Next thing you know, I was on my back on the living-room carpet.

We were both naked and Eileen was hunched over me, knees on the floor by my hips, hands clutching my shoulders, breasts swinging, head thrown back as she slid herself up and down on me, up and down.

We were still on the floor. Eileen was lying on top of me. We were sweaty and out of breath. I gently caressed her back.

She raised her head and looked me in the eyes. 'Told you there'd be good things.'

'Guess you were right.'

'Not the end of the world?' she asked.

'Nope.'

'Glad to hear it.'

Then she got off me, picked up her clothes and disappeared in the direction of the bathroom. When she returned a few minutes later, she was dressed. She had brushed her hair. Her face was still flushed and she had a sort of happy, dazed look in her eyes.

I'd gotten up and put my jeans on.

We met at the door.

'I'm gonna be a wreck tomorrow,' she said.

'You and me both.'

She put her arms around me and gave me a quick kiss. 'Gotta go.'

I nodded. 'See ya.'

'Tomorrow, okay?'

'Sure.'

I opened the door for her and watched her walk light-footed and bouncy through the dim, silent hallway. She swung her arms. Her hair danced and swayed. Her jauntiness reminded me of the mystery girl. At the top of the stairs, she turned and waved.

I waved back. Then I listened for a while to make sure nobody intercepted her.

When I heard the front door of the building latch shut, I realized that I should've walked her down and out to her car.

She'll be all right, I thought.

Worried, though, I hurried through my apartment to a window in my kitchen that had a view of the street. From there, I watched Eileen climb into her car and drive away.

I just stood there staring down at the empty street for a long time after she was gone.

Trying to make sense out of what had happened.

But mostly feeling empty and pleased with myself and astonished by Eileen, and more than a little bit worried about where it would lead.

Chapter Eight

I woke up in bed with my room full of daylight. The other half of my bed was empty where Holly should've been. I pictured her lying there asleep, curled on her side, loops of russet hair dangling across her face. On mornings before she woke up, her face always seemed soft and very young so that she looked like a sleeping child.

A feeling of sadness and longing came over me.

I wondered if there might be a way to get Holly back.

It didn't seem likely. But even if she gave up her Jay and returned to me, it wouldn't be the same. She was different now. Or maybe she was the same as she had always been, but now she had shown her true self.

Her true, horrid self.

The only good way to have Holly in my life from now on would be to remember how it had been before the summer came. When she was asleep in the bed beside me, for instance.

The telephone rang.

With a groan, I turned over. The alarm clock on my nightstand showed 11:48.

It was set to go off at noon.

As the phone kept ringing, I climbed out of bed and hurried into the living room. I was naked. But the sunlit rooms were warm, the curtains were shut and nobody was here to be shocked so I didn't bother to put anything on.

On my way to the phone, I stepped where I'd been down on the carpet last night with Eileen on top of me. I suddenly had a pretty good idea who was calling.

41

'Hello?'

'Hi, Eddie.' I wasn't wrong. 'Are you up and at 'em yet?'

'Oh, yeah.'

'I didn't want you to oversleep and miss your one o'clock. Horrible Hatchens would be devastated.'

I almost smiled. 'Oh, yeah, she'd miss me.'

'It's almost noon.'

'Getting there. I'd better put it in gear.'

Silence.

Here it comes.

'So,' she finally said. 'How *are* you this morning?'

'Not too bad, I guess. How about you?'

She hesitated, then said, 'Pretty good.'

Another silence.

After a while, Eileen said, 'So . . . do you want to get together later on?'

I tried to put some enthusiasm in my voice. 'Sure. That's a good idea.'

'Maybe we could go somewhere and get a burger or something.'

'Sounds good.'

'Why don't we meet at your place? I think it might look a little funny if you came over to the sorority . . . like I'm trying to take Holly's place, or something.'

And of course you're not.

'I mean, everyone knows everything about you two over here.'

'Ah. Yeah.'

'So it might be better if you and I keep things to ourselves for a little while. Don't you think?'

'Good idea,' I said.

'So why don't I come by your place at around five or six? Maybe we can drive somewhere far enough away so everyone won't know our business.'

Somewhere far away . . .

Suddenly, I was interested.

'There's an Italian place over by Dandi Donuts,' I said. 'How about there?'

42

'Great. So I'll pick you up around five and we'll drive out.'

'Sure.'

'Okay, great. I'll see you then.'

'Great.'

'Now don't be late for class.'

'Thanks for the wake-up call.'

'Bye-bye, Eddie.'

'So long.'

I hung up and headed for the bathroom. I used the toilet, then took a shower. In the shower, I tried to figure things out.

Mainly, what'll I do about Eileen?

I liked her and I *really* liked what we'd done in my living room last night. In fact, I started to get hard just thinking about it.

But I didn't love her. I didn't want her moving in with me. I didn't want to marry her. I didn't want her to bear my children . . .

What if she's already pregnant?

Nah, I thought. We only did it once.

Once can be enough.

I hadn't used a condom. Had *she* used anything?

Sweet, sensitive Holly's idea of birth control had consisted of good timing, pulling out, and luck . . . apparently she didn't want to dignify her lust by admitting it to a doctor or pharmacist. She wouldn't let me use condoms, either. According to Holly, she wanted to feel *me* inside her. That suited me fine, since I hated condoms, too. As a result, though, we'd had a couple of good scares when her period didn't show up on time.

Sharing such scares with Holly had brought us closer . . . or so I'd felt.

But I didn't want that sort of closeness with Eileen.

I've gotta get out of this, I thought.

Sure, but how?

I gave it all sorts of thought as I finished my shower, dried off, had myself a cup of instant coffee and a chocolate pop tart, then brushed my teeth, got dressed, gathered my books and headed for campus.

Some stuff just isn't simple.

Maybe she isn't after any sort of commitment, I kept telling myself. She knows how much I loved Holly. She must know I don't love *her*. Maybe she only did that last night to cheer me up.

Yeah, right.

I should be so lucky.

I never am.

By the time I entered Dexter Hall, generally called the English Building, I'd decided that honesty is always the best policy. I would simply have to confront Eileen and tell her my true feelings.

'I'm afraid I don't love you, Eileen. I wish that I could, but . . . I don't think I'm *capable* of love anymore . . . not after Holly.'

The words felt true to me.

But they sounded in my head like a crock of shit.

There's no good way out of this, buddy.

Entering the seminar room, I smiled at Dr Hatchens. She smiled back at me. It was one of those snide smiles. 'I'm glad you were finally able to join us, Mr Logan.'

I was two minutes late.

'I'm sorry, Dr Hatchens.'

'And so are we all,' she said.

And I thought, Things could always be worse. At least I didn't get maneuvered last night into fucking Horrible Hillary Hatchens.

I had a hard time paying attention. Focusing on Othello isn't so easy when you've got wench troubles of your own.

Dr Hatchens knew I was in trouble, too.

'Would you like to contribute an opinion, Mr Logan?'

'He loved not wisely but too well.'

I managed a feeble smile. Some of the other English majors laughed, but Dr Hatchens wasn't amused. 'It might behoove you to pay attention in the future.'

'I'm sorry.'

'We know.'

Shit.

Chapter Nine

While I waited for five o'clock, my stomach hurt. Not from hunger, though. From nerves.

I'd decided to break it off.

Not even go to the restaurant with Eileen. Just tell her quickly, as gently as possible, and get it over with.

I'd been ready for her ever since about four. From then on, I couldn't study, couldn't focus on anything except our approaching confrontation.

I practiced speeches in my head.

They all seemed amazingly lame.

Just tell her the truth, I thought. She'll understand.

She'll understand, all right.

In my mind, I could see the pain in her eyes. The tears. She said, '*But, Eddie, I love you. I thought you loved me, too.*'

Or, '*Isn't it a little late to be telling me this?*'

Or, '*Fuck me and dump me, is that it?*'

Or, '*Go to hell. You're a lousy lay, anyhow.*'

I imagined her saying plenty of other things, too . . . none of them pleasant.

Sometimes, I imagined trying to comfort her. Other times, I lost my temper. '*You seduced me last night. You plotted the whole thing. Now that Holly's out of the way, you made the big play to get me for yourself. I lost my head and gave in. Which is what you counted on. But it isn't going any further. It's over. It's finished. I don't WANT you.*'

Thinking that sort of thing, I cringed.

45

Five o'clock came and went.

I continued to stew.

Terrific. Now she's late. She doesn't even think enough of me to show up on time. This'll make it a lot easier.

At ten after, the buzzer rang and my stomach jumped. Heart hammering, I walked to the intercom. My legs felt weak. I seemed to be trembling all over. I pushed the button and said into the speaker, 'Yes?'

'It's me.'

'Okay, I'll buzz you in.' I pushed the button to unlock the building's front door. Then I opened the door of my apartment and waited for Eileen.

I heard a quiet 'Hi' from her, probably addressed to the Fishers as she walked past their open door. Then her footsteps were hurrying up the stairway. She appeared at the top of the stairs, gave me a smile and came striding toward me.

She wore a white blouse with the sleeves rolled up her forearms, a short tartan kilt that swished around her thighs, green knee socks and loafers.

'Missed you,' she said and stepped into my arms. She hugged me very hard at first, squeezing me against herself. Then she relaxed her hold and kissed me gently on the mouth.

'I'm really sorry I'm late,' she said. 'I couldn't get my car started.'

'That's all right.'

'I guess we'll have to change our dinner plans. Unless you want to walk out to the restaurant.'

'How did you get here?'

'Walked. That's why I'm a little late.'

'Oh.'

'I got an early start or I would've been *really* late.'

'What's the matter with your car?'

'Dead battery, I guess.' She gave me a grimace that was so exaggerated that I had to smile. 'I left my headlights on overnight.'

'How'd you manage that?'

'I had a lot on my mind.' She laughed softly and kissed me again.

46

'Anyway, we can walk out to that restaurant if you want to. Might be fun.'

'Seven miles,' I reminded her.

'Mmm. Maybe not so fun. A total of fourteen, right?'

'We could go someplace closer,' I said.

'What if we call out for pizza?'

Memories came pounding in. Many times, I'd phoned for a pizza delivery for Holly and me so we wouldn't need to go anywhere, just stay together, all by ourselves in my apartment.

We'd done it sometimes when Eileen was here, too.

'I guess we could do that,' I told her.

We decided on a large pepperoni pizza, and I made the call. 'It'll be half an hour,' I told her.

'I've got an idea. You wait here. I'll run out and pick up a bottle of wine. We'll make a party of it.'

'I'm under age.'

'Oh, I know. You poor, dear thing.' Smiling, she patted my cheek. 'That's what *I'm* for. I'll be back in a jiff.'

So off she went.

I found my wallet and took out enough money for the pizza and a tip. Then I sank onto the sofa and stared into space.

I can't just dump her, I thought. The least I can do is wait till after we've eaten. No point in ruining that. We'll have the pizza and drink some wine. It'll be easier afterward.

Soon, Eileen arrived with a bottle of Merlot *and* the pizza. 'We both got here at the same time,' she explained.

I tried to give her the money. She shook her head. 'It's on me.'

'No, it's not.'

'Hey, this was all my idea. It's my treat.'

'No, come on. Take it.'

'You can pay next time.'

As if there would be a next time.

'Well,' I muttered. 'Okay.'

I opened the bottle. Not having any wineglasses, I took out a couple of tumblers and half filled them.

'Where do you want to eat?' Eileen asked.

Holly and I always used to eat our pizza in the living room, sitting cross-legged on the floor. Eileen knew that.

'We can eat at the table if you want,' she said.

'The floor'll be all right.'

She frowned slightly. 'Are you sure?'

'If you'd rather sit at the table . . .'

'I always liked the floor.' She let out a quiet laugh. 'For eating pizza. That's what I meant.'

'Sure.'

She laughed again. 'The floor it is,' she said.

So we took everything out to the living room. Eileen placed the pizza box on the floor. She sat on one side of it and I sat across from her.

Glass in hand, she reached forward and toasted, 'To the good times that *aren't* all gone.'

'Okay,' I said.

We clicked our glasses together, then drank. Then Eileen opened the pizza box. As steam drifted up, we reached in and pulled out slices of pie that were dripping with strings of melted cheese.

The pizza was delicious. The wine was cool and slightly tart. While I ate and drank, I had a difficult time not staring at Eileen's legs. They were sheathed in the green socks nearly to her knees, then bare most of the way up from there.

'So how did Shakespeare go?' she asked.

'I was a couple of minutes late.'

'Uh-oh.'

'And then I couldn't think straight. My mind kept wandering.'

'Guess you didn't get enough sleep last night.'

'How about you?' I asked.

She shook her head. 'It was all I could do to stay awake during my ten o'clock. I tried to take a nap this afternoon, but couldn't pull it off. Too keyed up, I guess.'

'Keyed up? About what?'

'What do *you* think?'

I just looked at her.

Suddenly blushing, she said, 'I never meant for things to go that way last night. I keep thinking . . . it must've looked so *calculated*. But it wasn't. If you think I planned to . . .' She shook her head. 'I didn't. I just wanted to be your friend, try to help you. You were obviously so miserable about Holly . . . That's why I drove out to the donut shop. And then I really *did* need to use your john. It must've looked like an excuse to get inside your apartment, but it wasn't. I really had to *go*. But then . . . I don't know.' She took another drink of her wine, then shrugged. 'I just suddenly . . . I wanted to make things better. For both of us. I just suddenly *wanted* you. So I . . . you know, took off my stuff in the bathroom.'

'Well, it sure made *my* night.'

'Glad to hear it.' A sheepish look on her face, she said, 'Anyway, I just wanted you to know. In case you were wondering. You weren't the victim of a wily, plotting female. Not really.' Then she took another drink of wine.

'I never thought I was. Not really.'

Her smile lasted only a moment. Then she said, 'I also want you to know . . . I don't expect anything from you. I didn't do that last night to trap you. It just happened, you know? It doesn't mean we have to start *going* together, anything like that. I have no intention of forcing myself on you.' Her smile flickered. 'Not again, anyway.'

'It wasn't so bad.'

'Glad to hear it. But anyway, I know you're not in love with me. Okay? I don't expect you to love me. I can't take Holly's place. Not in your heart. I know that. It's not what I'm after.'

'What *are* you after.'

'I just . . .' Her eyes went shiny. 'I just don't want you to be miserable, okay?' With the back of a hand, she wiped her eyes. 'It hurts me . . . what she did to you. And to see you so . . . lonely and desolate. It just *hurts*. I want you to be *happy*, not . . .' She *really* started crying. 'Shit,' she gasped. Shaking her head fiercely, she set down her glass and got to her feet.

I stood up as she went to the door. 'Eileen . . .'

'I've . . . gotta go. I'm sorry.' She opened the door.

I hurried toward her, but she raised a hand.

'No,' she said. 'Don't.'

I stopped.

She stood in the doorway, her back to the hall, crying and shaking her head. 'I didn't come here to . . . Never mind. I feel like . . . such an idiot. I'm sorry. I don't know . . . what I was thinking.'

'Who does?' I said. 'Why don't you come back in? We'll have some more pizza and finish the wine . . .'

'No.' She raised her head, sniffed, and wiped her eyes. 'God. I'm sorry. I've gotta go.' She suddenly looked around. Then, raising her hand again like a cop halting traffic, she came forward and sidestepped over to where she'd left her purse. She picked it up. On her way back to the door, she said, 'See you sometime. I guess. If you want.'

'If you really have to go,' I said, 'let me at least walk you back.'

She shook her head. 'That's okay. No thanks. I wanta be . . . I never meant to . . . to *inflict* myself on you.'

'You haven't.'

'Oh, yeah. Oh, yeah.' Backing through the doorway, sniffing, she gave me a little wave with one hand. Then she turned and hurried down the hall.

I just stood there, gazing at the empty doorway.

I wasn't sure what had just happened. Eileen had certainly gone haywire. I'd never seen her that way before, and it left me feeling shocked and confused. And guilty.

Obviously, I should have stopped her from leaving.

She'd probably hoped I would stop her, but I hadn't.

I can still run after her.

But she'd told me not to.

Wants me to, anyway. She's probably expecting it.

'Not tonight,' I muttered, and shut my door.

Chapter Ten

I ate more pizza and drank more wine, wondering if Eileen would come back. She might walk a couple of blocks, change her mind and turn around. Who knows?

At any moment, the buzzer might ring.

If it did, Eileen would come up and apologize for her strange behavior and we would probably end up in bed. Imagining that, I thought about the look and feel of her last night and I hoped she would come back.

If I hadn't let her go, or if I'd run after her, we could've both been naked by now . . .

But then I'd be stuck with her.

At least for tonight.

If she rings the buzzer, I thought, there go my plans.

That might not be such a bad thing, either, because my plans frightened me.

There was still some wine left, so I knocked the cork back into the neck of the bottle. I put the bottle and the remaining pizza into my refrigerator. By then, Eileen had been gone for about twenty minutes.

I sat down and tried to read Coleridge for a while, but I felt groggy and my mind kept wandering. I was wasting my time, so I put the book away and went into my bedroom. The clock on my nightstand showed 7:10. I set the alarm for 11:00 p.m., then took off my clothes, shut off the light and climbed into bed.

*

ZZZZZZZZZZZZZZ!

I found myself in darkness.

My first thought was that someone was buzzing me to be let in. *Holly? Is Holly here?* Hope leaped up inside me, then fell. It can't be Holly, I realized. She's gone. It's Eileen. Eileen came back, after all.

I'll let her in and we'll make love.

Just about then, I realized nobody was buzzing to be let in. The sound came from my alarm clock.

Time to get up and start my adventure.

I reached out and killed the noise. Then I climbed out of bed. I shivered as I hurried across my room and turned on a light. The air felt cool on my bare skin, but the shivers probably had little to do with temperature, more to do with tension and excitement.

I dressed myself in undershorts, blue jeans, a dark-blue sweatshirt, socks and my brown leather high-top hiking boots.

As I sat on the edge of the bed to tie my boots, I changed my mind about them. They were excellent for long walks, but what if I needed to be swift?

So I took them off and put on a pair of Reebok running shoes instead.

I started to take my wallet, then changed my mind. It was loaded with identification: my driver's license, student ID, credit cards and so on.

What about money?

Nothing'll be open, anyway.

Dandi Donuts?

I took a ten out of my wallet, folded it and stuffed it into a front pocket of my jeans.

What else?

Nothing else from my wallet. But I pocketed my Swiss Army knife and my five-inch Maglite before leaving the bedroom. They both went into front pockets of my jeans. In the living room, I grabbed my keys.

Anything else?

A pen and paper in case I needed to take notes.

I pulled a full sheet of lined paper out of my notebook, folded it like a hanky and slipped it into a seat pocket of my jeans. Then I slid a couple of ballpoints into a front pocket.

What else?

A mask?

Why on earth would I need a mask?

Shaking my head, I left.

Downstairs, the Fishers' door stood open. I planned to ignore the old couple, but realized at the last moment that it might seem rude. So I turned my head as I walked by, nodded and smiled in.

No sign of Mrs Fisher, but 'the mister' looked up from his easy chair – positioned for a view of the hallway – and called, 'Hey there, Eddie.'

I had to stop. 'Hi, Mr Fisher.'

'How's things?'

'Not bad. How're things with you and Mrs Fisher?'

'Oh, can't complain. Saw your friend Eileen earlier. Had yourselves a nice pizza, did you?'

'It was pretty good. Well, I've got to get going. See you later, Mr Fisher.'

'Have yourself a good time, son.'

'Thanks,' I said, and took off.

It felt very good to be outside in the fresh October night. The breeze was slightly chilly. It carried a scent of chimney smoke and sent leaves drifting down sideways when they fell out of the trees along the road.

I made mental notes of my observations . . . partly because I fancied myself a writer and partly to keep my mind off my real reason for being out in the night.

When you're up to something iffy, it's better not to think about it or you might chicken out.

There's nothing *iffy* about this, I told myself. I'm taking a walk, that's all.

Over to Franklin Street.

It's a free country, I thought. The sidewalks are public property. I have every right to go over to Franklin Street. Nothing at all wrong with doing that.

I'm just a university student taking a late-night walk, minding my own business, maybe on my way to Dandi Donuts.

I'm not breaking any laws.

Nobody (except Eileen) knows I'm heartbroken. And nobody in the whole world (except me) knows how I hope in the chambers of my ruined heart to find a certain girl.

Last night, she'd simply come walking along. Her route had converged with mine as if by some miracle of timing and placement.

I was pretty sure it wouldn't happen again.

But I intended to be waiting, tonight, at the same time and place.

As I walked along, I kept a sharp lookout for trouble. In particular, I didn't want to be surprised by dogs or by the bike-riding hag.

She's probably a harmless old lady, I told myself. Maybe even nice if you get to know her.

Yeah, right.

She could be Mother Theresa, for all I cared: I didn't want her to *see* me, much less come wheeling up silently from the rear, startle the crap out of me with her ringer and speed by . . . close enough to touch me.

What if she *does* touch me?

It gave me the creeps just thinking about her and keeping watch for her.

As Falstaff says, 'The better part of valour is discretion; in the which better part I have saved my life.' Avoiding the bike hag wasn't likely to save my life, but it would do wonders for my peace of mind. Therefore, several blocks before the area where she'd put in her appearance last night, I cut over to Franklin Street.

I liked it much better there. Not only had I bailed out of the hag's territory, but I'd entered the mystery girl's.

Though I still kept a sharp watch, it was no longer just for signs of trouble; my watch now included the possibility of spying the girl.

I walked slowly, turning my head, often looking over my shoulder.

At length, I came to the sidestreet where I'd first seen her. I stopped at the corner and looked.

She wasn't coming.

Night In The Lonesome October

No one was coming, either afoot or by car . . . or by bicycle.

From where I stood, I seemed to be the only person out and about.

Though the hour was late, I was early. I hadn't kept careful track of time last night, but the girl had probably come walking toward this corner between about 12:15 and 12:30 a.m. My educated guess.

My wristwatch now showed 12:05.

At the earliest, she might not show up for another ten minutes.

Ten minutes. To most of us, ten minutes seems like a very brief period of time. Not long enough to do much of anything. However, ten minutes is ample time for a shower. A steak can usually be barbecued in ten minutes or less. And a healthy person can easily walk more than half a mile in ten minutes. At freeway speeds, ten minutes can take you more than ten miles.

But try waiting alone on a street corner in the middle of the night, and you'll discover that ten minutes can seem like a long, long time.

I only lasted five. During that period, six cars went by. A hairy man in shorts and running shoes, but no shirt, jogged up the middle of Franklin Street but paid no attention to me. I heard telephones in nearby houses ring on two separate occasions. I heard a woman shout, '*Don't you dare!*' Doors slammed shut three or four times. Two cats ran across the road. So did one opossum.

Then a gal came striding up the sidewalk, heading my way with two German shepherds trotting semi-loose around her. I couldn't tell for sure whether they were wearing leashes, but I didn't want to find out the hard way.

Abandoning my post, I turned right at the corner and headed eastward on the sidestreet.

It was Maple Avenue.

Last night, the mystery girl had come from this direction. With any luck, I might not only avoid the hounds but encounter her.

I followed Maple Avenue for about ten minutes. Though I saw no sign of the girl, the road led me into a shabbier section of town. Single-story houses with shingled sides, chain-link fences around their yards, barking dogs often *in* their yards along with collections of debris. People in this section of town didn't seem to throw anything away. Instead, when it ceased to be useful, they displayed it in their yards. Most of the yards were littered with such items as old chairs, old sofa cushions, old television sets, toilets, tires, and often entire automobiles.

God only knew what sort of *person* I might encounter in such a neighborhood.

Fortunately, none seemed to be outdoors at the moment.

At the railroad tracks, Maple Avenue descended into a dark underpass, so I turned around and headed back toward Franklin Street, walking more quickly than before.

It was 12:40 by the time I reached the intersection of Franklin and Maple.

Had I missed her?

Maybe she's just a little late, I thought.

Or maybe last night was a fluke; the one and only time she had ever, or *would* ever, walk that particular route at that time of night.

Then again, maybe she does it regularly, but only once a week.

I looked one way. I looked the other. I looked all around.

Where are you? Where are you?

You're somewhere, I told myself. And I'll find you.

If Ahab could find the White Whale, whose far-flung boundaries were those of the seven seas, I certainly should be able to locate one girl in the small town of Willmington.

Chapter Eleven

I approached her house from the opposite side of the street and looked at it casually as I strolled by.

The front porch and all the windows were dark, the same as last night.

Was the girl still on her way home?

Had she already returned from tonight's journey?

Maybe she'd stayed in and had gone to bed early.

Was she there in a dark upstairs room, fast asleep in her bed?

Not daring to stop and keep a vigil on the house, I continued to the corner. I crossed to her side of the street, went to the next corner, made a right and hiked southward along the back side of the block. At the corner, I made another right and returned to Franklin Street. This time, I walked up Franklin on her side.

As I neared her house, a light came on toward the rear of its ground floor.

My heart lurched. Then it pounded fast and sickeningly hard as I walked up the driveway of the house next door, glanced around to see if I were being observed, and slipped through a space in the bushes.

The glow from the window pulled me like a promise of treasure.

Never in my life had I crept up to a window in an attempt to spy on anyone. This is not to say I'd never been tempted to give it a try. In the past, however, I'd always fought off the temptation; my urge to sneak a peek was feeble compared to my terror of being caught at it.

Tonight was different. Not only had my world been blasted apart by the loss of Holly, but I was so vastly intrigued by the mystery girl that I *had* to look into the window.

As I neared it, I felt weak with fear. I trembled all over. Underneath my sweatshirt, perspiration poured down my torso. My underwear stuck to my sweaty rear end. My genitals felt as if they were trying to shrivel up and vanish.

Fear of being caught was certainly part of it. But so was fear of myself, that I should be doing this. And mixed with the fear was a horrible, nerve-racking anticipation of what I might see when I looked through the window.

Someone had turned on the light, and it was still on.

Someone was in the room.

The girl?

Breathless and trembling, I looked around to make sure nobody was watching me. Then I moved closer to the window. Because the house had a crawl-space, the windowsill was slightly higher than my eye level.

Standing close to its left-hand corner, I hooked my fingertips over the sill and raised myself on tiptoes.

What if she's looking straight at me?

She wasn't.

Peering through the glass at the bottom corner of the window, I saw a woman standing in the lighted kitchen, leaning back against a counter. In her left hand was a bottle of tequila. She held the bottle by its neck, took a sip, lowered it by her side, and just stared forward.

Not looking anywhere close to my window.

She didn't appear to be upset or nervous or troubled. Not like she'd come into the kitchen to sneak a few sips. More as if she'd simply found herself in the mood for a taste of tequila and wandered in. She seemed tranquil, almost languid.

Could this be the girl's mother?

Not likely. My mystery girl was probably at least eighteen years old, and this woman looked no older than thirty.

Her sister?

Whatever her relation to my girl, she was certainly pretty. Even with mussed hair and no make-up on, she looked a lot more attractive than most women. Also, she had a good figure and her white nightgown didn't hide much of it.

The nightie was very short, reaching only about halfway down her thighs. Its top was cut so low that I could see quite a lot of bare skin between her breasts, down to a couple of inches below her sternum.

Also, the gown was diaphanous . . . made of such fine, delicate material that I could see through it. Her nipples were large and dark and erect. She seemed to have a ladybug tattoo on her left hip. And to paraphrase Mickey Spillane, I saw that she was a natural blonde.

My genitals started to unshrivel. Rapidly.

She raised the tequila bottle and took another sip. When she lowered it, the strap of her nightgown fell off her left shoulder and down her upper arm. Without the strap for support, the gown slipped off her left breast.

I thought, *Holy shit!*

She didn't seem bothered at all that one of her breasts was naked. And why should she be? She was alone in her kitchen in the middle of the night and had no idea anyone might be watching her through a window.

No idea *I* was there, spying on her, getting harder by the moment.

As she raised the bottle to her mouth for another drink, her arm lifted the thin strap of her nightgown only slightly. While she held the bottle up, her arm obstructed my view of her breast. Then I could see it again.

I knew I should look away. *Look* away? I should *run* away.

I was violating this woman's privacy, ogling her body, *and* breaking the law.

I must've been nuts to come to her window at all!

But I'd done it in search of my girl, not to leer at this sultry stranger. *I've gotta get out of here!*

My eyes stayed locked on her.

I *can't* leave, I realized. Not as long as she keeps standing there, looking the way she does.

Then her head began to turn in my direction.

I sank out of sight and took my fingers off the sill.

What if she saw me?

I'd ducked pretty fast. Also, it's hard to see out of windows at night, especially if you're in a bright room and there isn't much light outside. Mostly, you only see your own reflection backed by darkness.

My face had been right up at her window, though, and probably illuminated by the light from the kitchen.

She *might've* seen me.

Staying low, I crept alongside the wall toward the front of the house. A safe distance from the kitchen window, I slipped into a gap in the bushes. Crouching there, I took a quick look around. I saw nobody, so I stepped out onto the neighbor's driveway.

At the foot of the driveway, I turned to the right . . . toward the house. It seemed like a wild, risky move. A person in my position should've gone the other way. I was feeling reckless, though. And lucky. And curious. So I stepped past the row of bushes.

Toward the rear of the house, light still glowed from the kitchen window.

Otherwise, the house remained dark.

Had she seen me?

I suddenly doubted it.

For a moment, I considered sneaking back to the window for another look.

Don't press your luck.

Already, I'd left the house behind.

As I neared the corner, a car turned onto Franklin a couple of blocks to the north.

A cop car?

My stomach went squirmy.

She *might've* called the cops. Or maybe one of the neighbors did.

No time to think.

I dodged up the nearest driveway, ran to the front of the car parked there, sank to my knees and hunkered down. Soon, the grumble of an engine intruded on the night's other sounds. It came from the north, growing louder, louder.

Though I cowered in hiding, excitement was mixed with my fear. I had an urge to scream, but also a strange inclination to giggle.

The car now seemed to be passing directly in front of the driveway. I heard not only its engine, but the hiss of its tires and a quiet song from inside, Garth Brooks singing 'The Dance'.

I took a peek.

The car was a large convertible with a guy behind the wheel.

False alarm.

Which didn't mean someone *hadn't* called the police. A squad car might be on its way this very moment. If I left my hiding place now, I might be caught out in the open.

I decided to stay put for ten minutes. If no cops came along by then, I could be fairly sure nobody had reported me.

My wristwatch showed 1:10 a.m.

The concrete was tough on my knees, so I turned my back to the car and sat down. And waited.

Ten minutes. Again.

I sat there with my legs crossed and thought about how strange it was that I should be hiding in front of a car in a stranger's driveway at such an hour. What would Holly think?

I'm here because of you, you filthy bitch. If I get caught by the cops . . . or killed or something . . . it'll be thanks to you.

I hoped she would cringe with guilt for many years.

Fat chance. She doesn't give a shit what happens to me. Probably never did.

That's not true, I thought. Be fair to her. She cared.

Only not very much. And not at all once she ran into Jay-Jay the Prick. May she rot in Hell.

You don't mean that, I told myself.

Sure I don't.

Look on the bright side, I thought. If she hadn't dumped me, I never would've gone out wandering last night, never would've seen *the girl.*

I wouldn't have seen *the woman* tonight, either.

The bitch did me a favor. I should thank her.

Even while I sat there thinking such things, part of me was appraising Ed Logan . . . finding him to be melodramatic and bitter and childish . . . and half mad.

Had I lost my mind?

Only a crazy person would set his alarm clock, get up in the middle of the night and go searching through town for a complete stranger he'd spent a while *stalking* the night before. And in the process, sneaking up to a window and spying on a half-naked woman.

All of a sudden, I'd turned into a Peeping Tom.

What next?

What had *better* be next, I thought, is home. Call the whole thing off. Go back to my apartment and go to bed. Get up in the morning and go to class. Get studious. Get serious with Eileen. Face it, she's probably better in every way than Holly *ever* was.

Images filled my mind of Eileen last night. The surprise of finding that she'd taken off her bra in secret. The delight of putting my hand down the front of her jeans, slipping my fingers into her juicy heat. And then how she'd felt gliding down, wet and snug, slowly impaling herself on me.

How can stalking an unknown girl compare to that?

How can peering through a window at a woman in a nightgown, even if one breast is showing, be more tempting than what I'd already seen and done with Eileen?

It's madness, I thought.

And this is the end of it.

I looked at my wristwatch. Twenty minutes had gone by, so I abandoned my hiding place. At the first corner, I turned right. At the next corner, I turned right again and walked to Franklin Street.

A turn to the left would take me back toward home.

A turn to the right would take me toward *her* house again.

Naturally, I turned right.

My heart beat faster as I neared the house.

If the light's still on, I told myself, I won't go over and look in. I'll just keep on walking. I won't look.

The kitchen light was off.

Relieved but disappointed, I walked on.

Chapter Twelve

Is that where she lives? I wondered as I continued northward on Franklin Street. It was almost certainly the house I'd watched her enter last night.

Later, though, I'd seen her several blocks away while Eileen was driving us back from Dandi Donuts. What was the girl doing out on the streets again no more than an hour after sneaking into her house?

Maybe it *isn't* her house.

Last night, I'd suspected she might be returning home from a rendezvous with her lover. But what if I had it the wrong way around? Maybe I hadn't seen her returning home, but sneaking *into* the house of her lover?

Certainly possible.

If so, who was her lover? The husband of the woman I'd observed in the kitchen? That could explain the drinking.

What if *they're* lovers?

My God.

There is no husband? The woman lives alone in the house, and the girl comes to her late at night. That might even explain why the woman had gone into her kitchen at such an hour; to have a few sips while she waited for the girl to show up. Or maybe the girl was late and the woman was worried.

Is she there now?

When I'd passed the house just a few minutes ago, the kitchen light had been off. Maybe the woman had simply decided to quit

64

drinking and go to bed. Or maybe the girl had finally arrived.

I imagined them together in the kitchen. The girl perhaps taking a sip of the tequila. Then kissing the woman on the mouth. Then putting a hand on her bare breast.

It got me pretty excited, thinking about that.

Should I go back to the house?

Are you out of your mind?

Forget about it, I told myself. *Especially* forget about it if they're a couple of lesbians; I wouldn't stand a chance with either one of them.

It's just as well, I thought. Quit all this nonsense before I end up in trouble.

Go home.

Why not go to Dandi Donuts first?

And eat a couple of those sweet, greasy donuts two nights in a row? Bad idea.

But the place seemed like a safe, peaceful refuge. I didn't *have* to eat donuts. Just sit there in the light and have a cup of coffee, rest for the hike back.

What if Eileen's there?

She won't be, I told myself.

She *might* be. It's a place she might go if she wants to find me.

I almost gave up on going to the donut shop. But I didn't. For one thing, Eileen wasn't very likely to be there.

I'll check before I go in.

But it might not be so bad if Eileen *is* there. She cares about me. She'll drive me home. We'll go up to my rooms and so what if she isn't Holly . . . so what if I'm not in love with her?

To avoid walking by the thrift shop's window, I stayed on Franklin and didn't cut over until I was past Dandi. I walked west on Dale, the sidestreet on which Eileen had parked her car last night.

Tonight, her car wasn't there.

I looked in Dandi's windows, anyway. Two customers were there, sitting far apart. Both were men. So I entered. As I walked toward the counter, my eyes slid over to the display case. Half a dozen glazed old-fashioneds were there, crusty and golden and glistening.

They looked luscious.

No way, I thought. I'll turn into a fat slob.

The clerk came up to the counter.

'What can I get you?'

'A medium coffee and two glazed old-fashioneds.'

So what if I turn into a fat slob?

Holly gonna stop loving me?

'For here or to go?' the clerk asked.

'For here.'

I wondered if he remembered me from last night. And if he did, was he curious about Eileen and why I'd come here without her tonight?

He must get all kinds, I thought.

I paid him, then turned around with my coffee and donuts. And wondered where to sit. I wanted to stay away from the two strangers. Neither of them, however, was sitting near the table I'd shared with Eileen last night.

Nor near the table where Holly and I had sat together the night we'd come here last spring.

I'll never leave you. You'll leave me.

The table would be haunted by her. The ghost of my lost love who wasn't dead but gone just the same.

Fuck up my appetite.

I went to a table at the opposite end of the room from where I'd sat with Holly . . . one table away from last night's table, which was straight in front of me. That was okay, though. The memories of last night didn't hurt.

In fact, they were pretty good.

I lifted my Styrofoam cup of coffee, gently blew the steam away, and raised it to my mouth. My nose and eyes felt the heat. When I took a sip, the coffee was too hot on my lips and tongue. I set it down.

Somebody stepped past me.

I looked up. The man stopped, turned around and smiled down at me. He wasn't one of the customers I'd already seen. Must've come in after I did.

'I could use a cup of coffee,' he said. 'Can you spare a buck?'

Clean and well groomed, he didn't *look* like a bum. Women would probably consider him handsome. With his golden hair and chiseled features, he might've stepped off the cover of a romance novel. He wore a blue chambray shirt that was partly unbuttoned, tucked into a pair of tight blue jeans.

Nothing at all threatening about him . . . except his request.

And maybe his eyes and smile. His eyes seemed too intense and his smile was too big, a little lopsided and twitchy. He had clean, straight teeth, but I felt as if I could see too many of them.

I suddenly wanted to get the hell away. But what about my coffee and donuts?

And what if this guy follows me outside?

'Sure,' I answered. Though he'd only asked for one dollar, I took a five out of my wallet. 'Have some donuts, too.' My hand trembled as I reached out and handed the money to him.

'Thanks, pal.'

He went over to the counter.

It's only five bucks, I thought. I can afford it.

In fact, my parents were fairly well off. Money had never been a concern of mine, but I didn't like being *asked* for it. People had no right to ask strangers for money. It was almost like a hold-up . . . using an implied threat instead of a gun or knife.

The man came back and sat across the table from me.

Shit!

With my money, he'd bought a cup of coffee, a jelly donut and a maple bar.

'What's your name?' he asked.

'Ed.'

'Thanks for the loan, Ed.'

Loan, my ass.

'You're welcome.'

Though his purchases hadn't cost more than two or three dollars, he didn't return my change. And I didn't dare ask him for it.

He raised his cup of coffee, squinting slightly as the steam got in his eyes. Then he took a few sips and set the cup down. 'You mind me sitting here?' he asked.

'No,' I lied.

'Glad to hear it. I like you, Ed.'

'Thanks.'

'My kind of guy.'

'Ah.'

Oh, shit. He's gay. He's putting moves on me.

There was nothing effeminate about him. If anything, he seemed perhaps *too* masculine.

Some of them are like that, I thought.

He was certainly fit. Not bulked up, but trim. A lot of them are like that, too.

'I'm Randy,' he said.

'Hi, Randy.'

He reached across the table to shake hands. I didn't want to offend him by refusing, so I shook his hand. It was bigger than mine. He squeezed hard. Hard enough to hurt.

Real nice, I thought.

After letting go, he asked, 'You live around here?'

He wants to go home with me?

'Not really.'

'Aren't you going to eat?'

Nodding, I took a bite of donut. The outside crunched. The donut probably tasted spectacular if I could taste it.

He took a bite of his jelly donut.

I drank some coffee.

'Thought maybe you lived around here someplace,' Randy said.

'Oh?'

'I've seen you the past couple of nights.'

'Really?'

What had he seen?

'It's the donuts,' I said, and took another bite. 'I've been coming out here for donuts the past couple of nights.'

'If you say so,' Randy said.

Oh, God! Why is he saying this stuff? What does he know? Has he been following me?

'Is there a problem?' I asked.

I don't like Peeping Toms, I expected him to say.

'No problem. I just want to talk.'

'Okay.'

'About that gal,' he said.

Oh, my God.

'What about her?'

'She your girlfriend?'

Is *who* my girlfriend? *What* gal? Is he trying to find out if I'm straight?

'Maybe,' I said.

'She's a real fox.'

I nodded slightly. Maybe Randy wasn't gay after all.

'She's got a real nice rack on her.'

Was he talking about Eileen? Sounded that way.

Leaning toward me, he stared into my eyes. His pale-blue eyes looked eager. 'Does she put out for you?' he asked.

Maybe they look that way, I thought, because of some medical condition.

Yeah. Lunacy.

I was not about to tell a stranger that Eileen had 'put out' for me. On the other hand, I didn't have the guts to tell him to mind his own business.

'No,' I said.

'You've got one of those *platonic* relationships?'

'Guess so.'

'Don't you *want* her?'

'I didn't say that.'

'A great-looking gal. And those tits. Terrific tits.'

'You don't have to talk about her that way. She's a nice person.'

'If she's so nice, how come you're not putting it to her? Bet she's really hot. Hot and juicy.'

'I wouldn't know.'

I'd hardly touched my coffee and donuts, but I would've gladly abandoned them to get away from this man. I didn't move, though. Far better to deal with him in Dandi Donuts than out on the empty streets.

'What's her name?' he asked.

'Sarah.'

'Sarah? Nice name. Suits her. What's her last name?'

'Lee' almost popped out of my mouth. I got as far as the L, so I finished up with, 'LaFarge.'

'Sarah LaFarge?'

I nodded.

'A very euphonious name.'

'Guess so,' I said. For some reason, this guy using the word euphonious bothered me.

'Why isn't Sarah LaFarge with you tonight?' he asked.

'She had other things to do. We're just friends. We don't . . . *go* together or anything like that.'

'Not your girlfriend, and yet she spent almost an hour in here last night waiting for you. Sitting over there all alone.'

'I didn't know it was that long,' I said.

He nodded. 'Then *you* had to show up and ruin my plans.'

Another sick feeling rushed through me. 'Plans?'

'You know.'

I shook my head.

'My plans for *her*. For Sarah.'

'Ah.'

'I had special plans for her. You ruined them last night, but now you're back. And so are my plans.'

'I see.'

'Do you?'

'You want to . . . go out with her?'

'Wanta go *in* her, Ed.'

'Hey, look . . .'

His smile spread, showing me his rows of straight white teeth. 'She'll love it. They all do. So where does she live?'

70

No harm in giving him a wrong address. So I said, 'I guess I can write it down for you.'

'I have a better idea. Why don't you *take* me there?'

Chapter Thirteen

'I don't have a car.'

'I do,' Randy said.

Apparently, he could afford a car but not coffee and donuts.

'Even if I took you there . . . she lives in a secure building. You wouldn't be able to just go in and get her.'

'She'll come out for you, won't she?'

'It's . . .' I looked at my watch. 'Two-fifteen.'

'She'll come out for you.'

Nodding, I said, 'Maybe.'

'Let's finish up our coffee and donuts.'

I resumed eating. So did Randy. He kept smiling at me as he chewed.

As *I* chewed, I tried to think. Mostly, I couldn't believe this was happening to me. Or to Eileen, for that matter.

I can't let this guy get her.

I took a deep breath and said, 'I'm not so sure it's a good idea to go over there, Randy.'

'Sounds like a good idea to me.'

'Not at this hour. Maybe you should give me your phone number. I can pass it on to her tomorrow, and . . .'

'I don't have a phone, Ed.'

'Well, maybe we can arrange for her to meet you someplace.'

'Do you think she'd do that?'

'Sure. I mean, probably. Maybe the three of us could get together for a lunch.'

He narrowed his eyes and nodded. 'Maybe, maybe. But I don't think so. What I really think, Eddie, is that you want to keep her for yourself. There won't be any lunch. You don't want me laying a finger on her. Isn't that right?'

'No. If she wants to have lunch with you, it's fine with me. She's *not* my girlfriend.'

'Really?'

'Really.'

'Let's go to her place.'

I looked at him.

'Right now.'

'But I told you—'

'I know what you told me. Let's go.'

I looked around the donut shop. Aside from me and Randy, only one customer remained. He had his back to us. The clerk wasn't behind the counter, either; he must've gone into the back room.

'Come on,' Randy said quietly.

I nodded. 'Okay. But I need to use the bathroom first.'

'Fine. I'll go in with you. We can compare sizes.'

I got to my feet. 'Let's just leave,' I said. 'I'll try to hold it.'

'Fine.'

He gestured for me to lead the way. I walked toward the door. The clerk was still in back. The customer didn't look around. I opened the door and walked out into the night.

Randy came out and grabbed my arm. Hard.

'I don't think we should be doing this,' I said as he pulled me along the sidewalk. Rhett and Zelda gazed out the thrift-shop window at us. 'I wasn't kidding about her being in a secure building. We won't be able to get in. I think you should let go of me and . . .'

'Think again.'

A Toyota pickup truck was parked at the curb. Randy towed me into the street, pulled open the driver's door and said, 'Get in and move over.'

He kept the tight grip on my upper left arm while I climbed into the pickup. Then he followed me in. When he was behind the wheel, he shut his door. Then he jerked my arm, pulling me toward him, and stuck his face up to mine. 'You gonna give me any trouble?'

'No.'

'Promise?'

'I promise.'

'Good boy,' he said and suddenly kissed me with his mouth open.

It's *me* he wants? The Eileen stuff was a lie?

He shoved his tongue into my mouth.

Groaning, I twisted my head away. His lips and tongue slid across my cheek. He laughed as I wiped his spit off.

'How'd you like it?' he asked. He still had that grip on my arm.

'Not much.' My voice sounded almost like a whimper.

'You'll get it again if you don't procure Sarah for me. Fact is, I'll give you the works. It's you or her, Eddie. Who will it be?'

'Her,' I said.

Randy let go of my arm, reached into a pocket of his jeans and pulled out his keys. The keys jingled a little while he searched for the one he wanted. Then he reached forward and slid a key into the ignition.

As he turned the key, I twisted sideways in my seat and pounded a ballpoint pen into him. It popped through his jeans and into the top of his right thigh.

He yelled, '*Yahh!*'

I flung open the passenger door and leaped out and ran. Not toward Dandi Donuts; I could too easily see Randy chasing me inside and dragging me out, nobody trying to help me. Instead, I ran past the rear of his pickup and poured on the speed. That's what they tell you to do so the driver can't chase you without going in reverse.

I glanced over my shoulder to see what was happening.

The back-up lights came on.

Eyes forward, I didn't watch the pickup speed toward me but I sure heard it.

To my right was Division Street, to my left a row of store fronts. Nothing was open. I ran past recessed entryways and display windows. If I could get across the next sidestreet, I would be on a residential block where I could cut across lawns . . . but the street was too far away. And if I did try to cross it, Randy might hit me with his truck.

His truck appeared beside me, moving backward, keeping pace with me. Its passenger door was still open. If he got any closer to the curb, it would hit a parking meter or light post.

I thought he might shout threats at me, but he didn't.

Didn't make a sound, just stayed even with me.

What if he's got a gun?

I did a fast stop and reversed my direction. He kept going backward.

Just as his brakes squealed, I turned my head toward the store fronts and saw a dark space between two of the buildings – a space too narrow for Randy's truck. I must've been looking the other way when I ran past it the first time.

I rushed in.

Behind me, brakes squealed again. Tires skidded. The engine shut off.

He's coming after me on foot?

A door slammed.

He is!

I picked up speed. The space between the buildings was only three or four feet wide and paved like a walkway. It had a pale area at the very end, probably where the buildings stopped. Down in front of my feet, however, was blackness. No telling what might be there. Invisible debris crackled and crunched under my shoes. Sometimes, my feet landed on small, hard objects. I kicked a can and sent it skittering away. I crunched broken glass.

At any moment, something might snag my feet and send me flying headlong . . .

I wanted to slow down, but didn't dare.

Randy was coming, all right. I heard the quick pounding of his boots on the pavement behind me. They had an uneven rhythm. Because of his wound?

The way I'd stabbed his leg, it was a wonder he could run at all.

I wished I'd gotten him with my Swiss Army knife. But the knife was in the left front pocket of my jeans. Randy would've seen me go for it. If he missed that, he definitely would've noticed me struggling to pry out one of its folding blades.

So I'd used a ballpoint instead.

Should've stuck it in his fucking throat!

At least he wasn't gaining on me. He didn't *seem* to be, anyway.

I'll be okay if he doesn't have a gun.

He must *not* have one, I thought, or he would've used it by now. Unless he's afraid of the noise.

I suddenly smashed full-speed into something. I didn't know what it was, at first. As I plowed it down and tumbled over it, though, the feel and sounds and aromas told me it was probably a shopping cart . . . a cart parked sideways in the narrow space and loaded past the brim with the treasures of its homeless proprietor.

I landed on *him*. He was cadaverous and stank of garbage and cigarette smoke and excrement and he screamed in my face. I tried to shove myself off him. His coat felt like sticky, moist tweed.

He clutched my shirt.

'*Gotcha!*' he gasped.

'*Let go!*'

He didn't. I slugged him in the face and he let go and I scurried off him and ran for the grayness at the end of the buildings.

Just as I got there, somebody either fell over the shopping cart or kicked it.

I broke into a lighted alley, cut to the right and ran hard for the cross-street at the south end of the block. Along the way, I glanced over my shoulder again and again.

No sign of Randy.

At the mouth of the alley, I dodged to the left and ran across the street.

No traffic anywhere in sight.

No people, either.

I ran farther to the left, rounded the corner of the block and raced past the first two houses. They had porch lights on, but the third house didn't. That porch wasn't screened in. It had no door, either, but was roofed and surrounded by a wooden railing about three feet high. The railing had a row of thick bushes in front of it.

I ran up to the porch, silently climbed its stairs and dropped to the floor behind the railing, totally hidden from anyone going by.

Chapter Fourteen

Every so often, a car passed. Or a truck. I didn't dare take a peek. I figured it might be Randy in his pickup truck, searching for me.

But I'd been on the porch about half an hour, and he hadn't found me yet. He probably *wouldn't* find me, either – at least so long as I stayed put.

I'll wait another hour just to make sure.

Ten minutes times six.

The hour would pass very quickly if I fell asleep. I was wide awake, though, sitting with my legs crossed, my back toward the front railing. From the half-hour I'd already waited, my butt ached and my back felt a little sore.

Off to my right, maybe eight feet away, the porch had an old-fashioned swing that hung by chains from a ceiling beam.

I could stretch out on that, I thought.

But it would probably make all sorts of noise if I put my weight on it. It was noisy enough *without* me.

The swing liked to move all by itself. With the help of a breeze, I supposed.

After long silences, it would stir, taking me by surprise with groans and creaking sounds.

But that wasn't my biggest problem with the swing.

About fifteen minutes into my first half-hour, I'd noticed something unsettling about it.

Though some areas and shapes on the porch looked black, there were also gray places. I couldn't always quite be sure what I was really seeing. Sometimes, when I looked at the swing, I thought someone was sitting on it. Just sitting there, not moving at all – and staring at me.

I knew nobody *was* on the swing, but it gave me the heebie-jeebies just the same.

I tried to stop looking at it, but it kept pulling my eyes back . . . almost as if part of me *enjoyed* the torment.

If I'm staying any longer, I thought, I'd better get it settled – crawl over, reach out and touch the swing to *prove* nobody's there.

But what if I reach out and my fingers meet someone's knee? Or what if a hand suddenly clutches my wrist?

Ridiculous. These were fears for a five-year-old, and I was twenty.

Amazing, though, how being alone in a strange place at three o'clock in the morning shaves the years off. I *felt* like a kid again. A kid in bed late at night, wide awake, gazing at the partly open door of his closet, waiting for a horror to spring out and come for him.

Forget Randy . . . who's that on the swing?

Nobody, I told myself. Nobody's there at all. It's just shadows.

Then 'nobody' struck a match.

In its flare, I glimpsed a leering, ancient face. An instant later, the match flew at me, followed by a quiet cackle.

Chapter Fifteen

As the match scratched a bright curve through the night and bounced off the sleeve of my sweatshirt, the sound I made was a quick, high-pitched, '*Eeeeeee!*'

Then I was scurrying up, twisting around and leaping from the top of the porch stairs. I hit the ground running. Without a glance back, I cut diagonally across the front yard. The sidewalk felt like a race-track. I sprinted, arms pumping, legs flying, clothes flapping, sneakers smacking the concrete.

At the corner, I sprang off the curb and dashed across the next street. Partway down the block after that, I slowed to a walk and looked back.

Nobody behind me.

I'd been chased this far only by my goosebumps. Though breath-less and sweaty, I still felt their chill. I was crawly almost everywhere: thighs, balls, spine, arms, nipples, nape of neck, scalp and forehead.

God Almighty, I thought. I must've been on that porch for thirty-five or forty minutes . . . with *him!* Why'd he just *sit* there?

What was he *doing* there?

Probably just likes to sit out on his porch at night and watch the world go by.

At three o'clock in the morning?

Hell, yes, I thought. That's when all the good stuff happens.

I chuckled nervously.

Continuing to walk, I turned halfway around to make sure nobody was coming toward me from the rear.

The coast looked clear.

For no good reason, it suddenly occurred to me that perhaps the old man was *stranded* on the swing. Maybe he was paralyzed from a stroke or something, and his family had put him outside after supper so he could enjoy the autumn evening. Then they'd forgotten he was out there and gone to bed.

He hadn't moved or spoken to me because he *couldn't*. He only had use of his hands. The match had been his version of an emergency flare.

But why the cackle?

Because he's a lunatic, that's why. This damn town is FULL of lunatics!

It isn't the town, I told myself. It's the hour. At this hour, probably *everyplace* is full of crazy people. All the sane citizens are either at night jobs or asleep in their beds. The loonies rule the town.

But what if the old guy *is* paralyzed? I wondered. Maybe he tried to ask me for help but the cackle was the best he could do.

Should I go back and check on him?

'Shit,' I muttered.

I sure didn't want to do that. But I felt that maybe I *ought* to.

No!

If he was capable of striking a match and *throwing* it at me, he could've let me know he was there when I first showed up. He wasn't stranded on the porch; he was just a nutty old shit with a mean streak.

I didn't go back.

Near the end of the next block, I heard the sound of an engine. I looked back. Headlights pushed their brightness into the intersection behind me. Not waiting to find out if they belonged to Randy's pickup . . . or whether it would turn in my direction . . . I ducked and plunged into a row of bushes.

On the other side, I found myself at the edge of a lawn. In front of me was a two-story house, all its windows dark.

Crouched and motionless, I listened.

The engine sound was gone. If not gone, it had faded with distance until it blended in with the rest of the night's quiet hum and buzz.

Unless perhaps the driver had stopped and shut his engine off.

Maybe nearby.

Maybe because he'd spotted me.

Staying low, I crept away from the bushes and hurried to the rear corner of the house. The back yard appeared to have a picnic table, lawn chairs and a barbecue. I didn't see any people, so I hurried across the grass . . . keeping my eyes on the chairs.

Nobody *seemed* to be in any of them. Looking at them gave me the creeps, anyway.

When I came to the cinder-block wall at the other side of the yard, I looked back.

I saw no one.

With nobody chasing me, climbing the six-foot wall held no appeal. So I walked alongside it, making my way slowly through the shadows between the wall and the house. Ahead of me, beyond the front yard of the house, was a sidewalk and a street.

What street? I wondered.

I had no idea.

I'm lost?

The notion gave me an uneasy flutter that was different from my fears of bodily harm by Randy, different from the eerie fright the old man had given me. This fear felt like a slip toward unreality.

What if I'm really lost and can't find my way home?

'Ain't gonna happen,' I whispered, trying to calm myself with the sound of my own voice.

Soon as I get to a corner and see the street signs . . .

On the sidewalk directly in front of me, maybe thirty feet away, the mystery girl sauntered by. Face forward, one hand stuffed into a seat pocket of her jeans, one hand swinging by her side, hips swaying, pony-tail flipping behind her head.

She looked as if she owned the night.

I didn't move, just stood there astonished and watched her.

When she was out of sight, I began to doubt my senses. Certainly, *someone* had just walked by. But *her*? It seemed too strange and wonderful.

I hurried to the sidewalk and looked to the right.

There she was! Almost to the next corner.

When she started across the street, I followed her.

All thoughts of going home were lost. I'd found her! She was in sight! If I ran, I could catch up to her in a matter of seconds, see her close up, talk to her . . .

Scare the hell out of her.

I didn't want to scare her, though. I didn't even feel up to meeting her. For now, all I wanted was to follow her and watch her. My mystery girl.

While earlier, I'd felt the terror of a child waiting in bed for the closet monster to come for him, now I felt like the same child on a wonderful Christmas morning at first glimpse of the tree's bright colored lights and the treasures brought by Santa.

Awestruck, shivery with an almost painful sense of pleasure, I followed her down the next block.

So far, she hadn't looked back.

I picked up my pace. The gap began to close. She grew larger, more distinct. The nearer I came to her, the nearer I yearned to be.

Careful! Slow down! Can't let her know I'm here!

We must've both heard the engine sound at the same moment.

Randy?

I froze.

The girl didn't freeze, didn't flinch, simply glided off to the side and vanished among the shadows of a lawn.

I rushed over to a tree in the grassy strip between the sidewalk and the curb. It had a trunk as wide as my body. I hid behind it, standing and ready to run.

Peeking around the side of the trunk, I saw a car cruise through the intersection. A car, not a pickup truck. But it had a rack of lights on its roof.

Cops!

The police car seemed to be in no hurry. It rolled through the intersection, crackles and beeps and senseless jabber coming from its radio, and kept on going.

Its sounds faded.

I watched the lawn where the girl had vanished.

And watched it.

Minutes went by, but she didn't reappear.

What's she waiting for?

While I waited, my mind replayed her vanishing act: the grace and speed with which she'd whirled and leaped and plunged into darkness. Like a ballerina. Like a sprite. Like a ninja.

Maybe she turned herself into a shadow.

Sure thing, I thought, scoffing at the notion even though it almost seemed possible given the strangeness of the night and the way I felt about the girl.

I continued to wait.

She didn't come out.

What if she knew I was back here and now she's staying hidden, waiting to see what I do?

Suppose I just resume walking and pretend I don't even know she exists?

Heart thudding, I stepped out from behind my tree. On the sidewalk, I looked all around as if afraid someone might be spying on *me* (in case she was watching). Then I followed the sidewalk toward the corner.

She's probably watching me right now!

My throat tightened. My mouth went dry. My heart beat even faster and harder.

Watching me, appraising me. Have I been stalking her? Am I a threat?

Soon, I was striding casually past the place where she'd vanished.

I kept my face turned away.

See? I'm not interested. I don't even know you're there. Besides, I'm harmless. You've got no reason to be afraid of me. Why don't you come out?

She didn't.

I reached the corner, stepped off the curb and walked across the street. I continued past the corner house, then doubled back in its yard and crouched in a dark place behind some bushes and waited for the girl to show herself.

I waited and waited.

And began to suspect that she wasn't even there anymore. Instead of hunkering down and hiding, maybe she had slipped off into the darkness and hurried to someplace far away.

I wanted to return and search the lawn for her.

But she *might* still be there, patiently waiting. My return would confirm she had a stalker.

It wasn't worth the risk.

At last, I gave up and headed for home.

Chapter Sixteen

I was lost for a while, and had to check the signs at three different intersections before I found a street name I recognized. That street would lead me back to Division, so I followed it. Not all the way, though. Often, I took detours in case someone might be tailing me. A few times, I ducked out of sight behind trees, bushes or fences.

The sky was gray with the approach of dawn by the time I entered my apartment building. The Fishers' door was shut. I made my way silently upstairs. The long, dim hallway was empty. I went to my door, tried to make no noise as I unlocked it, and stepped into my room.

I shut the door, locked it.

Safe!

It took me about five minutes to wash, brush my teeth, use the toilet, take off my clothes and climb into bed. Rolling on to my side, I reached out and picked up the alarm clock. And groaned.

If I set it for 7:00 a.m., that would give me almost two hours of sleep and leave enough time to work in a quick shower before heading off for my eight o'clock Romantic Literature class.

Oh, well. That's why I'd taken the nap last night.

I set the alarm, turned off the lamp, rolled over and shut my eyes.

Far as I know, I fell asleep right away.

And dreamed horrible dreams. Several times, I flinched awake with a frightened gasp, breathless, my body bathed in sweat, only to look at my clock and discover it was too early to get up. So I closed my eyes and tried again and fell into another nightmare.

I only remember the last of them.

I was lost among the dark streets of town, hurrying from block to block. Every time I found street signs, they bore strange names. *I'll never get back in time for class!* As I hurried along, I saw a girl at the next corner. She wore a loose, white gown that drifted behind her as she walked. *Maybe she knows where I am!* I hurried after her.

Is it *the girl*? I wondered. I couldn't tell.

But she was walking away, so I broke into a run. I quickly gained on her. As I closed in, I realized she might be frightened by my quick approach. So I called out, '*Excuse me, miss. I think I'm lost. Could you help me . . .?*'

She turned around.

She was an old, old man . . . the man from the porch. Cackling, he raised his arms and trotted toward me. I whirled around and ran.

He's an old bastard, I thought. He'll never catch me.

When I looked back, however, he was riding a bicycle and gaining on me fast.

I turned to face him. I wanted my knife, but when I tried to take it from the pocket of my jeans, I realized I was naked.

Where did I leave my clothes?

I couldn't even remember taking them off.

But there was no time to worry about them now, because the old man in the gown was speeding closer on his bike. He was hunched over the handlebars, grinning, a pencil clamped between his teeth.

Oh God, he's gonna get me with the pencil! I'll die of lead poisoning!

It isn't lead, I thought. It's graphite. I felt some slight relief at the realization.

'*Gonna shove it up your ass, honey!*' he yelled. '*Gonna give you the works!*'

If only I had my knife! I looked down again to make sure I didn't. I was still naked.

Damn! This is what I get for taking off my clothes! It's all Holly's fault!

I seemed to recall we'd been making love in a park somewhere, and that's why I was naked.

Where is she? I wondered. Maybe she can get this guy off me.

Did he get her first?

'*Got her right here!*' the old man answered from behind me as if he'd heard my thoughts.

How can he talk with a pencil in his mouth?

I looked back.

The pencil was no longer clamped between his teeth. It was in his hand, upright, poked into Holly's neck stump . . . He held her severed head high in his right hand like a big, all-day sucker on a stick. Her eyes were open, her hair flowing in the breeze. '*Hi, honey!*' she called to me. '*Stop running away.*'

I felt glad to see her, but also horrified.

'*What do you want?*' I asked.

'*The works,*' answered Holly's severed head. '*The whole works!*'

My alarm went off.

Thank God.

I shut it off, then flopped onto my back feeling nervous and exhausted and slightly nauseous.

How about cutting the eight o'clock?

And do what? Go back to sleep and have another nightmare or two? No thanks.

Besides, my teacher for Romantic Literature was Dr Trueman, a truly sweet and daffy old scholar who would take my absence as a personal affront. I *had* to go.

So I hauled myself out of bed, groaning, and stumbled into the kitchen. There, I peeled the plastic lid off the coffee can, held the can under my nose and inhaled deeply. The warm, calming aroma of French roast filled my head. My eyes drifted shut. I sighed.

I'll sleep all afternoon, I told myself. Just have to make it through my one o'clock, then I'll come back here and hit the sack till dinner time.

I spent a couple of minutes making the coffee. When it started dripping into the pot, I headed off to the bathroom to take my shower.

As the hot spray splashed against me, I tried to think about what had happened last night. Not the dreams, the real stuff. But the real stuff almost felt unreal and dreamlike. Almost. I knew what was real and what wasn't.

After pondering it all, I concluded that I'd been lucky. I'd accomplished part of my mission: got to see and follow the mystery girl again, even though she managed to disappear. I'd been treated to a good, long look at the woman in the kitchen and didn't get caught at it. The geezer on the porch had freaked me out but done no real harm.

Most important of all, I'd escaped from Randy.

He *kissed* me!

It disgusted me to remember it . . . and scared me to think about what he might've done if I hadn't gotten away.

I felt proud, though, of how I'd taken care of him. I'd been in minor scuffles from time to time, but I'd never really defended myself before . . . or needed to. I'd certainly never stabbed anyone until last night.

In my mind, I heard the *pop!* of the ballpoint punching through his jeans. I felt it go into him and the way the sides of the hole in his thigh held the pen upright and made it twitch in my hand.

I really nailed the bastard.

The pen *is* mightier than the sword, I thought, and smiled.

If only I'd *had* a sword!

But the pen had done just fine, and it seemed particularly appropriate since I considered myself a writer.

I'll have to write about all this someday, I thought as I climbed out of the shower. Maybe write a story about the woman in the kitchen. What was she really doing in there sipping tequila by herself at that hour of the night?

Was she waiting for the mystery girl?

Or maybe do a story about the old man on the porch. What was *he* doing there?

Call it 'The Old Man on the Swing'. I smiled at the thought and pulled my towel off its bar and began to dry myself. 'He was an old man who sat alone on a swing on his front porch and he had gone eighty-four days now without scaring the shit out of anyone.'

Or I could write about Randy and how he sat down across from me at Dandi Donuts . . . and how he'd kissed me and pushed his tongue into my mouth.

I won't write about that, I decided. I might write about everything else that happened last night, but not about that.

Maybe a story about the homeless guy sleeping in the space between the two buildings . . .?

No. I won't write about him, either.

What about the mystery girl?

Oh, yes.

Someday.

Maybe.

Done drying, I headed for the kitchen to get a cup of coffee and wondered if I would ever see her again.

Not unless she just pops up, I thought. I'm not gonna go out like last night again. No way. Never again. I must've been out of my mind. Lucky I survived.

Walking from my apartment house to the campus a few blocks away, I kept an eye out for Randy and for his Toyota pickup truck.

Would he look for me in daylight?

He might.

Might look for Eileen, too.

He'd only seen us far to the north, but it wouldn't take a genius to figure out we might be university students.

I'll have to warn Eileen.

Chapter Seventeen

My classes kept me on campus until three o'clock. Between them, I wandered around outside, sat on benches, had a burger and Pepsi in the student union, and spent a while reading in the library. I kept my eyes open for Eileen, but didn't see her anywhere.

After my last class of the day, I considered heading over to her sorority house. But it was out of the way and she might not even be there. Besides, I hadn't been able to figure out what to tell Eileen and I felt too tired to think straight.

So I walked back to my own place and went to bed.

When I woke up, my room was dark. I didn't know what was going on. My clock showed 8:15. That helped me figure things out, since the sun would've been up by that hour of the morning. Pretty soon, I remembered that I'd climbed into bed for the nap. Then I remembered the rest.

Something had to be done about Eileen.

After getting dressed, I went into the kitchen and microwaved the leftover pizza from last night.

While it was heating up, I checked my answering machine. No new messages. It hardly surprised me. Eileen didn't want me to think she was *forcing* herself on me, so she probably intended to leave the next move to me.

While I ate my pizza, I read some of Wordsworth's *The Prelude*, but couldn't concentrate very well. Maybe I would've done better with *The Prelude* if it had been a real barn-burner, but it wasn't. At best, it was quiet and lovely and nostalgic. At worst, boring.

My mind was mostly elsewhere while my eyes moved over the words. Just as I was about to give up, however, a passage caught my attention:

'Sometimes it befell
In these night wanderings, that a strong desire
O'erpowered my better reason, and the bird
Which was the captive of another's toil
Became my prey; and when the deed was done
I heard among the solitary hills
Low breathings coming after me, and sounds
of undistinguishable motion, steps
Almost as silent as the turf they trod.'

A couple of days ago, I wouldn't have given the lines a second thought; now, it was as if they'd been written *about* me – a night-wanderer whose desire overpowered his better reason. 'The bird' might be the mystery girl. And the final four lines hinted of danger from someone 'coming after me'. Someone like Randy, perhaps.

I read the passage again and again, feeling its deep mystery and magic, struck by the strange union of circumstances that had compelled me to discover it on this night of all nights.

After marking the passage with a yellow Hi-liter, I kept on reading. Wordsworth had my full attention for about ten more seconds. That's when he started rhapsodizing about bird eggs and I began wondering how to get in touch with Eileen.

Call her on the phone? More than likely, she wasn't in her room; she usually did most of her studying in the student union or the library. Even if I *could* reach her on the phone, I probably shouldn't; it might look as if I were trying to avoid her. Better to go out and find her in person.

I put Wordsworth and Fitzgerald (*The Great Gatsby* for my Twentieth Century American Literature class) into my book bag, slung the strap over one shoulder and left my rooms.

Downstairs, the Fishers' door stood open. They had their television on. Keeping my head straight forward, I walked as if I were in a big hurry and got past their door without being beckoned.

But the Fishers were a minor nuisance. Randy was a real threat, and he might be anywhere outside.

Cruising the streets, searching for me or Eileen.

Or parked and watching.

Or walking.

I looked for him constantly on my way toward campus.

Though I carried my Swiss Army knife in a pocket of my jeans, it didn't give me much comfort. Neither did my ballpoint pens. My assault on Randy last night had only succeeded because I'd taken him by surprise. Next time, he wouldn't let me get away with it.

There'd better not be a next time.

He might not even *try* to find us, I told myself.

The hell he won't.

But maybe he won't hunt for us this far south. Maybe he stays in his own area, and we'll be safe as long as we don't go there.

Maybe. But I doubted it.

Every so often, a pickup truck went by, putting fear into me. Each time, I got ready to run but the pickup kept on moving. Now and then, men who matched Randy's physical shape came walking toward me. One even had a limp. None, however, was him.

What if it goes like this from now on? I wondered. Watching for Randy all the time, everywhere I go, never knowing when he'll pop up and grab me . . . *give me the works.*

Or maybe he'll grab Eileen, instead. Drag her into his car and take her someplace desolate.

Where no birds sing.

What if he already has her?

My stomach cringed.

I should've *warned* her! What was I thinking? Why didn't I phone her room the instant I got back to my apartment this morning?

It hadn't even occurred to me.

She's probably fine, I told myself.

If she isn't, it's all my fault.

By the time I reached campus, I was frantic.

First stop, the student union. Otherwise known as the Tigers' Den. Willmington University's teams (and students in general) used to be known as the Braves. Then came the era of political correctness. 'Braves' was deemed to be a slur against Native Americans, so a new name had to be found. We chose to be Tigers. Our student union, the Braves' Cave, became known as the Tigers' Den.

It was crowded. Students sat at almost every table, some by themselves but most of them with friends. They were talking, laughing, eating snacks, drinking coffee or soft drinks, some even trying to study – books spread out on their tables. The food line was closed for the night, so several students were busy trying to buy refreshments from vending machines.

I knew many of the people I saw, and smiled and nodded at those who noticed me, even exchanged a few words with some of them.

'Hey, Ed, what's up?'

'Not much. How about you?'

'Hangin' in. Come on over 'n sit with us.'

'Can't. Thanks, though. I've gotta run.'

That sort of thing.

Several of Eileen's sorority sisters were in the Den. Among them, someone probably knew where to find her. I stayed away from them, though. For one thing, Holly would've come up. For another, they didn't need to know I had any interest whatsoever in Eileen.

I left the snack area of the Tigers' Den and wandered across the room to the lounge section. There, students sat in armchairs and on sofas. Many were by themselves, reading. Several couples occupied the sofas, talking quietly, some holding hands.

Holly and I had sat together on these sofas so many times last year . . . trying to study but never for long, soon holding hands and talking, staring into each other's eyes, often laughing at little things, giving each other a pat on the thigh or back. We'd probably been on every one of the sofas at one time or another.

We drank our coffee black. We often ate red vines. They were usually stale. Holly taught me how to make them soft and mushy by dunking them in coffee. Sometimes, we took turns eating the same vine and it excited me to know that my end of the candy had just been in Holly's mouth.

The memories made me feel hollow and hungry and sick.

The memories and the loss.

Lovers were here, but Eileen wasn't. I hurried away and was glad to get outside.

I headed for the library. Holly and I hadn't really spent any time there together, so it felt like safe ground. As I walked from the student union toward the library, the intensity of my loss slowly faded . . . to be replaced by worries about Eileen.

The worries felt better. But they grew stronger while I searched the library.

What if she's not here?

Then I'll see if she's in her room at the sorority house.

What if she's not there?

That's when to really start worrying, I told myself.

But even if she isn't in the library or her room, it won't mean that Randy got her. There are a lot of other places she might be.

Like where?

I found her on the second floor of the stacks in a far corner of the room at a study carrel reading *Crime and Punishment*.

Thank God, I thought.

It felt great to find her safe.

And I was struck by how wonderful she looked, sitting there in the light of a reading lamp. Her thick hair, which usually looked brown, shimmered with secret threads of gold and russet. Her face looked warm and smooth. She frowned as if concentrating deeply on her book. She wore the bright plaid chamois shirt that she'd had on the night we made love.

'Hi,' I said very quietly.

She raised her head, saw me, and smiled.

'Hi, yourself,' she said.

So that I wouldn't loom over her, I crouched. 'I've been looking for you,' I said.

'Really?'

'Yeah. Would you like to go somewhere?'

'Sure. But can it wait a while? I really need to get some reading done.'

'Same here.'

'How about an hour?'

'Fine. There're some empty carrels.'

'Okay. See you in an hour.'

I found a study carrel only a few away from Eileen's and along the same wall. With everything that had been going on the past few days, I hadn't actually started *Gatsby* yet. So I pulled it out of my book bag and started reading.

I got through about half the first page.

What sort of shit is this?

I knew it was supposed to be a great book. It'll probably get better, I told myself. And I tried to read more, but just couldn't.

Some other time.

For certain books, your mind has to be in just the right mood.

I put *Gatsby* back into my book bag and pulled out my volume of Wordsworth. I felt totally incapable of reading *that*, too.

'Screw it,' I muttered.

Then I reached into my bag again and pulled out a rather battered old paperback. *The Temple of Gold* by William Goldman. I always kept it in my book bag, just in case. It was like an old friend I could trust.

So I opened *The Temple of Gold* to the bookmark for my current reading of it, and jumped in.

A hand gave my shoulder a gentle squeeze. I looked. It was a girl's hand. Turning my head further, I found Eileen standing over me. Her left hand was still on my shoulder. Her right arm was busy holding her books and binders against her chest.

'Finish early?' I asked.

'It's been an hour and fifteen minutes.'

'Huh?'

'What're *you* reading?'

I held it up so she could see the cover.

She nodded and smiled. 'What class is *that* for?'

'None. I just like it.'

'All caught up with your assigned stuff?'

'You've gotta be kidding.'

'Anyway, if you can tear yourself away from it, I'm ready to go.'

'Let's go.'

I put the book away, got up and hung a strap of the bag over one shoulder. I walked ahead of Eileen down the narrow aisle toward the staircase, then opened the door for her.

Stepping past me, she patted me on the rear end and whispered, 'So what's the handle, Zock?'

'You've *read* it!'

'Hasn't everyone?'

'It isn't even in print.'

'I know. They've got nothing in print but *The Princess Bride*.'

I followed Eileen down the stairs, watching her long hair bounce and sway, thinking that Holly had never read *The Temple of Gold* and wondering what was wrong with me that I wasn't in love with Eileen.

Chapter Eighteen

As we walked down the outside steps of the library, she said, 'So, did you come by for your nightly dose of Eileen's insanity?'

'Can't live without it.'

She smiled at me. At the bottom of the stairs, we just kept walking, no discussion of where we were headed.

'My pleasure,' she said. 'Anything I can do to take your mind off you-know-who.'

'I've got other things on my mind.'

Though we were walking side by side, Eileen seemed to be leading the way. We went in the general direction of her sorority house. Was I simply walking her home?

Many other things were in the same direction.

It doesn't matter where we're going, I thought.

After a while, Eileen said, 'What sort of things *are* on your mind?'

'You.'

'Me?'

'I wanted to make sure you're all right.'

'I'm fine.'

'You didn't seem so fine last night. When you left.'

'Ah, well, that was simply a matter of self-preservation. Preserving my self-esteem. Getting out before I made an even bigger idiot of myself.'

Eileen was on my left and my left arm was free. Her arms were full of books and binders, so I put my hand on her back. She looked at me.

'You weren't making even a *small* idiot of yourself,' I told her.

'Yeah, I was. That's all I can ever do when I'm around you anymore . . . go off the deep end.'

'Nah.'

'Yeah.'

I caressed her side, feeling her smoothness through the chamois shirt.

Looking straight ahead, Eileen said, 'I should've just stayed away from you. The last thing you need is *me* messing up your life.'

'Funny you should mention it,' I said, my heart suddenly beating hard. 'Messing up people's lives. Because you've got it turned around. I'm the one messing up *your* life.'

'Well, you haven't made it any easier, but it's not your fault . . .'

'There's somebody after you because of me.'

Eileen stopped walking and we faced each other. 'What're you talking about?'

'There's this guy,' I said. 'He saw you in the donut shop when you went out to meet me. I guess he was about to make a move on you, but he backed off because I showed up. The thing is, he wants to meet you. He tried to get your name from me.'

'Did you tell him?'

'I gave him some fake name. Then he wanted to know where you live. I wouldn't tell him that, either.'

For a long time, Eileen just stood there looking into my eyes. Then she said, 'I don't get it. When did this happen?'

'Well, Monday night's when he saw you.'

'I got that part.'

'Well, I went back to Dandi last night. That's the first time I ever saw the guy. He sat down at my table.'

'You went there last night, too?'

I nodded. 'After you left, I started to feel pretty lousy. I needed to take a walk.'

'I wish you'd told me. I was feeling pretty lousy myself. I would've gone with you.'

'Thank God you didn't.'

99

'What possessed you to go out there again?'

'It was just a place to go. Someplace that's open.'

'But it's so far away. What time did you go?'

'I don't know.' Figuring the truth would make things worse, I said, 'I studied for a while after you left. So it was maybe around nine-thirty or ten.'

She shook her head. 'And you went by yourself, I take it.'

I nodded, shrugged.

'That's *so* dangerous, Eddie. Even a nice little town like this . . . it's probably not so nice in the middle of the night. Probably no place is. No place that has people, anyway.'

And places that don't have people, I thought, probably have other dangerous things roaming the night.

'Well,' I said, 'I don't plan to go out there anymore. But I'm afraid the damage is already done. This Randy guy . . .'

'Is that his name? Randy?'

'Yeah.'

She cracked a smile.

'What?'

'A guy named Randy with the hots for me.'

'He's not very amusing,' I told her.

'Is he handsome?'

'I guess so. In a Ted Bundy sort of way.'

'This guy sure rubbed *you* the wrong way.'

'Yeah, he sure did. You know what he said? I asked him, "You want to go out with her?" Meaning you. And he answered, "No, I wanta go *in* her."'

Her smile went away. 'Oh, swell,' she muttered.

'He's not a nice guy.'

'Not if he'll say a thing like that.'

'It gets worse.'

'What?'

'He made me get into his pickup truck. He wanted me to show him where you live.'

'He *what*?'

'He wanted to get his hands on you last night. And he tried to force me to help him.'

She grimaced. 'You're kidding me.'

'I was supposed to bring you out for him.'

'My God.'

'I wouldn't have done it.'

'I know.' Gazing into my eyes, she said, 'You *didn't* do it.'

'I got away from him. He chased me, but I lost him. The thing is, he's still . . .'

'The thing is,' she interrupted me, 'thanks.'

We were standing on a lighted section of walkway just north of the quad. Trees were all around us, their branches casting shadows on the pavement and grass. To my right was Donner Hall, one of the freshman dormitories. Just ahead was Division Street. To the left, out of sight below a steep embankment, was the Old Mill Stream.

'Come with me,' Eileen said.

I followed her to the left. We walked into the darkness of the trees. A couple of park benches were at the edge of the embankment above the stream, but nobody was using them. Eileen set her books and binders and purse on one of them. I put my book bag down beside her purse.

In front of the bench, we turned toward each other. She reached out, took the front of my shirt in both her hands and pulled me against her. She kissed me with her open mouth. As she rubbed herself against me, she let go of my shirt and wrapped her arms around my back.

Why here? I wondered. Did she have to lead me *here* of all places?

Last spring, more than once, I'd stood in this very place with Holly. Embracing her, kissing her, exploring her body.

I shut my eyes.

She *is* Holly, I told myself. Holly's right here with me now in my arms . . .

Yeah, sure.

I couldn't kid myself. The feel was all different, and so was the smell. Eileen was nearly my own size. I kissed her without bending over. Her breasts pushed against my chest, not my stomach, and they

101

were larger than Holly's. She wasn't pudgy like Holly, either. She felt firm in places where Holly was soft. And she didn't use whatever perfume Holly had always worn. Instead of Holly's sweet, heartbreaking aroma, Eileen simply smelled fresh and clean as if she'd just stepped out of a shower.

Why would I *want* to pretend she's Holly? I wondered.

The hell with Holly.

We kept on holding each other, kept on kissing. The feel and smell of her soon pushed all thoughts of Holly out of my mind and there was only Eileen, here and now, and fresh memories of her as she'd been on Monday night when we made love.

Tonight, she wore a bra. I unhooked its back. Then I moved my hands to her front, slipped them beneath the loose cups of her bra and filled them with the warm softness of her breasts.

Her mouth was slippery against mine.

Breathing hard, she used both hands to unfasten my jeans. When they were open, one hand pulled the elastic waistband of my shorts toward her and the other hand went down the front. Her fingers curled around my penis.

I pressed my hand against the crotch of her jeans. The denim felt warm and moist. She squirmed, rubbing herself against my fingers, and started to make quiet whimpery sounds.

Then she gasped, 'Wait.'

'What?'

'Wait. Not here.' She slid her hand off me, took my wrist and eased my hand away from her jeans. I still had one hand on her breast. 'We'd better not do it here,' she whispered.

'But . . .'

'Someone might see us.'

'Okay.' I fastened the waist button of my jeans, but didn't bother to pull up my zipper or buckle my belt.

Eileen didn't fix her bra, either.

'We'll go down there,' she said, and nodded toward the stream.

We hid our books underneath the bench, but Eileen said, 'I'd better take this along,' and hung the strap of her purse over one shoulder.

Taking my hand, she led me to the edge of the embankment.

'Let's try under the bridge,' she said. 'Nobody'll see us there.'

'What about the trolls?' I asked.

'Trolls my ass.'

I laughed. 'Okay. Let's do it.'

Chapter Nineteen

The slope was steep and slippery. On the way down, Eileen let go of my hand and put her arms out for balance. I thought about how her breasts were loose underneath her shirt. Not that I could see much; the heavy trees looming over us blocked out so much light that Eileen was nothing but a vague shape with the purse swinging by her side.

At the bottom of the slope, we walked carefully alongside the stream. Though we remained in darkness, pale light from the streetlamps above the bridge glowed ahead of us. A couple of times, I heard cars go by. I couldn't see them or even the bridge.

Soon, the bridge came into view through the branches . . . the Division Street bridge with its low stone parapet where Holly and I used to linger, staring down at the creek.

Don't start thinking about Holly, I told myself.

The hell with her.

At least we'd never gone *under* the bridge together. I'd wanted to. One night, walking Holly back to her sorority, we'd stopped along the bridge the way we nearly always did and I asked, 'Have you ever been under there?'

'No. Have you?'

'Just once.'

'How was it?'

'Nice and private.'

She'd given me a look. 'Oh, really?'

'Want to go down and take a look?'

'Now?'

'No time like the present.'

'It's almost midnight.'

'No time like almost midnight.'

'*I'm* not going down there.' Smiling, she'd said, '*Trolls* live under bridges.'

'Not this bridge. This one's troll-free.'

'So say you.'

'I could go down first and take a look around.'

'Oh, no you don't. What if they *get* you? And then I'm left up here all by myself while the trolls have you for a midnight snack. Thanks, but no thanks.'

'Then come down with me.'

'No no no no no.'

'Where's your sense of adventure?'

'It doesn't extend to sneaking under bridges at midnight. I mean, seriously. No telling *who* might be under there.'

'Well, okay.'

I'd been disappointed that night, but now I was glad Holly and I hadn't ventured under the bridge. It was one of the few places where I *hadn't* been with her.

But as Eileen and I walked closer to the bridge, I saw the darkness of the area down there.

'I'm having second thoughts about this,' I said. 'It might not be so safe.'

Eileen stopped, half turned, looked back at me and reached out her hand. I took it in mine. She didn't say anything, just gave my hand a squeeze and kept hold of it as she started walking again.

A car went over on the bridge, tires hissing on the tarmac, engine grumbling, radio heavy on the bass and giving out low *thump-thump-thumps* that I could feel in my chest. I looked up but couldn't see the car. Its sounds faded.

'Have you been down here before?' I asked.

'Never at night.'

'Me neither.'

'Good,' she said. 'This'll be a first for both of us.'

We were about to enter a clear area when Eileen suddenly stopped. Her back stiffened. With her right hand, she pointed up at the bridge.

A girl about halfway across stopped walking and leaned over the parapet. A moment later, a guy showed up beside her. He leaned over the low wall, too. They both gazed down toward the stream . . . and toward us.

I was fairly sure they couldn't see us. Not if we stayed put. But they probably *would* see us if we continued forward.

The girl turned her head toward the boy. He turned his head toward her and put an arm around her. Then they kissed. They kissed for a long time as if nothing else mattered in the world. I knew exactly how it was. It made me sad. Not just for myself, but for them, too.

Eileen and I stood motionless in the dark below them, watching.

A car went by, but it didn't disturb the two lovers.

Finally, they stopped leaning over the parapet. Standing up straight, they wrapped their arms around each other and resumed kissing.

'Okay,' Eileen whispered.

We hurried on.

The stream was about ten feet wide as it flowed toward the darkness under the bridge. On both sides of it were broad areas of dry, rocky ground littered with fallen branches and various items that had probably been thrown off the bridge: beer cans, a hubcap, an old bicycle wheel, a grimy white sneaker, a broken pair of sunglasses.

Eileen looked back at me. 'This place could use a clean-up,' she whispered.

'Yeah.'

'You okay with this?' she asked.

'Fine.'

She squeezed my hand, then faced forward. A few more steps, and we would be under the bridge.

I looked up, but couldn't see the lovers or anyone else.

'I'd better go first,' I said.

'Be my guest.'

Though she moved aside, she continued to hold my hand as I stepped past her. 'Maybe you'd better let go,' I whispered.

She released my hand, then took hold of the back of my shirt and walked behind me into the darkness.

Almost utter darkness.

To our left and right, I could see only black. Straight ahead of us was more black – about thirty feet of it – then a dim gray smudge where the underpass ended and the stream continued on toward the Old Mill a couple of blocks away.

'Who turned out the lights?' Eileen whispered.

'The trolls.'

'Very funny.'

I walked deeper into the darkness, moving slowly, Eileen still holding onto my shirt.

'Be careful,' she said.

Under here, the air seemed to have a moist chill and it smelled of old, wet things.

Rocks tipped and rolled under my shoes, scraping together, softly bumping. But I also stepped on soft objects that made squishy sounds. My shoe hit a can and sent it clattering. A couple of times, I crunched broken glass.

This reminded me of running through the narrow, dark space between the buildings last night, Randy chasing me.

The place where I'd fallen over a shopping cart, tumbled onto a bum.

Eileen tugged my shirt. 'This is good,' she whispered.

I started to turn. If I'd turned all the way around, Eileen would've had at least a hint of light behind her. But I only turned part of the way before her hands met my chest. I was facing the stream . . . and blackness.

'I didn't know it'd be so dark in here,' Eileen whispered.

Though I felt her breath on my lips, I couldn't see her at all. 'Do you want to leave?' I asked.

'Huh-uh.'

She touched her moist, warm lips against mine and began to unfasten the buttons of my shirt. While she worked on my shirt, I worked on hers. When both were open, we eased our bodies together.

I felt the cloth of her rumpled bra up near my collar bones. Below that, her breasts were warm and soft against me, her nipples stiff. Lower, she was warm smooth skin all the way down to the waist of her jeans.

We kissed with open mouths.

Her purse still hung from her right shoulder. I felt its straps when I reached around her. They didn't get in the way, though.

I ran my hands up and down her back, savoring her silken curves. She shivered and hugged me more tightly.

'Too cold?' I whispered.

'A little. And a little scared.'

'Wanta go to my place?'

'No. This is good.' Her arms loosened their hold on me. Then they went away. I felt her breath on my face and the warm pressure of her breasts against my chest and small pulling sensations at my waist as she unfastened my jeans. Reaching into my shorts, she caressed me. Then her breasts eased away from me. I felt her mouth kiss my chin, the side of my neck, my chest and my belly as she crouched, pulling down my shorts and jeans.

Then no part of Eileen seemed to be touching me.

I stood there alone, shivering.

What's going on?

I looked down, but couldn't see her . . . couldn't see anything in the darkness, not even my own bare legs.

'Eileen?' I whispered.

No answer came.

'What're you doing?'

A warm, wet something flicked against the front of my penis, then slid under it.

Felt like a tongue.

As it drew back, I was encircled by a moist, pliant ring. It slipped down me, taking me in.

Lips?

'I sure hope that's you,' I whispered.

In response, the mouth tightened its hold and sucked. Warm hands slid up the backs of my legs and cupped my buttocks. The mouth took me in deeper as the hands squeezed and pulled.

Then the mouth slid off me.

'It's only me,' Eileen whispered.

She slowly stood up, keeping her body close to mine so that her breasts rubbed me and my penis rubbed her.

When she was upright in front of me, I unfastened her jeans. I slipped a hand down inside the front of her panties. She was wet and slippery and hot. My fingers made her writhe and flinch. Whimpering, she took care of shoving down her jeans and panties. Her thighs parted.

I took my hand away. She guided my penis between her legs.

Between them, but barely into her.

We tried for a while. Then I whispered, 'This isn't working too well.'

'I should've worn a skirt. Damn. I've gotta get these jeans off. Hold onto me, okay?'

'Where?'

'My shoulders, I guess. Just don't let me fall. Gotta get my shoes off first.'

While I held her shoulders, she bent down in front of me. I felt her hair against my belly and penis. She twisted and swayed, rocked from side to side, and gasped a couple of times when she lost her balance. I held her steady, though, and kept her from falling. Finally, she whispered, 'There.'

She stood up and eased in against me. She was bare and warm and smooth. She'd removed her jeans and panties. Even her purse and bra were gone, though I didn't think she could've taken them off while I'd been holding her steady. All she still wore was her chamois shirt, which was wide open.

I was stiff against her belly. As we kissed, she rubbed against me, her hands roaming over my back and rump.

Then, almost as if we knew what we were doing, she parted her legs and I bent my knees. I felt the wet curls of her pubic hair along the underside of my penis, then only cool air when I was crouched enough to be under her.

Her fingertips found me, guided me. She eased downward and I felt her slick flesh open around me. I straightened my knees. Eileen dug her fingers into my back and moaned as I slid up high and deep.

She raised one of her legs and hooked it behind me and I went in deeper yet. I wanted the feel of both her legs up around me so I pulled at the back of her other thigh. She brought it up and I was in all the way.

Both feet off the ground, Eileen clung to me as if she were climbing a tree trunk while I clutched her buttocks. She grunted as I thrust. I could feel her breasts going up and down while I bounced her. They slapped the fronts of my shoulders. Whimpering, she clutched my head.

And suddenly she was twitching and grunting. I'd been trying to keep control of myself, but her frenzy pushed me over the edge. I started to jerk and throb inside her. As my semen spurted, she squeezed my head between her breasts.

And something went wrong.

She let out a frightened squeal as her weight shifted backward.

Gripping her buttocks, I pranced forward through the blackness in hopes of getting our balance back. But my feet tangled in something – her jeans? – and down I went, Eileen clinging to me, me clinging to her, me buried deep inside her.

I thought we would probably fall into the stream.

We didn't, though.

When her body struck the ground, she let out a hurt grunt. Her arms fell away from around my head. Under my face, her chest was heaving, her heart thudding.

As I started to push myself up, she clutched my shoulder. In a voice that was high and shaky and quiet, she said, 'Someone else is here.'

Chapter Twenty

I didn't want to believe her, but I did.

'Are you sure?' I whispered.

'Yessss. Oh, God.'

'It'll be all right.'

'He pulled my hair . . . made us fall.'

Someone in the dark with us, standing so near to us that he could reach up and pull Eileen's hair . . . someone so stealthy, so silent, that we'd been utterly unaware of his presence.

The fear made my skin crawl like last night when the old man on the porch struck his match. I wanted to leap up and run like hell.

I couldn't do it, though. My pants were down around my ankles. Eileen, under me, was naked.

And hurt? She'd taken a hard fall, gotten herself pounded against the ground with all my weight on top of her and God-knew-what underneath her.

'Are you hurt?' I whispered.

'Not that bad.'

'Bleeding?'

'Yeah. A little, anyway.'

'We've gotta get out of here.'

From somewhere off to my left came sniffy sounds like someone laughing softly through his nostrils.

Eileen's arms clamped around me and her thighs squeezed against my hips. Her body was trembling under me.

'It'll be all right,' I whispered, my lips against the side of her neck.

'I'm so scared.' She started to cry. Small spasms shook her body. Her hitching sobs sounded awfully loud in the dark.

I went, 'Shhhh.'

So did the person who had hissed his laughs.

So did someone else, over to the right.

Eileen gasped and went rigid.

In a secret corner of my mind, I'd suspected that the stranger in the dark might be Randy, that he'd somehow followed us down here. It had been my fear but also, in some way, my hope. Randy was horrible, but at least he was known to me. He had a name, a face . . . and I'd already hurt him once.

When I heard the second 'Shhhh,' I decided Randy had nothing to do with this. Also, I suddenly remembered the Swiss Army knife in the pocket of my jeans.

Jeans that were wrapped around my ankles.

'Let go,' I whispered against Eileen's neck.

She kept on holding me tight.

'Let go of me,' I whispered again.

Though I spoke softly, the strangers in the dark could probably hear every word. I didn't want to mention the knife.

'Please,' I said.

'You'll run away.'

'No, I won't. Just let go.'

'Promise?'

'I promise.'

She loosened her hold on me. With my hands on the ground on both sides of her, I pushed myself up. Then, holding onto my jeans and underwear, I rose to my feet.

'Eddie?' Eileen asked.

'I'm right here.' As I fastened my jeans, my belt buckle clinked.

'Get my clothes for me,' she whispered.

'I will.' But first I reached into the front pocket of my jeans and pulled out my knife. I shifted it to my left hand, felt the blunt edges of the closed blades and tools, and tried to catch the slotted side of a blade with my thumb nail.

'Eddie?' It was almost a squeal.

'Huh?'

'Where *are* you?'

'Right here.'

'He's *touching* me!'

Somebody slammed into me from the right. The impact twisted me and sent me stumbling sideways through the dark. I tripped over my own feet, fell as if making a dive into shallow water, and slammed against the ground so hard that I skidded.

In the distance past my feet, Eileen cried out, '*Eddie! Get him off me!*'

I heard a smack like a fist striking bare skin.

'Leave her alone!' I yelled.

As I struggled to get up, I realized that I'd lost my knife. I *had* to have it. Dropping to my knees, I swept my hands over the ground.

Eileen whined . . . part pain, part terror.

The hell with the knife.

I grabbed a heavy, jagged rock that was larger than my hand, scrambled to my feet and rushed toward the sounds from Eileen and what was happening to her.

The sounds sickened me. Sobs and giggles, punches and slaps, yelps of pain, gasps for air, muttered curses, wet slurps, frenzied grunts.

I expected to be taken down, myself, at any moment.

But then I came to where the sounds were.

I was glad I couldn't see what was being done to Eileen or who was doing it.

I piled on.

It *was* a pile on: me on top, the attackers underneath me, Eileen almost certainly on the bottom.

Heads, arms, asses everywhere.

More than two attackers. Three? Four? I couldn't tell.

I laid into them with my rock.

Their turn to cry out.

I couldn't see them and they couldn't see me. I think they hurt each other as much as I hurt them. During the minute or two it lasted, I got elbowed, punched, scratched and bit.

Then nobody was between Eileen and me. I lay gasping for breath on top of her sprawled, twitching body, the rock still clenched in my hand. Where my bare skin was against her, she felt wet and sticky.

'Are you okay?' I whispered.

Crying, she shook her head. I felt it against my cheek.

'Let's get out of here,' I said.

'Where . . . are they?'

'Gone. I don't know. I think they ran off.'

'Let's hurry,' she said.

I pushed myself up. When I was on my knees, I reached down and took hold of her wrists. 'Can you sit up?' I asked.

She started to rise, so I pulled her arms. She winced and whimpered.

Soon, we were both on our feet. She felt wobbly, though. I had to hold her up. 'I'll carry you,' I said.

'My clothes.'

'Let's get out of here before we get jumped again.'

Before she could argue, I dropped the rock and swept her up in my arms. She was too exhausted or hurt to fight me. I carried her, cradled against my chest, toward the gray blur at the mouth of the underpass.

With every step, I thought we might get attacked again.

Finally, I carried her out of the darkness. We were in the open for a few seconds, in plain sight of anyone who might be looking down toward the stream. I didn't look back, but nobody called out.

I hurried with Eileen into the shadows of the trees along the shore. There, I lowered her gently onto the grass. Then I glanced around.

'Looks like we're safe,' I whispered.

She squeezed my hand.

We were shrouded in darkness, but not total darkness. For the first time since venturing under the bridge, I could see Eileen. I thought she would at least still have her chamois shirt, but it was gone like the rest of her clothes. She seemed to be bloody in places.

'Can you tell if you're bleeding badly anywhere?' I asked. 'Like if an artery got hit, or something?'

'Nothing like that.'

'You sure?'

'I'm just . . . leaking a little here and there.'

'Okay. Good. Now, I guess we'd better get you up top and somewhere safe, and I'll go find a phone and . . .'

'We left my *purse*!' she blurted as if suddenly remembering.

'Oh shit,' I said.

'All my *stuff's* in it.'

Nodding, I took off my shirt. 'Put this on.' I gave it to her. 'I'll be right back.'

'No. You'd better not.'

'We can't leave your purse.'

'I can cancel the credit cards and—'

'*They'll* know who you are . . . where you live.'

In a very small voice, she said, 'But I don't want 'em to get *you*.'

'I'll be fast,' I said. 'If anyone comes after *you*, yell, okay? Yell or scream, and I'll come running.'

'Maybe we'd better get help.'

All I did was shake my head. There was not a moment to lose – not even in explanations – if we hoped to get her purse back.

I whirled around and raced toward the bridge.

Nobody was up top.

When the blackness swallowed me, I stopped running. I put myself backward in time and tried to retrace the route I'd taken with Eileen.

I heard nobody.

They probably ran off, I told myself. For all they know, the cops are on the way.

Crouching, I reached down and patted the ground. I felt moist earth, rocks and twigs.

Who says I'm even close?

I got down on my hands and knees and crawled. I wished I had gloves on. Not because of the cold, but because of the things I found

115

myself touching in the darkness. Some were sharp, some mushy, some hard, some slimy.

At last, I found a shoe. It felt and smelled like a fairly new athletic shoe.

After wiping my hands on my jeans, I continued searching in the same area and found the rest: Eileen's other shoe, her jeans, her bra and her purse. Her panties and chamois shirt didn't seem to be there.

Better get out of here while I still can.

But I liked Eileen's chamois shirt. I didn't want her to lose it and I sure didn't want someone *else* ending up with her panties.

On the chance that Eileen might have a flashlight, I put a hand into her purse and felt around. I touched her billfold, various cylinders and small cases, a hair brush, a pocket-sized spiral notebook, and several unidentified items wrapped in plastic and paper. No flashlight, though.

Digging deeper, I found a treasure trove of loose objects near the bottom of her purse: sticks of gum, coins, half-used rolls of something shaped like Lifesavers, a couple of condoms in plastic wrappers, an array of pens and pencils and markers, a couple of cigarettes and a book of matches.

Yes!

I pulled out the matchbook, flipped open the cardboard cover, tore out a match and struck it. The head flared, hurting my eyes. I was blinded for a second or two.

When I could see again, I yelped.

In the murky glow of the matchlight, I saw a bare foot on the ground just out of my reach.

Chapter Twenty-one

No one was standing on the foot.

It was toes up. The ankle and shin looked hairy. Just above the knee, the leg vanished into darkness.

Looking around quickly, I saw nobody else within the aura of light cast by my match.

The match was starting to burn me. I shook it out, struck another, then hurried over to the man. He was naked. He lay motionless on his back. He had long, wild, filthy hair. His eyebrows, mustache and beard were so thick that he hardly seemed to have any face at all. After a moment, however, I located his small, sooty nose. Then I found his deep-set eyes with their closed lids.

The hair on the right side of his head was matted flat, shiny red with blood.

Had I done that to him with my rock?

It seemed likely, but not certain. The mêlée had been chaos. No telling who had done what to anyone.

The man looked dead.

Serves him right, I thought. He attacked us. Probably tried to rape Eileen.

With that.

It was upright, big and glistening.

Did he rape her?

The match started to burn me, so I shook it out. I struck another.

The guy was still motionless on his back.

I went looking for my Swiss Army knife. It almost certainly carried my fingerprints, so I couldn't leave it down here with a dead man.

Finding it wasn't easy.

Two matches later, however, I spotted its bright red handle on the ground near a smashed Budweiser can. I hurried over to it and picked it up.

I shook out my match. Standing in total darkness, I pried open one of the blades. Then I held the knife in my left hand with the matchbook. With my right hand, I struck a fresh match.

I was too far away to see the body.

What if he's gone?

What if he's coming at me?

I walked in his direction. A few seconds later, the murky light from my match found him. He was still sprawled on his back.

I stepped up to him. His eyes were still shut. I stared at his filthy, hairy chest. It didn't seem to be moving.

He's probably dead, I thought.

But he's got a hard-on. Can a dead guy have a hard-on?

I had no idea. Seemed possible, but not likely.

It suddenly occurred to me that it looked bigger than before.

It's growing?

I muttered, 'Oh shit.'

What dreams may come when we have shuffled off this mortal coil . . .

Don't freak out, I told myself. He's probably not dead.

If he isn't, I'd better help him. Check his wounds. Call an ambulance.

Then I thought about what he'd done to us.

'Fuck it,' I muttered.

I lit a new match, then did a quick search for Eileen's chamois shirt and panties. Other clothes were scattered around: coats, shirts, trousers, shoes. Even a couple of hats. All of them looked filthy. Eileen's shirt and panties, however, didn't seem to be among them.

Fast as I could, I gathered up her purse, shoes, jeans and bra and hurried out from under the bridge.

No sooner did I escape from the darkness than I began to fear the worst for Eileen.

I shouldn't have left her alone.

The others probably got her . . .

I came to the place where I'd left her in the shadows, and she wasn't there. I crumbled inside.

They *did* get her.

'Eddie?'

Her voice came from the wrong direction. I jerked my head sideways and looked toward the stream. Still, I couldn't see her.

'Where are you?'

Several yards upstream, a pale arm lifted into the air. Below it, a face was a pale smudge against the black of the water.

I set down her things and walked toward her along the bank. 'You okay?' I asked.

'Not bad. How'd it go?'

'I got your purse and most of your clothes. Couldn't find your shirt.'

'Any trouble?'

I crouched down on the grass a few feet away from her. She was submerged to her neck in the stream. 'The creeps must've all run away,' I said. 'Probably figured the first thing we'd do is call the cops.'

'Why don't you come in and wash up,' Eileen asked. 'We can figure out what to do.'

Shaking my head, I said, 'I think we should get out of here. Get you to the student health center.'

'Not the health center.'

'The ER?'

She stood up, her body rising out of the black water pale and gleaming in the moonlight. 'How about your place?' she asked. Her torso ended at the water's surface. 'I don't much want to be alone right now . . . tonight. If it's all right with you . . .'

'You should probably see a doctor.'

'I'll see one if I need one. I can look myself over when we get to your place. Unless you don't *want* me to come over.'

'I want you to come over.'

'Thanks, Eddie.' She waded toward me, silvery where the moon lit her wet skin. I watched how her breasts moved. Their tips looked like large black coins. Her navel was a small black dot. With each step she took, the level of the water lowered.

Seeing the dark patch of her pubic hair, I thought about the guy under the bridge.

She'll tell me what she wants me to know.

When the water level was down around her knees, she shuddered and wrapped her arms around her chest. 'Do I still get to wear your shirt?' she asked.

'Sure.'

It was on the grass near my feet. I picked it up and handed it out to her. She put it on. 'Ah, that's better.' She fastened a button down near her waist, then climbed out of the stream.

I led the way back along the shore to the place where I'd left her purse and clothes.

'This is fantastic,' she said. She picked up her purse and took out her billfold.

'A reward won't be necessary,' I said.

'You'll get a reward, all right. I can't believe you actually went back under there.'

'I can't either,' I said.

'I was so scared. I was afraid they'd get you.'

'Still might,' I said. 'We really shouldn't hang around here any longer than necessary.' I looked toward the bridge. It was out of sight, hidden by the thick tangles of tree branches looming over the embankment.

'I think we're all right here, don't you?' Eileen asked.

'Never know.'

She looked inside her billfold.

'I didn't take anything.'

'I know *you* didn't.'

'I'm sure they didn't, either. If they'd seen your purse at all, they would've taken it.'

'That's probably true.' She put the billfold back into her purse.

'I did steal a matchbook,' I confessed.

She looked up at me. 'Went through my purse, huh?'

'For a good cause. I needed some light.' I took the matchbook out of a pocket of my jeans and dropped it into her purse. 'Thanks,' I said.

'Any time.'

She crouched and set her purse on the ground, then searched through her clothes. Soon, she looked up at me. 'You didn't happen to find a pair of panties?'

'They seem to be among the missing.'

'Oh, swell.'

'Sorry.'

'So one of those . . . *trolls* . . . took them?'

'Not necessarily. I might've just missed them.'

'Hope so,' she said. 'I hate to think that . . .' Shaking her head, she stood up and stepped into her jeans. 'We must've been nuts,' she muttered as she fastened the waist button.

'Yeah.'

She pulled up her zipper and smiled at me. 'It was sure something, though. Huh? I mean, *before* . . .?'

'It was something, all right.'

'I've never . . .' She shook her head again. 'It was *really* something.'

'I'll say.'

She bent down and picked up her bra. 'Want to wear this?' she asked.

'I don't think so.'

'Nor do I.' She stuffed the bra into her purse, then sat on the ground and started to put on her shoes.

'Are you okay?' I asked.

'Pretty okay, all things considered. We're alive, right? And not too badly hurt. Could've been a lot worse.'

'That's for sure.'

'What I really want to do is go to your place and take a nice hot shower and then get somewhat smashed.'

'I've only got about half a bottle of wine.'

'We can pick up something on the way over.' Shoes on, she stood up. 'You must be freezing,' she said.

'Just a little.'

'My poor sweetheart.' She opened the shirt wide and stepped against me and put her arms around me. The heat of her body seeped into my chilled skin. 'How's this?' she asked.

'Not bad.'

Chapter Twenty-two

At the top of the embankment, we retrieved our belongings from under the park bench. I wore my book bag like a small knapsack and carried Eileen's books and binders against my chest. That way, I didn't feel quite so cold or bare.

But shirtless I was. Scratched and bloody, too, as I found out when we entered the glow of a streetlight.

Because of her soak in the stream, Eileen wasn't bloody. Her face, however, looked somewhat battered. Also, her hair was wet and stringy.

To avoid being seen by campus security or by anyone we knew, we walked *around* the university campus instead of through it.

That's how we ran into Rudy Kirkus.

I'd known Kirkus since my freshman year. We were both English majors, so we'd spent quite a lot of time in the same classes. Also, we were both on the staff of the university's literary magazine, *The Roar*. A smug know-it-all, he seemed to consider himself God's gift to literature and good taste.

He was an easy guy to recognize at a distance. Well over six feet tall and skinny, he walked like a drum major at the head of his own parade. His uniform was a corduroy jacket with patches on its elbows, a blue chambray shirt, blue jeans, loafers and an ascot. He *always* wore a silk ascot around his neck.

If I'd seen Kirkus approaching us, I would've dragged Eileen in a different direction. Fast. But he came at us from around the corner of the bank at Ivy Street, a block south of campus.

'I *say*!' he said. He clapped me on the shoulder. 'Eduardo, old man. And Eileen! What ho?'

Kirkus was a native of San Francisco, but he affected a British accent and mannerisms. He'd probably picked up most of his act by watching those old Sherlock Holmes movies with Basil Rathbone and Nigel Bruce.

'How's it going, Kirkus?' I asked.

'It goes, it goes.' Nodding, he put his hands behind his back and began his usual routine of going up and down, up and down on the balls of his feet. Head cocked to one side, he eyed my chest. 'I say, old chap, a bit nippy to be roaming about the streets *sans* shirt.'

'Don't knock it till you've tried it,' I told him.

He cocked his head toward Eileen and eyed *her* chest. If another guy had stared that blatantly, I might've been miffed. But this was Kirkus. Her breasts, obviously braless under the shirt, would be of no interest to him . . . except perhaps as objects of disdain.

'Hello!' he exclaimed. '*You're* wearing his shirt. The plot does thicken, hey what?' He bobbed, grinning.

'I'm afraid I left home without mine,' Eileen told him. 'This chap was nice enough to lend me the use of his.'

Kirkus continued to bob, but his grin vanished while he hoisted an eyebrow. 'You're having me on.'

'Not at all,' Eileen said, appearing perfectly serious.

'And why are you wet?' he asked.

'A touch of rain, old bean.'

He still bobbed, but both his eyebrows lowered and crept toward the bridge of his nose. 'And your injuries?' he asked. He glanced from Eileen to me, bobbing and frowning, not so much a drum major, now, as a stern headmaster determined to get to the bottom of the mischief. 'Have ourselves a bit of a row, did we?'

Eileen looked to me for this one.

'A spot of trouble with a canine, I'm afraid. Out on the moor. A huge brute with glowing eyes.'

'I see.' He took a deep breath, began to sag, then straightened up again and threw back his head. 'Well, have your sport with me.'

I suddenly felt bad. Kirkus was a pretentious and arrogant boob, but that was no excuse for mocking him. 'Hey,' I said. 'I'm sorry.'

'Me, too,' Eileen told him. 'We've had a tough night.'

'Ah.' He seemed pleased by our contrition. 'Quite all right.'

'As a matter of fact,' I told him, 'we got jumped by a gang of teenagers a few minutes ago. They beat us up pretty good and tore off Eileen's shirt.'

'Rum go,' said Kirkus.

Shrugging, Eileen said, 'Well, we got away from them. *You'd* better watch out for them, though.'

'I'm perfectly capable of taking care of myself,' he said.

'Just be careful,' Eileen said. 'They're nasty bastards. They pissed in my hair.'

Kirkus eyed her hair, sniffed the air a couple of times, and took a step backward.

'We don't want everybody knowing about this,' I explained. 'In fact, we don't want *anybody* else knowing about it.'

'It's terribly humiliating,' Eileen added. 'And disgusting.'

'We've taken you into our confidence,' I said.

'We'd like you to respect it,' said Eileen.

'Righto.' Kirkus gave a stiff nod, bounced, and said, 'Mum's the word.'

'Thank you,' Eileen told him.

'Thanks, Rudy,' I said.

'And thank *you* for the warning. If the young hooligans have a go at me, they'll rue the day.'

I reached out and patted his arm. 'Knock 'em dead.'

'Where were they?' he asked.

Eileen turned sideways and pointed behind us. 'A couple of blocks back.'

The boarding house where Kirkus lived was in that direction.

Scowling, he asked, 'How many ruffians did you encounter?'

'Six or seven,' I said.

He nodded briskly.

'I guess you'll have to go past them to get home,' I added.

'Quite.'

'They might be gone by now,' Eileen pointed out.

Kirkus straightened up and tossed back his head. '"Danger knows full well that Caesar is more dangerous than she."'

'You say so,' I told him.

'Ta,' he said, and stepped past us.

'Good luck,' I told him.

'Give 'em hell,' Eileen said.

As Kirkus strode bravely down the sidewalk, we crossed the street. Halfway up the next block, we both glanced back. Kirkus was nowhere to be seen.

'Hope he doesn't hurt them,' Eileen said.

I chuckled and felt a little mean.

'Poor sod,' Eileen said.

We both laughed.

'You know,' I said, 'he might not be such a bad guy if he didn't go around acting like such a fucking know-it-all snob.'

'A *bloody* know-it-all snob.'

We laughed some more.

On the next block, we came to the Grand Market.

'You might want to wait out here,' Eileen suggested. 'I'll go in and get the stuff.'

I nodded.

'Don't go away.'

She went inside. I stepped around the side, away from the main street, and stood close to the wall. Though a few people went by, nobody paid attention to me.

Eileen was gone for a long time. That's how it seemed, anyway.

At last, she stepped around the corner with a brown-paper grocery sack in her arms. 'Ah, there you are,' she said. 'Look what I got for you.'

She set down the bag at her feet, reached in and pulled out something that appeared to be a black cloth. Grinning, she held it high and spread it open.

'A Dracula cape,' she explained.

'So I see.'

'A nice one, too. Put it on.'

'Now?'

'Come on. I know you're freezing.' She brought it toward me. 'It was the best I could do. They didn't seem to have any clothes in there. Lucky for you, they've got a great bunch of Halloween costumes.'

'I'm supposed to *wear* this?'

'You can throw it on over your book bag. Wrap it around yourself like a blanket.'

'Well . . .'

'Better than freezing.'

'I suppose.'

I set my armload of books and binders down on the sidewalk, then took the cape from Eileen. I swung it around behind me. It draped my book bag and shoulders. I wrapped it around my front. It felt smooth and warm. 'Pretty good,' I said.

'You look smashing, as Kirkus might say.' With that, Eileen stepped closer. She found a couple of dangling cords and made a bow of them at my throat. Then she slipped her hands inside the cape and caressed my chest. 'I should've bought you some vampire teeth.'

I bared my own teeth at her.

She laughed softly and kissed me.

When we resumed our journey, Eileen carried her own books and binders and purse. I carried the grocery bag close to my chest with one hand while I held the cape shut with the other.

In the bag were two cans of squirt cheese (sharp cheddar and sharp cheddar with bacon), a box of Ritz crackers and a liter bottle of dark rum.

Though most of the businesses along the street were shut for the night, people walked past us now and again. Some of them noticed what I was wearing, and smiled.

With a university in the middle of town, they were used to all sorts of antics. A guy in a vampire cape three weeks before Halloween was no big deal.

After we left the business district behind, the sidewalks seemed to be empty. Every so often, a car went by.

Richard Laymon

We were about two blocks from my apartment house when Eileen glanced over her shoulder. Facing forward again, she muttered, 'Somebody's back there.'

Chapter Twenty-three

I looked, but saw only the empty sidewalk stretched out behind us. I checked the street, then the sidewalk on the other side of the street. 'I don't see anyone.'

Eileen looked again. 'That's funny.'

'Maybe he went in a house,' I suggested.

'Or ducked out of sight.'

We kept on walking.

'What did he look like?' I asked.

'Just a guy. I *think* it was a guy. He was pretty far back and I only caught a glimpse of him.'

'Wasn't Kirkus, was it?'

'I don't think so.'

'Old guy, young guy?'

She shook her head. 'I have no idea. But whoever he is, let's not lead him to your apartment.'

I'd already thought of that. I nodded. At the next corner, instead of going straight onto Church Street, we turned to the left.

'What was he wearing?' I asked.

Eileen shook her head again. 'Something dark. A long coat, maybe.'

'Like a trenchcoat?'

'I don't know.'

'This really sucks,' I muttered.

'Think it's someone from under the bridge?'

'God, I hope not. But I guess it might be. Or that Randy guy I was telling you about. Or maybe it's just somebody who happened to be walking behind us.'

'Let's find out,' Eileen said.

We both glanced back. Nobody was behind us. Not yet, anyway.

'Come on,' I said.

Side by side, we ran up the sidewalk. The first driveway had a car parked in it. The house's porch light was on, but all the windows looked dark.

Our pursuer – if we had one – still hadn't rounded the corner. We rushed up the driveway and crouched in front of the car.

I'd been spending a lot of time, lately, hiding in front of parked cars.

But always alone.

This time, Eileen was hunkered down beside me, her upper arm lightly touching mine. I could feel its heat through my cape. She turned her face toward me. 'This is kind of exciting,' she said.

'If you say so.'

I felt mostly anxiety . . . bordering on dread. And I felt weary. Too much had already happened tonight. I wanted to be safe in my apartment with the lights on and the door locked. Underneath all that, however, I did feel a certain thrill at being crouched down and hiding with Eileen.

After a while, she said, 'What's taking him so long?'

'How far back was he?'

She shrugged, and I felt her arm move against mine. 'Just a block.' She straightened up slightly and peered over the hood. 'I don't see anyone.'

'We'll hear him when he goes by.'

She stayed up, half crouched, her books and binders clutched to her chest.

'We don't want him to see you,' I whispered.

She sank down beside me, and I felt the rub of her arm. 'I don't think he's coming,' she said.

'Let's wait a while longer. Maybe he's being careful.'

'We might've lost him.'

I nodded.

We crouched together in silence, waiting. Out on the street, a car went by. Its sounds slowly faded away. I listened for footsteps, but heard none.

Eileen turned her face toward mine. 'He probably wasn't following us in the first place.'

'Maybe not,' I said.

'Maybe he just happened to be going in the same direction as us.'

'Yeah.'

'Happens all the time.'

'Sometimes,' I said, 'they *are* following you.'

'Not this time, I guess.'

'Let's make sure,' I said. 'He might just be waiting for us to come out of hiding.'

'Guess you're more deeply paranoid than me.'

'More than likely,' I said.

'I don't like being on someone else's property.'

'We're not hurting anything.'

'They might not see it that way.' She twisted partway around and looked toward the house.

I looked, too. From where we were crouched, we couldn't see any of the windows.

'Guess they can't see us,' Eileen whispered.

I looked toward the house next door. 'Neither can they,' I said.

Eileen faced me. 'We're pretty well hidden, aren't we?'

'Pretty well.'

'Not as well as under the bridge, though.'

I wished she hadn't mentioned the bridge. 'This is sure better lit,' I whispered.

'I was so scared.'

'Me, too.'

She set her books and binders down on the concrete. 'Hold me,' she whispered.

I put down the grocery sack.

On our knees in front of the car, we turned toward each other.

Eileen spread my cape open and eased in against me. She put her hands on my back below the bottom of my book bag. I hugged her gently. She was trembling, but felt warm against my body.

'That was so terrible,' she whispered close to my ear.

'A lot worse for you.'

'They were all over me.'

And in you? I wondered. But I couldn't ask.

'You know what bothers me the most?' she asked.

'Huh-uh.'

Here it comes.

'They could see us.'

'I guess so.'

'They *must've* been able to see us,' she said. 'They knew right where we were . . . and where to grab and . . . or they couldn't have done all that. But it was pitch-black in there.'

'Not completely,' I said.

'We sure couldn't see them. Or even each other.'

'They'd probably been under there long enough for their eyes to adjust.'

'But it was *so* dark. God, it was dark.' She pressed herself more tightly against me. The concrete was hurting my knees. 'You can't see in that kind of darkness no matter *how* long you've been in it.'

'They must've.'

'I know. I know. They were probably there the whole time. Just standing there silent. You'd think we would've at least heard them breathing.'

Or undressing, I thought.

Unless they stripped before we got there.

Maybe they'd been skinny-dipping in the stream.

Didn't seem likely. Not on a chilly night like this.

'Or smelled them,' Eileen said. 'Did you smell them? They stank when they were on me, but I never smelled them till then.'

'I didn't, either.'

'I thought we were alone.'

'Same here.'

132

'I mean, we should've been able to *hear* them or something. It doesn't make sense.'

'Huh-uh.'

'And to think they were right there while we . . . did all that.' She shivered in my arms. 'And we didn't even know it.'

'Ninja bums,' I whispered.

She laughed softly, quietly, her breath blowing hot against the side of my neck, her body shaking. 'Very funny,' she whispered.

For a while after that, we didn't say anything. Just held each other. She stopped trembling. I could feel the slow, easy rise and fall of her chest as she breathed.

'We've probably been here long enough,' I said.

'My knees are killing me,' she said.

'Me, too.'

'My knees aren't even touching you.'

We both laughed a little at that.

'You're pretty funny for a scholar,' I told her.

'I'm no scholar. Kirkus is the scholar.'

'He just thinks he is.'

'Hope he got home all right.'

'Think he believed us?' I asked.

'The teenage gang attack? Yeah. He believed that, all right.'

'Nice touch, the pee in the hair.'

She laughed. 'Did you catch him sniffing? The look on his face, you'd think he smelled it.'

I put my face against her hair. It seemed damp and heavy against the side of her head.

'How does it smell?'

'Fine.'

'I hope nothing awful was in that stream.'

'You can take a nice bath when we get to my place.'

'Can't wait,' she said.

'Ready to go?'

'Hope I can still stand up.'

I knew just what she meant; my knees felt ruined, too.

We eased away from each other. Eileen picked up her stack of books and binders and clutched them to her chest. I grabbed the top of the grocery sack with one hand and held the front of my cape shut with the other.

My knees made crackling sounds when I stood up.

Eileen groaned. 'Next time we do this,' she said, 'we should bring kneeling pads.'

'That's a very good . . .'

Bring-bring-bringgg.

It was too late to duck.

She came coasting down the sidewalk from the left, a skinny old hag in black spandex, her ballcap turned backward, her bike tires humming softly, almost silent.

As she glided toward the driveway, her head turned toward us.

Her face was dark with shadows.

She sees us, I thought, though I couldn't see her eyes.

As her bike sailed across the end of the driveway, she turned her head even more so she wouldn't lose sight of us. She kept watching us until she passed the neighbor's hedge.

Eileen and I stood side by side, motionless and silent.

From the right came the *bring-bring-bringgg* of the bicycle bell.

Eileen looked at me. 'What the *hell* was that?' she whispered.

'The bike hag,' I said.

'You know her?'

'Not really.'

Bring-bringgg.

It came from farther away.

'I wanta get outa here,' Eileen said.

'Let's go.'

Chapter Twenty-four

'Oh God, the church,' Eileen said as we crossed the final street on our way to my apartment building. 'Nothing more fun than an old church late at night. I wonder who's waiting *there* to scare the crap out of us.'

'No one, I'm sure.'

'I'm not sure of anything,' she said.

'You want something good to worry about, how about Mr and Mrs Fisher?'

'Oh, they're harmless.'

'If they see us like this . . .' I shook my head.

'We'll tell them we were set upon by a gang of teenaged ne'er-do-wells.'

'Sure.'

'Worked on Kirkus,' she pointed out.

'Kirkus is an idiot.'

I stepped ahead of Eileen, unlocked the door and let us in. I shut the door silently. Leading the way, I crept through the foyer.

The Fishers' door was open, light spilling out into the gloom of the hallway. From where I stood, I could hear their television. The music sounded like *Halloween*.

'Great,' I muttered.

'It's okay,' Eileen whispered.

'I'm wearing a *vampire* cape.'

'They'll just think you're zany. Come on.' Eileen left me standing there. As she walked past the Fishers' open door, she kept her face forward and didn't look in.

I hurried after her.

On my way past the door, however, I had to look.

Mrs Fisher stood just inside the doorway, leaning forward on her cane. She stared at me through her thick glasses. Her eyes looked as big as eggs. I jumped and said, 'Oh, hi.'

'Hi back,' she said, grinning.

I had to stop.

'What's that outfit ya got on there, Eddie?'

'A vampire cape. It's for Halloween.'

'What's Holly got on?' she asked.

Holly?

I backed away as Mrs Fisher hobbled into the hallway. Eileen had stopped at the foot of the stairs.

'Hi, Mrs Fisher,' she said.

'Come on back and let me take a look at ya, Holly.'

Eileen smiled and approached.

'What sorta get-up's that?' Mrs Fisher asked her.

'Just my usual clothes.'

'If you say so.'

Mrs Fisher, herself, was wearing a huge gray sweatshirt with the old Willmington University logo on the front. Around the logo, purple letters read, HOME OF THE BRAVES. She had a white bath towel wrapped around her waist. It reached down almost to her knees like a skirt. From the towel down, her heavy legs were bare. She wore blue tennis shoes that didn't have any laces.

'Thought ya had on yer Halloween get-up,' she said.

'Not tonight,' Eileen said.

'Eddie, he's already got his.' Turning her giant eyes on me, she said, 'Come on in and show Walter.'

'We really have to get going.'

'It won't take but a second. Give him a laugh.' She reached out for me, but I sidestepped toward the stairway and she missed. 'Now don't be so shy, Eddie.'

'It's awfully late,' I said. 'I'll show Walter some other time, okay?'

'Well . . .'

'We'll see you later, Mrs Fisher,' Eileen said.

'Well, awe right. You two go 'n' run on along. Good seein' ya again, Holly.'

'Thanks,' Eileen said. 'Same here.'

'My, but you've grown.'

'Thanks.'

'Still just as nice as pie.'

'You, too. See you later.'

At the foot of the stairway, we looked back at her. She waved goodbye with her cane.

'Night,' I said.

'Don't let the bed bugs bite.'

We hurried upstairs. I felt squirmy from the encounter, but Eileen was smiling.

The second-floor hallway was murky with dim, yellowish light. All the doors were shut.

'She's not so bad,' Eileen whispered.

'At least she didn't make any trouble about you coming up here.'

'Maybe because she thinks I'm Holly.'

'She liked Holly a lot.' Unlocking my door, I added, 'Everyone did. Guess everyone still does. Except me.'

We entered my rooms and I shut the door.

'I'm not such a big fan anymore, myself,' Eileen said.

While she set her books and binders down on the coffee table in front of the sofa, I carried the grocery sack into the kitchen and put it on the counter. I reached under my cape and removed my book bag. As I swung it onto the table, Eileen came in.

'Okay if I take a shower?' she asked.

'Sure. I'll get you a clean washcloth and towel.'

She followed me to the bathroom. I flicked on the light, then went to the nearby linen closet. The washcloth and towel I took down were pink and soft. I'd bought them last year for Holly to use when she spent nights with me.

I carried them into the bathroom for Eileen.

'I might need some bandages when I'm done,' she said.

137

I opened the medicine cabinet and showed her where they were.

'I'll try to be fast,' she said.

'Take your time. No hurry.'

'Go ahead and help yourself to the rum. You don't have to wait for me.'

'Okay. See you later.' Leaving her in the bathroom, I shut the door.

But I didn't help myself to the rum. Instead, I went into my bedroom. With the light on, I turned to the mirror. My hair was mussed, my face dirty and scratched. Spreading the cape open, I bared my teeth and snarled at the mirror.

Big, bad vampire.

Sure.

I *did* look scruffy and a little scary, though.

Should've tried this with Kirkus.

Or the bike hag.

I almost smiled, but my mind suddenly hit me with a picture of the bum I'd found underneath the bridge. Feeling hot and sick, I turned away from the mirror and removed the cape. Then I took off the rest of my clothes, put on my robe and flopped down on my bed to wait for Eileen to finish her shower.

The guy's probably okay, I told myself.

He had that erection.

I should've checked his pulse.

If I'd tried that, he might've grabbed me.

Suppose he *is* dead?

He's not, I told myself. But if he is, they won't know we had anything to do with it.

We'll have to keep our mouths shut about what happened under there.

What about Kirkus? He knows we were in a fight. He might tell on us.

So who cares? It was self-defense anyway. It's not like I murdered the guy.

But I felt hot and sick from thinking such thoughts.

So stop it, I told myself. Think about something pleasant. Think about Eileen.

As I gazed at the ceiling and listened to the hiss of the shower, I pictured her standing under its spray. Steam swirled around her like hot fog. Water splashed her face, ran down her body. She was ruddy and gleaming . . .

Just like Holly.

I shut my eyes.

Holly and I had taken showers together sometimes. Stood facing each other beneath the hot spray, me sliding soapy hands over her breasts, Holly lathering my penis, her slippery hand gliding up and down.

Should I go to her?

It's Eileen, not Holly.

Holly wouldn't want me, anyway. The slut has her Jay.

It's Eileen in the shower now.

Maybe she wants me to be with her. Maybe she's hoping I'll come in, and she'll be disappointed if I don't.

No no no, I thought. She doesn't want me now, not after what they did to her. She wants her privacy while she cleans up and tends to her wounds.

In my mind, however, I go to her. I sweep aside the shower curtain and there she stands under the spray, looking at me and weeping and holding out her hands for help. She is scratched and scraped and gashed and chewed, blood spilling from a dozen wounds. Blood squirts from her nipples. It gushes from her vagina as hard as water from a garden hose, pounding the bottom of the tub and splashing against her ankles and shins.

Help me, she says.

I climb into the tub.

I'm bleeding to death!

And I say, *Maybe it's your period.*

No! They did it to me. Help! Please!

With my fingertips, I pinch her nipples to shut off the squirting blood.

Yes! But the other! The other! Plug it up!

With what?

I already know what. It's hard and ready. Keeping her nipples pinched, I position myself under the hot gusher and push up into her, stopping the rush of blood.

'Eddie!'

Did it!

'Can you come here!'

Where's she calling from?

Doesn't matter, I think. I can't go anywhere. If I pull out, she'll bleed to death. This was a really bad idea. Should've taken her to the emergency room. Never should've tried to plug her like this.

But it feels so good.

Too good. When I come, I'll get soft and she'll bleed out and . . .

'Eddie? Can you come in here?'

I woke up. I was lying on the end of my bed, my legs hanging off below the knees, my feet on the floor. Pushing myself up on my elbows, I saw that my robe hung open. I was stiff and hard, but not in Eileen.

Nobody in the room but me.

'Eddie?'

She IS calling!

I lurched up, ran to the bathroom and knocked on the door. 'Eileen?'

'You okay?' she called over the hissing, splashing sounds of the shower.

'Yeah. Fine.'

'I kept calling and you didn't answer.'

'I guess I drifted off.'

And dreamed a little dream of you.

'I thought something had happened.'

'No. Everything's fine.'

'Can you come in?' she asked.

I opened the door and entered.

The bathroom was hot and steamy. Eileen's clothes, including my shirt, were piled on the floor. I stepped over them and walked toward the bath tub. Through the frosted white plastic curtain, I could see the vague contours and color of her body.

I saw no red.

'Can you come here?' she asked.

'Sure.'

I stopped on the bath mat.

'You probably need a shower, too,' she said.

'Probably.'

'Want to come in now?'

I opened my robe and looked down. Still partly aroused from the dream, I was sticking out straight.

Embarrassing. But a little exciting, too.

Maybe it'll go down if I wait a while.

'Eddie?'

'Huh?'

'Coming in?'

'Just a minute.'

She was facing me through the curtain. One of her breasts seemed to be touching the frosted plastic.

I gave up any hope of shrinking.

So I took off my robe and tossed it out of the way. Eileen, obviously watching me, pulled the curtain aside. I climbed into the tub.

It wasn't much like the dream. Though her wet skin gleamed, no blood squirted or gushed out of her body. The injuries that I could see were contusions and scratches. She also looked as if she'd been bitten in several places. The teeth hadn't broken her skin, but they'd left marks.

'You don't look too bad,' I said.

'Neither do you.'

I had worse abrasions than Eileen. More scratches and bite marks, too.

She began to slide a bar of soap over my body. 'I'll get you all nice and squeaky clean,' she said.

She already looked squeaky clean, herself.

Her sliding hands made me soapy all over. Then she wrapped her arms around me, pressed her body gently against mine and kissed me with her mouth open. She moaned and squirmed. I was upright and thick against her belly. She felt slippery and soft all the way down to her knees.

A few times, she flinched when I touched bad places on her back and buttocks.

Soon, I was down on the bottom of the tub with Eileen straddling me, clutching my shoulders, her breasts wobbling and lurching as I drove up into her. Sometimes, the hot spray of the shower was blocked by her body. Other times, it got me full in the face.

Chapter Twenty-five

Standing outside the tub while I gently dried Eileen, I found that she did have a few cuts on her back and buttocks. They looked red and raw, but were no longer bleeding.

I put antiseptic and bandages on them.

Then she asked if I had a hair drier.

'Afraid not.'

'That's all right.' She held out her hands for the towel.

I gave it to her, then watched while she rubbed her hair vigorously with it, her arms high, her breasts shaking. Her breasts had marks on them. Not from me, but from what the others had done to her under the bridge.

What *had* they done to her?

'I'll be a few more minutes in here,' Eileen said. 'You want to run ahead and make the drinks?'

'Sure.'

'How about rum and Coke for me?'

'Coming right up.' I put on my robe and headed for the door.

'On the rocks,' she added.

I glanced over my shoulder at her. She looked wonderful standing there with her arms up, smiling at me from under the bunched towel.

'You can leave the door open,' she said. 'Let the steam clear out.'

Nodding, I turned away and went into the kitchen. I made the drinks. Then I carried them into the living room and returned to the kitchen for the Ritz crackers and squirt cheese.

When I came out, Eileen was standing in the living room. Her hair, still moist but neatly brushed, hung down to her bare shoulders. The pink towel was wrapped around her waist, one end tucked in at her hip.

'Wow,' I said.

'But a little nippy,' she said. 'Got anything for me to wear?'

'Oh. Sure. I'm sorry.'

'No problem.'

I hurried past her and she followed me down the hall to my bedroom. I took a cotton nightshirt out of a dresser drawer. Holding it up for her to see, I asked, 'How's this?'

It was red and had Goofy on it.

Eileen frowned slightly. 'Was this Holly's?'

'It's mine.'

'I bet she wore it, though.'

'Yeah.'

Holly had worn it a lot. The nightshirt had looked great on her, short and clingy.

'I can get you something else,' I said.

Shaking her head, she stepped forward and took it from me. 'No, this is fine.' She plucked the towel away from her body, tossed it onto my bed, then put the nightshirt on over her head. The thin cotton drifted down her body. It was shorter on her than on Holly.

She raised her arms to sweep her hair out from under the night-shirt's neck, and the hem lifted higher than her groin. When she lowered her arms, it descended.

Smiling, she asked, 'Do I look okay?'

'Great.'

'It's a little short.'

'I don't mind if you don't.'

She grinned. 'I'm ready for a drink. How about you?'

'Sure am.'

This time, she led the way. I walked to the living room behind her, my eyes on the smooth curves of her buttocks as they flexed under the clinging nightshirt.

We sat down beside each other on the sofa.

I picked up both drinks and handed one to her. She raised her glass toward me. 'To being safe and clean and together,' she said.

'I'll drink to that.'

We drank.

'Mmmm, good,' Eileen said. 'You make a mean rum and Coke.'

I laughed. 'It's not totally disgusting.'

After a few more sips, Eileen set down her glass and picked up the Ritz crackers. 'Let's dig in.'

While she opened the box of crackers, I peeled the seal off a canister of squirt cheese.

'Can't believe how hungry I am,' she said.

'We had an active night.'

'I'll say. My God. Here, give me.'

I popped the lid off and passed the canister to her. Upending it, she squirted a small pile of orange cheese onto a cracker in her hand.

'Open wide,' she said. I opened my mouth and she stuffed the cracker in. I chewed. The cracker crunched. The cheddar was creamy and tangy and I could taste the bacon flavor.

Eileen prepared a cracker for herself. She ate it while I drank more of my rum and Coke. As she chewed, she closed her eyes. She looked as if she were relishing a rare delight. After swallowing, she sighed. 'Fantastic.'

'Pretty darn good.'

Squirting cheese onto another cracker, she said again, 'I can't believe how hungry I am.'

'You go ahead and eat that one.'

'No, you.' She pushed it into my mouth, then took another drink and started preparing another cracker. 'It might have something to do with all that sex,' she said.

I nodded and chewed.

'But I bet it makes people hungry when they have close calls. All that adrenalin. Do you know any physiology?'

'Not much.'

'Me neither. But I've been in some earthquakes and I always feel hungry afterward.' A smile spread across her face. 'Horny, too.' She popped a cheese-loaded cracker into her mouth.

'You think we're so hungry because we got attacked?'

Chewing with her mouth shut, she nodded.

Though I felt the heat of a blush spread over my skin, I asked, 'And horny?'

She nodded some more.

'Those bums piling on you made you horny?'

Frowning slightly, she shook her head. She swallowed and took a long drink. 'Not that. Sur*viv*ing. Es*cap*ing. Getting away in one *piece*. That's what does it.'

'I thought you meant getting attacked.'

'God, no. You must be kidding.' She suddenly went silent and stared at me, looking appalled. 'You think I *liked* having those guys on me?'

'Not really, but . . .'

'They were vile. They stank. They were all over me, slobbering on me, groping me, hurting me. They were *naked*. I could feel their *cocks*. They were trying to *rape* me. And you think I *liked* it?'

Now or never.

'They *didn't* rape you, did they?' I asked.

She looked as if I'd slapped her. She gaped at me, her mouth drooping.

'I mean, if they did, you might need . . .'

'They didn't.' Her voice was low and steady, her eyes locked on mine.

'Are you sure?'

'I think I would know.'

'Okay.'

'You don't *believe* me?'

I didn't want to tell her about the bum I'd found when I went back for her purse and clothes.

'I believe you,' I said, trying to sound convincing. 'It's just that . . . they were on you for a couple of minutes . . .'

'Tell me about it.'

'I got to you as fast as I could, but they might've had time . . . maybe one or two of them . . .'

'Well, they didn't.'

'Okay.'

She looked shocked and sad. 'I can't believe you even felt it necessary to ask.'

'But if they did—'

'If they *did*, do you think for one second I would've invited you into the bathroom to *fuck* me? Do you think I would endanger your life that way?'

'No.' I sounded like a guilty kid on the verge of tears.

'You're damn right I wouldn't!'

'I'm sorry.'

'Not half as sorry as I am. I can't *believe* you, Eddie. My *God*!'

'I'm sorry.'

I reached out for her.

'Don't!' she blurted and scooted away from me, her glass and the squirt cheese in her hands, the box of Ritz crackers resting on her lap. The Ritz box tumbled off. Crackers spilled out on the cushion between us.

'I'm sorry,' I said. 'I shouldn't have asked.'

'But you did. You did.' Leaning forward, she slammed her glass and the squirt cheese onto the table. Then she got to her feet. 'I'll be going now.'

'No, wait. You can't . . .'

'Just watch.'

She hurried around the end of the coffee table, but I leaped to my feet and intercepted her. I grabbed her by both upper arms.

Instead of struggling to free herself, she stood motionless and stared me in the eyes. In a steady voice, she said, 'Let go.'

'I only asked because I care about you.'

'You think I'd *keep* something like that from you? You think I'd let you *touch* me if any of those filthy pigs had . . .'

'No. No, I don't.'

'The hell you don't. You must think I'm a real prize. Just 'cause I put out for you a couple of times, you've got me mistaken for some sorta hot-to-trot piece of ass like Holly who'd rather have a hot cock in her pussy than . . .'

147

She cut off her words and stared at me. Her mouth hung open. Her eyes glimmered with tears.

'I'm sorry,' she murmured.

Though stunned, I shook my head as if what she'd said about Holly didn't matter.

And it didn't matter nearly as much as what I needed to tell her: 'When I went back under the bridge to get your stuff, I found a body. One of the guys who attacked you.'

She gaped at me.

'What do you mean, "a body"? Like a *dead* body?'

'Or unconscious. I don't know. But he . . . he looked as if he'd . . . you know, *been* in someone.'

'What do you mean?'

'It was wet.'

'Didn't get that way from me.'

'Or from me,' I said.

She gave me a sad little smirk. Then she stepped against me. It was a good, familiar feel. Arms around me, she lowered her face into the curve on the side of my neck. I could feel the wetness of her tears.

Softly, she said, 'So you thought this guy had nailed me, but you went ahead and put *yours* in me anyway?'

'Well . . .'

'What kind of idiot are *you*?'

'An optimistic idiot?'

She laughed, her body shaking against me. Then she settled down. We held each other for a long time in silence.

Later, Eileen rubbed her face dry on the shoulder of my robe. She sniffed and looked at me. 'This guy under the bridge?' she said. 'Are you the one who put him out of commission?'

'Probably. When they were on top of you like that, I went sort of nuts with my rock. If he's dead, I'm probably the one who killed him.'

'Oh, boy,' she said. 'What'll we do?'

'Nothing.'

'Just pretend it didn't happen?'

I shook my head. 'We don't have to pretend anything. We just accept that somebody got hurt when we defended ourselves.'

'Got what he deserved,' Eileen said.

'Yeah.'

'But what about the police?'

'Want to report it?' I asked.

'No!'

'Didn't think so.'

'But we don't want them coming after us, either. What if we left something behind?'

Her shirt and panties.

'I don't think we did,' I said. 'I searched around pretty good when I went back.'

'I'm still missing a couple of things.'

'I know. But they weren't there.'

She stared me in the eyes and said, 'I think we'd better go back.'

That was not what I wanted to hear.

'It was pitch-black under there,' she said.

'I used your matches.'

'We've got to go back with a good flashlight.'

'Now?'

'The sooner the better. Before someone reports the body. In fact, what we *really* should do is get rid of it. Make it go away.'

'You're kidding, right?'

'If nothing else,' she said, 'we both *bled* down there. If the cops do any kind of real homicide investigation, they'll pick up samples of our blood. And your semen.'

I was feeling worse by the word.

'We probably left footprints, too,' she said. 'God knows what else. Like maybe your fingerprints on the murder weapon.'

'It was a rock.'

'Any smooth surfaces?'

'I don't think so. Anyway, maybe the guy isn't even dead.'

'But if he is, he's down there in a crime scene *jammed* with evidence against us.'

Chapter Twenty-six

For the next hour or so, we talked about what to do. We ate more cheese and crackers and drank more rum and Coke. Though I made the drinks light, I felt a little high by the time we were done talking.

In my bedroom, we got dressed. I had enough clean clothes for both of us. Eileen wore her own shoes, but brown corduroy trousers that belonged to me, and the same dark-blue sweatshirt that I'd worn during my adventures the night before. I dressed myself in a chamois shirt, jeans and the Reeboks.

I decided to leave my wallet behind, but I pocketed my Swiss Army knife. As I took my five-inch Maglite off the night stand, Eileen said, 'Too bad you didn't have *that* with you.'

'Didn't know we'd be going under a bridge.'

'Is this the best flashlight you've got?'

'The only one I've got. It's pretty good, though.'

I found a dark-blue knit cap for Eileen, a Yankee ballcap for myself.

'What about gloves?' Eileen asked.

'Ball mitts?' Like I said, I'd had a few.

'Like rubber gloves or something. Dishwashing gloves?'

I shook my head.

'Glove gloves?' she asked.

I shrugged.

'What do you do in winter?'

'Put my hands in my pockets.'

'Ah. Then that's it, I guess.' With that, she pulled her hat on.

We went to the door. Before opening it, I turned to her. 'We sure we wanta do this?'

'I think we have to.' She looked very cute in the stocking cap, her hair stuffed inside it so that she looked boyish. She had a pale crumb of Ritz cracker at the left corner of her mouth, adhering to the down above her lip. With a fingertip, I brushed it away.

She leaned forward and gave me a kiss that was brief but soft and warm.

'Let's get it over with,' she said. 'I don't want to be late for my ten o'clock.'

'I hope that's a joke.'

'No joke.'

'Whatever we're gonna do,' I said, 'we'd better have it done before sunrise.'

'Oh, I know that.' She opened the door.

We had the hallway to ourselves. On the way downstairs, I worried about encountering the Fishers. We found their door shut, however, and hurried past it and got out of the building without being seen.

We had already decided on a route . . . one that would keep us at least a block from campus until the very end.

We walked quickly.

A cool breeze was blowing. It had the strange, moist smell that only comes 'in the dead waste and middle of the night'.

I'd been out on the streets *last* night at this hour, and later. In trouble even then, but in more trouble now.

What the hell's happened to my life? I wondered.

The answer was easy.

Holly.

Holly had broken my heart. She was why I'd started my night wandering. She was why Eileen had come into my life, and Eileen had drawn in Randy and led me down into the darkness under the bridge where the trolls got us . . . and I got one of them.

Thanks a lot, Holly.

But maybe it's more Eileen's fault than Holly's.

151

Eileen's only in this because Holly dumped me.

Maybe I ought to be *thanking* Holly for bringing Eileen into my life.

Maybe not.

One thing's for sure, I thought; Holly deserves credit for the mystery girl. I never would've seen her if Holly hadn't smashed my world.

I wonder where she is?

Probably a few miles to the north.

Strolling down a sidewalk? Sneaking into a house? Maybe keeping her rendezvous with the tequila-drinking woman I'd watched in the kitchen?

What if Randy gets his hands on her?

It's Eileen he wants.

Too bad, asshole, the trolls beat you to the punch.

No, they only tried.

Where's *Randy* now? I wondered.

Right behind us.

Wouldn't that be terrific?

I had an urge to look over my shoulder, but fought it off. For one thing, Eileen would question me about it. For another, what if he's actually back there?

As I walked along beside Eileen, I felt more and more certain that someone was following us.

I dared not look back.

Words from a poem crept into my mind:

Like one, that on a lonesome road
Doth walk in fear and dread,
And having once turned round walks on,
And turns no more his head;
Because he knows, a frightful fiend
Doth close behind him tread.

How apt! I thought.

Wordsworth? No, I'd never read much Wordsworth till this semester.

Poe? I didn't think so. I'd memorized several of Poe's poems, but this didn't seem to be from any of them.

Coleridge!

Almost for sure. It *felt* like Coleridge. I knew only three Coleridge poems by heart, 'Christabel', 'Kubla Khan', and 'The Rime of the Ancient Mariner'. This definitely wasn't 'Kubla Khan'.

I gave Eileen's hand a squeeze. She looked at me, and I recited the verse.

'Thanks for creeping me out,' she said, smiling.

'It just popped into my head.'

'Can't imagine why.'

'Does it ring a bell?'

'"It is an ancient Mariner, and he stoppeth one of three."'

'Ah! Okay. Thanks. I thought it might be "Christabel".'

'"Mariner."'

'I should've known.'

'"Instead of the cross, the Albatross about my neck was hung."'

'Nice poem for a night I killed someone.'

Eileen squeezed my hand. 'If he's dead, we'll deal with it.'

'If you say so.'

'One way or another.'

'What do you mean?' I asked.

'Well, we'll have to see what's feasible. Maybe we can take him for a drive, dump him somewhere outside of town. Maybe in Gunther Woods.'

'Is your car working?'

'Got a new battery. It's fine now. I've been thinking maybe we bring him up closer to the road, then go get my car and put him in the trunk.'

I imagined us trying to carry the dead, naked bum up to the road. Without gloves.

'I don't know,' I muttered.

'We'll see,' said Eileen.

After taking a very circuitous route, we came upon the Old Mill Stream a block east of the Division Street bridge. As we descended its embankment, I realized I'd forgotten for quite a while to worry about anyone following us.

Nobody was following us, I thought.

Oh, yeah?

Now I was worried again.

When we reached the shore of the stream, I whispered, 'Let's wait here a minute and make sure nobody's coming.'

'Was someone behind us?'

'Not that I know of. Just wanta be careful.'

Nodding slightly, Eileen whispered, 'Nothing wrong with a healthy dose of paranoia when returning to a crime scene.'

We crouched among some bushes. Eileen put an arm across my back, and I could feel her breast against the side of my arm.

Breath tickling my ear, she whispered, 'If somebody's following us, I hope it ain't one a them frightful fiends.'

'You and me both.'

For a while after that, we were silent and listening. I heard the breeze in the leaves around us. I heard a car, but it sounded far away. Now and then, a bird twittered. An owl hooted. Something small scurried over the ground somewhere up the embankment from us.

I was aware, every moment, of Eileen's breast touching my arm. I could feel its warmth through the layers of my shirt and her sweatshirt. I felt its slight movement each time she breathed in or out.

Is she doing this on purpose to get me excited? I wondered.

At least it's taking my mind off our troubles.

'I don't think anyone's coming,' she whispered.

'Ready to go?'

'Might as well get it over with.'

When we stood up, the side of my arm lost her warmth and felt chilly.

I took the lead. We walked along a path by the shore of the stream. Though I held my flashlight ready, I kept it off.

We walked in silence.

Soon, the Division Street bridge came into sight. The area underneath it looked black.

We can't go under there, I thought. The others might've come back by now.

At least I've got a flashlight this time.

Not very far from the bridge at all, I stopped and studied the area. Because we were approaching from the opposite side, everything looked much the same, but reversed, as if I were observing my memories of earlier that night in a mirror.

It was different in other ways, too. No lovers were lingering by the parapet. No cars were going by. And the approach to the blackness below the bridge was more cluttered with foliage than it had been on the opposite side.

To enter, we would need to force our way through tangles of bushes. Or wade in the stream.

Either way, I thought, they'll probably hear us coming.

I turned to Eileen and whispered. 'How about calling it quits?'

'How about going to jail?'

'I just think we might be pressing our luck.'

'Just think how great we'll feel after it's taken care of.'

'I don't know. I have a bad feeling about this.'

'It'll be fine. We've got the flashlight.'

'Yeah.'

'If anyone's in there . . . anyone *alive* . . . we'll take off like bats outa hell.'

'I suppose.'

'It'll be all right.'

'I sure hope so.'

'Why don't you give me the flashlight and I'll go first?'

'Nah, that's all right.' Not waiting for any more suggestions, I turned away and headed for the dark passageway under the bridge.

I felt tight and heavy inside. My heart hammered. My penis retreated and my scrotum shriveled. My bowels squirmed.

This is *not* a good idea, I thought.

But I kept moving, anyway.

155

Richard Laymon

Being a guy isn't always a picnic. To keep women from thinking we're jerks or cowards – and consequently scorning or dumping us – we do what they want us to do. Even when we don't want to do it. Even when we know better.

I knew *this* was a bad idea.

But I'd already voiced my objections and Eileen still thought we should go through with it.

Okay. Let's just see.

I started trudging through a waist-high thicket. It snagged my jeans, rustled and crackled. Dry leaves crunched under my shoes. Twigs snapped.

They'll hear us coming a mile away.

I halted. Eileen put a hand on my back and stopped behind me. I turned the flashlight on.

Its beam drove a narrow, widening tube of brightness into the black, lighting air and ground, the stream, rags and an old mattress and mashed cans and broken bottles.

But no naked man sprawled on the ground.

No people at all.

Until I swept the beam a small distance to the left. Near the far end of its reach, it dimly illuminated a low, squatting circle of men. Hairy, filthy, bloody.

All of them looking at us.

Chewing.

Blood spilling from their mouths.

Behind my back, Eileen grunted with shock and despair and horror as if she'd just watched a panda get beheaded.

I shut off the flashlight fast.

Eileen whispered, 'Fucking shit.'

Whirling around, I gasped, 'Let's go!'

Chapter Twenty-seven

They didn't get us. I don't really think they tried very hard. We heard them scurrying and grunting behind us for probably less than a minute. When we climbed the embankment, they apparently quit . . . not willing to risk being seen by whomever else might be up and about at such an hour.

Eileen and I kept running. We ran for blocks and blocks, gasping for breath, often glancing back, our shoes slapping the pavement of sidewalks and streets. A few times, we ducked out of sight to hide from approaching cars.

Mostly, though, we just kept running. I hardly paid attention to where we were . . . just so we were running *away* from the bridge. Then Eileen hit my arm and pointed across an empty parking lot toward a Speed-D-Mart and laundromat, both open 24 hours a day.

'Come on,' she gasped.

As we ran through the parking lot, I thought she wanted us to go inside one place or the other . . . to get off the streets and hide? Then I spotted our destination; a pair of pay phones between the entrances.

The narrow walkway in front of them was empty.

Unusual, I thought.

Though I'd been disoriented for a while, I now knew where we were. I'd used this Speed-D-Mart myself many times. And there were usually panhandlers loitering nearby, shuffling along with hands out, murmuring requests for money.

Not tonight, though.

Bet I know where *they* are, I thought. Having a little midnight snack.

It's way past midnight.

Instead of snatching up one of the phones, Eileen turned around and slumped against the wall. She panted for breath. She wiped her face with a sleeve.

'You okay?' I whispered.

'You kidding? *Jeezus!* You see what they were doing?'

'I think so.'

'*Jeezus!*'

'Well, we left 'em in the dust.'

'They were *eating* him.'

'Looked that way.'

'*Yaaah!*'

'It's all right. We got away.'

'We've gotta call the cops,' she gasped. 'Maybe they can get 'em.'

'I hope so.'

'It's okay with you?'

'Yeah.'

'I don't think we . . . need to worry about . . . getting blamed.'

I nodded. Any evidence of me or Eileen at the crime scene would be insignificant, if not obliterated entirely by the gang of trolls.

'I'll do it,' Eileen said. She pushed herself off the wall and lurched over to one of the phones.

'I don't think we have any change,' I said.

'Doesn't matter. You can . . . don't need it to call the cops.'

'Oh.' I hadn't known that.

She picked up a handset and tapped 9-1-1 on the keypad.

'Anonymous?' I asked.

She nodded. 'Is this a bad idea?'

'I think we have to.'

'Yes,' she said into the mouthpiece. 'Somebody's getting murdered down by the Mill Stream under the Division Street bridge.' She hung up. 'There.' She picked up the handset again. Holding it in the sleeve of her sweatshirt, she quickly rubbed its surfaces. Then she hung up again. With a sleeve, she wiped the keypad. 'Let's get out of here.'

We ran around the nearest corner and down the block. After turning the next corner, we slowed to a walk. We were both huffing for air. Eileen took hold of my hand. We walked quickly, not talking, keeping watch on the area around us.

Once, we hid when a car approached. We didn't hide again, however, until we were just around the corner from my apartment. Beside us was the churchyard's wrought-iron fence. 'Let's go in here,' I whispered.

Eileen looked behind us.

'Come on.' I pulled her hand.

'What?'

'Just wanta make sure.'

I thought she might resist, but she stayed with me as I led her through the gateway of the old cemetery. The church in front of us looked dark at every window. The graveyard was illuminated only by the dim glow from nearby streetlights. Through the bars of the fence, I could see the sidewalk where we'd just been.

'What're we doing?' Eileen whispered as we hurried among the tombstones.

Most of them weren't large enough for us to hide behind.

'Here.' Near the fence was a vault the size of a small shed. We crouched down behind it.

'What're we doing here?' Eileen asked again.

'Just want to make sure nobody's following us.'

'Did you see anyone?'

'No.'

'Thank God for that, anyway.'

In silence, she looked around the graveyard. We had our backs to the vault, but both of us were squatting like catchers behind home plate, not leaning against it.

Though I didn't watch the sidewalk, we were near enough to hear anyone walking by.

Or pedaling by?

It isn't the bike hag I'm worried about, I thought. It's the trolls from under the bridge. Or Randy.

'We could've picked a different place,' Eileen whispered.

'Sorry.'

'Bone orchards aren't my idea of a good time.'

'Lots of good hiding places, though.'

'Yeah. No telling who *else* might be hiding here.'

'We'll be fine,' I told her.

We went silent. She put a hand on my back. It felt warm through my shirt. After a while, she said, 'I wonder what's happening under the bridge right now.'

'Cops must be there.'

'Yeah.'

'Hope they went in force.'

'The trolls are probably long gone.'

I nodded, certain Eileen was right.

'Think they were really eating him?' she asked.

'Looked that way.'

'How *could* they?'

'It happens.'

'Right under the bridge? That's on *campus*, for godsake.'

'It probably doesn't happen every night.'

'Nobody's *missing*,' she said. 'Not that *I* know of. We'd hear about it if anyone disappeared.'

'Maybe they only eat their own.'

'Ooof.'

'Anyway, maybe that's *not* what we saw. We only got a glimpse.'

'I guess it'll be on the radio first,' she said. 'The radio gets everything first.'

'Can't wait.'

'Whatever happens,' she said, 'we play ignorant.'

'Right.'

'The cops have no reason to suspect us of anything.'

'We're a little beat up,' I reminded her.

'If they question us, we'll give them the story we gave Kirkus. But they won't. Nobody'll even notice we're banged up except a few students and maybe some faculty, and we can tell them anything we want.'

'Sounds good.'

'But we'd better work on the story we told Kirkus. Come up with details so we'll be able to get our stories straight.'

'Where'd we say it happened?' I asked.

'Let's wait till we get inside.'

'Sure.'

'Can we go inside *now*?'

'Maybe give it a few more minutes.'

'I have to pee *really* badly, Ed. And I'm wearing your pants.'

'Ah. Okay. I guess we can go in.'

We stood up and looked around. Then, holding hands, we walked through the graveyard to the place where we'd entered. I leaned out the gateway.

Nobody was in sight.

So we left and went around the corner and past the front of the church and up the walkway to the front door of my apartment building. I unlocked the door. We went inside.

The Fishers' door was shut.

The upstairs hallway was dim and deserted. I unlocked my door and we entered my room. When the door was shut, Eileen wrapped her arms around me and whispered, 'Safe.'

Chapter Twenty-eight

When I woke up Thursday morning, I raised my head off the pillow and looked at the clock on the nightstand.

10:32.

I rolled the other way. Eileen's side of the bed was empty.

Considering what we'd been through last night, I'd thought she might cut her ten o'clock class. She must've gotten up and gone to it, though.

I imagined her sitting at a desk in the English building. I wasn't sure which class she had, so I didn't imagine a teacher. Just Eileen sitting there, her face bruised and scratched. I pictured her rubbing her eyes. Yawning. How much sleep did she get, maybe three hours?

I wondered what she was wearing. Had she gone back to the sorority house for clean clothes of her own? Or did she go to class in my corduroy trousers and sweatshirt from last night? With no bra on?

Imagining her breasts loose under the sweatshirt, I started getting hard.

No panties, either?

A troll got her panties.

Trolls suddenly swarmed through my mind, sickening me, scaring me, shrinking me. Knowing the torment would continue so long as I remained in bed, I threw the sheet aside and climbed out.

As I put my robe on, the comfortable aroma of coffee reached me. Eileen must've brewed a pot before leaving.

I went into the bathroom, used the toilet, then hurried to the kitchen.

On the table, a sheet of lined notebook paper was standing up like a pup tent. The side facing me had handwriting on it.

I picked up the paper and read it:

Dear Eddie,

As you may have realized by now, I decided not to miss my ten o'clock class. We must keep up appearances so as to avoid arousing suspicion.

We ought to go about our respective lives as if nothing has happened. (In other words, you should attend your regular classes, too.)

For the sake of not drawing any undue attention to ourselves, I think it would be best if we stay apart for a period of time. Let's give our faces an opportunity to heal before we allow ourselves to be seen again side by side.

This won't be easy, but I think it might be the smart thing to do, as we do NOT want anyone to suspect we were involved in any way with what happened last night.

I will miss you so much, Eddie. Please do not mistake this note for any sort of 'brush-off.' In no way am I trying to dump you. I feel so very good when we're together.

Hope you sleep late and wake up missing me. Talk to you later.

All my love,

Me

PS Burn after reading.

I smiled when I read the PS. Then I filled a mug with coffee, sat at the table and read her note again. It made a lot of sense to go about our lives as if nothing were wrong. It also made sense to stay away from each other until our faces looked better.

But her denial that this was a 'brush-off' made me worry that it might be exactly that, or a preliminary move in that direction.

Why did she even bring it up?

Just to reassure me, probably. Just to remind me that she's not Holly.

Several times, I reread the line, 'I feel so very good when we're together.'

She'd closed the letter, 'All my love.'

It's pretty obvious how she feels, I thought. She loves me. She doesn't want to stay away from me, just thinks it's necessary to avoid arousing suspicion.

Unless she's lying.

She's not lying, I told myself. She's not Holly. If I start thinking they're all like Holly, I'm screwed.

Eileen means what she says.

Probably.

I hid her note, then came back into the kitchen, turned on the radio and poured myself another mug of coffee. Rush Limbaugh was on, talking about Bill and Hillary and obstruction of justice.

We'd done a little obstructing of our own, I thought . . . at least to the extent that we didn't report everything we knew. We'd conspired to do more, but the trolls had saved us from that.

Oughta send them a thank you.

Dear Friends,

Just a quick note to express my gratitude for the way you all pitched in and cleaned up our mess last night. Next time, I'll provide the wine. Perhaps a nice Merlot.

Bon appétit!

Eddie

I smiled, but felt raunchy about it.

Next time?

There won't be a next time, fellows. You're probably all in jail by now.

Rush's program broke for news, weather, and a load of commercials. I sat at the table and stared at the radio, listening, hardly daring to breathe.

The news at the top of the hour regularly covered major late-breaking stories on the international, national, state and local levels.

For a local story, half a dozen homeless guys cannibalizing one of their pals under a campus bridge ought to qualify.

There was no mention of it.

At six minutes after eleven, the break ended and Rush came back.

I gaped at the radio.

How could they not cover a story like that?

All sorts of possibilities swirled through my mind: the cops had kept quiet about it (possibly to avoid freaking out the good citizens of Willmington); nobody had been sent to the scene in response to Eileen's call; she hadn't actually talked to a 911 operator; the cops had gone to the wrong bridge; or they'd gone to the correct bridge, but found no mutilated body, no evidence of murder.

Another possibility: a couple of cops might've gone to the correct bridge and gotten ambushed by the trolls. I strongly doubted that one, though. The dispatcher would've known where they went. If they failed to report in, all sorts of back-up would've poured into the area.

The news story then would've been enormous.

So what *is* going on? I wondered.

I had a couple of hours before my Shakespeare seminar, so I decided to head for campus early and do some looking around.

It was a wonderful October day, chilly and fresh, sunny, the air carrying a scent of woodsmoke. I wore jeans and a chamois shirt, my Yankees cap and sunglasses. The cap and sunglasses made me feel like a cliché. They did, however, conceal some of my injuries.

Most of the people I passed on my way to campus and then through the quad paid no attention to me: they were hurrying toward urgent destinations, or ambling along and chit-chatting with friends, or dwelling deep in their own thoughts of glory, disgrace, nooky, or what have you. A few of them noticed me and nodded. I nodded and smiled in return.

Walking through the campus, I looked for signs that an alarming story was on the loose. I saw only the usual. Some students and faculty bopped along eagerly. Others seemed blasé. This one looked frantic, that one smug, this one blissful, that one petulant, this one cheerfully confident.

Nothing out of the ordinary seemed to be going on.

Then Stanley Jones came striding my way. He was a fellow English major, so we'd been in several classes together. I'd even visited his apartment a few times last year when we were collaborating on a project about Edgar Allan Poe. He lived on the same block as Kirkus. Therefore, he couldn't reach campus without crossing Division Street.

As he approached, I said, 'Hey there, Stanley.'

Though he'd been looking glum, he raised his head and smiled when he heard my voice. 'Hey, Ed.'

'How goes it?'

'SOS.' (Translation: 'Same old shit.') Then his eyebrows flew up. 'What happened to *you*?'

'What do you mean?'

'You get stomped or something?'

'"My head is bloody, but unbowed."'

'Shit, man.'

'Actually, I crashed and burned playing Frisbee yesterday. Ran into a tree.'

'It messed you up, man.'

'You should've seen the tree.'

Stanley laughed and shook his head. Then he frowned. 'Hey, tough about Holly.'

I hadn't expected that. It felt like a heat bomb exploding in my chest. 'Thanks,' I muttered.

'Really sucks.'

'Yeah.'

'Shit.'

'Yeah.'

Grimacing, he said, 'But you know what they say: can't live *with* 'em, can't shoot 'em.'

I'd heard it before, but I laughed a little anyway. Then I asked, 'Who says so?'

Which got a pretty good laugh from Stanley.

'Right on,' he said. 'Anyway, I gotta haul ass over to the library. See you later, huh?'

'Right.'

'Watch out for low-flying aspens.'

'Good one, Stan.'

He continued on his way.

Tough about Holly.

Thanks for the reminder, pal.

He was just trying to be nice, I told myself. But I felt the loss of her all over again for a while. It might've lasted a lot longer, but the bench came into sight.

The bench, nearly hidden among the trees, was where Eileen and I had left our books last night before descending the embankment and going under the bridge.

Give it a quick look, make sure we didn't forget anything.

I started toward it, then changed my mind.

I've gotta act like everyone else. The worst thing I can do is draw attention to myself.

I stayed on the walkway and continued striding along as if I had someplace to go. Someplace east of campus. Someplace on the other side of Division Street.

I looked straight ahead. I looked to my right. I looked up and down. But I didn't look to the left.

Not until I stood at the curb of Division Street.

Before crossing, a person is *supposed* to look both ways.

I did so. And when I finally turned my head to the left, I saw not a single police car.

No cars or vans or trucks or vehicles of any kind at all were stopped on the bridge or anywhere near it.

Chapter Twenty-nine

I saw Eileen once that afternoon. I was on my way to Shakespeare, climbing the stairs toward the second floor of the English building when she came trotting down the stairs, her books and binders hugged to her chest.

She was indeed wearing my university sweatshirt and corduroy trousers. No hat, no sunglasses. She'd made no attempt at all to hide her injuries.

She had one black eye. She wore a small bandage above her left eyebrow, another on her right cheekbone, another on her jaw. She had a swollen, split lip, a bruise on her chin and a bruise on her left cheekbone.

When we converged on the stairway, others were above and below us. She met my eyes, flashed me a quick smile and trotted on down. I felt a soft puff of breeze as she passed me.

I wanted to turn around and watch her a while longer, but resisted the urge.

The afternoon edition of the local newspaper mentioned nothing about a murder under the Division Street bridge or anywhere else in town.

The five o'clock news said nothing about any killing whatsoever in the peaceful community of Willmington.

What gives? I wondered. It *did* happen, didn't it?

At about seven o'clock that evening, I was studying at my kitchen table when the telephone rang. I jumped. My heart lurched. Frightened, I hurried to the phone and picked it up. 'Hello?'

'Hi, honey.' Eileen's voice.

Honey. 'Hi. How's it going?'

'I don't know. Not bad, considering. Strange, though. I'm glad I at least got to *see* you today.'

'Same here. You had my clothes on.'

'Hope you don't mind.'

'I like it.'

'They're nice and comfy. My own things are all messed up . . . what's left of them. I threw them in your hamper, by the way.'

'Fine. Maybe I'll do a wash tonight.'

'Do you know how to get bloodstains out?'

'Not exactly.'

'Maybe I'd better take care of it.'

'Coming over?' I asked.

'Not tonight. Did you read my note?'

'Yeah.'

'I think the less we're seen together, the better. I mean, we're both pretty messed up. Our faces.'

'What've you been telling people?'

'My boyfriend beat me up.'

'Huh?'

She laughed. It sounded good. 'What about you?' she asked.

'I've been saying Kirkus tried to bugger me.'

She laughed even harder. 'Oh, that's awful, Eddie. You should be ashamed of yourself.'

'Oh, I am, I am. What I actually said is that I ran into a tree chasing a Frisbee.'

'That's pretty good. In my story, I fell out of a tree.'

'What were you doing in a tree?'

'A kid's kite got stuck in it. Over at the park? So I climbed up to set it free for him.'

'That was very heroic of you.'

'I know. I'm a wonderful person.'

'We both have a tree motif,' I pointed out.

'Great minds,' she said.

There was a pause.

'So,' she said, 'do you suppose anyone's listening in?'

'Not likely.'

'Not that it matters. I mean, we didn't really do anything wrong. Right?'

'Right,' I said.

If you don't count me probably killing a guy. Plus a small conspiracy to destroy the evidence.

'Have you noticed,' she asked, 'that nobody seems to know anything about it?'

'I noticed, all right.'

'"'Tis passing strange."'

'More than "passing".'

'Maybe the cops thought my call was a prank.'

'Maybe that's it.'

'I mean, I've thought about this *a lot*,' she said, 'and nothing makes sense. I think they either didn't *send* any cops to the bridge or the cops showed up but couldn't find anything wrong.'

'A good chance it's one or the other,' I said.

'You know . . .? Shit! This isn't good. I wanted those guys in jail, you know?'

'Me, too.'

'That bridge . . . I go across it every day . . . two, four, *six* times a day. And at *night*. Are they under there every night?'

'I don't know.'

'I took the long way around to get home this afternoon. I mean, I don't want to walk across that bridge anymore. But they might be under *any* bridge, you know? And where are they during the *day*?'

'Wandering around begging for money, I suppose.'

Eileen was silent for a few seconds. Then she said, 'What're we going to do?'

'Well, they don't seem to be grabbing people off the streets. We would've heard about it.'

'We haven't heard about *this*,' she said.

170

'I know, but the guy last night was one of their own. If a student got snatched, we'd never hear the end of it.'

'That's true, I guess.'

'So I don't think we need to worry too much. As far as we know, the only reason they . . . *bothered* that guy was because he was already dead.'

'If he *was* dead.'

'Yeah.' It was nice to think that maybe I *hadn't* killed him.

I'll never know for sure.

'So what should we do about them?' Eileen asked.

'Stay out from under bridges.'

'That's a given. But do you think we should try calling the police again?'

'If you want to. I don't see much point in it, though. We called last night when it mattered. If they didn't take care of it then . . . maybe we oughta just figure they missed their chance. At this point, we're probably better off if they *never* find out about last night.'

'You think we should just stay out of it?'

'Pretty much. It was one thing, you know, when they had a chance of catching the trolls red-handed. That won't happen now. Too much time's gone by.'

'They probably scattered right after we got away,' Eileen said.

'Right. And by now, there's been time for them to go back and clean the place up.'

What if they left the remains of the body, cleaned up after themselves but left Eileen's shirt and panties there for the cops to find?

Would they be sneaky enough to do a thing like that?

'I just hate to leave it this way,' Eileen said. 'What if somebody else goes under the bridge like we did, and *they* end up getting . . . you know, attacked by those people?'

Something suddenly occurred to me. 'You know what? "Those people" will probably stay away from there for *months*. They know they were seen.'

'That's true,' Eileen said. 'I bet you're right.'

'Wanta go under and look around?'

'Oh, sure, the very moment hell freezes over.'

171

I wondered if I should go under just to see what they'd left behind. The idea of it terrified me.

Not a chance, I thought.

But I *should*.

I won't.

'Not to change the subject,' I said, 'but how long do you want to stay away from me?'

'I don't *want* to stay away from you at all. I just think it'll be the wise thing to do. Don't you?'

'I guess so.'

In a voice lower than before, she said, 'I already miss you.'

'I miss you, too.'

'We'll have to just be phone friends for a while.'

'It's not the same,' I said.

'I know. I'm sorry.'

'Not your fault.'

'In a way, it is. It was my big idea to go under the bridge last night. If we hadn't done that, none of this would be happening.'

'It was worth it.'

She made a quiet laugh. 'Think so?'

'Sure.'

'You're so . . .' The way her voice went, I knew she was starting to cry.

'It's all right,' I told her. 'Everything's fine. We'll just stay apart for a few days . . . till our faces heal up, right?'

'Right,' she said.

'Then we'll be back together and everything will be fine and we'll stay out from under bridges forever.'

'Uh-uh.'

'In the meantime,' I said, 'this'll give us a chance to catch up on our studies.'

She sniffed. 'And our sleep.'

'Exactly.'

By the time we hung up, we were both still in agreement on the two major issues: we wouldn't give the police another call and we would stay away from each other for the next several days.

I stared at the phone and sighed.

I missed Eileen badly. I missed the sound of her voice and the look of her and the feel of her. I wanted her here in my apartment. Sitting on the sofa with me. Sipping wine. Wearing maybe my robe and nothing at all underneath it.

But since that was not to be . . .

My heart racing with excitement, I went into my bedroom and set my alarm clock for 11:00 p.m. Then I shut off the light, took off my clothes and climbed into bed. The sheets were cold at first, then warm.

For a while, I felt too agitated to sleep. Too many thoughts, some exciting, some unpleasant, were swirling through my mind.

Calm down, I told myself. Just settle down and fall asleep and eleven'll be here before you know it.

Chapter Thirty

I slept hard. When the alarm blared at eleven o'clock, I shut it off and considered getting out of bed.

Forget it, I thought. I need a full night of sleep. I need *several* full nights of sleep.

Anyway, it's too dangerous out there.

> And every fiend, as in a dream,
> Doth stalk the lonesome night.

I didn't know where the lines came from, but they sounded like Coleridge.

Eileen might be able to identify them.

She's not here.

That's the point, I realized. That's why I set the alarm, to wake me up to go wandering, to go looking for the mystery girl.

Do I really want to do that? It's bad out there.

Too damn many fiends. I just need to go back to sleep.

Go out tomorrow night. Better yet, don't. Who needs it?

If I keep going out, they'll get me.

But if I *don't* go out, I'll never see *her* again.

I didn't see her last night. I won't see her tonight, either, if I stay in where it's nice and safe.

Suddenly, sleepy no more, excited and frightened instead, I climbed out of bed. My room was chilly. I shivered as I hurried into my clothes.

Downstairs, the Fishers' door stood open.

Oh, great.

What am I, their entertainment?

I ought to move out, I thought. Find myself a place where I can come and go without a couple of spies keeping track of my every movement.

Face forward, I raised my hand in greeting and walked quickly past their doorway. On my way by, I heard Andy Kaufman doing his Latka voice. A *Taxi* rerun.

When their doorway was behind me, I picked up my pace. I didn't look back. As I turned the corner to the foyer, however, my peripheral vision picked up someone back near their room. A Fisher – I couldn't tell which – was watching me from the doorway. He or she didn't speak.

Take a picture, I thought. It lasts longer.

I hurried through the foyer, worried that the Fisher might ask me to come back.

No call to go rushing off. Come on back and chat a spell.

Thanks, but no thanks.

I got outside. Even as I put space between myself and the building, I imagined being called back to their door.

Say, what're you up to, going out at this hour? Say, what happened to your face there?

'None of your business, folks,' I muttered.

You shouldn't oughta go off roaming by yourself this time of night, I imagined the old man warning me. *Ain't safe. That's when all the fiends come out, you know, and they're lookin' to give you the works.*

Thanks for the warning, I thought. You're telling me nothing I don't already know.

In truth, I'd already taken certain fiends into consideration, choosing a route that would keep me west of Division Street until I was well north of the bridge.

I would not only stay away from Division until I was past the bridge, but also past the sorority house. I didn't need memories of Holly inflicting themselves on me. Nor did I need Eileen to look out a window and see me walking by.

The road I followed northward was Fairmont Street. Like Division, it passed over the Old Mill Stream. Its bridge looked almost the same as the other, but older and shabbier. Four light posts were built into the parapets, two on each side of the street. They had old-fashioned white globes over their bulbs. All the globes were intact, but three were dark.

No cars were coming. No people were anywhere in sight.

They're all *under* the bridge, I thought.

The Division Street bridge might've been better than this.

I considered turning back, trying another route.

Don't be a wuss.

Approaching the bridge, I quickened my pace.

They probably *are* under this one, I thought. Or maybe hunkered down, clinging to the other side of the parapet, waiting to leap over and grab me when I go by.

Why don't I just run across it?

Not unless something happens.

As I started across the bridge, I stepped off the curb and took a diagonal route to the middle of the street. Then I walked the center line to keep a lane of pavement and a sidewalk between me and either side of the bridge. Space to see them coming.

Of course, I might get hit by a car.

Nothing was coming, but that could change in a matter of seconds.

I'll have plenty of time to get out of the way.

I hurried over the bridge with long, quick strides, swinging my arms high, watching both sides and straight ahead, glancing over my shoulder every few seconds to make sure I was safe from behind.

So far, so good.

I was halfway across when, a couple of blocks up the street, headlights brightened an intersection. My stomach tightened.

The unseen car was on a sidestreet. It might continue straight ahead, turn left or turn right. Only a left hand turn would bring it in my direction.

The car stopped at the corner. I could see its front bumper, but no more. Too many trees and bushes stood in the way.

Couldn't tell if it was a police car.

Couldn't tell if it was a pickup truck.

If it was either, I didn't want to be seen walking down the middle of the street. I hurried to the left.

The vehicle moved forward and its headlights swept an arch of brightness through the intersection as it turned left.

Not a patrol car or pickup truck, thank God.

Some sort of dark, medium-sized van.

Hugely relieved, I hopped the curb and strode along the sidewalk, too close to the parapet for comfort.

Almost across.

The van was rumbling closer.

I glanced over my shoulder. Nobody was sneaking up behind me.

The parapet ended. I'd reached the other side of the bridge slightly nervous but safe and sound.

The van, slowing down, eased toward the curb in front of me and stopped. In the glow from a nearby streetlight, I could see that it was black. Its front passenger window glided down.

Oh, God, what now?

I stopped, remaining on the sidewalk.

The passenger seat appeared to be empty. The driver leaned toward it, looked out at me and spoke. Because of the engine noise, I couldn't make out her words. I shook my head.

'. . . over here,' she called.

Shaking my head some more, I took a couple of steps closer to the van.

'. . . find . . . street . . . know . . . it is?'

Asking directions? It might be a trick.

The whole town isn't crazy, I told myself. Maybe this person is really lost.

I stepped to the curb and leaned forward. The woman behind the wheel had a thin, pale face. Hair as dark and sleek as oil hung to her shoulders. She seemed to be wearing a shiny black blouse.

'Sorry,' I said. 'I couldn't hear you too well. Where are you trying to go?'

'Why don't you climb in?'

Confounded, I didn't know whether to be flattered or frightened . . . or neither.

'I thought you needed directions,' I said.

'Just climb in. I want to ask you something.'

'I can hear you from here.'

'Come on,' she said. 'What's the matter with you? I just want to talk to you.'

'About what?'

She unfastened the top button of her blouse. 'Get in, then I'll tell you.'

'I don't think so.'

'Please?' She unfastened another button. Then another. 'Scared?'

'No.'

Then another. 'I bet you're lonely, aren't you?'

'No.'

'Walking out here all by yourself at this hour.'

'I've got to get going.'

'Why don't you just climb in here with me?' She slid the blouse aside.

Everybody's nuts!

I stared at her pale breast and its dark nipple.

'*Now* will you climb in, honey?'

'Uh, no thanks.'

Through the quiet rumble of the engine noise, I heard soft laughter. It didn't come from the woman, though. It came from somewhere behind her in the van and it sounded like men.

I think I squealed.

I know I ran like hell.

Chapter Thirty-one

I expected the van to speed after me in reverse, just as Randy had done a couple of nights earlier. Then the gal would hit the brakes and the side door would fly open and her hidden men would leap out and chase me down.

Nothing like that happened.

As I dashed for the nearest corner, I glanced back and saw the van take off . . . driving forward, its doors still shut.

Just some sort of prank? I wondered. Give the kid a scare?

Sure.

Afraid the van might return, I ran across the street and around the corner and hid behind the trunk of a tree. Several minutes went by.

Maybe I should head for home as soon as it's safe, I thought. One close call is enough for one night.

And miss the girl?

I might not be able to find her, anyway. Besides, it's not worth the risk.

What if I'd gotten into the van?

Don't even think about it, I told myself. I *didn't* get in; that's what matters.

On the other side of the street, a man walked by with a Great Dane on a leash.

That's what *I* need, I thought. An enormous, dangerous dog. Keep the fiends at bay.

The man and his dog vanished around a corner, but I remained in hiding. The van didn't return. No other vehicles went by, either. I finally stepped away from the tree and began to walk in the direction from which I'd come.

Discretion being the better part of valour . . .

What is *wrong* with this town, anyway?

Maybe there's a lunatic asylum nearby and they open its doors at night, let all the inmates run loose in the streets. *Have a good time, darlings. Raise some hell. But you must be back before sunrise.*

Nice.

Might make for an interesting story, I thought. Sort of far-fetched, but a situation like that would explain what's wrong. Something *has* to be wrong with this place. Every town isn't like this at night.

Or maybe they are.

Soon, I found myself approaching the Fairmont Street bridge. It stood between me and home. I looked at its empty, shadowed street, its low stone parapets, and the darkness on both sides.

I would have to cross it sooner or later. This bridge or another, and God only knew what might be lurking under any of them.

Nothing will happen, I told myself.

I'd walked across such bridges hundreds of times in the past couple of years – often late at night – without any trouble.

That was before I knew.

We used to joke about trolls lurking under the bridges, but we never *knew.*

Well short of the bridge, I halted, suddenly reluctant to cross it again.

Aside from whatever fears I had in regard to the bridge, I hated the idea of being a quitter. I'd set out to search for the girl. Was I really going to call it quits because some creeps in a van scared the hell out of me?

If I quit tonight, I may never see her again.

I *have* to see her, I thought. And talk to her. And find out her name and why she roams the streets at night and whether she's lonely and what it's like to be with her.

Shaking my head, I turned my back to the bridge and left it behind.

I kept a sharp watch. Every so often, the approach of a person or vehicle forced me to duck out of sight. As time went on without any more troubling incidents, however, my courage seemed to grow. I spent less time hiding, more time hurrying from block to block.

After making my way northward on Fairmont for nearly an hour, I turned right on a sidestreet. I followed it to the east and came upon Division Street, then continued eastward until I arrived at Franklin.

As I found myself nearing the region of the mystery girl, my fears seemed to fade beneath the excitement of possibly encountering her. Instead of watching all around me for dangers, I watched for her.

She's *somewhere*, I told myself. If not on this sidewalk, on another. Or she might be in one of these houses. Or even crouching behind bushes somewhere, hiding from a suspected threat.

She might even be hiding from me.

Perhaps I had already walked past her and she'd watched me from the shadows.

Please don't hide from me, I told her in my mind. *I'm nobody to fear. I would never hurt you.*

At length, I came upon the house that she'd entered on Monday night . . . the house where, on Tuesday night, I'd watched the tequila woman. I looked toward the kitchen window, but it was dark.

From what I could see as I walked by, the entire house was dark.

At the end of the block, I crossed Franklin. I came back on the other side of the street and hid among bushes in a front lawn directly across from the house.

My wristwatch showed 12:40.

Everyone's probably asleep in there, I thought.

But who?

The tequila woman almost certainly lived in the house.

What about the mystery girl? I'd seen her go in, but she'd shown up later the same night over on Division Street. Had she only come here to visit the tequila woman or some other member of the household?

Perhaps, I thought. Or perhaps this *is* her house. Monday night, she might've returned home for something that she needed, sneaked in and grabbed it, then headed off for her main destination.

I could see a problem with that theory, though. After watching her go in, I'd hung around for a while, then walked to Dandi Donuts and spent time there with Eileen . . .

Where Randy watched *us*.

Don't start thinking about him. Get back to the problem.

Where was I? The girl. The time lapse.

Between the time she entered the house and when I later saw her on Division Street, more than an hour had gone by.

Her two locations were only about a five-minute walk from each other.

An hour, maybe longer, was unaccounted for.

If she'd spent it inside the house, she hadn't just rushed in to grab something . . . or change shoes or go to the bathroom or take care of some other simple matter. She'd been inside too long for anything of that sort.

Why would someone return home in the middle of the night, stay an hour, then leave? What did she do in there? Take a nap? Take a shower? Bake a cake?

Make love?

Making love in her own house, then leaving within the hour, didn't make sense to me.

I couldn't think of *any* good reason for her to sneak into her own house at that time of night, stay an hour, then leave.

It's not her house?

But that doesn't mean she isn't in it. She might be inside right now. Or she might be on her way over.

I made up my mind to stay put. There was a good chance she would either show up or leave before too long. All I needed to do was wait.

I waited. And waited.

Of course, she might be fast asleep in her own house on some other block. Or she might be having a maple bar at Dandi Donuts or roaming along a sidewalk miles away. She might be almost anywhere.

What if Randy snatched her, gave her the works?

She's fine, I told myself.

Or she's dead under a bridge . . .?

She's fine.

Or captured by the van people . . .?

No. She's fine. But she isn't likely to *stay* fine if . . .

I heard a distant engine. It slowly grew louder. From the rough grumbly noise, it sounded powerful. It might belong to a truck. Or a pickup truck.

Randy on the prowl?

Maybe it's the van.

Though I was well hidden among the bushes, my heart pounded hard as I watched the street in front of me.

Headlights brightened the pavement.

A police car passed by, moving slowly.

Keep going! I told it. *Keep going! Keep going!*

It did.

When it was gone, I crouched there trembling and sweaty and breathless.

Oughta be glad it was cops, I thought. They might be the ones to save my ass if things go really wrong.

A lot of good they did last night.

What *did* they do last night? Did they even *look* under the bridge?

Maybe they're in cahoots with the trolls.

That seemed awfully far-fetched, but sometimes far-fetched stuff is true.

When they pick up suspects at night, maybe they take them underneath one of the bridges and turn them over to the trolls.

Ridiculous. But it might make for a story.

Why would the cops do something like that? For a bottle of wine? For a piece of the action? A piece of the person pie?

Got it! The cops kill two birds with one stone: they eliminate suspects permanently, plus they keep the trolls from going after decent folk for fresh meat.

But what do *they* get?

The satisfaction of a job well done.

I chuckled softly.

That makes *two* story ideas. Not bad for one night.

Even if I don't find the girl, this has been a pretty worthwhile . . .

Across the street, a dark shape drifted down the porch stairs and cut across the lawn toward the sidewalk. Out of the shadows, the shape had a light, springy stride. Behind it, a ponytail bounced and swung.

Chapter Thirty-two

I gaped at her, astonished. Though I'd hoped very much to find her, I hadn't really expected to have an easy time of it. The search might have taken three or four nights, or even a week or two. It might've taken a month. There had also been a real possibility that I would never see her again at all.

And here she was, coming out of the very house I'd seen her enter on Monday night.

At the sidewalk, she turned to her right and headed north on Franklin Street. When she reached the end of the block, I scurried out of my hiding place.

What if tequila woman's watching?

Nobody seemed to be on the porch. The front door appeared to be shut. All the downstairs and upstairs windows that I could see were dark, and nobody was visible at any of them, looking out.

If she saw me, it's too late to do anything about it.

Staying on my side of Franklin, I walked toward the end of the block.

Tomorrow night, she'll tell the girl.

If not sooner. Maybe she'll tell her on the phone tomorrow. Or in class. Or at work. *Honey, when you left the house last night I observed a stranger creep out of the bushes across the street and commence to follow you.* In my mind, she spoke with a mellow drawl like a Tennessee Williams character. *You'd best take care. Perhaps you should stay away from here until the matter has been resolved.*

Then again, there was no good reason to assume she'd seen me.

When the time came for the girl to leave, she might've remained in bed. Or perhaps she had gone to the kitchen for a nightcap.

In fact, she might've slept through everything. For all I really knew, someone other than tequila woman was the object of the girl's visits to the house.

What if *that* person looked out and saw me?

Nobody saw me!

Probably not, I told myself. But if someone *did*, the girl will probably find out about it tomorrow. Tonight might be my only chance.

I crossed the street, and we were both on the same sidewalk. Though we walked nearly a block apart, the narrow, straight strip of concrete joined us.

Her pace was more gradual than mine. She strolled along as if out for no other purpose than to savor the night. For a while, I allowed myself to close the gap. Then I slowed down.

As on the night of our first encounter, I felt the strange awareness that in all the vast reaches of time and space, she and I were now occupying the same moment and place.

In so many different ways, we might've missed this rendezvous.

And yet, here it was.

The forces of chance or nature or God had drawn us together on this night of all nights of the year. With a little help from my own determination to find her.

Now what? I wondered.

I wanted to *know* her, not just follow her.

I've gotta get closer.

How? So far, she seemed unaware of my presence. That wouldn't last for long, however, if I tried to catch up.

She sees me coming, she'll take off.

Not for the first time in my life, I wished I were invisible. I would hurry up the sidewalk, stay only a stride or two behind her for a while to watch the way she moved, then rush ahead and walk backward to study the front of her. Unseen, I would be free to stare at her for as long as I wished. I wouldn't have to go away, not even when she reached her home. I could simply go inside and stay with her. Perhaps she would take a bath before going to bed.

I imagined standing nearby in her bedroom while she pulled her sweatshirt off.

Yeah, right, I thought. *In my dreams.*

On the off-chance I can't turn invisible, I thought, what *should* I do?

Instead of closing in from behind, how about making my approach from the front? That would be less likely to spook her. Run around the block and get ahead of her. Maybe even start walking *away* so she's behind *me*. Then I slow my pace. I slow it way down and she closes in. Maybe.

Great plan, I thought. Better, anyway, than trying to turn myself invisible.

Moving in the right direction.

Only one little problem. In putting my plan into effect, I would make the detour and return to Franklin Street and the girl would be gone. That's how things work in real life.

Looked good on paper . . .

In fact, she might *not* be gone. There was a good chance she would continue to walk north on Franklin for a while.

Not if I try to circle around. I'll lose her for sure.

Better just to hold back and follow her at a safe distance. See what happens. With any luck, maybe she'll lead me to her home.

A few minutes later, she crossed Franklin Street.

Good thing I'd decided not to circle around. She would've been gone, just as I'd suspected.

Leaving Franklin behind, she headed westward on the sidestreet. After she walked out of sight, I ran across Franklin. I slowed to a casual stroll as I approached the corner. When I came to the end of the block, I casually turned my head to the right, then to the left.

The sidewalk was clear.

I lost her?

Before I had time for dismay, a stir of motion drew my eyes to her.

She was crossing the street, almost to the other side. Fearing she might glance back, I looked for cover. The streetlamp posts were too narrow. So was the trunk of the nearest tree. But a car was parked at the curb, so I rushed over and crouched beside it.

A lousy place to hide. It offered me concealment from the girl, but not from much else.

Peering over its hood, I saw her walk across the front lawn of an old, two-story house by the alley. No lights shone in any of the windows. The porch, too, was dark.

In the glow of the streetlights, she climbed the porch stairs. Then the shadows consumed her. I watched for the front door of the house to open. Perhaps a strip of gray would appear and widen, such as I'd observed on Monday night.

Perhaps not.

I detected no sign of the door being opened or shut.

There would be nothing to see, I told myself, if the house is as dark inside as the porch.

Maybe, however, she didn't open the door at all.

What if she's still on the porch?

Maybe this isn't where she lives, and she's hiding on the porch because she fears she's being followed.

> Because she knows, a frightful fiend
> Doth close behind her tread.

Caught a glimpse of me following her, maybe, and thinks *I'm* a fiend.

It made me feel ashamed.

I'm not a fiend, I told her in my mind. *I would never do anything to hurt you. There's no reason in the world for you to be afraid of me.*

Sure, I thought. Right. No reason? How about I'm *stalking* her? Why shouldn't she be afraid of me? For all she knows, I might be hoping to abduct her . . . take her into the woods somewhere (or under a bridge), and rip off her clothes and do things to make her scream.

I imagined her in a dark place, hanging by her wrists, naked and writhing.

I would never do that, I told her in my mind.

But she had no way of knowing. She couldn't be blamed for fearing me.

Is she watching from the porch?

I felt terribly vulnerable, crouched beside the car. Somebody might come along. Even now, someone in a nearby house might be watching me. Maybe the cops had already been called.

If they don't come out for bloody murder under a bridge, I thought, they won't come looking for me.

Think not?

I needed to find a better place to hide. But if the girl was watching from the porch, she would see me abandon my place by the car and her worst fears would seem justified. I would lose any chance of befriending her.

She's probably in the house, I told myself. I missed her opening the door, that's all.

But if she's on the porch . . .

I heard a car coming. It sounded far away. I couldn't figure out which direction it was coming from.

Just what I need!

Anyone driving by on Franklin to my right or on the north-south street to my left (its name escaped me) would have a chance to see me hiding behind the parked car.

But if I run off, *she* might see me.

What'll I do?

The sound of the engine grew louder.

Shit oh shit!

The parked car giving me such limited shelter was low and close to the curb. I couldn't possibly crawl under it, not from this side.

As headlights brightened the intersection of Franklin Street, I lay down flat on the grass by the car and lowered my face against my crossed arms.

Along with the engine sounds and the hiss of the tires on the pavement, I heard familiar music. Warren Zevon. 'Excitable Boy'. The sounds grew louder as the car moved through the intersection.

I raised my head.

A small, pale pickup truck just like Randy's.

Chapter Thirty-three

I dropped my head and shut my eyes. The pickup continued through the intersection, heading south on Franklin.

It might not be Randy's, I told myself. I hadn't seen the driver, and he probably hadn't seen me. There must be lots of compact, light-colored pickup trucks in a town the size of Willmington.

It was Randy, all right. He's cruising the streets, looking for me. Looking for Eileen.

How about the mystery girl? I wondered. Would she do?

It sickened me to think of what Randy might do to the girl if he ever got the chance.

Does she know about him? Does she watch out for him? She probably watches out for everybody . . . including me.

Suddenly realizing that Randy (if that was him) might circle the block and come for me, I shoved myself up and ran. I ran across the street and across the lawn and up the porch stairs. Breathless, heart thudding, I halted in the darkness of the porch.

The girl didn't seem to be there. Remembering the old man who'd frightened me so badly, however, I tiptoed around and checked the porch swing and in all the patches of blackness where a person might be hiding. Nobody was on the porch except me.

Afraid that Randy might drive by at any moment, I sank down in a dark corner with my back to the railings.

He'll never see me here.

Listening for the approach of his pickup, I heard only a faint *shhhh* that might've been the noise of distant engines. The sounds were so indistinct that some might not be coming from cars or trucks or vans. Perhaps an airplane was going by, high and far away. Perhaps some of the sound was the hiss of breezes passing through treetops all over town.

Randy's pickup was certainly nowhere nearby.

Unless he'd killed the engine.

Maybe he did see me and he's coming back on foot.

I wished I hadn't thought of that.

I sat motionless and frightened for a while, hardly daring to breathe. After maybe ten minutes, however, it began to seem that Randy wouldn't show up.

He probably hadn't seen me, after all. Maybe the pickup truck wasn't even his.

As my fears of Randy faded, I turned my mind to thoughts of the girl. She had gone into this very house. She was somewhere inside it at this very moment.

If the walls and floors were invisible, she would be in plain sight. Upstairs, probably. Maybe in the bathroom, or maybe in her bed.

Had she gone to bed without washing her face? Or brushing her teeth? Or going to the toilet?

From my corner of the porch, I should have been able to hear water running through the pipes. I'd heard nothing of the sort.

Maybe she finished in the bathroom before I came over. I'd watched the porch from across the street for at least five minutes, maybe even ten. Plenty of time to scrub the face, brush the teeth and use the toilet. She could've done all that before I arrived.

While I'd been searching the porch and sitting in a corner and worrying about Randy, she might've gone into her dark bedroom, taken off her clothes, put on whatever she liked to sleep in, and climbed into her bed.

She's probably in bed right now, I thought. Curled on her side, covered to the shoulders by a sheet and blanket. Wearing what? She didn't seem like the sort to go for a frilly nightgown or teddy. More likely, she wore pajamas or a simple cotton nightshirt.

How about nothing at all?

A little chilly for that.

And so I imagined her under the covers in a white nightshirt. I could see her under there. The way she was curled on her side, half her face was buried in her pillow and her rear end showed below the nightshirt's hem.

If I were invisible, I would sneak into the house and find her bedroom. I would stand by her bed and watch her sleep and listen to her breathing. I might even draw the blanket and sheet carefully down her body, let them drift to the floor at the foot of the bed in order to see her uncovered.

Her white nightshirt almost glows in the darkness. Her skin looks dusky. I can see the curves of her bare buttocks, the shadowy cleft between them.

Maybe she doesn't sleep in a nightshirt, after all. Maybe she sleeps in the nude.

Much better.

Moaning in her sleep, she rolls onto her back.

As if stumbling out of my fantasy, I suddenly wondered if the front door was locked.

The girl might've forgotten to lock it after sneaking in. Also, from what I'd heard and read, a fairly large percentage of people rarely lock the doors of their cars or homes at night. Especially in small towns.

What if this door isn't locked?

I could open it and sneak in. In the darkness of the house, I would be *almost* invisible. I could go to the girl's bedroom and stand by her bed and . . .

Not a chance. Not me.

But I could.

I *could* do plenty, I thought. But I'm not *going* to. I must be losing my mind to even *think* about it. For one thing, I might get caught. For another, I wouldn't do it even if there were no chance whatsoever of being caught.

Is that so? I thought. Then why the fantasies about being invisible? The only reason to be invisible is to do whatever you want without getting caught.

Well, I'm *not* invisible. If I go sneaking into the house, somebody might catch me in the act. Clobber me. Shoot me. Hold me for the police. And what'll the girl think? She'll figure I'm a criminal or a pervert. She'll *never* have anything to do with me after that.

But if everyone is sleeping and I'm very quiet . . .

Again, I imagined myself standing over the girl's bed, staring down at her.

I'm *not* going in, I told myself. Besides, the door's probably locked.

If it's locked, that settles it.

That would settle it, all right. Opening someone's unlocked door was one thing – and maybe within the realm of possibility – but *breaking* in was totally out of the question.

Just see.

My fear and excitement began to grow.

No big deal, I thought. Just get up and go to the door and see if it's locked. Why not? What's the worst that can happen? If I get caught at it, I can play drunk or confused and pretend I'm at the wrong house. Anyway, it's probably not a crime to try a door.

No crime, but wrong. I knew it was wrong, knew it was a bad idea (like going under the bridge last night), but got to my feet anyway. Standing motionless in my corner of the porch, I looked around the neighborhood. Here and there, the streets were well lighted. Trees, however, cast shadows on the pavement and lawns. In every direction, the lighted places were surrounded by motes of darkness.

Anyone might be lurking in those dark places, watching. Or watching from behind a parked car. Or from behind bushes. Or from inside a house across the street.

I was in darkness myself, however, and probably almost unseeable.

So I made my way toward the front door, walking slowly, putting my feet down gently. A couple of times, floorboards creaked under my weight. The sounds made me cringe, though they were so quiet that nobody else could've heard them.

I'm not really doing this, I thought.

And yet, I was.

My journey to the door seemed to take ages. I couldn't even see it, though I had a general idea of where it ought to be . . . a straight shot from the top of the porch stairs.

Reaching through the darkness with one hand, I touched a stiff, tight screen.

Two doors, not just one. Doubles my chance of being locked out.

Feeling my way downward and sideways, I found the handle of the screen door.

Don't do it.

I pulled gently and the screen door swung toward me. Its hinges, apparently well lubricated, made almost no sound at all.

One down, one to go.

What am I doing?

Propping the screen door open with my shoulder, I touched the inner door. Smooth wood, slick with layers of varnish. Its handle felt like thick, cool brass. With my thumb, I pressed down slowly on the lock release. It sank down and down and I heard the bolt slide back.

I pushed forward slightly. The door eased away an inch or two.

Holy shit, it opens!

Now shut it and get the hell out of here!

I pushed the door open a few more inches. Though I knew it was open, I couldn't see the jamb, the door, or the gap between them.

Dark as hell in there.

I really *would* be invisible.

Don't even think about it.

I had never in my life entered anyone's place without being invited. I had never cheated, never shoplifted, never driven a car through a stoplight (on purpose), never told a major lie, never bullied anyone, never started a fight, never in fact done *anything* particularly immoral, unethical or illegal . . .

Oh, yeah, killed that guy last night.

If I *did* kill him, it was self-defense. Stabbing Randy in the leg had been self-defense, too.

Oh, yeah, and I spied on the tequila woman. That was pretty bad. Not nearly as bad, however, as sneaking into a stranger's house in the middle of the night.

Do this, I thought, and I'm really crossing a line. And where will it end? Maybe it won't stop with watching the girl sleep. Maybe I'll feel compelled to remove her covers, and after that I'll . . .

No! All I'll do is look.

Don't even do that! Shut the door right now and get the hell out of here!

Before I could pull it shut – or open it wide – the handle was jerked from my grip.

Chapter Thirty-four

I gasped with surprise. So did someone inside the house and close in front of me.

The girl?

A low, husky voice murmured, 'House inspector.'

'Huh?' I asked.

A hand pressed against my chest. 'No need to be alarmed,' the girl said, pushing me aside. As she stepped by me, she added, 'You passed with flying colors.' Then she lurched forward, raced across the porch and leaped from the top of the stairs. Silhouetted by the streetlights, she seemed to hang in midair for a moment, arms spread out wide, her right leg thrown forward, her ponytail high behind her head. As she dropped, her sweatshirt lifted, baring her midriff.

The screen door banged shut.

Her sneakers clapped against the walkway and she took off running for the street.

I didn't leap from the porch, but descended the stairs in a couple of quick bounds and sprinted after her – chasing her, but also fleeing from the house because someone *must've* heard the door slam.

The girl was fast. Not as fast as me, though.

I narrowed the gap between us, but didn't try to stop her. We were still too close to the house.

We raced across a street, dashed around a corner, ran down a sidewalk, cut across another street in the middle of a block, then ran down another stretch of sidewalk.

I remained four or five strides behind her, listening as she panted for breath, hearing the smack of her sneakers, watching her ponytail leap and swing, her bulky sweatshirt flop, her arms pump, her legs fly out one after the other.

It was wonderful to be chasing her. But awful, too. She must've been terrified.

'Hey,' I said.

'I didn't steal anything.'

'I'm not chasing you,' I blurted. 'We're just . . . fleeing in the . . . same direction.'

'I didn't hurt . . . anyone.'

'I just . . . want to talk.'

'Leave me alone.'

'Stop running. Please.'

'Get outa here.'

I stayed a few strides behind her until she ran into the next street. Then I picked up speed, caught up to her and ran alongside her. She turned her head and scowled at me.

Even in the poor glow of the streetlights, I could see that she looked younger than me. Maybe eighteen, maybe as young as fifteen or sixteen. And far more beautiful than I'd imagined.

'Can't we . . . just talk?' I asked.

Matching strides, we leaped over the next curb. The narrow sidewalk forced me closer to her.

'Stop, okay?' I asked. 'You can't . . . outrun me. Why not just—?'

She rammed me with her shoulder. As the impact knocked me to the right, I reached out and grabbed a handful of her sweatshirt. I kept hold of it as I raced off the edge of the sidewalk. My feet hit the lawn. My legs crossed. Then came a wild, twisting dive.

My side slammed the damp grass. I slid, tumbling, holding on tight to the girl's sweatshirt, bringing her down with me. She landed on me, squirmed and rolled off. I scrambled onto her, sat on her and pinned her arms to the ground. She grunted and writhed. I held on.

'Not . . . gonna hurt you,' I said.

'Get off.'

'Calm down. Please. Just . . . lie still.'

She thrashed and bucked, but couldn't throw me. Finally, she stopped. She lay beneath me, chest rising and falling as she fiercely panted for air.

'Just . . . take it easy,' I said. 'Okay? Not gonna hurt you.'

Gradually, she regained control of her breathing.

'Are you all right?' I asked.

'Let me up.'

'You'll make me chase you again.'

'I've had enough running.'

'So you won't try to run away?' I asked.

'You're too fast for me, anyhow.'

I was too fast for her, but she would probably try to run again, anyway, if I let her up. We were in the front yard of a house, however, quite close to the sidewalk and street. We weren't in shadows, either.

'Look,' I said, 'we can't stay here. Somebody'll see us.'

'So let me up.'

'I don't want you to run away.'

'I won't. Okay? Let me up.'

I wanted a friend, not a captive. So I climbed off her and stepped back. She said, 'Thanks.' Her sweatshirt was twisted and rumpled, her belly bare. She sat up, straightened her sweatshirt, then got to her feet. Reaching back with both hands, she brushed off the seat of her jeans.

'I'm sorry you fell,' I said.

'I didn't exactly fall, now, did I?'

'Well, I helped.'

'You grabbed hold and took me with you.'

Reminding her that she was the one who had shoved me off the sidewalk didn't seem like a great idea, so I answered, 'I was afraid you'd get away.'

'You claimed you weren't chasing me. We were "fleeing in the same direction"?' A corner of her mouth curled up.

'Sorry.'

'You didn't want me to get away, but you weren't chasing me. How does that work?'

'It's complicated.'

'Why don't you just let me go, okay? I didn't steal anything. I didn't hurt anyone. Your family's fine.'

Not wanting to lie, I avoided the word *my* when I said, 'And the house passed inspection with flying colors?'

A slight smile drifted across her face. 'It's splendid. Come on, let me go. Please? I can tell you're a nice guy. You don't want to get me in trouble, do you?'

I can tell you're a nice guy.

Maybe she'd only said it to soften me up, but it gave me a pleasant, warm feeling.

'I don't want to get you in trouble,' I said, following her to the sidewalk. 'I'd like to help you, if . . .'

'Then just let me go.'

'Tell me one thing and I will,' I said. 'What were you doing in the house?'

'Okay. But let's get away from here first.'

We walked side by side to the end of the block and around the corner. Then she stopped, turned to me and said, 'It's sort of embarrassing. I needed a bathroom. Very badly. I knew I wouldn't be able to get to my own house in time. There aren't any public facilities for miles, and I didn't want to do it outside. That'd be too gross. So I decided to try a house. I went to three or four . . . they had locked doors. But yours didn't, so I let myself in.'

'You could've rung the doorbell and asked permission.'

She grimaced. 'I know. But it's . . . what, about one-thirty? Nobody wants someone ringing the doorbell at this hour. Besides, it was so *embarrassing*. Can you imagine going to the door of a stranger's house and asking to use their bathroom?'

I was embarrassed to be *hearing* about it. Even though I knew she was lying, my mind gave me images of her entering a bathroom and pulling down her jeans. Then I remembered that Eileen had gotten herself invited into my apartment Monday night by claiming a need to use the toilet.

What is it, some sort of standard ploy?

Maybe it's chapter twelve in *The Girl's Guide to Male Manipulation*. ('As the male animal is naturally both embarrassed and aroused – and embarrassed *by* his arousal – when confronted with the elimination processes of the female, the "bathroom" gambit is a surefire winner . . .')

'Can you?' she repeated.

'Can I?'

'Imagine the embarrassment?'

'Oh. Sure. It'd be terrible.'

Nodding, she said, 'So I just snuck in and took care of it. All I did was use the toilet. I didn't bother anyone. I didn't take anything. Do you want to check my pockets?' She pulled her sweatshirt up a few inches higher than the waistband of her jeans.

I saw the skin of her belly. 'I don't have to check,' I told her.

'You believe me?'

'I'll take your word for it.'

'Thanks.' She lowered the sweatshirt. 'Can I go now?'

'If you want. I won't chase you.'

'Will you *flee* in the same direction?'

'I *was*,' I said. 'The slamming door probably woke up everyone in the house.'

She looked perplexed.

'I don't live there.'

'What?'

'It's not my house.'

'Not your house. Then what were you doing there?'

'Hiding,' I said, and began to walk again. She stayed with me, walking slowly by my side.

Chapter Thirty-five

'Hiding from what?' she asked as we strolled together down the sidewalk.

'A guy in a pickup truck. He's after me.'

'Why's he after you?'

'I'm not sure, but . . . He saw me at Dandi Donuts a few nights ago. I was there with my girlfriend.'

'You have a girlfriend.'

Eileen was part of the story and had to be mentioned, but I could've referred to her as a 'friend' or a 'former girlfriend.' Calling her anything other than a girlfriend or lover, however, would've been like a lie. I didn't want to betray Eileen that way. Nor did I wish to lie to this girl.

Plus, the mention of a girlfriend was sure to make me seem less threatening.

Maybe it's Chapter Twelve in *The Guy's Guide to Female Manipulation*. ('As the female animal naturally suspects that all males are predators, many of their basic fears are allayed by the belief that the man in their presence has his eyes and penis set upon different prey.')

'Her name's Eileen,' I said. 'We're students at the university.'

'Willies,' she said.

I nodded, smiling. I'd heard the term before: it was what townies often liked to call us.

'Wet Willies,' the girl added.

'That's us.'

'So the two of you were at Dandi . . .'

'Yeah. And this guy saw us together. Apparently, he liked the looks of Eileen.'

'Is she pretty?'

Not as pretty as you, I thought. Would've been dumb to say it, though. Better if she thinks I'm totally devoted to Eileen. 'Very pretty,' I said.

'So what did he do? This guy?'

'Nothing at the time. That was Monday. We didn't even know he'd seen us. But I went back to the donut shop on Tuesday night and he was there. He wanted me to take him to Eileen.'

'She wasn't with you?'

'Not on Tuesday.'

'Why not?'

I left her behind so I could spend the night hunting for you.

That would go over big.

With a shrug, I said, 'She wasn't feeling very well.' A lie? Not necessarily. Not exactly the truth, either. 'So she stayed behind.'

'Where?'

'In her sorority house.'

'Which one?'

'Alpha Phi.'

The girl nodded.

'You know where that is?' I asked.

'I know where everything is. Everything in *this* town, anyway. So you were at Dandi Donuts without Eileen, and this guy . . .'

'He made me go outside with him and get into his pickup truck. He planned to drive me over to the sorority house, and I was supposed to bring Eileen out so he could take her off in his truck. He said he wanted to "give her the works."'

The girl wrinkled her nose.

'But I got away from him. That was Tuesday night, and I guess he's still after me. I saw his pickup go by tonight, so I ran over to that house and hid on its porch. That's why I was there when you came out.'

'You were about to go in.'

Taken by surprise, feeling caught, I felt myself blush. Luckily, we were walking through a patch of shadows just then. Even though the girl was looking at my face, she probably couldn't see that it was red.

'I wanted to find out if the door was locked,' I explained.

'So you could hide from him in the house?'

Trying not to lie, I said, 'Any port in a storm.' Before she could hit me with another question, I said, 'The guy's name is Randy, by the way. He drives a light-colored Toyota pickup truck. You should watch out for him when you're out at night. He might try to get you.'

'I'll be careful.'

'My name's Ed, by the way. Ed Logan.'

'Okay.'

'It's fine if you don't want to tell me your name.'

She just looked at me.

'I guess there's no point in knowing your name, anyway, if you're leaving.'

'I can stay a while,' she said.

'Really?' I almost blurted, *Great!* Not wanting to seem too excited, though, I simply smiled and said, 'Good.'

'But I'm not going to tell you my name.'

'No problem.'

'You can call me whatever you want.'

'Okay. How about . . .' The name 'Holly' almost leaped out. *Are you nuts? Don't call her that!*

'How about what?' she asked.

'Bertha.'

She laughed. 'Thanks anyway.'

'Esmeralda?'

'Give me a break.'

'Rumplestiltskin?'

'Oh, sure.'

'I'm doing the best I can.'

'You get one more chance.'

'How about Chris?' I suggested.

'With a C-H or a K?'

'C-H.'

'Not bad,' she said. 'But how about Casey instead?'

'The initials or the word?'

'C-A-S-E-Y.'

'"Oh, there is no joy in Mudville,"' I said.

She smiled. 'This Casey doesn't strike out.'

I laughed. 'Glad to hear it. And I'm glad you know the poem.'

'Doesn't everyone?'

'Probably not.' She would be a lot more likely to know it, however, if Casey was her actual name. 'It's pretty popular, though,' I admitted.

Up the street several blocks ahead of us, headlights appeared.

'Uh-oh,' I said.

Smiling, Casey gave me a Clint Eastwood squint and asked, 'Feeling lucky, punk?'

'Huh?'

'Want to ride it out?'

'Huh?'

As the vehicle kept coming toward us, its headlights seemed to grow larger and farther apart.

'Ride or hide? Do we stand our ground and hope for the best, or duck out of sight?'

Was she serious?

'Might be cops,' she said. 'Might be that fellow Randy. Might be worse. No telling what we might get. That's part of the fun.'

'You do this a lot?'

'All the time. Only at night, though. You'd have to be nuts to play it in daylight.'

I laughed.

Though the vehicle was a lot closer now, I still couldn't make out its shape. The engine sounded grumbly and low.

If we wait much longer . . .

'What's it gonna be?' Casey asked.

I was pretty sure what *she* wanted. 'Ride it out,' I said.

'Good man.' Grinning, she patted me on the back like a pal.

So we went on walking side by side. I felt very brave and daring and eager to run like hell.

Casey smiled at me. 'Fun, huh?'

'Oh, yeah.'

At the end of the block ahead of us, the vehicle came through the intersection. I could see it well in the glow of the streetlights. It was a Jeep . . . or one of those imitation Jeeps . . . with an open top and roll bar.

'Ah,' said Casey. 'It's the Wigginses.'

We couldn't see the occupants yet, so she must've recognized their Jeep.

As it neared us, the Wigginses came into view. The driver had blonde or gray hair in a flat-top crew cut. She wore shorts and a sleeve-less tan shirt as if she were driving through a desert at high noon. Her arms and legs looked powerful. She seemed to have a tattoo on her thick upper arm, but I couldn't make out its details.

The passenger looked like a slender replica of the driver. She had a matching crew cut. Her outfit was the same except for its smaller size and the fact that her shirt had short sleeves rather than no sleeves at all.

Going past us, the driver glanced our way. I expected Casey to wave, but she didn't. Nor did the driver wave at us. She simply gave us a glance, then returned her gaze to the road ahead. The passenger never seemed to notice us at all.

After they went by, Casey smiled at me. 'That's how we play Ride or Hide.'

'Ah.'

'It's always more exciting when you ride it out.'

'I'm sure.'

'Admit it, you liked it.'

'I'm just glad it was only the Wigginses.'

'Could've been worse,' Casey admitted.

'They didn't seem very friendly.'

'We're not precisely on speaking terms.'

'Or waving terms,' I added.

'Waving is against the rules.'

'Really?'

'Of course.'

'So who are they? The Wigginses.'

'Sisters. Walinda's the big one. Linda's her kid sister.'

'Linda and Walinda Wiggins?'

'That's them. Ever hear of them? They used to be pro wrestlers.'

'You're kidding.'

She shook her head. 'They were in the ring for about five years. Even won some championships. They've got the trophies to prove it.'

'They don't wrestle anymore?'

'They gave it up after Linda lost her arm.'

'Lost her *arm*?' I realized I'd only seen her right arm.

'Not in the ring. Here in town a couple of years ago. Nobody knows how it happened. Walinda drove her to the emergency room at about two in the morning. Her left arm was gone at the shoulder.'

'Nobody knows *how* she lost it?'

'Well, I guess Linda and Walinda know, but they wouldn't say.'

'Weird,' I muttered.

'Lotta weird stuff goes on around here,' Casey told me.

'I've noticed.'

'Wanta know what's *really* weird?'

'What?' I asked.

'They've *got* the arm. It's in their house. They keep it in like a fish tank – an aquarium – only the tank doesn't have any fish in it. Just Linda's arm. In some sort of preservative. Formaldehyde or something like that.'

'You're kidding.'

'I've seen it with my own eyes.'

'Holy . . . cow.'

'It's exceedingly gross,' Casey said.

'I can imagine. Are Linda and Walinda nuts or something?'

'Either nuts or zany. Sometimes, it's hard to know the difference.'

Chapter Thirty-six

I could hardly believe the mystery girl and I were walking along together, talking and laughing and she actually seemed to like me. It may seem strange, but even though I wanted to leap for joy, I somehow also felt a little like crying. I struggled, however, to keep it all to myself.

I needed to be very careful about everything I said and did, or risk scaring her off.

As we continued our way up the sidewalk, Casey said, 'Maybe you can teach Eileen how to play Ride or Hide.'

'She's not much of a night owl.'

'You have to get her out really late, after midnight at the very *least*, or Ride or Hide isn't worth playing.'

'And why is that?' I asked.

'You know why.'

'Because that's when everyone who comes along is either crazy or zany?'

'Yep, you got it. Not *every*one, though.'

'Not you and me.'

She laughed. 'Speak for yourself, Chucky.'

'It's Ed.'

'I know. Anyway, I think maybe *half* the people out at an hour like this are normal. You've got some people, it's their job to be out. Like cops, for instance. And truckers. A *lot* of stuff gets delivered at night. And a lot of cleaning up gets done. And fixing up. You've got maintenance crews on the streets sometimes, repairing sewer lines or traffic lights, stuff like that. Then there're also some people whose lives are reversed because they've got a late shift or early shift where they work. You see some of them out at night. It's sort of like daytime for them. Plus, there are a few who just go out wandering because they love what it's like at night.'

'Like you?' I asked.

She tossed me a quick smile. 'Maybe. Anyhow, that pretty much accounts for the half that *aren't* crazy. Just about everyone else *is*, which is why you only play Ride or Hide at night. Somebody comes toward you, you've got a fifty-fifty chance of running into trouble.'

'You've given it a lot of thought,' I said.

'I pay attention, that's all.'

'Do you come out every night?' The question was asked before I realized it might be a mistake.

She answered, though. 'Pretty much. How about you?'

'Off and on,' I said. 'Not very often, really, until this week. This makes four nights in a row.'

'You're getting hooked.'

'Looks that way.'

'What does Eileen think about it?'

'She doesn't always know. She doesn't know I'm out tonight, for instance.'

'Will you tell her about it?'

'I don't know. Probably not. She wouldn't be thrilled that I went off in the middle of the night without her. She might feel left out. Plus, she knows it's dangerous. And if I told her about you . . .' I shook my head. 'She probably wouldn't take it very well.'

'Think she'd be jealous?'

'More than likely.'

'Even though we aren't doing anything?'

'Well, we're spending some time together and she's not here.'

'I'd better leave,' Casey said. She hurried ahead of me, turned around and walked backward. 'Nice to meet you, though. Maybe we'll run into each other . . .'

'No, don't go. Please. Not yet.'

'I'd better. It's been fun, though.'

209

'How about one more round of Ride or Hide?' I asked.

'I don't know, Chucky. It might be a long wait.'

'Might be a short one,' I said.

A corner of her mouth tilted up. She kept walking backward. 'I don't want to get you in trouble with Eileen.'

Maybe telling her about Eileen hadn't been such a hot idea, after all.

'There won't be any trouble,' I said. 'She doesn't have to know about any of this. So how about it? One more round?'

She seemed to think about it for a few seconds. Then she said, 'Okay. Sure. As long as we don't have to wait too long.'

'Great.'

She stopped and waited for me. When I caught up to her, she turned around and walked beside me. 'I suppose we can give it fifteen or twenty minutes,' she said.

'Do you need to be home by a certain time?'

She looked at me and chuckled. 'What do you think?'

'Well . . . you're obviously not out here at *this* hour with anyone's permission. You look pretty young to have a place of your own, so you probably live at home with your parents. Or parent. My guess is, you sneaked out of the house after they went to sleep. How am I doing?'

'Very logical,' she said.

'Accurate?'

'Maybe.'

'If I'm right, then you probably need to get home before your parents get up in the morning.'

'Very good. I can see you're a brain.'

Laughing, I said, 'Thanks. So. Is dawn your deadline?'

'Maybe.'

'What about school?' I asked.

'What about it?'

She seemed cheerful, not at all reluctant to discuss the situation, so I pressed on. 'Are you still *in* school?'

'Do I look like I'm in school?'

'Not at this exact moment . . .'

'You *are* sharp, Ed.'

'Have you got classes in the morning?'

'Maybe. Do you?'

'An eight o'clock.'

'Are you sure *you* have time for another round of Ride or Hide?'

'I don't mind missing a little sleep.'

'Neither do I,' said Casey. We walked along in silence for a short time. Then she smiled at me and asked, 'Do you want to guess my grade?'

'A-plus.'

She shook her head. 'Something needs to be done about your sense of humor.'

'Wonderful, isn't it?'

She laughed. 'Sure. If you prefer to think so.'

'You wanted me to guess your grade level? Like freshman, sophomore . . .?'

'There you go.'

'Well, I'd have to say you must be a senior.'

'Why's that?'

'Your obvious maturity, intelligence and wit.'

She bounced her knuckles off my upper arm.

'Your physical strength,' I added.

She laughed.

'So, am I right? Are you a senior?'

'Maybe.'

'*Maybe?* You aren't going to tell?'

'You're assuming I even *go* to school.'

'You said you do.'

'Did I? Really?'

'I thought so.'

'Think again, Chucky.'

'Are you saying you *don't* go to school?'

'Not admitting to anything.'

'How about your age?'

'How old do you *think* I am?'

Grinning, I shook my head. 'Lotta good it'll do. Even if I guess right, you won't admit it.'

'Are you sure?'

I laughed. 'No, I'm not sure.'

'Can't hurt to give it a try.'

'Okay. I'll say eighteen.'

'Wishful thinking.'

I blushed, taking her remark as a reference to the state's legal age of sexual consent.

'Try again,' she said.

'Younger?'

'I'm not giving clues.'

'Okay.'

'Put your powers of reason to work.'

'Unless you're extremely mature for your age, you're probably no younger than fifteen. You have awfully well developed verbal skills for any sort of teenager at all.'

'Why, I'm flattered, sir.'

'From your physical appearance, I'd say you're definitely under twenty-one. I'd probably rule out twenty, too.'

'If I'm under twenty-one, I'm obviously not twenty-two.' She grimaced. 'Cripes, your humor is rubbing off on me.'

'It's an improvement.'

She blurted out a laugh, then glanced around as if afraid she might've given away our presence. I looked around, too. I had no idea where we were. The houses on both sides of the street were looking shabbier and farther apart than those that had surrounded us earlier. The street seemed darker. But I saw nobody watching us, no traffic coming.

'So how about my age?' Casey asked in a hushed voice.

'Okay. Probably somewhere between fifteen and nineteen. Am I close?'

'Maybe.'

I growled. She laughed. Then she said, 'Look. You're such a brain.'

'Not really.'

'Sure you are. So try this out. Take your own age, double it, divide by two, then subtract the number of your feet.'

'My shoe size?'

'How many *feet* do you have at the end of your legs?'

'Okay.' I gave it some thought, then gave her my answer. 'Eighteen.'

'Ah!'

'You're eighteen?'

'Don't you remember, I told you there wouldn't be any clues?'

'But the *formula*!'

'That was for me to find out *your* age. Which is twenty. Am I right?'

Chapter Thirty-seven

'Right.'

Casey laughed. She looked wonderful laughing. Though I ached to put my arms around her and hold her close to me, I only smiled and shook my head.

'Anything else you'd like to know?' she asked.

'As if you would *tell* me.'

'Give it a try.'

'I don't have a clue in the world as to where we are.'

She looked around. 'No problem. I know precisely where we are.'

'If you're going to take off pretty soon, how would you like to lead me somewhere familiar?'

'Where *is* familiar?'

'Well, I know Division and Franklin fairly well.'

'Let's head back,' she said. 'But we'll use a different route. It's always more interesting that way.'

'Good idea.'

We continued walking in the same direction. At the end of the block, however, we turned right at the corner. We made another right at the next corner, too, and headed back in the direction from which we'd come, but one street over.

'Just so you'll know,' Casey said, 'Franklin and Division are straight ahead.'

'Thanks.'

'In case we get separated.'

'I hope that doesn't happen.'

'One never knows. If we have to hide, we might lose each other.'

'How'll I find you again?' I asked.

She turned her head and stared at me. 'Maybe you won't.'

'If you don't want me to . . .'

'We'll see.'

Don't push it, I told myself.

'Want to check out the park?' she asked.

'Sure.'

'This way.' We cut across the street. At the corner, we went to the left. We followed the sidewalk to the end of the block. There, cater-corner from us, was what appeared to be a public park.

We trotted through the empty intersection.

Just on the other side was a baseball field. Nothing fancy, just a backstop behind home plate, one small set of bleachers along the first-base line and another set along the third-base line. The field was equipped with banks of lights for night games, but the lights were dark.

'I don't see anybody,' Casey said. 'Do you?'

'Looks deserted.'

'Keep your eyes open.'

We stepped around one end of the backstop.

'There's a playground over that way,' Casey said. She pointed toward the far end of the park. I could make out the vague shapes of monkey bars, swing sets, slides and other equipment. 'Want to go over and look?' she asked.

'Sure,' I said.

Side by side, we walked up the middle of the baseball diamond, over the pitcher's mound and on past second base. The base bag was missing. So were all the others. 'I wonder where the bases go at night,' I said.

'Home,' Casey said.

I laughed, but not loudly. It felt strange to be walking across a base-ball field at such an hour.

Leaving the diamond behind, we headed out through center field. The grass whispered under our shoes. Though there seemed to be no light except for the glow of the moon, we both cast shadows ahead of us.

There were no trees nearby.

I looked over my shoulder just to make sure nobody was watching us.

Casey looked, too.

'So far, so good,' I said.

'Hardly anyone's ever around here after dark. Not unless there's a night game. It's too exposed.'

'I've noticed that.'

'The night loonies get nervous when they're out in the open.'

'Night loonies?'

'You know.'

'I guess so,' I said. 'The town's full of 'em.'

'Half full,' she corrected me.

'Aren't you afraid of them?' I asked.

'They don't hurt anyone,' she said.

I couldn't believe my ears.

'They *don't*?'

She gave me a one-sided smile. 'They don't hurt anyone they can't *catch*. If they catch you, though, forget it.'

'What do they do?' I asked.

'They *get* you. And that's all she wrote. You're gone. Unless you manage to escape. They almost got me once. It was pretty soon after I started coming out at night. I didn't know any better and tried to help this guy. Must've been three o'clock in the morning. He looked like your typical homeless guy, going down the middle of the street with all his stuff in a shopping cart. I was on a sidewalk and we went past each other heading in opposite directions. I was all set to run, but he kept going. You know how noisy those shopping carts are?'

'Oh, yeah.'

'All of a sudden, his wasn't. I turned around to see what was going on, and the guy was down, just lying there on the street, not moving. So I went running over to see if I could help.' She shook her head. 'Stupid move.'

By this time, we'd left the outfield behind and were approaching the children's playground area. Studying the shadowed darkness, I saw nobody wandering about, no strange shapes on the park benches, nobody on the swings or monkey bars or slides or teeter-totter or carousel, nobody anywhere else in the area.

'When I bent down to help the guy,' Casey said, 'he bashed me on the head with a bottle. Anyway, I think that's what he did. The seizure . . . whatever . . . it'd been a fake-out to lure me over and get me. He knocked me out. When I woke up, I was *in* his shopping cart. It *had* been piled up to the top, so he must've gotten rid of most of the stuff to make room for me. Guess he figured I was a better class of junk.'

We walked over to a swing set. Casey sat on one of the swings. I stood in front of her, but off to one side.

'He hadn't taken out *all* his crap,' she explained. 'I could feel some of it under my back.'

'How did you fit in?'

'It was a pretty big cart,' she said. Smiling, she pushed her feet at the ground and moved herself back and forth a little. 'I only fit in from my head to my butt. My legs were sticking up over the top of the basket and my feet dangled in front. Anyway, I was pretty shocked to find myself in a predicament like that . . .'

'I'll bet.'

'When you're stuck in a grocery cart, there's no easy way to escape. I couldn't just leap out and run away, so I played possum.'

'You must've been scared to death.'

'I sort of was and sort of wasn't. I'd been in some bad situations before and I'd gotten out of them in one piece . . . more or less. So I figured I'd get out of this one, too.'

'I guess you did,' I said.

'Guess so.' She smiled up at me. 'I'm here.'

'How did you get away?'

'Well, I kept *hoping* someone would see us and stop him. Like a cop, for instance? I mean, nobody could exactly look at us without seeing me in the shopping cart. He didn't even bother to cover me. I was right there in plain sight.'

'At three o'clock in the morning,' I added.

'Right. But it's not as if *nobody's* out at that hour. You know that.'

'I know, all right.'

'I heard a jogger once. And I thought I heard a bike go by. Even a few cars, too. I think the jogger and bike went right past us on the same street. None of the cars did, but I heard them go through intersections pretty close to us. Nobody said anything or did anything. They just kept going.'

'Maybe they didn't see you.'

'Half of them were probably weirdos, themselves.'

I smiled. 'Yeah.'

'Anyway, the guy finally got where he was taking me. He turned the cart over and dumped me out, but he must've already figured out I was playing possum. When I tried to get up and run, he grabbed me and pounded me half senseless. Then he swung me over his shoulder and carried me down a slope. I had a pretty good idea where we were, and figured he was taking me down by the stream where we'd be good and hidden. I figured he planned to molest me, you know? For starters.'

I nodded. My mouth was dry, my heart pounding hard.

'When we got down to where the stream was, I thought he would throw me down and do it. I wanted him to try. That's when they're easiest, when they're all hot and ready to stick it in. Only thing is, he didn't stop and put me down. Instead, he turned and carried me along the shore. He was gonna take me under the bridge.' Casey frowned up at me. 'One thing about bridges, Ed. You don't want to go under them at night.'

'I've noticed,' I muttered.

'I figured I'd better do something real fast and get away. Before I had a chance, though, he calls out, *"Come 'n get it!"* And he gets *answers* from under the bridge. Like a bunch of guys are already there waiting for him. Maybe a couple of gals, too.' Shaking her head, Casey muttered, 'Damn. *That* scared me. I thought my skin was going to crawl off my bones. It scares me just remembering.'

'It scares me just listening,' I said.

'Well, I wasn't about to let him take me *under* there. The way he had me, I was sort of drooped over his back with my legs down his front, and he had just one arm across my legs to hold me steady. His other hand . . . well, it was feeling up my rear end. I hadn't fought him, so far, just stayed limp and kept my mouth shut, so he wasn't expecting anything.

'All of a sudden, I grabbed hold of his trousers with both hands and kicked my legs up for all I was worth . . . like unbending myself. He couldn't hold on. For a second, I was straight up, teetering on the back of his shoulder. Then I flipped the rest of the way over and dropped to the ground behind him. I landed on my feet, but just barely. I was so off balance I fell back against him . . . which steadied *me* but knocked him flying. I think he actually bumped into some of the others. Sounded like one or two of them went down. And maybe they blocked the shore for a few seconds so none of the others could get by very fast. I don't know what really happened, just that I ran like my ass was on fire and nobody ever caught me.'

'Thank God for that,' I muttered.

'I don't like to think about it much . . . what they might've done to me. I sure didn't like the way he called, "Come and get it." That's what my mom used to say when it was time for supper.'

'What do you think he meant?' I asked.

Swaying back and forth, Casey looked up at me and sounded almost amused as she said, 'He took me most of the way there in a grocery cart. I guess that's a clue.'

Chapter Thirty-eight

'Where'd this happen?' I asked. 'What bridge?'

'I'm not sure. It was before I knew the town very well. I do know it was one of the bridges that crosses over the Old Mill Stream.'

'On Division?'

She shook her head. 'No. That's right by the campus. This was a pretty good distance to the west. Maybe over near Fairmont or . . .'

She mentioned a couple of other street names, but I only heard Fairmont; the street I'd taken north earlier that night to avoid Division.

'I live near there,' I said. 'Near Fairmont.'

'Well, don't go under the bridge. I'm not sure that's where the guy tried to take me, but it doesn't matter much. You never know which bridge they'll be under.'

'You've studied them?' I asked.

'I sees what I sees.'

'You think they . . . eat people?'

She shrugged. 'Whatever they can get into a shopping cart.'

I nodded.

'At this point,' Casey said, 'you're supposed to tell me I'm nuts. People don't eat people.'

'People eating people,' I said, 'isn't as unusual as most people would like to believe.'

'Well, they seem to do it around here. The night loonies, anyway. How about giving me a push?'

'Sure.'

I stepped behind Casey's swing. Bending over slightly, I put my hands behind her shoulders and gently pushed. She glided forward, the chains creaking.

'Harder,' she said.

When she came back at me, I thrust harder and she went higher. I took a couple of steps away so she wouldn't collide with me on her return. Her back pressed against my hands and I shoved again.

'Harder,' she said.

Next time, I shoved harder. My hands were lower on her back. There seemed to be nothing between the sweatshirt and her skin. I felt the curves of her ribcage.

'You're doing good,' she said.

'Thanks.'

Soon, I had her flying. On her upward course, she leaned far back, pulling at the chains, her legs out straight, her ponytail hanging toward the ground. On the way down, she sat up and bent her knees, bringing her feet up close to the bottom of the swing, and her ponytail went in against the back of her neck.

I had to keep moving farther away to avoid being struck. As she went higher, my contact with her back traveled lower and lower. My open hands pushed at her flanks, then her hips, then the sides of her jean-clad buttocks, and then the edge of the swing seat.

Finally, she went so high that slack came into the chains. She and the swing fell for a moment. Then the chains went taut, the swing lurching and jerking and going crooked. Casey laughed. She swept downward, twisting.

'Want me to . . .?'

'I'm fine,' she said.

I moved out of the way. Casey began to pump, and soon she had the swing gliding along on a steady course.

'Nicely done,' I said.

'Thanks.'

'You didn't really need a pusher.'

'No, but I liked it. Why don't you grab a swing?'

I'd rather watch you, I thought. But I didn't say it. Instead, I sat on the swing next to hers. The wooden seat and cool chains felt good and familiar.

Too familiar to be memories from childhood.

I suddenly remembered that I'd been at a playground last spring with Holly. On a warm, scented night near the end of the semester, we'd sat side by side on swings very much like these. Neither of us had done any real swinging; we'd just sat and talked softly for a very long time.

I could picture Holly sitting there in the darkness, her head turned toward me, her hands on the chains, her bare feet in the sand under the swing. She'd been wearing white shorts. Her skin had seemed much darker than the shorts.

Was *this* the playground where we'd been? I couldn't be sure.

I realized that I didn't much care.

Nor did I feel the sadness and longing and bitterness that usually came with memories of Holly.

'*Gerrr-onimo!*' Casey called, but not very loudly.

Her voice pulled me into the present and I raised my eyes in time to see her leave the swing at the height of its arc. She seemed to let go of its chains and remain high in the air as the seat fell away from under her, twisting and flopping. After a moment poised in midair, she dropped as if she'd stepped off a high dive.

Legs straight, arms spread out, she plunged toward the ground. The image reminded me of her earlier jump from the porch. This, however, was a straight decent and a much greater fall. Her ponytail flipped up higher than the top of her head. Her sweatshirt flew up to her armpits. I saw her bare back. I glimpsed the side of her left breast.

The ponytail and sweatshirt leaped down. Her knees bent. As if shoved from behind by an invisible bully, she stumbled forward very fast for a few paces then fell to her hands and knees.

I jumped off my swing. Hurrying toward her, I asked, 'Are you okay?'

'I'm splendid.' She tumbled over and rolled onto her back. Smiling up at me, she put her folded hands underneath her head and raised her knees. 'It's like flying,' she said.

'And crashing.'

She laughed softly. 'It didn't hurt much.'

'You like pain?'

'I'm not a big fan, but I'm not scared of a little. It was worth some pain to fly like that.'

Smiling down at her, I shook my head.

'You think I'm nuts.'

'A trifle peculiar, perhaps.'

She chuckled. Then, in a low and raspy voice as if imitating an old geezer – probably one of her relatives – she said, 'That's a peculiar one, that Casey. Been a touch daffy ever since she fell on her head.'

'You fell on your head?' I asked.

'Oh, sure,' she replied in her usual voice. 'A few times. And I've gotten clobbered on the noggin plenty of times, too. Good thing it's so hard.' She took a hand out from under her head and knuckled her brow as if rapping on a door. Then she frowned.

'What?'

'Nobody home.'

I grinned.

Casey sat up. She reached out a hand the way people do when they want a pull to their feet. I took hold of it. As I tugged her up, glad for the feel of her hand in mine, I watched her face. She seemed to be looking into my eyes.

When she was standing, I tried to let go of her hand. She kept hold of mine. Neither of us moved. We stood there, holding hands and gazing into each other's eyes. My heart pounded harder and I felt a tightness in my throat.

She squeezed my hand.

I started to pull her toward me, but she shook her head and put her other hand against my chest. 'Just friends,' she said. 'Okay?'

Though I sank inside, I also felt a certain joy that she had accepted me as a friend.

'Sure,' I said. 'Friends.'

Still holding hands, we shook on it as if making a deal. 'Don't look so glum,' she said.

'I'm not glum.'

'We hardly even know each other. Besides, you've already got Eileen.'

Was Eileen the *real* reason Casey intended to be 'just friends' with me?

I almost told her that Eileen and I had broken up. It wouldn't exactly be a lie; we had agreed to stop seeing each other – at least for a few days, to avoid arousing suspicion about our injuries. But it would be a betrayal of Eileen. A lie to Casey, too, whether or not I preferred to call it that.

Besides, maybe Casey only considered me 'safe' because of my relationship to Eileen.

'I'm happy just to be your friend,' I said.

'Good.' She shook my hand again. 'I'm glad that's settled. Now we can just have a good time and stop thinking about that other stuff.'

Had *she* been thinking about that other stuff?

Obviously! I suddenly felt almost gleeful.

Just as suddenly, fear swept through me.

'What?' Casey asked.

I let go of her hand and pointed. She turned around.

'Where?' she asked.

'On the backstop.'

When she saw him, she didn't make a sound, but her head moved slightly up and down.

Past the playground, beyond center field and second base and the pitcher's mound and home plate, perhaps three feet off the ground, someone was clinging like a monkey to the chain-link backstop.

He seemed to be on the other side of it, facing our way.

My skin crawled.

'Anyone you know?' Casey asked. She sounded calm.

'I don't think so.'

'Isn't Eileen, is it?'

'I think it's a guy.'

She turned her head and smiled at me. 'I think so, too.'

'A *big* guy,' I pointed out.

'Isn't Randy, is it?'

'Looks too big to be Randy.'

Her smile grew bigger. 'Wanta go find out?'

'Not especially. Aren't you scared?'

'He's pretty far away. And he seems to be happy just watching.'

As if the man had heard Casey and wished to prove her wrong, he scurried down the backstop.

My stomach seemed to flip.

He dropped to the ground.

'Shit,' I muttered.

He trotted around one end of the backstop then turned our way and broke into a run.

'Oh, dear,' said Casey. Then she faced me, smiling, and asked, 'Ride or Hide?'

Chapter Thirty-nine

'Run,' I suggested.

'Good thought,' Casey said. 'Let's go.' She whirled around and took off across the playground. I ran close to her side, but slower, letting her stay in the lead. She knew the area better than I did. Also, I wanted to stay slightly back to guard her rear.

When I looked over my shoulder, the man was still chasing us. He seemed to be dressed in black, floppy clothes. He chugged along with his head down, his heavy legs moving fairly well for such a big guy, his hands punching at the night. There was something off-kilter about the way he ran. That Hemingway character from 'The Battler' came into my mind. Not Nick Adams, but the crazy boxer, Ad Francis. Paul Newman played him in the movie, but this guy was a lot bigger than Paul Newman and I had a feeling he was no Ad Francis. I *wished* he were Ad Francis.

At the other side of the playground, I looked back again. He was still pounding after us.

Not gaining on us, though.

We leaped off the curb and took a diagonal course toward the other side of the street. No cars were coming. None was even in sight except for those parked along the street and in driveways.

We ran up a driveway to the sidewalk and swung to the right. The sidewalk was narrow, so I dropped back. Running directly behind Casey, I matched her stride for stride and watched her ponytail prance.

As we neared the end of the block, I looked over my shoulder. I couldn't see our pursuer at first. Then I spotted him way back, pounding his way past a teeter-totter.

'We're leaving him in the dust,' I gasped.

'The game's not . . . Ride or Run,' Casey said. 'It's Ride or Hide.'

'Yeah, but . . .'

'Like this.' She suddenly veered to the left. I followed her off the sidewalk, onto the grass of a lawn, and up half a dozen wooden stairs to the front porch of a house.

The porch was dark. It had a swing and I hoped an old man wasn't sitting there, watching us in silence.

We're nowhere near that house, I thought. But I wasn't sure. I had only vague notions about our location.

'Be very quiet,' Casey whispered. Then she opened the screen door of the house.

'What're we—?'

'Shhhh.' She opened the main door.

I followed her in. Standing on the other side of the threshold, I eased the screen door shut. Then I stepped out of the way and Casey closed the solid wooden door very quietly.

She took hold of my arm. I looked at her, but could hardly see her at all.

Off to one side, a dim gray luminescence seemed to be entering the living room through a large window. I could make out the vague shapes of furniture over there, but the foyer where we stood was almost black.

Though Casey's hand remained in the same position on my arm, I could tell that she was moving. She pulled slightly. I leaned toward her and she whispered, 'We'll stay here till he's gone.' Her breath was soft and warm against the side of my neck.

'Whose house is this?' I whispered.

'Ours.'

The news came as a vast relief, and also brought a sense of joy that she trusted me enough to bring me to her home.

If she was telling the truth.

It seemed like quite a coincidence, Casey's own home just happening to be across the street from the playground and such a handy place to hide when we suddenly found ourselves being chased.

Or maybe not such a coincidence. After all, ever since I'd joined Casey, she had been leading the way. She'd brought me into this area of town, taken me to the playground, led me to this house.

Maybe the man chasing us was incidental and Casey had meant to bring me here all along.

'We'd better take off our shoes,' she whispered, her breath stroking my neck.

She let go of my arm.

Balancing on one foot, then the other, I removed my shoes.

'Give them to me,' Casey whispered. 'I'll put 'em with mine.'

I reached out with a shoe in each hand. She touched my hands, found my shoes and took them away. Stepping by, she brushed against me.

Moments later, she took hold of my arm again. 'Let's go upstairs,' she whispered.

Upstairs. To her bedroom?

What had happened to just being friends?

I felt stunned, thrilled and scared.

Calm down, I told myself. Just because we're going upstairs doesn't mean we'll make love.

'We've gotta be very quiet,' she whispered. 'Don't wanta wake anyone.'

'Who else is here?'

'Let's take a look.'

'Don't you know?'

'Shhhh.'

Casey in the lead, we sneaked through the foyer and climbed a stairway. The darkness was so deep that having my eyes open or shut made no difference. I kept them open anyway. Casey kept hold of my right arm. I slid my left hand up the banister. We moved very slowly, very quietly. Every so often, a stair creaked or groaned.

My God, I thought. I'm sneaking upstairs with Casey, the mystery girl.

My excitement was nearly unbearable. So was my fear.

What if her parents catch us?

What if they don't, and she takes me into her bedroom and we make love?

What if our pursuer saw which house we ran to, and comes in to get us?

I was pretty sure Casey hadn't locked the front door.

I imagined the big man lumbering up the stairs, pulling out a knife as he reached the second floor.

Fee, fi, fo, fum . . .

Shit.

At the top of the stairs, Casey guided me to the left. We moved along silently on the carpet. Ahead of us, a window seemed almost bright with the gray of the night outside. The gray seeped in, filling that end of the hallway but dimming away as it neared us, leaving most of the corridor black.

A growly sound sent shivers up my spine.

Casey halted.

She'd stopped us in front of a doorway. The growly sounds came from that direction, and I realized they were snores from someone sleeping. No, from *two* people sleeping. To our left was a doorway. The room beyond it was slightly less dark than where we stood.

Casey pulled gently on my arm and I followed her into the room. It had a very large bed between two windows. The window curtains were shut, but light from outside came through them and from spaces at their edges.

There seemed to be two people asleep on the bed. Their heads were on pillows. One person was covered to the shoulders with blankets, while the other, curled on her side, had no sheet or blanket on her at all. She seemed to be wearing dark pajamas, but her feet were bare. The room was chilly. I thought her feet must be cold.

I supposed these two people must be Casey's mother and father.

Strange that she would bring me into their bedroom while they slept.

She must have her reasons, I thought.

Though I wanted to get out of the room, Casey still held my arm. She led me past the right side of the bed, all the way to the window. There, she let go of my arm. With both hands, she parted the curtains. Light from outside poured in. At first, it seemed so bright that I feared it might disturb the sleepers. But they continued to snore and I realized that the light from outside was not very bright, after all.

As Casey spread the curtains all the way open, quiet, skidding sounds came from the top.

The sleepers went on snoring.

Casey moved sideways to make room for me at the window. I eased over until my arm touched hers. Looking down through the glass, we had a fine view of the area in front of the house.

That's why she'd brought us into this room.

Except for shadowed places, the lawn and sidewalk and road were well lighted by streetlamps. We could even see portions of the neighbors' property to both sides of Casey's house and across the road.

Nobody was in sight.

Where is he?

Maybe, having no idea where we'd gone, the chaser had run on by to search for us on different streets, different blocks. Maybe he'd quit and wandered off.

Or maybe he knew exactly where we'd gone. He might be hiding down there, waiting for us to come out. Maybe in those bushes across the street. Or behind one of the parked cars. Or behind the trunk of the tree in Casey's front yard. Or on the porch of this very house, *or already inside.*

If only we could *see* him!

Suddenly, I wondered if he could see *us*. Standing this close to the glass, we might be visible to someone looking up at the window.

As if Casey shared the thought, she bumped gently against my side. I moved out of the way. She reached high with both hands and slid the curtains shut.

Taking me by the arm, she led me toward the bedroom door. About halfway there, however, she stopped. She gave my arm a squeeze, then let go. I slowly turned and watched her drift through the darkness to the side of the bed where the uncovered woman was sleeping.

She draped a blanket over the woman's bare feet.

The woman kept on snoring.

Casey came back to me. Her hand found my forearm and she led me out of the room.

Chapter Forty

She guided me down the hallway and into another bedroom. I hoped it might be hers, but the curtains were open. In the glow from outside, I saw the shape of someone on a single bed beneath one of the windows. A head lay on the pillow. The rest of the body was hidden under a blanket.

For a moment, I thought this might be a fake person – a dummy put there by Casey before she crept out of the house. But sounds of slow, steady breathing came from that direction. Unless Casey's ruse was sophisticated enough to include sound effects, the shape on the bed was a real person.

Beneath the other window was a second bed. Empty.

Was *this* Casey's bed? Did she share the room with a sister?

Its blankets looked smooth and straight. If Casey had gone to bed earlier in the night, she'd apparently made the bed before departing for her adventures.

Breath soft against my ear, Casey whispered, 'We'll wait here for a while.' Then she stepped away from me and silently shut the bedroom door.

After that, she led me by the hand to the empty bed. 'Lie down,' she whispered.

Heart thudding wildly, I sank onto the bed. It made some quiet creaking sounds. I scooted over to the far edge to make room for Casey. On my back, I watched her sit on the edge of the mattress, swing her legs up, and lie flat. She turned her face toward me. 'You can take a nap if you want,' she whispered.

I found her hand and held it. She gave my hand a squeeze.

'I don't think I can sleep,' I said, hoping my quiet voice wouldn't disturb the other girl.

'Why not?'

'I'm a little nervous.'

'About what?'

'Everything.'

She turned onto her side, facing me. I turned onto my side, too. The mattress shook slightly as she scooted closer to me. She put an arm behind my back. I felt her breath on my lips, her breasts touching me through soft fabrics, the warmth of her thighs touching mine. I reached over her side and laid my hand on her back.

'You don't have to be nervous,' she whispered. 'We're safe here.'

I almost mentioned that she hadn't locked the front door. If I'd said it, though, she might've gone downstairs to correct the situation. I wanted her to stay just where she was.

'Try to sleep,' she whispered.

'That'd be a good trick.'

'All you've got to do is relax. Think nice thoughts.'

I closed my eyes. My thoughts were nice, all right. All about Casey on the bed with me.

From the feel of her breath, her lips were only an inch or two away from mine. I longed to kiss her, to scoot closer and hold her body tightly against mine, to slip a hand up the back of her sweatshirt.

Is that what she's hoping for? I wondered.

Back in the playground, she'd stopped me when I made a move to kiss her. *Just friends*, she'd said. And, *We hardly even know each other.* And, *You've already got Eileen.*

Had she changed her mind?

Not likely.

Then what're we doing in her bed?

It's just a place to stay while we wait for things to get safe outside.

Really? The living room would've been fine for that. But we're not in the living room, we're in her bedroom.

Suppose she *does* want me to make a move? If I don't do it, she'll think I'm either a chicken or I'm not interested in her.

But she's already told me *not* to. If I go ahead and try it anyway, she'll think I'm a jerk. I imagined her saying, *What part of the word 'no' don't you understand?*

Casey would never say such a thing. No halfway considerate person would *ever* say such a crappy thing to someone. She might like me less, though.

'Maybe I'll try counting sheep,' I whispered.

She didn't answer.

My comment, pretty inane if I do say so myself, hadn't required an answer. Still, her silence seemed a little odd.

'Casey?' I whispered.

Her warm breath blew against my lips and chin. The breeze went away as she slowly filled her lungs. Then the air returned to my face.

She's asleep!

She breathed with an easy, peaceful rhythm that sounded much the same as the breathing that came from the other bed.

How could she let herself fall asleep? She and I were supposed to be in this together.

I felt abandoned and disappointed.

And worried.

After all, I was a stranger in this house. Casey was my host, my guide, my protector. So long as she remained asleep, however, I was on my own.

I can wake her up.

The way she'd dropped off so fast, it was obvious that she needed sleep. I probably needed it, myself, but I was too keyed up.

I'd better *not* fall asleep, I thought.

I pictured myself waking up in daylight with Casey in my arms, her parents and sister standing over the bed, glaring down at me.

Wouldn't that be lovely?

It won't happen, I told myself. The moment I start to get drowsy, I'll wake Casey up and tell her I have to leave. She can either see me to the door or stay here. In the meantime, I'll just let her sleep.

But what if I drift off?

That sort of thing can sneak up on you. I might just close my eyes thinking I'll rest them for a few moments . . . and not wake up till six or seven.

I thought about setting my wristwatch alarm. Unfortunately, the watch was on my left wrist, and my left arm was trapped underneath me. Just as well, probably. Though the alarm's noise was a quiet beep, it might be loud enough to wake up the girl in the other bed.

Casey squirmed in her sleep. Her back slid under my hand and she made a soft 'Mmm' sound as if she liked how my hand felt. When she quit squirming, I went on rubbing her back. I caressed her in slow, gentle circles, making the sweatshirt move over her smooth skin.

I didn't intentionally work the sweatshirt upward. After a while, however, it got rumpled. Feeling my way downward, I discovered that the sweatshirt no longer overlapped the top of her jeans. A distance of two or three inches separated them. In the space between them was Casey's bare skin.

I put my hand there. She continued to sleep. Her skin felt smooth and slightly cool.

At the very back, the waistband of her jeans was pursed out slightly. Probably something to do with the way she was curled on her side.

I turned my hand and eased my fingers in. An inch or so down, I felt the thin elastic band of her panties. Keeping my fingers outside the panties, I stroked the top of her buttocks through the slick fabric.

Her breathing stayed the same, so I knew she still slept.

I thought how easy it would be to slip my fingers *under* the elastic. Just a little bit.

I knew I shouldn't do it.

What'll it hurt? She's asleep. She'll never even know I did it.

It's wrong.

But I was already pretty excited by that point. Unwilling to stop myself, I went ahead and snuck my hand down under the back of her panties. I slid my fingers slowly across her buttocks and stroked the smooth, warm valley between them.

Casey still slept.

Fearful of disturbing her if I explored too deeply, I kept my hand fairly high on her rump.

When she moaned, I moved my hand higher – and out from inside her panties.

Moments later, her breathing returned to the slow in and out of her sleep rhythm.

'Casey?' I whispered.

She didn't respond, so I slipped my hand beneath the bottom of her sweatshirt. She felt good and warm under there. My hand glided slowly, savoring her smoothness and curves. I caressed her from side to side, slowly making my way upward all the way to the backs of her shoulders.

And now the front?

I wanted badly to do it. I was hard and aching.

My hand continued to caress her back. The way she was curled on her side, her left breast still pushed against me.

It's already touching my chest, I told myself. What's the difference if it's touching my hand?

Plenty.

Underneath her sweatshirt, my hand moved slowly downward until it almost came out. Then I eased it up her side, feeling the curves of her ribcage. Her arm, draped over my side, wasn't in the way. I stopped my hand on the warm skin just below her armpit.

She still breathed slowly, deeply.

The ball of my thumb rested against a rising smoothness that was probably the side of her breast.

Now all I needed to do was bring my hand toward me.

Are you out of your mind? What if she wakes up?

I'll tell her I thought she was awake the whole time.

You wanta blow everything just to cop a feel? Are you nuts? Go find Eileen, you can mess with her tits to your heart's content.

I didn't care about Eileen's.

I ached to touch Casey's. Especially the one I could feel against my chest and against the side of my hand.

If she catches me, she'll hate me.

If she doesn't catch me, I thought, I'll hate myself. I saw nothing particularly wrong with caressing her back while she slept – or even her *low* back – but to feel up her breasts was crossing the line.

If I don't draw the line at that, what next? Unfasten her jeans and put my hand down the front of her panties? Slip a few fingers into her?

I imagined myself doing just that.

Aching with lust, I gritted my teeth and slid my hand downward, out from under her sweatshirt.

I placed my hand safely in the middle of her back and sighed.

Casey went on sleeping.

I don't know how much time went by – perhaps five minutes, maybe ten – before I realized that sounds of slow, steady breathing no longer came from the direction of the other bed.

Casey's head blocked my view. I raised my head enough to see over her with one eye.

While I watched, the girl in the other bed turned on to her side and pushed herself up on one elbow.

Chapter Forty-one

'Hey,' the girl said, her voice a fairly loud whisper.

Going squirmy inside, I didn't say a thing. I didn't move.

'Is that you?' she asked.

Time to call in the troops. I grabbed Casey's arm and shook it. 'Mmm?'

Lowering my head, I whispered, 'She's awake.'

'Mmm?'

'Who *is* that?' the girl asked. She sounded somewhat concerned, but not alarmed.

Casey made another quiet, 'Mmm,' sound. Then her lips pushed softly against mine. They were open and warm and moist and too quickly gone.

Moaning again, Casey rolled onto her back and turned her head toward the girl. 'Hi, Marianne,' she whispered.

'Is someone with you?'

'Yeah.'

'A *boy*?'

'Yeah. His name's Ed. He's my new friend.'

'Hi, Marianne,' I whispered.

'Hi, Ed.'

Casey sat up and swung her feet to the floor. 'Ed's a student at the university.'

'Cool,' said Marianne.

'Marianne's in the eighth grade,' Casey explained.

'Cool,' I said.

Marianne laughed softly.

'Ed's real nice,' Casey explained to her, 'but he already has a girl-friend so I guess I'm out of luck.'

'I wouldn't say that,' I whispered.

She looked around at me, then stood up and moved silently across the floor to Marianne's bed. There, she said, 'How're you doing, honey?'

'Oh, not so bad.'

Casey bent low over the bed. She put her arms around the girl, who then reached up and embraced her. They clung to each other and didn't let go. After a while, someone began very quietly to sob.

'It's all right,' Casey whispered.

'No it's not.'

'Sure.'

'I thought . . . you weren't coming back.'

'I'm here.'

'Thought you . . . didn't care about me . . . anymore.'

'I'll always care about you.'

'But you . . . didn't come.'

'It hasn't been that long, has it?'

'Yes it has.'

'A week?'

'Longer,' Marianne said, and sniffed. 'Almost two. Twelve nights.'

'I'm sorry.'

'I've missed you so bad.'

'I've missed you, too.'

'Then why didn't you *come*?'

'I have lots to do.'

'Was it 'cause of *him*.'

'No, no. I only met Ed tonight. But I have lots of places I need to go. I come here as often as I can.'

'I wish you'd come more.'

'I know. So do I. But I'm here now.'

'Yeah.'

239

They released each other. Marianne scooted over. Casey lifted the covers and crawled into the bed.

After a few minutes, she eased herself out of Marianne's bed and came toward me. By the sounds of the breathing I heard, Marianne must've fallen asleep.

Bending over me, Casey whispered, 'We can go now.'

I made my way slowly across the mattress. Then Casey took my hand and pulled. I stood up. Keeping hold of my hand, she led me out of the room and down the dark hallway to the top of the stairs, then down the stairway.

At the bottom, we put on our shoes. Though I expected Casey to lead me straight to the front door, we turned away from it. In a corridor that was nearly pitch-black, she whispered, 'Do you want to use the bathroom?'

'Here in the house?'

'Yeah.'

I had to go fairly badly, but I said, 'I don't think so.'

'Okay. I'll be right out.' She let go of my hand. I heard a few soft footfalls. Then, just to my right, a door bumped quietly shut. A moment later, a strip of yellow light appeared across the bottom of the door.

Maybe this *is* her house, I thought.

From the sound of her urine drilling the water, she must've had to go very badly. It went on for a long time. After it stopped, I heard a faucet come on. She was washing her hands, but she hadn't flushed yet.

Under the circumstances, maybe you *don't* flush.

She opened the door a crack. The bathroom light was still on. Her face close to the crack, she whispered, 'You sure you don't want to go?'

'I'm sure.'

She nodded, then stepped away from the door. After the toilet flushed, she came back and turned off the light. I heard the door open. She found my arm, then my hand. Her hand felt cold from the faucet.

Instead of turning us around and heading for the front door, she led us toward the back of the house. The carpet ended. In the vague light from the windows, I saw cupboards, counters, a stove and a refrigerator.

'Thirsty?' Casey asked.

'I don't think so.'

'Hungry?'

'Shouldn't we get out of here?'

'Why?'

'This isn't really your house, is it?'

While she continued to hold my hand, her free hand patted me on the chest. 'So that's the problem.'

'Yeah.'

'Don't worry about it.'

'It isn't your house, is it?'

'Not exactly.'

'I didn't think so.'

'But we've got permission.'

'Whose?'

'Marianne's. We're like her guests.'

'What about her parents?'

'They're asleep.'

'God, I hope so.'

She laughed softly.

'Do they know you sneak into their house in the middle of the night?' I asked.

'God, I hope not.' She patted my chest again, then released my hand and walked over to the refrigerator. She opened it. Light flooded out. Looking over her shoulder, she asked, 'What'll you have?'

'Nothing.'

'A Coke? A beer?'

'No! Are you nuts? We've gotta get out of here.'

'How about a maraschino cherry?'

'No!'

She removed a jar of the bright red cherries from a shelf in the refrigerator door, unscrewed the lid and held out the jar toward me. 'Come on, help yourself.'

'It's stealing.'

'Nah.'

I shook my head and refused to take a cherry, so she turned away and set the lid down on a shelf inside the refrigerator. Going into the jar with her thumb and forefinger, she pinched a long stem and lifted a cherry out of its clear red juice. She let a few drips fall into the jar, then tilted back her head, opened her mouth and lowered in the cherry. She brought her teeth closer together. A small tug jerked the cherry up against them and the stem came off. She chewed and I heard the wet squishy sounds and could almost taste the cherry's sweetness.

I liked maraschino cherries very much, but not enough to take one that didn't belong to me.

'I *know* you want one,' Casey whispered.

'No thanks.'

'Come on.' She inserted her thumb and forefinger again and fished for a stem. 'It's okay with Marianne. She says I should make myself at home.'

'But her parents.'

'The hell with them. They're creeps. They're horrible to her.' She caught a stem and lifted out a cherry. Holding it above the jar, she whispered, 'Open up.'

I opened up and tilted back my head. Casey raised the cherry above my mouth. Then she teased me with it, bumping it against my lips a few times before lowering it into my mouth. I brought my teeth closer together and she plucked the stem off. The loose cherry rolled around inside my mouth. I got it between my molars and squeezed it a little. It felt springy. Juice seeped out of it. Then I chomped and the cherry exploded, flooding my mouth with sweet juices.

'You've eaten of the forbidden fruit,' Casey whispered. 'Now your ass is doomed.'

I almost burst out laughing. I fought it back, though. 'Thanks a lot,' I said.

Laughing softly, Casey screwed on the lid and returned the jar to its place on the shelf of the refrigerator door.

'Now can we go?' I asked.

'Whenever you're ready, Eddie.' She shut the door, and darkness clutched the kitchen.

Chapter Forty-two

The kitchen had a door to the back yard, so we used it. After the darkness inside the house, the night seemed very bright. We stood on the elevated deck just outside the door and looked all around.

No sign of the man who had chased us.

No sign of anyone else, either.

We descended a few stairs to the yard, then went around the side of the house. At the front corner, we stopped in the shadows and stood motionless for a long time.

Nobody was in sight.

'I guess the coast is clear,' I said.

'Looks that way.'

Still keeping careful watch, we made our way to the sidewalk. 'I'll stick with you for a while,' Casey said. 'Then maybe we'd better call it a night.'

'You have lots of other places to go?'

She took hold of my hand. We started walking toward the end of the block. 'I have certain things to do,' she said. 'Places I go.'

'Like Marianne's house?'

She shrugged. 'Marianne's my friend. I visit her when I can.'

'Not often enough.'

'Her house came in handy, didn't it?'

Nodding, I asked, 'Does she leave the front door unlocked for you?'

'Doesn't have to. Her parents never lock it.'

'They have no idea you sneak in?'

'Haven't got a clue. If they ever found out, they *would* start locking the door. Not that it'd keep me out.'

'You also go through locked doors?'

She beamed a smile. 'They're my specialty.'

'You're a very bad girl.'

Her smile went slightly crooked. 'Think so?'

'Not really.'

'Good. I don't think so, either.'

'How come locked doors are your "specialty"?'

'I'm good at opening them.'

'And going into places where you don't belong?'

'People don't necessarily lock their doors to keep *me* out. They're more worried about burglars and killers and other assorted denizens of evil.'

'Or maybe to keep out everyone who isn't *invited* inside.'

She smiled at me. 'They might invite me in if they knew me.'

'I'm sure they would.'

'Marianne would.'

'Not her parents, though.'

'Not hardly. But you can't please everyone, and I don't even try. That's a nice thing about night roaming; you're mostly on your own and don't have to deal with people. You can watch them. You can hide from them. You can even get to know them pretty well if you want, but they never have to know *you*.'

'Like going around invisible.'

'Precisely.'

'And being invisible, you make a habit of sneaking into people's houses?'

Her smile broke out again. 'It's been known to happen.'

'Why do you do it?'

'Why not?'

'It's against the law. It's dangerous.'

'It's exciting.'

'Is that why you do it?' I asked.

'I just do it. I like to do it and I do it. *You* did it tonight. What'd you think?'

'I thought you lived there. In fact, you *said* it was your house.'

She gave my hand a squeeze. 'I was speaking figuratively, college boy.'

'How is someone else's house yours *figuratively*?'

Not even pausing to consider her answer, she said, 'It's *like* mine while I'm in it.'

Laughing, I said, 'That's a stretch.'

'Perchance.'

Suddenly, a thought struck me with concern and sorrow. 'Do you *have* a home?'

'What makes you ask?'

'You're roaming around all night, obviously going into *other* people's homes.'

'Does that mean I don't have one of my own?'

'It might.'

'But not necessarily.'

'Where *do* you live?'

Her smile died. 'Wherever I want.'

'You don't *have* a place?'

'Of course I do.'

'I mean a place of your own. Not somebody else's house. Your own house or apartment or something.'

'Maybe I do and maybe I don't.'

'You don't,' I said.

'Think not?'

'Where are your parents?' I asked.

'Who says I have any?'

'Are you an orphan?'

'That'd make them dead.'

'So you *do* have parents.'

'Somewhere.'

'But not here?'

'Let me ask *you* something,' she said.

'Okay.'

'Do you want to see me tomorrow night?'

'Sure.'

'Why?'

'Why? Because . . .' Be careful, I warned myself. 'I like being with you.'

'Why?'

'I don't know. Because you're interesting. And funny.'

'Isn't Eileen interesting and funny?'

'Sort of. Not like you, though.'

'But she's your girlfriend. You said so yourself. Don't you want to be with *her* tomorrow night?'

'Which night is that? This is already Friday morning . . .'

'To me, it's still Thursday night.'

'When does it become Friday?'

'Sunrise.'

'So "tomorrow night" is Friday night?'

'Exactly.'

'I'm free,' I said.

'What about Eileen? Friday night, shouldn't you be seeing your girlfriend?'

Oh, boy.

'We agreed to stay away from each other for a few days.'

'How come?'

I wanted to tell Casey the truth. Easy enough to explain about getting attacked and probably killing a guy and the rest that happened Wednesday night; my real problem would be admitting that I'd gone under the bridge to have sex with Eileen.

'I think I mentioned she hasn't been feeling very well?'

Casey nodded.

'It's probably nothing serious, but she doesn't want *me* to catch it. So we definitely won't be getting together tomorrow night.'

'Are you sure you didn't have a fight with her?'

I frowned and said nothing.

'You look like you were in a fight with *some*body.'

I almost cringed. I'd forgotten about the bruises and scratches on my face. 'Oh, that,' I said.

'You didn't beat her up, did you?'

'No!'

'What happened to you?'

Stalling, I shrugged. Then I thought of something. 'There's this guy I know, Kirkus. He's a real jerk.' So far, I wasn't lying. 'We're both on the staff of the university's literary magazine. We get together a couple of times a month to read the stories and poems that people submit. Anyway, Kirkus read this story of mine . . .'

'You wrote it?'

'Yeah. Anyway, Kirkus read it and said it was lousy. "Pedestrian and sophomoric, full of gratuitous violence and sex," he said. So I called him a tight-ass, illiterate old prig and one thing sorta led to another.' Still the truth. 'Next thing you know, I said something he *really* didn't like and he punched me in the face. So I punched him.' I smiled and shook my head. 'It was all pretty dumb. We threw a lot of punches and both of us got bruised up a little. It was no big deal.'

All the truth.

But it had happened the previous May.

'So you and Eileen didn't have a fight?'

What if Casey sees her?

We *didn't* fight.

'No,' I said. 'We've never had an actual fight.'

'Do you ever hit girls?'

'Not if you don't count Kirkus.'

'I thought he was a guy.'

'Nobody's absolutely sure. Anyway, I think Eileen's just down with a bug. Like maybe the flu or something.'

'What happens when she gets well?'

I took a few moments, trying to think of a good answer. Then I said, 'She's never up past eleven or twelve, anyway. And she lives over at the sorority house, not with me. So I can come out whenever I want to.'

'On the sly?'

'She doesn't have to know everything I do. We're not . . . engaged or anything. We haven't even been going together all that long.'

'How long?'

Since Monday night. And this was Thursday night, by Casey's calculations.

'Well,' I said, 'we got to know each other last spring, but we didn't really start going together until this semester.'

'So that makes it okay to see someone else behind her back?'

'I'm not exactly *seeing* you. We only met . . . what, a couple of hours ago?'

'But we're getting together tomorrow night, aren't we?'

'I hope so.'

'Will you tell Eileen about it?'

'Probably not.'

'So you *will* be seeing me behind her back.'

'Yeah, but we're not doing anything.'

'We're doing *some*thing.'

'Well, yeah, but not—'

Casey stepped up against me, wrapped her arms around me and kissed me on the mouth. As the kiss went on, I put my arms around her. We were pressed tightly together. I could feel her breasts and ribcage against my chest, her belly against mine, the curve of her mons pushing against my crotch.

Her mouth eased away. 'Are we doing anything yet?'

'Sure are.'

'Just so you know,' she said. Then, 'See you tomorrow night.'

'You're leaving?'

She walked backward, smiling. 'Going, goinggg . . .' She whirled around. As she ran down the sidewalk, she called over her shoulder, '*Gone!*'

'But where'll . . .'

. . . she dodged out of sight behind a hedge . . .

'. . . we meet?'

She didn't answer.

I ran past the hedge, but she wasn't there. I couldn't see her anywhere.

'Casey?' I called.

She didn't answer.

I wandered around looking for her, thinking that perhaps she was playing a small prank and might turn up again. Finally, I realized she was gone for the night.

Giving up, I took a few moments to figure out which way to go for Division Street, and commenced my journey home.

A few times, I had occasion to play Ride or Hide. Each time, I hid. I watched from my hiding places.

A police car cruised by. So did a moving van. And Linda and Walinda Wiggins in their Jeep. (Why were *they* still out?) But I didn't see Randy's pickup truck or the van I'd encountered at the Fairmont Street bridge.

A guy in a sweatsuit ran down the middle of the street alongside his Doberman, which may or may not have been on a leash. I heard the tinny rattle and clank of a shopping cart somewhere nearby, but saw neither the cart nor the person pushing it.

I didn't see any trolls at all . . . 'night loonies', as Casey called them.

I didn't see the bike hag, either.

Most of all, I didn't see Casey.

When I came to the Franklin Street bridge over the Old Mill stream, I ran across it.

Soon after that, I was safe inside my apartment.

Chapter Forty-three

After a couple of hours of sleep, a shower and a cup of coffee, I left the building to head for my eight o'clock Romantic Literature class and found Eileen coming up the sidewalk toward me.

I felt a moment of alarm. But she looked cheerful. Seeing me, she smiled and waved and quickened her pace.

It was a windy autumn morning. Her thick hair blew, some of it flying across her face. She wore a green sweater, a plaid skirt and green knee socks. Her breasts went up and down inside the sweater with the motions of her walking. The wind flung her skirt against her legs.

She looked wonderful.

Except for her face. Even her face, however, looked better than when I'd seen her yesterday morning. She still had bandages above her left eyebrow, on her right cheekbone and on her jaw, but her eye and lip were less puffy. Nor did her bruises show. I guess she'd covered them with makeup.

'Good morning,' she said.

'Hi.'

'Surprised to see me?'

'Yeah.' Surprised and disoriented. Though I'd only been with Casey for a couple of hours last night, Eileen now seemed a little foreign to me: bigger, heavier, older, more steady and mature, more stable, less dangerous and less exciting.

All she carried was the purse hanging from her shoulder. When she opened her arms, I swung my book bag down to the sidewalk. We embraced. She squeezed herself against me and I felt the soft push of her breasts. Her cheek was cool against my face.

'I've missed you so much,' she whispered.

'Me, too.' Then I added, 'Missed you.'

Then she eased her hold, moved her face back and kissed me on the mouth . . . a gentle touch to avoid hurting her split lip. Stepping away, she said, 'I just thought I'd come by and see you safely to your eight o'clock.'

'Good deal.' I shouldered my book bag and we started walking. 'Anything going on?' I asked.

'Not a thing. It's like nothing ever happened Wednesday night.'

'Let's hope it stays that way.'

'I'm halfway thinking nothing *did* happen. Except I can feel the aftereffects. And *see* 'em when I look in a mirror.'

'You're looking a lot better.'

'You, too. But I still *feel* like a disaster.'

'You got it a lot worse than me,' I said, and wondered again if her injuries included rape.

'The worst part was staying away from you yesterday. I hated that.'

'Me, too.'

'And I got to thinking it was really sort of pointless. I mean, what've we got to hide?'

'Murder.'

'You didn't murder anyone. Even if you *did* kill that guy, it was self-defense. But there doesn't seem to be any sort of investigation going on. I don't think they've even found his body. As far as the cops go, nothing happened. So I don't know if we really need to stay away from each other any more.'

'I don't know,' I said. 'People see us side by side, they've gotta figure we got hurt together.'

'We have our tree stories,' she said. Though she smiled, she looked troubled. Apparently, she had expected me to go along with her new idea.

It took me a few moments to remember the tree stories. 'I ran into one chasing a Frisbee, and you fell out of a tree rescuing a kitten?'

'A kite.'

'Yeah. In my professional opinion as an amateur writer, the two stories are somewhat lame and marginally believable, taken separately. Put them together, though, and *no*body'll believe them.'

'Do you really think it matters?'

'It might matter if the body turns up.'

'Maybe,' she said. 'But Kirkus saw us together right after it happened, anyway. He knows we got beaten up.'

'He won't tell.'

'He won't?'

'Nah. If he thought I killed someone, the last thing he would do is turn me in. He might threaten to, but he wouldn't actually do it. He'd keep what he knows a secret and try to control me with it.'

She smiled. 'You really think so?'

'Pretty sure.'

'Why on earth would he do that?'

'He's got the hots for me.'

'Wooo!' she blurted, and laughed. Then she said, 'You're awful.'

'I might be awful, but I think I'm right. He's careful not to let it show too much . . .'

'Disguises it with overt hostility?' Eileen suggested, smiling and nodding.

'Exactly.'

'I'd never thought of it that way. I've always just seen him as a self-important pain in the ass, but you might be right.'

'If I am, we probably don't need to worry about Kirkus tipping off the cops.'

'He might do it in a fit of jealous rage.'

'Nah.'

'Or good citizenship might overcome his lust for you.'

'I doubt it.'

'Anyway,' said Eileen, 'it's a moot point since there's no body and no investigation.'

'Yet,' I added.

'I don't think there *will* be. Those awful creeps under the bridge must've done something . . . hidden the body somewhere . . . maybe buried it.

'Or devoured it completely,' I threw in.

'All but the bones.'

'*Even* the bones, maybe. Dogs eat bones down to nothing.'

'Ug.'

Closer to campus, the streets and sidewalks were busy with students and faculty members. I recognized most of them. So far, however, nobody seemed to be paying attention to Eileen or me.

'Maybe we'd better split up,' I said.

'Do we have to?'

'If we don't, we'll have to start fielding questions about our faces. And it's the sort of thing people will probably talk about and remember.'

'I don't think it'll matter.'

'I'm the one who killed the guy.'

'You don't know that for sure.'

'Let's just play it safe. Okay? Just for today, let's keep our distance. It's Friday, so we'll have the whole weekend to heal up some more before everyone starts seeing us together.'

We both stopped at the corner.

Eileen's smile was gone. 'You think we should stay away from each other till *Monday*?'

'It might be a good idea. Just to play it safe.'

Frowning, she asked, 'Is something going on?'

'It was your idea in the first place, you know. Staying away from each other till our faces heal. Remember your note?'

She nodded, but she didn't look happy.

'And we discussed it last night.'

'I know,' she said.

'I thought we'd agreed that we shouldn't be seen together for . . . I don't know, *several* days.'

'I guess we did,' she admitted.

'So if we just wait till Monday . . .'

'Being *seen* together isn't the same as *being* together. We can still be together if nobody's around to see us, can't we? What would that hurt?'

My chances of being with Casey tonight.

Realizing I was in hazardous territory, I said, 'You're right,' and tried to look pleased. 'The thing is not to be *seen* together. So how about coming over to my place later on?'

'You don't sound very sure.'

'No, I'm sure. Yeah! It'll be great. We'll need to stay in, but . . .'

'No problem.' She seemed happier. 'I tell you what; I'll bring everything over. Drinks, food. You won't have to do anything but be there.'

'Great!' I said.

'What time should I come by?'

The earlier, the better.

'How about five?'

'You got it. See you then.' Smiling, she whirled around and went striding off down the sidewalk, hair and skirt blowing in the wind.

I muttered, 'Just great.'

Chapter Forty-four

Kirkus intercepted me as I walked past the student union. Raising a hand, he called out, 'What ho, Eduardo!'

Speaking of the devil, I thought.

I wasn't surprised to see him, though; like me, he was in Dr Trueman's eight o'clock Romantic Lit class. More often than not, he met me along the way to it, suddenly popping out of a door or out from behind a nearby tree as if he'd been waiting in ambuscade.

'Hey there, Rudy,' I called to him.

He came striding toward me, bouncing on the balls of his feet. Around his neck was a tangerine-colored ascot. He wore his usual corduroy jacket, blue chambray shirt and blue jeans. Though just about everyone else on campus lugged book bags on their shoulders, jaunty Kirkus carried a large leather briefcase.

I hadn't seen him since Wednesday night, but I'd spoken badly about him much more recently . . . to both Casey and Eileen. He had no way of knowing about any of that. I felt a little guilty, anyway.

'How you doing?' I asked as he caught up with me.

'Tip top, old bean.'

'Glad to hear it. No trouble with the ruffians Wednesday night?'

For a moment, he seemed at a loss. Could he possibly have forgotten the incident? Before I had a chance to kick myself for mentioning it, he tipped back his head and said, 'Ah! None at all. No, indeed, I glimpsed neither hide nor hair of the hooligans. I'd rather hoped to retrieve Eileen's blouse, but they must've gone off with their prize.'

He looked pleased, no doubt with his choice of *gone off*. 'And how fares the fair Eileen?' he asked.

'Fairly well.'

He rolled his eyes upward to disparage *my* word play.

'She's improving,' I added.

'Looked as if she'd had a bit of a rough go.'

'She's pretty embarrassed about the whole thing.'

'Eileen embarrassed? I say, *you* were the chap without the shirt.'

'Right. By the time *you* saw us.'

'Ah, yes. You'd lent your garment to the damsel. Quite the chivalrous gesture, what?'

'I couldn't let her walk around half naked,' I said. Discussing the matter with Kirkus made me feel squirmy, but I had a plan growing in my mind. 'After those creeps tore off her blouse, she was . . . she had nothing on up there.'

'Braless in Gaza, was she?'

Nodding, I said, 'Must've been six or seven guys got to see her . . . you know.'

'Her precious boobies.'

'I shouldn't be telling you this.'

'Oh, please do.'

'They touched her, too. Some of them . . . you know . . . felt her up.'

'Oh, dear. Before or after they whizzed on her hair?'

I'd forgotten that part of Eileen's story. 'Before,' I said. Shaking my head, I went on. 'She's *really* embarrassed by the whole episode. She doesn't want anyone to know about it. If people hear about that sort of thing, they picture it in their minds. And they talk. Pretty soon, everybody's thinking about Eileen without a top on and guys groping her and pissing on her and all that.'

'Quite so.' He smiled. '*I'm* thinking about it even as we speak.'

Maybe he's not so gay, after all.

I said, 'Eileen sure doesn't want everyone on campus picturing her like that.'

'Certainly not.'

257

'So maybe you could just forget you saw us.'

'Hardly possible, dear fellow, to forget such a rare and wondrous sight.'

Wondrous sight? *I* was the shirtless one.

'Okay,' I said, 'you don't have to *forget* it. How about just keeping it to yourself? Eileen and I would both be very grateful.'

The corners of Kirkus's mouth turned upward and his eyes sparkled. 'Mum's the word, old sport.' With that, he pressed his lips together and locked them with an invisible key. He tossed the key over his shoulder and brushed off his hands.

'Thanks,' I said.

'You're quite welcome, really.'

'And don't let Eileen know we had this talk, okay? She'd be really upset if she found out I'd blabbed to you.'

'Righto.' He clapped me on the back.

Side by side, we climbed the concrete stairs toward the side entrance of the English building. Suddenly I noticed, a few steps above us, the backside of Horrible Hillary Hatchens. Her head with its pixie haircut looked very small up there. She wore a white pullover sweater, a tight gray skirt, and cowgirl boots. For a woman with such a slight build, she had a remarkably broad rear end.

Luckily, I wouldn't be sitting in her class again until the following Tuesday, which seemed like years away.

As Hatchens entered the door at the top of the stairs, Kirkus asked, 'When shall I join you for dinner?'

'Dinner?'

'How about tonight?'

'I'm seeing Eileen tonight.'

'Splendid! We'll make it a threesome!'

The top stair had a dip worn into its concrete by the tread of countless feet. It was generally considered special. I considered it mostly a safety hazard, and carefully stepped around it.

Inside, the building smelled like floor wax and old wood. It was also quite dark. Daylight had a way of refusing to enter the old windows.

I spotted Hatchens strutting down the first-floor hallway. She seemed to be predominantly butt.

Kirkus and I started climbing the stairs toward the second floor. The stairwell above us appeared to be deserted. The way sounds traveled and reverberated, however, voices and tromping feet and the creaking sounds of stairs and banisters seemed to be coming from all around us. Kirkus's voice joined them. 'Dinner?' he asked.

'What about it?'

'You, me and Eileen. Tonight.'

I shook my head. 'I don't know if she'll like that idea.'

'Oy, vaht's not to like?' he asked, switching from his phony British voice to his phony Jewish-mother voice. Kirkus was a man of numerous, if feeble, talents. 'A nosh, a nosh, my kingdom for a nosh!'

'Jeez.'

'Your shiksa, she von't even know I'm there.'

'Yeah, right.'

'So, vee haff a date?'

'Now you're starting to sound like a Nazi.'

'Yah? Vee haff *vays* to make you talk, yankee dog!'

At the top of the stairs, we turned to the right and headed down a wide hallway toward our classroom. The hall was nearly deserted. I glanced at my wristwatch. Five till eight. Though class rarely began on time, most of the other students were probably already seated and ready.

'Zo,' said Kirkus. 'Dinner tonight?'

'I guess so, but only if you swear you'll never tell anyone about Eileen . . .'

'Unt her vunderbar boobies unt zee pee in her hair.'

'Right.'

Smiling, Kirkus patted me on the back. 'I'm quite looking forward to our engagement, Eduardo.'

'My place at five.'

'And your place is where?'

I told him the address. 'Do you know where that is?'

'I'll find it.'

'I'm sure you will.'

I hardly dared hope otherwise.

Stepping aside, I let Kirkus enter the classroom first. I followed him through the doorway. Just as I'd thought, nearly everyone had already arrived. There must've been fifteen of them. They were gathered rather loosely at the seminar table, some talking to friends, a few using the time to catch up on Wordsworth, some drooping in their seats as if barely conscious.

'What ho!' Kirkus greeted the whole gang.

He was ignored by many, groaned at by several. A few other students rolled their eyes upward in despair.

'"Awake!"' Kirkus proclaimed. '"Arise! Or be forever fallen!"'

'You and the horse you rode in on,' muttered Connor Blayton, a gruff and whiskered aspiring playwright.

I went to my usual place on the left side of the table. My chair was between Stanley Jones and Marcia Palmer. Stanley smiled at me as I pulled my chair away from the table. 'How goes it, man?' I asked.

'SOS.'

'You said it.' I sat down. 'Good morning, Marcia.'

Not looking away from her open book, Marcia nodded.

'Is that the one where he wanders lonely as a cloud?' I asked.

'Grow up,' Marcia said. She wasn't among my fans.

'I'm working on it,' I said.

'Work harder.'

'Pithy.'

She turned her head and scowled at me. She was a senior, probably the smartest of all the current English majors, beautiful and blonde and a grade-A bitch. At the moment, she looked ready to seethe. 'What did you say?' she asked.

'Pithy.'

'That'd better be what you said.'

'It thertainly ith what I thaid.'

'Know what?'

'What?'

'Get fucked.'

I gave her my warmest smile.

'Cretin,' she muttered, and turned away.

'That hurt,' I said.

She ignored me.

Into the room bounded Dr Trueman, silver-haired, ruddy of cheek, dressed in a trim tweed suit and red bowtie. He carried a weathered brown briefcase with wide leather straps and large buckles. Stopping at the head of the table, he regarded us with his sparkling eyes. 'Fresh faces, newly scrubbed! Youth! Passion! Love!' He fixed his merry eyes on me. 'King Edward of Willmington!'

'Sir?'

'For godsake, what befell your face?'

'Mayhem, sir.'

'I hope you saw to it that your enemy paid dearly for his insolence.'

'I destroyed him entirely, sir.'

'Bravo!' Dr Trueman plonked his briefcase on the table and applauded me. So did about half the students in the room, while others shook their heads and rolled their eyes. Marcia hung her head and shook it slowly. Kirkus was among those who joined the applause.

Only I knew I'd told the honest truth.

Chapter Forty-five

About halfway through Dr Trueman's class, I realized that I'd invited Kirkus over to my apartment for a supper that was being provided by Eileen.

I'll bring everything over, she'd said. *Drinks, food.*

She would bring them for two, not three. And she wasn't likely to be delighted by the presence of Kirkus.

She needed to be told of the additional guest.

Warned.

Around noon, I saw her at a distance. I didn't call out or go after her, though. For this sort of news, I preferred the telephone.

Back in my apartment shortly after three o'clock that afternoon, I made a call to Eileen's room. I hoped to get her answering machine, but she picked up the phone herself.

'It's me,' I said.

'Hi, me.'

'About dinner tonight . . .'

'Uh-oh.'

'I'm afraid Kirkus has invited himself over.'

'Kirkus? Are you kidding?'

'It's sort of an extortion thing. I had a little talk with him about Wednesday night and he agreed to keep his mouth shut. Thing is, dinner seems to be part of the deal.'

'Wow. Maybe he *does* have the hots for you.'

'Maybe he just wants a free dinner.'

'Well, you caught me just in time. I was about to head for the store. I'll pick up a little more of a few things.'

'I'm really sorry about this.'

'Oh, don't be. It's not your fault he finds you irresistible.'

'Very funny.'

'I guess he and I will be vying for your attention.'

'Won't be any contest,' I said.

'Just the same, I'll dress for the occasion.'

The words sank in. My imagination took over and my body reacted.

'What do you have in mind?' I asked.

'You'll just have to wait and see. I'd better get going. See you around five.'

'See you.'

Suddenly, Kirkus or no Kirkus, I was eager for five o'clock to arrive.

By about four, I'd finished showering and dressing. I sat at the kitchen table to study Chaucer, and had just about worked my way to the end of 'The Prologe of the Wyves Tale of Bathe' when my buzzer went off.

I marked my place and glanced at my wristwatch. Four-thirty.

At the speaker, I said, 'Who's there?'

'Your intellectual and moral superior.'

'Impossible,' I said.

'Open up, old boy.'

Leave it to Kirkus to arrive half an hour early.

I buzzed him in. Then I just stood there, annoyed. I soon heard footfalls coming up the hallway, but waited for his knock before I opened the door.

He'd changed clothes for the occasion. His blue jeans looked brand new. He also wore a white shirt instead of the usual blue chambray. Instead of his corduroy jacket, he wore a jacket of light brown suede. He now sported a royal blue ascot, not the tangerine one he'd worn to Romantic Lit.

Head tilted back, he smiled in at me and bobbed up and down on the balls of his feet. 'I'm early,' he announced.

'No problem.'

'And I come bearing gifts.' He held out a bottle of white wine.

'Thanks.' I accepted it, stepped out of the way and said, 'Come on in and take a load off.'

He entered my apartment and looked around. 'The beckoning fair one isn't here yet?'

'Not yet. Would you like some of this wine?'

'We might prefer to save it for dinner.'

'Eileen's bringing something to drink. I could open this now if you want.'

'If you like.' He went to a window and looked out. 'How inspiring to dwell in such proximity to a church.'

'It has a nice little graveyard,' I said, taking the bottle into the kitchen. 'You can't see it from here.' I almost told him that my bedroom had a view of the graveyard, but the less said to Kirkus about my bedroom, the better.

While he continued to stare out the window, I opened the bottle. I located a couple of water glasses. As I poured wine into them, I asked, 'So how'd you lay your mits on the wine? Not twenty-one yet, are you?'

'Certainly not. Are you?'

'Not till next year.'

'Then why would I be twenty-one while you're not? We're both juniors.'

'Maybe you had to repeat the fourth grade,' I suggested, carrying the glasses into the living room.

He turned away from the window and faced me. 'In fact, I *skipped* a grade.'

'Wow! Really? So you're only nineteen?'

'A mature nineteen.'

'If you say so.'

He smirked at me. 'Considerably more mature than you, I dare say.'

'Well, shit yeah. I don't even *own* an ascot.' I put a glass into his hand, then said, 'Thanks for bringing the wine,' and took a drink from my glass. It didn't taste bad.

'No toast?' he asked.

'No toast, no bacon, no eggs.'

'And little or no wit,' he added.

I almost laughed, but didn't want to give him the satisfaction.

'Good wine,' I told him.

'Thank you.'

'Who picked it out for you?'

'Ah, Logan.'

'Ah, Kirkus. Why don't you have a seat?'

'*Merci*,' he said, and wandered over to the armchair. Stopping in front of it, he turned around and faced me. He took a sip of wine. Then he said, 'I'm really quite overwhelmed by your generosity in inviting me to dinner.'

'I'm pretty sure you invited yourself.'

'Did I?' Smiling, he sat down.

'That's how I recall it,' I said, and sat on the sofa a safe distance from him.

'As I recall, you requested a service from me and kindly invited me over to show your gratitude.'

'Something like that.'

'You *are* grateful for my pledge of silence, I take it?'

'The pledge doesn't interest me much, but the silence does.'

Smiling unpleasantly, he took a sip of wine. 'If you hope for my cooperation, it might be*hoove* you to treat me with a certain amount of consideration.'

'Be*hoove*?'

'There you go again.'

'A thousand pardons.'

Raising both eyebrows, he asked, 'Would you prefer that I leave? I could, you know. I could quite easily remove myself from the premises . . .'

'"And take thy beak from out my heart . . ."'

He stood up.

Staying seated, I patted the air and said, 'Down, boy. Down. Just kidding. Stay. I promised you dinner. Eileen's expecting you. She's even picking up extra groceries. We'd both be *très* disappointed if you force us to eat without the glory of your presence.'

Kirkus sat. He smiled. He said, 'You are such a wad.'

'Want to call a truce?' I asked.

'Calling a truce would presume we're at war. Are we at war, Eduardo?'

I shrugged. 'Not really. A war of wits, maybe.'

'For which you are sadly lacking in weaponry.'

I tried to think of a comeback, but nothing worthwhile popped into my mind – tending perhaps to prove his point.

He sipped his wine and looked smug.

I said, 'Actually, I used to be marvelously intelligent, witty and urbane – but then they stole my ascot.'

'Oh, how droll.'

'Noël Coward and Somerset Maugham chased me three blocks for it.'

Looking singularly unamused, Kirkus set his glass on the lamp table, reached to his neck with both hands, untied his ascot and held it out to me. 'Perhaps you would like to borrow mine,' he said.

Three big, blue letters were tattooed across his throat.

FAG

Chapter Forty-six

'Is it real?' I asked. 'A real tattoo?'

'Of course it's real.'

Maybe real, but amateurish. The sort of tattoo that a person might do to himself with a sharp instrument and ink, shaky hands and no artistic talent at all. 'Oh, man,' I said. 'What were you thinking?'

'I hardly did this to myself, dear fellow.'

'Somebody *else* did it to you?'

'Oh, yes.'

I must've been gaping at Kirkus like a stunned fish.

'Perhaps you would enjoy hearing about it,' he said. 'You seem to have a special fondness for the morbid and *outré*. Perhaps you'll enjoy putting me in one of your stories.'

I shook my head. 'No, that's all right. Really. Why don't you go ahead and put your ascot back on?'

'Let it replace the one stolen by Coward and Maugham,' he said, and tossed it to me. Halfway between us, the silken cloth fluttered open and drifted to the floor.

I went over to it, crouched and picked it up. Taking it to Kirkus, I said, 'I had no idea you've been wearing these things to hide your tattoo.'

'Is that why?'

'Isn't it?'

'For that and for the style.'

Laughing softly, I reached out with it. He plucked it from my fingers.

On my way back to the sofa, he said, 'I won't tell you the whole sad tale; I'll make it brief.'

'You don't have to tell me anything,' I said, and sat down.

'Oh, but you'll find it "right up your alley", so to speak. Lurid, brutal, sordid and trite.'

'Oh, thanks. In that case, I've *got* to hear it.'

'I know.'

'If it's such a good story, maybe you should save it until Eileen gets here.'

'That would hardly be appropriate.' He wrapped the ascot around his neck and began to tie it. 'This is for your ears only.'

'Are you sure you want to tell me?'

'We'll *both* have secrets to keep.'

'You said I could write about it.'

'Someday.'

I looked at my wristwatch. A quarter till five. 'Maybe you oughta just skip it.'

'Oh, no. I insist.' He took a drink of wine, then commenced. 'I'm sure the basics are all quite familiar to you: the overly sensitive, father-less boy with the relentless and irrepressible mother; the boy being picked on by Neanderthals at school; taking refuge in the safety of books. All terribly trite and predictable . . .'

I took a drink of wine and wished I were elsewhere.

With any luck, Eileen would show up immediately.

'The other kids used to laugh and call me names.'

Like Rudolph the Red-Nosed Reindeer, I thought, and felt a strange urge to laugh. Then I realized *his* name was Rudy, short for Rudolph. His name seemed like a bizarre and not-so-funny joke.

'I could never walk down a hallway at school,' he explained, 'without someone tripping me or bumping into me or knocking the books out of my hands. During recess and lunch, a great sport was to grab me and stuff me into a trashcan. Sometimes, a group of jocks would jump me and run off with my pants. And of course I was regularly beaten up. In short, I grew up friendless, trusting no one, fearing and despising my tormenters. Not unlike the childhood of countless other chaps.'

'I knew a few,' I told him. During my schooldays, I'd only been a level or two higher on the social scale, myself, and I'd befriended guys who were worse off than me. I couldn't tell Kirkus that, however. You can't say 'one of my best friends was a geek . . . or gay . . . or black . . . or Jewish . . .' It might be true, but you can't say it. There's a lot you can't say.

So I kept my mouth shut about the cool band of social rejects with whom I used to hang out.

After a deep sigh, Kirkus resumed. 'Ironically, they were calling me a queer, a homo and a fag long before I'd ever engaged in any sexual activity with *anyone*: boy, girl or aardvark. Apparently, my appearance and manner were the only oddities they required.'

'It's pretty rotten,' I said.

'You may not believe this, Ed, but I was a *nice* young lad. I'd yet to develop my aloof and cynical demeanor, nor the smug pomposity that you seem to find so irritating.'

'Hard to imagine you without 'em.'

'Oh, I was a dear.'

I laughed softly.

'However, they hated me anyway. My chief oppressor was a chap named Dennis Grant, a rather typical high school bully: strong, fat, ugly and stupid. He tormented me constantly – usually in front of his friends, of course, in order to show off his toughness. Then one afternoon, I stayed at school late to help one of the teachers. By the time I'd finished, the hallway was deserted. Except for Dennis. He was waiting for me with his knife. He pulled me into one of the bathrooms and made me get down on my knees. Then he opened his fly and hauled out "George". Why he called it George, I have no idea.'

Kirkus tried to smile, but couldn't manage it. His eyes were suddenly shiny.

'I said to Dennis, "What am I supposed to do with that?" He said, "You know what to do with it, you fuckin' fag." I said, "Look who's calling who a fag." That, as it turned out, was a vast error.' A couple of tears leaked out of his eyes. He rubbed them away with the back of a hand. 'At any rate, after pounding me to a sticky pulp, Dennis gave me my first taste of George there on the filthy bathroom floor. And thus was I introduced into the joys of the gay lifestyle.'

All I could say was, 'Jeez.'

'It lacked a bit in the way of romance and comfort.' He pulled out a handkerchief, blew his nose, then sighed and put his hanky away. 'We *did*, however, have a smoke afterward.'

'Did he do the tattoo?'

Kirkus shrugged. 'I've never learned whether the artistry was performed by Dennis or by his buddy, Brad.'

'This Brad was there, too?'

'Oh, no. Not at all. Dennis and I were quite alone that day in the school bathroom . . . and quite alone on every occasion afterward. Or so we thought.'

'It happened more than once?'

'Oh, my dear Eduardo, Dennis got together with me almost daily after that.'

'You couldn't stop him?'

'I saw no point in trying. He'd done what he'd done. I'd done what I'd done. It did seem horrid at first. Before long, however, I found myself looking forward to our sessions. Dennis was rather magnificent, really.'

I tried not to look aghast.

'Unfortunately, his friend Brad caught us in the act one fine evening in Dennis's garage. In a valiant attempt to maintain his dignity, Dennis pretended to be the victim of an unwarranted assault by yours truly and they *both* beat me senseless.' Lightly stroking the front of his ascot, Kirkus said, 'I returned to consciousness the next morning naked in a dumpster behind a 7-Eleven store . . . tattooed with perhaps the only three-letter word Dennis and Brad were capable of spelling correctly.'

'My God,' I muttered.

'And that's my tale. Lurid enough for your taste?'

'It's awful, Rudy. Jeez.'

'It isn't the worst thing that has ever happened to me, but it *is* the tale of my tattoo.'

'What happened to Dennis and Brad?'

'I haven't a clue,' said Kirkus. 'I left all that behind when I came to Willmington. I brought nothing of it with me except the memories, the scars and the tattoo.'

'You could probably get the tattoo removed.'

'Oh, certainly.' Again, he stroked his ascot. 'Unfortunately, I'm rather fond of it.'

'If you're fond of it, why do you hide it?'

'It's private. I share it only with certain special friends. Friends like you.'

'Ahh.'

'You *are* my friend, aren't you?'

'I guess so,' I said, feeling slightly sick. 'In a way. I mean, you're okay except when you're being a pompous, smug asshole.'

'You're such a dear,' he said.

'I can do without you calling me that. And I don't want you trying any funny stuff with me, either.'

'Have you ever given it a try?'

'No, and I don't aim to, either.'

'As the sage says, "Don't knock it till you've tried it."'

'Sometimes, the sage is full of shit.'

'Ah, Logan! You never cease to astonish me. Is *anyone* more plebian than you?' Chuckling, he picked up his glass. He drank it empty, then held it out in my direction. 'More, please?'

Chapter Forty-seven

A few minutes later, Eileen arrived. I buzzed her in, then opened the door and stood at the threshold to watch for her. She soon appeared at the top of the stairs, a grocery bag hugged to her chest. She wore a yellow windbreaker, but it reached down only to her waist. It seemed to be covering the top of a forest-green evening gown. The gown's skirt was clingy, reached down to her ankles, and had a slit up the left side.

'Back in a minute,' I said over my shoulder.

Kirkus answered, 'No rush, old man.'

I hurried down the hall. As Eileen walked toward me, her left leg came out of the slit, went back in, came out again. She obviously had no stocking on. Her leg looked very bare.

When I took the bag from her, she put a hand behind my head and I leaned toward her. The bag was between us. Our bodies crunched its paper, squeezed whatever was inside it and made a couple of bottles clink softly. We kissed. Her face felt cool from the weather outside. I took it easy on her lips, but then she slipped her tongue into my mouth and we really went at it for a while, Eileen moaning and me growing stiff.

Too soon, she eased away from me. She was wet around the mouth. She smiled. 'I've been wanting to do that.'

'Me, too.'

'Guess we'd better not keep Kirkus waiting,' she said. 'What did he do, get here early?'

'Half an *hour* early.'

'Was it edifying?'

'Oh, yeah.'

I carried the groceries. As we walked side by side, she said, 'It's a little warm in here for this,' and took off her windbreaker. Her gown had a plunging neckline; it plunged nearly to her waist, her long V of bare skin gradually narrowing on its way down.

'Wow,' I said.

She smiled. 'Like it?'

'You look fantastic.'

Putting a hand on my shoulder, she leaned toward me. Breath tickling my ear, she whispered, 'If Kirkus has on the same outfit, I'll just die.'

'Oh, you bitch.'

We both laughed, but it tapered off before we reached the doorway of my apartment.

As we entered, Kirkus stood up.

'Hi, Rudy,' Eileen said.

'Eileen. Aren't *we* looking splendid tonight!' He bobbed on the balls of his feet, tilted his head to one side and said, 'On our way to the prom, are we?'

'Just an old frock,' Eileen said. 'Glad you could join us tonight.'

'My pleasure.'

'Do you like Mexican?'

'Mexican of what variety?'

'Of the food and drink variety,' Eileen said. 'Such as beef fajitas and my infamous *Hoocha de los Muertos*.'

'What's that?' I asked, grinning.

'Let's go in the kitchen and I'll show you.'

I followed Eileen into the kitchen, Kirkus tagging along behind us. I set the grocery bag onto the counter. Eileen peered inside, then reached in and took out a quart bottle of Cuervo Gold tequila. Next, out came a somewhat smaller bottle of Triple Sec.

Holding a bottle in each hand, she turned around and assumed a serious demeanor. 'This,' she said, 'and this. A glass, some ice, and a *lot* of this.' She gave the tequila bottle a shake. 'Then a wee tad of this.' She shook the Triple Sec. 'Stir briskly with a coffin nail.'

'A cigarette?' I asked.

'Don't be absurd. The nail from a coffin.'

'Ah. Well, I don't think I have one of those.'

'In that case, a finger will have to do. But don't worry, I'll take care of it. Ed, why don't you get down the glasses?'

I removed three glasses from the cupboard. Eileen instructed me to add ice cubes. Then she instructed Kirkus and I to wait in the living room. 'Too many people in the kitchen! I'll be out in a minute with the drinks.'

'Which you fully intend to stir with your finger?' asked Kirkus.

Smiling, she twirled her forefinger in the air.

'How sanitary,' he said.

'The alcohol kills the germs,' she explained. 'You know that, don't you?'

Laughing, I left the kitchen.

Soon, we were all in the living room, sitting around the coffee table, sipping our *Hoocha de los Muertos* and munching on tortilla chips dipped in salsa. Eileen was beside me on the sofa. Each time she leaned toward the table, slack came into the top of her gown, letting me see most of her right breast . . . including a bruise near the front that couldn't be seen when she was sitting up straight.

The smooth, pale breast, smudged by the bruise, excited me and reminded me of what we'd gone through together and made me feel closer to her. It also made me feel like a louse. Eileen was too beautiful, too smart and funny and good, to deserve having me slip away at night to seek out Casey.

Luckily, with the drinking and talking, I didn't have a whole lot of time to dwell on how I was betraying her.

When our glasses were empty, Eileen took them into the kitchen. She came out with two fresh drinks. I vowed to take things more slowly with my second *Hoocha*. They were nothing but booze – margaritas minus the citrus additives – and my head already felt light.

Her back to Kirkus, Eileen bent over at the waist and set both the glasses on the table. The front of her gown loosened and drooped. I could see her entire left breast. It was swaying slightly. Its nipple was erect. From her smile, she knew exactly what I could see. Remaining bowed, she asked, 'Should I bring you in some more chips?'

'I can come out and get them.'

'No, no, stay right where you are. I'll bring them in.' She straightened up and turned toward Kirkus. 'How you doing, Rudy?'

He grinned. 'Tip-top.'

'Hand me my glass?' she asked me.

Hers wasn't quite empty. I picked it up and gave it to her.

'*Gracias*,' she said.

'*Da nada*,' said I, and immediately wondered whether I'd responded in Spanish or French. It shouldn't have been a problem; I'd had only one drink so far.

As Eileen went into the kitchen, I tried to think of 'you're welcome' in French. *Da Nada?* Or was that Spanish, as I'd intended? Then I thought of Hemingway. 'Our nada who art in nada.' So it *is* Spanish. But no, maybe not. He'd spent all that time in Paris.

'Something amiss, old boy?' asked Kirkus.

He was about the last person to whom I would confess such befuddlement. 'Eileen is a miss,' I said, making an effort to speak clearly.

'I heard that,' she said, coming out of the kitchen with the bag of tortilla chips. 'Hell, I was hoping to be a hit, not a miss.'

'Miss as opposed to Mrs,' I explained.

'So you say,' she said, and bent over the table just as she'd done before and shook more chips into the bowl. Just as before, I gazed at her breast. 'Can I get you anything else?' she asked, remaining bowed. I met her eyes. She looked vastly pleased with herself.

'You're driving the poor lad to madness,' said Kirkus. Though he couldn't see what I could, he obviously realized what was going on.

Eileen's smile widened. 'Am I?' she asked me.

'I'm fine,' I said.

'Good.' She straightened up. 'Now you two boys will just have to get along without me for a while. My fajitas are beckoning. Just give a shout if you need anything.' She turned toward the kitchen.

I didn't want her to go. 'Could you use a hand?'

'Nope, thanks anyway. You stay out here and entertain our guest.'

'You might not be able to find everything.'

'If I get stuck, I'll give you a shout.' She went on into the kitchen. A few moments later, the sounds of her activities were joined by Willie Nelson and Ray Charles singing 'Seven Spanish Angels.'

I took a drink and smiled at Kirkus. 'Great music,' I said.

'Once again confirming your pedestrian taste, good fellow.'

'Up yours.'

'Don't say it if you don't mean it.'

I laughed and shook my head. 'That'll be the day.'

'"The lady doth protest too much, methinks."'

'I ain't no lady.'

'Ah, and *vive la différence.*'

Though I understood the French (or was it Spanish? – damn the *Hoocha de los Muertos*!), I wasn't quite sure what he meant by that. I scowled at him.

'Oh, don't pretend to take offense. You're flattered and you know it.'

'Huh? Flattered?'

Leaning forward, speaking quietly, Kirkus said, 'And well you *should* be, here in your apartment with *two* beautiful people, both of whom would simply love to eat you alive.'

For an awful moment, it ran through my mind that perhaps Eileen and Kirkus had set a trap for me, that they intended to have *me* for dinner. After what I'd seen under the bridge Wednesday night – and what I'd heard from Casey – it didn't seem terribly far-fetched.

Yeah, right.

Of course, I knew full well what Kirkus had really meant.

'Don't even think about it,' I told him.

'I can hardly resist *thinking* about it, dear boy. You're so luscious.'

'You wanta knock it off?'

'Oh, lighten up. I'm not about to pounce on you. I am a gentleman, after all. I've never forced myself on anyone.'

'Glad to hear it.'

'If you want me, though, just whistle. You know how to whistle, don't you? Put your lips together . . .'

'Give me a fuckin' break.'

Eileen came out of the kitchen. She was wearing my one and only apron – which I had never worn, myself. 'Eddie, you want to come in here and clear off the table?'

'Saved by the belle,' I said.

Kirkus smirked. 'You're excused.'

Chapter Forty-eight

After removing my computer and books and papers from the kitchen table, I put out the place mats, napkins and silverware.

'Won't be long, now,' I said to Kirkus.

At his seat facing the coffee table, he raised his drink toward me, winked, and took a sip.

I went over to Eileen. She was standing in front of the stove, an area of the kitchen that couldn't be seen from the living room. She held a spatula in one hand and her drink in the other. I stepped behind her, slipped my hands underneath her apron, wrapped my arms around her waist, and looked down over her shoulder. On the burner was a skillet full of sizzling strips of marinated steak.

'Smells great,' I said.

She finished her drink, then set down her glass. 'How goes it with Kirkus?'

'He wants me.'

'Don't we all.'

'But he promises to leave me unmolested unless I whistle.'

The way Eileen's cheek pressed against my face, I figured she must be smiling. 'Do you know how to whistle?' she asked.

'You were eavesdropping?'

Her head shook. 'Saw the movie.'

'That wasn't in the book, you know. *To Have and Have Not*. The whistling business.'

'I didn't know that.'

'Now you do.'

'It feels wonderful to be well informed,' she said, and pushed her rump against me and moved it from side to side, rubbing my groin.

I whistled softly, close to her ear.

She asked, 'Was that for me or for Kirkus?'

I tried to put a hand inside the front of her gown, but she clutched my wrist through the apron. 'Not now, honey. You better go on back and keep our friend company.'

'I can help you.'

'I'll take care of everything. It'll just be a couple more minutes. Go on, okay? It's not polite to leave him alone.'

'All right.' I gave the side of her neck a kiss, then returned to the living room. 'What's up, Rudolph?'

'Oh, please.'

I went to the sofa, sat and picked up my drink. My glass was still half-full of my second *Hoocha de los Muertos*, but the ice had melted. I took a sip. It was still fairly cold.

On the radio, Randy Travis was singing 'Heroes and Friends.'

'It's almost ready,' I said.

'I'm in no hurry,' Kirkus said.

'Are you having a lovely time?'

'Quite.'

'Glad to hear it.' I dipped a chip into the salsa, then maneuvered it into my mouth without dripping.

As I crunched the chip, Kirkus said, 'We should do this more often. Next time, I'll host the affair at my place.'

I almost said, 'Don't hold your breath,' but I was feeling too good to be mean . . . even to Kirkus. The aroma of the fajitas was wonderful, Eileen was wearing the wonderful dress, I'd had fine views of her wonderful breasts, I planned to go out later and have a wonderful time with Casey, and I was wonderfully, mildly high from the *hoocha*. 'Well,' I said, 'just let us know when you want us.'

He raised both eyebrows. 'Will you really come?' For a moment, I glimpsed hope and sadness in his eyes. They were quickly hidden, however, behind his usual haughty demeanor.

'Maybe,' I said. 'I guess it'll depend.'

'On what, dare I ask?'

'Let's just see how things go tonight.'

'I shall be on my best behavior.'

From out in the kitchen came the beep of the microwave.

'I'll prepare my specialty,' Kirkus said.

'What's that?' I asked him.

'Pork roast.'

'Not *long pork*, I hope.'

He frowned. 'Long pork?'

Eileen appeared in the kitchen entryway. She had taken off the apron and she was smiling. 'Come and get it, guys.'

Kirkus and I went to the table and sat down. Eileen took our glasses. 'Go ahead and get started,' she said. 'I'll make refills.'

'What should we do?' I asked.

'Grab a tortilla, spread it with sour cream or avocado or whatever, throw on some meat and cheese and lettuce, whatever, roll it up and chow down.'

'Easy for you to say,' I said.

Soon, she came over with all three glasses full of her special concoction. Then she sat down. She raised her glass and said, 'Good for what ails ya.'

Kirkus and I picked up our glasses. We all leaned forward and bumped each other's glasses.

Kirkus sipped his drink. '*Grande*,' he said. '*Mucho grande*.'

I sipped mine. '*Rio Grande*.'

Eileen sipped hers and said, 'Mississippi.'

I hoisted my glass. 'To Mark Twain.'

'Oi,' said Kirkus.

'You got a problem with Mark Twain?'

'He's *so* plebian. No wonder you adore him, Eduardo.'

'*Huck Finn*'s the greatest novel ever written.' I felt a moment of guilt over betraying William Goldman. But if I'd tried to claim *The Temple of Gold* or *Boys and Girls Together* as the greatest novel . . .

'Oh, please,' Kirkus said.

'It is.'

'American,' Eileen said. 'Greatest *American* novel, maybe. Gotta leave out the British and the Irish and the Russians and the French . . .'

'What'd the French ever write?' I asked.

'Dumas?' Eileen said. 'Hello? *The Three Musketeers*. And De Maupassant.'

'Let's not forget Sartre and Camus and the great Simone,' Kirkus said.

'*I* like Simone,' I proclaimed. 'He's good.'

'She,' said Kirkus.

'I like that detective of his, Maigret.'

'That's Simenon,' Eileen corrected me. 'Georges Simenon.'

'I was speaking, old boy, of Simone de Beauvoir.'

'Oh. Of course you were. She sucks.'

Eileen laughed.

'You must simply adore playing the fool,' Kirkus told me.

'Anyway,' I said, 'if we can get back to *Huckleberry Finn*, the greatest American novel . . .'

'Highly overrated,' said Kirkus.

'Hemingway says it's the best.'

'Proving my point,' said Kirkus.

'I'd have to go with *Atlas Shrugged*,' Eileen said. 'That's the best book I've *ever* read, and they don't even teach it in school.'

'They don't?' I said.

'No school I've ever heard of. That's 'cause all the teachers hate her. They lie about her. They won't teach her books.' Scowling, Eileen spread some sour cream on a steaming, flour tortilla. 'They're afraid of every damn thing she ever wrote. Most teachers are commies, in case you haven't noticed.'

This was a side of Eileen I'd never seen before – the intoxicated side, I suppose.

'Commies?' said Kirkus. 'Dear me.'

Narrowing one eye at him, Eileen said, 'My dad fought the goddamn commies in Vietnam. You think there's something *funny* about that?'

'I apologize if I've tread on your toes, my dear . . . or the toes of your father's combat boots. But really, *communism*? You must admit the subject is a trifle *passé* these days. Which also makes Ayn Rand's books *passé*.'

'Ever read one?' she asked.

'I wouldn't waste my time,' Kirkus said.

She pointed her fork at me. 'How about you, Eddie?'

'I'm afraid not. I'd like to, though.'

She turned her fork to the steak platter and placed a few strips of meat on her tortilla. '*Atlas Shrugged, The Fountainhead, We the Living.* We're forced to read every goddamn book that ever came down the pike by the *chosen* few. *The Great Gatsby*, for godsake. *The Pearl*, for godsake.'

'*The Scarlet Letter*,' I joined in.

'Not to mention *Madame Ovary*,' she said. 'What the fuck is *that* about.'

Kirkus shook his head and looked very disappointed in us.

'*Hundreds* of books,' Eileen continued. 'Books by every Tom, Dick and Charlie that ever put pen to paper, but Ayn Rand? Huh-uh. Not Rand. She's better than most of them, *nobody's* better, but they try to keep her away from us 'cause they hate her message.'

'Her message is selfishness, my dear,' said Kirkus.

Eileen sprinkled grated cheese on top of her beef, then began to roll her tortilla. 'That's what they want you to believe, 'cause they don't want you reading her. Know what her real message is?'

'I fear you're about to tell us.'

'Nobody has a single goddamn right,' she said, 'to take what doesn't belong to them. Like a government, for instance. The government's got no right to make us do *any*thing . . . not even for what they call "the common good." We're nobody's slaves. We have an absolute right to the fruits of our own labor and we don't owe jack-shit to society. You ever hear of John Galt?'

'Of course,' said Kirkus, and sighed. '*Who is John Galt?*'

'Who *is* John Galt?' Eileen asked him.

'He's obviously a creation of your literary goddess.'

'*He turned off the lights of the world.*' As she spoke the words, her voice went husky and tears glimmered in her eyes.

'And that means?' asked Kirkus.

'That's what they don't want you to find out,' said Eileen. She wiped her eyes, then took a drink, then said, 'Read the book' and picked up her rolled tortilla.

'*Atlas Shrugged*?' I asked.

She nodded and sniffed.

'Perhaps I'll give it a try,' Kirkus said. 'A novel capable of reducing the stout Eileen Danforth to tears . . .'

'Watch that "stout" business,' Eileen said.

'It was a reference to your character, not your physique.'

'Something wrong with my physique?'

'Not at all, deary. From the standpoint of *this* observer, it's really quite spectacular.'

'Thanks.'

'Is it not truly spectacular, Eduardo?' he asked me.

'I'd say so,' I said. A little worried about his negative, I added, 'It is.'

'Of course, he *has* to say so, being your boyfriend *cum* loverboy – pun intended, of course – whereas *I* am truly disinterested and speak the truth without fear of reprisal. From a perspective of complete objectivity, I can say that your physique is truly extraordinary. At least what I've seen of it. I'm sure Edward has the advantage over me in that regard.'

I muttered, 'Jeesh.'

He eyed me. 'You do have a flair for words, old boy.' To Eileen, he said, 'Speaking of which, I understand that the entire gang of ruffians Wednesday night had the pleasure of feasting their eyes on your undraped titties. Seems that everyone has seen them but me.'

Staring at him, she tilted her head sideways. 'Where did you pick up that bit of news?'

Kirkus looked at me and smiled. 'Was I not supposed to tell?'

'Whatever happened to "mum's the word"?' I asked.

'I wasn't aware you meant it to apply to the fair Eileen.'

I groaned.

'No problem,' Eileen said. Then she shoved some of her tortilla between her teeth and tore off a mouthful. As she chewed, her eyes again became shiny. She swallowed and wiped her mouth with a napkin. Then she said, 'Excuse me.'

She shoved back her chair, stood up, and walked out of the kitchen.

From where I sat, I watched her stride across the living room and enter the hall. Moments later, a door shut. She had apparently gone into the bathroom.

'Oh, dear,' said Kirkus, and smiled. 'Do you suppose it was something she ate?'

Chapter Forty-nine

'Probably something *you* said,' I told him.

Looking delighted, he said, 'Woe is me.'

'Asshole.'

'Don't be too quick to blame me, old boy. She might simply be hurling. Those are powerful drinks. I'm more than a trifle smashed myself.'

'I'd better go check on her.'

'Oh, don't be too hasty. Give her some time. Whatever her problem may be, she would probably rather not have an audience quite yet. Why don't we both stay here and enjoy the repast before it gets cold? Give Eileen an opportunity to recover in private.'

'Maybe you're right,' I said.

'I most frequently am.'

'When she does come out, keep your mouth shut about Wednesday night, okay? The last thing she needs is to have you rubbing it all in. We're trying to put it behind us.'

'Quite so,' said Kirkus. 'My mistake.'

We both commenced to eat our fajitas. By the time we were done, perhaps ten minutes later, Eileen still had not returned to the table.

'I'm going to check on her,' I said, scooting back my chair.

'Give her my regards,' said Kirkus.

As I'd suspected, the bathroom door was shut. I knocked gently.

'What?'

'Eileen? It's me.'

'Leave me alone.'

'What's wrong?'

'Just go away.'

'Is it what Kirkus said?'

The door suddenly opened. Eileen grabbed the front of my shirt and pulled me in and shut the door. Her eyes were red and wet, her face streaked with tears.

Still clutching my shirt, she said, 'What did you tell him? Did you tell him *everything?*'

'No.'

'It was supposed to be our secret. How could you *blab* to him?'

'I didn't tell him anything. Not about what really happened. Nothing about under the bridge. All I told him was the stuff we made up about the gang of teenagers jumping us. The same thing we told him Wednesday night.'

'Oh really? Know what? I don't recall telling him they ripped off my shirt and feasted their eyes on my undraped titties.'

'That's just Kirkus. The undraped stuff.'

'What else did you tell him?'

'I think . . . well, *you* told him they pissed in your hair, remember?'

'Of course I remember.'

'I reminded him of that. And I told him that you felt really humiliated by the whole thing and that's why you didn't want anyone to know about it.'

'What else?'

'That's about it.'

'*About* it?'

My face heated up.

If she didn't hear it from me, she might hear it from Kirkus. 'I think I mentioned something about them touching you.'

'Touching me?'

'Fondling you.'

'Where?'

'I guess your breasts.'

'You told Kirkus they fondled my breasts?'

'I think I mentioned something along those lines.'

'Thanks a lot.'

'He's gay.'

'That makes it all right?'

'It was just so he'd understand why he has to keep his mouth shut.'

'Well, thanks a lot.'

'I'm sorry. If I'd known it would upset you like this, I never would've told him *any*thing.'

'What else *did* you tell him?'

'Nothing. That's it.'

'Are you sure?'

'Pretty sure.'

'You didn't figure it would make a better story if they fucked me?'

'No.'

'Well, I appreciate your restraint.'

'Come on, Eileen, don't be this way.'

'And what way am I being?'

'You're blowing it all out of proportion. I mean, the whole idea was to make him realize how humiliated you'd feel if he told anyone . . .'

'Really should've had me gangbanged.'

'Cut it out.'

'What'd you tell him about *you*? You've got a bunch of creeps ripping off *my* clothes and feasting their eyes on *my* undraped titties and groping *me*, what'd they do to *you*? Seems sorta one-sided if you ask me. You're making stuff up, why not have them tear off *your* clothes and grope *you*. Hell, that would've made a *better* story, don't you think? Considering Kirkus.'

'Maybe.'

'I mean, *you're* the one he's got the hots for.'

'*You* were the one wearing *my* shirt when we ran into him Wednesday night.'

Her eyes widened slightly. Her mouth opened as if she were about to say something. She blinked a few times. Then she said, 'Oh.' Then she said, 'That's a point.' Then she said, 'Even still.'

I put my arms around her. 'I'm sorry I told him all that stuff.'

'It's just . . . if it just wasn't Kirkus. He's such a shit. I don't like him knowing stuff like that. Or thinking stuff about me. Thinking about me naked.'

'He's gay,' I said again.

'Maybe he is and maybe he isn't.'

'I'm pretty sure he is.'

'Even still.' She pushed her face against the side of my neck. It felt warm and wet. She sniffed. 'And I've gotta be wearing this stupid dress.'

'It's a wonderful dress.'

'In front of him.'

'He doesn't care.'

'Oh, I bet.'

'Shall we go out and ask him?'

She shook her head. 'I'm so embarrassed.'

'You shouldn't be.'

'And I drank too much.'

'We all did.'

'But I'm the one who fell apart right in front of God and everyone.'

'I'm sure God forgives you. I know I do, and who cares if Kirkus does?'

She stroked the back of my head. 'I love you so much, Eddie.'

'Now I *know* you're drunk.'

'I do. I've loved you from the very start, even when you were going with Holly. Did you know that?'

'Not really.' The sound of Holly's name gave my stomach a twist.

'You never even suspected, did you?'

'No.'

'I know. I never let anyone know how I felt. It was just for me to know. But I ached inside. I ached for you. It hurt so much to see her with you that way. I wanted so much for it to be me.'

'And now it is,' I said. The words made me feel like a louse.

Eileen hugged me hard and kissed the side of my neck. 'I'm so glad,' she said. 'I'm so glad.'

'We should probably get back to the kitchen,' I said. 'You'll feel better after you've had some more to eat.'

She nodded. Then she took a deep breath and sighed. 'Okay,' she said. 'But I . . . I need to change first.'

'Change how?'

She laughed and sniffed. 'My clothes. I don't want Kirkus seeing me in this again. Even if he *is* gay.'

'He is.'

'Can I wear something of yours?'

'Whatever you want.'

We let go of each other. I opened the bathroom door and Eileen followed me into the hallway.

'I'll just be a minute,' she said, and headed for my bedroom.

'See you later,' I said.

I found Kirkus on the living room sofa, the remains of a drink in one hand, his legs crossed. At the sight of me, he said, 'I was beginning to feel abandoned.'

'Eileen'll be along in a minute.'

'How is she?'

'Pretty upset.'

'Not with me, I hope.'

'With both of us. She didn't like me telling you that stuff. She thought it was too personal.'

'We embarrassed her?'

I nodded.

'How peculiar.'

'What do you mean?'

'Did you by any remote chance happen to notice what she's wearing? And she's thrown into a tizzy by a few words regarding the very assets she is so brazenly displaying for all the world to see?'

'It's two different things,' I said.

'A left and a right?'

'Knock it off.' I sat in the armchair. 'She'll be out in a minute. She's changing clothes.'

'Oh, pity.'

'When she does come out, how about . . .?'

'I'll be an angel,' he said. 'For you.'

289

'Thanks.' I would believe it when I saw it.

We sat there for a few minutes and didn't talk much. Every so often, I glanced toward the hallway.

'She doesn't appear to be appearing,' Kirkus said.

'I'd better see what's going on.'

Chapter Fifty

I went down the hallway to my bedroom. The door was shut. I knocked softly, but Eileen didn't respond so I eased it open. The light was on.

Eileen, still in her gown, was lying on my bed, snoring. Her arms were limp by her sides, her legs hanging off the edge of the mattress, her feet not quite touching the floor. Her left leg, free of the slit in her skirt, was bare all the way up to her hip.

I took a step toward her, then changed my mind. Leaving the lamp on, I stepped into the hallway and silently shut the door.

When I entered the living room, Kirkus raised his eyebrows.

'She's out,' I said.

'Out?'

'Asleep.'

'Passed out, you mean.'

'I don't know. Anyway, I decided not to wake her up.'

'Good idea.'

Shrugging, I said, 'So I guess that's about it. Thanks for coming over, Rudy. Maybe we'll do it again sometime.'

'But the night is young.'

'Well, I'm a little tired myself. I'll probably take a nap, then try to hit the books for a while.'

Instead of getting up, Kirkus smiled and spread out his arms along the back of the sofa. 'I really shouldn't leave without properly thanking the hostess.'

'You can thank her tomorrow.'

'Oh, that would never do. I'll stay. She's bound to wake up sooner or later.'

'Kirkus.'

'Be nice, Eddie. I am, after all, your guest.'

'The party's over, okay? Time to go.'

'Now, now. You don't want to ruin a beautiful evening by turning surly at the end, do you? Why don't you offer me another drink? Those *Hooches* are certainly tasty. We'll both partake of another while we have ourselves a nice chat, and then I'll be on my way.'

I was about to protest.

'Pleeeease,' he said, and batted his eyelids.

'Don't do that.'

'One more itsy-bitsy drink. For the road.'

'Then you'll go?'

'Cross my heart and hope to die.' With an outstretched forefinger, he grandly crossed his heart.

'All right.' I started toward the kitchen. 'We'll have one more drink, then you'll leave. No ifs, ands or buts.'

'I shall hightail my tail out the door.'

'Okay.'

In the kitchen, I took our glasses off the table and put ice into them. I didn't want another drink, myself. I'd had more than enough already, and was afraid that one more might knock me off my feet.

I had plans for those feet.

But I couldn't figure an easy way to fake the look of a *Hoocha*, so I went ahead and made two real ones. I carried them into the living room.

Kirkus patted the sofa beside him. 'Sit here.'

'Thanks anyway,' I said.

'I'm not a leper, old boy.'

'I know.'

Keeping the coffee table between us, I set down his glass.

'Please.' Again, he patted the cushion by his hip. 'Don't worry, I won't molest you.'

'Glad to hear it.' I took my own drink back to the armchair and sat down.

He smirked slightly. 'You're afraid of me.'

'I'm not afraid of you.'

'Then sit with me.'

'I'm fine here.' I took a small sip of my drink, then put it down on the lamp table.

'Actually,' Kirkus said, 'though I've often assailed you for various aspects of your rather unfortunate personality, I never dreamed you were a homophobe.'

'A homophobe? Is that something like a xylophone?'

'I'm not amused.'

'Neither am I, as a matter of fact. All of a sudden, you're calling me names.'

'If the shoe fits . . .'

'I would really expect a more original figure of speech, Kirkus, from someone of your erudition.'

He chuckled softly, shook his head, and took a drink. 'Sit where you like,' he said.

'Thanks for the permission.'

Slumped on the sofa, he took another drink. Then he stared at me. Then he sighed. 'Eduardo, Eduardo.'

'Rudolph, Rudolph.'

'What must you think of me?'

'Right now, I just wish you'd leave so I can take a nap.'

'I'm rather sleepy, myself.' He yawned elaborately and patted his mouth. 'And I've such a *long* walk home. Perhaps I should take a brief nap here before I leave.'

'Yeah, sure.'

'We'll *both* nap.'

'Right.'

'No?'

'No.'

'My God, man, what are you afraid of?'

There was no answer that wouldn't either offend Kirkus or cause him to mock me, so I simply shrugged.

'You're afraid I'll molest you while you snooze,' he said.

Bingo.

'I didn't say that,' I said.

'I would never do such a thing.'

'If you say so.'

His eyes suddenly twinkled. 'Shall we give it a try?'

'No.'

He laughed. 'Coward.'

'Gimme a break.'

'No,' he said, frowning. 'You give *me* a break. Don't automatically think the worst of me. What have I ever done to make you suspect I would molest you in your sleep?'

'Nothing I can think of at the moment,' I admitted.

'And I *would* never do it.' Breaking into a smile, he said, 'Tempted though I might be.'

'Well, I aim to save you from the temptation. Drink up, okay?'

'You're a hard man, Eduardo.'

'Yeah.'

'Of course, I *adore* hard men.' With that, he raised his glass as if toasting me, then drank the rest of his *Hoocha de los Muertos*.

I stood up and went to the door and opened it.

'So it's the bum's rush, is it?'

'I wouldn't put it that way. Party's over, that's all. Time to fold your tent like the Arab and silently steal away.'

'How poetic,' he muttered.

'Knew you'd like it.'

He struggled off the sofa, stretched and yawned, then came to the door and stopped in front of me. He bobbed up and down a couple of times on the balls of his feet. Then he said, 'Well, old man, it's been a slice.'

'Yep.'

'Please inform Sleeping Beauty that I adored the repast and her cocktails were marvelous.'

'I'll tell her.'

He stuck out his hand. I shook it. When I tried to let go, he held on.

'Until next time at *my* place,' he said.

'We'll see.'

He released my hand. Backing into the hallway, he said, 'Still mates?'

'Mates?'

'Friends, laddie.'

'I guess so.'

'Jolly!' He twirled away and strolled down the hallway.

I shut my door.

'All right!' I whispered.

Though glad to be rid of him, I also felt slightly ashamed of myself. I'd treated him badly. He'd brought it on himself, but that didn't make me feel any better about it.

I carried our glasses out to the kitchen. His was empty, but mine was nearly full. I poured the remains of my drink into the sink. Then I cleared off the table and started to do the dishes.

For a long time, I couldn't take my mind off Kirkus. In some ways, I felt sorry for him. He'd had some tough times in his life. There was no excuse for the way kids had abused him in school . . . and the *tattoo*! The last thing he needed was *me* adding to his grief.

I should really be nicer to him, I thought. I ought to be his friend.

Then I thought, How can I be his friend when he acts like a total asshole half the time?

For a while, I wondered *why* he was such an asshole.

He really isn't one, I thought. It's an act. A very obvious act.

Which made it even more strange. Why would he or anyone else put on an elaborate performance designed to annoy people? Did he *want* everyone to despise him?

Apparently.

Some sort of self-destructive thing?

Maybe it's to keep people at a distance so he doesn't get attached to them. Get attached, and they can hurt you.

Dump you.

Like my good old friend, Holly, hurt me.

As I scrubbed the skillet in which Eileen had prepared the fajitas, I wondered what Holly was doing at the moment. I glanced at my wristwatch. A quarter till eight. Maybe on her way to the movies with Jay-Jay the Wonder Boy.

Or are they in bed?

I pictured Holly on her back, a handsome strange boy on top of her, plunging into her . . . and I felt no jealousy, no bittersweet longing for Holly, no pain, no anger, not much of anything at all.

I didn't really *care* what Holly was doing. Didn't care at all.

As I dried the skillet with a dish towel, I wondered what Casey might be doing at the moment. Not even eight o'clock yet. Was she in a house somewhere? Her own, or someone else's? Or was she outside, roaming the dark streets?

If I went out now, would I have any luck finding her?

I can't go out now, I reminded myself; Eileen's here.

She's asleep.

Is she?

I finished the dishes, then went down the hall to my bedroom. Gently pushing open the door, I saw that the lamp was still on. I opened the door wider and saw Eileen. She was still crooked on my bed, her legs hanging off. She didn't look as if she'd moved at all since the last time I'd seen her.

Dead to the world, but snoring up a storm.

She's so out of it, I thought, she probably won't wake up for hours. If left alone, she might sleep through the entire night and halfway through tomorrow morning.

She'll never know I'm gone.

I can't just go off and leave her, I told myself. It wouldn't be fair. She came over to be with me. She made those great drinks and the dinner. She loves me. I can't just *abandon* her.

She's asleep.

But what if she wakes up later? She might. And then she'll know I went away.

Leave her a note.

Chapter Fifty-one

Sneaking around the bedroom, I gathered my blue jeans, chamois shirt, sneakers, knife and flashlight while Eileen continued to snore.

I carried them into the hall and set them down. Standing in the doorway, I watched Eileen for a while. Especially the skin revealed by the plunging top of her gown. And her left leg outside the slit.

Exposed to the hip, and no sign of panties.

Isn't she wearing any?

I could find out . . . simply sneak over to the bed and ease my hand through the slit.

She isn't.

But if she does have panties on, I thought, she would be glad to have me take them off.

Except she's asleep.

Asleep.

Staring at Eileen, I remembered being in the bed with Casey last night. The feel of her warm breath on my face as she slept. The feel of her breast. And how I had furtively explored her . . .

I suddenly ached to be with Casey.

No matter that Eileen loved me, that Eileen was sprawled on my bed, that Eileen's body was almost within sight and touch beneath her gown. No matter that she was beautiful and passionate and smart and wonderful. No matter any of it; I needed to be with Casey.

I was tempted to turn off the bedroom light. In the dark, Eileen would probably sleep longer. Again, however, I feared that a sudden absence of light might wake her. So I left it on and silently shut the door.

In the living room, I changed into my dark clothes and slipped the knife and flashlight into my pockets. Then I went into the kitchen to write my note.

It wasn't easy. The first version had so many words and entire sentences scratched out that I finally threw it in the wastebasket and started over again.

Come on! I thought. She'll wake up and I'll *never* get out of here.

Finally, it was done.

Dear Eileen,

Your dinner was great! Kirkus loved it, too, and he thanks you profusely. (I finally got him to leave.)

Hope you had a good sleep. I didn't want to disturb you, so I left you as-is.

I'm feeling a little restless, myself, and am going for a walk. The walk is why I'm not here, in case you're wondering.

Please don't leave. You're welcome to stay all night. I'm counting on finding you here when I return. Tomorrow's Saturday. No classes. We can sleep in. Maybe I'll bring us back some donuts for breakfast.

Done except for the closing.

It required, 'Love, Ed,' but I was reluctant.

Go ahead, I told myself.

I *could* just sign it, 'Me.'

She'll hate it if she doesn't find 'love' at the bottom of the note.

But what if I don't love her? Should I write it anyway?

Not writing it would be like a blatant denial that I love her. I don't want that.

Why not?

Maybe I *do* love her.

Then why am I sneaking out to find Casey?

Muttering, 'Screw it,' I signed, 'Love, Ed.'

298

I gave the note a final, quick proof-reading, then folded it in half and stood it up like a tent in the middle of the kitchen table. On my way to the door, I was tempted to look in on Eileen again to make sure she was still asleep.

If she's awake, I'll call it off. I'll stay. We'll make love and . . .

Forget it, I thought. If she *is* awake, I don't want to know it.

I stepped out into the hall, eased my door shut, made sure it was locked, then headed for the stairway. My heart was beating fast. My legs felt shaky.

How can I do this to her?

Easy, I told myself.

But it wasn't easy, not really. I knew it was wrong to sneak out, leaving Eileen on her own. *Especially* wrong because I was abandoning her to go on a quest for Casey.

I'm stabbing her in the back.

No, I'm not, I thought. More than likely, she'll be asleep the whole time I'm gone.

Is she *less* stabbed in the back, I wondered, if she doesn't know about it?

Probably not. I've *done* the deed whether Eileen's aware of it or not. I'm just as much of a bastard either way.

No better than Holly.

So *don't* go, I told myself.

I started making my way slowly, quietly down the stairs.

Go on back, I told myself. Destroy the note . . .

I can't.

I can't give up Casey. Maybe it won't work out, anyway, but I have to see it through and find out. Can't just quit on her when we've only just gotten started. Not out of some stupid loyalty to Eileen.

What did I really owe to Eileen, anyway? I'd no sooner been dumped by Holly than Eileen had jumped all over me.

I'm not her lover, I'm her prey.

With those thoughts racing through my mind, I felt justified and liberated and rotten as I hurried down the final stairs and heard voices from the Fishers' room.

One voice belonged to Mrs Fisher.

The other came from Kirkus.

Yellow light was spilling onto the carpet runner in front of the Fishers' doorway.

I stopped.

My chances of sneaking past the door without being seen were pretty much zip.

Just great, I thought.

Maybe it's a sign; I'm not *meant* to leave the building. I'm not meant to go out and see Casey tonight. I'm meant, instead, to return to my apartment and be with Eileen.

'Fuck what's meant,' I muttered.

I strode forward. My heart pounded faster. The voices from inside the room grew louder, more distinct.

'. . . sure it will be splendid,' Kirkus said.

'Well, come on by tomorrow and I'll . . .'

I walked past the doorway. In my peripheral vision, I glimpsed the back of Kirkus. He seemed to be well inside the room.

'There goes young Logan, now,' said Mrs Fisher.

Shit.

'Where's *he* off to?' inquired Kirkus.

I kept moving, faster than before.

I rounded the corner, then rushed across the foyer to the building's front door. As I pulled it open, Kirkus called out, 'Eduardo!'

Caught!

Briefly, I considered bolting.

Play it cool!

Holding the door wide open, I looked around and smiled at Kirkus. 'I'm just on my way out,' I said. 'You coming?'

He nodded and hurried toward me. I held the door for him, then followed him outside.

'Waylaid by the landlady?' I asked.

'Not at all,' said Kirkus. 'Agnes is a dear. We've been having a marvelous time, and it appears that I'll shortly be your neighbor.'

'What?'

'They have a vacancy upstairs, a mere two doors away from you.'

'And you're thinking about moving in?'

'It's very nearly a done deal, old boy.' He slapped me on the back. 'Isn't it wonderful?'

'Wonderful.' I tried not to sound aghast.

'I'm so thrilled.'

At the sidewalk in front of the building, I stopped and faced him. 'We can talk about it tomorrow,' I said. 'I have to get going.'

'Decided against the nap, did we?'

'I felt like getting some fresh air.'

'Well, allow me to accompany you. Together, we'll drink deep of the brisk October night.'

'I was hoping for some peace and quiet.'

'I'm fine with that,' said Kirkus. 'Mum's the word.'

I turned to the right and started walking. Kirkus stayed by my side.

After a couple of minutes, he said, 'Does the fair Eileen realize you've deserted her?'

'She's asleep.'

'And so you availed yourself of the opportunity to sneak away.'

'Give it a rest, huh?'

'Did you sneak out in hopes of finding *me*?'

'In your dreams, Kirkus.'

He laughed softly. 'One can hope.'

'Don't you need to be getting home?'

'Not at all.'

What does it take to get rid of him!

'Nothing would tickle me more,' he said, 'than to while away the night with you, Eduardo.'

'I'd really prefer to be alone.'

'You're just saying that. *Nobody* likes to be alone.'

'Speak for yourself.'

'Where are we going?' he asked.

'*I'm* going this way,' I told him.

'*I'm* going this way, too.'

So far, we were both walking northward along Fairmont Street.

Even though I'd come out much earlier than usual, it made sense to start heading in the right direction.

'Such a splendid night,' Kirkus soon said. 'The chill October breeze, the blowing leaves, the dancing shadows. I feel as if I'm in the midst of a Ray Bradbury story.'

'I feel like I'm in a Gore Vidal.'

Kirkus let out a whoop of laughter and patted me on the butt. 'Naughty boy!'

Chapter Fifty-two

When the Fairmont Street bridge came into sight, Kirkus asked, 'Where *are* we going, old boy?'

'Onward,' I said.

'Beyond the bridge?'

'Far beyond the bridge.'

'You must have a destination in mind.'

'Dandi Donuts.'

'You jest.'

'Nope.' If he stays with me, I thought, that's exactly where I'll go. Maybe have a couple of donuts and a cup of coffee, pass some time with Kirkus, then lose him and go looking for Casey.

'That's *miles* away.'

'"I have miles to go before I sleep."'

'Oh, dear.'

'You can come along if you want, but it's up to you. With or without you, I'm going to Dandi Donuts.'

'You must be mad.'

'"TRUE! – nervous – very, very dreadfully nervous I had been and am; but why *will* you say that I am mad?"'

'Delightful! A quote for every occasion.'

'Just trying to impress you, old bean.'

'If you hope to impress me, quote Camus.'

'In that case, you'll have to remain unimpressed.'

We began to make our way over the bridge. Of the four old-fashioned lamps by its sides, three of the globes were dark and one glowed with murky light. The same as last night.

We were about halfway across when Kirkus said, 'Don't you just adore the Old Mill Stream?'

'It's pretty nice.'

Saying, 'So picturesque and romantic,' he turned aside and stepped over to the parapet.

Though I halted, I didn't join him.

He glanced back at me. 'Are you in such great haste for donuts that you have no time to linger and enjoy the beauties of the night?'

'Pretty much.'

'I should think a setting such as this would have a special appeal for you. It's so . . . Poe-ish.'

'The stream?'

'The old, gloomy bridge. Don't you think so?'

'I suppose.'

He beckoned to me. 'Please.'

I just stood there and looked at him.

He shook his head. 'I promise not to molest you.'

'Comforting. Are you coming?'

'You come here.'

'I don't think so.'

'My God, man. All I want to do is linger here for a few brief minutes and enjoy the view.'

'I'm not stopping you.' I started walking away. Glancing back, I said, 'See you later.'

'I wouldn't go off and leave *you*, old man.' Though he sounded nearly as smug as usual, I heard a note of pain in his voice.

'Okay,' I said. 'I'll wait for you.'

'Thank you.' He turned away. Bending over, he put his elbows on the parapet. His head moved slightly from side to side, up and down. Then he looked back at me. 'It's a splendid view,' he said.

'I've seen it.'

'Come here and see it with me.'

'Thanks anyway.'

He muttered, 'It's thrilling to be loathed,' and turned away.

Oh, great.

His back to me, his elbows on the parapet, he lowered his head. I watched him for a while. Then I asked, 'You okay?'

He neither answered nor moved.

'Rudy?'

Still no response, so I went over to him. Close by his side, I bent over and put my elbows on the parapet. The area below us was so dark that I could hardly see the stream. 'Nice view,' I said. 'I can't see a thing.'

He didn't look at me, just leaned there with his head drooping and stared down.

'Hey,' I said. 'Cheer up, okay?'

He kept staring down for a while. Then he said, 'Perhaps I should jump.'

'Up and down for joy?'

'You're *so* amusing.'

'You mean "jump" as in *off the bridge here*?'

'It seems like a fine idea.'

'A *smashing* idea,' I said.

'Asshole,' said Kirkus.

'I wouldn't do it if I were you.'

'If you *were* me, you might.'

'Well, shit yes. Put it *that* way.'

He laughed, but it sounded dreary. 'Edward, Edward.'

'Is there something going on that I don't know about?'

'I don't believe so.'

'No hideous, fatal disease?'

'My health is splendid.'

'Won't be if you jump off this bridge.'

'Ever the wiseass.'

'I'm not kidding, man. It might *look* like a long way down, but it isn't. You might break a couple of bones, but it isn't likely to kill you.'

'Perhaps we should find out.' With that, he flung a leg up and over the parapet.

Instead of trying to grab him, I said, 'I wouldn't.'

He swung his other leg up and over, then sat there, his feet hanging toward the stream, his hands flat against the concrete on both sides of his rear end.

'If you fall,' I said, 'it's gonna really fuck you up.'

'I'm already fucked up.'

'Be that as it may . . .'

'Besides, I have no intention of falling.'

'Best laid plans . . .'

'The plan is to jump, not to fall.'

'You don't want to do that.'

'We shall see.' With more agility than I expected from Kirkus, he rose from his sitting position and stood up. The top of the parapet was plenty wide enough to stand on, but I wouldn't have wanted to do it myself. It made my stomach feel funny to see Kirkus up there. He stood fairly straight, but with his knees bent slightly and his arms out for balance.

'Okay,' I said. 'Great. Now come on down.'

'You don't believe I'll jump?'

'I believe it. Come on down, okay?'

'Why?'

'You're scaring me.'

'You *care* if I jump?'

'Of course I care. Come on, Rudy. I don't want you to get hurt.'

'You do nothing *but* hurt me.'

'It isn't . . . I don't *mean* to. It's just . . . you can be real annoying sometimes and it's fun to give you a hard time. It's nothing to jump off a bridge about. Especially a *low* bridge.'

'You bastard.'

'I'm *sorry.* Okay? Just come on down. I tell you, you don't want to jump. *I* don't want you to jump. We're friends, aren't we?'

'Would that we were.'

From somewhere beyond Kirkus – and below him – came a couple of fast claps. A husky voice called, 'Come on 'n' jump, Tinkerbell. We gotcha.' Another two claps.

Kirkus looked down and squealed, 'Oh, dear God!' and lost his balance. He swung his arms, trying to steady himself.

The audience below him – five or six spectators, by the sounds of them – whistled, cheered and clapped.

I grabbed Kirkus around both thighs and jerked hard. With another squeal, he fell.

Chapter Fifty-three

Onto me.

His weight rushed me backward until I fell off the curb and into the street and he smashed down on top of me. My back slammed the pavement. Then my head hit. *Clonk!* The impact seemed to shake my brain. I saw a brief, dazzling display of fireworks.

Kirkus rolled off. On hands and knees, he looked down at my face and gasped, 'Are you okay?'

I groaned.

'Oh, dear God.'

'I'll live,' I mumbled.

'What've I done to you?'

'Never mind. Just . . . help me up.'

'No, no, you shouldn't move. I'll go call an ambulance.'

'Don't. I'm okay.'

'You might have a concussion or . . .'

I reached up and grabbed his arm. Hard. 'Just help me up. I'll be okay. I'm sure as hell not gonna . . . *wait* here while you . . . run off to call an ambulance. Not gonna let *them* get me.'

'They did seem rather . . . unsavory.'

'We've gotta get outa here.'

He raised his head and looked around. 'Perhaps you're right.'

Letting go of his arm, I shoved at the pavement and braced myself up on my elbows. Though my head ached and felt too heavy for my neck, it didn't seem to be bleeding. Nothing, at any rate, was running down my scalp or the back of my neck.

I turned my head slowly. A car was coming, but it seemed to be a couple of blocks away. No sign of the group from under the bridge.

Kirkus crouched behind me, grabbed my sides just below my armpits, and helped me sit up. Then he held on while I struggled the rest of the way to my feet.

'Thanks,' I said.

He still held on.

'You can let go.'

'You won't fall?'

'We need to get out of the street.'

He moved to my side and clutched my upper left arm. I staggered to the curb and stepped onto the sidewalk. With my free hand, I reached up and fingered the back of my head. I had a big lump there. Touching it, I winced.

The car was almost to the bridge.

I muttered, 'Ride or Hide?'

'Pardon?'

'Nothing.' Immediately, I wished I hadn't mentioned the game. It was Casey's and mine, and I felt cheap for speaking of it in front of Kirkus.

The car came closer. Its headlights made me squint. I looked away. Soon, the car passed us. It kept on going.

Still clinging to my arm, Kirkus turned me southward and guided me along. We'd taken several steps before I realized what was going on. 'Hey,' I said. 'Whoa.'

He didn't stop, kept pulling me.

'Wrong way,' I said.

'I'm taking you home.'

'No. Huh-uh. I'm not going back.'

'I'm afraid you are, old boy. You're in no condition to be hiking anywhere, much less to some donut shop on the outer edges of nowhere.'

I jerked my arm from his grip.

'Edward!'

I dodged around him and headed north. Of course, he hurried after me. Not looking back, I raised my hands and said, 'Don't touch me.'

'Please. This is no time to be foolish.'

He reached for my arm, but I knocked his hand away. 'Don't mess with me!' I walked as fast as I could, though every stride pounded jolts of pain up my neck and into my head.

Kirkus kept after me, staying a couple of paces back. We left the bridge behind, but I didn't slow my pace. 'This is madness,' he said. 'You can't simply continue on your merry way; you're *injured*.'

'Thanks to you,' I reminded him.

'It was your own fault. You should've let me jump.'

'You weren't jumping, you were falling. And those guys down there would've had a field day with you.'

For a while, we didn't talk. Kirkus simply remained behind me, silent as I walked northward. A couple of blocks later, he said, 'I suppose I ought to thank you.'

'Don't bother.'

Quickening his pace, he came up alongside me and put a hand on my back. 'You saved my life, Eddie.'

'More than likely.'

'And now you're hurt, and it's my fault.'

'Looks that way.'

'I'm so sorry.'

'Hey,' I said, 'it's all right. Okay?'

'I owe you my life.'

'You don't owe me anything.'

'I do. I do. Not only because you saved me, but because you *cared* enough to save me. Cared about *me*. Nobody has ever cared about me before.'

'I don't care *that* much.'

Laughing softly, he patted my back. 'Enough to reach out and drag me back from the brink of destruction.'

'Forget about it, okay?'

'I'll never forget about it.'

'Just do me one favor, then,' I said.

'Anything.'

'Don't try something like that again. Next time, I'll let you fall.'

He patted my back some more. 'Oh, Eduardo, you're so *tough*.'

'Hands off, okay?'

His hand stopped patting me, but remained on my back. 'And how's the head?'

'Not great.'

'Shall I kiss it and make it better?'

'No.'

He chuckled. 'I thought not.'

'I really don't need this, Kirkus.'

'Don't need what, old boy?'

'I'm in no mood to be fending you off.'

'Then don't.'

Whirling, I knocked his hand away from my back. 'Just *stop* it! Stop touching me! Stop *flirting*, or whatever the hell it is you're doing. I don't appreciate it. Just leave me the fuck alone.'

'Oh, dear.'

'Know what?' I asked.

'I sense you're about to enlighten me.'

'We might actually stand *some* chance of being friends if you'd stop acting like such a fag all the time.'

'Oh, my. Aren't *we* distraught.'

'Just leave me alone. Go home.' I turned and walked away from him. He came striding after me.

Over my shoulder, I said, 'Get outa here. I've had it with you. Go find someone else to bother.'

'Very well,' he said.

'Good.'

He halted. 'Perhaps I'll wake up Eileen and bother *her*.'

I stopped and turned around to face him. 'Leave Eileen out of this.'

'*You* obviously hope to leave Eileen out of this . . . your peculiar little adventure. Exactly why *did* you sneak out of your apartment tonight? Don't tell me you're on a quest for donuts. Even if *I'm* gullible enough to believe such rot, I doubt that Eileen is. She'll more than likely suspect the worst.'

'I should've let you fall.'

'Now, don't be surly. Eileen needn't know anything.' Smiling, he came up the sidewalk. He stopped in front of me and reached out and patted my shoulder. 'Your secret is safe with me,' he said. 'Shall we be off?'

'Extortion must be a way of life with you.'

'I prefer to think of it as persuasion.'

Side by side, we resumed our northward walk.

'Don't you simply *love* autumn?' he asked after a while. 'The crisp, fresh wind, the blowing leaves? The tang of woodsmoke in the air?'

'It's adorable,' I said.

'Oh, dear. You're in a snit.'

'I just wanted to take a walk.'

'I know, I know. And you're *having* your walk.'

'It's not the same.'

'It's ever so much better,' he said. 'You have *me* along for companionship.'

'Whether I want you or not.'

'Of course you want me. You're simply too plebian to admit it.'

'Oh, yeah.'

'Deny it all you please. We both know that you find me desirable. Deep down, you want me. The thought of kissing me makes your little heart go pitty-pat.'

'The thought of kissing you makes me want to barf.'

'Shall we experiment?'

My heart didn't go pitty-pat, it thudded.

'Don't even think about it,' I said.

'One little kiss. I know you want to.'

'No.'

He forced me off the sidewalk. Grabbing both my arms, he turned me and pushed my back against a tree.

'Don't.'

'You'll like it. I know you will.'

'No.'

'Yes.' His face moved in closer to mine. 'Yes,' he said again.

I turned my face away.

Lips brushing my cheek, he said, 'Just one kiss.'

'No.'

'You want me to leave, don't you?' he whispered. 'I'll leave if you kiss me. I'll leave and I won't go to Eileen. I'll go back to my own apartment and you'll be free to meet with your secret flame and nobody will ever know any of this happened.'

'I haven't got a secret flame.'

'Liar, liar, pants on fire.'

'And I'm not gonna kiss you.'

'Afraid you'll enjoy it?'

'Fuck you.'

'Certainly, if you'd rather.' One of his hands turned my face toward him and he planted his mouth on mine. I pinched my lips tight together. Moaning, he tried to push his tongue in. And then I felt his other hand against the front of my jeans, rubbing me.

My fist got him in the solar plexus. He *whooshed* against my mouth, folded over. Stumbling backward, he crossed the sidewalk and dropped onto his ass on someone's front yard. He sat there, hunched over, hugging his belly and wheezing.

'You got your kiss,' I said. 'Now go home.'

He didn't even lift his head.

I wiped my lips with the back of my hand, turned away from him and broke into a run. At the end of the block, I glanced back. He was on his hands and knees on the sidewalk, looking at me.

Chapter Fifty-four

I cut across Fairmont, raced up a sidestreet and turned left at the next corner. The running made my head hurt worse, made it throb with pain. Also, I knew I looked conspicuous. When people run for excercise, they wear proper outfits: shorts or warm-up suits or sweatclothes, not jeans and a chamois shirt.

Late at night, my clothes hadn't mattered very much; almost nobody was around to see me. But this was well before the bedtime of most adults. It was also a Friday night, so many of them had probably gone out to movies or friends' houses. Plenty had remained at home, too. Nearly every house was well lighted. Through picture windows, I glimpsed people in their living rooms. Some were watching television or reading. Others appeared to be having parties.

Few of those inside the houses probably saw me run by. I was definitely noticed, however, by some who were outside. They seemed to be everywhere: on their way to or from cars; taking walks, alone or in couples; taking their dogs for a stroll; walking or running for exercise – in proper attire, of course; standing outside their houses while they puffed at cigarettes; driving by in cars and vans and SUVs and pickup trucks.

It crossed my mind that Randy might drive by and recognize me, but the thought didn't bother me much. For one thing, my head pounded so badly that I couldn't be bothered. For another, I was more worried about being spotted by Kirkus.

He was probably coming after me. Maybe I'd lost him, but I couldn't count on it. I needed to get out of sight. Find a place to hide, to rest, to wait. Give Kirkus time to give up and go home.

I stopped running. Though I panted for air and poured sweat, my head didn't feel quite so horrible.

If I could just lie down for a while . . .

But where?

A few hours from now, most of the lights would be off. Most of the people would be in bed. I would be surrounded by good, dark places were I could hunker down and rest unseen. Now, however, the night seemed alive and terribly crowded.

I've *got* to go somewhere, I thought.

If only I knew where to find Casey. This early, she might be anywhere.

Probably in her own house, I thought. If she has one.

I had no idea where that might be, or whether it even existed.

She must live somewhere.

Doesn't matter, I told myself. I'll find her later. At the usual time. I hope. For now, I just need a place to hide and rest.

Marianne's house?

The extra bed in her room would be wonderful. At this hour, however, her parents would probably still be up and around. Marianne might welcome me, but her parents certainly wouldn't.

How about the park across the street from her house? I could go to the playground area and lie down on the grass for a while.

I remembered Casey on the grass after her jump from the swing.

Nice to be in a place where I'd been with her.

But then I remembered the man leaping down from the backstop and running toward us. The memory of him sent chills crawling up the back of my neck. My head began hurting worse.

Forget the park.

I wondered if the tequila drinking woman over on Franklin Street would let me in. I could ring her doorbell, explain that I'm Casey's friend and need a place to rest for a while.

No way.

First, I would never have the guts. Second, she might not be the one to answer the door. Third, I had no idea what sort of relationship – if any – she had with Casey. Unlikely as it seemed, maybe she wasn't even aware of Casey's visits to her house.

She *must* be aware of them. Twice, I'd seen Casey either entering or leaving the woman's house.

I started walking in that direction.

Not with any intention of ringing the doorbell or attempting to enter. But it was where I would probably start looking for Casey later on, so why not go there now? I was just as likely to find a hiding place near that house as anywhere else. Maybe in the backyard, or behind a neighbor's house, or across the street.

It seemed like a fine idea.

It was a long way off, though. Could I go that far without Kirkus spotting me? And with such a stiff neck and throbbing head?

If I could just take something for the headache and lie down for a while!

No doubt Casey would be able to get me some aspirin.

Hours from now.

So *many* hours, I suddenly realized, that I could walk back to my apartment, take some aspirin, lie down for a while, and be back out on the streets in plenty of time to start searching for her.

Only two problems with that: Kirkus and Eileen. Kirkus might intercept me. At my apartment, Eileen might already be awake. Or she might wake up before I could leave again.

Better to live with the headache than to risk losing a night with Casey.

A couple of minutes later, grimacing and rubbing my neck and turning my head, I looked toward a house and realized it had no lights on. All the windows were dark and so was the porch.

No cars were parked in the driveway. The stretch of curb in front of the house was also empty.

By all appearances, nobody was home.

In my imagination, I saw a medicine cabinet loaded with pain relievers. I saw a bedroom with a king-sized bed.

If nobody *is* home . . .

Don't even think about it, I told myself.

Casey would do it.

By the time I reached the front porch, I was so frightened that my heart was thudding wildly and my head felt as if it might explode.

The area near the welcome mat was littered with fliers and brochures. They looked as if they'd been piling up for several days, maybe longer.

Nobody *is* home.

Just to make sure, I pressed the doorbell button. From inside the house came a faint sound of ringing.

Nothing more.

I rang again, waited a while longer, then reached forward and found the screen door's handle. I pulled and the door swung toward me. Bracing it with my body, I reached for the handle of the main door.

What if Casey opens it from the inside? I thought. And comes out and says, *House inspector.*

The memory made me smile.

Of course, Casey didn't come out of this house. Its door was locked.

Good, I thought. That's that. I wanted aspirin and a bed so badly that I might've *gone* in, had the door been unlocked, but I certainly wouldn't *break* in.

It's not exactly breaking in if I use a key, I thought.

Not that I'll find one.

I didn't find the key under the doormat.

I did find it on a thin ledge above the door.

Why anyone would lock a house then leave its key near the front door is beyond me. But some people do. Maybe they have an overpowering fear of locking themselves out. Who knows? People do plenty of strange and foolish things.

Hand trembling, I pushed the key into the lock and turned it. The latch clacked back, very loud. I flinched. Then I waited, listening. No sounds came from inside the house or from anywhere nearby. I heard only my own quick breathing, my own pounding heart. So I eased open the door and looked in.

Darkness.

Nobody's home, I told myself again. I can just walk in, find the medicine cabinet and help myself to a couple of aspirin.

It's no big crime.

Take some aspirin. Forget about lying down, just take the aspirin and get out fast before someone comes home. In and out in two or three minutes.

But I couldn't move. I just kept standing there, staring into the darkness.

Do it, I told myself. Don't be such a chicken. The place is empty.

What if someone comes back?

I'll be in and gone in two minutes.

I can't do it. It's wrong.

Not *that* wrong. If Casey were here, she would've gone in by now.

Whatever, I'd better stop standing here on the porch *thinking* about it. Someone'll come along and see me.

The tension was making my head throb with pain.

I really need some aspirin!

I imagined Casey smiling at me, shaking her head, saying, *You could've been in and out in the amount of time you've been standing here worrying about it.*

Chapter Fifty-five

I entered the house, shut the door, stood motionless and listened. Silence except for some electrical hums and a quiet, clicking sound that probably came from a clock.

The air felt warmer than outside. Much warmer.

Apparently, the owners had forgotten to turn down the thermostat before going away.

Unless someone's here.

The thought made my head hurt worse.

Nobody's here, I told myself.

I pulled the Maglite out of my pocket, but didn't turn it on. Even if the house were empty, someone outside might notice my light if I used it.

But I kept it in my hand, just in case, and started walking slowly through the house. Because of dim light coming in through windows, I could make out the general shapes of things well enough to avoid falling over furniture. And well enough to find doorways.

I made my way through the living room. Here and there, small dots glowed in the darkness from the television, the cable box, the VCR. Bright green numbers near the floor showed 9:20.

What if they've got an alarm?

Again, pain soared into my head.

Half the people in this town don't even lock their doors. The odds of anyone having an alarm . . .

Just get it done and get out!

At the rear of the living room, I hurried through the dark rectangle of an entryway. In almost total darkness, I twisted the head of my flashlight and the bright, narrow beam leaped out. I was in a hall with doorways on both sides. Framed pictures hung on the walls.

The nearest loomed near my shoulder. I glanced at it and saw a hideous face. For just an instant, I doubted it was just a painting. I gasped and leaped away. Then I found it with my flashlight.

Wild red fright-wig, enormous crimson nose, white-painted skin and a gawdy, scarlet smile. A clown face. It looked demented.

I hurried forward, glimpsed another clown painting, then swept my light through a doorway and discovered a bathroom. I ducked inside and closed the door.

And felt – stupidly – as if I'd shut it to keep the clowns out.

Trembling, I stepped away from the door, turned around and swept the bathroom with my flashlight: toilet, tub with shower doors, counters, and a mirror above the sink. The mirror reflected the flashlight beam and my haggard face. They swung away when I pulled at one side of the mirror and it opened on hinges.

Behind it was the medicine cabinet. Shelves lined with medications and ointments. Including Tylenol and Extra Strength Bufferin.

I snatched down the Bufferin, fought open its 'child-proof' cap and shook a couple of tablets into my trembling hand.

Holding them, I closed the plastic bottle and returned it to the shelf. I shut the medicine cabinet, then turned the cold water on.

What if somebody can hear it?

Nobody's in the house, I told myself again. Nobody but me.

(And those damn clowns.)

I tossed the pills into my mouth. Bent over the sink. Cupped water into my mouth and swallowed them.

After they were down, I drank more water. Then I shut off the faucet. I dried my hands on my jeans. I wiped my wet mouth on my sleeve. And sighed. Still frightened, but pleased with myself.

Now get out of here fast.

Turning away from the sink, I realized I needed to urinate.

It's not that urgent, I told myself. Just hold it and go later.

I'm in a bathroom, for Pete's sake!

Last night, I'd been in worse shape but I'd refused to use the toilet in Marianne's house.

That was different. That house had *people* in it.

I stepped over to the toilet and lifted its lid and seat. The bowl looked reasonably clean. Holding the flashlight in my teeth, I unzipped and pulled out and started to go. It sounded very loud in the silence. Like Casey last night.

Is anybody listening?

Stop it. Are you *trying* to scare yourself?

Done and zippered shut, I considered leaving the toilet unflushed. It was sure to make a lot of noise. But I'd already made plenty of noise, so why worry about a little more? Besides, it would be crude not to flush.

I wanted to leave the house exactly as I had found it – minus a couple of Bufferins.

So I pushed the handle down. With an explosive gush of water, the toilet flushed.

Time to get!

I took the flashlight out of my mouth. Holding it in my left hand, I opened the bathroom door with my right. I stepped out and looked both ways. To my right were the living room, the foyer and the front door. To my left, the hall continued on another twenty feet or so. More doorways in that direction. And more wooden picture frames on the walls.

Did every frame contain a painting of a clown?

Take a look and see.

Oh, sure.

I was tempted, though. And excited by the idea of *not* fleeing from the house.

I'm already in, I told myself. I've taken care of business. I can leave any time I want. So why not check the place out for a minute or two?

At least check the rest of the paintings, I thought. See if they're *all* clowns. I can tell Casey about it. I can write about it.

(What sort of person collects clown paintings? A clown, himself. Or a circus fan. Or a John Wayne Gacy fan.)

Heart thudding fresh waves of pain into my head, I turned to the left and made my way silently up the hallway. Each time I approached a painting, I aimed my light at it. Every painting depicted a different clown. They *all* looked slightly mad.

Afraid of making noise, I didn't try to open either of the closed doors that I came upon. Two more doors, however, stood wide open.

I stepped into the first doorway, shined my light around and felt as if I'd entered a one-room museum devoted entirely to clowns. In one corner stood a life-size mannequin in full clown makeup and costume. Along the walls were glass-fronted cases displaying clown dolls, circus posters, old newspaper articles, and items of clown gear such as wigs and rubber noses and floppy shoes and baggy trousers. I made my way quickly along the cases, shining my light through the glass, excited by this strange discovery.

Most of the newspaper clippings, brown with age, had to do with Clement O'Toole, who portrayed a clown called Sunny Boy. None of the hallway paintings had shown Sunny Boy. He was a large, fat clown. Wearing a straw hat and baggy overalls, he resembled an oversized Tom Sawyer. He had the standard enormous red nose, but his white-painted face had yellow streaks radiating away from his eyes and mouth – the rays of Sunny Boy's sun, I suppose.

The clippings had dates from the 1950s through the 1980s. Not daring to stop and read them, I only glanced at some of the headlines and dates. Clement must've been a real star. But in 1988, he'd nearly died in a circus tent fire. He'd survived his burns, but was horribly disfigured and Sunny Boy never put in another appearance under the Big Top.

Clement must be at least seventy by now, I thought. If he's still alive.

Almost ready to move on, I turned my flashlight to the mannequin in the corner of the room. It was dressed and made up to look like Clement's Sunny Boy.

Someone had gone to a lot of trouble and expense.

Sunny Boy looked as good as what you might see in an actual wax museum, except something seemed to be wrong with its face. Some of the wax had apparently melted, bubbled, flowed into odd shapes.

Too much heat somewhere along the line, I thought. A shame. It wasn't very noticeable from a distance, but up close . . .

And up close, the dummy's eyes looked old and bloodshot.

Goosebumps started creeping up my spine. Keeping my flashlight on the dummy, I backed toward the door. I wanted to whirl around and run, but was afraid to take my eyes off it.

Don't be ridiculous. It's just a dummy. A very lifelike dummy.

In the hallway, I swung my light out of the room and walked away. *Enough of this place.*

I was almost to the living room when a frail, reedy voice – like the voice of an old, old man – tremored down the hallway from behind me. It quietly sang, '*Oh, Sunny Boy, the pipes, the pipes are calling . . . from glen to glen, and down the mountainside . . .*'

Chapter Fifty-six

I ran through the house, somehow managing not to crash into furniture or walls. Outside, I leaped off the porch, ran to the street and across the street, and kept on running. I raced around a corner, crossed another street, turned another corner, kept on running, and finally, in a neighborhood of expensive-looking homes, came upon a two-story house with a lighted porch but dark windows.

The area behind the house was enclosed by a fence, but the gate wasn't locked. Quietly, I entered. Then I crept alongside the house. In back, I found a swimming pool.

The pool wasn't lighted. Neither was the patio or any rear window of the house.

The patio had a barbecue grill, a glass-topped table surrounded by iron chairs, a couple of aluminum patio chairs, and a lounge with a small table beside it. On that table was a drinking glass. I picked it up. It was made of sturdy plastic, and had a puddle of liquid in the bottom. Probably from melted ice cubes. Someone must've enjoyed a cocktail out here earlier.

Had he or she also gone swimming? It had been a nice, sunny day, warm for October.

Bending over, I swept a hand over the plastic tubing of the lounge. It felt smooth and cool and dry. The tubing sank under my weight as I sat on it. I lowered the backrest and lay down.

Pale, moonlit shreds of clouds were scooting across the sky. The night breeze carried a chimney scent of burning wood.

This is nice, I thought.

Hands folded on my belly, I shut my eyes.

Though the breeze felt cool against my face, I was snug in jeans and my thick, soft shirt.

The tightness and pain began to drain away.

This is so nice, I thought. Now if I just don't get caught back here.

My luck, some withered old zombie'll climb out of the pool and come slouching over to me.

What *is it* with this town? I wondered. Everywhere I go, creeps and weirdos.

Not everywhere, I told myself. Don't forget Casey. Neither a creep nor a weirdo. And Marianne seemed nice. Bet the tequila woman's nice, too.

How about one of *them* climbing out of the pool?

Which one?

As I imagined the side of the pool, someone boosted herself out of the water and climbed onto the edge. The tequila woman, slender and beautiful in the moonlight. Her hair wasn't wet, but her nightgown was. The pale gown clung to her body and ended high on her thighs. She came toward me with slow, graceful strides. Along the way, though, she changed into Casey.

Good, I thought. I don't even know the tequila woman really.

Casey was dressed in jeans and a baggy sweatshirt. I tried to imagine her in the wet, clinging nightgown that showed everything, but couldn't make it happen. Still, she sure looked good.

She crouched beside me and reached over and stroked my brow. *You had yourself a nasty knock on the bean, Chucky.*

Kirkus fell on me.

I'll kiss it and make it well.

Unfortunately, the bump was on the back of my head. *I'll turn over*, I said. But I didn't move. Though I definitely wanted Casey to kiss my bump, I felt very comfortable on my back.

I'll turn over in a little while, I thought.

The next time I thought about turning over, I felt calm and well rested and alert. I opened my eyes. A few pale rags of clouds were rushing across the sky. The full moon was high and very bright. Apparently, I'd been asleep.

325

An area at the back of my scalp felt stiff and sore, but my head felt pretty good inside. The nap had apparently given the aspirin a chance to do its job.

I raised my left arm above my face and pressed the button to light my wristwatch. 11:10.

Not bad!

Wary of my head, I sat up slowly. Then I got to my feet, and still felt fine.

Very good.

I looked around. All the lights were out, just as they'd been before my nap.

My lucky night, I thought.

Yeah, right. Lucky if I don't count Sunny Boy or the creeps under the bridge or Kirkus falling on me or my head getting bounced off the street.

Ah, well, I thought. After all that, things can only get better.

Oh, yeah?

Let's hope so. Let's at least hope I've lost Kirkus for the night and let's hope I don't have any trouble finding Casey. That's all I really want. Simple, really. Casey and no Kirkus.

I went around the side of the house, let myself out through the gate, then stopped at a corner of the front lawn. The neighborhood didn't look familiar. It was darker than when I'd arrived. I saw nobody wandering about. For a while, no cars went by. Then two came along, one after the other, and kept on going.

Eleven-fifteen on a Friday night. A lot of people are already in bed. Some are on their way home from movies or parties. Others are still out, living it up.

And where's my good buddy Kirkus? I wondered. Back in his own apartment by now? Or did he return to mine and wake up Eileen so she could fully appreciate my disappearance?

If he did that . . .!

Maybe, saints preserve us, he went back to the damn bridge and jumped off. And wouldn't that be a pity?

I felt guilty for thinking it.

He wouldn't, I told myself. He never meant to jump in the first place, just climbed up there for the drama of it. He wouldn't have done it at all if I hadn't been there.

Did it to get my attention.

Well, he got it, all right.

I suddenly remembered the feel of his open mouth, the feel of his hand. It made me a little sick, the way you might feel if you accidentally stepped on a dead baby bird.

I wiped my lips on my sleeve, then started walking. At the sidewalk, I turned to the left and headed for the end of the block.

You try to be friends with a guy, I thought, and he does that to you.

'What do you expect?' I muttered.

When I reached the corner, I looked up at the street signs. Olive and Conway? I'd never heard of either of them.

Where the hell *am* I?

After running away from Kirkus, I'd concentrated (to the extent that I'd been able to think at all) on making turns and losing him. I hadn't paid much attention at all to my actual location. Nor had I kept track of my route after running away from Sunny Boy's house.

Doesn't matter, I told myself. I'm not actually lost, just temporarily vague about my position. No cause for alarm.

I was obviously somewhere north of the Fairmont Street bridge. That was my impression, anyway. After ditching Kirkus, I'd headed generally to the north and east. I think.

I knew where I *wanted* to be . . . at the tequila woman's house on Franklin Street to begin my watch for Casey.

So which way is that?

Farther north, probably.

But which way is north?

Standing on the corner, I turned around in a full circle. I looked up and down the roads. Saw headlights, parked cars, trees and houses. Nothing, however, stood out as a landmark.

Terrific.

It's all right, I told myself. I've got plenty of time.

Pick a direction, any direction. Doesn't matter. Whichever way I go, I'll soon run into a street I recognize. Then I'll be set.

I turned to the right and walked quickly. The faster I walked, the sooner I would find a street I recognized and the sooner I could calm down.

It didn't feel good, not knowing where I was. It gave me an uneasy feeling as if I'd wandered into the *Twilight Zone*.

I half expected Rod Serling to step out from behind a tree.

Offered for your consideration . . . one Edward Logan . . . He went out on a fine October night in search of his true love but found, instead, that streets don't always lead where you expect and that love may not always 'find a way,' especially in that region of uncertain boundaries we call . . .

The sound of an engine broke into my thoughts. I looked over my shoulder. Headlights. Coming on fast.

Ride or Hide?

Too late to hide.

So I stood motionless on the sidewalk and watched the headlights grow larger, brighter.

A pickup truck.

It raced by.

As it passed me, I saw that it was a compact pickup truck, pale in color. I couldn't see the driver, but I saw the passenger for a couple of seconds.

Her head was drooping as if she'd fallen asleep. It wobbled with the motions of the truck. So did her shoulders. She probably would've fallen over if not for her seatbelt.

The way her head hung down, most of her face was shrouded by her hair.

She seemed to be wearing a dark, skimpy garment with a plunging neckline. It was open very wide, showing an expanse of dusky skin and much of her left breast.

Eileen?

In Randy's pickup truck?

The truck must've been fifty feet away by the time I got over my shock enough to give chase. I gained on it for a few seconds while it waited at a stop sign at the end of the block.

Then it took off and left me behind.

Chapter Fifty-seven

Though I kept after the pickup truck, it was soon a block ahead of me. Then two blocks. Then it turned left. By the time I reached the corner where it had turned, it was nowhere to be seen.

Exhausted, head pounding again, I quit running. I leaned back against a tree and tried to catch my breath. And tried to talk myself out of what I'd seen.

Maybe it *wasn't* Eileen. I hadn't gotten a very good look at the passenger's face – only glimpsed it, and the light had been bad, and her hair had been in the way. She might've been a stranger who bore a certain resemblance to Eileen.

And wore Eileen's dress?

It wasn't necessarily Eileen's dress, I told myself. Obviously, its top had a similar (*identical, who am I trying to kid?*) design to Eileen's dress. But who knows what it might've looked like from the chest down? And was it even green?

The pickup truck wasn't necessarily Randy's, either. It had looked similar, but there must be a lot of light-colored compact pickup trucks around town. And I hadn't even gotten a glimpse of the driver.

What I'd seen might easily have been a local couple, strangers to me, a guy and his girlfriend on their way home from some sort of formal occasion: a dance, a dinner party, maybe even a wedding.

Sure thing.

It was Eileen, all right. Asleep or unconscious (*dead?*) in the passenger seat of Randy's pickup truck. Somehow, he had found her and grabbed her and now he was taking her someplace.

I had special plans for her, he'd said at the donut shop.

You want to go out with her?

I want to go in *her.*

He's taking her someplace to do that, I realized. Someplace private where he can go *in* her. Where he can *give her the works.*

Or maybe she's still back at my apartment, asleep in my bed.

Fat chance.

She *might* be, I told myself. Maybe it really and truly wasn't Eileen in the pickup.

It was.

But I had to know for certain.

Call. Find a phone and call. If she answers . . .

. . . she won't . . .

everything's fine.

There might be a pay phone over near Dandi Donuts. Though I couldn't specifically recall seeing one in the vicinity, it seemed like a good place to try.

If I can find my way there.

I had stopped at a corner with a signpost, but hadn't checked it yet.

Let's hope.

I looked up at the signs: Olive and Franklin.

Franklin!

Somehow, in my confusion, I must've crossed Division without even knowing it.

I looked up and down Franklin Street. The houses seemed vaguely familiar. More than likely, I was still south of the tequila woman's house.

North should be to the left . . . the same direction Randy had gone.

He's taking Eileen someplace north of here.

As I started hiking up Franklin Street, I realized that Randy's destination might be nearby. Maybe he'd kept driving or turned onto a different road, but maybe he'd stopped at a curb along Franklin . . . or pulled into a driveway. So I slowed down and kept watch for his pickup.

I also kept watch for the tequila woman's house. And for Casey.

Casey'll get me to a phone, I thought. She'll probably take me into the nearest dark house . . . or maybe into the home of a 'friend' such as Marianne or the tequila woman.

Now that I *really* need Casey, I probably won't be able to find her.

I'll just go on to Dandi Donuts. By the time I get to the tequila woman's house, it won't be much farther to Dale. Take Dale on back to Division, and I'll be at the donut shop.

What's the point? I wondered. Eileen *isn't* going to answer the phone.

She might.

She really might, I told myself. The mind can be a tricky thing. It sometimes shows you what you're expecting to see, not what is actually in front of your eyes. Maybe the girl in the pickup truck looked very different from Eileen. The 'plunging neckline' of her gown could've actually been something like a V-shaped design on a sweater.

Possible.

Stopping at a corner, I looked both ways. No traffic. No sign of Randy's pickup truck parked along either side of the street or in any nearby driveways. No sign of any pedestrians in the distance.

I hurried across.

The porch and windows of the corner house were dark.

Why go all the way to Dandi Donuts?

I pictured myself sneaking into the corner house, creeping through its darkness, finding a telephone . . .

'Not a chance,' I muttered, and kept on walking.

But what if I can't find a pay phone?

There has to be one over by Dale and Division.

Doesn't *have* to be. And if there is, it might be out of order.

I'm not going to sneak into another supposedly empty house! Not tonight, not ever!

(Not by myself, anyway.)

When I reached the next corner, the home of the tequila woman came into sight. I forced myself to look away from it and check in both directions for Randy's pickup truck and for Casey. No sign of either. So I crossed the intersection.

Keeping Franklin Street between me and the tequila woman's house, I continued northward. Slowly.

For a while, I had a view of the kitchen window. It was dark. But the porch lights were on. Light also showed through the curtains of the large front window.

She – they – apparently hadn't gone to bed yet.

I checked my watch again. 11:48.

Instead of going on to Dandi Donuts, why not hide and wait here for Casey to show up?

Might take hours.

What if she's in the house right now?

Even if she isn't, the tequila woman probably is. Maybe she'll let me use her phone.

I stepped off the curb, made sure no traffic was coming, and walked to the other side of Franklin Street.

My mouth was dry. My heart thudded. Fresh pain began to pulse inside my head.

I can't be doing this, I thought.

Sure I can. Why not?

I climbed the porch stairs.

I've lost my mind. The bump on the head must've scrambled my brains.

I stood on the welcome mat and pressed the doorbell button. A sound of chimes came from inside the house. I had a strong urge to run away.

What'll I say?

I had no idea.

On the other side of the screen door, the main door opened a few inches, letting out a vertical strip of light. At about my neck level, a guard chain pulled taut. Then a face appeared in the gap.

Tequila woman's face.

It was prettier than I remembered it. And younger.

Her large blue eyes looked out at me.

'Yes?' she asked. She sounded neither frightened nor angry, but somewhat puzzled.

'My name's Ed,' I told her. 'I'm very sorry to bother you, but there's some trouble and I'm wondering if I might be able to use your phone.'

Narrowing her eyes, she tilted her head sideways and seemed to be considering my request.

'I know it's almost midnight,' I said, 'but it's sort of an emergency.'

'Your name is what?' she asked.

'Ed,' I repeated.

'Ed Logan?'

Stunned, all I could do was gape at her.

She shut the main door. A moment later, it swung wide. She reached forward, pushed the screen door open and said, 'Come on in, Ed.'

Chapter Fifty-eight

She *knows* me? It didn't seem possible.

As I entered her house, she backed into the foyer. I saw that she was barefoot, wearing tan corduroy trousers and a long-sleeved white blouse. The blouse was untucked. It wasn't completely buttoned.

After shutting the door, she offered her hand. 'I'm Lois,' she said.

'Hi, Lois.' I shook her hand. It was warm and smooth. I could hardly believe I was shaking the hand of the woman I'd spied on. And she *knew my name*!

'Are you okay?' she asked.

'You know who I am?'

'I believe we have a friend in common,' she said. 'She's all right, isn't she?'

'As far as I know. I haven't seen her tonight. I just came here because your lights are on and I really need to use a phone.'

Whether or not she believed me, she said, 'It's over here,' and turned away.

I followed her into the living room. Nobody else was there. The television was off. No music was playing. In the silence, I could hear our footsteps on the carpet. The tail of Lois's blouse draped the seat of her corduroys.

She walked to a lamp table at the end of the sofa, picked up a cordless phone, turned around and handed it to me, saying, 'Here you go.'

'Thank you.'

As I tapped the numbers in, Lois wandered out of the room. Probably to give me some privacy. It seemed very trusting of her.

A book lay open on her lamp table, face down, probably to keep her place. She must've been reading it when I rang the doorbell. *Light in August* by Faulkner.

After several rings, my answering machine took the call. My own voice told me, 'This is Ed. I'm not in right now. Please leave your name and number at the beep.' Along came the beep.

'Eileen?' I asked. 'Are you there? It's me. It's Ed. If you're there, I need to talk to you.' I waited for a few seconds, then said, 'Eileen? Are you there? It's really important. I *have* to talk to you. *Please* pick up if you're there.' After waiting a while longer, I returned Lois's phone to its cradle.

This is bad, I thought. This is really really bad. It wasn't someone else in the pickup, it was Eileen.

Of course. It was *always* Eileen.

But if she'd answered the phone . . .

There was never much chance of that.

Lois came back into the room. 'Is everything okay?'

'Not really. But thanks for letting me use your phone.'

'Is there anything I can do?'

I sighed. 'I don't know.' It was hard to concentrate.

'You look beat. Why don't you sit down and relax? Would you like some coffee? A drink?'

'I don't think I want anything.' I sank onto the sofa and leaned back. It felt good.

Lois sat down beside me. Turning toward me, she tucked one leg under the other and rested an arm across the back of the sofa. The way she sat, her blouse was drawn up against the underside of her left breast. The same breast I'd seen naked on Tuesday night.

I was blushing, and knew it.

'You seem very upset,' Lois said.

Not knowing what to say, I just nodded.

'I'll help you if I can,' she said. 'My friend thinks the world of you.'

The words warmed and thrilled me. 'She does? We only met last night.'

'She couldn't wait to come here and tell me all about it.'

'When was she here?'

'This morning. Early this morning. She was very excited. She couldn't stop talking about you.'

'That's . . . great.'

'You must be a pretty special guy.'

'Not really.'

'She thinks you are. That's enough for me.'

'Well. Thanks.'

'I'll help you if I can.'

'Thanks.'

'What can I do for you?'

'I'm not sure.'

'Do you want to tell me about the problem?'

I said, 'Uh,' and thought, Do I?

'Does it have to do with the man who's been after you? What was his name, Ralph?'

'Randy. She told you about him, too?'

'She tells me pretty much everything.'

'Do you know about Eileen?'

'Your girlfriend?'

'Yeah. Eileen. I don't know if she's exactly my girlfriend anymore . . . but I think I saw her tonight. Just like ten minutes ago. This pickup truck went by. It looked like Randy's, and this girl in the passenger seat looked like Eileen. And she didn't seem to be conscious. Maybe she was just sleeping, I don't know. Maybe she wasn't even Eileen. It might not've been Randy's pickup, either. But what I'm afraid of is that he got his hands on Eileen and he's taking her somewhere.'

'You think he kidnapped her?'

Nodding, I said, 'But maybe it wasn't really Eileen. That's why I wanted to call, to see if she was still at home. I got the answering machine, but she didn't pick up. So it probably *was* her in the pickup. Unless maybe she slept through the phone call . . . the ringing and everything. Or maybe she was in the bathroom. I just don't know. What I think, though, is that Randy has her.'

'Did you leave my number on the message machine?' Lois asked.

'No.'

'Why don't you call again? Maybe she *is* there, but just couldn't reach the phone in time.'

'Okay. Good idea.' Though I didn't hold much hope, I reached over to the lamp table and picked up the phone. I punched the redial button. After a quick, musical series of beeps, my home phone rang. Just like last time, my machine picked up and delivered my message. Then came the beep. 'Eileen,' I said. 'It's Ed. Are you there? This is pretty urgent, so please pick up if you're there.'

Lois patted my thigh. 'Leave my number,' she whispered.

'Are you there?' I asked again. Then I said, 'Okay. Anyway. You can call me back at . . .' I found Lois's number above the keypad, and read it off. Then I repeated it more slowly. 'Get back to me as soon as you can,' I said, and hung up.

Lois gave my leg another pat. 'If she calls while we're gone, my machine'll take it.'

'While we're gone?'

'Let's drive over to Eileen's place and see if she's there.'

'I don't have a car.'

'I do. Let's go.' She sprang up from the sofa. As I followed her across the living room, she said, 'Wait by the door. I'll be right back.'

While I stood in the foyer, she hurried toward the rear of the house. A couple of minutes later, she returned with white sneakers on her feet and a purse hanging from her shoulder. She walked so fast her hair shook. So did her breasts, but I tried not to watch them. 'All set,' she said, and swung open the door.

I stepped outside. She came after me, shut the main door, and hurried down the porch stairs. I rushed after her, letting the screen door bang shut. Her car was in the driveway.

We both climbed in. As she keyed the ignition, she said, 'Toward campus?'

'Yeah. At Fairmont and Church.'

'Got it.' Watching over her shoulder, she backed down her driveway. Then she shifted and started driving south on Franklin.

'I really appreciate this,' I said.

'No problem. I just hope it turns out to be a false alarm.'

'Me, too. But I'd be surprised.'

'If she isn't there, we'll take the next step.'

'What'll that be?' I asked.

'Let's worry about that if we come to it.'

'Okay.'

Lois looked toward me for a moment. 'How do you think you'll handle your situation?'

'What do you mean?'

'You seem to be involved with two women simultaneously.'

'Yeah. I guess I am.'

'That sort of thing always ends badly for someone.'

When she said that, I remembered my own feelings when I'd read the letter from Holly: my disbelief, my ache of loss, the pain of imagining her with Jay. I'd felt as if my heart had been torn apart. I'd thought my happiness was gone forever.

I can't put anyone through that.

But the letter had come only last Friday, one week ago. The real devastation had only lasted a few days. I'd started getting better on Monday night – the night Eileen met me at Dandi Donuts and drove me back to my apartment and we made love on the living-room floor – also the night I first saw the mystery girl and followed her, wondering about her and longing to meet her.

One of them had given the world back to me.

One, or both.

'Someone's bound to get hurt,' Lois said. 'Someone *always* gets hurt in deals like that.'

'I know.'

'What're you going to do?'

'I'm not sure yet.'

'You don't want to hurt Casey.'

'I don't want to hurt anyone.' Then I realized she'd called the girl Casey. 'So that *is* her name? Casey? She was kidding around about making up a name for me to call her, but I *thought* it was really Casey.'

'It is.'

'Casey what?'

'Just Casey.'

'You don't want to tell me her last name?

Lois glanced at me again. 'I'd be glad to tell you, Eddie, but I don't know it myself.'

Chapter Fifty-nine

'What *do* you know about her?' I asked.

'I know what I need to know.'

When she said that, I couldn't stop a single, quiet laugh from coming out.

'What?' she asked.

'You must be the one who taught her how to talk in circles.'

Lois turned her head. We were passing a streetlight, and I saw the smile on her face. 'Maybe she taught me.'

'Does she come to your house *every* day?'

'I wish. Sometimes, it's every day for a while. Then I might not see her for a few days . . . or longer.' She glanced at me. 'I can't stand it when she doesn't come. I always think the worst. That something's happened to her. That I'll never see her again.' On the last word, her voice broke. She took deep breaths. Then she asked, 'How's that for straight-forward?'

'Good.'

Holding the steering wheel with one hand at a time, she wiped her eyes.

'Doesn't Casey have a place to live?' I asked.

'She is not without places to live.'

'What do you mean?'

'It's just a guess – she doesn't tell me everything – but I think she probably has houses and apartments all over town.'

'But not a place of her own?'

Lois shook her head. 'I've asked her to live with me. She *will* sleep there sometimes, come by for meals . . . but she never stays for long. Sooner or later, she always says, "Gotta go. See you around."'

Going, going, gone, I thought.

'And then she's off.'

I asked, 'Why?'

'Other places to go. Other people to see.' Voice breaking again, she said, 'I hate it. But what're you gonna do? It's just Casey. If she weren't that way, she wouldn't be Casey. You know what I mean?'

'I guess so,' I said, though I really wasn't sure.

'I'd hate for her to change.'

'Yeah,' I said.

Then I saw my apartment building just ahead. 'That's it next to the church,' I said.

Lois pulled to the curb and stopped. 'Do you want me to go in with you?'

'I can just run up and check. Be right back.'

As I swung open the passenger door, she said, 'Good luck, Eddie.'

'Thanks.'

I hurried around the front of her car. As I ran across the street, I noticed Eileen's Saturn parked halfway up the block. It had the Willmington University sticker on the rear window and the Jack in the Box clown head atop its radio antenna.

Her car's still here. Maybe she is, too.

The front door of the apartment building was locked as it should be. I let myself in. Turning the corner on my way to the stairs, I saw light from the Fishers' doorway. Voices were coming from their television.

Eyes forward, I walked quickly and quietly past their door. Nobody called out. I hurried up the stairs, reached the landing without being accosted, and climbed to the second floor. The hallway was deserted. I went to the door of my apartment.

Shut. Locked.

Please let her be here!

My hand trembled so badly that I had a hard time getting the key into the lock. At last, it slipped in and I opened the door.

My living room was lighted, but silent.

I glanced around. Nobody there. The kitchen lights were off. The hallway to my bedroom was dark.

Had I left the lights like this? I couldn't remember.

On my way down the hall, I passed the bathroom. Its door was open, its light off.

Up ahead, I could see darkness through the doorway of my bedroom. The sight made me sink inside. I'd left that door shut, the light on. I was certain of that.

She is gone. Randy has her.

Entering the room, I flicked the light switch. The bedside lamp came on. The bed was empty, as I'd known it would be. The covers were a little rumpled.

I remembered Eileen lying crooked, her legs hanging off the edge, her left leg bare to her hip. I remembered my urge to go over to her and put my hand inside the slit of her dress.

I should've done it. Should've stayed. She'd still be here.

'*Eileen?*' I called out. Loud enough to be heard throughout the rooms of my apartment, but probably not loud enough to disturb other tenants on the floor. I didn't want to alarm my neighbors. Besides, what was the point in calling at all?

I called her name once more, anyway. Again, she didn't answer.

What'd you expect? She's miles away.

Feeling horrible, I hurried to the bathroom and took two Excedrins. Then I used the toilet, flushed, gave my hands a quick wash, and hurried to the kitchen.

My note to Eileen was flat on the kitchen table. I turned it over. She'd written a message on the back. A very simple message scratched with black ink in large, sprawling letters.

I'm outa here.

That was it. Nothing more.

I groaned.

'Nice job, Logan,' I muttered. 'Real nice job. Fuck.'

I stumbled around the apartment for a couple of minutes. Eileen's purse and bright yellow windbreaker were gone.

The girl in the pickup hadn't been wearing a windbreaker.

Maybe she *wasn't* Eileen.

She was Eileen, all right. Randy probably tore the windbreaker off her so he could enjoy the view while he drove. Probably put his hand inside her dress . . .

He's got her completely naked by now.

Feeling bludgeoned, I left my apartment and hurried downstairs.

The Fishers' door was still wide open. Voices still came from their television. This time, I looked in as I walked by.

Mr Fisher, in his chair, raised a hand and said, 'Hold on there, young fella.' I waited while he pushed himself out of his chair and came to the door. He wore an old blue bathrobe and slippers. The robe wasn't closed very well. 'Case you're wondering,' he said, 'your gal took off on you.'

'When was that?' I asked.

'Oh, say . . .' He narrowed his eyes, nodded. 'Yep, *Nash* was just about over with.'

'Nash?'

'*Nash Bridges*. You know. Has that Sonny Crockett in it, and that Cheech fella. Well, it gets over at eleven, and I had to miss me the end of the show 'cause of Holly coming by.'

Holly? She'd been here?

My heart thudded. I shriveled inside.

Not quite 'over' Holly, after all?

'Reckon they likely caught the bad guys. Always do, you know. Show has that *Baywatch* gal in it. Now *that's* a hot tomato.'

Did she break up with Jay?

'Holly?' I asked.

'Nah, the name's Yazzmeeeeen, something along those lines.'

'You said Holly came by.'

Does she want me back?

'Oh, her. Sure did. Your gal, Holly. Came by here all dressed up to beat the band . . .'

'Wearing what?' I asked, already suspecting the truth. He'd seen Eileen, not Holly. I felt a strange mixture of relief and disappointment.

'Well,' he said, 'that spiffy green dress. You know the one.' He touched his bare belly. 'Open down to here. I tell you, that's a dress. She wasn't too keen on *me* getting a good look at it, though . . . put on her jacket pretty quick when she saw me.'

'Was anybody with her?' I asked.

'Nary a soul.'

'Are you sure?'

'I stood right here talking to her.' He stomped a slippered foot on the floor. 'She stood right where you are. Reckon I'd of known if she'd had someone with her. She didn't.'

'How was she?'

'Mighty upset. She'd had herself a cry. You could tell 'cause of how her eyes was red. I says to her, "What's the matter, Holly?" And she says, "Eddie up and left me all by myself."'

I doubted that was what she'd said, exactly.

'So she gets her jacket zipped up good and high and then she asks if I know when you took off on her. Well, I must've missed you going by, and told her so. Then I says I'll keep an eye out for you when you come back, and does she want me to give you a message?'

'What'd she say?'

'Nothing right off the bat. She stands there and sorta thinks it over for a spell. Then she up and says, "No thanks, Walter" . . . using my name like that. "No thanks, Walter," she says, "I reckon I know where to find him." Then she tells me "Goodnight," and goes on her way.'

'She was going to look for me?'

Walter nodded. 'I'd say so.'

I muttered, 'Shit.'

'Give you a piece of advice, there, Eddie. That Holly, she's a humdinger. Know what I mean?'

'Yeah.'

'Gals like that, they don't come around every day.'

'I know.'

'Gotta treat 'em right.'

'I try.'

'Fucked up pretty good tonight, though, didn't you?'

'Sure did.'

Smiling at me like I was an old buddy, Mr Fisher gave me a none-too-gentle punch on the upper arm and said, 'Go on out and find her, boy.'

Chapter Sixty

I climbed into the passenger seat and shut the door. 'She's gone,' I said. 'Her car's still here, but she isn't. I saw the landlord and he says she left the building a little before eleven. That's about twenty minutes before I saw her in Randy's pickup.'

Lois pulled away from the curb. 'Do you know Randy's last name?'

'No. I don't even know if his name's really Randy.'

'What about his truck?'

'A light-colored Toyota pickup. White, I think.'

'License plate number?'

'Never got a look at it.'

'Do you know where he lives?'

'Where he *lives*?'

'Yeah.'

'How would I know that? I don't *know* the guy. I've certainly never been to his house – if he even has one. I saw him for about ten minutes Tuesday night. That's all. He forced me into his pickup and wanted me to take him to Eileen, but I got away from him. He chased me and I lost him and I haven't seen him since . . . not till tonight when he drove by with her.'

Listening to myself, I thought, It's all real. He really does have her. I muttered, 'God.'

'What does Randy look like?'

'I don't know, like he could be a male model or something. Like on the cover of a romance novel.'

'Don't read the stuff, myself.'

'It ain't Faulker,' I said.

She turned her head and smiled. 'Nope, it ain't. But I know the look you mean. Bronze skin. Granite features. Muscles. Flowing mane of hair.'

'That's about it.'

'What's his hair color?'

'Blond.'

'Ash blond . . .?'

'Golden.'

'How old is he?'

'I don't know, thirty?'

'Size?'

'Bigger than me. Maybe six-two. And heavier, stronger.'

Nodding, Lois flicked on her turn signal. 'He doesn't sound like anyone *I* know.'

'You wouldn't *want* to know him.'

'No, but I'd sure like to know who he is . . . where to find him.' She slowed down and made a right turn. 'Any thoughts as to where he might take Eileen?'

'Not really. Last I saw, they were just south of your house, heading north on Franklin. If he has a place in town, I guess it's probably on the north side. The night he spotted me with Eileen, we were at Dandi Donuts. Maybe he lives near there. Or maybe he lives out of town and just drives in sometimes. Even if he does live in town, he might not take Eileen to his house. I mean, I wouldn't.'

'Where would you take her?' Lois asked.

'If I wanted to do really bad stuff to her?'

'Is that what you think Randy has in mind?'

Feeling grim, I said, 'I'm pretty sure it is.'

'So where would you take her?'

'Maybe into the woods. That way, I wouldn't have to worry about neighbors hearing or seeing anything. I wouldn't have to move her body after I'm done with it. And I wouldn't end up with traces of evidence in my house for the police to find.'

Lois turned her head toward me. 'You're not a killer yourself, are you?'

'Nah. But I'm trying to be a writer. Apparently, I lean toward the morbid and grotesque. I suppose I think about murders and things like that more than most people.'

'Well, if he took her into the woods, we'll never find them.'

'It's just what *I* might do. Maybe Randy doesn't like the woods. Or maybe he has good reasons to take her to his house or to some other building . . . anyplace that's closed at night. They'd at least be *warmer* than the woods. Not that it's very cold tonight, but you might *want* to be in a nice, warm place if you're going to . . . you know, mess around with someone.'

Nodding, Lois turned a corner. Now we were northbound on Franklin Street. 'We'll stop at my house for a minute,' she said. 'Pick up a few things. Then we'll drive around, see if we can spot Randy's truck.'

'What about calling the police?' I asked.

Lois was silent for a few seconds. Then she said, 'Not me.'

I remembered Eileen's nine-one-one call on Wednesday night . . . and the strange lack of results.

'They *might* be able to help,' I said.

'I have some things in my past.'

'Oh.'

'They don't like me much.'

Smiling, I asked, '*You're* not a killer, are you?'

'Yes.'

She seemed serious. Still, I said, 'You're kidding.'

'No.'

'You *killed* someone?'

'My husband.'

'My God.'

'He was also the brother of a local cop.'

'Oh, my God.'

But wait, I thought. She's not in prison. She's sitting right next to me. 'You weren't convicted?' I asked.

'The charges were dropped. It was self-defense. But a lot of people think I should've gotten nailed for it. Particularly Joe's family and his brother's cop friends. So they haven't got much use for me. If *you* want to call the cops, I can drop you off at a pay phone. Just please don't bring me into it. Or Casey.'

'Casey?'

'They'd *love* to get their hands on her.'

'What do you mean?'

Lois swung to the curb in front of her house and stopped the car. She kept it running, though. 'What do *you* think?' she asked. 'You think girls her age are *allowed* to do what she does?'

'Not really, but . . .'

'At the very least, they'll put her in a foster home. At worst, she might be sent to a juvenile detention center. I *hope* that's the worst. She doesn't tell me everything. For all I know, she could end up in prison.'

'I sure don't want anything like that to happen.'

'So if you bring the police into this situation, be very careful what you tell them. Leave me and Casey out of it.'

I nodded.

'Should I take you to a phone?'

'I'm not sure.'

'I know you want to help Eileen.'

'I've got to. I've got to save her. If I can.'

'What I've seen of the cops in this town,' Lois said, 'they're not so great. It's like we've got the bottom of the barrel. We *used* to have some good ones, but they left because it's such a shitty department.'

'You think I shouldn't call?'

'If you do, you might end up waiting on a corner all night. Or they might show up in an hour and not take you seriously, might figure you're trying to make trouble for Eileen because maybe she went out with another guy. Or they might think *you* did something to her. That's the way this bunch operates.'

'From what I've seen,' I said, 'they aren't very good.'

'They're fuck-ups. And even if a miracle happens and one of these guys believes your story, you've got nothing much for him to go on. You've got a description of the suspect, but no name, no address, no license plate number. The cops *might* be able to help somehow, but it's not likely. The main thing is, Eileen has to be found fast. Here's what *I'd* do. You and me, we go looking for the pickup truck. Maybe we'll be lucky. If not, I'll drop you off at a phone and you can go ahead and call the cops. How does that sound?'

'Okay, I guess.'

'You don't sound very sure.'

'I'm not.'

It seemed wrong not to bring in the police right away. They were professionals. They had the manpower to conduct a thorough search. Hell, one of them might *know* Randy, know exactly where to find him.

On the other hand, according to Lois, they're fuck-ups.

I tended to believe her; apparently, they hadn't responded at all to Eileen's call on Wednesday night. A call reporting a *murder*.

If I get the cops involved, I'll have to do it without Lois. I'll be on my own. And they'll force me out. As soon as they get my statement, they'll be done with me.

We'll take it from here, Mr Logan. You can go on home, now.

'Let's do it,' I said.

Chapter Sixty-one

'Wait here,' Lois said. 'It'll be faster. I'll be in and out.'

'Sure.'

She climbed out of her car and ran to her house. She took the porch stairs two at a time.

Seeing a strip of light appear and widen when she opened the front door, it struck me this was the same house Casey had entered the first night I followed her. Hidden in the darkness of the porch, she'd opened the door with great stealth as if breaking in . . . or sneaking back into her parents' house after a late-night rendezvous.

Why had she been so furtive about it? Who had she been trying to hide from? Certainly not from Lois.

Maybe Lois doesn't live alone.

She *seemed* to live alone.

Maybe Casey sneaked in to surprise her.

On the other hand, perhaps her secretive behavior had nothing to do with who was *in*side the house, but rather with who might be *out*side.

Outside watching her.

Me?

Maybe not me in particular, but anyone who might be looking out a window or driving by or roaming the streets. She wanted nobody to know about her visits to Lois. Or about *any* of her activities, more than likely.

Where is she now? I wondered.

Doesn't matter. What matters is saving Eileen. Take care of this, and there'll be plenty of other nights to be with Casey.

I missed her, though. I'd wanted so badly to see her tonight.

Too badly. That's why this happened. I should've stayed with Eileen.

She wasn't supposed to wake up!

And if she did, she wasn't supposed to leave.

I'm outa here.

Real nice.

Out of my apartment and into Randy's pickup. He must've spotted her immediately after she came out of the building, before she could get to her car.

Did he just happen to be driving by?

Maybe he'd seen her earlier and followed her. Or seen me, for that matter. Found out where I lived. Staked the place out and bided his time, waiting for just the right moment.

However he did it, he did it. He got her. And now he's going to give her the works.

He's probably already doing it, I thought.

I looked at my wristwatch. 11:58.

What time had I seen them go by? Somewhere around 11:15 or 11:20. They were still on the road at that point. So if he took her someplace in town, they probably would've arrived there no later than 11:30.

So maybe he'd been at her for half an hour, so far.

Less time, if he took her farther away.

They might *still* be on the road, on their way to a secluded place in the woods or maybe a farmhouse outside of town or . . .

If they are, I thought, she might be all right so far but we'll never find them in time.

I heard the thud of Lois's house door bumping shut. Then she bounded down the stairs. She hadn't changed her clothes. Instead of her purse, however, she now carried an overnight bag. She hurried around to the driver's side of her car, opened the door and swung her bag in. Its buckles jangled. I smelled leather. 'Wanta put this on the floor?'

I took it from her. It was heavy. Leaning forward, I set it on the floor near my feet.

Lois climbed into the car, shut her door and started the engine. 'I was hoping Casey might be there. She knows this town inside and out. Not to mention, she can get through doors like they aren't even there.'

'Any ideas where she might be?' I asked.

'Sure. In somebody's house. Unless she's roaming the streets or fooling around in a park or . . . she might be almost anywhere. Most likely in a house, though.'

'Like whose?' I asked.

Shaking her head, Lois pulled away from the curb. 'No sense in sitting still while we talk. Keep your eyes open for the pickup. I'll check the parked cars on both sides of the street. You check the driveways the best you can. It was heading north on Franklin when you saw it, right?'

'Right.' I started watching the driveways.

'So we'll try going north till we hit the city limits, I guess, then maybe work out some sort of east-west pattern on the way back, try to hit every street. Of course, if he put his truck in a garage or something, we're screwed.'

'Or if he took her out of town.'

'Well, this is what we can do. Like I said, maybe we'll be lucky. If we strike out, I'll drop you off at a pay phone and you can call the cops if that's what you want to do.'

'Sounds good,' I said. 'But what about Casey? Do you have any idea which houses she goes to?'

'She's told me about some of them. She has regulars. Certain houses – certain people – she visits from time to time. But I think a lot of it's random. I can't imagine she has any sort of fixed schedule. She's what you might call a "free spirit".'

'I noticed.'

'Maybe a little nuts.'

I smiled. 'Think so?'

'Who knows?'

'Do you know why she does it?'

'Why she goes into the houses?'

'Yeah.'

'I know it started one night when she was out roaming and someone went after her. She ran into a house to hide. Thought nobody was home, but she was wrong. They were home, all right, but asleep in the bedrooms. So she started to explore the house. God only knows what sort of buttons *that* pushed. Here's a girl with – far as I know – no family at all, no home, and she's in someone else's home in the middle of the night. Almost like part of the family, but *not* part of the family. They're asleep and she's not. She's sneaking around, looking at them, at what they've got in their closets and drawers and medicine cabinet and kitchen, looking at their books, their mail . . . secretly participating in their lives.' Lois shook her head. 'I don't know exactly how one thing led to another, but I know she got hooked. Pretty soon, it became her way of life.'

'She's actually friends with some of the people,' I said.

'Yeah. Every so often, somebody wakes up. Or comes home and catches her. She's made a lot of friends. Me, for instance. I was having a pretty rough time a while back . . . I'm *still* having a rough time, but it's not so bad anymore. Mostly thanks to Casey. Have you ever had one of those dreams where you wake up crying?'

'I don't think so.'

'I did. I used to have them a lot, especially right after what happened with Joe. Anyway, I woke up sobbing one night and someone was standing over me, stroking my face, saying, "It's all right. Everything's fine." I guess I should've been terrified, waking up with a stranger in my room. But I didn't feel that way at all. I felt . . . peaceful and safe. That was the first time I ever saw Casey.'

'Must've been nice,' I said.

'It was wonderful. She's wonderful. But she's also . . . in such danger. Always in such danger. Things happen to her. They're bound to, the way she wanders around all night and sneaks through houses. She's had some terrible beatings. She's been . . . it's not for me to tell you these things. She might not want you to know. But awful things have happened to her. You can imagine. And she's had so many narrow escapes. I worry so much about her. But she is who she is. I wouldn't want to change her.'

'It would sure be nice,' I said, 'if we could find her tonight.'

'She'll probably turn up at my house sooner or later, but I don't know when. For now, we'd better keep looking for Eileen.'

'Yeah,' I said.

Just about then, we drove past a house with a pale pickup truck parked in its driveway.

Before I could speak up about it, Lois hit the brakes.

'Think that might be it?' she asked.

'I'll take a look.' I threw open the passenger door, leaped out, and ran toward the pickup.

A Nissan, not a Toyota.

I hurried back to Lois's car and we resumed our search.

Chapter Sixty-two

'This is probably far enough,' Lois said. We'd left the town behind –
along with all the streetlights and most of the houses. Even the paved
sidestreets had disappeared. Woods were on both sides of us. Every
so often, a dirt road led into the darkness.

'He probably didn't go this far,' I agreed. And hoped.

No other headlights were in sight, so Lois slowed almost to a stop
and made a U-turn. We were just into the city limits again when we
came to a cross-street. Lois turned right on it. 'Not many houses,' she
said. 'But maybe we'd better go for a while just in case.'

'Good idea.'

She drove fast. We kept our eyes open for pickups that might be
Randy's. After heading west for about a mile, she made a left turn,
then another left and we headed east again, back toward Franklin.

A couple of blocks after Franklin, Lois made a right turn, then
another right and we went west for a mile or so before cutting over
to the next street and heading east.

Always watching.

Every so often, we came upon light-colored pickup trucks. Most of
them were parked alongside the street or in the driveways of houses.
Sometimes, I could tell from a distance that a certain pickup wasn't
Randy's. Other times, I had to climb out of the car for a closer look.
None was his. They were always the wrong make, or an older model,
or had some sort of peculiarity: a bumper sticker or windshield deco-
ration – dice or a troll or a graduation tassel hanging from the rearview
mirror – that Randy's pickup didn't have.

A couple of times, we encountered light-colored pickup trucks in motion. One came toward us. Just as it went by, we could see that its driver was a husky man with a beard. Approaching another pale pickup from the rear, we saw that it had a built-in toolbox behind the cab.

Lois kept driving. We both kept looking. I watched for Casey as much as for Randy's truck.

Then a pickup crossed an intersection a block in front of us.

'Did you see that?' I asked.

'I saw it.' Lois stepped on the gas. 'Didn't get a good look, did you?'

'Huh-uh.'

'Anything off about it?'

'Not that I could see. It *might* be his.'

'I couldn't tell about the size, could you?'

I shook my head.

'Looked white, though.'

'If it's Randy, why's he still driving around town? I mean, he's got her.'

'Maybe he's looking for you,' Lois said and took the corner fast. The tires sighed. Almost tipping over, I grabbed the seatbelt strap up near my shoulder and held on tight.

When we came out of the turn, I could see red taillights far ahead of us, but not the vehicle itself. 'Hope that's it,' I said.

'Let's find out.' Lois sped up. At the next corner, we had no stop sign so we raced through the intersection. No traffic in either direction. Lois accelerated even more. We were gaining on the taillights.

I began to see the general shape of the vehicle. 'It's a pickup, all right.'

'Thought so.'

'What if it's him?'

'I've got a couple of guns in my bag.'

The leather satchel was on the floor between my feet. I remembered its weight.

'The first thing we need to do,' Lois said, 'is see if it's really him. Then we'll—'

Out from between two parked cars just ahead of us came a bicycle.

Lois shouted, '*Shit!*'

Bright in our headlights, the old woman turned her head and grinned at us.

The bike hag!

Lois swerved.

But not in time. Not possibly in time. The bike hag was a dead woman. I imagined her coming at me over the hood, diving headfirst with her backward ballcap tight on her skull, her leering, whiskered face smashing through the windshield . . .

Suddenly, she was no longer in front of us.

A van was. A parked van.

We crashed into its side with a roaring chaos of noise. I felt myself starting to fly forward, but was suddenly slammed back, bludgeoned across the chest.

Through the ringing in my ears, a voice. Lois, sounding like someone who'd just been beaten to the ground and kicked a few times. 'Least I missed her.'

I grunted.

'You okay?' she asked.

I was still strapped in the passenger seat. Just in front of me, a limp cushion was sagging out of the dashboard. An air bag? Was that what had pounded me?

The windshield was still intact, somehow, but the front of Lois's car was smashed and crumpled against the caved-in side of the van. Steam or smoke was rising from the engine area. I heard hisses, pings and clanks.

I looked at Lois. 'Guess I'm okay. How about you?'

'Just shaken up, I think. You gotta get outa here.'

'Huh?'

'Go. Take the bag.'

'The bag?' Did she mean the air bag?

'The *bag*. On the floor.'

'Uh.'

'Hurry,' she said.

I unlatched my seatbelt. Hunkering down, I found the leather bag near my feet. As I picked it up and set it on my lap, Lois opened her door.

'Get going,' she said, and climbed out. 'Quick. Run.'

I opened my door. 'What about you?'

She bent over and leaned in. 'I can't leave the scene. But you get outa here. Go. There'll be cops. I don't want 'em seeing what's in the bag.'

I suddenly, finally, understood. So I climbed out with the bag, swung the door shut and turned around. Lois was staggering toward the rear of her car. 'Sure you're okay?' I asked.

She said, 'Come here. Help me.'

I hurried around the rear of her car. She hobbled toward me as if hardly able to stay on her feet. Though her hair was mussed, I saw no sign of blood or any other injury. Her blouse dropped off one shoulder.

'Help me over to the curb,' she said.

I put an arm around her. Supporting much of her weight, I walked her away from the wreckage.

All around us, people from nearby houses were rushing down their porch stairs, running across their lawns. Many of them wore robes. Some of the women had curlers in their hair. I spotted three people with cellphones.

In a quiet voice, Lois said, 'You came by after the crash. You're just a good Samaritan. Blend in, then disappear before the cops show up.'

'Okay.'

'Anybody still in the car?' a man called out from somewhere behind me.

'It was just me,' Lois told him.

A woman with a cellphone yelled from her front lawn, 'Police and ambulance're on the way!'

'Anybody hurt?' asked a husky man running toward us from the other side of the street.

'The woman might be hurt,' I answered.

'I'm okay,' she protested. 'Just . . . shaken up.'

'What about the van?' an elderly woman asked. 'Anyone in it?'

'Somebody better check.'

'It's mine,' a man said. 'Nobody *better* be in it. How the hell'd *this* happen?'

'Herman, it doesn't matter.'

'Gonna matter to my insurance company. Anyone see how this happened?'

He was answered by a chorus of 'No,' and 'Didn't see a thing,' and, 'Heard this awful crash.'

'Let me help,' a man said, hurrying over to us.

'Here,' said someone else. 'Here.'

I relinquished my hold on Lois and two men hustled her over to the curb and eased her down on the grass.

Someone far away yelled, 'Has anyone called nine-one-one?'

Different people shouted, 'Yes!' and, 'Taken care of,' and 'Already done.'

'Nobody saw how it happened?' The man sounded peeved.

'Oh, hush up, Herman.' The woman had to be his wife.

On the strip of grass between the curb and the sidewalk, a small crowd was gathered around Lois.

'Where do you hurt?' someone asked.

'An ambulance is on the way,' said someone else.

'You'll be fine.'

'Don't try to get up.'

'Just lie still, dear.'

'Any broken bones?'

'Would you like me to call anyone for you?'

'I'm sure the ambulance'll be here any minute.'

'I'll go get her a blanket.'

That last voice was mine. Nobody looked at me, but I heard a couple of people say, 'Good idea.' Then the voices faded as I hurried across the street with the leather satchel swinging by my side.

By the time I heard any sirens, I was more than a block from the scene of the accident.

Chapter Sixty-three

Safely away, I had no idea what to do next. My head was aching again, my chest hurt from being struck by the air bag and my legs were shaky. I felt weak and trembly all over.

I was on my own. No companion. No car. Little or no hope of rescuing Eileen.

Thanks to the bike hag.

Miserable bitch!

Almost as if she'd pedaled in front of us on purpose to make us crash.

Nobody's that nuts. It's a miracle she wasn't killed.

Good thing she wasn't, though. Lois would've *really* been in trouble if she'd struck and killed an old woman on a bike. Hitting the parked van wasn't nearly so serious. She might get cited for speeding. Her insurance rates might go up. No big deal.

Hope she's all right.

She probably is, I told myself.

But what am I going to do?

Hurting and depressed, I longed to return to my apartment and go to bed.

Can't give up.

Besides, even if I *had* to go home, I didn't know where to find it.

Let's figure out where I am.

I walked to the next corner and looked up at the street sign.

Beaumont and Pittman.

'Huh?'

I didn't know *either* street.

'Shit.'

Standing at the corner, I looked in all four directions. The streets were bordered by lampposts and large trees. A wind was blowing the trees. The pavement was alive with waving shadows. I saw no approaching vehicles, no people. The houses looked pretty much like hundreds of others I'd seen while roaming the town. Old, middle-class homes, a mixture of one and two stories. Most had lights on, if only at their porches, but several were dark.

Where the hell am I?

I'm not lost, I told myself. This just happens to be the intersection of a couple of streets I've never heard of. Pick a direction, any direction, walk another block or two, and I'll find myself back in familiar territory.

What if I don't?

Left seemed like a good way to go, so I crossed Pittman Street and began walking up Beaumont. Or down Beaumont, perhaps, since I didn't know whether I was going north or south.

Maybe I can figure it out.

Yeah, sure. The way my head hurt, the way I ached and trembled all over, I hardly felt capable of thinking at all.

But I tried.

Before our brief pursuit of the pickup truck, we'd been cruising the east-west streets, making our way gradually southward. After Lois took off chasing the pickup, she'd made a right turn. But which way had we been going just before that? East? Seemed like east, but I wasn't sure. If it *had* been east, a right turn would've taken us southward.

But if we'd been heading west, the turn would've taken us to the north.

So which way?

Doesn't matter. Even if I could figure out where we'd been at the time of the crash, I'd fled from the scene in a daze, focused only on getting away, paying no attention to my route.

Don't worry about it, I told myself. I won't be lost for long.

Not far ahead was another intersection.

362

I came to it and stopped. Still no traffic, no people. Only the shadows moved. And the limbs of the trees. And the leaves in the trees. And the leaves that had fallen off and were blowing through the night, some flying by as if on missions, some skidding and tumbling along the pavement.

I stepped closer to the signpost, shifted Lois's heavy leather bag to my other hand, and tilted back my head.

Beaumont and Johnson.

Johnson?

I'd never heard of that street, either.

Moaning, I stepped off the curb. Might as well continue in the same direction.

This can't go on much longer, I thought. It's not a huge town and I've explored most of it. I'm bound to reach a familiar area pretty soon.

Familiar? It's *all* familiar. Just not familiar enough.

I'd probably been on Beaumont Street before, but hadn't paid attention to its name.

I'll recognize the next one for sure.

I got there. To the left, a truck was parked at the curb. Not a pickup, but a large, boxy Ryder truck that blocked much of my view in that direction. To the right, the street had shadows and blowing leaves and parked cars and houses and nothing that gave away my location. So I lifted my gaze to the street signs.

Beaumont and Hamner.

Impossible. *Another* street I'd never heard of?

Where am I? What if I'm not in Willmington anymore?

Don't be ridiculous, I told myself. But chills crawled through me and my skin stiffened with goosebumps.

Take it easy, I thought. I'm still in Willmington. Nothing weird is happening. I temporarily don't know where I am, that's all. It won't last much longer.

I stepped off the curb and began to walk across Hamner Street.

Bring-bring-bringgg!

I jerked my head to the left, toward the sound of the bicycle bell. Saw the Ryder truck. Took a step backward as the bike came out from beside it, speeding toward me, the grinning old crone hunched over the handlebars, her bony knees pumping up and down as she cranked the pedals.

Bring-bringgg!

She'd come out of nowhere, this hag, this witch in her spandex and ballcap, and now she was suddenly bearing down on me like a nightmare phantom, awful as what lurks under the beds of terrified children, freezing my blood, bringing a scream up my throat.

The scream was nearly out when her hand came off the handlebars and flapped, waving me back. 'Outa my way!' she squawked.

Outa my way?

Outa my WAY???

Not a nightmare phantom, a pushy old bitch!

She zipped past me, missing me by inches, leaving in her wake a cloying scent of rose perfume.

'Look out where you're going!' I shouted.

She raised her right arm, middle finger extended toward the sky.

That did it.

I shouted, '*All right!*'

She glanced back just in time to see me sling the long strap of the bag over my shoulder and break into a run. '*Yeeeee!*' she squealed. Facing forward, she raised her skinny butt off the seat and pumped faster.

I dashed after her, the heavy leather bag swinging beside me, bouncing against my flank. At first, I gained on her. Then she was picking up speed, pulling away from me.

That's it, I thought. She's gonna get away. I must've been nuts to think I could outrun someone on a bike ... especially hauling luggage. Whatever Lois had in her bag – guns, flashlights, ammo? – must've weighed a good fifteen pounds.

Nuts, all right. I'm chasing an *old woman*! What if I *do* catch her? Do I beat her up? Turn her in to the police for causing Lois's crash?

Moot point, I thought. I don't stand a chance ...

The distance between us seemed to be shrinking.

She's slowing down?

Of course, I thought. She's an old woman. She's wearing out. Down on her seat again, too tired to keep standing on her pedals.

I was still probably fifty feet back when she turned a corner. With a detour across the corner of a lawn, I cut her lead in half. I ran harder. Closed in. Harder. I was fifteen feet behind her. Ten. I poured it on, got closer to her and closer, my feet flying out, almost touching the rear tire of her bike.

I'll give it a kick, I thought. A good, hard kick on the side of the tire and down she'll go.

Don't do it! She's an old woman!

She made us crash! Made it so we can't save Eileen! It's all her fault and it was all on purpose!

Just as I kicked out at her rear tire, she sped up. My kick missed. My foot went out too far and came down crooked and somehow I tripped all over myself and went down.

Chapter Sixty-four

The worst part wasn't my fall. The worst part wasn't the jarring pain of my body striking the pavement or the burning in my hands and elbows and knees as I skidded. Nor was the worst part my blazing, thudding headache.

The worst part was after I'd pushed myself up to my hands and knees, when I raised my head and saw the old woman turn her bike around in a small, wobbly circle and start pedaling toward me.

Out of breath, I couldn't curse or yell. I did, however, hear myself make a panicky, whimpery sound.

She pedaled harder, picked up speed, squealed, '*Wheeeee!*' as she raced toward me.

I grabbed the leather handles of the bag and scrambled to my feet.

Guns in the bag, according to Lois. But it was shut with half a dozen zippers. No way to pull out a weapon in time.

Wouldn't shoot the old bitch if I could.

Probably.

Hunkered over her handlebars, grinning like a lunatic, she looked as if she had every intention of running me down with her bike.

Bring-bringgg! Bring-bring-bringgggg!

As she bore down on me, I readied myself to make a last-instant dodge to one side or the other.

She'll have a fifty-fifty chance . . .

I launched the bag straight at her face and leaped to the right. The bike would've mowed me down, anyway, but it swerved aside at the

366

very last moment as the old woman caught the heavy leather bag – not in her face, but in her two hands.

I stumbled, steadied myself against a parked car, and turned around.

Sitting up straight in her seat, the bike hag coasted away down the middle of the street not touching the handlebars at all – holding Lois's bag high above her head like a trophy.

I had enough breath to cry out, '*NO!*'

The hag answered with a distant, '*Hee-heeeee!*' and lowered the bag in front of her.

I was in no shape to chase her. My fall to the street had damaged me more than the car crash. The knees of my jeans were torn. So were the elbows of my shirt sleeves. My knees, elbows and palms felt as if they'd been smacked with bats and scraped raw. They burned. My head pounded and blazed. But I *had* to go after the old woman. I couldn't let her get away with Lois's bag – and guns.

About fifty yards ahead of me, she began to pedal. Though I ran as fast as I could, it wasn't fast enough. I could feel blood trickling down my shins.

The gap between us grew and grew.

Off in the distance, she glided around a corner without even touching her handlebars, the bag clutched to her chest.

By the time I turned the corner, she was gone. I stumbled along for about half a block anyway, then slowed to a walk.

I'd lost her.

Lost Lois's bag and guns.

Now the hag is armed.

I groaned.

I'd thought the heavy satchel would smash her in the face and knock her off the bike for sure.

Didn't think, just reacted.

At the end of the block, the intersection grew brighter.

Headlights.

Not waiting for the vehicle to appear, I rushed over to the curb. I was on the sidewalk by the time the lights swung toward me. A tree hid me from them. After the lights swept by me, I peered around the side of the trunk.

A black van.

It looked exactly like the van from last night, the one that had stopped for me near the Fairmont Street bridge, the one with the woman behind the wheel and the men in back.

The van moved slowly along the street in my direction.

It's probably not the same one, I thought.

Then I thought, what if the driver spotted me and she stops and the whole gang leaps out and comes after me?

Wouldn't that be sweet?

Though the van moved slowly, it drove past my tree and continued along the street.

I stared at its rear, expecting the brake lights to come on.

Please please please.

They came on, glaring bright red, and my heart almost stopped. The van slowed down. Then turned right.

Yes!

But what if it's a trick? Maybe I should stay with my tree for a while in case they circle back.

Good idea, I thought.

Rest.

I turned around and leaned my back against the tree and shut my eyes.

Just give it a minute or two, I told myself. Can't go on like this, anyway. Besides, what's the point? I don't know where I am. I don't know where Randy took Eileen. The hag rode off with the guns and I don't know where *she* is. I don't know where *anyone* is. Everything's all fucked up.

And where, oh where, is Casey? If only Casey were here.

She's not.

Oh, there is no joy in Mudville.

At least I can rest.

Lying down would be better. Lying on the nice soft grass. But I couldn't do that without moving and I didn't want to move. Being slumped against the tree was fine.

Night In The Lonesome October

> I think that I shall never see
> A bed as comfy as a tree . . .

I've got to get going.
Gotta find Eileen.
But how?
No idea.
Better find a phone and call the cops. Maybe they can find her.
If only I can find a phone.
Why not do it Casey's way – sneak into the nearest house?
No no no no no no no.
Remember what happened last time.
Probably a pay phone over by Dandi Donuts. But where is Dandi Donuts?

> Where Alph, the sacred river, ran
> Through caverns measureless to man
> Down to the sunless sea.

No sacred rivers around here. Just the Old Mill Stream, and it's miles and miles from Dandi Donuts.
And I have miles to go before I . . .
Don't fall asleep!
I won't. Just resting.
Stop resting and go find Eileen. *Randy's got her.*
I know I know I know. What I don't know is what I can do about it!
Get moving, for starters.
I can't.
Yes I can. Just push away from the tree and start walking.
In a second. Just give me a second.
Okay, maybe not right now. But pretty soon.
Soon.
Then I felt hands on my shoulders. Moments later, warm, moist lips kissed me on the mouth.

This is nice, I thought.

It got nicer.

Breasts pushed softly at my chest. Her flat belly met mine. She was pressed to my groin. Her legs were warm against my inner thighs. She seemed to be standing between my legs, leaning forward against me.

I moaned with pleasure.

I grew hard.

Her tongue slid along my lips, pushed into my mouth.

Who could this be? I wondered.

It's no one. I'm dreaming.

Am I? It didn't quite seem like a dream. The lips and tongue felt so real and wet and pliant. The breasts felt so springy, the belly so warm.

If it is a dream, I thought, it's a very good one. Don't wake up and ruin it. Whatever you do, don't wake up. If you wake up, she'll vanish.

Who'll vanish?

The bike hag!

Chapter Sixty-five

Erupting with a squeal of horror, I shoved her away and opened my eyes and saw not the bike hag stumbling backward across the sidewalk, but Casey. She sat down hard on the grass of someone's front lawn.

I gawked at her.

'Ow,' she said. The word didn't come out like a gasp of pain, but like a comment.

'Oh, my God! I never . . . I had no idea it was you.'

She smiled up at me. 'Good thing. Otherwise, I'd be offended as *well* as having a sore butt.'

I pushed away from the tree. Before I could reach her, she was already on her feet and rubbing the seat of her corduroys.

'My God, I'm glad to see you.' I pulled her gently against me. Her arms wrapped around me. I caressed her back through the softness of her chamois shirt.

As we held each other close, she asked, 'What's happened to you, Eddie?'

'Rough night.'

'I hardly recognized you.'

'You go around kissing strangers?'

'Oh, sometimes. I saw you from pretty far off . . . this guy drooping against a tree. A wreck. I came over for a closer look. Couldn't believe it was you. What's going on?'

While I tried to figure out where to start, Casey eased away from me. Hands warm against my flanks, she stared into my eyes. She had no smile now. She looked serious, concerned.

'A lot's happened,' I said. 'I'll tell you everything, but . . . the thing is, you know that guy Randy I was telling you about?'

'How could I forget *him*?'

'He took Eileen. I saw his pickup go by and Eileen was in the passenger seat.'

Casey winced. 'Are you sure?'

'I'm not completely sure of anything. But it looked like his truck and I'm almost positive it was Eileen. She wore the same dress . . . She was sort of slumped in the seat like she was unconscious.'

'When was this?'

'I don't know . . . maybe an hour ago. Maybe longer.' I took my hands away from Casey and tried to check my wristwatch. When I pressed the button to light its face, nothing happened. I moved the watch around until it caught the glow from a streetlight. The digital numbers were gone, the face blank. 'Out of commission,' I said.

'But about an hour ago?'

'Something like that.'

'Which way was the truck heading?'

'North,' I said. 'On Franklin Street. I ran after it for a while. Then Lois and I drove around looking for it in her car.'

'Lois?'

'Your friend Lois.'

'*My* Lois? You know her? How on earth . . .? Never mind. It'll keep. So you and Lois drove around?'

'She was helping me try to find Randy and Eileen, but then we crashed.'

'Oh, no.'

'She's okay. Neither of us really got hurt, but she had to stay at the scene of the accident. She sent me off . . . didn't want to get caught with guns in her car.'

'Guns?'

'The plan was to rescue Eileen if we could find her. So I took off and then I had a run-in with the bike hag and *she* ended up with the guns.'

'Bike hag?'

'This loony old woman . . .'

'Oh. Old Missy.'

'You know her?'

'We've had encounters. I don't know her name. She always calls me "Missy". As in, "Move it or lose it, Missy", when she suddenly shows up out of nowhere. So that's what I call her, Old Missy.'

'She's the one who made Lois crash. Then later I chased her and tripped. That's mostly how I got so messed up.'

'She didn't run you down with her bike?'

'She tried.'

'She's hit me a couple of times,' Casey said. 'On purpose. Sweet thing.'

'When she tried to run me down, I threw Lois's bag at her. But she *caught* it. So now I've lost Lois's guns unless we can find her again – Old Missy.'

'Don't worry about it. I can always get the guns back. Maybe not tonight, but . . .'

'We planned to use them for the rescue.'

'There won't be any rescue. Not unless you know where Randy took her.'

'We were driving around looking for his pickup. But I guess that's the end of that. Do you have any ideas? With all your night roaming . . .'

She shook her head. 'From what you told me, he doesn't sound like anyone I know . . . Maybe some guys I've seen around, but nobody in any of my houses. And pickups like his, there're lots of those around.'

'We noticed that.'

'You and Lois?'

I nodded.

'She's a pretty cool gal, isn't she?'

'Sure is,' I said.

'Any ideas about what to do next?'

'I was thinking about calling the police. They might not know how to find Eileen, either, but at least . . .'

'You don't want to call the police.'

'That's what Lois said.'

'Let's go over to Dandi Donuts.'

'Glad to. Do you know where it is?'

'Don't you?' she asked.

'I'm all turned around. I don't know *where* I am.'

'Come on. It's not very far.' She took my hand and led me along the sidewalk. 'That's where Randy saw you with Eileen, right?'

'Yeah. Monday night.'

'And that's where you had the run-in with him the next night, isn't it?'

I nodded.

'So that's two nights he was at the donut shop. Maybe the counter guy knows who he is. Maybe he even lives somewhere near there.'

'He was driving in that general direction when he went by with Eileen.'

'So we'll check it out.'

'Worth a try,' I said.

As we walked along, Casey moved closer to me and put her arm across my lower back. She rested her hand on my hip. I put my hand on her back and she smiled at me. 'I've been missing you,' she said.

'I've been missing you, too. A lot. That's why I came out tonight in the first place – to find you. I just wanted to be with you. I never thought all this other stuff would happen.'

'When you go out at night in *this* town, stuff always happens.'

'It wasn't like this last year. Last spring. We hardly ever ran into trouble.'

'Well, it does get worse in October. Seems to. October's always the creepiest month.'

'April is the cruelest month; October's the creepiest? Maybe it's because of Hallowe'en.'

'The whole month's weird.' Casey smiled up at me. 'Course, I sort of like it that way.'

'I'm sure.'

'Keeps life interesting. So who were you roaming around with last spring?'

'This girl, Holly.' I felt no ache of loss or longing when I said her name. Maybe because I was saying it to Casey. 'We were out pretty late sometimes.'

'Holly last year, Eileen this year. You're a busy fellow.'

'She was the first girl I ever . . . really cared about.'

'You loved her.' She didn't ask, but stated it like a fact.

'What makes you think so?'

'I can just tell. The way your voice got funny when you started talking about her.'

'Anyway, she dumped me.'

We walked in silence for a while. Then Casey said, 'That wasn't very nice of her.'

'Well . . .'

She looked at me. 'I'll help you get her back.'

'What?'

'I'll help you get her back. Holly. I'm good at that sort of thing.' She cast a wry smile at me. 'It's what I do.'

'What's what you do?'

'It's one of my specialties. Fixing things up for people. Making things better. Maybe I can get you and Holly back together again.'

'She's in Washington.'

'That might complicate things.'

'Besides, I don't *want* her back. I want *Eileen* back. Not that I'm in love with Eileen.'

'You're not.'

'I just don't want her to get hurt.'

As we approached the next corner, I looked up at the street sign. The intersection was Beaumont and Division.

Division!

A block to the right on Division, headlights were coming our way.

'Ride or hide?' asked Casey.

It might've surprised me that someone would think of playing a game while Eileen urgently needed to be rescued – but this was Casey.

Hiding would delay our journey to Dandi Donuts.

'Ride,' I said.

Chapter Sixty-six

Casey and I stood side by side on the corner, holding hands as the headlights approached.

Soon, I could make out the shape of the vehicle. Not a pickup, not a van. Just an ordinary midsize automobile. As it came nearer to us, however, it began to slow down.

The corner had no stop sign.

Slowing because of us.

'Now what?' I muttered.

Casey gave my hand a squeeze. 'All part of the fun,' she said.

'Oh, yeah.'

She chuckled.

The car abruptly veered in our direction, crossed the center line and entered the lane beside us – meant for oncoming traffic.

'Do you know who it is?' I asked.

'I don't recognize the car.'

'Wonderful.'

The windshield must've been tinted. I could see nothing through it except the dim, vague shape of the driver.

'Be ready to run,' Casey said. 'Just in case.'

The car stopped by the curb. The driver's window, tinted like the windshield, showed little more than a reflection. But it slowly glided downward.

A familiar voice called out, 'I say, old bean, you do look a trifle the worse for wear. May I offer you a lift?'

'Kirkus?'

His face appeared in the open window. 'At your service, Eduardo. And *yours*, fair maiden. Rudolph Kirkus, here. My mates generally call me Kirkus. Or Captain Kirkus, if they're feeling droll.'

'I'm Casey,' she said.

'Casey, Casey. You must be the beckoning fair one who has stolen Eduardo's heart! And lovely you are. 'Tis no wonder he's mad for you.'

'What are you doing here?' I asked.

'Matters this night are passing strange.'

'I've noticed.'

'How's the old noggin?'

'Not great.'

'My vast apologies.'

'What do you want, Rudy?'

'Come with me.'

'We're in a hurry,' I said. 'We don't have time for any games.'

'I don't know what's going on,' he said, his phony voice gone so he sounded like an ordinary guy. 'But I need to show you something. Come on. Get in. Both of you. I'll take you there.'

I looked at Casey.

She nodded.

I hurried to the car's back door, pulled it open and climbed in. Casey came in after me and shut the door. Kirkus glanced over his shoulder at us, then faced forward again and started driving.

'I felt miserable after our . . . our little tiff earlier tonight. I'm so ashamed of myself.'

'No problem,' I said.

'Oh, it is a problem.' He seemed to be gradually regaining his usual Kirkus persona. 'I know it is. I was simply devastated after you left . . . after you *escaped* from my clutches, if you will. So I hurried on home to lick my wounds and . . . to make a long story short, I found myself possessed by an urge to apologize, to put matters right between us, if possible . . . and as soon as possible. You'd mentioned Dandi Donuts as your destination. Hoping to intercept you among the crullers, I borrowed a friend's car and drove to the donut shop. You weren't there, of course.'

'We were on our way just now.'

'Well, I arrived at the shop some time ago. Expecting you to appear at any moment, I sat myself down with a cup of tea and a croissant and waited. And I waited and I waited and I waited and still no Eduardo.'

'I had delays,' I said.

'So it would seem. Well, I could only wait there so long. People were giving me odd looks. Bizarre individuals were coming and going. It's really quite a dreadful place, you know.'

Looking out of the window, I saw that we were only about a block away from the donut shop. 'Is that where you're taking us?' I asked.

'More or less,' Kirkus said. 'You see, I finally quit my vigil. As I was walking back to my car, however, I came upon a most peculiar sight.'

'What was it?'

'See for yourself.' Slowing, he swung toward the curb. He drove close to it, moving past a lamppost and parking meters and the narrow dark gap into which I'd run to escape from Randy on Tuesday night.

Nearing the rear of a parked car, he stopped.

'Out,' he said. His door flew open and he leaped into the street.

I swung open the curbside door, stepped onto the sidewalk, then held the door while Casey emerged.

'Hurry, old man.'

When Casey was out, I shut the door. Then I took her by the arm and we turned toward Kirkus.

He stood facing the thrift shop's display window.

Gazing in.

Staring in at the old mannequins that had disturbed me so much in the past. Rhett and Scarlet, frozen in time. Always the same, almost, while always gradually deteriorating. Rhett with half his mustache gone. Scarlet standing beside him in her gawdy red dress looking less like Scarlet O'Hara than a flapper from the Roaring Twenties . . . more Zelda than Scarlet.

But tonight she didn't wear the fringed and glittery red dress.

She wore a clingy gown of emerald green. Its neckline plunged almost to her waist, revealing a long V of bare skin that narrowed on its way down. Her left leg showed through a slit up the skirt.

'That's not her normal dress,' Casey said.

'It's the same as Eileen's,' I muttered.

'It *is* Eileen's,' said Kirkus. 'It's identical.'

'There might be others . . .'

'Oh, puh-leease. This is not an identical dress; it's the very same gown that she was wearing at dinner tonight. And now it's adorning a store-window dummy. What, as they say, gives?'

I shook my head. I kept staring through the window, hardly able to believe what my eyes were showing me – and not *wanting* to believe what it seemed to mean.

'Ed?' Kirkus asked. 'Do you know something about this?'

Feeling dazed, I answered, 'I saw her. An hour . . . more than an hour ago. She had the dress on. Went by in a guy's pickup truck.'

'She got snatched,' Casey explained. And went around me and Kirkus and stepped into the entryway of the shop. A CLOSED sign was hanging inside the glass door.

Except for the lights of the display window, the shop was dark.

'What're you doing?' I asked.

She tried the door. 'Isn't locked,' she said. 'It's *always* locked at night.'

Kirkus glanced at me.

'She knows these things,' I explained.

Casey opened the door.

'What're you doing?' I asked.

'Going in.'

'No, wait.'

She waited, holding the door open, while I hurried over to her.

'You're *not* going inside,' Kirkus said.

Casey gripped my forearm. Speaking in a hushed voice, she said, 'This might be where he's got her. There's an apartment upstairs.'

'Do you know who lives in it?'

She shook her head. 'I haven't been up there in a long time. It's been a year, maybe longer. Nobody was living in it then. Looked like it was being used for storage. A lot of junk all over the place. But I don't know . . . people might've moved in since then.'

'Maybe Randy,' I said.

'Could be.'

'We're right next door to the donut shop.'

Casey nodded. 'Whether he moved in or not, he might have Eileen up there. It's just the sort of place you'd want to take someone if . . . you know . . . you wanted to mess around with her. We'd better go in and see.'

'Wait wait wait,' Kirkus said, coming closer to us. 'You can't simply sneak into a store in the middle of the night. It's a criminal offense.'

'Not if we're invited,' Casey told him.

Speaking as if he considered her mentally challenged, he said, 'If this chap *has* absconded with Eileen, he isn't likely to invite you inside.'

'Already has,' said Casey.

'An unlocked door hardly suffices as . . .'

'It isn't just the unlocked door. Why do you suppose he put Eileen's dress on the dummy?'

'Why, indeed?'

'*That's* the invitation. Addressed to us. To Ed, in particular.'

'Oh God,' I muttered. 'You're right.'

Casey gave a brisk nod. 'He wants us to go in and look for her.'

'All the more reason not to do it,' Kirkus said.

I scowled at him. 'What am I supposed to do? Just let him keep her and do whatever he wants with her?'

'Call the police.'

'No,' I said.

Kirkus bent close to me. Speaking quietly and fast, he said, 'It's what's *done* in such circumstances. One does not simply charge willy-nilly to the rescue. Not in real life, Eduardo. You're not Joe Hardy. You're hardly John Wayne. You'll be breaking the law if you go in there, *and* you might very well get yourself killed. *Especially* considering that Nancy Drew here is so certain the dress was put in the window to lure you in.'

'You don't have to come with us,' I said.

'That's not the point, dear fellow. The point is, *you* shouldn't go in. *Nobody* should go in. Let's find a telephone, instead, and ring up the authorities.'

'I'm going in,' Casey said. 'You coming, Ed?'

'Yeah.'

I followed her inside. Before shutting the door, I said to Kirkus, 'Coming?'

'I should say not.'

'The game's afoot, Watson.'

'Fuck you and the horse you rode in on, Sherlock.'

Almost smiling, I said, 'Well, you might want to ring up the authorities if we're not out in fifteen minutes.'

'And have them arrest you for breaking in?'

'Whatever.'

'Ed, don't be an imbecile.'

'Later,' I said.

Leaving him outside, I pulled the door shut.

Chapter Sixty-seven

We walked deeper into the thrift shop, leaving behind the glow of light from the display window. In the darkness in front of me, Casey halted and turned around. She put a hand on my arm and whispered, 'Shoes.'

We both removed our shoes. Then she put her hands on my shoulders and leaned close to me. 'You wait here,' she whispered. 'I'll go upstairs and . . .'

'Not without me.'

She squeezed my shoulders. 'I do this sort of thing all the time.'

'But if Randy's waiting for us . . .'

'He'll never know I'm there.'

Her statement seemed more like pride – or wishful thinking – than fact. 'I should go up with you,' I said.

'Better if you stay down here. I'll just go up and scout around, find out what's going on. Then I'll come back and we'll figure out what to do.'

'God, I wish I hadn't lost those guns.'

'I don't need a gun. I'll be fine. But you wait here. Promise?'

I hesitated.

'Promise,' she said.

'Okay. I promise.'

Leaning forward, she kissed me gently on the mouth. Then she whispered, 'See ya,' and slipped away from me. Standing motionless, I watched her glide away like a black shadow. She made no sound at all. In moments, she disappeared entirely.

Feeling sick inside, I turned around. Lights from the display window cast a yellow glow over the clutter of furniture and clothes racks between me and the front of the shop. I saw rocking chairs, piles of books and magazines on shelves and tables, dolls, old-fashioned kerosene lamps, statues, vases and all sorts of nicknacks. Hanging on the wall behind the cashier's counter were velvet paintings of Jesus and John F. Kennedy and Jerry Garcia, along with a stuffed 'jacka-lope,' the head of a deer, and a barn owl with a snake clutched in its beak. A variety of swords and spears were also mounted on the wall.

While making my way toward the counter, I looked out the display window. The mannequins and some other items blocked only a small part of my view.

Kirkus seemed to be gone, but his car was still parked at the curb. Maybe he'd decided to wait for us in the donut shop.

Or had he gone off to phone the police?

No, I thought. Whatever else is going on with Kirkus, he won't do anything that might get me arrested.

I stepped quietly around one end of the counter, reached high up the wall with both hands and lifted a katana off its hooks. Silently, I drew the Samurai sword out of its sheath. I set the sheath on the counter, then carried my new weapon toward the rear of the store.

Halting in the darkness, I listened for Casey.

What's taking her so long?

I stood motionless and barely breathed.

Sounds seemed to be coming from all around me. Quiet sounds. The ticking of clocks. The soft hums, perhaps, of various electrical appliances. Along with barely perceptible sounds I couldn't recognize – perhaps old things slowly drying up, coming apart a little bit at a time: threads of old coats popping, book paste cracking, maybe the stuffed head of the deer decomposing ever so slightly, the shop itself creaking as its boards aged and loosened.

For the first time, I noticed the aroma of the place. It smelled of old clothes and older books. And stale cigarette smoke. And pine-scented floor wax and dust. I caught whiffs of cloying sweetness, too.

Underlying all the other odors seemed to be a sour fragrance of sweat and urine.

I should sneak upstairs and find Casey, I thought.

No. I can't go back on my word.

What if Randy got her?

I could at least look for the stairway. That wouldn't be breaking my promise, would it?

Holding the katana with both hands and upright in front of my shoulder – rather like a batter with my Louisville Slugger, relaxing a bit before the next pitch – I walked slowly toward the back of the shop.

I was making my way through almost total darkness when someone touched my chest. It surprised me, but didn't frighten me. I knew who it had to be. 'Eddie,' she whispered.

'Yeah.'

'I found her. She's upstairs.'

'Is she okay?'

'You'd better come up and see.'

'She isn't dead, is she?'

'No.'

'What about Randy?'

'I looked around the best I could without showing myself. If he's up there, I didn't see him. Maybe he's gone. I don't know.' She patted my chest. 'Come on, and bring the sword.'

'You can see it?'

'You're backlit.'

'Oh.'

'Can you hold it with one hand?'

'Sure.'

'Then give me your other.'

I gripped the sword with my right hand and reached out into the darkness with my left. Casey took hold of it. She gave it a squeeze. 'Ready?'

'Yeah.'

She led me forward. We walked slowly through the darkness, taking a route with so many turns I quickly lost track of our direction.

385

It's like a maze in here, I thought.

No wonder Casey had been gone so long.

Though I held her hand in mine, I couldn't see her in front of me. *Why aren't we crashing into things?*

She must have spectacular night vision, I thought. Probably comes from spending her nights sneaking around in people's dark houses.

Every so often, a floorboard creaked. Otherwise, we moved in complete silence.

'Stairs,' she whispered.

We began to climb a steep, narrow stairway. It had a banister on the right side. I couldn't hold on to the banister, but my hip kept bumping against it. Sometimes, my left shoulder nudged the other side of the staircase. We were surrounded by utter silence, utter darkness. The air itself seemed heavy and hot and black.

At a landing, we turned a corner and light appeared above us. A murky, shimmering, ruddy glow in the shape of a rectangle – a doorway?

Casey blocked much of the glow as she climbed toward it. Near the top, she released my hand. Crouching lower and lower, she climbed the final stairs. Then she crept through the doorway, crawled to the left and stopped when only her bare feet were still in sight.

I moved up silently. Squatting, I looked through the doorway. The staircase apparently opened into the corner nook of a room. I could see little more than three poorly lit walls and Casey, on her hands and knees, peering around the corner.

I set the sword down silently on the floor between us, then crawled forward, staying so close to Casey that I brushed against her side.

Just when I realized her head might be in the way of my view, she eased herself down flat against the floor.

I peered around the corner.

The only light seemed to come from burning candles. I could see plenty of them, but had no doubt there must be others out of sight. They filled the room with a golden, trembling glow, shadows that shifted and writhed, and scattered swaths of darkness.

Even in good light, I probably couldn't have seen much of the room; the clutter got in the way. It was like looking into a dense forest of statues, chairs, coat racks, tables, mirrors, figurines, lamps, chests of drawers, storage cartons, vases, mannequins and a thousand other things.

Someone, however, had cleared a wide pathway through the junk.

The pathway led straight to Eileen.

She stood near the middle of the room, about twenty feet in front of us, facing our way, naked, surrounded by a couple of dozen burning candles. Her arms were stretched out to either side, elevated slightly higher than her shoulders and secured by handcuffs to a couple of thick upright posts that were just beyond her reach. She was neither blindfolded nor gagged. Her feet weren't tied at all. She stood on them. Though her head was drooping so she couldn't see us for the moment, she seemed to be conscious, standing upright rather than hanging by her wrists.

Her wet skin gleamed in the candlelight. Most of her scrapes and scratches and bruises looked like those she'd sustained Wednesday night when we were attacked under the bridge. I saw no fresh blood, but she had ruddy areas on her breasts and belly and thighs that looked recent.

'Eileen?' I called.

As Eileen raised her head, Casey squirmed backward to get out of sight.

'It's me,' I said.

Eileen started to weep.

'Are you okay?' I asked. Dumb question.

'Not really.'

'Where is he?'

'I . . . I don't know.'

'Is he up here somewhere?'

'I think so. I'm not sure. I think he's . . . hiding someplace.'

'*You bet I am, pal.*' Randy's voice came from somewhere deep in the room, somewhere in the region near Eileen.

Chapter Sixty-eight

'I'm glad you found us,' he said. 'I was hoping you would. It took you a while, though. I'm afraid we had to go ahead and start without you.'

'What do you want?' I asked.

'I've already got *half* of what I want. The other half's you.'

'Okay, I'm here.'

'Did you come alone?'

'Yeah.'

I glimpsed a flick of movement. Crying out, Eileen flinched and twisted and jerked her knee up, losing her balance. She would've fallen if not for the handcuffs securing her to the posts. As she stood there on one foot, I saw she had a dart in her leg. A small, feathered dart – the sort they use in pubs – was sticking out from the side of her left thigh.

'Hey!' I yelled.

'You told me a fib. You're quite the liar, Ed. I learned, among other things, that your lady friend's name is not Sarah LaFarge. Is it, dear?'

'No,' Eileen said, her voice high and trembly. A thin line of blood was now dribbling down her leg from the dart wound.

'And she does indeed put out for you. She puts out for me, too. Don't you, Eileen?'

'Yes.'

'And now, Ed, you're telling me that you came here alone when I happen to know otherwise. Tell me about your friends.'

Friends. Plural. It wasn't simply that he'd spotted Casey when she came up to scout around. He must've seen us arrive in the car.

'Casey and Kirkus,' I said.

'Which one's the fag?'

'Kirkus.'

'That would make the other one Casey. Looked like a real honey, what I saw of her.'

Casey, still by my side but farther back than before, pushed herself silently to her hands and knees.

'I'd like to see the rest of her. I wanta see the fag, too. Fact is, how about all three of you stepping out where I can get a good look at you?'

'They aren't here.'

Another dart flew out of the shadows and hit Eileen. This one stuck in her ribcage just below her left breast. She flinched and squealed and went up on her tiptoes, twisting, jerking at the cuffs.

'Stop that!' I yelled.

'You lied.'

'I did not! Kirkus . . . he didn't come in with us. He was scared. I don't know where he went, but he stayed outside.'

'And what about Casey?'

'She's downstairs. She never came up. She's my lookout. She's supposed to warn me if anyone shows up. Cops or something.'

No more darts flew out at Eileen. Not for the moment, anyway.

'You'd better be telling the truth,' Randy said.

From the direction of his voice and the darts, he was apparently somewhere to Eileen's left and slightly in front of her. So much junk stood between us, however, that I couldn't see him. Nor did I stand any chance of reaching him quickly.

'I'm telling the truth,' I said.

'You'd better be.'

'I am.'

'If there are any untoward developments . . . the unexpected arrival of your fairy friend, for instance . . . or the cops . . . Eileen's situation will deteriorate rapidly. Do you see how I have her cuffed?'

Two sets of handcuffs. One bracelet of each encircled each of Eileen's wrists. At the end of their short chains, the other two bracelets were fastened to thick steel rings that seemed to be bolted into the posts on each side of Eileen, slightly higher than her head.

'Setting her free won't be fast and easy, will it?'

He was right about that. I answered, 'No.'

'And do you see the candles surrounding her?'

The candles that I could see formed a rough circle around her feet. They were close enough that she could kick them over if she tried . . . or by accident. Each slender candle, standing by itself in a small holder, was eight to ten inches tall.

'I see them,' I said.

'Easily tipped over, don't you think?'

'Yeah.'

'Now note what I've put under them.'

Spread out beneath the candle holders – and Eileen's feet – was what looked like an old-fashioned patchwork quilt.

'A quilt,' I said.

'Yes it is, Ed. And I took the trouble of dousing the quilt with lamp oil.'

'Lamp oil?'

'An odorless petroleum product. We sell it in the shop to go with various kerosene lamps. It's highly flammable. If just one candle should happen to fall over . . . *whoof!* Poor Eileen.'

'You're up here, too,' I said. 'I'm between you and the stairs.'

'I have other ways out, stupid. Eileen, however . . . she'll have only *one* way out if a fire starts . . . *up in smoke!*' As if surprised by his own wit, he laughed. Then he muttered, 'Good one.'

In my mind, I saw flames erupting around Eileen. I saw a sudden look of horror in her eyes. I watched her writhe in agony and struggle against the handcuffs. I heard her screams. I saw her hair catch fire. I watched her skin blister and crack, heard it sizzle.

'Just tell me what you want,' I said. 'Okay? Just tell me, and I'll do it.'

'First, no surprises. Complete cooperation from you and your friends.'

'I don't know where Kirkus is.'

'Just so he doesn't interfere.'

'If he tries to interfere,' I said, 'I'll take care of him. Just don't go starting any fires, okay?'

'We'll see. Now, you told me that the girl is keeping lookout downstairs. Casey?'

'Yeah.'

'Go down and get her. Bring her up here.'

'What for?'

Another dart hit Eileen. The point of this one sank into the side of her left breast. She cried out, '*Ah!*' and thrashed with the sudden pain, her breasts swinging and leaping. The rough motion only went on for a few seconds. When she settled down, the dart was still in her breast but it dangled as if almost ready to let go.

Sounding patient and slightly amused, Randy said, 'Go downstairs and get Casey. Bring her up here. We'll be waiting. Won't we, Eileen?'

Sobbing, Eileen blurted out, 'Yes.'

'Okay,' I said. 'I'll do it. Might take a few minutes.'

'Remember, no surprises.'

'I know.' I crawled backward.

Casey, already on her feet, pulled my arm and helped me stand up. As I turned toward her, she touched a finger to her lips. Then she moved ahead of me through the doorway. I followed her.

Making no sound that I could hear, she vanished down the dark stairs. I went down after her, one hand on the railing.

At the bottom, I felt a tug on the front of my shirt. Casey pulled me along behind her on a twisting route toward the front of the store. When we reached the glow from the display-window lights, she stopped and faced me.

'What was he doing to her?' she asked.

Staying out of sight, Casey hadn't been able to watch.

'He threw darts at her. He got her three times.'

'Oooo.'

'Maybe you'd better get out of here,' I said.

She wrapped her arms around me and hugged me tightly. I stroked

391

her hair. It was damp, and so was the nape of her neck. 'I don't think so,' she whispered.

'I can't have you getting hurt.'

'Eileen's up there because of us,' she whispered.

'It's not your fault,' I said.

'Sure it is. You weren't with her tonight because of me. Anyway, it doesn't matter whose fault anything is. What matters is, we have to save her.'

'I don't know how.'

'A good fire extinguisher might help. There *must* be one. They're required, a place like this.'

'Are you sure?'

'I'm the house inspector, remember?'

'Oh, yeah.'

'Store inspector, too. You can't have a store without a fire extinguisher.'

'I don't know how we'd find it in time,' I said. 'And there might not be one, anyway. Even if this place *had* one, I don't think Randy did all this on the spur of the moment tonight *after* he grabbed Eileen. He probably got most of it ready in advance. And I bet he didn't leave any fire extinguishers lying around.'

'Maybe he took one up with him,' Casey said, 'just in case.'

'Maybe.'

She let go of me and stepped away. 'We'd better get back up there.'

'Not you.'

'Yes, me.'

'Casey . . .'

'Don't worry.'

'Don't *worry*?'

'I can take care of myself.'

'Famous last words.'

'Been doing it for eighteen years and I'm still here. Still hail and hearty – mostly.'

'Jesus, Casey.'

'Let's go.'

I reached out to grab her, but my hand found empty darkness. I tried to go after her, but bumped into something that fell with a clatter. When that happened, I remembered the flashlight in my pocket. I pulled it out, twisted its front, and a narrow beam of brightness reached out.

I couldn't find Casey with it, though.

Chapter Sixty-nine

With the flashlight to show me the way, I hurried through the labyrinth of the thrift shop, found my way to the rear, discovered the staircase and started to climb. At the landing, I saw Casey in the shimmery glow of the upstairs doorway. She stood there, apparently looking down at me. I pocketed my flashlight and climbed toward her, but she backed away.

'Wait,' I whispered.

Before I could reach the top, she turned her back to me and stepped around the corner. 'Here I am,' she said, her words loud and meant for Randy.

The katana was still on the floor where I'd left it. I walked past it, went to Casey and stopped by her side.

Straight ahead of us was Eileen. While we'd been downstairs, the dart in her breast must've fallen out. It lay on the quilt by her left foot. The other two darts were still embedded in her. She looked much the same as before. A little bloodier, though. And she had probably been crying the entire time we were gone. Her eyes were red, her face shiny with tears, her nose running. She sniffed and blinked as she stared at us. Then she shook her head slightly, but I'm not sure what she meant by it.

'How are you doing?' I asked.

A corner of her mouth twitched as if she were trying to smile. 'Been better,' she said. Her tongue came out and licked at the mucous dribbling toward her upper lip.

'I'm sorry about all this,' I told her.

'Thanks for . . . trying to help.' She looked at Casey. 'You, too. Thanks.'

'We'll get you out of here,' Casey said.

'Bravado from the cutie!' Randy's cheerful voice came from somewhere beyond Eileen's right side. While we'd been downstairs, he had moved. 'And what a cutie you *are*! No wonder Ed dumped Eileen for you.'

'Nobody dumped anyone,' I said.

'Casey, let's see what *you* look like without your clothes on.'

The request didn't surprise me much. Something like this was to be expected, considering Randy's treatment of Eileen. But it made me go cold inside.

Casey, staring in the direction of the voice, was frowning slightly and breathing hard.

'You don't have to,' I whispered. 'Just go. Run. Get outa here.'

In a loud voice, she said, 'No problem.' Then she started to unbutton her shirt.

'I'm all eyes,' said Randy. 'Are *you* all eyes, Ed?'

'Go to hell,' I said.

My words bought Eileen a dart. It stuck in her right side, just below the armpit. She yelped and jerked.

I shouted, 'No!'

She shouted, '*Fuck!*'

'I'm *sorry*!' I blurted at her.

She cried out, 'Don't piss him *off*!' Then she broke down sobbing.

'Okay,' Casey called out, and dropped her shirt to the floor. She didn't have a bra on. Making no attempt to cover herself, she stood there with her arms down. Beside and slightly behind her, I couldn't see her front. But Randy probably could.

'*Very* nice,' he said.

The tops of her shoulders were golden in the candlelight. Her bare back was in shadow. She didn't have a belt on. Her tan corduroy trousers were low around her hips.

'Now let's see you feel yourself,' Randy said. 'We'll pretend your hands are mine. Do something nice with them.'

She nodded slightly. I saw her right arm bend at the elbow. From elbow to hand, it disappeared in front of her. Disappeared from my view, though certainly not from Randy's.

Her upper arm and shoulders moved. Though I couldn't see for myself, I knew she must be using both hands to fondle her breasts. She was squirming slightly, almost as if she enjoyed it.

'You don't wanta be missing this, Ed. Get around in front of her and watch.'

I didn't want to. I knew it would be wrong to observe Casey as she debased herself for Randy's enjoyment. Besides, if I moved to the front of Casey, she would be able to see that I was erect.

But if I don't do it, I thought, he'll get Eileen with another dart.

Before I could move, Casey turned around and faced me. She met my eyes. Then her tongue slid across her lips and I looked down at her hands. They were cupping the undersides of her breasts, her thumbs rubbing her nipples.

'You've got yourself a hot one, Ed.'

Casey slid her right hand down her belly, pushed it under the waistband of her corduroys and it went lower until her hand was gone to the wrist. It moved around down there, disturbing the front of her pants with fingers and knuckles. Her other hand pulled at the nipple of her left breast. She stared at me, her eyes half shut, and slowly squirmed.

'Girl,' called Randy, 'take those pants off.'

She pulled her hand out. With shiny wet fingers, she unfastened the button at her waist. Then she drew the zipper down. Bending at the waist, she lowered the corduroys to her ankles.

She remained bent over.

'Casey?' Randy asked.

She straightened up and looked in the direction of his voice. Her corduroys were piled around her feet. She still wore a pair of powder-blue panties. Down low at the crotch, they were soaked and clinging to her.

'Very good,' Randy said. 'This is going just fine. You're really a great looking kid, Casey.'

'Thanks.'

'Don't you think so, Ed?'

My throat was tight and dry, but I said, 'Yeah.'

'Now it's your turn.'

'Me?'

'Off with the clothes, pal.'

'What . . .?'

'*For godsake do it!*' Eileen snapped.

Casey nodded at me and said softly, 'Go ahead.'

'Then we'll *all* be naked and happy,' Randy called out in a cheery sing-song.

Casey turned her head. 'Should I help him, Randy? It'll speed things up.'

'Sure. Why not. No tricks, though. We wouldn't want anything to get in the way of our wonderful time and turn it ugly, would we?'

'No, we wouldn't,' said Casey.

She stepped up to me, actually smiled, then sank to her knees. Facing the bulge in my pants, she said. 'You get your shirt off, I'll take care of the rest.'

While I worked at the buttons of my shirt, Casey unbuckled my belt, opened the waist of my jeans and slid the zipper down.

It seemed impossible that such things could be happening. Such wonderful things, such awful things. I felt as if I were caught between the horrors of a nightmare and the astounding lust of a wet dream.

As Eileen watched, I took my shirt off.

Casey slid my jeans and underwear down my legs.

Unconfined, I relished the feel of air against my rigid tightness. And felt a mixture of shame and delight at having Casey's face inches away.

'Wow,' she said.

'Wow what?' Randy asked.

'It's a beauty.'

'Oh?'

'You wouldn't believe the size of this thing.'

'You sound as if you've never seen it before.'

'I haven't.' Tilting back her head, Casey smiled up at me. She slid a finger up the underside of my penis, and I shuddered.

'Don't tell me he's never fucked you.'

'Never,' Casey said. 'Not yet.' Leaning forward, she opened her mouth. I felt her moist lips.

Eileen stared at us, blinking rapidly. Even though Casey's head was in the way, she must've had a pretty good idea what was going on.

We're doing it to save you, I told her in my mind. *It doesn't have to mean anything.*

But it does, I thought. Oh, it does.

Casey's lips glided, slippery, down my flesh as she sucked me deep into her mouth.

'What's going on there?' Randy asked. He sounded a little worried.

'She's, uh . . . she's . . .'

'*Is that little scamp giving you head?*'

'Uh.'

I was about to explode into her mouth, but suddenly it slid away with a quiet slurpy sound. She again smiled up at me for a moment before dropping gracefully backward and catching herself with stiff arms.

Only her hands and feet touching the floor, her knees wide apart, she scuttled away from me, silently moving head first toward Eileen.

What's she . . .?

I suddenly understood.

When Casey had bent over to pull down her corduroys, Randy had called out her name – because he'd no longer been able to see her.

After she'd stood up again, Randy hadn't ordered her to remove her panties. He'd assumed she was naked.

He hadn't been able to see my erection, or even Casey's head as she sucked me.

He can't see that low!

Based on that conclusion, Casey was now off to the rescue.

And it was my job to play along.

I watched how her breasts jiggled and wobbled. I watched the shiny dark crotch of her panties.

Moaning, I writhed and reached down as if stroking her head, as if she were still kneeling in front of me, sucking.

Eileen watched both of us, a strange look on her face.

I gasped, '*Uh! Uh! Yes!*'

Randy called out, '*Whooeee, go for it!*'

I grunted and squirmed.

'*Suck him, honey! Suck him good 'n' get ready for me!*'

Though half dazed with lust and hope, I suddenly realized that Randy's voice had come from a different location.

Somewhere nearer than before.

Chapter Seventy

I continued my mime, acting as if Casey were still on her knees in front of me even as I watched her scurrying closer and closer to Eileen.

At the edge of the quilt, she stopped the strange crab-walk, lowered herself to the floor and rolled over. She squirmed onto the quilt on her belly like a soldier going under barbed wire.

Braced up on her left elbow, she reached forward with her right arm and pinched the wick of the nearest candle. The flame died between her thumb and forefinger.

'*Oh, cute.*'

Randy's voice. Behind me. I whirled around. The aisle of cleared floor between me and the corner was empty at first. Then Randy leaped out from the side. He slid on his bare feet, stopped himself and turned toward me. He wore a bandage on his right thigh where I'd stabbed him with the pen on Tuesday night. Otherwise, he wore nothing.

Naked and happy.

He was aroused, smiling and holding a pistol in his right hand.

Eileen shouted, '*Watch out!*'

He raised the pistol. It looked like a small semi-automatic. 'Outa the way,' he told me. 'Move!'

Straightening up, I glanced over my shoulder. Casey was still on her belly, busy snuffing candles. Many were already out, but others still burned. Down like that, she would be a hard target. But Eileen would be easy, upright and shackled between the two posts.

I faced Randy and spread my arms like a basketball player trying to block a shot.

Still smiling, he said, 'Dumb fuck,' and shot me.

The noise was a quick, flat bang. A .22? The pain was a sting on the right side of my ribcage.

I ran at him.

Through the ringing in my ears, I heard him say, 'All right.' He aimed at my face as I rushed him, then smirked and lowered the pistol and shot me in the thigh. My leg went out from under me. I slammed against the floor in front of him. Then he fired twice more, but nothing else hit me.

Somewhere behind me, a girl cried out in pain.

Randy laughed. 'There,' he said.

Eileen cried out, '*You fucking bastard!*'

'You should thank me,' he said. 'She was your competition, stupid.'

I lurched forward and tried to grab Randy's feet, but he easily stepped out of the way. 'You want me, Ed?' he asked. 'The feeling's mutual.' Suddenly, he leaped past me. Crouching over me, he pulled at my arms, turned me, rolled me onto my back. He no longer held the pistol. I wondered where it was.

Then he was kneeling above me, stretching my arms out, pinning me to the floor. 'Gonna give you the works, Eddie boy. Just like I promised.' He lowered himself on to me. I felt his erection against my belly, his mouth on my mouth, his tongue pushing in.

Suddenly, he pushed himself up. Braced above me on his hands and knees, he said, 'We'll have us a real good time. But first things first. Gotta get me a taste of the honey while she's still fresh.'

Casey.

'No,' I said.

'Don't worry, I'll be back.'

Then he stuck his forefinger into the hole in my thigh. Pain blasted through me. I must've blacked out, but not for long.

I returned to consciousness with Eileen's voice ripping through my head. '*Let go of her you fucking bastard! Leave her alone! Don't! Stop that!*'

401

I sat up and saw Randy staggering backward, dragging Casey by her ankles. Apparently, he wanted her clear of the fuel-soaked quilt before having his fun with her.

She'd done a good job, but several candles still burned.

Eileen, sobbing and grunting, thrashed between the posts like some sort of female Samson trying to stop the horror by bringing down the building. But the posts held firm. So did the handcuffs.

Though pain soared through my body, I struggled to my knees. I tried to stand up, but my leg wouldn't let me. So I crawled.

I crawled toward them as Randy, with his back to me, dropped to his knees between Casey's legs and tore off her panties. Crawled toward them as Eileen bucked and thrashed between the posts, specks of sweat flying off her hair and off her gleaming skin, three darts still protruding from her body.

'*I'll kill you, Randy!*' she cried out. '*Leave her alone or I'll kill you!*'

He didn't leave her alone.

I crawled as fast as I could. I tried to stand up, but I fell. Disturbed by the sound, Randy looked over his shoulder. Seeing me down, he laughed. 'Gee, guy, I don't think you're gonna save the day after all.'

Then he turned his head away and sank down on top of Casey.

I shouted, '*NO!*'

Eileen cried out, '*Don't!*'

Randy's white ass flexed as he thrust. Each time he pounded into her, Casey's small, bare feet jerked slightly.

Then I heard quick, soft thumping sounds and felt the floor shaking under my body and wondered what was going on. Eileen stopped moving. Randy stopped thrusting. Pushing at the floor, he arched his back and looked over his shoulder.

This time he didn't laugh.

Someone leaped over me.

Ran straight at Randy.

My view was partly blocked by the tall, running man, but I saw plenty.

Saw that the running man was Kirkus. Saw Randy try to climb off

Casey. Saw Kirkus swing the katana. Saw Randy raise an arm to block it and saw his upraised hand leap off and fly into the clutter, spraying blood, waving goodbye to us all.

Chapter Seventy-one

Kirkus, as if shocked and exhausted by what he'd done, lowered the sword.

Eileen swayed on her feet, panting for breath.

Randy, on his knees between Casey's legs, held up the spurting stump of his arm and cried out, '*I need help! Somebody help! Call an ambulance!*'

'Fuck you,' gasped Eileen.

Groaning, I pushed myself up to my hands and knees.

And saw one of Casey's small, bare feet lift off the floor. Her knee came up. Then her leg swung out of sight in front of Randy.

He said, 'What . . .?'

Then he was hurtled backward. He landed back-first on the floor not far in front of me. His head thudded. As he lay there squirming and groaning, Casey stood up. She was splattered with blood, some of it probably Randy's, but it must've been blood of her own dribbling down her inner thighs.

Head down, she hobbled over to Kirkus.

'Mind if I borrow this?' she asked, her voice low and husky.

He gave it to her.

Randy squealed, '*You're dead! I shot you!*'

'Yeah, right,' she said.

She stood over him.

'*NO!*' Up on his elbows, he tried to scoot away from her.

I planted my right foot against the top of his head, stopping his retreat.

Somehow, even after getting his hand lopped off, he still had an erection. At least until Casey swung the sword.

Randy shrieked.

Then he passed out, and the silence seemed strange.

Kirkus, Eileen and I all stared at Casey as she walked toward Eileen. Her back, dusky with shadows, seemed free of blood or wounds of any kind.

'I thought he shot you,' I told her, my voice shaking.

She didn't look at me, but said, 'He missed.' Then she halted in front of Eileen, reared back with the sword and swung it with both hands. The blade chopped through the handcuff chain and thudded into the post. Eileen's left arm dropped to her side.

As she swayed on her feet, right arm still raised and cuffed, Kirkus went to her.

'Watch out for the candles,' I warned him. 'The quilt's soaked with oil.'

All he said was, 'Okay.' Then he pulled the darts out of Eileen's body. Each time, she flinched and winced.

After letting the darts fall to the quilt, Kirkus wrapped his arms around her. Then Casey chopped through the chain of the other cuffs. Eileen's right arm fell. She sagged, but Kirkus held her up. Clinging to each other, they staggered off the quilt. Kirkus eased Eileen down to the floor.

Casey had already put the sword down. She was crawling on her hands and knees, puffing out candles. As she did so, the room slowly darkened.

Kirkus came over to me. 'How's the leg?' he asked.

'Shot.'

'I heard the gunfire,' he said.

'That why you came up?'

'Let's say it hastened my decision.'

'Glad you came along,' I told him. 'Thanks.'

'The least I could do, old chap. Looks as if I arrived slightly later, however, than the proverbial "nick of time".'

'You did pretty good, Rudy.'

He crouched beside me and explored my bare thigh with both his hands. A couple of times, one of his hands brushed against my genitals. Accidentally, I'm sure.

'I can't seem to find an exit wound,' he said.

'The bullet's probably in my bone.'

'In your bone,' he said, and I half expected a quip. He didn't come out with one, though. Instead, he took a folded handkerchief out of his pocket. 'Don't worry, it's clean.' He pressed it against the hole in my thigh. 'Hold it there,' he said. 'I'll wrap my belt—'

'Help,' Randy murmured. 'Help me. Please.'

In the dimming light, I saw him raise his head.

'Not dead yet?' Kirkus asked. 'Give it time.'

'Please,' Randy murmured again.

'I'll help him,' Casey offered.

She came hobbling toward us, a lighted candle in each hand. Behind her, the room was in darkness. These were apparently the last two burning candles.

Naked and bloody in the glow of the candles she carried, Casey looked like a teenaged savage girl playing her part in some sort of pagan ritual.

She stopped beside Randy and looked down at him.

'We'd better stop the bleeding,' she said, her voice soft and husky.

'Let him die,' Eileen said.

'I concur,' said Kirkus.

'I have to do what I can,' Casey said. She sank to her knees, next to Randy's bleeding wrist but not very far from me. In the fluttery light, I saw semen trickling down through the blood on her thighs. 'These wounds need to be cauterized,' she said. 'Let's see if candles will do the trick.'

A soft chuckle came from Eileen.

'I say,' said Kirkus.

Then came the screams from Randy. And the stench.

Chapter Seventy-two

Later, we lit more candles. We were careful to keep them away from the quilt.

Kirkus used his belt to secure the handkerchief over my wound. I didn't complain about the way he sometimes just happened to touch me; after all, he'd saved our bacon.

While Casey and I put on our clothes, Kirkus ran downstairs. He returned a few minutes later with Eileen's gown. A while after that, the three of us were dressed and ready to go.

I put Randy's pistol in my pocket, figuring I would probably tell the authorities (doctors are required to report gunshot wounds) that it was my own weapon and I'd shot myself in the leg by accident. This might work, at least if the gouge across my side from Randy's first bullet went undetected – somewhat more difficult to explain away *two* gunshot wounds.

'I guess that's about it,' I said.

'What'll we do about all this?' Eileen asked. 'The crime scene?'

'We simply tell the truth,' Kirkus pointed out. 'Eileen was kidnapped and brutalized by this horrid man and we came to the rescue. *Voilà*. It was all quite justifiable.'

'Only one problem with that,' Casey said.

'And that is?'

'No way in hell,' she said. 'You try bringing the cops into this, I'm gone. They're not gonna find out what happened to me tonight. Or what I did to *him*. Or who I am. Or *anything*.'

'I'm with Casey,' Eileen said. 'Even if I thought she was wrong, I'd be with her. She almost got killed for me. But this bastard . . . the things he did to us . . . I don't want to be telling cops about it or have it show up in the news and be all over campus.'

'I'm not exactly eager, myself,' said Kirkus. 'After all, I'm the chap who lopped off his hand.'

'For which I'm forever grateful,' I told him.

'Same here,' said Eileen.

'You bet,' said Casey.

'Thank you,' Kirkus said, and I heard a choke in his voice. 'Sorry I wasn't in time to stop him from . . . violating you.'

'You saved my life,' she said. Then she handed her candles to me and hugged Kirkus and kissed him.

When she stopped, he said, 'I say. Glad I could help.'

After that, we stood around in the candlelight, silent for a while, looking down at Randy.

Eileen broke the silence. 'We've got to do something about him . . . about all this. We can't just walk away. Must be all kinds of evidence they'd be able to use against us.'

'We might torch the place,' Kirkus suggested.

'No,' Casey said. 'Even if Randy did work here, I'm pretty sure someone else owns the shop. Besides, a fire might spread to other stores . . .'

'Wouldn't wanta burn down Dandi Donuts,' Eileen said. I couldn't tell whether she meant it sarcastically.

'And somebody might get hurt if we start a fire,' Casey added. 'A fireman or an innocent bystander.'

'We have to do something,' I said. 'We've *all* bled up here.'

'Not me,' said Kirkus.

'Your fingerprints are on the sword,' I pointed out.

'Won't be,' he said, and wandered off with a candle.

'What we need to do,' Casey said, 'is get Randy out of here. Take him out to the car. Clutter this room up so it looks pretty much like normal, then drop Randy off somewhere.'

'Like at a hospital?' Eileen asked. Again, I wasn't sure whether she was being sarcastic.

Casey said, 'That's not exactly what I have in mind.'

Chapter Seventy-three

Because of my leg wound, I missed out on the cleanup and heavy lifting.

Kirkus helped me downstairs and out to the car. I sat in the back seat and waited, once in a while ducking out of sight when a car or pedestrian came along.

After about half an hour, the shop's front door opened and Casey came out. She looked around, then walked over to the car and opened its trunk.

Out of the shop rushed Kirkus carrying a big, rolled rug over his shoulder.

Nice touch, I thought.

Eileen came out after Kirkus. She had a large coil of rope hanging from her shoulder.

When Kirkus flung the rug into the trunk, the whole car shook.

Eileen sat up front with Kirkus. Casey sat in back with me.

As Kirkus swung away from the curb, Casey squeezed my hand. 'How are you doing?' she asked.

'Not bad. How about you?'

'I think everything'll be all right.'

I squeezed her hand and said, 'Hey, Rudy, who you got in the rug?'

'Not Cleopatra.'

'I thought not,' I said.

Kirkus stopped his car halfway across the Fairmont Street bridge – the same bridge where he had almost jumped/fallen and I'd saved him and smacked my head on the street.

We all climbed out, even me. With Casey and Eileen holding me up, I made it to the parapet. I leaned against it and they let go of me.

They all hurried over to the trunk of Kirkus's car.

I kept watch. So far, no traffic was approaching from either direction. I saw no people, either, except my friends.

The rug stayed in the trunk.

Randy didn't.

Nobody had bothered to put clothes on him. But his thigh was still bandaged and there were white rags tied around both his stumps like two peculiar, blood-stained flags of surrender.

Kirkus wrapped one end of the rope around Randy's waist and knotted it. Then all three picked him up.

Randy regained consciousness while they were hauling him over to the parapet. He started whimpering and mumbling.

'What's . . . going on?' he asked.

Nobody answered him.

'I need help,' he said.

No response.

'Where are we?' he asked.

They put him over the low concrete wall of the bridge.

'*No!*' he squealed. '*What're you doing?*'

My leg had been shot, but there was nothing much wrong with my arms. I took hold of the rope, along with Kirkus and Eileen and Casey, and helped to lower Randy slowly toward the Old Mill Stream.

'*Hey, no!*' he cried out. '*What're you doing?*'

We lowered him slowly. He squirmed and bucked on the rope. It felt like having a very large fish on the line.

Near the top, the structure of the bridge held him fairly steady. Lower, clear of the bridge, he began to spin and swing.

'*What're you doing!*' he called out again.

'This seems about right,' Kirkus said.

The glow of the bridge's single functioning lamp didn't reach down far enough to light Randy. Peering over the parapet, however, I was able to see him in the moonlight – hovering four or five feet above the surface of the stream. 'Looks good to me,' I said.

We tied off our end of the rope to the base of the nearest lamp-post.

Still, no traffic was in sight.

We all leaned over the parapet and looked down. Randy was slowly swinging and twirling above the water.

'What if nobody's down there?' Eileen asked.

'It'll be fine,' said Casey.

A couple of dim shapes waded slowly out from under the bridge.

'See?' said Casey.

'Dear God,' Kirkus muttered.

Randy didn't seem to be aware, yet, of the approaching trolls.

'Let's get out of here,' I said.

The girls were helping me back to Kirkus's car when Randy's very frightened voice said, 'Hey, who're you? What're you guys—'

Then Randy let out a scream I'll never forget.

We all looked at each other. I had goosebumps. I wouldn't be surprised if they did, too.

Eileen muttered, 'Holy shit.'

The next day, while I stayed in bed, Kirkus drove over to the bridge. He came back and reported that even the rope was gone.

Chapter Seventy-four

It wasn't my own bed, by the way.

After disposing of Randy, we had a discussion about where to go and Casey suggested Lois's house. 'She's probably home by now. She'll take care of us.'

By the time we reached her house, Lois had been home for more than an hour. She seemed overjoyed to see us . . . though upset by our condition.

As it turned out, I didn't need any excuses for my gunshot wounds. Around dawn, Casey showed up in the bedroom with a doctor. He was one of her special friends, one of those souls she'd drawn to her during the night roaming. A friendly, elderly man, he removed the bullet from my leg and patched me up. He also bandaged Eileen's dart wounds. He injected both of us with tetanus boosters and gave us antibiotics.

I missed a week of classes because of my leg wound, but Eileen and Kirkus continued on as if nothing had happened, and kept me up to date on various assignments.

I had lots of time for reading and writing.

'If you're writing about *us*,' the one I call Eileen said when she caught me at it, 'make sure you change the names.'

To which I responded, 'Never fear. They're changed already.'

'What're you calling me?' she asked.

'Hillary.'

'You lookin' to die?'

'Just kidding. I'm calling you Eileen.'

She frowned and nodded, thinking about it. Then she said, 'Not bad. Not bad at all. What about the others?'

I told her.

She laughed about one of them.

'Think I should change it?'

'Oh, hell no. It suits him.'

After I'd been at the house for a few days, Lois asked me to stay on as sort of a permanent guest. I explained that her house was too far from campus, but she offered to let me use her new car. So I moved out of my apartment building (pleased to leave the Fishers behind) and into Lois's house.

Kirkus moved into my old apartment.

It is all fairly strange, really.

I'd gone out for a walk through the streets of town on a night in early October, the most lonesome night of my life . . . heartbroken, bitter and desolate. Within a week, three women had entered my life and taken away the loneliness and I found myself happier than I'd ever been.

I still am.

As for Lois, Eileen and Casey, we're taking things a step at a time. Lois and I, sharing the same house, have grown to be very close. Eileen often comes over, and sometimes we go out together. Casey sleeps in my bed. When I wake up late at night and discover that she's gone, I don't mind . . . but I worry about her.

I don't know where it all may lead, but I do love the journey.

As for Kirkus . . . Well, Kirkus is Kirkus. He's an emotional wreck with the hots for me. Sometimes, we get along fine. Every so often, I have to fight him off. We really need to find him a new boyfriend.

As for Holly, who dumped me for the summer camp counselor – fuck her.

No Sanctuary

Chapter One

Saturday, May 24

The sound of breaking glass shocked Rhonda Bain awake. She went rigid on the bed and stared at the dark ceiling.

She told herself it *wasn't* someone breaking into the house; a framed picture or a mirror had fallen off one of the walls.

She didn't believe it.

Someone had smashed a window. She'd heard glass hitting a floor, so it was the kitchen window; the other rooms had carpet.

Rhonda imagined herself bolting from the bedroom, racing for the front door. But as she rushed past the kitchen, a dark shape would lurch out and grab her.

I can't just lie here and wait for him!

She flung the sheet aside, sat up, snapped her head toward the bedroom window. The curtains were open, stirring slightly in the breeze. She shivered and clenched her teeth, but not because of the mild night air on her bare skin.

I've gotta get out of here!

The window was no good. The damn thing was louvered. There wouldn't be time to pull out enough slats, remove the screen and climb through. If she barricaded the bedroom door and smashed an opening with a chair . . .

She flinched at the sound of a footstep – a shoe crunching broken glass. He's still in the kitchen.

If I try smashing the slats, he'll know I'm here, and what if he gets to me before I can—

He doesn't know I'm here!

Rhonda swung her legs off the bed. She rose slowly. The boxsprings squeaked a bit, but then she was standing. She turned to the queen-sized bed. With trembling hands, she smoothed her pillow, drew up the top sheet, then the electric blanket, then the quilt. A few tugs and the bed looked as if it hadn't been slept in.

She crouched. She sat on the carpet. She lay back and squirmed sideways, the hanging quilt brushing across her body. It passed over her face. She kept moving. It slid over her left breast, then her shoulder. She scooted in farther. Stopping, she fingered the hem of the quilt. It was five or six inches beyond her left hip and about two inches short of touching the floor.

Good enough.

She lay still, hands pressed to the sides of her thighs. She was trembling badly. She heard her quick thudding heartbeat. She heard herself panting. But she didn't hear footsteps.

He's probably out of the kitchen, walking on carpet. Where?

Turning her head, Rhonda could see out with one eye. She watched the bottom of the doorway.

Calm down, she told herself.

Oh, sure thing.

Want him to hear your damn heart drumming?

She let go of her legs, rested her hands on the carpet, and concentrated on letting her muscles relax. She filled her lungs slowly and let the air out.

Calm, she thought. You're not even here. You're lying on a beach. You're at the lake, stretched out on a towel. You can hear the waves lapping in, kids squealing and laughing. You can feel the sun and the breeze on your skin. You're wearing your white bikini.

You're naked.

Her stomach twisted.

You're naked and hiding under a bed and somebody's in the goddamn house.

She suddenly felt trapped. Though the bed didn't touch her, it seemed to be pressing down, smothering her. She struggled for breath. She wanted out. She ached to squirm free, scurry to her feet and make a dash for safety.

Calm down. He doesn't know you're here.

Maybe he does.

The pale beam of a flashlight danced through the darkness beyond the bedroom door. Rhonda glimpsed it. Then it was gone. She held her breath and stared through the gap, waiting. The beam scrawled a quick curlicue, darted high and vanished again.

He'll come in soon, Rhonda thought. He'll find me. God, why didn't I make a run for it when the window broke?

Why didn't I go with Mom and Dad to Aunt Betty's?

She forced herself to take a breath.

The beam of the flashlight slanted through the doorway, swept toward Rhonda and up.

He's checking the bed, she thought.

See, nobody's here. So get on with it. Rob the place. Take whatever you want, you bastard, just don't look under the bed.

With the snap of a switch, the lights came on.

Rhonda's fingernails dug into her thighs.

Her one eye saw a pair of old jogging shoes in the doorway. The ragged cuffs of blue jeans draped their tops and swayed slightly as the man walked forward.

The shoes stopped, turned, moved toward the closet. Rhonda watched the closet door swing open. She heard some empty hangers clink together. A loop of threads hung from the back of the jeans' frayed left cuff, dangling almost to the floor.

The shoes turned again. They came toward her, veered away, and passed out of sight as the man walked toward the end of the bed. She heard quiet steps crossing the room.

A sudden clatter and skid of metal made Rhonda flinch.

He must've yanked the curtains shut.

What for? The backyard is fenced. Nobody can see in. Maybe he doesn't know that. Or he knows it, but isn't taking any chances. Not with the light on.

The bed shuddered. It kept shaking above Rhonda. The edge of the bedspread trembled. She turned her face up. There was only darkness above her, but she pictured the man crawling over the mattress.

What's he *doing*?

He's right on top of me!

The bed squawked as if he'd suddenly flopped down hard. Something wispy – the fabric under the boxsprings? – fluttered briefly against Rhonda's nose.

She heard a click.

What was that?

Rhonda suddenly knew. The stem on the back of the alarm clock. She'd pulled it after getting into bed, wanting to wake up early for *Jurassic Park Marathon* on a cable channel.

He knows I'm here.

Rhonda squeezed her eyes shut. This isn't happening, she thought. Please.

The bed shook a little. Turning her head, Rhonda watched fingers curl under the edge of the quilt near her shoulder. The quilt lifted. There was more rustling above her. The quilt stayed up. Hands lowered and pressed flat against the carpet. Then an upside-down head filled the space between the bed and the floor.

A man, perhaps twenty-five or thirty years old, stared in at her. His light brown hair was cut short. Even though his face was upside-down, he looked handsome. In other circumstances, Rhonda might have found herself attracted to him. But she felt only revulsion.

She squirmed sideways, moving toward the center of the bed.

'Go away!' she gasped.

The man did a quick somersault off the bed, landed lightly on his back, rolled over and peered in at her. One hand darted out like a paw. The hooked fingers missed her upper arm by inches and raked back along the carpet.

Pushing himself up, he crawled on hands and knees toward the end of the bed.

Heading for the other side?

Rhonda heard nothing. She turned her head to watch the quilt along the right side of the bed. It was lower there, touching the floor.

She shrieked as cold hands grabbed her ankles.

They pulled. Rhonda skidded, the carpet burning her back. She swept her arms away from her sides, reached up and clung to the metal bedframe. The pulling hands stretched her. She kicked, barking a shin on the end of the frame. The hands tugged. Her body jerked, leaving the floor and pressing the underside of the boxsprings for an instant before she lost her hold and dropped.

The carpet seared her buttocks and back. She clawed at the bed, ripped the flimsy cloth, tried to grab springs, curled fingertips over the edge of a wooden cross-slat. But the man was dragging her too hard and fast. Nothing could stop her rough slide.

The quilt flapped her face.

Clear of the bed, she squirmed and tried to kick her feet free of the man's grip. He clamped her ankles against his hips. He smiled as if he enjoyed watching her struggle.

Finally, exhausted, she lay still and panted for breath.

The man kept smiling. He kept her feet pinned to his sides. His head moved as he inspected her with wide, glassy eyes.

Rhonda pressed a hand between her legs. She crossed an arm over her breasts.

The man laughed softly.

He said, 'No need of modesty, Rhonda.'

He knows my name!

'Who are you?' she gasped.

'I've been watching you. You're very beautiful.'

'Leave me alone.' Her voice sounded whiny, scared. She didn't care. 'Please,' she said.

'Don't worry. I won't hurt you. Just don't cause any trouble and do exactly what I say, and you'll be fine.'

Rhonda started to cry.

The man kept smiling.

421

'Okay,' she finally said through her sobs. 'I'll . . . just don't . . . hurt me. Promise?'

'Cross my heart and hope to die.'

Rhonda's body was found three days later and far from home.

Chapter Two

Saturday, June 21

The jangle of the telephone forced its way into Rick's dream and woke him up. Moaning, he rolled onto his side. The lighted dial of the alarm clock on the nightstand showed five o'clock.

Braced up on an elbow, he reached over the clock and lifted the phone's handset. As he brought it to his face, the uncoiling cord nudged the clock off the stand.

'This is obscene,' he muttered.

'How did you guess?' Bert started breathing heavily on the other end of the line.

'It's still night,' Rick interrupted. 'That's the obscenity. Human beings weren't meant to get up before dawn.'

'There are human beings who do it every day.'

'Not when they're on vacation.'

'Speaking of which . . .'

'Must we?' Rick asked.

'Don't be so negative. You're going to love it. The fresh mountain air, the grand vistas, not to mention the peace and quiet . . .'

'I've been camping before. It's not my idea of—'

'Never with me.'

'Right. Bertha Crockett, Queen of the Wild Frontier.'

The sound of her husky laugh reminded Rick of just why he had allowed Bert to talk him into a week of backpacking. 'Are you still in bed?' he asked.

'I've been up for an hour. I'm all packed and showered.'

'Dressed yet?'

That laugh again. 'Wouldn't *you* like to know.'

'Matter of fact . . .'

'Come on over and find out.'

'Bye.'

'Hey!'

'Huh?'

'I called for a reason.'

'I thought it was just to interrupt my sleep.'

'You'll be passing some doughnut shops on the way over. Why not pick up a dozen? We can eat them in the car. I'll fill a Thermos with coffee.'

'Okay, fine.'

'See you later.'

'Half an hour. So long.' He hung up, swung the sheet away, and sat on the edge of his bed.

We're actually going to do it, he thought. The realization made him tight and shaky inside. Leaning forward, he propped his elbows on his knees and stared at the floor.

It's today. Christ.

When they'd decided to make the trip, when they'd outfitted him, even last night while he was packing, the journey seemed somehow distant and vague, as if it were a concept, not an event that would actually occur.

Like having a will drawn up, he thought. You do it, but you don't quite figure on having any real need for it.

Then one fine morning . . .

You can still back out.

Hell I can.

Should've just refused when it first came up.

He had suggested alternatives: the MGM Grand in Las Vegas, the Hyatt on Maui, a tour of Ireland, a cruise on a luxury liner to Acapulco, even a steamboat trip down the Mississippi. But Bert had her heart set on backpacking in the Sierras. Somehow, she'd let two years slip by without roughing it, and she *needed* time in the wilderness. She *had* to go, with or without Rick.

And who would she go with, if not with Rick?

Myself, she'd answered. I find myself excellent company, but you're pretty excellent, too.

That had settled it. The thought of Bert going alone was intolerable.

And what was true three weeks ago was still true. Rick was sure of that. If he backed out, Bert would make the trip alone.

He flinched at the sudden blare of his alarm clock. Reaching down, he picked up the clock and silenced it. He placed it on the nightstand. Hard.

Okay. You're going. So relax and enjoy it.

He put on a robe, walked down the hall to the room he thought of as his 'entertainment center', and stepped behind the wet bar. There, he made himself a Bloody Mary with a double shot of vodka, light on the tomato juice, heavy on Worcestershire and tabasco. He twisted a wedge of lemon over the drink, added ground pepper, and stirred.

It tasted tangy and good. He carried the glass into the bathroom. After using the toilet, he took a shower. He wanted to linger under the soothing hot spray. After all, there would be no showers for the next week.

No soft bed.

No safety of walls and locked doors.

No Bloody Marys.

At least you've packed a fifth of bourbon and a revolver, he thought. Those'll help.

Bert'll crap when she finds out.

Tough. Not going into the wilderness without my peacemakers.

Rick turned off the water and climbed out of the tub. He quickly dried himself. He took a long drink of his Bloody Mary, then rolled deodorant under his arms. The shower hadn't lasted long enough to steam up the mirror. He lathered his face and shaved. Though his hand trembled, he managed not to cut himself.

Back in the bedroom, he tossed his robe aside and stood in front of the full-length mirror on his closet door to comb his hair. At least you're in good shape, he consoled himself. You were a wimpy teenager last time around.

Last time around . . .

His scrotum shriveled tight. In the mirror, he saw his hanging penis shrink.

Turning away from his reflection, he stepped into his underpants and pulled them up. The hugging fabric took away some of the vulnerable feeling. He took another drink, then finished dressing.

Bert had selected the outfit: a camouflage shirt with epaulets and pocket flaps, and baggy olive green trousers with pockets that reached down almost to his knees. He fastened the web belt, put on his socks and boots, and stepped in front of the mirror again.

All you need is an ascot and a red beret, he thought, and you'll look like a paratrooper.

Appropriate. You sure as hell feel like one – like a paratrooper about to take the big step without benefit of a 'chute.

Rick made his bed. He checked the bedroom windows to be sure they were shut and locked.

He finished his Bloody Mary on the way into the kitchen. There, he rinsed out the glass and put it into the dishwasher.

Then he went into the living room.

His backpack was propped upright against the front of the sofa. On the nearby table were his sunglasses, handkerchief, wallet and keys, Swiss Army knife, matches and a pack of thin cigars. He loaded them into his pockets. Then he mashed a battered old cowboy hat onto his head. He stepped over to his pack.

Forgetting anything? he wondered.

He had double-checked Bert's instructions while packing last night. He knew he was missing nothing on her list.

What else?

Curtains all shut. Lights off. The timer set for the living-room lamp so that it would come on at eight each night and go off at eleven. Doors and windows locked. Newspaper delivery stopped. Mail put on vacation hold.

That seemed to be everything.

Rick hoisted the backpack and slipped his arms through its straps. It felt heavy, but had a comfortable fit.

He turned around once.

What are you forgetting?

Rick entered the courtyard of Bert's apartment building. On his way up the outside stairs, he paused and stepped aside while a man in a sport coat and necktie came down.

Lucky guy, Rick thought. *He's* on his way to work. Wish I was.

But that feeling changed when Bert opened her door. Rick stepped inside and into her arms, felt the moist warmth of her mouth, her tight hug, her breasts and pelvis pressing against him. He slipped his hands beneath her loose shirt-tails and caressed her back. It was smooth and bare. He moved his hands all the way up to the sides of her neck and slid them out along her shoulders. He was always amazed by her shoulders; they were slender but wide, giving her body a tapered look and feel. As he stroked them, Bert squirmed against him and moaned.

'How about one for the road?' she whispered.

'You're kidding,' Rick said.

'Well, if you're in a big hurry to get going . . .'

'I think we can spare a few minutes. Or a few hours. Or a few days.'

'However long it takes.'

Straddling Rick on her hands and knees, Bert stared down into his eyes. Her mouth was open. She was still breathing heavily. 'Well,' she said.

'Well.'

'Guess we'd better get a move on.'

'Yeah.'

She lowered herself and kissed his mouth. He felt her nipples brush against his chest. Then she pushed herself up. 'I guess that'll hold us till tonight,' she said.

'Isn't it customary to sleep after all this exertion?'

'If you want me to drive, you can sleep in the car.'

'How about a shower first?'

'Already had one this morning.'

'So did I. But this was a messy job, and—'

'I'll keep my mess, thank you. Something to remember you by,' she added, smiling down at him. 'You may feel free to take a shower, however, if you make it quick.'

'Without you?'

Nodding, Bert climbed off him.

'I'll pass,' Rick said.

He got out of bed and followed her. The air stirred against his damp body, cooling him. He watched Bert. Her short blonde hair looked brown in the dim light, her skin dusky. She walked with easy strides. Rick's gaze slid down her wide shoulders, her back, her slim waist, and lingered on the smooth moving mounds of her buttocks.

When we're on the trails, he thought, I'll let her take the lead.

He tightened inside. He wished he hadn't thought about being on trails.

We're not there yet, he told himself.

He stopped in the entryway to the living room and leaned against the cool wood.

Bert continued into the room. Her head lowered as she looked at the discarded clothing. She was in profile when she bent at the waist, and Rick stared at the side of her breast. She picked up her panties. Her breast swayed slightly as she shifted from one foot to the other and stepped into them. The panties were little more than a white elastic waistband. When they were on, she turned toward Rick.

'Am I the only one getting dressed around here?' she asked.

'Yep.'

'Anything to stall.'

'Magnificent view. Mount Bertha.'

'That's twice.' She raised an eyebrow. 'Once more and you've had it.'

'Bert's a boy's name. You quite obviously are no—'

'Bertha's a cow's name. My parents were mad.' After a glance at the

428

floor, she ducked down and picked up a white sock. She bent over, raised a foot, and started to put the sock on.

'What name would you have liked?' Rick asked.

'Maybe Kim, Tracy, Ann. But they didn't ask. How about you?' She stretched the sock almost to her knee and picked up its mate.

'Ernie,' Rick said.

'Ernie's a trucker's name.'

'We'd be Bert and Ernie. We could move to Sesame Street.'

Bert shook her head. She lost her balance and hopped on one foot to steady herself. Rick watched her breasts shake. She finished with the second sock and straightened up. She looked at Rick's penis, then at his face.

'You missed your calling,' she said. 'You should've been a peeping Tom.'

'Doesn't pay as well as ophthalmology.'

'Taking care of other people's peepers.'

'So they won't miss out on the glories of observing the human form.'

'You're a humanitarian.' She picked up her tan shorts and stepped into them. They were loose-fitting, with deep pockets and button-down flaps like the trousers she had picked for Rick. After belting them, she sat on the floor and began to put on her boots.

She was deliberately leaving her shirt for last.

'What I like about you,' Rick said, 'you're so considerate.'

'Maybe I enjoy being looked at as much as you enjoy the looking.'

'Impossible.'

'Then just consider it a perk. I know you're not thrilled about spending your vacation in the boonies. Anything I can do to make it more bearable . . .'

'So far, it's just great.'

When Bert finished tying her boots, she reached around, picked up Rick's socks, and tossed them to him.

'I usually start with my shorts,' he said.

She grinned. 'Not this time.' She leaned back, braced up on straight arms, and watched. Rick couldn't take his eyes off her. After his socks were on, she threw the shirt to him. Then his shorts, and finally his trousers. While he fastened the belt, Bert slipped into her faded, blue chambray shirt. Leaving it open, she rolled the sleeves up her forearms. Then she buttoned the front.

Show's over, Rick thought.

A sudden rush of panic squeezed him.

Bert frowned. 'What's wrong?'

He shook his head.

'What is it?'

'Just butterflies.'

'You look like you got kicked in the nuts.'

Feel that way, he thought. 'I'm fine,' he said.

Bert got up. She put her arms around him. 'What kind of butterflies?'

'Mallards.'

'Mallards are ducks.'

'I'll be all right.'

'It's about camping?'

Rick nodded.

'I thought you just didn't want to go without the comforts. It's more than that.'

'I had some trouble the last time.'

Bert stroked the hair on the back of his head.

'I was fourteen. I was packing with my father out of Mineral Springs. We were in deep. Nobody else was around. I stumbled going across some rocks and stepped into a crevice. It was so dumb. I should've looked where I was going. Anyway, I sustained fractures of my left tibia and fibula. Dad left me alone to go for help. It was three days before I got air-lifted out. Not such a big deal, I guess, but I was fourteen and it was a pretty desolate area like some kind of Dali nightmare landscape, and I felt . . . vulnerable. There were coyotes around. I'd see them slinking over the rocks near the camp and I figured I was probably on the menu. Hell, I was scared shitless the whole time. The end.'

Bert held him tightly.

'No major deal in the scheme of things,' Rick said. 'But enough to dampen my enthusiasm for roughing it.'

'You must've been terrified,' Bert said.

'It was a long time ago.'

'I shouldn't have pushed you into this. I mean, I knew you weren't eager to go, but I never suspected . . .'

He patted her rump. 'We'd better get a move on.'

'Maybe we should change our plans.'

'Call it off?' Rick asked.

'Sure. It's okay with me.'

Go for it, Rick thought. This is just what you've been waiting to hear.

'What about the call of the wild?' he asked.

'I'll answer it some other time.'

'Without me?'

He felt her shrug.

'I'll go. You know what they say about falling off a horse. And about lightning striking the same place twice.'

'Are you sure?' Bert asked.

'Absolutely.'

She squeezed him. 'I'll make you a promise. If you break a leg this time out, I'll stay with you. We'll stick it out together until somebody comes along, and send *them* for help. I'll stay and take care of you. If we run out of food, I'll fish and set traps. And I'll shoo the coyotes away.'

It was the last thing Rick wanted to hear. 'A deal,' he said.

Chapter Three

Gillian O'Neill stared at the ringing telephone. She didn't want to pick it up.

This time, she thought, I won't.

If I don't pick it up, they'll be all right.

But as she watched, the handset rose into the air.

No!

She had a pair of scissors in her hand. She rushed forward, ready to cut the cord, but she wasn't in time. A voice boomed out of the phone as if from a loudspeaker: 'Guess what happened to your parents!'

The mouthpiece sprayed blood. The red shower splashed Gillian's face, blinding her. She shrieked, lurched backward, tripped and began a long fall, and jerked awake.

Gasping, she rolled onto her back.

The bell rang again.

Not the telephone; the front door.

Trembling, Gillian used the top sheet like a towel to wipe her sweaty face. Then she scurried off her bed. At the closet, she grabbed her robe. She put it on as she rushed from the room. It clung to her skin. She got the belt tied on her way down the hall.

'I'm coming,' she called when she reached the living room.

'Okey-doke.' It was the voice of Odie Taylor.

She slowed down. Just Odie. Good.

She opened the door.

Odie smiled nervously. His head bobbed and swayed, as usual, like the heads of the toy dogs Gillian sometimes saw in the rear windows of cars. As usual, he didn't look her in the eyes. His gaze stayed level with her neck.

'Wake you?' he asked her neck.

'I'm glad of it. I was having a bad dream.'

'Gee, I'm sorry.' He hitched up his sagging jeans. 'You been gone.'

'I took a little vacation. Want a Pepsi?'

'Thank you.'

He stayed on the balcony outside the door while Gillian hurried into the kitchen and took a can of soda from the refrigerator. She knew better than to ask Odie in. The only time she had invited him into the apartment, he had gone wild-eyed and started stuttering, scared as a trapped animal until he was outside again.

She handed the can to him.

'Thank you very much,' he said. He held it and stared at her neck. His head weaved and nodded.

'Is there a problem? My rent late?'

'Heyuh.' It was Odie's way of laughing. 'You're trying to joke me, Miss O'Neill.' Odie seemed as nervous about calling her Gillian as he was about entering her apartment. 'You don't pay no rent, you own the place.'

'Oh, that's right. I forgot.'

'You didn't forget, you're trying to joke me.'

'*Is* there a problem, or . . .'

'Gee.' He bit down on his lower lip.

'What is it?'

'I'm gonna have to go on back home. Pa took a spill off the barn roof.'

'God, I'm sorry.'

'Well, he ain't dead or nothing but he got busted up some. Me and Grace, we're gonna have to go on back home. I'm sure sorry.'

'Will you be coming back?'

'I jist don't know. I jist might stay. I been thinking maybe with the baby coming we oughta stay at the farm. City's not a good place for a kid.'

'Or for anyone else,' Gillian said. 'I'm really sorry to have you and

433

Grace leave, you've done a great job managing the place.'

'I'm sure sorry. You've sure been nice to us. I don't know what we'd of done . . .'

'You're good people, Odie. I'll miss you and Grace. But I bet you'll be glad to get back home.'

'Well . . .'

'When will you be leaving?'

'Friday, I guess. The rents're all paid up for last month and everything's tip-top around here. Want me to bring the stuff over?'

'No, that's fine. Just leave it all in your apartment so it'll be there for the new people.'

'Okey-doke.'

'I might not be around for the next few days, so hang on a second and I'll get you your pay.'

Odie stayed in the doorway while Gillian returned to her bedroom. Her handbag was on top of the dresser. She took out the checkbook and wrote a check.

Odie was drinking his Pepsi when she reached the door. She handed the check to him.

'Thank you very much,' he said. Then he glanced at it. He raised it close to his face and peered at it. His head stopped moving. He looked at Gillian, looked into her eyes. 'You made a mistake here, Miss O'Neill. You got a zero too many.'

'It's no mistake, Odie.'

'This says five thousand dollars. We get five hundred, not five thousand.'

'It's a bonus for you and Grace being such good managers.'

'Holy cow.'

'If I don't get a chance to see you again before you leave, have a good trip.' She held out her hand. Odie gripped the check in his teeth and pumped her hand. 'Drop me a line sometimes, let me know how things are going.'

His head started bobbing again. He took the check out of his teeth. 'Sure will, Miss O'Neill. Gillian.' His voice was high-pitched. He grimaced as if he were in pain. He fluttered the check under his face.

'Grace, she's gonna lay a brick when she sees this.' He shrugged.

'Take it easy, Odie.'

'Yeah. Holy cow.' Rubbing the back of his hand under his nose, he turned away and started along the balcony toward the stairs.

Gillian shut her door. She went into the kitchen to make a pot of coffee.

She would miss Odie and Grace. She had managed the twenty-unit apartment complex herself for almost a year before they showed up in their lopsided pickup truck. Odie was unemployed, but Grace had already lined up a book-keeping job that would bring in enough money to cover the rent and little else.

Gillian not only liked the two at once, she trusted them. She gave them an apartment rent-free and hired Odie, overjoyed to be released from the burden of running the place.

Now they were leaving.

I'll have to get someone else, she thought as she poured a mug of coffee. No way am I going to start managing again.

Sliding open the kitchen door, she stepped onto the sundeck and sat down on a padded chair. She stretched her legs out, propping her feet on a plastic table. She took a drink of coffee.

Damn.

Her stomach hurt. It wasn't just losing her managers, it was liking them and knowing she would never see them again after they left.

They weren't exactly *friends*. But she had cared about them, and now they'd be out of her life forever.

That's life, she told herself. That's why you shouldn't start caring.

She drank some more coffee. She rested the mug on the arm of the chair, closed her eyes and tilted her head back to feel the sun on her face.

How's about bugging out? she thought.

I don't know.

She'd only come back yesterday. The need wouldn't start getting strong for a week or two.

Right.

But with Odie and Grace taking off, she might be stuck here after

Friday – at least until she could find someone to replace them.

If you wait, you might have to go without for a whole month. Maybe even longer.

You'll be climbing the goddamn walls.

Better go for it while you've got the chance.

Her decision made, Gillian felt a familiar stir of excitement.

Get a move on, she thought. If you don't have any luck today, you'll have to wait for Monday.

She finished her coffee and went inside.

Gillian drove to an area in Studio City where the homes were nice but not elaborate. Rarely did she venture into truly exclusive neighborhoods – except on occasions when she wanted a special treat. Not this time. She had no taste today for the luxuries of a million-dollar home. Nor for dallying with such frills as elaborate alarm systems and private security patrols. A nice home in a middle-income neighborhood was all she desired. This area was just right.

Gillian had spent a terrific week in a house not far from here. The Jenson place. Murray and Ethel, away on vacation to Boston, had been good enough to leave their calendar clearly marked with their departure and return dates. Gillian had simply cleared out the day before they were scheduled to return. That had been back in February. This was June, so plenty of time had passed. She never liked to return to the same general area unless at least three months had gone by.

After cruising the streets for a while, she spotted one of the white Jeeps with red and blue stripes used by mail carriers. It was parked near a corner.

Gillian left her car on the next block, then began to wander the streets in search of the mailman.

Within ten minutes, she found him.

She walked slowly toward him. With his detours to front doors, she soon overtook him. She left him behind. At the end of the block, she crossed to the opposite side of the street and watched him from there.

When he made no delivery to a house, Gillian wrote the address on a note pad.

She spent nearly two hours observing the mailman. By then, she had five addresses on her list.

She returned to each house.

At one, she heard voices through the front door. She walked away and scratched that address off her list.

At another, a surly old man came to the door when she rang the bell. He glared at her. 'I ain't buying. I ain't donating, I ain't signing shit. Get outa here 'n stop annoying me.' Gillian smiled at him. 'Are you saved?' she asked. 'Get fucked,' he said, and slammed the door.

Gillian scratched that address off her list. Her hand shook when she did it.

At the other three homes, nobody answered the doorbell.

One of these had an alarm system, two didn't. She scratched off the one that had the alarm.

In an alley behind one of the remaining homes, she peered through a narrow gap between the fence and gate. There was no swimming pool, but the back yard had a nice patio area and a hot tub.

She walked two blocks to the other house. On close inspection, she found that it had a swimming pool. A definite plus.

Gillian returned to her car.

On the way back to her apartment, she weighed the choices. A pool was preferable to a hot tub. However, the place with the hot tub had a vacant house next door with a For Sale sign in front. That would mean one less next-door neighbor who might get suspicious of her sudden presence.

Gillian decided on the hot-tub house.

Chapter Four

They had set off with Bert driving. After the coffee and doughnuts, Rick nodded off and dozed for an hour. When he awoke, they were on the Grapevine, heading down through the Tehachapis. The valley below them looked flat and endless.

In Bakersfield, they stopped at a filling station. The gas tank was only half empty, but their bladders were full. Bert used a restroom while Rick pumped gas at the self-service island. When she returned, he hurried to the men's room.

He came back and offered to take over the driving, but Bert said that she wasn't tired yet. 'Why don't I drive till Fresno?' she suggested. 'That's when we start east. I'll let *you* experience the joys of the mountain driving.'

'Fine. And you can navigate, since you're the one who allegedly knows where we're going.'

When they reached Fresno, they were ready for lunch. Bert took an off-ramp. Along the sideroad were several restaurants. Bert said that a Burger King would do nicely, but Rick talked her into Howard Johnson's. 'I've really got a craving for fried clams,' he told her, 'and that's a specialty at Howard Johnson's.'

'You interested in the clams or the bar?' Bert asked.

'Both,' he admitted.

'Just remember you'll be driving.'

Inside, they each drank a Bloody Mary while they waited for the meal to be served. Then Bert had iced tea with her clams and French fries, and Rick had a beer. He nursed the beer along, wanting another but holding back so Bert wouldn't start to worry.

The car was stifling when they returned to it. Rick put on the air conditioner, and soon cool air was blowing against them.

Though the alcohol made him groggy for a while, it blunted his apprehension as the valley was left behind.

The land changed quickly. For a while, the road rose and dipped through brown foothills where cattle grazed. There were few trees, and only a scattering of rock. Then the rolling fields became littered with rock, and clumps jutted up like broken knobs of bone that had split the flesh of the earth. The road curved upward, a granite wall on their right, a ravine on the left. Then trees on both sides cast their deep shadows onto the pavement.

Bert asked Rick to turn off the car's air-conditioner. They both rolled their windows down. Warm air that smelled of pine rushed into the car. 'Delicious,' Bert said.

She rested her elbow on the window sill, and Rick stole glances at her as he steered around the curves. Her forearm was sleek and tanned. Her face was tilted toward the window. The one eye he could see was half shut and her mouth was open slightly, smiling. The wind ruffled her hair and fluttered the open neck of her shirt.

God, she was beautiful.

In Rick's imagination, she opened more buttons and the wind flapped her shirt open.

Then his mind strayed away from her beauty. He found himself wishing he *were* Bert, face to the wind, relishing the scented mountain air. She seemed untarnished, pure and free, enjoying herself like a child. Rick longed to be inside her and feel the way she must feel. There would be no worries, no knot in his stomach, only the thrill of being in the mountains at the very start of a vacation.

He could remember the way it felt to be that way. The memories made him hurt for what had been lost.

Maybe I can get some of it back, he thought. Maybe some of Bert will rub off on me.

Just don't let me rub off on Bert. Don't, for godsake, ruin it for her.

Bert turned her head. 'I once hiked three days,' she said, 'and never saw anyone. Can you imagine that? Nobody else on the trails. We camped by lakes and had them all to ourselves.'

'That does sound nice,' Rick said. 'I hope we get a lake to ourselves.'

'Yeah, I bet I know what you've got in mind.'

'You can freeze your nuts off in those glacial lakes.'

'Not me.'

Rick laughed.

'It's not so bad,' Bert said, 'once you get used to it.'

'I was never in that long.'

'One does tend to take on a lovely shade of blue.'

'I guess we'll find out,' Rick said. 'You swim, I'll watch you turn colors.'

'Chicken.'

'I'll be your towel holder.'

'One doesn't use a towel. One lies out in the sun on a flat rock.'

'That's how it's done, huh? Does one wear a swimming suit?'

'Not if one can help it.'

'This is sounding better and better.'

'But you've got to be somewhere isolated for that, so I wouldn't count on it.'

'You mean we won't be isolated? I thought that was the whole idea.'

'It'll be in an area that's pretty out of the way. I know the popular places that'll be swarming with campers, and we've steered clear of those. But we won't be in deep. Even if you do go in deep, that's no guarantee. Just means you meet a hardier breed of hiker. We'll probably have some company, but not much.'

'Be great if it was just you and me.'

'That, of course, is what we'll be shooting for.' She ran a hand down his thigh, gave him a pat, then reached to the glove compartment. She took out a map. As she unfolded it, the wind snapped it taut. She lowered it against her legs.

'We almost there yet?'

'Not by a long shot. The fun hasn't even started.'

'Which fun is that?'

440

'About thirty miles on an unpaved road.'

'I can hardly wait.'

'That's the part that keeps out the riff-raff.' She spent a while studying the map. 'It's not even on here,' she said.

'Maybe it doesn't exist.'

'Jean at the office was there last summer with her husband. They stumbled onto the road by accident and thought the area was great. I've got her directions.' Bert patted her breast pocket. 'We'll find it.'

A while later, dwellings began to appear among the trees on both sides of the road. Some of them looked like summer cottages Rick had known as a boy. There were a few log cabins and several A-frames. He heard the sputter of a distant chainsaw.

A sign read: BRIDGER CREEK, POPULATION 63, ELEVATION 7,300.

'We're getting up there,' Bert said.

Bridger Creek had a crossroads. On two of the corners stood A-frame real estate offices. On another corner was the B.C. Bar with a few pickup trucks and motorcycles and off-road vehicles parked in its lot. The fourth corner was occupied by a general store with gas pumps in front.

Rick stopped beside one of the pumps. A skinny teenaged boy in bib overalls trotted down from the porch. He wore a cap with its bill at the rear. He smiled through the window at Rick. Two of his upper front teeth were missing. 'Help ya?' he asked.

'Fill it up with unleaded,' Rick said.

The kid went over to the pumps.

'"Duelling Banjos", anyone?' Rick asked.

Bert gave the side of his leg a gentle punch.

After paying for the gas, Rick moved the car to the end of the lot. They went inside the store and used the restrooms. Before leaving, they bought a bag of potato chips and two bottles of cream soda.

He drove with the bottle of soda clamped between his legs. It was cold through his trousers. The open sack of chips rested on the seat. He took turns with Bert reaching into it. Sometimes, when he was concentrating on the road, his hand collided with hers.

Soon after the chips and sodas were gone, the road narrowed. It curved along the side of a mountain. Beyond the other lane was a sheer drop to a wooded valley. Rick's hands tightened on the steering wheel and he slowed down and edged to the right each time he met a descending vehicle. There were pickup trucks, Jeeps and vans, a few RVs. The big campers barely had room to squeeze by. Rick began pulling onto the gravel shoulder and stopping each time one of them appeared around a bend.

After the fourth time he did that, he slid a thin cigar out of the pack in his shirt pocket.

'Uh-oh,' Bert said. 'The man's getting serious.'

'They help calm me down.' He held the cigar out to Bert. 'Want one?' he asked.

'Why not?'

Though she had never complained of his cigars, she had never smoked one, either. 'You are in a festive mood,' Rick said. He took one out for himself. His hands shook badly as he unwrapped it.

Cigar jutting from her pursed lips, Bert leaned toward Rick for a light and wiggled her eyebrows like Groucho.

Rick lit it for her. 'You're a regular guy,' he said.

'If I'm a guy, I'm irregular.'

He grinned and fired up his own cigar. He checked the road. Then he eased off the rough shoulder and picked up speed.

Smoking the cigar helped his nerves. So did watching Bert with hers. She didn't smoke it so much as fool with it: she held it out daintily between two fingers; she stretched out her lips and sucked it like a monkey; she talked with the cigar clamped in her side teeth; she tapped off ashes with her pinky; looking at Rick with half-shut eyes, she licked its blunt wet end and slid the shaft deep into her mouth and out and in again.

'You're going to make me crash,' he said.

'You're doing fine.'

Long after the cigars were snuffed out in the ashtray, Bert unbuttoned the flap of her breast pocket and took out a folded yellow sheet from a legal pad.

'Does this mean we're almost there?'

'Time to start thinking about it,' she said.

She spread the paper open across her thighs. There was no map, just handwritten directions. She looked at it briefly, then put it away and patted it. 'There'll be a road on the right with a sign for Jacktooth Mountain.'

'And we take it?'

'Nope. We check the odometer and go about twelve miles more. There'll be a big rock on the left.'

'A rock? That's a great landmark.'

'Some lovebirds painted "Bill & Marie, 69" on it surrounded by a heart.'

'Romantic. Do you think that's a year or their favorite pastime?'

'If it's a year, it's been around a long time.'

'Maybe they make annual pilgrimages to touch it up.'

'At any rate, after the rock we go about two hundred yards and there'll be an unmarked road on the right. We take that and follow it to the end. Then we'll be there.'

Rick looked at his wristwatch. 'Almost three,' he said.

'Jean said it's about two hours from the Jacktooth Mountain sign.'

'Lordy. I hope we spot it soon.'

They passed it forty-five minutes later. Rick checked the odometer, added twelve to the mileage, and kept an eye on the slowly turning numbers.

Eighteen miles later, they spotted the rock. Bill and Marie had not been the only artists to leave their mark on it, but they'd been the most ambitious. Their heart, names and number were faded but twice the size of the surrounding graffiti.

'Two hundred yards,' Bert said.

'Want to get out and pace it off?'

'Thanks anyway. It might be a mile the way Jean gives directions.'

Rick slowed the car. The area to the right was thickly wooded, the spruce and pines brilliant green in the sunlight but dark in the shadows beyond the edge of the road. It looked foreboding.

Rick flinched at the blare of a honking horn. He checked the rearview. A van bore down on them. Without slowing, it veered into the other lane and rushed by. It had a mountain landscape, red in the sunset, painted on its side panel. Rick watched it speed around a bend.

'There!' Bert stuck an arm out of the window and pointed.

Rick eased off the road and stopped. He peered through Bert's window. 'You think that's it?' he asked.

'Must be.'

All he saw were tire tracks like parallel walking paths leading into the woods. Between the tracks was a hump with foliage growing on it.

'Fondly referred to as "the fun part",' Rick said, and steered onto the twin paths.

Only a few dusty shafts of sunlight slanted down and mottled the forest floor, not enough to dispel the gloom of the heavy shadows. The car rocked and bounced along. Sometimes, the springy limbs of nearby saplings brushed the sides of the car or scraped along with squealing sounds like fingernails on a chalkboard.

Rick wondered vaguely if they were scraping the paint.

The least of my worries, he thought.

'What happens if we meet another car?' he asked.

'It'll get interesting,' Bert said.

'Or have a breakdown?'

'We'll call the Auto Club.'

'Yuk, yuk.'

'You worry too much.'

A rock on the center hump scraped and clattered against the undercarriage.

Rick took one hand at a time off the steering wheel and wiped each dry on his trousers.

The tracks rose up a gentle grade and dipped on its other side. At the bottom, the tire ruts were puddles. The water whooshed as Rick drove through.

'Thirty miles of this?' he asked.

'Maybe it gets better,' Bert said.

Around the next curve, the way was blocked by a fallen branch. Bert shrugged.

'You don't suppose,' Rick said, 'someone put that there to discourage us?'

'Could be an ambush.'

Rick smiled, but he scanned the nearby trees before climbing out. Quickly, he walked in front of the car and stopped at the broken end of the limb. He crouched over it. The branch had neither been sawn off nor hacked with an axe.

Of course not. Rick felt a little silly for even suspecting such a thing. There was a long split up one side. The limb had simply been torn from a tree by its own weight or a strong wind or a burden of winter snow.

He lifted it with both hands and stepped across the tracks, swinging it out of the way. He gave it a shove and let go. The limb dropped with a soft thud onto the brown mat of pine needles. There was sap on the index finger of his left hand. He bent the finger and felt the skin stick. He sniffed the brown stain. It smelled like a Christmas tree.

Turning back toward the car, he saw Bert behind the steering wheel. He went to the passenger door and climbed in.

'Mind if I drive?' she asked.

Bert seemed to enjoy it. Rick enjoyed watching her. She sat forward, away from the seat back, and peered intently out of the windshield. She held the steering wheel with both hands. Sometimes the tip of her tongue appeared at the corner of her mouth.

As time passed, however, Rick found himself watching the woods more often than he watched Bert. He gazed out the windows, half expecting to spot someone in the deep shadows sneaking around among the trees. He saw no one. But the farther they traveled along the dirt tracks, the more certain he became that they were not alone. Once, a sudden moving shape deep in the woods made his heart jump before his mind registered that the shape was merely a deer.

This is going to be a long week, he told himself, if you don't settle down. Nobody's out there. Nobody's stalking you.

But he wished his revolver were close at hand, not in the car's trunk at the bottom of his backpack.

He kept watching the trees. Sometimes, he looked over his

shoulder and gazed out the rear window. If they were being followed, the man or vehicle was not in sight. Could someone looking closely at the tracks tell that their car had recently made the passage? He remembered the limb that he had lifted out of the way and wished he'd had the sense to place it back across the tracks after they'd gone by.

'What are you doing?' Bert finally asked.

'Just enjoying the scenery.'

'You look like a cemetery guard keeping an eye out for spooks.'

'Just a little edgy,' he admitted, and made a weak smile.

'Hey, if there was anything to worry about, do you think *I'd* come out to a place like this? I'm the world's greatest chicken. I get the willies all the time. You should see me when I get back to my apartment at night. Especially after I've been with you and it's late. I check behind the furniture, look in closets. I've even been known to look under the bed. And I've usually got a great case of the shivers till I've made sure nobody's lurking around.'

'Really?'

'Absolutely. I always figure some drooling maniac has gotten in, somehow, and is just waiting for a chance to rape or murder me. Or both.'

'You're kidding. You?'

'Had me figured for a fearless Amazon?'

'Something like that.'

'Disappointed?'

'Well, I knew you were no Amazon. You've got two boobs.'

Bert grinned. 'But really, the way I see it, a certain percentage of people are criminals or dangerous nut cases. Therefore, the smaller the population, the less danger of running into one. When you get out in a place like this, there's almost nobody so your chances of meeting a creep diminish to almost nothing.'

'On the other hand,' Rick said, 'the larger population works to your advantage in that the nut has a larger pool of victims to choose from. Start decreasing the population, you might have fewer nuts but it also knocks down the odds that someone *else* will be the victim.'

Bert nodded. 'So if there *is* a nut out here, we win by default.' In a teasing voice she added, 'Better keep a sharp eye out.'

Though Bert was making light of it, Rick wished he hadn't pointed out the less comforting side of her argument. Getting her worried would serve no purpose. He should've kept his mouth shut.

'I've spent a lot of time in wilderness areas,' Bert said after a while. 'I've never run into trouble so far.'

'Well . . .'

'That probably hurts the odds on this time out, huh?'

'Don't be such a pessimist,' Rick said.

She laughed.

In the silence that followed, Rick's uneasiness came back. He felt a strong urge to resume his watch of the surrounding forest, but he fought it. He watched Bert instead. Then he lay down on the seat and rested his head on her lap. Drawing up his knees, he propped his feet on the window sill.

Bert smiled down at him. 'Comfy?'

'Very nice.'

Rick felt her warmth through the fabric of her shorts. Her flat belly eased against his cheek sometimes when she inhaled. The front of her loose shirt, jutting out like smooth hills just above his eyes, stirred slightly as the bouncing, rocking motions of the car shook her breasts.

'Down there,' she said, 'you can't keep a look-out.'

'The view's fine.'

She let go of the wheel for a moment and brushed a hand through his hair.

'If you're nervous about going back to your apartment at night,' Rick said, 'how come you won't stay over at my place?'

'I believe we've been over that ground.'

'Well, you could do it sometimes. Maybe just on weekends.'

'It might start with just weekends, but pretty soon that wouldn't be enough. I know men, and I know myself. Before long, you'd be pointing out with infallible logic that keeping my apartment is a wasteful expense, that I should move in with you and get rid of it.'

'And you,' Rick continued for her, 'value your independence too highly—'

Bert stopped the car.

'What's wrong?'

'We're there.'

Rick's stomach did a small flip, but he managed a smile. 'And I was just getting comfortable.' He sat up slowly, keeping the side of his face against Bert. His cheek nuzzled her breast. He turned his head and kissed it. Her nipple was stiff under her shirt. He opened his mouth wide and ran his tongue over the fabric.

Bert slapped his stomach gently. 'Stop it,' she said. 'People are watching.'

Rick stopped. He bolted upright and looked out the windows. Perhaps he'd *sensed* rather than seen somebody back there in the trees. He stared. Hard. Nothing moved.

'Just kidding,' she said. She pinched the cloth away from her breast. 'Look what you did.'

His mouth had left a dark wet patch on the blue pocket. 'But it felt good, right?' he asked.

'Feels damp.'

'Better get into a dry shirt.'

She gave him a smirk, then took the key from the ignition and rolled up her window. She punched the lock button down. Rick watched her climb out. The back of her shirt was wet and clinging, though not as wet as he'd made the pocket. She swung her door shut.

The car had stopped in a clearing. Rick saw no tire tracks ahead. There was a heavily wooded slope, dim with shadows. Looking out of his window as he cranked it up, he saw that the clearing provided enough room to allow the car to be turned around. He elbowed down his lock button, then checked the rear doors. They were secure.

He joined Bert behind the car as she opened the trunk. She gave the key case to him. 'Don't lose it,' she said.

Her comment triggered new worries. What if he lost the keys? What if they came back here, ready to depart, and the battery was dead? What if the car had two flat tires? What if it was vandalized or stolen while it sat here unguarded for a week?

So many things could go wrong. They might get through all the camping unscathed only to find themselves stranded when they were ready to leave. By that time, their food supplies would be depleted . . .

Bert reached into the trunk.

'I'll get it.' Rick lifted out her pack. He held it while she slipped her arms through the straps. Then he propped his own pack on the edge of the trunk. Bert held it steady. He crouched and found the straps. Standing, he felt the solid weight pressing his shoulders and back.

Bert took their hats from the trunk and shut the lid. She plopped Rick's hat onto his head and put on her own. It was a tan, Aussie hat with one side of the brim turned up. It might look silly on some people, Rick thought. On her, it looked great.

'Now what?' he asked.

'Now we find the trail and start walking.'

'Maybe we should spend the first night here.'

'Sleep in the car?'

'There's a thought.'

'Jean said there's a nice area near a stream about half a mile from here.'

'The way she gives directions, it's probably two miles.'

'We'd better get moving, then. Need to get there before dark.' Bert dug deep in a pocket of her shorts. She came up with a compass, held it flat in her open hand and studied it. 'Trail should be thata-way,' she said, and pointed to the left.

Rick followed her past the front of the car.

'Ah-ha!' she said.

At the edge of the clearing, nailed to a short brown post, were two slats of wood with carved messages. One pointed to the left and indicated that Mosquito Pasture was two miles distant. The other pointed straight ahead. Dead Mule Pass was eight miles in that direction.

'Encouraging names,' Rick muttered.

Bert smiled back at him. 'You'll be glad to know we're not heading for Mosquito Pasture.'

'Dead Mule Pass doesn't sound like the Garden of Eden.'

Bert tucked a thumb under each of her shoulder straps. She flexed her knees and pulled the straps as if to adjust the fit of the pack.

The wet patch on her pocket was still dark.

She turned away and started walking down the trail.

Rick looked back at the car. Then peered into the deep shadows among the trees. Get a grip, Rick. There are no boogey men out there. Believe me.

Hurrying to catch up with Bert, he began to sing. 'Please Mr Custer, I don't wanna go.'

Chapter Five

The parking area under Gillian's apartment building was deserted. She slid her suitcase onto the floor of the car in front of the passenger seat, set down her purse, then went around to the rear and opened the trunk. Reaching inside a nylon satchel, she took out a pair of license plates. It was one of six sets she had removed, late one night last month, from cars parked along a secluded lane in Brentwood. She had used WonderGlu to fix strong magnets onto the back of each plate.

She covered her own plates with the stolen ones, and drove out.

She shivered as she drove. The tremors seemed stronger, less pleasant than usual.

Maybe this is too soon, Gillian thought. Maybe I'm pressing my luck.

Nothing to worry about, she told herself. You've never been caught, and there was only that one close call.

That, and the house on Silverston.

The 'close call' had happened nearly a year ago. She'd been swimming in the pool at the Farnsworth house in Rancho Park when car doors thudded shut nearby. Thrusting herself out of the water, she ran dripping to the corner of the house. From there, she saw the roof of a van beyond the top of the gate. She heard quiet voices. The Farnsworths weren't due home for two more days, but they must have cut their trip short. In seconds, they would find themselves prevented from entering the front door because of the burglar bar. When that happened, they were bound to come through the gate to try a back door. Gillian, choked with panic, raced around the end of the pool.

451

At the rear of the yard, she sprang at the redwood fence, boosted herself up and squirmed over the top, scraping her thigh in the process. She dropped into the alley on the other side.

Fortunately, she'd left her car parked around a corner from the Farnsworth house, with an ignition key in a magnetized compartment under the rear bumper.

That wasn't good fortune, she thought, that was good planning.

The good planning also paid off in that Gillian had taken nothing into the house that could be used to identify her. She lost her suitcase, clothes, security bars, purse and camera (along with a roll of film in the camera that must've given the Farnsworths food for thought if they had it developed), but nothing to give them any clues as to who the owner might be.

Still, it had been a narrow escape. She'd sworn off intrusions for good after that.

As time passed, however, the urge had grown. Three weeks later, she was inside another house. It had been scary for a while, but soon the fear of being discovered had faded and she'd had no more problems.

So why, tonight, was her usual anticipation tainted by a shadow of dread?

Gillian parked in front of the house. Light shone through the closed draperies of the living room, but that was normal; most people had timing devices to activate a lamp and make their homes look occupied while they were away.

She shut off her engine and headbeams, and got out of the car. As she walked around to the passenger door, she eyed the next-door houses. The one with the realtor's sign was dark. The other had lights on, but no car in the driveway. The owners might be home, but there was a good chance they were out enjoying themselves.

Ten o'clock on a Saturday night was the ideal time for Gillian to make her entries: too early for most people to return home from movies or dinner parties; not so late that her arrival, if noticed by a neighbor, would draw much suspicion.

Especially not the way she was dressed.

Gillian opened the passenger door. She took out her purse and suit-case, and walked casually toward the front porch, confident that anyone who might spot her would assume she was a legitimate visitor. Burglars, after all, do not usually wear heels, a skirt, and a turtleneck sweater.

If questioned by a neighbor who'd been alerted that the owners were off on a trip, she would simply claim to be the niece who'd come to house-sit. That had happened a few times. Usually, they bought the story. If not, Gillian was ready to cover herself. 'Uncle Henry insisted that I—'

'No Henry lives here.'

She would frown. 'Sure. Henry Wadsworth.'

Assured that no Henry Wadsworth resided here, she would act perplexed and show the suspicious neighbor a slip of paper on which she had written Uncle Henry's name and address. The neighbor would then explain that she was at the wrong address. 'This is 8322, not 3822.' Grateful for having her error pointed out, she would depart.

Tonight, Gillian had no use for the slip of paper on which she had reversed the first two numbers of this address. Nobody questioned her. She saw no one on her way from the car to the porch.

The light above the front door was dark. She listened for a few moments and heard no voices from inside. Ringing the doorbell went against procedure. Though that was a good way to make sure nobody was home, the sound of a doorbell could sometimes be heard by neigh-bors. Also, it went against the logic of her cover; a niece coming to house-sit would hardly ring the doorbell.

Setting down her suitcase, Gillian opened the mailbox. It was empty except for a flier. She quietly lowered the lid.

The porch was an L-shaped concrete slab with a waist-high wall, and extended around the corner of the house. Its front was concealed from the street by a pair of geraniums. The house windows that looked onto the porch were dark.

Gillian carried her suitcase and purse around the corner and set them down. From there, she could see the high redwood fence that ran alongside the property. The next-door house had a single story, and only the very tops of its windows were visible above the fence. Lights shone through the windows.

It was all right, though. Not only were the curtains shut, but anyone inside would have to stand on a chair to see over the fence.

After slipping out of her shoes, Gillian stepped barefoot to the low wall and peered down. In the space between the house and the fence was a driveway that extended from the gate to a two-car garage. The porch was elevated leaving a drop of about six feet from the top of its wall to the driveway. There was no opening at the rear of the porch wall. She would have to jump.

Gillian opened her skirt and stepped out of it. She folded it, set it on the edge of her suitcase, then pulled off her sweater. Shivering in her gym shorts and tank-top, she opened her handbag and removed a small leather satchel. Then she climbed onto the side wall of the porch and pushed off. Her feet slapped the pavement, a quiet sound that could certainly not be heard inside the neighbor's house.

She walked quickly up the driveway, noting that all the windows along this side of the house were dark. At the rear was a sliding glass door, then more windows. The concrete slab of the sundeck had a single lounge, a glass-topped table, a Weber grill, and a square platform surrounding the covered hot tub.

Gillian stepped around the corner of the house. She walked along the dewy grass strip between the wall and the fence, checking the windows and listening for sounds from inside. The last two windows showed light through their curtains, undoubtedly from the same source that illuminated the picture window she'd seen from the street. On this side of the house, there was no gate at the front.

Completing her rounds, Gillian felt sure that the house was deserted. She returned to the rear deck.

At the sliding door, she took a small flashlight out of her leather case. Shining its beam downward through the glass, she checked the runner. No rod had been placed there to prevent the door from being opened. She inspected the inside handle. It was one of those with a simple lever. A downward flick would disengage the lock.

With the flashlight clamped between her teeth, Gillian started to work. An open square of duct tape on the glass in front of the lock lever. A circle of tape stuck to the center for use as a handle. A careful line with her glass cutter along an inside border of the tape. Three more slices through the glass, completing the square. A few gentle taps at the edges. Finally, a pull at the tape in the center. The square of glass came out.

A cinch, Gillian thought.

She set the small section of glass on the table.

Reaching through the opening, she lowered the lock lever. She removed her hand and pulled the aluminum handle. The door slid open with a low, quiet rumble.

Gillian left her leather case on the table. She entered the house. The warm air had a closed-in, stuffy heaviness; one more indication that nobody was home.

Shining the flashlight around, she saw that she was in a den or recreation room. It had a couch, a couple of easy chairs, lamps and tables, a television with a large screen and VCR, a stereo, bookshelves along the wall in front of her and a built-in bar at the other end of the room. The floor was hardwood.

Very nice, Gillian thought.

Especially the bar and the VCR.

Pointing her flashlight at the bookshelves, she found that the owner had an extensive collection of tapes for the video recorder.

Gillian turned around and went through a doorway. Ahead was the dining room. To the right was another entryway. She stepped through it and found herself in the kitchen. After a quick look around, she backtracked, passed the door leading into the den, and entered a hallway on the left. A short distance down the hallway, she came to a wide arch that opened onto the living room. She switched off the flashlight. Then she peered around the corner of the arch. Satisfied that the room was deserted, she continued her search.

Just beyond the arch, she found a closet, then a bathroom. Farther down the hall, on the left, was a small room with exercise equipment. Squinting into the darkness, she saw a Nautilus, treadmill, rowing machine and weights, a mat on the floor and a wall of mirrors.

Then she came to the bedroom. Standing close to the open door, her back pressed to the wall, she held her breath and listened. No sounds came from the room. She wiped her sweaty hands on her shorts. Flashlight still off, she stepped away from the wall and moved in front of the doorway.

In spite of the closed curtains, the room had a dim gray glow. Gillian peered at the bed. Its cover was flat except for the bulge of pillows near the headboard.

That's that, she thought.

Suddenly exhausted, she sagged against the doorframe.

End of Phase One, she told herself. You're safely in and nobody's here.

Of course, someone *could* be here, hiding. It was unlikely, though. So unlikely that it wasn't even worth worrying about.

Even if all the other indications were misleading, the stuffy air of the closed-up house was sure proof.

After a while, Gillian thrust herself away from the doorframe and walked toward the bed. She turned on her flashlight. Though it was aimed at the kingsized bed, a bright beam streaked across the ceiling.

She flinched and looked up.

Mirrors. Mirrors on the ceiling above the bed.

Well now, Gillian thought. Whoever lives here must be quite a sport.

Turning around, she found the light beam ricocheting off mirrors on the wall. Even the shut door of the closet had them.

Grinning, Gillian went to the bed, sat on it, and gasped as she sank into the mattress. Waves rolled back against her rump.

A *water bed*!

This is going to be terrific.

She flopped down on the undulating softness, felt herself rise and fall on the gently moving surface, stared up at her reflection in the mirrors.

She'd been in a few houses with water beds but none with mirrors like this. It would be strange, trying to sack out with images of herself on the ceiling and wall.

The sport who lives here must get quite a kick out of looking at himself . . . or herself. Could be a woman, she thought. But definitely not married. Definitely on the make.

Her curiosity aroused, Gillian went to the closet and opened it. The inside of the door had a necktie bar. On the floor were men's shoes. The hanging clothes were shirts, slacks, and sport coats.

Our Narcissus, she decided, is definitely a guy.

Gillian shut the closet. Beyond the end of the bed was a bureau. She could inspect its contents later. Beside it was another television. This TV, like the one in the den, had a VCR attached.

Leaving the room, Gillian went to the front door. She opened it, looked around, then stepped out on the porch. She gathered up her shoes, clothes, purse and suitcase, and carried them into the house.

Then she headed back into the den. She spent the next few minutes gluing the square of glass into its original place in the door. She taped it there to hold it while the glue had a chance to set. Then she packed up her tool satchel and entered the house.

She locked the sliding door.

In the living room, she opened her suitcase and took out her burglar bar. She extended its telescoping rod, fitted its V-shaped end under the doorknob and jammed its other end against the carpet at a wide angle.

'All right,' she said. 'The house is mine.'

Chapter Six

Rick woke up. The tent was dark. He pulled an arm out of his mummy bag and fingered a tab at the side of his wristwatch to light the digital numbers. Eleven-fifty. He grimaced. He'd been asleep less than two hours, and now he felt wide awake.

Bert, in her own bag alongside his, breathed slowly in and out. She was deeply asleep, gone, and Rick felt abandoned.

Trying to find a more comfortable position, he rolled onto his side. The rubber mat under his bag helped a little, but it was thin and the cold earth was unyielding. Too much weight bore down on his shoulder, upper arm and hip.

They'll fall asleep before I do, he thought.

He rolled the rest of the way over and crossed his arms beneath the makeshift pillow of his rolled coat. This was better; the ground felt fine under his thigh muscles. But he was pressing down hard on his lower ribs. His penis, sideways against his groin, felt mashed. He turned slightly to relieve the pressure. Now his knee pushed against the ground and there was more weight on the left side of his ribcage. After a while, the knee and ribs began to ache.

Muttering, 'Shit,' he rolled onto his back again and gazed at the slanted walls of the tent.

This is madness, he thought. I could be home in my own soft bed, instead of out here in the wilderness scared out of my gourd. Like last time . . .

He listened to Bert's slow breathing, and resented her. This was all her fault.

'Get off it,' he told himself. 'You didn't have to come. And she's been great.'

Rick wished he'd had a couple of shots before turning in. He'd been reluctant, however, to let Bert find out that he'd brought the bourbon along. She might not complain, but she would certainly disapprove. She *did* complain about her parents' drinking, whose cocktail hour had stretched into two hours on the several occasions when she and Rick had dined at their house. She didn't complain to them. She complained to Rick later on. By implication, her comments seemed directed at Rick since he had matched her parents drink for drink. 'Can't people have a good time,' she would say, 'without trying one on?'

Rick had seen opportunities to sneak a couple of slugs after dinner tonight when Bert left camp to gather firewood. But he'd resisted the urge, knowing that she would smell it on his breath later when they made love.

I should've brought vodka instead of bourbon, Rick thought. Hell, she would've smelled that, too. Its odor is faint compared to bourbon, but distinctive.

He thought about the bottle. It was near the bottom of his pack.

They had left their packs outside the tent, resting atop slabs of rock on the other side of the campsite and covered with ponchos.

Not only was his bourbon out there, but so was his revolver. A lot of good the gun would do them some forty feet from the tent, but Rick didn't want Bert to know about that, either. The gun was a double-whammy; she hated firearms in general, and Rick bringing one on the camping trip would probably be seen as an act of cowardice.

If I'd had a gun the last time . . .

Maybe I should've told Bert the whole truth this morning. Giving her that sanitized version probably just made me look yellow – like I was a kid back when it happened, scared of my own shadow.

Rick had never told the whole truth about that camping trip to anyone.

When they first came upon the lake, Rick had wanted to keep moving. It was a deep shade of blue, itself beautiful, but trapped in a landscape of such desolation that Rick felt the skin crawl on the back of his neck in spite of the heavy sun.

Steep canyon walls loomed over the lake on three sides. High up were gray stretches of glacier shaded by overhangs so that they probably never melted completely, year after year. There were a few scraggly patches of foliage on the rock walls, trees stunted and twisted into grotesque shapes. Otherwise, the slopes were bleached tumbles of broken granite.

The trail down from Windover Pass led to a small oasis that looked alien in the midst of the otherwise bleak surroundings. The oasis, a shady clearing near the lake shore, had a campsite.

A *nice* campsite, probably added on to over the years by many people who had stopped there after the exhausting trek down from the pass. There was a stone fireplace with a heavy steel grill that must've been brought in by mule. Surrounding the fireplace were several flat-topped rocks that could be used as either seats or tables. Here and there were walls of stone, no doubt constructed to hold back the winds that must rip through the canyon at night. The site even had a few flat areas, mostly near walls, that looked as if they had been carefully cleared of rocks and leveled.

Dad swung his backpack to the ground and stretched. The armpits of his tan shirt were dark with sweat. 'Fantastic, huh?' he asked.

'I don't like it,' Rick said.

'What's not to like?' Dad asked.

'This place gives me the creeps.'

'It is a little . . . barren,' Mom admitted. 'They built those walls. The wind must be awful.'

'Well, folks, it might be a long trek to the next decent spot. Even if we move on, there's no guarantee we'll find any place better than this. Might even be worse.'

'It's still pretty early in the day,' Mom said.

Dad showed her the topographics map, pointing out what lay ahead. Mom grimaced. 'I guess we stay,' she said.

They set up camp, pitching the larger tent in the flat area between two of the stone walls, setting up Rick's tent in a naturally sheltered area beside a high clump of rock. After arranging their gear, they rested for a while. Dad sat on a rock near the shore and smoked a corncob pipe. Mom sat cross-legged under a tree and read, and Rick lay down inside his tent. The tent was hot in spite of the shade, but he liked being enclosed, hidden away from the bleak landscape.

Later, Dad suggested that they take a hike to 'explore the environs'.

Rick wanted no part of the environs. 'Let's not and say we did,' he suggested.

'Stay if you want,' Dad told him. 'We probably won't be gone more than an hour.'

'Mom, are you going, too?'

She crawled out of the bigger tent, stood up and nodded. She had changed into a tube top that wrapped her breasts and left her midriff bare, and cut-off jeans so short that the ends of the front pockets hung out below the frayed leg holes. She had abandoned her hiking boots for a pair of ragged tennis shoes. 'You want to come,' she asked, 'don't you?'

Rick certainly did not want to stay by himself. 'Sure,' he said.

They started out, Dad leading the way. It soon became clear that his plan was to hike entirely around the lake. Though the lake was not large, maybe a couple of hundred yards from one end to the other, the shoreline trail petered out on the other side of a rushing stream just beyond camp. After that, the lake was bordered by rocks: tilted pale slabs, chunks the size of cars, piles of smaller blocks, some that wobbled or slid underfoot.

In spite of the rough terrain, the going wasn't difficult. Rick felt amazingly light and springy in his sneakers and without the burden of his pack. He leaped from rock to rock, strode easily across slanted sheets of granite, hopped over crevices.

Mom, just ahead of him, sometimes looked back to see how he was doing.

He watched her feet, and stepped where she stepped. Now and then, his gaze wandered higher. Her slender legs looked dusky through his sunglasses. Her shorts were cut so high in the rear that he could see the creases where her buttocks joined the backs of her thighs. Isn't

461

she wearing panties? he wondered. He felt himself getting hard, and guilt swarmed through him.

She's my mother, he warned himself.

Not really. His real mother had left Dad when Rick was six. Two years later, Dad married Julie.

That doesn't mean you can get the hots for her, Rick thought.

But sometimes he did. He just couldn't help it.

He looked away from her. He watched the rocks in front of his feet.

Soon, however, his eyes found their way back to her. He stared at the faded seat of her shorts, at the way the curves under her rear pockets took turns rising and falling with the movements of her firm rump as she walked. He stared at the exposed crescents of her buttocks. There was little more than a narrow strip of denim passing between her legs. If she got high enough above him, maybe he would be able to see up inside the shorts and—

Rick yelped with surprise as his foot came down. Rock was supposed to be there, but wasn't. He glanced down. Saw his shoe and jeaned shin drop into a crevice. Tried too late to push out with his other foot. Fell forward. Shrieked out his pain as the bones snapped.

Mom threw her arms around him, catching him in time to prevent the bones from ripping through muscle and skin. Then Dad was there. They eased his leg out of the fissure and lowered him onto the rock.

They both knelt over him. Dad, who never seemed to lose his calm, had a frantic look in his eyes. Mom's face was twisted with fear. 'Are you okay?' she asked. 'It's not broken, is it?'

Rick, teeth clenched in pain, nodded.

'Let's get those jeans off,' Dad said.

As Mom unfastened his jeans, Rick noticed that her tube top was askew. It must've been pulled when she stopped his fall. On one side, a smooth half-moon of dark skin showed above the fabric hugging her breast.

He was in too much pain for the sight to arouse him.

But he remembered where he had been looking when he stepped into the crack.

He shouldn't have been looking there. It was dirty of him, even though she wasn't his real mother. The fall had been a punishment.

'I ruined everything,' he muttered.

'Could happen to anyone,' Dad said, and pulled the jeans down Rick's legs. His left leg, below the knee, looked swollen and slightly bent. Dad ran his hand along it. 'There's a break, all right.'

'What're we going to do?' Julie asked.

That was when Rick stopped thinking of her as Mom. It didn't seem quite so terrible to have gloated over a woman who was not Mom, just Julie.

'Hold his knee,' Dad said.

Julie clutched his knee with both hands, and Dad tugged sharply on his ankle. Rick flinched rigid as white-hot pain streaked up his body.

Dad fingered the shin again. 'I think that set it. You okay?'

Rick nodded.

Dad stood up, looked around, apparently didn't spot whatever he wanted, then crouched and pulled off Rick's sneakers. Following his instructions, Julie pressed the soles of the shoes flat against both sides of Rick's shin. A little more of her nipple was showing. Rick forced himself not to look at it. He watched Dad instead. Soon, the shoes were strapped tightly into place with two belts.

'That ought to hold it,' Dad said.

They helped Rick up. Julie suggested they support him under each arm and walk him back to camp, but Dad said that it would be easier, and less risky, if he carried Rick piggy-back.

'You might hurt yourself,' Julie said.

'You kidding? The man of iron?'

Dad didn't feel like a man of iron as he carried Rick over the rough terrain. He felt like oak, thick and solid and resilient. He wasn't even breathing heavily by the time they reached their campsite.

Instead of putting Rick down, he waded into the lake.

'What're you doing?'

'I want you to soak that leg for a while. The cold'll keep the swelling down.'

'Do I have to?'

Dad crouched. The icy water soaked through the seat of Rick's cotton underpants, shocking his anus and biting into his genitals. Then the water numbed his legs. Julie, behind him, clutched him under the armpits.

'Okay, I've got you,' she said.

Releasing his father, he eased backward against Julie. She lowered him deeper. Dad let go of his legs, then moved around to where Julie was. Together, they guided him closer to the shore. They found a flat rock for him to sit on.

Both legs were still submerged below the knees, but the agony was gone. Rick felt as if his balls had been released from a vice. He took a deep breath.

Dad and Julie both stood in front of him, thigh deep in the lake. Didn't the water hurt *them*?

Julie had Rick's jeans with the crotch at the nape of her neck and the legs draping her front.

'You should probably soak that leg a few times a day,' Dad said. He looked at Julie. 'You make sure he does.'

'You're going for help?' she asked.

'Don't see any way out of it.'

'You're going to leave us alone?' Rick was stunned.

'There's no reason to worry. You've got plenty of food. Shouldn't take me more than about two days to reach the ranger station. They'll probably bring in a chopper.'

'God almighty,' Rick muttered.

'It won't be so bad,' Julie said, and showed him a smile.

'Let him have some bourbon,' Dad told her. 'That'll help if the pain gets too bad. I'd better get a move on.'

Rick and Julie both tried to talk him into staying the night, but he argued that there were still several hours of daylight and he'd better get to the ranger station as fast as possible.

They left Rick.

Turning sideways on his tiny island of rock, he watched his father pack a few things in his rucksack, kiss Julie goodbye, wave, and start striding briskly up the trail toward Windover Pass.

No Sanctuary

That night, the wind woke Rick. It howled and shrieked through the canyon. It shook the tent in spite of the protective stone walls on either side. He was glad that Julie had moved his sleeping bag into her tent, but she seemed to be sleeping through the uproar. His leg throbbed. He began to weep. The pain was bad, but the fierce noises were worse. He felt as if their presence had somehow offended a monstrous thing that dwelt in the canyon; it hated intruders in its domain and wanted to crush them. Finally, unable to bear the terror, Rick shook Julie awake.

'Huh? What . . . Jesus, what's going on out there?'

'Just the wind,' Rick said, trying to keep his voice steady so she wouldn't know he was crying.

'Sounds like the end of the world.'

'My leg hurts awfully bad,' he said.

'Maybe we should break out the booze. Do you think that'd be a good idea?'

'I guess so.'

'I could use some myself. What's going *on* out there?'

Rick rubbed his eyes. He saw Julie sit up in the darkness. A moment later, light stung his eyes. She had turned on the dry-cell lantern hanging from a joint of the aluminum tent poles near her head.

She crawled out of her mummy bag. She was wearing a T-shirt, baggy gray sweatpants and wool socks. She put on her down parka. 'Right back,' she said. On hands and knees, she made her way toward the front of the tent.

'Where are you going?'

'The bourbon's in my pack.'

'Don't go out there,' Rick said. There was a whine in his voice.

'I'd send you, but you're gimped.' She opened the tent front and crawled away.

Braced up on his elbows, Rick stared at the shuddering flaps. He thought he heard a scream. Maybe it was only the wind.

Julie didn't come back. The packs were only a few feet from the tent. Even if she had trouble finding the bottle, it shouldn't take this long.

Suppose she *never* comes back!

He called out to her, but she didn't answer.

It got her! Whatever it was out there shrieking like a demon, it got Julie and ripped her apart and next it would come after Rick!

The tent flaps whipped inward and a scream stuck in his throat as Julie crawled in, her hair a tangle and the bottle in her hand.

'Where were you!' he raged through his sobs.

'Hey, calm down. What's the matter?'

'You didn't come back! I yelled and . . .'

'I was out there anyway so I took a pee. Calm down, for godsake.' She sat cross-legged beside him and combed fingers through his hair.

Slowly, he regained control. He sat up, keeping his splinted leg straight inside his mummy bag, bending his other at the knee and turning so he could face her.

'Better?' she asked.

Rick nodded.

She unscrewed the cap of the bottle, took a sip, and handed it to him. He had tried wine and beer a few times before, but never whiskey. He drank some and winced. It tasted like medicine and scorched his throat, but then it felt warm and nice in his stomach.

'Like it?' Julie asked.

He wrinkled his nose. He took another swallow. 'It's okay.'

He gave the bottle to Julie and she drank. 'Nasty out there,' she said.

'I knew this was a bad place to stay.'

'I wasn't too happy about it myself, but we didn't have much choice. We would've had to go over another pass to get out of here.'

'I wish we had've.' Rick accepted the bottle, took another swallow, and handed it back. His cheeks felt a little numb and there was a mild, pleasant fogginess inside his head.

Though the wind still howled and shook the tent, it soon stopped bothering Rick. It was outside and couldn't get in, couldn't hurt them. In here, talking with Julie and sharing the bottle, his worries slid away. He even found himself feeling glad that he'd broken his leg; otherwise, he wouldn't be here with her. Dad would be here instead, and Rick would be off alone in the other tent.

'When I get older,' he said, 'I hope I get to marry someone like you.'

She smiled. 'The booze must be getting to you.'

'No, I mean it. Honest. You're really neat. For a mother,' he added, just so she wouldn't get the wrong idea.

'You're pretty neat yourself. Even if you don't clean up your room.' After capping the bottle, she placed it near the head of the tent and said, 'We don't want hangovers in the morning. You think you'll be able to sleep now?'

'Maybe.'

She took her parka and rolled it up. 'Any more problems, just wake me up.' She leaned forward and kissed him gently on the mouth. 'Sleep tight,' she said.

Rick settled down into his bag. He watched Julie reach up to turn off the lantern. A side of her T-shirt rose, showing a wedge of bare skin. He saw the way her nipples made the fabric jut. He felt a warm, heavy stirring in his groin.

The light went out. He closed his eyes. His mind held the picture of Julie reaching up toward the lantern. He knew he should feel guilty, but he didn't. He felt only languid and peaceful and pleasantly aroused. Soon, he fell asleep.

The next day, the men came.

There were two of them.

Rick was in his swimming trunks and wearing no shirt. He had just finished soaking his leg in the frigid lake. Julie, crouched in front of him, was using belts to strap the splints to his shin. She had made the splints yesterday, soon after Dad's departure, by chopping a length of dead branch into a pair of thin slats and padding each of them with one of Rick's undershirts.

Rick didn't hear the men coming. Suddenly, they just appeared among the trees behind the tent. He flinched. Julie looked up at him. 'Someone's here,' he said.

Julie made a final adjustment to the bindings, then stood and turned around.

'Morning,' one of the men said in a cheerful voice. He and his friend came forward. He had a thick, shoulder-high walking stick. He wore a faded Dodger cap with sweaty blond hair sticking out like spikes around its edges. He wore sunglasses with silver lenses that hid his eyes. He looked as if he hadn't shaved for a couple of days. The sleeves of his filthy, plaid shirt had been cut off at the shoulders. A big sheath knife hung from the belt of his jeans.

His friend looked a couple of years younger, maybe eighteen. He was shorter and heavier, but not fat. His T-shirt bulged with muscles and was cut off just below his ribcage. For a hat, he wore an army helmet liner. Around his waist was a wide web belt with a canteen hanging at one side and a knife at the other. He wore plaid Bermuda shorts. He looked slightly ridiculous, but Rick didn't feel like smiling.

'You got some trouble there?' asked the thin one.

'My son broke his leg yesterday.'

'Bad place for a thing like that.'

With the help of a crutch Julie had made for him after preparing the splints, Rick pushed himself up. He stood beside Julie, most of his weight on his right leg, using the crutch for balance.

'We're getting along okay,' Julie said. 'Did you come down from Windover Pass?' she asked.

'Nope. Heading that way. Mind if we rest up for a minute?'

'Help yourselves.'

They lowered their backpacks to the ground, but didn't sit down. 'Nice camp,' the lean one said. 'Just the two of you?'

'My husband's around here someplace,' Julie said. She looked off toward the outcroppings beyond Rick's tent. 'Dave?' she called.

Rick, already concerned by the presence of the two men, was frightened by Julie's lie.

'I'm sure he'll be along in a minute. He just went after some firewood.'

'Right.' The lean man turned to his friend. 'Dave went after firewood. How many packs you see?'

The stocky one smiled. 'Just two. I'll just bet Dave hiked out to get help for the kid.'

Rick felt as if his lungs were caving in. He swayed on his one leg and crutch.

It's okay, he told himself. They're jerks, but nothing's going to happen.

Julie shook her head. In a voice that sounded calm, she said, 'My brother-in-law hiked out. Dave's just over—'

'Hey Dave!' the heavy one yelled. 'Yoo-hoo, Daaavy! Where arrre you?' He shrugged. 'Gosh, Jiff, I don't know where he could be.'

Jiff, grinning, took a step toward Julie.

Julie's back stiffened. 'Now don't . . .'

He barely moved, just reached his left hand across to the walking stick by his right leg and rammed it upward with both hands. The point caught Julie under the chin. Her head snapped back. Her arms flew up. She was still falling when Jiff pivoted and swung the staff at Rick. It smashed him above the ear.

There was a terrible, roaring pain in his head. He thought, I shouldn't have drunk so much booze last night. If this is what it means to have a hangover . . . Groaning, he opened his eyes.

He wasn't in the tent. Above him, the leaves of trees were shivering in the wind. He lifted his head off the ground, felt himself spinning, and twisted onto his side. The sudden motion shot pain through his head and leg. Vomit erupted out of him.

Good thing I'm *not* in the tent, he thought vaguely.

When he was done vomiting, he wiped his teary eyes. He pulled a handkerchief out of his pocket, blew his nose, and cleaned his mouth and chin. Then he sat up.

He saw Julie naked on the ground.

He remembered.

The men!

He looked around quickly, making his head whirl. The men seemed to be gone.

'Julie!' he yelled.

She didn't move. She was sprawled on her back a few yards away. She still had her knee socks on. And one shoe. Her blouse lay in a heap near her head. Her shorts were on the ground close to the shoe that was off.

Don't look at her, Rick warned himself. She's naked. God, naked.

You might get turned on, and if you hadn't been looking at her yesterday, trying to see up her shorts . . .

As sick as he felt, and as guilty and frightened, he realized there was little need to worry about becoming aroused.

From where he sat, Rick didn't see any blood on her. But she didn't look right.

'Julie?' he asked again.

She's just out cold, he told himself. Like I was. That's good. Maybe she'd been unconscious while the men did things to her. They *must* have done things to her, or why were her clothes off?

When she woke up, she would know.

It'll be all right, Rick thought. I'll take good care of her. I'll cover her first. That's the first thing I'll do, so I won't keep looking at her.

Cringing as the pains in his head and leg punished him with burning throbs, he thrust himself up with his crutch. Another wave of dizziness came. He swayed, barely staying up as the ground tipped and turned. When the dizziness passed, he hobbled over to Julie.

She had a dark bruise where the walking stick had hit her under the chin. Her eyes were shut. Her lips and cheeks were crusted with something, as if white glue had been squirted around her mouth and dried. Rick wondered what it was. Then he knew.

Gagging, he turned his eyes quickly away from her face. But what he saw only added to his disgust and horror. The skin of her shoulders was bruised and dented from bites. Her breasts still held the imprint of fingers, as if they had been fiercely squeezed. Fingernails had left tiny, crescent-shaped impressions. Her nipples looked chewed. Rick covered his mouth and shut his eyes. But he had to look again. Lower, she was caked with dried blood and more semen. Rick had never seen that part of a woman before, just in a few pictures.

Embarrassment suddenly pushed its way through Rick's other agony. Even though he wasn't turned on, what if Julie woke up and saw him staring there?

He bent over and lost his balance. Though he waved an arm to steady himself, he knew it was useless. He flung the crutch from his other hand and reached beyond Julie as he fell. For a moment, he was braced above her like a bridge. But his left leg gave out as pain blasted up it. He collapsed. He fell on Julie.

He started to cry.

She was naked, and Rick had nothing on but swimming trunks, and he was lying on her. Her bare skin against him. He could feel the jut of her hipbone, her flat belly, her ribcage. He could feel a breast against his side, just below his armpit.

If she comes to now . . .

There was no movement under Rick.

No rise and fall of Julie breathing.

Of course she's breathing, he thought.

But she wasn't . . .

Rick's mind seemed to freeze. He shoved himself off Julie, rolled onto his side with his head resting on her outstretched arm. He saw his hand reach out as if it belonged to someone else. It curled around her throat. His fingers searched for the feel of blood pumping through arteries and veins below her jaw.

Then he was up on an elbow, sobbing as he shook Julie by the shoulder. Her head wobbled from side to side. He waited for her eyes to open.

They didn't.

They never would.

Chapter Seven

Gillian's first task, after securing the house, was to determine the name of its owner.

On the coffee table were several magazines: *People*, *Playboy*, *Los Angeles* and *Newsweek*. They had apparently been bought in stores, and bore no subscription labels.

Gillian went into the den. She shut the curtains across the glass door, then turned on a lamp. On top of the television, along with two remote control units, was a copy of *TV Guide*. It had a label with the address of this house.

The owner, therefore, was undoubtedly Fredrick Holden.

So, she thought, I'm house-sitting for Uncle Fred. Or is it Uncle Rick? I'd better just stick with Uncle Fredrick till I find out what he goes by.

With the lamp off, she stepped under the curtains and slid the door open. She carefully peeled off the duct tape she had used to hold the glued section of glass in place. She wadded it in her hand, shut and locked the door, turned on the lamp again, and tossed the tape into a waste basket she found behind the bar.

The bar had a refrigerator. Inside was a nice selection of soft drinks and beer, and a couple of jugs of wine. Gillian lifted out a jug of Blanc de Blanc. She chose a good-sized brandy snifter from a shelf of glasses, twisted out the bottle stopper, and filled her glass. She took a sip. The cold wine had a subtle, fruity flavor, and was not too sweet.

With the glass in one hand and her flashlight in the other, she went into the kitchen. The windows there faced the side of the house and the front porch, as she searched the kitchen in darkness except for the glow from outside. A bulletin board hung next to the wall phone. Some notes were pinned to it. Gillian decided to wait until morning to read the notes. Beside the bulletin board was a picture calendar. Flashlight tucked under her arm, she lifted the calendar off its small nail and carried it into the den.

She sat on a soft recliner chair, took a sip of wine, and studied the calendar. The top portion had a glossy color photo of a slender young woman posing beside a pool. She wore a string bikini and her skin was shiny with oil. Just what Gillian expected of a fellow who had mirrors on his bedroom ceiling.

The lower portion of the calendar was devoted to the month of June. Today was Saturday the 21st. The square block for the 21st had no writing on it. Neither did any of the squares for earlier in the week. On the 13th was written: '7:30 Stewardess; 9:05 Passion'. The 7th had similar notations: '7:10 Elena; 8:50 Crazy'. Gillian guessed that these were the starting times for double-features, the movie titles abbreviated. The rest of the dates for the month of June had no writing in their spaces. She glanced at July, then shook her head.

'You're no help,' she muttered at the calendar.

Apparently, Fredrick Holden needed no reminders of when he was leaving on his trip or returning. Maybe Gillian would turn up some information later. She was in no mood to continue investigating the matter now. She wanted to settle in and relax.

One final chore.

After taking the calendar back into the kitchen, Gillian went to the front room. She stepped into her skirt again and pulled the sweater over her head, but decided not to bother with her heels. Car keys in hand, she removed the burglar bar and unlocked the door.

Outside, the night air was cool and fresh after the stuffy warmth of the house. The grass was dewy under her bare feet. Down the street, a car swung into a driveway. A man and a woman climbed out and walked toward their front door. Nobody else was in sight.

Gillian climbed into her car. She drove it to the end of the block, turned the corner, and parked at the first empty stretch of curb. She walked back to the house.

At the driveway, she stopped.

Something looked different.

She frowned. What was . . .?

Light no longer glowed through the living-room curtains.

The nape of Gillian's neck went tight.

Someone inside the house? Had someone been in there all along?

No. Probably the lightbulb burnt out.

But what if someone *is* . . .?

She suddenly knew. Shaking her head and smiling at her foolishness, she checked her wristwatch. Eleven o'clock. Though she hadn't seen the timer, hadn't even bothered to look for it, the living-room lamp was obviously equipped with one. It would be set to turn on the lamp after dark and kill it around bedtime.

Nobody in there after all.

Hearing the grumble of a car engine behind her, Gillian looked around. A Corvette. Slowing down as it approached.

Her heart lurched.

Oh Jesus, no!

But the car didn't swing into the driveway. It went by and turned onto the driveway of the house next door.

Gillian hesitated.

She must've been seen.

Okay, she thought. Fine. Great, in fact.

As the Corvette stopped in front of the gate at the far side of the neighbor's house, she cut across the lawn, heading for it. The engine went silent. The headbeam died. A man climbed out from the driver's door, swung it shut, and walked around the low front of the car.

'Hi,' Gillian called.

'Hello,' he said. He was slim, dressed in dark slacks and a sport shirt, and appeared to be in his mid-twenties. He had a friendly smile.

'I'm Gillian,' she said. 'Glad you came by. I'll be staying at Uncle Fredrick's place till he gets back. You know, house-sitting?'

'Didn't know he was gone,' the man said.

'Well, I was afraid he might've mentioned he'd be away, and maybe forgot to tell you I'd be watching the place for him.' She grinned. 'Didn't want you thinking I was a burglar or something.'

'You don't look much like one,' he said. 'I'm Jerry Dobbs.'

Gillian offered her hand, and he shook it. 'Nice to meet you, Jerry.'

'From around here?'

'I've got a cramped little studio apartment in West LA. Which is why it'll be so nice spending a few days here.'

'I can imagine. I was an apartment dweller myself till I scraped up enough to get this place. Hated every minute of it. Confining, no privacy . . .'

'Exactly,' Gillian said. 'Well, I'd better let you go. It was nice meeting you.'

'Same here. Look, you need anything, just drop over.'

'You mean like a cup of sugar?'

'Or company. Whatever.'

'Thanks. Maybe I will.' She backed away, raising a hand in farewell. 'I'll see you around, Jerry.'

'Right. So long.'

Gillian headed across Jerry's lawn. She felt him watching, so she glanced over her shoulder and smiled, then continued toward the house. That had turned out great. Seemed like a nice guy, Jerry. If he'd been suspicious at all, he sure hadn't shown it.

Now, Gillian would be able to make herself at home without worrying about what the next-door neighbor might see or hear. A terrific development.

Inside the house she made her way through the darkness to a table lamp. After turning it on, she knelt on the floor beside the lamp that had gone off. She followed the cord, pulled the plug from the small plastic timer unit and inserted it into the wall socket. The lamp came on again. She turned off the other one.

After securing the door, Gillian carried her suitcase, purse and high-heeled shoes into the bedroom. She removed a few items from the suitcase, then packed her sweater and skirt.

She made a detour into the living room to pick up her wine glass.

In the bathroom, she had a few sips while she undressed and waited for the tub to fill.

She set the glass on the edge of the tub. She stepped into the water, sat down, and sighed with pleasure as the heat wrapped her to the waist. She stretched out her legs.

Flinched rigid as a bell jangled somewhere in the house.

Someone at the door?

Oh, Christ. And me in the tub.

She braced herself, ready to spring out, but the ringing came again and she realized it was the telephone.

A call. At this hour.

Her skin crawled. She saw goosebumps rise on her submerged thighs, felt her nipples tighten and pucker.

Calm down, she told herself. One thing's certain, it isn't for me.

Unless it's Jerry.

But it's not, she thought.

Each bray of the phone scraped her nerves.

It's not for me. That's the main thing. It's not bad news. Shit, there's nobody to get bad news *about*.

Maybe a neighbor, someone from across the street who saw me come in. Maybe just a wrong number.

At her apartment it was almost always a wrong number when it rang late at night.

Why doesn't it stop!

Gillian gritted her teeth.

Maybe an obscene caller, she thought. Maybe a burglar checking to find out if anyone's home before dropping by.

Maybe Fredrick Holden, calling in to ask what the hell I'm doing in his house. A pretty thought.

Gillian realized that a few seconds had gone by since the last ring. She sat motionless in the tub, her back rigid, her heart thudding, and listened. There was silence except for the slow drip of water near her feet.

Okay, she thought, he finally quit.

Or someone picked up the phone.

Charming idea.

Absurd.

She strained to hear a voice.

Your damned imagination is running haywire tonight. What are you, going paranoid? The house is empty, *empty*. Nobody home but me. The caller hung up, that's all.

Shit.

Gillian thrust herself up and climbed out of the tub. She rushed to the bathroom door, jerked it open, then ran dripping through the dark hall.

This is great. If someone *is* . . .

Even before she reached the kitchen, she could see the pale shape of a wall phone just beyond its entrance. Nobody there. Of course.

But the house had phones in the den and bedroom.

She reached for the handset. Stopped.

Drips of water trickled down her legs.

What if you pick it up and hear voices?

That's easy. You beat it the fuck out of here.

Or drop dead of cardiac arrest.

She snatched up the phone. A dial tone buzzed in her ear.

Of course.

Still shaking, Gillian returned to the bathroom. She locked the door, then stepped into the tub and sat down. She took a few swallows of wine.

Now just relax, she told herself. Nothing's wrong.

She set aside the glass and lay back. The water washed over her, covering her to the neck, its warm caress soothing, but not enough to make the gooseflesh go away. She rubbed her thighs. The skin felt tender and achy at first, then better. She rubbed one arm, then the other. She massaged the back of her neck. She covered her breasts until the tightness faded and the flesh was smooth again. Letting her arms sink into the heat, she closed her eyes. She took a deep breath.

As the fear seeped away, a heavy weariness settled into Gillian.

She moved her arms and legs, sending gentle currents rolling against her body. Her mind seemed vague. She could almost fall asleep. The water bed would be nice.

She was back in her own apartment, lying on the sofa.

Feeling pleasantly warm, her limbs all lazy and limp. Suddenly, she was flotsam; drifting, floating beneath clear sparkling water. She felt so-ooo peaceful . . . Sunlight glittered like diamonds through the rippling waves above. Below, a mass of dark swirling weeds undulated in the current. Reaching up, but not *quite* touching her.

With a gasp of fear, she swam up toward the sunlight.

She was back on the sofa, the TV on, the sound turned low. Shadowy images flickered across her vision. Her eyelids closed . . .

And snapped open again.

In one limp hand she held a glass of wine. The wine was red and dark. Staring into its ruby depths she saw . . .

But the glass slipped from her grasp and fell to the floor. Rising up on an arm, she looked down at it. Watched the stem snap away . . .

Click.

Smoothly. Neatly.

Like a slender neck, broken by a strong, practiced hand.

She stared at it for what seemed like an age. Then her eyes slid beyond the glass to the patch of spilt wine spreading around it.

Blood.

Whose?

Her face felt taut, expressionless. As if her skull was hard, moulded wax. She glanced down at her arms, turning them over, this way and that. Studied her hands.

No blood there.

Her arms fell, heavily, and her eyes strayed down the length of her body. It came as no surprise to see that she was naked. Naked and glistening with sweat. It was so hot.

I need air!

She opened her mouth to scream but nothing came.

Then, like angry snakes, cords and wires whipped themselves around her ankles. Cutting into her flesh. At the same time, her wrists crushed violently together. She jerked with the shock and pain. Beads of sweat and blood eased out of her pores.

Aaaghhh!

A strangled scream broke from Gillian's lips.

And another one. Louder this time.

In a frenzy of fear, she kicked and floundered in the tub; her body thrashed, the water heaving around her like a storm at sea. Her wrists, mashed tight together, were thrust up high before her.

She came to with a jolt.

Her hands hit water, hard. With a tremendous splash, waves of it smacked her face, stung her eyes . . .

Ugghhh. How long had she been out of it? She shivered and shook her head, spraying droplets all around. The water was barely warm and goosebumps crawled all over her skin.

No blood. No cords. No wires.

'No panic, Gilly-babes. Just your friendly neighborhood nightmare,' she muttered, clutching her arms across her breasts and shivering some more.

'So I dropped off in the tub. Lesson to be learned there. Never relax on the job, babe. Take a tub, sure. But *don't* fall asleep in it!'

Toweling herself dry, she dwelt on the mystery telephone caller. Who could it have been? She shrugged and slipped into a long, hooded terry-cloth robe she found hanging on the back of the bathroom door. Maybe she would never know.

Tying the belt tightly around her waist, she dug her hands deep into the pockets. A grateful smile curved her lips. So long, nightmare. Time for beddy-byes.

She felt warmer already.

Snuggling between the satin sheets on Uncle Fredrick's Amazing Wonderbed, she curled up into a fetal ball. Undulating gently with her movements, the bed reminded her of the bath she'd just climbed out of.

She still felt shaky after her weird experience.

After falling asleep in the tub.

That, and her scary dream or nightmare, whatever it had been. She told herself that similar slip-ups must never, ever happen again. Her intrusions were based on perfect planning. No, she prided herself on being the consummate strategist, right?

So no more sloppy hiccups. Okay?

She shuddered and shook her head, making the bed bounce some more. What if Fredrick Holden had come home early and found her hallucinating in his tub?

Yeah. *What if?*

Chapter Eight

Sunday, June 22

When Gillian woke up in the morning, a mild breeze was stirring the curtains. She squirmed a little, enjoying the feel of the satin sheets sliding against her bare skin and the way the water-filled mattress undulated. Turning over, she saw herself on the ceiling. She drew the sheet away, stretched, and folded her hands under her head.

Fredrick Holden might have a few quirks, she thought, but she had to admit that the combination of water bed, satin sheets and mirrors was rather appealing. She wouldn't want to have such things herself, but they would be nice for the few days she hoped to stay here.

Gillian was in no rush to leave the bed.

Soon, she found herself sliding around, rolling, savoring the smooth feel of the sheet and the warm breeze from the window. She tried every position she could think of and watched herself in the mirrors, at first with simple curiosity about how she looked from the different angles. Then she imagined a man being with her, a man admiring her display. He had the face of Jerry from next door. She twisted and writhed and contorted herself into erotic poses for his benefit, and suddenly blushed with shame.

For godsake, she thought, what am I doing?

She sprang from the bed. She was sweaty and breathing hard.

The blue satin bottom sheet, dark in places from her moist body, swelled and sank like the skin of something alive and panting.

Fredrick's Amazing Wonderbed. Too true, Gillian thought. Climb aboard, folks. See the astounding Miracle Mirrors transform you before your very eyes into lusting slaves of carnality.

Come one, come all.

Who're you kidding? Gillian thought. It's not the bed and mirrors, it's me.

Been alone too much.

She opened her suitcase, took out her white bikini and hurried to the bathroom. She dried herself before putting it on.

In the kitchen, she made coffee. While she waited for the pot to fill, she went to the den, opened the curtains, and slid the glass door wide. Most of the concrete slab behind the house was still in shade. The breeze felt good on her hot skin. She returned to the bedroom for her sunglasses and book, then poured herself a mug of coffee and stepped outside.

The redwood lounge chair needed a pad. She found one in a storage room alongside the garage. Then she sat down, crossed her legs, and drank coffee while she read her Simon Clark paperback.

When the mug was empty, she wandered over to the fence. On tiptoes, she peered into Jerry's back yard. He wasn't there. He had a big pool that shimmered in the morning sunlight, a patio set with an umbrella over the table, a couple of loungers and a barbecue.

It was against procedure, she reminded herself, to get involved with neighbors. It was risky. Too much danger of letting something slip. You make the brief, initial contact to allay their suspicions, then you stay away from them.

Curious that Jerry had wandered into her Wonderbed fantasy.

A little disturbing.

Disturbing, too, that she had hoped to see him when she looked over the fence.

The last thing you need is to get interested in some guy, she thought. All they do is mess you up.

Gillian went into the house for more coffee, then resumed reading until the mug was empty again.

She took the mug and book inside.

Then she went to the bedroom for her camera.

*

It had all started when Gillian was seventeen.

On her way home from school, she was walking past the deserted house when John Deerman called out to her. She stopped and waited for him to catch up.

'Look at this! Look!' He tugged a typed sheet out of his binder and waved it in front of her face.

She took it from him.

The title page of his term paper: 'The Whiteness of Moby Dick'. It had a big red 'A' beside his name. The teacher had scribbled, 'Wonderful job. A vast improvement.'

'That's nice,' Gillian said.

'Nice? It's *great*! I got an "A"!'

'Somebody did.' The 'A' called for a ten-dollar bonus in addition to the twenty-dollar advance John had paid her for writing the paper. She held out her hand.

Smiling, John produced his wallet. 'You're terrific, you know that?' As he slipped out a ten-dollar bill, a sudden gust of October wind snatched it from his fingers. Gillian made a quick grab for the tumbling bill as it fluttered past her face. She missed. It sailed over the battered picket fence.

'Shit!' John yelled.

Several yards beyond the fence, weeds in the overgrown yard snagged the bill.

'Don't stand here like a numbnuts,' Gillian said. 'Go get it.'

'No way. I'm not going in there.'

Gillian sighed, set her binder and books on the sidewalk, and rushed toward the gate.

'I wouldn't do that!' John called.

'Obviously,' she said. The gate hung crooked, held up only by the single hinge at the bottom. She lifted it, shoved it inward, then ran through the weeds. She plucked the money off a sticker bush.

'Boy, that was stupid,' John said when she returned to get her books.

'The only stupid thing was that you made *me* go after it.'

'That's Mabel Brookhurst's place.'

'So? Who's she?'

John's eyes brightened as if he were thrilled to meet someone who hadn't heard the story. 'She was a lunatic. My dad's a paramedic, you know. He was one of the guys that went in and got her. She'd been dead like three weeks, hanged herself. The stink was so bad the neighbors had started complaining. That's how come she got found.'

'Pleasant,' Gillian muttered.

'They say there's no way to get the smell out. That's how come nobody's bought the place. And there's the writing. Dad said she'd written weird shit everywhere – all over the walls and ceilings. With a marking pen. You can't just paint over a marking pen, it comes right through the paint. So even if they could get rid of the stink . . .'

'What sort of stuff did she write?'

John shrugged. 'Who knows? Weird shit. She was cracked.'

'Didn't anybody read it?'

'I don't know. Dad didn't. I mean, the place *reeked*. He didn't stick around any longer than he had to.'

'I wonder what she wrote,' Gillian said.

Grinning, John said, 'Why don't you go in and find out?'

'Sure thing,' Gillian said. 'You think I'm nuts?'

It was a Friday. Before her parents went to bed, Gillian told them she would be staying up late to watch TV. It was not exactly a lie. At that time, intrigued as she was about the writing Mabel Brookhurst had left on the walls and ceilings before hanging herself, she doubted that she actually had the courage to sneak over to the old house for a look.

After an hour of staring at the television movie, wondering about the Brookhurst house and trembling, she made up her mind. She left the TV on with its volume low. She turned on the light in the downstairs bathroom and shut the door to make it appear that she was inside – just in case one of her parents should come downstairs and wonder why she wasn't in front of the television.

In her bedroom, she changed from her nightgown into jeans, a chamois shirt and sneakers. She picked up her Polaroid camera and tiptoed downstairs and out of the house. In the garage, she found her father's flashlight and a screwdriver.

No Sanctuary

The walk to the Brookhurst house took no more than ten minutes. She stopped in front of it. Her mouth was dry, her heart thudding. She felt the wind under her shirt-tail, chilling her back.

Lights were on in some nearby houses, but she saw no one.

And no one sees me, she thought.

The Brookhurst house looked dismal. The weeds in front shifted and crackled in the wind. One of the front windows was broken, a star of blackness on the reflecting sheen of its pane.

I must be nuts, Gillian thought. I'm not going in there.

She walked past the crooked gate and kept on walking, and felt her fear slide away.

I'll just go back home and forget it. Nobody will ever know. It was a stupid idea.

Instead of relief, Gillian felt a sense of letdown.

What's the worst thing that could happen if I *did* go inside, she asked herself. The cops might get me. Can't be much of a crime, sneaking into an abandoned house. They'd take me home. I'd have some explaining to do, but Mom and Dad are okay. They'd think it was a weird move, but . . .

What's *really* the worst thing that could happen?

I'm not, for godsake, going to meet Mabel's ghost.

The worst thing, she finally decided, would be to sneak in and get herself nailed by some kind of creep or pervert. A deserted, run-down place like that, *anybody* might be staying there.

She began to feel the fear again. This time, she recognized that part of it, at least, was excitement.

Just watch your step, she thought, and get the hell out if there's any sign the place is occupied.

Gillian had already reached the corner of the block. She turned back. On her way toward the Brookhurst house, she watched the neighboring homes. Most of the draperies in the lighted windows were shut. Someone might be peering out a dark window, but she was willing to take the chance. If the cops grabbed her, too bad, but so what? A little embarrassment. She could live with that.

She swung open the gate and ran through the weeds to the side of

485

the house. Ducking around the corner, she leaned against the wall and tried to calm down. For a few moments, she couldn't get enough air. This seemed strange to Gillian. She was in good shape; running such a short distance shouldn't have winded her at all. It had to be nerves.

Soon she was breathing more easily but her heart continued to race. Though she was no longer cold, she felt shivery inside. She noticed a tingling tightness in her chest and throat – a peculiar cross between pain and pleasure that she associated, somehow, with sliding down a rough hill on her rump. Her skin was crawly with goosebumps. Her nipples felt stiff and sensitive, alive to every touch of her blowing shirt. The inseam of her tight jeans pressed against her like a finger. The denim was moist.

For a long time, she didn't move. She simply leaned against the wall, hidden by a thick hedge along the neighbor's property line, and wondered what was going on with her body. It had to be a combination of fear and excitement – the thrill of doing something forbidden and a little bit dangerous.

I'd better get on with it, she finally told herself.

Easing away from the wall, she walked alongside the house. The weeds crunched under her feet. She crouched each time she came to a window. At the rear of the house was an overgrown yard.

She found a back door. Stepping up to it, she tried its handle.

The door was locked. Good. If it hadn't been, she might have given up, figuring that somebody else might be inside. She realized that she hadn't tried the front door.

Too late for that now.

With the screwdriver, she dug into the doorframe beside the lock plate. Bits of wood broke off. Splinters tore loose. Finally, she worked back the lock tongue and opened the door.

She entered the house.

The stale air was warm and had a faint, sweetish odor that Gillian found a little sickening, but not so bad that she needed to gag.

She was in the kitchen. For a while, she stared straight ahead into the darkness and didn't move. She heard the rush of her heartbeat, the sounds of her shaky, ragged breathing. She tried to hold her breath, but couldn't. She still trembled. The current sizzling through her body seemed even stronger than before; it made her ache for release, to cry out in terror or quake in orgasm.

Get moving, she told herself.

She turned on the flashlight and swept its beam through the kitchen. There was no writing. Maybe John had it all wrong.

Then Gillian stepped into the hallway. The ancient wallpaper, yellow with age and peeling in places, looked like the canvas of a crazed graffiti artist. So did the ceiling. Amazed, she swung her light beam along the multi-colored words and drawings.

All the drawings seemed to feature an obese woman. They were as primitive as the artwork of a four-year-old: bloated bodies, pumpkin heads with scrawls of orange hair and faces composed of bright slashes and circles, oval legs and arms, stick fingers. There were pictures with colors scribbled on to represent clothes. In many of the pictures, the woman was naked, with mammoth, pendulous breasts and huge red nipples. Here and there were drawings of a rump that looked like a pair of clinging balloons.

Must be self-portraits, Gillian thought. She felt a little sorry for the woman, but her pity was mixed with astonishment.

As if she had discovered a hidden treasure.

She read some of the scrawled messages:

> Mabel Mabel, big as a stable,
> Finished her meal
> So she ate the table.

> I think that I shall never see –
> my feet!

> Blubber. Blub blub blub.

> It is no fun
> To weigh a ton,
> It is no fun at all.

It'll take a crane
As big as a train
To pick me up if I fall.

Deader is bedder.

I have no kids,
No Mary or Bill.
It's just as well.

I have no kids,
No Bonnie or Jim.
If I had kids
I'd eat them.

Wingle wangle
Hang and dangle.

Why me?

Gillian didn't read any more. She had brought her camera along, intending to take photographs of whatever she might find interesting in the house, but she wanted no reminder of this woman's torment.

She didn't explore the rest of the house.

She left.

Would've been fine, she thought as she walked home, if the woman hadn't put such depressing shit on her walls and ceilings.

What d'you expect? The gal committed suicide. You're lucky you didn't find something a whole lot worse.

Depressing.

Interesting, though.

Sneaking in that way, spying into her life.

Next time, don't pick a goddamn suicide.

Next time?

Gillian wanted to feel that way again, to feel as she did before the gloomy drawings and messages ruined it for her.

The next day, she called John on the telephone. 'Guess what I did,' she said.

'Finished my history paper?'

'I had a look inside Mabel's house.'

'Sure thing.'

'I wanted to see what she wrote all over the place.'

'Yeah. And what did you find out?'

'She was fat. A blimp. Apparently, that's what drove her crazy enough to kill herself.'

'I *knew* you didn't go in there. You kidding? She was nothing but skin and bones. Dad said she looked like one of those pictures you see of Auschwitz survivors.'

'That's impossible.'

'Hey, she was always that way. I used to see her around. She'd turn sideways, she'd disappear.'

'No way.'

'Ask anyone.'

The revelation astonished Gillian. She couldn't get over it. Though Mabel's problem certainly seemed tragic, she felt as if she'd made an amazing discovery.

What if every house held strange secrets?

And even if they didn't, there was the thrill of sneaking in to explore.

That night, after her parents had gone to bed, she broke into the house of Ralph and Helen Norris, friends of her parents who were in Las Vegas for the weekend.

She felt a frenzy of fear and excitement.

She searched their closets and drawers.

Though she made no startling discovery, it didn't seem to matter. All that mattered was being there.

She tried their bed.

She took pictures and notes of every room.

What else? She wasn't ready to leave. Not yet.

She drank a cold beer and ate potato chips at their kitchen table, sitting in the darkness, hardly able to swallow because of her thudding chest.

Still unwilling to leave, she went into the master bedroom. There was a huge sunken tub. She filled it, took off her clothes, and climbed in. Except for the dim light from the window, the bathroom was dark.

I can't believe I'm doing this, she thought. I must be nuts. What if they come home and find me naked in their tub?

Hi, folks. I'm Goldilocks.

With a trembling laugh, she slipped down into the deep, hot water.

The Norris experience had been the start of something big. A life-changing event. The beginning of a series of adventures that led to a weird kind of addiction. It set in motion within her a yearning desire to discover the innermost secrets of other people's homes. In doing this, Gillian found an immense sense of fulfillment. A *needy* gratification that was almost sexual.

The highlight of it all, though – the cherry on top of the proverbial cake – had been bathing in the Norrises' tub. After that, the ritual bath had been the highlight of every one of her intrusions.

Later. Two years and forty or so intrusions later, she'd tried to reason out, *why baths*? Why this fetish with other people's bathing arrangements? That first glimpse of the bathroom itself, the tub and the accessories that went with it: oils, shampoos, talc, deodorants, perfumed soaps. They all played an important part, leading up to the real climax. The shivers of excitement, the thrill of *invading* the inner sanctum of some unknown person.

Then. Easing into those hot bubbles.

As good as an orgasm.

The sensual release of some kind of mental climax. Lying naked and up to the neck in some guy's hot, foaming bubbles, she'd come, no problem.

Other girls had sex with strangers. Just for the thrill of it. Wham bam, thank'ya ma'am. And goodbye forever. No hassle. No hangups. No long-winded affairs to cool off, or drift into indifference. Two ships that passed in the night.

For Gillian, it was like: who needs a man when you can have it all in a stranger's tub?

You get it *off* in a hot tub? In somebody else's bathroom? D'you get all of your kicks this way? Like as in some kind of *titillation*? The whole experience is a *come-on*?

No shrink had heard of this one.

Climaxing under water.

Sure we're not talking *masturbation* here?

We're not? Er, well, Miss O'Neill. Must admit your problem *is* er . . . rather unusual, to say the least. But hey. People get their kicks lotsa ways these days.

Maybe we should edit all of this down to one root cause. In your childhood, you were deprived of nice hot baths and have felt guilty about enjoying them ever since? A classic example of the 'naughty but nice' syndrome!

It's not uncommon for people to become addicted to things they like, things with *forbidden* connotations. Things which are often socially unacceptable. Such as alcohol, drugs, certain foods. Shopping.

But hot baths . . .?

Mmmm-huh. I think we've found the answer to your problem, Miss O'Neill. Deprived childhood and no mistake. Good day to you. Oh, and please leave your check for $3000 with the clerk on your way out . . .

Of course, she hadn't seen a shrink. First off, her little jaunts had not only 'forbidden' connotations. They were illegal. Her intrusions were a criminal act. But she'd been addicted to them for too long to stop now. She knew that. *This thing will be with me forever*, she told herself. *Like some kind of disability.*

She'd tried to put a stop to it. Seriously. For weeks at a time she'd abstained. Then, like a reformed junkie offered a free trip, she'd feel the old familiar sequence moving neatly into action. Just like a clock-work train.

It was all there. Again. The adrenaline rush as she eased open the front door. The sweats, the soaring, nerve-wracking excitement, wondering if the house owner really was home. Upstairs taking a nap? On their way to the Speed-D-Mart for aspirin? Or Pizza Hut for a takeaway?

Or would she be met in the hallway by the occupant? Fearful, trembling, finger poised. About to dial 911.

But she knew that, cool as ever, she'd pass off her intrusion by saying she'd mistaken the house number. She'd express frustration at her own stupidity. I'm *so* sorry . . . What*ever* must you think of me?

Yes, she was plausible, she knew that. She had her performance down to a fine art. After all this time she could play to packed houses. Fill theaters up and down the country. Her sudden warmth, charm, *ingenuousness*, would have people eating out of her hand in no time at all.

But it hadn't ever come to that.

So far, so good.

But only because she did her groundwork like a true pro.

Yeah, sure. She was good. Just as well, since her intrusions were food and drink to her now. A major part of the thrill was paying minute attention to detail – at every stage of the game. The reconnaissance, the illegal entry.

Then, the *prize*.

Eating and drinking *their* food. Watching *their* TV. Sleeping in *their* bed. And the kick of it all – entering *their* private domain. *Their inner sanctuary*.

Unknown to them.

She used their bathroom; their tub; their toilet. *And they knew fuck all about it*. She invaded their most private places without their knowledge.

That was the kick.

Gillian smiled softly. She didn't need the help of an expensive shrink to work that one out.

She got off on it is all.

Hey. Tubs she had known . . .

About sixty-six in total?

She could write a book.

Or a screenplay.

Miss O'Neill, talented winner of the Golden Goblet Screenwriter of the Year Award, please tell our viewers – your fans – which, in your experience, has been the most fascinating tub of all?

Her camera and notebook were ready. But instead of taking shots of Fredrick Holden's artifacts, as planned, she returned to the concrete sundeck and flopped back onto the lounge chair.

So, which *was* the most fascinating tub? Gillian thought hard about that one. But, damn it, she decided, she didn't need to give herself such a hard time. Because, like a flame among dying embers, one occasion stood out from all the rest.

Yeah. That one on Silverston. West of Studio City.

No shit, that's been the most fantastic tub so far.

She'd done her routine check. No one around. No snoopers. No dog-walkers. No mailmen . . .

The absence of human life, or of any other type of life on that street, come to that, was in itself unusual.

The house fascinated her from the start. The neighborhood was maybe too upmarket for her liking. But, in some strange way, she knew that the old place *needed* her.

And Christ, she knew about *need*, all right. She was here, wasn't she? Cruising around, searching for places to satisfy *her* need.

Looks like I've found it . . .

Too upmarket? Okay, Miss O'Neill, so break a few rules.

This one's going to be your special treat!

It was as if that lonely old house, set back against dark shadows, was crooking its finger and beckoning to her. She imagined its whispering voice, mingling and swishing with the windblown palms lining its path.

Hey, girl. Come on in. You want tales? I got tales a-plenty to tell – and a thousand secrets to share . . .

That clinched it. The white stucco house, detached and with around two, three hundred yards of driveway leading up to it, was her target for tonight. Tall, dark palms ran either side of the driveway. The rustling trees almost blocked out all of the remaining daylight until they looked like one long, dark, moving tunnel.

Leading to what?

The house. Secreted away in the background. Looming like a forgotten ghost; silent and forbidding.

Scary.

I must be nuts.

No possibility of nosy neighbors. Unless they used a pair of step-ladders, the tall yew hedges either side would obscure the driveway from view. And when she'd driven past earlier, she'd seen a For Sale sign sticking up out of next-door's front lawn. *That* house had looked dark and empty too.

The gravel leading up to number 1309 crunched loudly under her feet. This place, with its flaky, white-painted exterior, exuded an air of loneliness.

But not emptiness.

The driveway, the gardens, the long green lawn in front of the house, were neat and well-kept. A sure sign that a gardener or handyman had recently been at work. By the time she reached the three shallow steps curving up to the arched front door, she knew there was no one around to halt her progress.

In some strange way, this knowledge was a *certainty*.

Gillian smiled.

The house was hers.

Alarm system?

Yeah. Alarm system . . .

She looked around for tell-tale electronic devices. Wires. Anything. Nope.

Crazy, but true. There were no alarm devices that she could see.

So, go for it.

She did.

Gaining access was easy. In the studded dark wood door a rectangular window gleamed. It was small, narrow and about two thirds of the way up: a nice stained-glass affair showing a white, stylized lily, cupped by two long green leaves. The background was bright blue. A quick glance around assured her there was no one immediately in sight. Taking her small leather tool satchel from her purse, Gillian paused for a moment, head tilted, listening intently to sounds from within.

Like someone running to open the door.

The click of a telephone being lifted off the hook.

Nothing.

She stretched out a length of duct tape and stuck it around the window. She stuck a circle in the center of the window to use as a handle. It's an old window, she thought with satisfaction. Should drop out okay.

She set to work with her glass cutter. When she'd finished she tapped the glass. It came away in her hand.

Easy as drawing breath.

Too easy?

She reached her hand through the space and felt around with her fingers. The door handle was just below the space. It was large and heavy and she could move it up and down with her fingers. But the door wouldn't give.

A bolt?

Yeah. She reached inside, felt below the window space and found the bolt.

Slid it back.

It moved smoothly, in double quick time.

Freshly oiled.

Especially for her?

The door swung open.

Briskly, and with a pounding heart, she returned her tools, and the small piece of window, to the satchel, slid it into her purse and picked up her suitcase. She stepped inside and closed the door behind her.

Taking her tools out again, Gillian worked quickly, replacing the window in the door and returning her tools to the leather satchel. She placed the satchel into her purse.

Then looked around her.

Thirties Hollywood. That was her first impression. Maybe not so big as some of those deco places out in the hills. But in its own faded, still glamorous way, this one was just as tasty.

White marble entrance hall. Light streaming through looped drapes at the long windows either side of the tall white studded door. A white staircase rose before her. It branched off, right and left, each section winding upward and then back on itself. Both sets of stairs met on a white and chrome balcony, the entire width of the house. Just like the prow of a cruise liner.

The Busby Berkeley Babes.

Dick Powell and Ruby Keeler.

'Yessir,' Gillian breathed. 'The place has style, all right.'

She shivered. It was this air of loneliness, inside the house as well as out. It hung about the place like some long-forgotten melody. It made her want to cry, it was so sad.

The emptiness made her think that maybe this house, too, was up for sale. But once again, she had this deep down certainty that it wasn't.

A quick check on all the rooms told her that the house *was* lived in. It was tidy; not a magazine out of place. Garden flowers were still fresh in the tall white vases.

Black and white studio shots of a blonde with cupid bow lips and provocative, dark-lashed eyes smiled archly from the walls. In one photograph, she was dressed up like Heidi, complete with pigtails, accompanied by a mustachioed guy in Bavarian fancy dress.

Gillian recognized the woman – though from where, she couldn't say. *Some old-time movie star. All alone with her memories. Alone, except for a maid coming in twice a week to keep the place straight . . .*

She inspected the first bedroom she came to. White quilted satin on a large, circular bed. Flimsy white drapes drawn aside from the heart-shaped quilted satin headboard. Flimsy white drapes at the windows, too. Built-in wardrobes. A curved white dresser covered in glass gewgaws and perfume and stuff. Matching nightstands stood either side of the bed.

A movie set from years ago.

Gillian stepped inside the adjoining all-white bathroom. And gasped with pleasure as her eyes took in the round sunken tub and ornate gold taps shaped like dolphin heads. Slender bottles filled with colored oils and unguents were set neatly at intervals around the rim.

Claudette Colbert in *Cleopatra*.

Only thing missing was a Nubian slave girl.

Excitement stirred, touching her spine with soft, seductive fingers. The tingly feeling teased her stomach and goosebumps rose on her skin. She couldn't wait to undress.

But first off, had she missed anything? Like some vital clue telling her that the owner was home, after all? To be safe, Gillian called out, 'Hello? Anybody home?'

If somebody answered she could always say . . . hell, what *could* she say? The usual excuses, like she'd been asked to call around, to check on . . . who? That she was a relative come to stay? All seemed woefully inadequate.

An escapee from the local psychiatric unit seemed more plausible, she remembered thinking.

Okay. Weak wasn't the word. Especially if she was discovered upstairs already. She'd have to come up with a pretty good answer. Bluff her way out of a tricky situation.

Or just make a break for it.

Let's hope it doesn't come to that.

Silence.

No reply.

Thank God.

She was safe. Although . . .

Do it now. Do it. I dare you . . .

The short hairs on the back of her neck began to rise.

Hey. Live life on the edge, Gilly baby. Why not?

She cocked her head. Listening for sounds. Any sounds.

None.

The familiar tingle of excitement teased her center. Her pubic mound throbbed until the ache became unbearable. A low giggle burst from her lips. She slipped off her shoes and undressed.

A flicker of fear came and went. *Wait*, a small voice whispered. *Forget the tub. Go explore. Make sure it's safe . . .*

Against her better judgement, she ran water into the tub. Steam curled into her face, making her gurgle with excitement. Selecting a long-stemmed container of bath oil, Gillian took off the stopper and poured it into the tub. Fascinated, she watched the amethyst fluid flow into the bubbling torrent.

The delicate scent of lilacs met her nostrils. Mmmm . . . Stepping into the fragrant water, she hummed a tune:

'*Keep young and beautiful . . .*'

Yeah. That was the most fascinating, the most luxurious, most memorable tub she'd *ever* taken.

All round, her most fascinating, memorable intrusion so far.

And the briefest, so it turned out.

Chapter Nine

Bert wasn't in the tent. Rick told himself there was no reason to worry, but he scurried out of his sleeping bag, needing to see her, needing to banish his sudden fear. He swept aside the tent flap.

She was nowhere in sight.

The fire crackled. Its pale flames fluttered in the morning sunlight. A distance beyond the fire were their packs. The ponchos had been removed and the red nylon top of Bert's pack was open.

Rick sat down just inside the tent and pulled on his running shoes. His fingers trembled as he tied the laces.

She's all right, he told himself. Probably down by the stream.

On her back. Wearing one knee sock.

Rick shook his head sharply to dislodge the thoughts, and winced. His head had a dull ache, thanks to the bourbon. He got to his feet, looked around, and walked across the campsite.

She'll be down by the stream, he thought. When I get to the top of the embankment, I'll see her. She's fine.

God oh God, why had he let himself remember all that last night? Over the years he'd become talented at turning his mind away from the memories whenever they started. But lying there in the dark tent, he'd dwelled on them, wallowed in them. He hadn't even tried to fight the memories.

He suspected that he knew the reason why – because he had a *need* to remember what happened last time. He was out here again. Probably a hundred miles from the place where Julie was murdered, but *here*, in the mountains, in the wilderness. He needed to relive the horror.

He needed it fresh in his mind. A cautionary tale. Watch out, be ready, it could happen again.

Shaken by the memories, he had crawled from the tent last night, stirred the smoldering fire to life, gone to his pack and taken out the bottle and revolver. The pocket of his parka was deep enough to hold the revolver. Its weight felt good. He sat on a stump close to the fire and drank. The heat of the bourbon swept through him. He wished he had brought two bottles, not just the one. He had six more nights to go. He needed to hold back, to drink no more than a seventh of the bourbon, or he might run out.

But a seventh of a quart wasn't much at all.

There were bound to be nights when he wouldn't need to drink, nights when he would sleep through till morning.

Now is when I need it, he thought.

When a quarter of the bottle was gone, he forced himself to quit. Hoping that would be enough to help him sleep, he put the bottle away and returned to the tent. He rolled his parka into a pillow. In spite of its thickness, he could feel the revolver under his head. He didn't mind.

Nobody gonna fuck with us this time, he thought vaguely, just before falling asleep.

Rick reached the edge of the embankment. For a moment, he didn't see Bert and something clamped tight in his chest. Then he spotted her. She was off to the right, sitting cross-legged on a rock near the middle of the stream.

'Morning,' he called, climbing down the slope.

She looked over her shoulder at him and smiled. 'Afternoon,' she said.

'Oh, it's not that late.'

She got to her feet, hopped across the stream, and stepped into her sneakers. She was wearing baggy tan shorts and a white T-shirt. She looked fresh and wonderful. She came to Rick. He put his arms around her. She pressed herself against him.

'How come you didn't invite me to your party?' she asked.

She knew. Of course she knew.

'You were asleep,' Rick said.

He felt her shrug.

'You didn't miss much. I woke up and couldn't get back to sleep. So I knocked back a few. They helped.'

'The first night out can be tough,' she said. 'It'll get better.'

'God, I hope so.'

'Good thing I didn't light a match this morning, the tent would've blown up.'

Rick laughed softly. 'Sorry.'

Her hands slipped inside the seat of his sweatpants. They were warm on his buttocks. 'If you have trouble sleeping again, how about waking me up? I don't want you to suffer alone.'

'All right.'

She patted his rump, then stepped away. 'Let's get some breakfast. I'm starving.'

Back at the camp, Rick heated water on the fire for instant coffee. Bert dumped powdered eggs into her pan, stirred in water, and used her sheath knife to scrape chunks of meat off a bacon bar. She cooked the meal over the burner of her small propane stove.

Rick normally abhorred instant coffee. This morning, however, it seemed to taste great. He drank it eagerly while he lingered over the scrambled eggs with bacon.

And he watched Bert sitting on a log across from him, eating from the pan. Her hair gleamed like gold over one ear where the sunlight fell on it. Her white T-shirt, so bright that it almost hurt his eyes to look at it, hung loosely over her breasts. Her nipples made it jut and he could see a hint of their darkness through the fabric. The pan was on her lap. Her legs, long and sleek, were stretched out and crossed at the ankles.

Finishing first, Rick got up and went to his pack. He took out his Polaroid camera.

'Come on,' Bert said, 'my hair's a mess.'

'You look great. Just keep eating.'

She shrugged and rolled her eyes upward. Rick took a shot as she lifted the fork to her mouth. With a buzz, the camera ejected the photo.

Rick crouched beside Bert and they watched the picture appear, faint at first, growing sharp, finally showing every detail in rich clarity. 'I told you my hair was a mess.'

'Now let's get one with your shirt off.'

'Up yours.'

'I'll wait till you go to change it.'

'Who says I'm going to change it?'

Rick tried to keep his tone light. 'You show through, you know.'

She grinned. 'Is that a problem for you?'

'I love it. But we might meet someone on the trails.'

'Ah.'

'Or you could put on a bra.'

'If I'd brought one.'

'I just don't think . . .'

'I know. You don't want some stranger getting an eyeful. Rather selfish of you, don't you think?'

'Yep.' Not just selfish, he thought. Seeing her nipples through the shirt might give people ideas. Such ideas might lead to . . .

'Well, I suppose if it's going to bother you. But no pictures, or I'll change in the tent.'

'A deal.'

'Why don't you get some shots of the campsite before we tear it down?'

Rick obliged, then put the camera away.

They took the cook kits down to the stream. After cleaning them, Rick remained to brush his teeth and wash. He returned to camp. Standing in a patch of sunlight, he changed out of the sweatsuit he had slept in. Bert doused the fire and watched him. Then she pulled off her T-shirt, walked over to her pack, and took out the faded blue chambray shirt she had worn yesterday. She buttoned it up, and gave Rick a coy smile as she fastened the button at her throat. 'Is this modest enough for you?' she asked.

'Well, you don't have to overdo it.'

She smiled and opened the top two buttons. 'Okay?'

'Fine.'

She went inside the tent. Rick watched while she forced her sleeping bag into its stuff sack. 'Want me to do yours?' she asked.

If she started touching the things on his side of the tent, she might find the revolver in his coat.

'No, fine. I'll take care of it.'

She crawled out.

Rick entered the tent, rammed his sleeping bag into its tiny sack, and brought it out along with his rolled parka. Bert stayed beside him, rearranging the contents of her backpack. He wanted to put the gun into a side pocket of his pack where it would be easy to reach, but that was impossible with Bert there. So he left it inside his parka. His sleeping bag went on top of it.

So much for easy access, Rick thought.

They struck the tent. They were both on their knees, folding it, when Rick heard voices. His stomach clenched. Head snapping to the side, he saw three figures moving through the trees, coming down the trail that ran past their campsite. He looked at Bert.

She was watching them, too. Her hands were on the tent. The way her loose shirt hung toward the ground, Rick could see the shadowed slope of a breast. He felt as if his head were being squeezed. He wanted to shout for her to button up, damn it! Then the shirt swayed back and concealed her breast as she raised herself.

She waved at the strangers. 'Morning,' she called.

Shit!

They might've gone on by if she'd kept quiet. Why did Bert *do* that?

The young man in the lead called, 'Hi, there,' and turned off the trail. He stepped between a couple of saplings and came toward them, followed by his two companions.

Bert stood up. She brushed dirt and pine needles off her knees.

Numb and shaking, Rick got to his feet. He forced himself to smile and say, 'Hello' to the three approaching men.

Men? Boys. They were teenagers, seventeen or eighteen years old.

That's worse, he thought.

Three of them. God.

He strolled over to his pack, lifted out his sleeping bag, and set it on the ground. There were voices behind him, but he didn't listen. Fingers trembling, he plucked at his down parka, turned it until the pocket was on top. He slipped his hand in, pulled out the revolver and shoved its barrel down the front of his pants. He untucked his shirt, looked down at himself to make sure the gun handle didn't show, then took a cigar from his shirt pocket and faced the intruders.

They're not intruders, he told himself. Bert *invited* them over for godsake.

She was still beside the collapsed tent. The three guys stood in a semi-circle, facing her.

He ripped off the cigar's cellophane wrapper as he walked toward them. 'Hello, fellows,' he said, and clamped the cigar in his teeth.

As he lighted up, Bert smiled at him. 'They spent the night at Mosquito Pasture,' she said.

'Sure did,' said the leader, smiling. He was bigger than Rick and had a body that looked solid. 'They damn near carried us off. Wally got messed up real good.'

Wally, a fat kid in glasses who wore cut-off jeans that hung low and appeared ready to drop around his ankles, turned and pointed to red weals on the backs of his legs. He pointed out others on his neck, on the inner sides of his forearms and the crooks of his elbows. 'They murdered me,' he said in a dismal voice.

'Don't you have insect repellent?' Bert asked, sounding concerned.

'Who wants to stink?'

'That's a good one,' said the third boy, a lanky, freckled kid in white-rimmed sunglasses and an olive green beret.

Wally sneered at him.

'Have you tried Cutters'?' Bert asked. 'It doesn't smell bad.'

Wally shook his head.

'I've got some left in my old bottle,' she said. 'Why don't you take it?'

'Gee . . .'

Bert headed for her pack.

Wally scratched the side of his neck and watched Bert. The leader watched her, too. Rick couldn't tell where the guy in the sunglasses was looking, but he could guess.

They were all three staring at the way she moved inside her shorts.

'How long you fellows been in?'

'Three nights,' said the leader, still looking past Rick. He licked a corner of his mouth. Then he took a pack of Winstons from the pocket of his sleeveless shirt, shook out a cigarette, and poked it into his mouth. 'Borrow a light?' he asked.

Rick slipped a book of matches from his pocket. He pictured the guy grabbing his hand when he reached out, yanking him forward and driving a knee into his guts. So he tossed the matches.

The guy caught them, muttered 'Thanks', and lit his cigarette. He tossed the matches back to Rick.

'Where are you folks heading?' asked the one in sunglasses.

'Granger Lake,' Rick said. He'd never heard of such a place.

'Yeah? That anywhere near the Pylons?'

'Is that where you're going?' Rick asked. 'The Pylons?'

'Yeah.'

Rick heard footfalls behind him. Bert was coming back, and the eyes that he could see were on her. She stepped past Rick and handed a squeeze-bottle to Wally.

'Thanks a lot.'

In her other hand was a plastic tube. 'Here, put some of this on your bites. It should help with the itching.'

Wally nodded. He uncapped the tube, sniffed its opening and wrinkled his nose.

Bert let out her husky laugh.

'Can't smell any worse than your pits,' the one in the sunglasses said.

'You and the horse you rode in on, Bugger.' He started dabbing the pink ointment onto his bites.

'Bugger?' Bert asked, smiling.

'It's *Burgher*.' He spelled it. 'Luke Burgher.'

'Also known as Ham, Cheese, and McDouble,' Wally said, leering as he got in his digs.

'So it's Wally, Luke and . . .' Bert looked at the leader and raised her eyebrows.

What *is* this, Rick thought, a goddamn cocktail party?

The guy blew out smoke and said, 'Jase.'

'Jason?'

'Just Jase.'

'He's sensitive,' Luke said.

'You know,' Wally said. 'Jason. *Friday the Thirteenth.*'

Bert smiled at Jason. 'I didn't recognize you without the hockey mask.'

He blushed. Then he smiled.

'I'm Bert. Nobody calls me Bertha and lives.' She shook hands with Jase. The cigarette drooped in his lips, and his eyes glazed over as if she were holding his cock instead of his hand.

'My silent partner here is Rick,' she said.

Rick nodded, but didn't offer his hand. Jase made a feeble smile, and his eyes stayed on Bert as she sidestepped to Wally.

'Bert,' Wally said. He wiped his pink fingertip on his shorts, then shook her hand. He grinned and blushed. Watching, Rick half expected the kid's glasses to fog up.

She moved on down the line.

'Pleased to make your acquaintance, Bert,' Luke said, and gave her hand a quick, stiff shake. Rather formal. Rather mocking, as if he thought she was weird for shaking hands with them all.

Good for him, Rick thought.

Wally resumed smearing goo on his bites.

'Are you guys heading up over Dead Mule Pass?' Bert asked.

'Yeah,' Jase said. 'How about you?'

'Same here.'

Great, Rick thought. Why don't you break out the map and show them our whole route?

'Maybe we'll run into you up ahead,' Bert continued.

'Yeah. Could be.'

Next, she'll be inviting them to hike along with us.

'We'd better finish getting our stuff together,' Rick said, 'or we'll be here all day.'

'Need a hand with the tent?' Jase asked, looking at Bert.

'We can take care of it,' Rick said. 'Thanks anyway.'

Wally twisted the cap back onto the ointment.

'Better?' Bert asked him.

'Yeah. Thanks. And thanks for this.' He patted the shirt pocket where he'd put the mosquito repellent.

'It was nice meeting you,' Jase said. Then, he stepped over to the muddy ashes of the fire and tossed in his cigarette butt.

'Well,' Bert said, 'if we don't run into you fellows up ahead some-where, have a real good trip.'

Don't worry, Rick thought. We'll run into them again. They'll see to it.

'Yeah,' Jase said. 'So long.'

'Nice meeting you,' Wally said.

'See you around,' said Luke.

'Take it easy, guys,' Bert told them.

'Yeah,' added Rick.

He watched the three turn away and head for the trail. Wally looked back and waved. Jase glanced back a couple of times. Luke didn't.

'Nice kids,' Bert said.

'That remains to be seen.'

She looked at him. 'Did I miss something?'

'Hell, they were drooling all over you.'

'Drooling?'

Rick nodded. For a moment, he couldn't see the three boys. Then they appeared on the other side of a rock cluster. 'Looks like they're leaving,' he muttered.

'Expect them to circle around and jump us?' She sounded amused.

'It's a possibility.'

'My protector,' she said, and patted his rump.

Rick was tempted to lift his shirt and show her what was in his belt.

Protector, all right.

He fought the urge. If Bert found out that he had a gun, she would go into shock.

507

She'll find out if I have to use it, he thought. Then she'll be damn glad I was scared and crazy enough to bring it along.

'Want to stand guard while I pee?' Bert asked.

'Why don't you wait a few minutes?'

The smile left her face. 'They're gone, honey.'

'Maybe.'

Frowning, Bert gently stroked his cheek. 'I wish you wouldn't worry so much.'

'Me too.'

'There's honestly no need for it. We're perfectly safe out here. We left all the nutcases behind in LA.'

'I hope so.'

'Anyway, my teeth are floating.'

The trail looked deserted. There was no sign of the boys. 'Okay, go ahead. But stay out of sight.'

She turned away and walked toward her pack.

Rick shifted his attention from the trail to Bert until she wandered into the trees with a roll of toilet paper in her hand.

The moment she was gone, he rushed over to his pack. After a quick search, he found a T-shirt. He wrapped it around his revolver and stuffed them in a side pocket of his pack. He zipped the pocket shut, patted it, and felt the hardness of the gun inside.

Now he'd be able to get at it without taking his pack apart.

Still wouldn't be as fast as he'd like.

He only wished he could wear the gun on his hip.

Chapter Ten

Gillian took photographs of every room in Fredrick Holden's house for her scrapbooks. When shooting the bedroom, she was especially careful to avoid catching her reflection in the mirrors. In the past, she had sometimes taken pictures of herself, either in mirrors or using the camera's delayed timing device. Fortunately, she hadn't done that at the Farnsworth house, where the family returned home early and she left everything behind, camera included. After that, she stopped taking self-portraits.

Once every room of Fredrick Holden's house had been photographed to her satisfaction, Gillian began to investigate.

She started with the kitchen. The notes on the bulletin board by the phone provided no information about Uncle Fredrick's trip. There were scribbled names and telephone numbers, nothing of much interest.

The refrigerator was well stocked, but Gillian noticed that it held no milk or cream. A good sign. Fredrick had removed the perishables, not wanting to return home and find his refrigerator stinky. He wouldn't have tossed such things if he planned to be gone for only a couple of days. If Gillian could just find out the date he left . . .

The freezer section was full of goodies: steaks, lamb chops, chicken breasts, bags of onion rings and Golden Crisp Potato Nuggets, two sausage pizzas, chocolate-chip ice-cream, a box of tacquito hors d'oeuvres, and a dozen TV dinners such as veal parmesan, lasagna, fried jumbo shrimp, and lobster Neuberg.

Gillian decided she was hungry.

She turned on the oven, tore open a box of pizza, and slid the frozen slab onto the oven tray. After setting the timer for ten minutes, she took a lamb chop from the freezer and set it aside to defrost for dinner.

The pleasant odors of the pizza stole her concentration as she inspected the drawers and cupboards. When the dinger sounded, she opened the oven door. The heat washed over her. She breathed deeply of the rich, spicy aromas. The tomato sauce and cheese bubbled, but the crust needed to darken some more. Leaving it in the oven, she went into the bar and got herself a bottle of Corona beer.

She checked the pizza again. The rim of its crust was golden brown, nearly black in places, just the way she liked it.

She cut out several large wedges, put them on a plate, and sprinkled them with salt and pepper.

She ate outside, sitting cross-legged on the lounge chair with the plate on her lap. The sun felt uncomfortably hot on her bare skin. The pizza, in spite of its wonderful look and smell, was more of a disappointment than a pleasure.

If I'd wanted the taste of cardboard, Gillian thought, I would've eaten the box.

But the beer was cold and tasted terrific.

Her hand was wet from the bottle. She rubbed it over her shoulders, sighing as the cool moisture soothed her hot skin.

I ought to get Jerry to invite me over for a swim, she thought.

Forget it. No fraternizing with the neighbors.

She looked over at Fredrick's spa. The water in there was probably cool.

Later, she told herself. I have more snooping to do before I can flake out.

The second and third slices of pizza didn't seem as awful as the first. Gillian supposed that they *were* no less awful; that they only seemed better because she was growing accustomed to the lousy flavor.

When her plate and bottle were empty, she stood up. She was streaming with sweat and the seat of her bikini pants clung to her buttocks. She plucked the fabric away as she walked over to the fence. On tiptoes, she gazed into Jerry's yard. No sign of him. His pool looked delicious.

He should be in it, Gillian thought. *I* should be in it.

Back in the house, she peeled off her bikini, went into the bathroom, and took a brief, cool shower. It felt great. In the bedroom, she put on a lightweight sleeveless shirt that draped her thighs. She buttoned it at the waist, and returned to the kitchen.

She wrapped the left-over pizza in aluminum foil and put it in the refrigerator. It would make a decent snack, cardboard taste or not, for tonight when she planned to watch movies on the VCR.

With another beer from the refrigerator behind the bar, Gillian sat down at a small desk in one corner of the den. The top of the desk was clear. She searched the drawers.

Fredrick had left behind his checkbook, which seemed a little odd. The balancing was up-to-date. His account had a total of $1,248.60.

The last check had been written on June 20.

Friday.

Jesus!

Gillian grinned.

He was still in town on Friday, day before yesterday. I got here yesterday.

He'd stopped his mail, tossed his milk so it wouldn't go sour.

I bet I could stay two, three more nights. Maybe longer if I want to push it.

The check dated June 20 had been made out to 'cash' in the amount of $2,000.00.

He took that kind of money, he might be gone *weeks*.

Just because he withdrew that much, Gillian thought, doesn't mean he plans to use it all for his trip.

She looked at the earlier stubs. Most of the checks had been written to pay supermarkets, auto insurance, the monthly mortgage, utilities and credit card companies. None of the checks had been made out to an airline or travel agent.

So he'd probably used part of the two thousand dollars to pay for his transportation to wherever he went.

Unless he drove.

His car is probably parked at the airport, Gillian thought.

She snapped the checkbook shut and slid it back inside the drawer.

Awfully strange that he left it behind. Who would go on a trip without taking his checkbook along?

With that kind of cash, who needs a checkbook?

In the same drawer, Gillian found Fredrick's savings account passbook. It showed a total of $156,835.46. 'Not bad,' she whispered. She had twice that in her own passbook and nearly as much tied up in stocks and bonds, but not everybody gets two wrongful-death settlements to build up that kind of nest egg.

Whatever Uncle Fredrick does for a living, she thought, he does pretty well for himself. Maybe he's a doctor or a lawyer.

He certainly had quite a modest house considering his income.

'You'd think he could afford a goddamn pool,' Gillian muttered.

She put away the passbook and looked through the rest of the drawers. They held nothing of much interest until she slid open the bottom drawer and found a .357 magnum Colt Python. Whistling softly, she lifted it.

The thing was loaded.

Obviously Uncle Fredrick was prepared to blast away intruders.

That's me, Gillian thought.

Though she didn't expect to be taken by surprise, she saw no point in leaving a loaded gun around where it might be used on her.

She broke open the cylinder and tilted the barrel up. The cartridges slid out, dropping into her palm. She dumped them into her shirt pocket and returned the revolver to its drawer.

Finished at the desk, she wandered over to the bookshelves. Three of the shelves were taken up by boxed video tapes. Though tempted to explore the collection, she decided to wait until later and check them out when she was ready to settle down and watch a few.

The books looked fairly normal. At first. The reference collection included a set of the *World Book* encyclopedia, several atlases, a dictionary, *The People's Almanac*, *Gray's Anatomy*, and a couple of motion picture encyclopedias. He had several books about body-building, but none that might indicate his profession. Unless he's a photographer, Gillian thought. There were fifteen or twenty books on that subject, most of them expensive, large format and with glossy pages. Most of them featuring nude women.

His hardbound fiction ran toward best-sellers by Joseph Wambaugh, Robin Cook, Lawrence Sanders, Dean Koontz, Stephen King, and so on. He had rows of paperbacks, mostly suspense and horror novels.

And one entire shelf of non-fiction that made Gillian wonder about Fredrick Holden. She felt a chill on her back as she inspected the books: volumes about Jack the Ripper, Albert Fish, Ed Gein, Charles Starkweather, Richard Speck, the Boston Strangler, the Manson family, John Wayne Gacey, the Skidrow Slasher, the Hillside Strangler, and Theodore Bundy. Many of the books contained photographs of the dead victims.

What's with this guy? she wondered.

Maybe he's a suspense writer, she told herself, and just had these books around for reference.

Then where's his computer?

Maybe he's a true crime buff, into police procedure and that kind of thing.

Sure. What he is, he's crazy about homicidal maniacs.

And he's got a water bed. And mirrors all over his bedroom.

'I really picked a good one,' Gillian muttered.

After sliding a copy of *Helter Skelter* back onto the shelf, she headed for the bathroom to wash her hands.

She was reminded of the Benning house, where Bill and Andrea had shelves of sex manuals, stacks of nudie magazines, an assortment of dildos and vibrators, various devices for which Gillian could only guess at the purposes, numerous oils and lotions, and erotic wardrobes: transparent negligees, G-strings (Bill's with a leopard-cloth pouch that opened like curtains), loin cloths, frilly garter belts, leather undies and bras, and bras with open fronts.

Gillian had inspected the Bennings' collection, intrigued and a little embarrassed. Though she'd considered trying out some of the devices and clothes, she'd found the idea more repellent than exciting.

She'd washed her hands after touching the things, just as she was washing her hands now.

All you touched this time were books, she thought as she rinsed off the suds. Hardly the same.

But what kind of person would enjoy reading that kind of junk?

Gillian recalled the uneasy feelings she'd had last night before even arriving at the house. Were they premonitions? Nonsense.

How about the way she reacted when the telephone rang? Phones had rung at odd times when she was staying at other places, but she hadn't panicked.

It was as if a shadowy corner of her mind knew she'd picked the wrong house this time.

'Bullshit,' Gillian said. She dried her hands and stepped into the hall. 'So what if the guy's a little bent.'

That's what keeps it interesting, she told herself. Discovering the hidden quirks.

She took her Minolta from the bedroom and returned to the den and touched the books again. After arranging them on the floor with their front covers showing, she snapped a close-up. She put them away. Just to be thorough, she then grouped the photography books on the floor for a shot, then the body-building books.

That, she thought, takes care of his peculiar reading habits.

In books, at least.

The search for Fredrick's magazine collection took about two minutes. She found it in the bedroom in the bottom drawer of his nightstand, pretty much where she expected it to be. The magazines were neatly arranged in two stacks. True-crime magazines.

Kneeling on the floor, Gillian lifted out half a dozen. Most of the covers featured a woman in peril, usually sprawled at the feet of a man. Only the back of the man was shown. The woman invariably gazed up at him with terror in her eyes. She was dressed in scanty undergarments or a revealing negligee or a torn blouse. More often than not, her hands were tied.

Gillian looked through a few of the magazines. The stories had lurid titles: 'Weird MO of the Sorority Killer', 'Death of the Gang-Sex Beauty', 'Rampage of the Peeper'. There were grainy photos of murder weapons, cops investigating cases (usually in wooded areas), apprehended killers and their victims (before and after).

The advertisements seemed as strange as the stories. They pushed pamphlets revealing the secrets of how to build the body you've always wanted, how to earn big bucks at home in your spare time, how to become a detective, how to hypnotize girls 'Secretly!' so they'll obey your every command. There were several ads for trusses. Other ads urged readers to buy pellet guns, tear-gas guns, 'authentic badges' and 'durable, reliable' handcuffs.

Gillian had seen such magazines at news-stands, never suspecting they contained such garbage: stories to titillate you with the details of sex killings (including hints on police procedure to help you avoid capture), followed by those ads.

The crime books in the den were sophisticated literary endeavors compared to these rags.

Who reads this shit? she wondered.

Fredrick Holden, for one.

He's starting to look like a real sicko.

Gillian lifted more magazines out of the drawer. More of the same.

Then she came to the sex magazines.

'Surprise,' she muttered.

Already feeling disoriented and revolted by the crime magazines, Gillian could only stand to look at a few of these. The photos didn't depict beautiful women in seductive poses.

The last magazine Gillian inspected dealt with bondage and sado-masochism. The men and women pictured wore chains and leather. Some wore black leather masks that made them look like medieval executioners. The victims were tied spread-eagled to a bed or shackled to a wall or suspended from a ceiling beam. Gillian flipped the magazine shut. She closed her eyes and took deep breaths.

She felt as if she had descended into a dark world of perversity.

A world in which Fredrick Holden loved to wallow.

Any *more* nasty little secrets? Gillian wondered. She bent over the drawer and glanced at the covers of the remaining magazines. Most of those near the bottom of the drawer appeared to be S&M. She left them there.

She spread half a dozen of the crime magazines on the bed and took a photograph. She did the same with several of the sex magazines. After putting them back in the drawer, she returned to the bathroom and once again scrubbed her hands.

Enough goddamn exploration for one afternoon, she thought.

Keep it up, you might find something *really* nasty.

She gave a sour laugh. In the mirror above the sink, her face looked a little bloodless, her eyes glassy. There were specks of sweat above her lip. She hadn't taken pictures of the S&M stuff at the bottom of the drawer. Hadn't wanted to.

She felt nauseous. Needed fresh air.

Gillian changed into her damp bikini, grabbed a bath towel, and went to the den. She took a beer from the refrigerator behind the bar.

The hot concrete sundeck hurt her feet as she turned toward the spa. Setting her beer and towel aside, she started to remove the cover.

She hesitated.

So you really want to go in this guy's hot tub? Especially after that *dream* . . . God only knows what's gone on in it . . . who might be in the water.

Yuck.

She picked up the cold bottle of beer and took a drink.

Maybe I should get the hell away from here, she thought, while the getting is good.

'Hey there!'

Gillian whirled around.

Chapter Eleven

'Why don't we take a breather?' Rick suggested.

Bert grinned along with her frown. 'You can't be pooped again already . . . a strong fellow like you.'

'Must be the altitude.'

'Okay. Five minutes.'

He stepped backward to a waist-high boulder, eased his pack down, and sighed as the straps went loose on his shoulders. The sigh was for Bert's sake. He'd found the hike rather easy so far and his occasional pleas for rest stops had nothing to do with the effort of lugging his pack up the trail. His only motive was to slow their progress, to avoid overtaking Jase, Luke and Wally.

So far, fine. He hadn't seen them since that morning.

The boys had had a fifteen-minute lead by the time the tent was rolled, the packs were ready, and they started out. Fifteen minutes, Rick quickly realized, was too short a gap. Bert didn't hike with a leisurely stroll; she took long, sure strides that ate up the trail. Though Jase and Luke might be fast on their feet, Wally had seemed like the type who would hold them back. Rick felt sure that, without the frequent stops, they would've caught up with the boys by now.

There was also the possibility that the boys would take it slow or even stop and wait to make sure of another encounter with Bert. If that was their game, Rick's delays would only postpone the meeting, not prevent it.

Rick opened a side pocket of his pack and took out his plastic water bottle. He unscrewed the cap and took a drink, then passed it to Bert.

The shadow of her bush hat left her face as she tipped back her head. She shut her eyes and drank.

'I'm wondering if we really want to go over Dead Mule Pass,' he said. 'Are we locked into that?'

'It's the route I planned,' she said, and returned the bottle to him. 'That's how we'll make a circle and get back to the car without backtracking. What've you got against Dead Mule Pass other than its name?'

'Sounds like a tough climb.'

'That's a good one. All of a sudden you're pooped at every turn and worried about a little climb. Aren't you the same guy who did a 10K run last month?'

'That was different.'

She lifted an eyebrow. 'I *am* onto you, y'know. You don't have to pretend with me. Took a while, but I figured it out after about the third rest stop. You just don't want us running into our friendly neighborhood teen trio.'

'Maybe.'

'Maybe, my ass.'

'It's your ass I'm worried about,' he said, forcing a smile. 'And other nearby areas.'

'You still think they want to jump my bones.'

'You think it hasn't crossed their minds?'

Bert shrugged. 'I suppose it probably has. That hardly means they'll try it, though. There's an enormous gap between wanting something like that and actually trying it.'

'Maybe. I just think we're better off avoiding those guys. I mean, we're out here in the middle of nowhere and they've got us outnumbered. Why tempt fate?'

'Rick, they're three guys on a camping trip. They seemed perfectly normal to me.'

'Even Jase?'

She hesitated. Frowning, she said, 'Jase I could do without. If I were alone out here and he showed up, I might be a little concerned. But you're with me, and Jase has Burgher and Wally in tow. Those two guys wouldn't try anything.'

'If they thought they could get away with it, they might.'

'Would you? Suppose the situation were reversed, and you're out here with a couple of buddies and run into someone like me? Would you and your pals try to rape me?'

'Of course not.'

She put a hand on his thigh. 'Sure about that? You're talking as if it's inevitable that all guys would try it in a situation like this.'

'It would occur to most guys. It would occur to me, I'm sure. But I wouldn't do it.'

'Why not?'

Rick shrugged. 'Aside from being a decent guy with moral scruples, I suppose I'd be chicken.'

'Afraid the cops'd get you?'

'That'd be a major deterrent. Thing is, and why I'm so worried, this area isn't exactly teeming with fuzz. We're pretty much beyond the reach of the law out here. A guy could get away with most anything.' Rick went cold inside. 'Especially if he didn't leave witnesses.'

'Plot thickens,' Bert said. 'Now we're talking murder.'

'You rape someone, you don't want a prison stretch, nobody knows you did it except you and the victim. Even if you're not a cold-blooded killer, you're scared. The thrill is over and you realize what you've done – the consequences if you get caught.'

Bert's fingers tightened on his thigh.

'You take these three,' he went on. 'Jase wouldn't kill us out of panic. He'd be more likely to do it for kicks, or just to be on the safe side, or just for the hell of it.'

'You don't even know the guy,' Bert muttered.

'I know his type. Burgher, he seemed aloof. The rational sort. He'd see the logic of eliminating us and that might override his qualms about it. Wally, he'd panic. He'd no sooner get his pants up than he'd start seeing himself getting gang-raped in prison.'

Bert looked into his eyes. 'You're scaring me,' she said.

'I just think we need to realize the—'

'I mean *you're* scaring me. What the hell is going on inside your head? We meet three guys who don't give us any trouble at all. Next thing you know, you've got them raping me. Jase kills us for kicks, Burgher kills us because it makes good sense, and Wally kills us so he won't get sodomized in prison. My Christ! Your imagination is revolting.'

'I read the newspapers,' he muttered, stunned by her reaction.

'Sounds to me like you're projecting your own fantasies onto those guys.'

'My fears,' he said.

Her eyes seemed to soften. 'Oh, Rick.' Her hand lifted to his face, gently stroked his cheek. 'I shouldn't have dragged you out here, should I?'

'I was doing all right till those three came along.'

'Doing all right? That's why you got yourself shit-faced last night?' Her tone was sympathetic, not accusing.

'I didn't get shit-faced.'

'Maybe we'd better hike on back to the car and get out of here.'

'Hell,' he muttered.

'It's no good if you're a basket-case the whole time. It isn't fair to you.'

'I'm sorry. I promised myself that I wouldn't ruin things. But I won't get this stuff out of my head.'

'I'm the one who pushed you into this. I knew you hated the idea.' A corner of her mouth curled up. 'Guess we should've gone to Maui after all.'

'I'd feel awful if we quit,' he said.

'You'd feel worse if we stayed. Besides, you might be right about those guys. I mean, I don't really expect them to attack us or anything, but just the fact that they're around – truth is, I've had some of the same thoughts as you.'

'Really?'

She nodded. 'My thoughts didn't go quite as far as yours. But it crossed my mind that Jase might talk the others into jumping us.' Her smile widened. 'In my version, they thumped you on the head with a rock, but I fended them off with my knife.'

'Always the optimist.'

'That's me. Anyway, all things considered, I won't be too disappointed if we leave.'

'I guess we could head over to Lake Tahoe, check into a nice hotel . . .'

'Nothing to wear.'

'They've got stores.'

'Sounds good to—'

Her voice stopped.

Rick heard faint, distant talking. Fear clamped his chest. He handed the water bottle to Bert. Standing, he slipped his arms from the pack straps. He turned to his pack, reached for the side pocket where he'd put his revolver, and pulled at the zipper with trembling fingers. It was half open when he realized that the voices were female.

He glanced at Bert. She was watching him. With a shake of his head as if he were confused, he shut the zipper. He took the water bottle from Bert and slipped it into the other pocket.

'Afraid they'll try to bum our water?' Bert asked, grinning.

'Exactly. Wouldn't be sanitary.' He rested against his pack again. He still heard the voices, but he saw nobody on the trail.

'From the sound of them,' Bert said, 'they're either girls or sissies.'

They were girls. They came striding, side by side, around a bend in the trail.

The one on the right looked up, saw them, smiled and said, 'Howdy.' The other, flushed and panting, nodded a greeting.

'Hi there,' Bert said.

'Hi,' said Rick.

'Let's take a load off,' the girl said to her haggard friend. She stepped to the side of the trail across from Rick and Bert, swung her pack down, and boosted herself onto a hip-high shelf of rock. The other girl kept her pack on. It scraped against the vertical block of stone as she sagged. Her rump met the trail and she stretched out her legs. She sighed.

Her slim legs were tanned, her shins mottled with trail dust that had turned dark on her sweaty skin. She wore faded blue gym shorts and a gray T-shirt that read UCSC. Her shirt had a wet V, wide at the crew neck and narrowing as it descended between her breasts. Her chest rose and fell as she fought to catch her breath. The bill of her ballcap was tipped upward. A fringe of blonde hair clung to her forehead and glossy wisps curled around her ears. In spite of her grimace and sunglasses, Rick could see that she was a beauty.

'From Santa Cruz?' Bert asked.

'I shoulda boogerin' stayed there,' said the one on the ground.

The one sitting on the rock laughed. 'We just got done with finals,' she said.

'Great way to start the summer break.'

'Andrea isn't used to this sort of thing.'

'Neither am I,' Rick said.

'I love it.' The girl swept off her straw cowboy hat. Her thick, brown hair was pinned up except for bangs that fluttered in the breeze. Unlike Andrea, she looked cool and dry. She wore no sunglasses. Her brows were thick, her eyes bright green. Though she lacked Andrea's delicate features, she had a fresh, athletic look that Rick found appealing.

She tossed her hat. It landed on her pack, slid off, and dropped onto the trail. Leaning back, she braced herself with straight arms. She was wearing a yellow blouse. The sleeves were cut off, and it was unbuttoned and tied below her breasts. From the yellow cord across the gap, Rick guessed that she was wearing a bikini. Her flat belly was tanned. She wore jeans, the legs cut off so high that the ends of her front pockets hung out white against her thighs.

The way her jeans looked disturbed Rick. For a moment, he didn't know why. Then he remembered that Julie had worn jeans like these, cut so short the pockets showed. He'd been watching her instead of the trail.

My fault, he thought as a warm wave of shame swept through him. If I hadn't been trying to see up her pants . . .

It's not my fault, he told himself. She shouldn't have worn something like that if I wasn't supposed to look. A guy will look. Any guy will look. It was her fault more than mine.

'. . . your car we parked next to this morning,' the girl in the cutoffs was saying. Rick realized he had missed some of the conversation.

'A blue Pontiac?' Bert asked.

'Yeah, that's the one.'

'So you just got in this morning?' Rick asked.

'Seems like a century ago,' Andrea said. Still on the ground, she had slipped out of her pack straps without Rick noticing. Her gray T-shirt was dark around the armpits. She was no longer panting. 'Bonnie doesn't believe in resting. You ask me, I don't know what's the big rush.'

'I thought we'd make it over the pass today,' Bonnie said, 'but that's starting to look doubtful. There's a lake just this side, though. Fern Lake? I suppose we'll wind up there. What about you?'

Bert shrugged. 'We're not too sure at this point.'

'Are you going over the pass?' Bonnie asked.

'We might head back,' Bert told her. 'I'm not feeling too swift.'

Bonnie frowned. 'That's too bad. You might just pack it in?'

'We're considering it.'

'That'd be a shame, you came this far.'

'Sounds like a good move to me,' Andrea said. She raised one knee and folded her hands around it. Her other leg was still extended. Through the gaping leg-holes of her shorts, Rick saw her shadowed thigh. He looked away.

Bonnie had her ankles crossed.

'There are some guys up the trail,' Rick said. 'You may run into them.'

'Guys?' Bonnie asked.

'Three of them,' Bert said. 'They're probably about your age.'

'Oh great,' Andrea muttered.

'What sort of guys?' Bonnie asked.

'How many kinds *are* there,' Andrea said.

Bonnie uncrossed her feet and swung a boot sideways as if to knock her friend in the head. She missed. 'Did they seem all right?' she asked Bert.

'I guess so.'

'They're not a contingent from Stanford,' Rick said, with a smile in Andrea's direction. Bonnie threw him a challenging look. He could've been mistaken, but he thought it said, *Get off my patch, mister. And lay off Andrea. She's mine.*

Andrea looked up at Rick and wrinkled her nose. 'They're a contingent from like where?'

'The Youth Authority.'

'I'm gonna barf.'

'They aren't that bad,' Bert said. 'One of them did seem rather hard, but the others were okay. We had a chat with them back at our camp. They didn't give us any trouble.'

'Sure they didn't,' Andrea said. 'You've got *him*.'

'Rick,' he told her, pleased that the girl believed his presence had prevented trouble.

'Yeah, you had Rick.'

'How far ahead are these guys?' Bonnie asked. Leaning forward, she hunched over and put her hands on her knees. The front of her blouse bunched outward. Rick saw the side of her left breast. The yellow bikini looked too small to hold it all.

'Who knows?' Bert said. 'We've been stopping a lot. They might be half an hour up the trail, maybe farther.'

'Or they might be just around the bend,' Rick said.

'Just what we need,' Andrea muttered. 'Hassled by a trio of cretinous thugs.'

'Who says they'll hassle us?' Bonnie said.

'They're guys, aren't they? No offense, Rick,' she added, and grinned up at him with one side of her mouth. 'I'm talking mostly your basic teenage toad. They got just one thing on their minds, and we all know what that is. Fucky-wucky.'

'You're gross,' Bonnie said.

'But perceptive.' Andrea twisted her head around and peered up at her friend. 'You think these guys are gonna just ignore us, we meet up with them?'

'You can level them with your tongue.'

'Yeah, that'd be sure to save the day. Get the scrotes pissed at us.' She turned to Rick. 'Maybe the four of us oughta stick together for a while. You mind us tagging along?'

'They're leaving,' Bonnie reminded her.

'Oh, yeah. Shit soup. You guys sure about that?'

'It's not definite,' Rick said.

Bert looked at him. 'We'll have to discuss it,' she said. 'If we change our minds, we won't be far behind you.'

'Well,' Bonnie said. 'We'd better get moving.' She leaped from her perch, picked up her hat and dusted it off. 'If we don't see you again, have a good trip back.'

'Thanks,' Bert told her. 'You too.'

'I was just getting comfortable,' Andrea complained, reaching behind her for the pack straps.

Bonnie lifted her pack off the trail without apparent effort, swung it onto her back, and slipped her arms through the straps.

Andrea struggled with hers. First, she clutched both straps and tried to rise from a squatting position. That didn't work, so she lurched forward onto her hands and knees, then thrust herself up.

'So graceful,' Bonnie said.

Grimacing, Andrea rubbed her hands on her shorts. They left dust smears on the faded blue fabric. She turned her palms up. 'Never gonna be clean again,' she muttered.

'The pleasures of roughing it,' Bert told her.

'Yeah. You guys really serious about leaving?'

'We'll see,' Bert said.

Andrea grinned at her. 'Want to loan us Rick for a few days? We'll make sure we get him back to you in good condition.'

She caught Bonnie's sour look and rolled up her eyes in a gesture of mock despair.

What's with the attitude all the time, Bonnie? Can't take a joke? Loosen up for godsake, we're on vacation here.

Rick laughed. 'I could go for that.'

He was joking. Almost.

Bert slapped his leg. 'Sorry,' she told Andrea, 'I'm afraid I can't do without him. He's my love-slave.'

The girls, including Bert, laughed it up.

'Real cute,' Rick said, smiling but embarrassed.

525

Still laughing, Bonnie and Andrea raised hands in farewell, turned away, and began striding up the trail. Rick and Bert watched until the two girls disappeared around a bend in the trail.

'Nice kids,' Bert said.

'Yeah.'

'So what about it?' she asked. 'Do you still want to split?'

'I don't know,' Rick said. 'Maybe not.'

Bert looked amused.

'You have to admit, they change the picture somewhat. In terms of the guys,' he added.

'I'd say so,' Bert agreed. 'Substitute victims. If the boys are so inclined. Which would let us off the hook.'

'They must be out of their gourds, coming out to a place like this. Two girls.'

'Dykes,' Bert said.

'You think so?'

She laughed. 'Maybe. On the other hand, maybe not. Not fully fledged yet, anyway. Borderline in my opinion. Bonnie's the pushy one and Andrea's playing hard to get. But don't quote me on that. And I don't think they're out of their gourds. They're probably safer out here than they'd be on the streets of Santa Cruz.'

'That's not saying much.'

'So what are we going to do?' Bert asked.

'I think they're worried about running into the guys.'

'Of course they are. You made the fellows sound like escapees from a chain-gang.'

'What do *you* want to do?' Rick asked.

'Let's stay. We'll give the girls a good long lead. The guys can jump them and fuck their brains out, and be too pooped to care by the time we go by.'

'Sometimes,' Rick said, 'you're very strange.'

She contorted her face and rolled her eyes.

'Does this mean you think we should join up with them?' Rick asked.

'I'm not thrilled by the idea, but I guess it makes sense. I get my camping trip, the girls get our protection, and you get to continue drooling over a couple of nymphets young enough to be your daughters.'

'I wasn't drooling,' Rick protested. 'And I'm not that old.'

She arched an eyebrow.

Rick grinned. 'Maybe we'd better forget it. I just might lose control and go for them.'

'I'm worried.'

'Obviously.'

'You get the urge, buddy, just remember something.'

'What?'

Smiling, Bert gently squeezed him through the front of his pants. 'They ain't me.' She let go and patted his leg. 'Come on, we'd better catch up with the children.'

Chapter Twelve

Jerry Dobbs was smiling at Gillian over the top of the fence. 'Sorry,' he said. 'Did I startle you?'

'That's all right.' The jolt of alarm she'd felt at first hearing his voice faded, but her heart still raced from the shock of it. She managed a smile.

'A little warm today for the hot tub, don't you think? How about coming over here and joining me in the pool? I was just about to go in myself.'

Gillian, surprised and delighted by the offer, didn't hesitate. 'That sounds great.'

'Come around to my driveway, I'll open the gate for you.'

'Be right there,' she said.

His face disappeared, and Gillian went into the house.

She knew she was breaking her rule against fraternizing with neighbors, but she didn't care. Ever since meeting Jerry so briefly last night, she'd hoped to see more of him. He must've felt drawn to her, also. A guy doesn't invite just anyone over to use his pool.

I'll have to watch what I say to him, she cautioned herself. Wouldn't do, at all, to slip up and let him find out I'm not Fredrick's niece.

Fredrick, the sicko.

The house, though pleasantly cool after the heat outside, seemed forbidding to Gillian as she hurried toward the bedroom.

She dreaded the thought of spending another night in it.

I won't, she told herself. After I leave Jerry's, I'll pack up and get out of here.

In the bedroom, she set her beer bottle on the dresser and slipped into sandals. She turned to the wall of mirrors. And shook her head in dismay. The bikini was little more than cords that tied at her hips and behind her back and neck. Strung from the cords were flimsy, meager swatches of snug white fabric. Gillian felt naked. This was an outfit for wearing in private, not in front of strangers. She had a modest one-piece swimsuit for beaches and pools, but it was back in her apartment; she hadn't foreseen any need to bring it along.

That's because you don't go swimming with neighbors, she thought. Right.

She considered changing into shorts and a T-shirt.

He already saw me in this. He'd think I'm nuts.

With a sigh, she put on her shirt as a cover-up. The shirt was long enough to drape the scanty bottom of her bikini. She buttoned it, brushed her short hair, then picked up her beer bottle and headed for the front door.

She removed the burglar bar. Having no key, she left the door unlocked.

She walked across Jerry's yard and found him waiting at the open gate of his driveway. He was lean and dark. Instead of trunks, he wore an old pair of tan corduroys with the legs cut off.

'Glad you could come over,' he said.

'Who could refuse a swimming pool on a day like this?'

He shut the gate. Gillian walked with him toward the rear.

'Enjoying the house-sitting?' he asked.

'It sure beats staying in my little apartment.'

'Does your apartment have a pool?'

Gillian nodded. 'I never use it, though. There could be thirty people watching you from their windows. Not to mention an assorted variety of tenants who might decide to join in the fun.'

'Yeah. Know just what you mean.'

His pool was shimmering and clear, its surface flat in the still afternoon.

'Feel free to dive in,' Jerry said. 'I think I'll get myself a beer. Could you use another?'

Gillian squinted at her bottle. It was half-empty. 'Sure, why not?'

She sat at the table under the shade of its broad umbrella while Jerry went into the house. She sipped her beer. Her hand trembled slightly and she felt her heart thumping. She looked at the house. From the rear, it seemed similar to Fredrick's.

Bet it doesn't come with a collection of sick magazines, she thought.

Or mirrors on the ceiling.

Not that I'd mind the mirrors.

She wished her heart would slow down.

Take it easy, she told herself. Relax.

The rear door slid open and Jerry came out with a bottle of beer in each hand. He sat at the table. He pushed a bottle across to her.

'Beck's,' Gillian said, reading the label. 'I like it.'

'What's that you're drinking?'

She slid the bottle toward him. 'Corona. Have some. It's okay, I don't have any diseases.' As the words came out, she felt herself blush. That's certainly laying the cards on the table, she thought.

Jerry drank from her bottle and nodded. 'I'll have to pick up some of this stuff.' He passed it back to her.

She drank the rest of it. 'Uncle Fredrick has good taste in beer,' she said. 'I can't say the same for his taste in reading matter.'

'Oh?'

Careful, she thought. 'He seems to go in for some pretty gruesome stuff.'

'I guess we all have our quirks.'

'Does he seem all right to you?'

Jerry shrugged. 'I'm embarrassed to admit it, but I really don't know the man at all. I've said hi to him a couple of times when we've crossed paths, but that's about the extent of it. He keeps to himself pretty much. So do I. Comes from all those years of apartment living, I think. The less I see of my neighbors, the better.'

'That's why you poked your head over the fence and asked me over,' Gillian said, smiling.

He laughed. 'That's different.' He took a drink of beer and flinched slightly as the bottle dripped water onto his chest. Gillian watched the clear bead trickle down his skin, leaving a shiny trail. He smeared it with the flat of his hand.

'Are you on vacation?' he asked.

'Me? I'm on permanent vacation,' Gillian said. 'I don't do much in the way of work.'

'How nice for you. Wealthy family?'

'Dead family.'

His eyes widened.

Gillian felt a little shocked herself. Why am I telling him the truth about my family? she wondered. Would've been easier to lie. She always lied about her background.

'I shouldn't be flippant about it. I'm sorry. But it's been a few years and I usually don't . . . I usually just make up a story. The fact is, my parents were killed in a traffic accident. A deputy sheriff's car lost its brakes while it was in hot pursuit of a robbery suspect and smashed into them. My parents' attorney filed a wrongful-death suit on my behalf, and it was settled for a good sum. I'm pretty well set up.' Gillian shrugged.

'I'm sorry about your folks.'

'Well, thanks. What is it that you do?'

'I design computer programs.'

'Ah, you must be a brain.'

'That's me.' He laughed and took a drink of beer.

'What kind of programs?'

'I specialize in weapons systems.'

'You mean like for missiles?'

'Something like that.'

'Yikes. Guess I'd better stop asking questions or you'll put the FBI on me.'

'That's right.' He set down his bottle. 'Well, I'm about ready to go in for a dip. How about you?'

'Sure.' Gillian lingered at the table, taking another sip of beer while Jerry rose from his seat. He hitched up his shorts and turned toward the pool. Gillian pushed her chair back. He looked around at her. 'You don't have to wait for me,' she said, and crossed a foot over her knee to remove a sandal. Nodding, Jerry headed for the deep end of the pool. Gillian slipped off her other sandal and stood up. She slowly unbuttoned her shirt. As Jerry dove, she took it off. She draped it over the chair and stepped quickly to the pool, watching him skim beneath the surface to the opposite side. He was just coming up for air when she leaped. She hit the water in a shallow dive. For an instant, the chill was an agony. Then it felt good as she glided along through the silence. Her fingers touched the tile wall. She bobbed to the surface and stood. The water covered her to the shoulders.

She spotted Jerry near the middle of the pool, treading water, watching her. 'I missed your dive,' he said.

'Too bad. It was a ten.'

'Let's see you go off the board.'

'Thanks, anyway.'

'I'll go first.'

'I'm not stopping you.'

He swam to the side and boosted himself up. His sodden shorts hung low. Gillian saw a pale band of skin where his tan stopped, the top of his buttocks. He tugged the shorts up as he walked toward the diving board. Pausing at the end of the board, he rubbed his hands together. 'I'll now perform my world famous triple somersault.'

He bounced on the board, springing higher and higher, his firm body shining in the sunlight. Suddenly, he tucked and hugged his knees. Gillian winced as his head barely missed the tip of the board. Midway through the first somersault, his back slammed the surface. A geyser of white water exploded.

He came up grinning foolishly, and Gillian clapped. 'Bravo!' she called.

'Do I get a ten?'

'I'll give you a three on the grounds that you survived at all.'

'Okay. Let's see how an expert does it.'

'I don't know.'

'Come on. I'm sure you can do better than me.'

'I'm sure not much into diving.'

'You're too modest.'

That's about right, she thought.

Jerry side-stroked to the opposite side of the pool. Facing Gillian, he boosted himself up and sat on the edge. He grinned and wiped the water from his eyes. 'I'll make you a deal. One dive will get you a steak dinner tonight. Barbecued by the master chef, me. How about it?'

'Shameless bribery,' Gillian said.

'Naturally, the offer includes cocktails and hors d'oeuvres.'

'What about dessert?'

'Ice-cream, followed by after-dinner drinks.'

'And all I have to do is one dive off the board?'

'That's all.'

'How come you're so eager for me to go off the board?'

'So I can get a good look at you,' he said. His smile vanished. 'And so you can stop being nervous about your bikini.'

'You noticed, huh?'

'Yep. You came over here in a shirt. That was my first clue. Then you kept it on.'

'I don't usually parade around in something like this.'

'But remember, I've already seen you in it.'

'You took me by surprise.'

'Nevertheless, the damage is done. I've seen what there is to see.'
Gillian grimaced.

'I think we'll both enjoy ourselves a lot more once you get over the self-consciousness. You can stop worrying about what I might see, and I can stop worrying about *trying* to see what you're hiding.'

'Makes sense,' she muttered. She rolled her eyes upward and sighed. She wished she had left the shirt back at the house. Drawing attention to her timidity had turned out to be even more embarrassing than if she had simply shown herself from the start. 'I feel like an idiot,' she said.

'Don't. There's nothing to be ashamed of. If I were in your place, I would've been reluctant, myself, about going over to a stranger's pool in an outfit that exposed every intimate detail of my anatomy.'

The remark stunned Gillian for an instant. Then, bursting into laughter, she cried out, 'You bastard!'

He rocked, clutching his knees and grinning, delighted.

Gillian whirled around, still laughing, and thrust herself out of the pool. She strode toward the far end, scowling over her shoulder at him. 'Every intimate detail, my ass!'

'That's included!' he called. He wasn't laughing anymore. His smile was slipping. He stared at her.

Gillian looked away from him.

It's all right, she told herself. Plenty of women wear as little as this to the beach. Why should it bother me?

Her wet feet slapped the concrete. Water trickled down her body. The cling of the bikini kept her terribly aware of how little there was of it. Her breasts, though firm and not very large, jiggled and swayed as if they were bare. Without looking down, she knew that her nipples were erect and that the fabric of the bikini was too flimsy to hide the fact.

At the end of the pool, she turned toward the diving board. Jerry was still sitting with his legs in the water. He was gazing straight ahead.

He's not even looking at me!

Gillian felt a mixture of relief and annoyance.

She stepped onto the diving board. Jerry kept staring into space.

She walked to the end of the board. It was springy under her feet. She stood straight, toes curled over the edge, and waited for the board to stop moving.

What's with this guy? she wondered. He bribes me to climb out of the pool so he can get a good look at me, and then it's like I'm not even here.

'Yoo-hoo,' she called.

His head turned. 'Oh,' he said, as if mildly surprised to see her.

'Welcome back.'

'Guess I was daydreaming for a second there.'

'Gee, thanks. I thought you couldn't wait to ogle my marvelous, semi-nude body.'

His eyes slowly roamed down Gillian. 'And a fine body it is,' he said. 'Now, let's see if you can top my dive.'

'That'd be tough,' she said. What do you want? she asked herself.

Do you want him to gape and pant in awe? Lick his lips? Drool? The bastard *could* show a tiny bit more interest.

Maybe he's gay.

Wouldn't that be a joke?

With a sigh, Gillian hopped. Her feet hit the board. She leaped as it flung her up. Soaring over the pool, she arched toward the sky, bent quickly at the waist and touched her toes, then straightened her body and knifed down into the water. When her fingertips brushed the bottom, she pushed herself away and glided to the surface.

Jerry held up both hands with their fingers spread. 'Definitely a ten,' he said. 'I had no idea I was in the presence of a champion.'

'I think it was a seven,' Gillian told him. 'But thanks.'

'I knew you looked familiar. I saw you in the Olympics.'

'I'm not that good,' she said.

'Could've fooled me. And you claimed you weren't into diving.'

'It was an easy one.'

'Well, don't stop now. Let's see another.'

'Okay, one more.' She boosted herself out of the pool. 'Don't expect anything spectacular,' she cautioned him. 'I'm a little rusty.'

She was standing at the end of the board before she realized that she had forgotten to be self-conscious about her bikini. Jerry was watching her. He had an eager look on his face.

What the hell, she thought. He thinks I'm a great diver.

She bounced high, tucked, somersaulted, and went in straight and clean.

Jerry was clapping when she came up. 'An artist!' he proclaimed. 'A virtuoso. You could win trophies for that kind of performance.'

'I've got a few,' Gillian admitted, treading water just in front of his submerged feet.

'I don't doubt it. Let's see another one.'

'I think two's enough,' she said. 'I don't want to press my luck. Next time, I might belly-flop and embarrass myself.'

'Just one more?' he asked.

What's the point of refusing? she thought. He really wants to see me dive again, and I've got no good reason to disappoint him. 'Okay,' she said. 'One more, and that's it. For now, anyway.'

'Terrific.'

Instead of crossing the pool to climb out where she had before, she swam to Jerry's side. He watched as she placed her hands on the edge next to him and thrust herself up. Gillian stayed there for a moment, braced with stiff arms. She saw him glance at her breasts, then look into her eyes. 'I'll do a really hard one this time,' she said. 'My grand finale.'

Jerry made a thumbs-up sign.

Gillian swung her leg up, climbed from the pool, and hurried to the diving board. She walked out to the end of it, stood motionless until the board stopped shaking, then did an about-face.

Her back to the pool, she stood erect with her arms at her sides. She jumped, bounded straight up, came down again and bounced higher. On the third leap, she shot herself away from the board, did a quick somersault and snapped rigid, coming down fast with the board at her back and her arms stretched toward the water.

She had an instant of stabbing fear when she realized she had come out of the tuck too late.

Her head missed the end of the board. So did her upper back. It caught her just above the buttocks. She gritted her teeth as the board pounded her, scraped her and knocked her forward. She glimpsed her bare legs kicking against the pale sky. Then the water blurred her view.

She blew out air through her nose. Plunging toward the bottom of the pool, she wondered how badly she was hurt. She clawed at the water.

Then she felt a hand on her back. The hand found her arm and pulled her. She reached out and grabbed the side of the pool. Jerry was beside her.

His face looked pale. 'My God,' he gasped, 'are you okay?'

She shook her head. Her heart was slamming with fear and her throat felt clamped tight. Tears filled her eyes. She crossed her arms on the tiles, and rested her face on them. Jerry's hand gently rubbed her back.

'I'm sorry,' he whispered. 'I'm so sorry. I shouldn't have made you do it.'

'It's what I get . . . for showing off.'

'Damn, I bet that hurt.'

'I feel . . . like I got . . . kicked by a mule.'

'You ever been kicked by a mule?'

'Don't be a wiseguy.' She managed to swallow. She took a deep breath. She wiped a wet forearm across her eyes, then reached down and carefully fingered a raw area near the top of her right buttock. She could feel loose edges of skin that had been peeled down. Her left buttock was in better shape. It felt battered and slightly scuffed, but not flayed.

Suddenly alarmed, Gillian reached lower. Her bikini pants.

'Oh shit,' she muttered.

'What?'

'I lost something.'

'Don't worry about it.'

'Easy for you to say,' she told Jerry. She thought she was done crying, but her voice broke and her eyes flooded. '*Damn* it!' she gasped.

'I'll find them for you.'

Jerry was no longer beside her. She wiped her eyes and turned around. He was far below the surface, kicking his way toward the bottom of the pool.

Gillian pushed away from the edge. She swam toward the shallow end, then stood. She was shoulder-deep. She peered down. The water blurred the view, but not enough.

Jerry was swimming toward her, well below the surface, the white rag of her bikini pants fluttering in his grip.

She drove her hands down quickly to cover herself.

Jerry veered off. So he has his eyes open under there, Gillian thought. Wonderful.

He swam toward the left, moved past her, and stood up. He lifted her pants out of the water. 'Here you go.'

He looked into her eyes. He didn't look down.

Gillian uncovered herself. She took the garment from him. The cords on both sides dangled, torn loose from the seat. 'It's ruined,' she muttered.

'You can't put it on?'

She shook her head. She sighed. She felt as if she might burst into tears again.

'I'll get you something to wear,' Jerry said. He turned away, waded to the side of the pool, climbed out, and hurried across the sundeck to the rear of his house.

While he was gone, Gillian moved to the pool wall. She pressed herself to it, feeling the slick tile against her belly and hips and pubic mound and thighs.

The initial pain had been replaced by a dull ache. Even the skinned areas no longer hurt much.

What hurt was the humiliation.

It wasn't much different from the time, a few years ago, when she got plastered at a party and barfed on the floor in front of everyone.

That was worse, she decided. This time, at least, it was an accident. It wasn't exactly my fault.

If I hadn't been showing off . . .

Jerry came out of the house with a blue terry-cloth robe. 'This should do the trick,' he said. He dropped it onto the pool deck in front of her, then turned away.

Gillian climbed out, hoping he wouldn't take advantage of the opportunity to look at her. She put on the bulky robe, and belted it shut. 'Okay,' she said.

He faced her. He was frowning. 'Better?' he asked.

Gillian nodded. 'Thanks.'

'You really caught it.'

'Yeah. I noticed. Thanks for pulling me out.'

'Do you think you need a doctor? I could drive you to an emergency room.'

'No, it's not that bad. I'll have an ugly ass for a couple of weeks, that's all.'

Jerry smiled a little sadly. 'It's a shame for something that gorgeous to get banged up.'

Heat rushed to Gillian's face. 'I'd better get going,' she muttered. Stepping over to the table, she slipped into her sandals and picked up the shirt she had worn as a cover-up.

'You'll come back for the barbecue, won't you?'

'I don't know, Jerry.'

'You earned it. The hard way.'

'I don't know. This is all . . . pretty embarrassing.'

'Yeah, I guess it would be.' He lowered his voice. 'Look, the invitation stands. I'd really like you to come over. But I'll understand, if you'd rather not.'

'If I do come, are you going to make me dive?'

He looked up at her. 'Certainly. If you won't dive, forget it. Stay home and starve.'

'What time do the festivities start?'

'Say five?'

Gillian nodded. 'We'll see. I'll bring you back your robe, anyway.'

He walked with her to the gate, and opened it. 'I'm awfully sorry you got hurt.'

'I'm awfully sorry I lost my pants.'

'I'm not.'

'Screw you, buster.'

He patted her gently on the arm. She stepped through the gate and walked down his driveway, trying hard not to limp.

Chapter Thirteen

'I think we should push on,' Bert said. 'It's still early, and Dead Mule Pass is only two miles.'

'Two miles straight up,' Andrea pointed out. 'I don't know why we want to push it. This looks like a perfectly good place to spend the night.'

Rick thought so, too. The lake was surrounded by trees, and the shady place where they'd stopped was close to the shore and had a rushing stream nearby. There were flat areas where they could pitch their tents, a ring of stones for a campfire, and sawn-off logs for seats.

Nobody was using the seats. All four had dropped to the ground and were resting against their packs.

'Let's go on,' Bonnie said, looking up from a map spread across her legs. 'It shouldn't be more than a couple of hours to the top. We'll come into a whole string of lakes just on the other side of the pass.'

'Bug squat,' Andrea muttered.

Bert smiled at her. 'Look at it this way. If we don't go over the pass this afternoon, we'll be hitting it first thing in the morning. Wouldn't you rather get it over with?'

'Maybe it'll flatten out overnight. Maybe we'll die in our sleep. Maybe . . .'

'What do you think, Rick?' Bonnie asked.

'Yeah, Rick,' Andrea said. 'How about it? Which'll it be, the Bataan Death March with yours truly more than likely turning toes up along the way, or a pleasant afternoon relaxing here by the lake, possibly going in for a dip?'

'Well,' he said, 'it's two against one.'

'Make it two against two. I'll give you my first-born.'

'No fair bribing,' Bert told her.

'It's nice here,' Rick said. And it would be very nice indeed if the ladies decided to take a dip in the lake. 'Also, the chain-gang is probably up ahead somewhere. I'd prefer not to run into them.'

'Right,' Andrea said. 'We stay here, we won't meet up with The Three Thugateers.'

'But I think we should keep moving,' Rick finished.

'Stabbed in the back!' Andrea blurted.

'Sorry. I just think it'll be nice to get the hard part over with.'

Sure I do, he thought.

He wanted to stay here. But Andrea wanted to stay and Bert didn't. He had to side with Bert, damn it. Because Andrea was young and beautiful, and it wouldn't look right if he didn't.

'Guess I'm out-numbered,' Andrea said. 'You guys'll regret it when I drop dead of heat prostitution.'

'Prostration,' Bonnie corrected.

'You die your way, I'll die mine.'

They got up, shouldered their packs, and hiked up the path that led from the lake to the main trail, leaving the shade behind. Ahead was the barren, rocky side of a mountain with switchbacks zigzagging up its slope and no top in sight.

Rick supposed that Jase, Luke and Wally were up there someplace. But he wondered if he had misjudged them. If the guys had any plans for staging a confrontation, they probably would've done it by now.

Unless they're biding their time, he thought, waiting for just the right opportunity.

Maybe waiting for nightfall.

If we'd just stayed at the lake, we might've lost them for good.

There are four of us now, he told himself. We've got them out-numbered. That should give them second thoughts. But the temptation might be greater. Three gals instead of just one. Three times the temptation. Might be too much for them. Take me out of the picture, they'll have a field day.

Hell, they might not even know about Bonnie and Andrea.

I hope not.

Bonnie, in the lead, came to the first turn in the trail. She rounded it and kept walking, facing them now as she started up the next level. She swung her arms. Her stout legs took powerful strides. She looked as sturdy as a tugboat.

Andrea, behind her, hesitated when she reached the turning place. Tilting back her head, she peered at the trail and bared her upper teeth. Her chest rose. Rick could almost hear her pained sigh as her chest deflated. Clutching the straps at her shoulders, she leaned forward and started trudging. Her legs looked too slim and frail to support her under the weight of the big pack.

Bert, just in front of him, seemed neither as fragile as Andrea nor as solid as Bonnie. Lithe and graceful, that was Bert. Rick watched her slender legs swing out, watched the way the seat of her loose tan shorts moved with each step.

Here I am, he thought, one guy with the three of them. Not bad. Better make that two of them, though. Count Bonnie out. Try anything with her, you'd probably get a right hook for your trouble. Or a rock to the head. Good looker, though. So, count your chickens, Ricky baby, it's not all bad – three gals and one guy. Know some dudes who'd give their eye teeth . . .

If I just didn't have to worry about those other guys . . . and make sure Bert doesn't catch me eyeing the other two. Especially Andrea. Wouldn't mind seeing a lot more of that one. And she's available, looks like. Maybe she's straight after all.

Bert looked back at him. 'You hanging in okay?' she asked.

'No problem. How about you?'

A corner of her mouth twitched. She turned around and walked backward. 'It's starting to get to me,' she admitted. She took off her hat and rubbed a sleeve across her brow. Fringes of hair were clinging in damp curls around her face. Her faded blue shirt was dark around the collar. All but the lower two buttons were unfastened. Her skin in the opening gleamed as if it were oiled. She was breathing hard, and Rick could see a glossy patch of skin below her sternum throb with her pulsebeat.

'Maybe we should take five,' he said.

'Let's keep at it a while longer. Gotta get this over with.' With a wry smile, she shook her head and raised her arm, pointing at something behind Rick.

He looked around.

Bert was pointing at Fern Lake. It looked clear blue and cold below them. 'And to think we could be there right now,' she said. 'Maybe Andrea had the right idea.'

'No pain, no gain.'

'Wise-ass. Why didn't you talk me out of this?'

'Would've looked like I was siding with Andrea.'

'Long as that's all you do with her.'

'She's an eight, you're a ten.'

Bert huffed out a laugh without much breath behind it. 'I'd say she's more of a six, but that's in the eye of the beholder.' Grinning, she turned away.

She walked slowly, staying a few strides ahead of Rick. Even though the hike was beginning to take its toll on her, she could easily have passed Andrea. She was probably even capable of leaving Bonnie in her dust, if she had the inclination. Ever since they had joined up with the girls, however, Rick had kept to the rear and Bert had remained in front of him like a barrier. When Andrea slowed down, Bert slowed down even more. When Andrea stopped to rest, Bert stopped too, and the three of them waited until she was ready to move on.

Protecting her interests.

Just as well, Rick thought. It keeps the burden off me.

If Bert went on ahead at her normal pace, he would need to choose between trying to keep up with her (and letting Andrea disappear behind him), or staying back with Andrea (which would look as if he were choosing to desert Bert). Either way, it would've been lousy.

This was better.

A lot to be said for hiking behind the three of them. Nice view.

Too bad they aren't naked, he thought. On the other hand, that'd be rough. Then I'd feel compelled to take over the lead. The front view could be far superior to the rear. Rick smiled. Every silver lining has its cloud.

Be worth the effort, though. Plug on ahead. No pain, no gain. Get up in front for the view. Walk backwards the way Bert was doing a while ago, careful not to fall on your ass or step off the side of the mountain. They'd be hiking toward him single-file.

Rick stopped smiling.

They'd still have on their hats, their socks and boots. They'd still be lugging their packs, the straps pulling their shoulders back and thrusting their breasts forward. Their breasts would jiggle and bob as they walked. Their skin would gleam with sweat. Their muffs would be powdered with trail dust.

'How about a little fucky-wucky?' Andrea called to him.

'Don't be so gross,' Bonnie told her.

He asked Bert for permission. 'Long as I'm first,' she replied. Then all three gaped in alarm. Rick whirled around. Jase smashed his head with a rock.

He came to. The guys were gone. The girls lay sprawled along the trail in motionless heaps. He rushed down to them and crouched over Bert. Her throat was split as if slashed by a razor. She had blood in her open eyes. Whimpering, Rick backed away and tripped over Bonnie. He rolled off her without looking and found himself on his hands and knees, staring at Andrea. She was staked to the trail, spread-eagled. Her neck was a pulpy red stump. Her head was between her legs, peering at him over the bloody mat of her pubic hair.

'It's all right.' It was Bert's voice. He opened his eyes. His head was on her lap. Her throat was healed. She was in her clothes again, though her shirt gaped open and he could see the side of a breast above his face. She was mopping his forehead with a cold, wet rag.

Andrea and Bonnie were also alive again, both kneeling beside Rick. They wore clothes, but no packs. They were staring at him.

He suddenly had to vomit.

He lurched up and scurried away on hands and knees, but didn't get far before spasms wracked him and he heaved. When he finished, he crawled backward away from the mess. He turned around and met Bert's gaze. She looked worried.

'What happened?' Rick asked.

She shook her head. 'I heard you groan. I looked back just in time to see you fall flat on your face.'

'Christ,' he muttered.

Bert passed a water bottle to him. He gulped the cold liquid.

'What was it?' Andrea asked.

Yeah, he thought. What was it? Exhaustion? Dehydration? The heat? He'd been feeling just fine before it happened. Having quite a pleasant, erotic daydream and suddenly it turned on him, twisted into something hideous.

As if all his worries about Jase, Luke and Wally had blasted to the surface and knocked him out.

Some kind of paranoia attack?

A premonition?

Rick felt a sudden chill.

That old John Newland show, *One Step Beyond*. People were always having dreams or visions foretelling disaster. ESP.

I've never had any ESP.

This was just my imagination taking a nose-dive.

'I don't know what happened,' he said. 'I guess I just passed out.'

'Did you feel it coming on?' Bonnie asked.

'No, I was fine.' He shrugged. 'I feel all right now.'

'We'd still better rest for awhile,' Bert said. Putting a hand on his shoulder, she guided him down. He stretched out on the trail and laid his head on her lap. She smoothed the damp cloth over his brow.

'Maybe we'd better turn back,' Bonnie said.

'If we'd stayed at the lake in the first place,' Andrea said, 'this wouldn't have happened.' She sounded angry, as if she held Bonnie and Bert responsible. 'He could've fallen over the friggin' side and broken his neck.'

'I'll be all right,' Rick protested. 'We can go on in a minute.'

'We're still a long way from the top,' Bert told him. 'I think Bonnie's

545

right. We should go back down to the lake. We can tackle this again first thing in the morning when everybody's fresh.'

'Before it gets so hot,' Bonnie added.

'Really, I . . .'

'It's settled,' Bert said.

Rick closed his eyes.

We're going back down to the lake, he thought. I wanted to stay there in the first place.

He wondered if a scheming corner of his mind had staged the nasty little skit in hopes of getting the group to turn back. Slap Rick off his feet, everyone gets worried, hy-ho, hy-ho, it's back to the lake we go.

It's what you wanted. It's safer there. The guys are up ahead, and it's the guys you want to avoid, so it's all working out great.

Great, except I conked out like a wimp, then barfed right in front of everyone.

Shit.

Way to go, Ricky-babes.

Hearing movement, he opened his eyes. And figured he saw a shadow. A darting figure disappearing behind a rock.

Gone.

A scrawny leafless tree dipping over the rock made short, jagged patches of shadow.

He peered into the shimmering heat. Nothing but rock and goddamn tree. He groaned, snapped his eyes shut and shook his head. When he opened them he saw that Bonnie and Andrea were both on their feet, turning away from him. Bonnie strode up the trail toward her pack. She must have thrown it down and come running back when he passed out. Andrea's pack was next to Bert's, only a couple of yards away. As she went to it, Rick lifted his head off Bert's lap, hoping to orient himself because they didn't seem to be on the trail.

They were at one of the hairpins where the trail turned back on itself. One wing of the trail stretched downward along the mountainside, one angled upward to meet another juncture far beyond the place where Bonnie was swinging her pack off the ground. Rick raised his eyes. The side of the mountain seemed to go on forever. The higher switchbacks were barely visible, faint pencil lines zigzagging upward.

He looked at Andrea as she sat down. She leaned back against her pack and stretched out her legs. She folded her hands behind her head. The side of her gray T-shirt, from armpit to waist, was dark with sweat. Turning her head, she smiled at Rick. 'Too bad you didn't flop a little sooner.'

'I don't think it's something to joke about,' Bert said.

'Who's joking? Felt like I was crawling up the bung-hole of the universe. A couple more minutes, they could've renamed it Dead Andrea Pass.'

Rick smiled at her, then put his head down. Bert's hip bone was against the nape of his neck. She turned slightly, and the knob went away. She felt good under his head. He pressed his face against her, then winced and turned away as the hot belt buckle stung his nose. Bert laughed softly. 'Not your day,' she whispered.

Nice view, though, he thought. If her shirt was open about one more inch, he'd be able to see her left nipple. If Andrea and Bonnie weren't around . . .

You'd better just forget about the goddamn nice views, he warned himself. They get you into nothing but trouble.

Bonnie appeared. She swung her pack to the ground not far beyond Rick's feet, then sat down on a boulder with her back to the mountainside.

'That lake does look nice down there,' she said.

'Too bad we're not in it,' Andrea muttered. 'But at least we don't have to—'

'What?' Bonnie asked.

'Something flashed up there.'

Bonnie twisted around and tilted her head back. 'Where?'

'Way up. There it is again.'

Rick felt a clutch in his chest. He sat up, scooted himself around in the dust until he was beside Bert, and searched the mountainside.

He too saw the flash. It was followed by a second blink of brilliant glare. Double-barreled, he thought.

'It's the sun hitting something,' Bonnie said.

'A piece of glass?' Bert suggested.

'How about binocular lenses,' Rick said.

Bert moaned and started to fasten a button.

'Cripes,' Bonnie muttered.

'Those fuckheads are *spying* on us!' Andrea blurted. 'Spy on *this*, you jack-offs!' She jammed her middle finger into the air.

Bonnie saw her do it. 'Don't!'

'Maybe it's someone else,' Bert said.

'I don't care who it is,' Bonnie said. 'They shouldn't be watching us with binoculars.'

'Scumbags.'

'It's them, all right.' Rick had hoped that the boys didn't know about Andrea and Bonnie. But they knew. And they were very interested, or they wouldn't be studying the group with field glasses.

Andrea got up. She walked in front of Rick and sat down near the end of the lower trail, her back to a cluster of rocks so she would be out of sight from above. 'Aren't gonna get their kicks looking at me,' she muttered.

Bonnie shoved herself off the boulder and squatted. 'Maybe we ought to start down.'

Bert nodded. 'I don't like this at all.'

You and me both, Rick thought. 'Let's get moving.'

Chapter Fourteen

Gillian woke up. She was sprawled on the water bed. Lifting her head off the pillow, she looked at the alarm clock on the nightstand. Three-twenty. That left more than an hour and a half before it was time to go over to Jerry's.

If I'm going, she thought.

She groaned as she climbed off the undulating bed. Her back ached, and her rump felt stiff and sore. Standing up straight, she turned her back to the wall of mirrors. She looked over one shoulder. Her right buttock had a three-inch band of shiny red near its top. Some curls of white skin rimmed the lower edge of the scrape. She picked at one of the larger pieces, thinking she might peel it off like the dead skin after a sunburn, but pulling it hurt so she stopped. The left buttock, now so raw, looked as if someone had taken a hard swipe at it with sandpaper. The skin around both abrasions had a rosy glow. That's where the bruises will come, she thought. That's where I'll be black and blue.

Could've been a lot worse, she thought.

The rosy glow suddenly spread. Even her face took on a deep red hue.

God, why couldn't I just get bashed up? Why did I have to lose my pants?

Talk about your Stupid Human Tricks.

Jerry was good about it, though. Hell, he was terrific.

He really wants me to come over.

And I told him I'd bring his robe back.

She lifted the robe off the foot of the bed where she had tossed it before flopping down. It was still damp inside. She didn't see any blood on the dark blue fabric, but maybe she ought to throw it into the washing machine, anyway.

She tossed the robe down, stepped into her sandals, and slipped into her shirt. The shirt felt fine. The way it draped her rear end, it didn't even touch the wounds as long as she stood very straight.

When she bent over to pick up the robe, the shirt fell lightly against the raw place. It stuck to moisture there when she straightened up. She plucked it away, thinking she had better bandage that side, at least.

First, I'll throw this in the wash.

She carried Jerry's robe outside.

On her way to the laundry room, she looked at the high redwood fence and listened for the splashy sound of swimming. There was only silence from the other side. Maybe Jerry had gone inside. Or maybe he was stretched out, sunbathing.

I might still be there, she thought, if I hadn't crashed and burned.

She saw herself lying on one of his loungers. She felt the heavy heat of the sun, and then Jerry's hands sliding over her skin, spreading oil on her back and legs.

It might have gone that way, she thought. With a sigh, she entered the laundry room.

In spite of the light coming in through the curtained windows, the room seemed dark after the brightness outside. Next to a large basin stood a drier. On the other side of the drier was a top-loading washer. A nearby shelf held a collection of detergents and bleaches.

Gillian lifted the lip of the washing machine and peered inside. The drum appeared to be empty. She stuffed Jerry's robe inside, sprinkled it with soap powder, and closed the lid. She changed the temperature setting to cold, and turned the dial to regular. The machine started with a rush of shooting water.

Jerry'll think I'm terribly domestic, she thought, returning the robe to him all freshly laundered.

Smiling, she looked away from the washing machine. At the end of the room stood a white-painted cabinet. Its doors were shut.

Normally, Gillian's curiosity would have been whetted by the sight. She would've hurried to inspect the contents.

But the urge wasn't there.

She realized that she'd had enough of Fredrick. She didn't want to inspect any more of his possessions, didn't care to discover any more of his secrets.

She left the cabinet unexplored and went out the door.

Walking into the driveway, she angled toward Jerry's fence.

Don't be a ditz, she told herself.

Why not?

On tiptoe, she peered over the top of the fence. The pool was deserted. Jerry was nowhere to be seen. Feeling a small tug of disappointment, Gillian turned away. She cut across the driveway and entered the den through its sliding glass door.

In the bathroom, she searched the medicine cabinet. She found adhesive tape and a roll of gauze. And three straight razors, one with a scrimshaw handle depicting an old-fashioned sailing ship. She picked that one up. Holding it carefully, she fingered a trigger-like lever and the blade flashed up.

She grimaced and muttered, 'Yook.'

Fredrick Holden *would*, she thought, have a collection of straight razors. The way his taste seems to run, he probably daydreams of slicing up naked women.

Maybe he does slice up naked women.

Goldilocks and the homicidal maniac.

Cute thought, that.

She looked closely at the white handle of the razor. Any bloodstains? Didn't seem to be.

She set the razor down on the edge of the sink, then took off her shirt. There was only enough gauze to make a bandage for her main scrape, so she didn't need the razor to cut it off the roll. Lucky me, she thought. She folded the netty fabric into a pad. Then she stripped off two lengths of tape to secure its edges. She used her teeth to rip the tape off the spool.

I could've gotten by, she thought, without even touching the damn razor.

She picked it up and carefully folded the blade. She put it back into the medicine cabinet, set the remaining tape inside, and shut the mirrored door.

Her face in the mirror looked flushed. Specks of sweat glistened on her forehead, under her eyes, over her lip. A hand towel hung from a bar beside the sink, but the thought of wiping her face on one of Fredrick's towels was repulsive.

She used her shirt to mop the sweat off her face.

Then she stepped in front of the full-length mirror on the bathroom door. She turned around. Peering over her shoulder, she pressed the bandage into place.

She put on her shirt as she walked to the den. She went directly to the bar, opened the refrigerator, and took out a bottle of beer. After a few swallows, she sighed.

Now what? she wondered.

The washing cycle wouldn't be finished yet.

She wished she could take her suitcase out to the car. That way, there would be no need to return here after leaving Jerry's house tonight. But he might see her carrying it out.

I'll get it all ready, she decided, and leave it by the door when I go over. Then I'll just have to reach in, grab it, and take off.

Beer in hand, she stepped around the end of the bar and glanced at the digital clock on the VCR. Three thirty-eight. Christ. Only eighteen minutes had gone by since she woke up from her nap.

Give yourself about twenty minutes to get ready, you've still got an hour to kill.

Read? She felt too restless to read.

So watch the tube, she thought.

She wandered over to the shelves and looked at Fredrick's collection of video tapes.

Should've known, she thought, as she started to read the titles: *Maniac, Texas Chainsaw Massacre, Halloween, Friday the 13th, 2000 Maniacs, Psycho, Dressed to Kill, Badlands, Visiting Hours, Mother's Day,*

Body Double, Sleepaway Camp, Return to the Valley of the Dolls, Ten to Midnight, The Ripper, I Spit on Your Grave, and a lot more. Gillian had seen several of the movies in Fredrick's collection. Most of them featured nude women and nasty murders.

This guy has a real bent, she thought.

Crouching to inspect a lower shelf, she found some titles that were more to her liking: *Back to the Future, E.T., Star Wars, Alien, The Howling, The Snows of Kilimanjaro,* and about a dozen others. She'd never seen *The Howling.* She'd enjoyed the book, and the movie was supposed to be good. There wouldn't be enough time to watch all of it, but she could take a look at the first half, then rent the tape later and watch the rest back at her apartment. So she slipped its case off the shelf and carried it over to the television.

The VCR was a different make from hers. She studied it for a few moments, then turned on the television, pressed a button marked Power and another marked Play. The machine came on. She took her beer to the easy chair and sat down.

The movie opened with a young woman standing under a shower. She turned slowly, humming as she soaped herself and the camera roamed her body.

Werewolf victim number one, Gillian thought.

She was a little surprised by the explicit nudity. They even showed a close-up of the girl's vagina as she stroked it with a sudsy hand. The picture quality was poor, too. It looked grainy and cheap.

Suddenly, the shower curtain shot open. The girl yelped in surprise as a hand grabbed her hair and jerked her backwards. She fell over the edge of the tub and landed with a slap of wet skin against the tile floor. Kicking and whimpering, she was dragged out of the bathroom by her hair.

The screen went dark.

Against the black background appeared the words: *Torture Slave.*

What's going on? Gillian wondered. She glanced at the plastic box on the floor. It clearly belonged to *The Howling,* not something called *Torture Slave.*

Credits were still showing on the television. Screenplay by Tryon

Cleaver, directed by Otto Keller. Obviously pseudonyms created by guys with terrific senses of humor.

Must be some kind of porn, Gillian thought.

The credits ended.

The girl from the shower was hanging by her wrists from ropes attached to ceiling beams in the living room of a house. She squirmed and screamed while a man in black clothes stood nearby. His back was to the camera. He was facing a fireplace, holding a wrought-iron poker.

Gillian muttered, 'Oh, shit.'

She rushed from her chair, stopped the tape and ejected it. Her hands trembled as she placed the cassette into the box labeled *The Howling*.

What kind of sick crap is this? she wondered.

She stepped over to the shelves and scanned all the titles on the three rows of video tapes. No *Torture Slave* in the whole collection.

She slipped the cassette back into its place and pulled out *Star Wars*. She opened the box. The cassette inside had no label at all.

She took it to the television. Crouching there, she inserted it in the VCR and pressed the Play button. For a few seconds, the screen was blank.

Then a young woman inside an elevator approached its opening doors. Before she could step out, two thugs in leather jackets rushed in, knocking her backward. She slammed against the rear wall of the elevator. Laughing, one of the men tore open her blouse. The other yanked her skirt up.

Gillian stopped the show. She ejected the cassette and took it back to the shelves.

Probably, *E.T.*, *Back to the Future*, and the rest of them in this section of Fredrick's collection were more of the same. The popular titles on the containers were camouflage for his secret library of sick videos.

Where did he even *get* such things? Gillian wondered. Maybe he ordered them through one of those S&M magazines he kept in his bedroom. Did they come packaged as legitimate films? That hardly seemed likely. Pretty expensive, though, if he bought all those popular videos just for their cases.

The guy's loaded. He can afford to squander money when he has that much of it.

Why would he even bother? He could keep the things in a closet, or something. Maybe he enjoys having them hidden in plain sight. His little secret.

A guy like this, his mind's warped. He probably has plenty of strange games. I'd just as soon not run into any more of them, Gillian thought.

She wondered if she should get her camera and snap some photos of his video tape collection. She didn't much care to have such a reminder; it would be like taking a little of Fredrick the Gross home with her. On the other hand, she already had shots of his book and magazine collection – with the exception of S&M and child porn. If she left without taking pictures of his tapes, she might regret it later. Besides, she had time to kill.

She went to the bedroom for her camera.

I don't have to put any of these in my scrapbook, she thought. Just throw them in the back of a drawer if I don't want to look at them. But at least I'll have the things.

Back in the den, Gillian removed *Psycho*, *I Spit on Your Grave*, *2000 Maniacs*, and several more from the shelf of legitimate videos and arranged them on the floor. She took a close-up showing their covers. As she put them away, she wondered if even these were what they seemed to be. Probably. But she opened the case of *I Spit on Your Grave*. The label on the cassette inside had the same title. So the psycho/slasher movies were for real. Naturally.

Crouching, she took down a dozen of the videos with the phony cases. She spread them on the floor, took a shot, and returned them to the shelf.

She wondered when she'd find time to put all this down into note form – but maybe she wouldn't want to; the pictures would speak for themselves. She returned to the bedroom with her camera and put it into the suitcase. The clock on the nightstand showed five minutes after four.

The washing machine had probably stopped by now.

Gillian hurried through the house.

I won't wait for five o'clock, she decided. As soon as the robe's in the drier, I'll come in and get ready. By the time I'm set to go, the robe should be pretty dry. Jerry won't mind if I show up a little early.

Outside, she resisted the urge to peer over the fence again. She walked straight to the laundry room. The washing machine was silent. She opened the lid, reached inside, and lifted out the heavy, sodden robe. She dropped it on top of the drier.

Bending over, she opened the drier's door.

And groaned.

Fredrick had gone off and left laundry in the machine.

Just what I want to do, Gillian thought. Touch his stuff. At least it looks dry.

Reaching into the drum, she pulled out a washcloth, a shirt, some white socks and a few pairs of brightly colored bikini underpants. She tossed them on top of the drier beside Jerry's robe. When she dragged out a large blue bath towel, the machine was empty.

Except for a book.

It was oversized, with a brown leatherette cover, and looked like a photo album.

So what's it doing in the drier? Gillian wondered.

She supposed that Fredrick had put it there as a precaution, to save it in case the house burnt down while he was away.

She removed it, set it on top of the drier, and stuffed Jerry's robe into the machine. She closed the door. She pushed a button to start the drying cycle.

Then she stared at the album.

My big chance, she thought, to see what Fredrick looks like. A guy with mirrors all over his bedroom would probably have quite a collection of photos featuring himself.

It's more likely crammed with Polaroids of his girlfriends in the raw. That would be his speed.

Do I really want to find out? I doubt it.

Gillian left the album on top of the drier, turned away, and walked to the laundry room door. She stepped outside into the sunlight. Then she halted. She sighed.

If I look in the album, I'll regret it.

She muttered, 'Shit,' turned around, strode to the drier and picked up the album. Holding it under one arm, she walked quickly to the lounge and sat down. She rested the book on her crossed legs and opened it.

There were no photographs on the page. Pressed beneath the clear plastic sheet was a newspaper clipping. There was nothing to indicate the name of the paper or the date. Gillian read the story.

U of A CO-ED VANISHES

Foul play is suspected in the disappearance, Saturday, of 19-year-old Candice Fairborn, a University of Arizona co-ed, from her apartment on Spring Street.

According to police authorities, the roommate of Miss Fairborn returned to the ground-floor apartment Sunday evening after a weekend outing to find a rear window open. Further investigation led to the discovery of an upset lamp in the victim's bedroom along with the torn remnants of her nightgown.

Being sought in connection with the disappearance is Miss Fairborn's former boyfriend . . .

The story continued, but Gillian didn't bother to finish it. She turned the page. And found another clipping.

MYSTERY BODY GREEN BAY
HOUSEWIFE

The partially decomposed body discovered Thursday by hikers in the Bagley Rapids area has been identified as Kathy Ellen Warnack, the 22-year-old wife of Ronald Warnack, who disappeared from their Jackson Avenue home on August 4.

According to the coroner's report, the slain woman had been sexually molested and died of multiple stab wounds . . .

Gillian had a tight, cold feeling in her stomach.
Why did Fredrick Holden keep these clippings? Why, indeed?
Her hand trembled as she turned the page.

GRISLY DISCOVERY

Saranak Lake – The remains of an unidentified female were found Saturday in a densely wooded area north of Saranak Lake . . .

She glanced at the next page. Eighteen-year-old Pam Jones had vanished from her parents' home in Park Ridge while they were out playing bridge. On the next page was the story of Maggie Drukker, a twenty-three-year-old housewife who disappeared from her New Orleans apartment while her husband was working the graveyard shift at the airport.

The raped and mutilated body of a Seattle secretary was found in the woods near Salem, Oregon, two weeks after her disappearance.

Remains, partially devoured by wildlife, were found in the bayou and identified by dental charts as belonging to Maggie Drukker, who had disappeared from her New Orleans apartment on November 2nd.

Page after page, the stories went on. Young women mysteriously vanishing from their homes or apartments. Corpses found in secluded, wild areas. On four occasions, stories of the discovered bodies matched earlier stories of disappearances. Gillian turned several pages and came to one without a clipping. The remaining pages of the album were bare.

She turned back to the final story.

MISSING TEEN FOUND SLAIN

Underhill – The raped and savagely mutilated body discovered Friday by hikers in the Smuggler's Notch area of Mt Mansfield has been identified as that of 17-year-old Rhonda Bain, who was abducted May 24 from her parents' home in Burlington.
The nude corpse of the teen was found . . .

Gillian didn't read the rest of it. Numb and confused, she flipped to the front of the album. She counted the clippings. Twenty-six of them.

She looked again at each.

Most of the stories contained references to locations. Some of the areas were unfamiliar to Gillian, but she knew enough geography to realize that the disappearances and murders had taken place in states all over the country.

None in California, though. That was interesting.

She shut the album and stared at it.

Why, for godsake, did Fredrick Holden have a scrapbook like this? Yeah, why?

Why do I keep my photographs and stuff?

To look at them and remember.

Chapter Fifteen

'You guys should get first choice of where you want to set up your tent,' Bonnie said.

'I think we'll do some scouting around,' Bert told her. 'You can have this campsite. I'm sure we'll find a good one.'

Rick felt something collapse inside. Oh no, he thought. Bert, no.

Andrea pulled a boot off and looked up, perplexed. 'What do you mean?' she asked. 'You aren't leaving, are you?'

'There's plenty of room here,' Bonnie added. 'There's no reason to go.'

'I'm sure we won't go far,' Bert said. 'You girls didn't come out here to be stuck with us.'

'And vice versa,' Andrea muttered.

Bert didn't respond to that remark. 'Maybe we can get together later on, tell stories around the campfire or something.'

'Whoopee.' Andrea looked at Rick. 'I thought we were all going to stick together.'

'Yeah. Well. I guess it doesn't really matter. We'll be close by, in case anything happens.'

'Nothing's going to happen,' Bert said. 'I'm sure Jase and the others are over the pass by now.' She turned to Rick. 'Why don't we leave our packs here until we find a place? No point in lugging them around any more than necessary.'

Andrea peeled a sock off her foot and threw it down.

Rick followed Bert to a path near the shore of the lake. 'There are probably a lot of good campsites,' she said.

'This one has the stream. We want to have running water, don't we?'

'Maybe we'll find another stream.'

They walked only a short distance before Rick spotted a clearing with a fire ring. 'Let's check this place out,' he suggested.

Bert scanned it from where she stood. 'We can do better,' she said.

It's too close to the girls' camp for her taste, Rick thought. Great. Wonderful. Shit.

They kept walking. Soon, they came to a clearing with a built-up fireplace that had a grate. There were logs for seats, even a makeshift table. The area had high clusters of rock on three sides that would provide a natural barrier against the wind.

It was probably not much more than a five-minute hike from the girls' camp.

'This looks perfect,' Rick said.

'Not bad,' Bert agreed. 'Why don't we keep going, though? There's no big hurry. Maybe we'll run into something even better if we keep looking.'

'Okay.'

'Maybe we'll find a stream.'

They found a stream.

But not before they had rounded the end of the lake.

Standing on a small rise, they stared down at it. The stream by the girls' camp was a trickle compared to this. The wide band of water rushed down over bare rocks, white and frothy in places; in other places gleaming like clear glass. Not far from where it spilled into the lake, the stream formed a wide pool.

'Oh, this is fabulous,' Bert said.

Rick tried to spot the girls' camp. He couldn't. The stream emptied into an inlet with a rim of rocky, wooded land across the front. There was only a narrow opening between a high outcropping on the shore and the end of the sheltering arm. Bert couldn't have found a more secluded spot. And there was a camping area on the other side of the stream, down near the inlet.

She smiled at Rick and squeezed his hand. 'Come on.' She led him down the slope. She had a spring in her step. She really loves this place, Rick thought. And he couldn't blame her. But it was too far from Andrea and Bonnie.

When they reached the stream, Bert stopped at its edge. She stood there, turning her head, smiling as she watched it rush and swirl. It sounded like a strong wind, and a hint of coolness seemed to rise off its surface.

'What do you think?' she asked. She looked eager. And she looked ready for disappointment.

'It is nice,' he admitted.

'I know we're a long way from the girls, but this is *so* beautiful and we'd have it all to ourselves. It's the kind of place I was hoping we'd find, even before we started out.'

'Okay,' Rick said.

'You *want* to camp with the girls, don't you?'

'No, of course not. It's just that we told them . . .'

'We don't owe them anything. Hell, we spent the whole day with them. We didn't come on this trip to have a foursome. We came to be with each other.'

'It's just that I'm worried about them.'

'The guys are long gone, Rick. The girls don't need our protection.'

'No, I suppose not. I *said* we could stay here.'

'Your heart wasn't in it. Do you *want* Andrea? Is that it?'

'Don't be ridiculous.'

'Because if you do, just say so. I'll camp here, out of your way. Maybe we can even get Bonnie to come over, so she won't . . .' her voice snagged. Her eyes glimmered wet. She turned away.

Rick put his hands on her shoulders. 'For godsake, Bert.'

'I'm sure she'd be . . . more than happy to oblige you.'

'It might be nice,' Rick said. He felt Bert stiffen under his hands. 'But she isn't you.'

'Oh, I'm sure she has pretty much the same parts.'

'So do a Volkswagen and a Rolls-Royce.'

'Christ, you're going *automotive* on me?'

'Four wheels and an engine, but there's a difference.'

'You don't even have a Rolls-Royce.'

'Got you.'

She sniffed and rubbed a shirtsleeve across her nose. 'Yeah, you got me. Still want me to move in with you?'

'Will you?'

'No. But I'll think about it.' She turned around. Her dirty, tear-streaked face wore half a smile.

'Your mascara ran,' Rick said.

'What mascara?' The other half of her smile came up.

'You need to wash your face.'

'Thanks, buster. You seen yourself lately?' She kissed him on the mouth. 'Anyone for a bath?' she whispered.

'We'll freeze our nuts off.'

'You may.'

'We'd better get back,' Bert said. 'The girls might think we're lost and come looking. If they see you like this . . .'

'They'd go apeshit, but they'd be tough out of luck. I couldn't get it up now if my life depended on it.'

'Wouldn't bet on that,' Bert said.

He felt her hand.

'Ah, I was right.' She patted his belly. 'But enough of this. We'd better get dressed.'

She sat up. Her back was speckled with grit. The smooth face of the rock still bore her wet imprint.

They both stood. Rick used his open hands to brush off her back and rump. Then he turned around, and she did the same for him. 'For a man,' she said, 'you have a very nice ass.'

'Well, don't beat it to death.'

She squeezed it and stepped away.

When they were dressed, they crossed the stream, leaping from rock to rock, and made their way down to the campsite. The shaded clearing had a fireplace with a grate, and a good flat area where they decided their tent would go.

'Looks fine to me,' Rick said.

'Any more qualms about abandoning the girls?'

'They'll be all right.'

'Would you feel better if we asked them to come over here? I'm not willing to give up this place, but if they want to bring their stuff over . . .'

'You've sure changed your tune.'

Bert shrugged. 'I guess Andrea doesn't seem like such a big threat anymore.'

'I guess she wouldn't,' Rick said.

Bert reached forward and clasped her hands behind Rick's neck. 'So, what do you think? Should we allow them into our nice little hideaway?'

He slipped his hands inside her open shirt. He curled them over her breasts, lightly caressing the smooth skin and stiff nipples. 'I don't think so,' he said. 'They'd just be in the way.'

'Let's bring our packs over.' She tipped back her head and squirmed against his moving hands.

'What's the hurry?'

'I want to . . . lie out on the rocks again . . . while the sun's still on them.'

'That's certainly worth hurrying for.'

She swallowed. 'Thought you might think so.'

Rick drew the front of her shirt together and fastened the middle button. She released his neck. Her hands glided down his shoulders, then dropped away.

He followed Bert across the clearing and up the rock slabs to the stream. They hopped across it. The flat surface on the other side, where they had made love, was dry now.

Rick remembered how her wet skin had been cold at first, and stippled with goosebumps.

Then he remembered what his mind had done.

How could he have let himself imagine such things?

It had been Bert under him, but sometimes it was Andrea; Andrea naked on the trail to Dead Mule Pass, but not dead, not decapitated,

564

alive and writhing, gasping and clutching at him as he rammed; and then she was Julie sprawled beneath him in nothing but her knee socks, Julie his stepmother, but she was no more dead than Andrea or Bert and those were her hands tugging at his buttocks to urge him deeper into her wet, hugging heat. Rick had thought, this is wrong, this is bad. But he couldn't help it. He loved it. He was having Bert and Andrea and Julie all at once.

It's these damn mountains, he thought, ashamed now that he'd allowed such fantasies to take hold. It's the mountains and not enough sleep last night and hiking all day in the heat. It's what happened with Julie all those years ago. It's Jase and Luke and Wally and knowing what they'd do to the women if they got the chance. Or is it what *I* would like to do to them?

Hadn't Bert suggested as much this morning?

You're scaring me, she'd said. *What the hell is going on inside your head? Your imagination is revolting.*

Sounds to me like you're projecting your own fantasies onto those guys.

Yeah? And what was I projecting when we caught them spying on us with their binoculars? Was that my imagination, too?

But you have to admit, he thought, your imagination's been throwing some real curves lately. Some wild stuff. Dreaming up that slaughter on the trail, turning Bert into Andrea, which was bad enough but understandable; turning her into Julie, which was sick.

Need to get home. All this will stop when I'm home.

God, we almost turned back this morning before the girls came along. We'd be home tonight, or at least out of the damned mountains, maybe in a hotel at Tahoe, but I had to open my big mouth and talk Bert into staying. To watch out for the girls. To *watch* them, more like it. Had nothing to do with protecting them.

What did I think, I'd get in their pants? Fat chance of that, unless I bashed in Bert's head . . .

Or slit her throat.

'Oh my God!' Bert gasped. She stopped abruptly and grabbed his arm.

Rick felt a surge of dread that she'd somehow read his mind. His face burned. She's not psychic any more than I am, he told himself. And I'm not. That trail massacre was mind garbage, paranoia, not a premonition.

But it came roaring back through his head – the sprawled naked bodies, the mutilations, the death – when he saw what Bert was pointing at.

Jase, Wally and Luke.

The three were crouched side by side among the rocks of an outcropping that jutted into the lake.

They had their backs to Rick and Bert.

The way they peered over the top reminded Rick of old westerns, of outlaws waiting to ambush a stagecoach.

'Those bastards,' Bert muttered.

Rick pulled her off the path and into the trees, where they couldn't be seen if the boys should turn around.

'Those assholes are spying on the girls,' she said. Her eyes looked fierce and unafraid.

'Close up, this time.'

'Can you imagine? If that was them with the binoculars, they actually came all the way back down.'

'Obviously liked what they saw.'

'The nerve of those . . .' A red hue washed over her face. 'You don't think they watched *us*, do you?'

Rick shook his head. 'No. They don't know where we are.'

'They would've, though. If they'd known.'

'Yep.'

'I'd like to rip out their eyes.'

'It could come to that,' Rick said. 'They might not be happy, just looking.'

'We'd better do something. Maybe we can sneak up and take them by surprise.'

'And then what? I forgot to bring my black belt.' *And my revolver's in my pack.* 'I don't think this is the right time to confront them. We'd be . . . catching them red-handed. I don't think they'd like that at all.'

'Screw what they'd like.'

'If they feel cornered, they might decide to go for broke and have at us. I seriously doubt that we'd come out on top. Let's just stay out of their way. If we circle the lake, we can come around from the front and join up with the girls, and those three scums won't know that we're onto them.'

'That makes sense,' Bert said. 'Yeah. That's what we'll do.'

'Guess we can write this place off,' Bert said when they came to the stream. 'Now we've gotta stick with the girls.'

'Maybe we can all come over here.'

'Doesn't matter,' she muttered. 'It's no good now, anyway.'

'I'm sorry.'

She shrugged and looked at him. 'It was nice, though, wasn't it?'

'Fantastic.'

'At least we had that.'

They hiked through the trees, staying away from the shoreline path, until they heard faint splashing sounds. Then Rick led the way to the edge of the lake. They ducked behind a deadfall and peered out through the rotted limbs.

'Oh great,' Bert said. 'Just great.'

Andrea and Bonnie were directly across the lake from them, knee-deep in the water near the shore. Bonnie, in her yellow bikini, was bent over and splashing herself. Andrea, in a black bikini, stood closer to the shore, rigid and hugging her chest as if she were freezing.

Rick turned his eyes to the jut of rocks where the boys had been. He couldn't see them.

'So where are the guys?' Bert asked.

'Still there, probably. Enjoying the view.'

'Nice of the girls to be so obliging.'

'They don't know they're being watched,' Rick said.

Bonnie waded farther out. The water climbed her stout legs. Her lips peeled back in a grimace when the cold lapped her groin. She turned to face Andrea. She spoke, but Rick couldn't quite make out her words. When Andrea replied, her voice carried clearly across the water. 'Yeah, sure it's not so bad. Tell me that when you're pissing icicles.'

'Come on,' Bert said. 'Let's get going.'

Rick glanced toward the rocks. This time he did see a shadow. Small. Fleeting. Even imagined a low, cackling laugh. He exhaled slowly and shook his head in disbelief. What was the *matter* with him? The place was giving him the creeps, that was the matter. At least The Three Thugateers were flesh and blood. He could handle them okay. But skinny shadows? No way.

Bert was moving forward. Had she seen him staring at the rocks like some crazy lunatic? In case she had, Rick said, 'I wish the guys would show themselves.'

Andrea turned around and waded toward shore. Her hips swayed. Her small, firm rump flexed with each step. Her bikini pants were low enough for Rick to see the shadow of cleavage between her buttocks.

'Quit stalling,' Bert said. 'You're no better than those peeping Toms.'

'I just hope they don't do anything but look,' he said. 'We'd better get over there fast.'

'Before the girls get dressed,' Bert added.

She *is* psychic.

With Bert in the lead, they stayed away from the shore, and only pale bits of the lake were visible through the dense trees to the right. A few times, Rick heard the girls' faint voices. There were occasional splashing sounds.

Finally, Rick saw bright orange in the distance. 'Looks like a tent,' he said.

Bert nodded.

They made their way into the clearing. Their own packs were on the ground near the side of the tent. The girls' packs were propped up against rocks, and open. Rick saw no one, not even when he turned toward the lake. He felt himself knot up.

Oh my God, he thought.

We would've heard shouts, he told himself.

Not necessarily. If the guys took them by surprise . . .

He headed for his pack.

'Going for your camera?' Bert asked. The smile fell off her face when she saw Rick's expression. 'What's wrong? You don't think . . .?' Her head snapped toward the lake. 'Bonnie?' she called. 'Andrea?'

'Over here,' Bonnie called from the direction of the lake.

'You guys get lost or something?' Andrea asked.

Bert looked relieved. She glanced at Rick and rolled her eyes upward.

'False alarm,' Rick muttered.

He followed Bert to the lake shore and they found the girls on a sunlit slab of rock that slanted gently into the water. They had their towels beneath them. Bonnie was sitting up, hands on her raised knees, looking over her shoulder as they approached. Andrea was stretched out, face resting on her crossed arms. Her bikini top, untied so the strings wouldn't leave marks across her back, was pressed between her body and the towel. The side of her breast was bare and pale. Rick forced himself to look away. He glanced to the left. The cluster of rocks where the boys had been lurking was farther away than he had supposed – maybe fifty yards off. With the binoculars, though, they'd still have a fine view.

'Don't look around or anything,' Bert told the girls. 'Try not to show any reactions.'

Frowning, Bonnie turned herself around to face them.

Andrea lifted her head. She glanced from Bert to Rick.

'The guys are here,' Rick said.

'You're shitting me,' Andrea muttered. '*Our* guys? The chain-gang?'

'They're down the shore a ways,' Bert explained. 'Or they were, when we saw them about half an hour ago. They were hiding behind some rocks, watching the two of you while you were in the water.'

'*Jesus.*'

'You're serious?' Bonnie asked. 'They're right here at the lake?' She kept her eyes on Bert. Rick admired her restraint in not trying to spot them. 'They were *way* up the trail above us,' she said. 'They came all the way down just to . . .'

'Must've really liked what they saw,' Andrea said.

'Where are they?'

569

Bert turned so her body would block the boys' view, raised a hand to her belly, and pointed.

Bonnie still didn't look that way. Andrea tried, twisting her head to look over her shoulder and rolling just a bit. Her right breast unmashed and lifted partway out of the limp bikini. Bert sidestepped into the path of Andrea's view. Unable to see past her, Andrea eased down again. She picked up the ends of her bikini strings, bent her arms up high behind her back, and started to tie them.

'To get over there,' Bonnie said, 'they had to go right past us.'

'You know, this really sucks.' Andrea finished tying her bikini. She sat up, adjusted her top, and crossed her legs. 'Do you realize how much this sucks? These scrotes came all the way down the trail. They were almost to the *top*. They came all the way back down and snuck past and spied on us like a bunch of fucking voyeurs. And we're not supposed to know they're around. What are they planning on, anyway? They obviously aren't gonna leave, not this late in the afternoon. It not only sucks, it's extremely creepy.'

'Aren't they going to pitch tents or build a fire or anything?' Bonnie asked.

'If they do that,' Rick said, 'they'll give away that they're here.'

'What they're gonna do,' Andrea said, 'is keep hidden and some-time during the night they're gonna move in.'

Bonnie looked up at Rick. 'What are we going to do?'

He thought about the gun in his pack.

'I'll tell you what I think,' Bert said. 'Why don't you two get into some clothes, then the four of us will take a walk and pay the guys a visit.'

Andrea grinned. 'Fuckin' A, right!'

Bonnie looked grim. She nodded. 'Yeah, let's face the bastards.'

'I agree,' Rick said. 'If there's going to be trouble, better to get it over with. While it's still light out and we can see what we're doing.'

'What *they're* doing,' Bert added. 'And let's not go empty-handed.'

Chapter Sixteen

'Damn it,' Bert said. 'I have to pee.'

'Pick a tree,' Rick told her.

She scanned the woods around the clearing. 'What about our three friends? I certainly don't need an audience.'

'They're probably still near the place where we spotted them. I don't think they'd come in close. Not while it's still light out.'

'Want to come along?'

'I thought you didn't need an audience.'

'You don't have to watch.'

How do I get out of this? he wondered. The girls were inside their tent getting dressed. Bert going off to urinate would give him just the chance he needed to grab his revolver out of the pack.

Bert reached a suitable clearing, well away from the trail, bent over her pack and took out some toilet paper and a small plastic shovel. She frowned. And bent her head to get a closer look at what she saw on the ground.

A paw print. A large one.

'My God,' she breathed, almost forgetting why she was here in the first place. Her stomach lurched and a warm patch began to spread between her legs. She clamped her muscles tight to stop the patch getting any bigger.

Bert rocked back on her heels. Trying to come to terms with what this new danger would mean to them. She leaned forward to examine the palm-size pawmark imprinted in the sand.

Relatively new. A few hours old at the most. Another one, to the right of the first, lay about eight inches ahead. She looked back and saw two more.

'My God,' she whispered again. Cougar, by the look of it – and one helluva size. It's in the vicinity. Or was last night. Just passing through? Or is this its patch?

No sign of it now, anyway. She got to her feet. Slowly. Thinking, one cougar and you got more cougars . . . Great. That's all we need. Should've listened to Rick and gone to Maui instead.

Scooping up her pack, paper and trowel, Bert raced back to Rick.

'Hey,' she panted, pulling up short. She took a couple of deep breaths to steady the tremor in her voice. 'Looks like we got company, Rick. Big cat type company . . .'

'Oh yeah?'

'Sure. Come see for yourself. I know cougars are around in the mountains, the Rockies, mainly. But let's hope this is a one-off that's strayed from home . . .'

She tried, but she couldn't convince herself that this cougar was a one-off. One vacation she'd helped out at a feline breeding center in Rosamund. From her time there, she'd learned enough about big cat behavior to know that there was probably a mom cougar, and a bunch of kitty cougars holed up in the rocks somewhere near.

Rick followed her back to the clearing.

Apart from coyotes and maybe the occasional wolverine, he'd discounted other wildlife. Keep to the track, he'd thought. No problems if we keep to the track. But if it looks like we got mountain lions tracking us down as well as the teen trio, then maybe it's time to bring out the gun . . .

'We better keep our eyes peeled. For cats – and for The Three Thugateers,' Bert said. 'And tell the girls, too. Better safe than sorry. Anyway, we keep to the main trail, cougars won't bother us.'

'Okay. But you said we shouldn't confront the guys empty-handed,' Rick said. 'What did you have in mind?'

'Weapons.' She patted the sheath knife on her belt and eyed Rick's. 'The girls have knives, too.'

Rick opened the side pocket of his pack. He pulled out the T-shirt and unwrapped his revolver.

Bert gazed at it. 'My God,' she muttered.

'Just in case there's real trouble,' he said. He lifted the back of his shirt and pushed the pistol under his belt. Its barrel slid down cool between his buttocks. He let his shirt-tail hang out to conceal the bulge.

'I don't believe this,' Bert said.

'I knew you wouldn't like the idea. That's why I kept it out of sight. But it'll do us a lot more good than knives and a hatchet.'

'You wouldn't shoot anyone?'

'If we're attacked . . . This isn't fun 'n games, Bert. We've got to be ready to protect ourselves.'

'But a gun.'

'They've got knives, too, you know. You actually think we'd stand a chance if it came to a fight?'

'I don't want anyone getting killed.'

'As long as it's them and not us.'

'You and Dirty Harry. Maybe we shouldn't take any weapons at all.'

'Are you looking to get yourself gang-raped? Or chewed up by a cougar?'

'Yeah. Cougars.' The color drained from her face.

'It'll stay in my belt unless they try for us.'

'Promise?' she asked in a small voice. 'You won't wave it in their faces and threaten them?'

'They'll never know I have it. If I pull the gun, it comes out firing.'

'Don't let the girls know about it, either. Andrea – she might start something with the guys if she knew you had it.'

'It'll be our secret. You and me.'

'I wish it was just *your* secret.'

'Well, now at least you know we've got some protection.'

'A real comfort. You didn't happen to bring along a nuclear warhead?'

'Wouldn't fit in my pack.'

Bert sighed. 'Let's go. My teeth are floating.'

He followed her out of the clearing. They leaped the small stream. A distance beyond it, he stopped and Bert went ahead. She stepped behind a tree. Rick heard her belt buckle, the rustle of fabric as she lowered her pants.

She didn't take it well, he thought. But at least she didn't go ape. She'll be damn glad I've got the gun if things get so bad that I have to use it. The look on her face when I mentioned getting gang-banged. Hell, she'd probably use it herself before she'd let that happen.

Give the gun to *her* if she's so afraid of what I'll do with it.

I don't think so. No, I don't think so. Not such a hot idea. She might not even know how to fire the thing, and even if she did, she might chicken out until it's too late. Too late for all of us.

I'll just keep it, thanks.

Just let them try something, they'll be dead meat.

Dead meat.

The words had a chilling ring to them.

Rick began to tremble. His breath hissed through his clenched teeth.

If I'd had a gun last time, Julie would still be alive. They wouldn't have fucked her and killed her. I'd have blown their heads off and saved her and we wouldn't have been alone together until Dad got back with help and Dad wouldn't have acted like *I'd* killed her and he wouldn't have turned into a drunk and killed himself and my life wouldn't have turned to shit.

All because I didn't have a gun.

Well, I've got one now.

Bert came out from behind the trees, fastening her belt. When she saw Rick, her face darkened. 'What's wrong?' She looked around as if expecting to spot the guys.

'Everything's fine,' Rick said.

'Is it?'

'I'm just worried about what might happen.'

'What's to worry about? You've got your equalizer.'

'Thank God.'

They returned to the clearing. The girls were out of their tent.

Both had changed into jeans and jogging shoes. Bonnie wore a sweat-shirt, Andrea a red plaid shirt with long sleeves. It looked too big for her, and it wasn't tucked in.

'Do you have knives or something?' Rick asked.

Nodding, Bonnie patted a bulge in a front pocket of her jeans. Andrea lifted the front of her shirt. Sheathed at her hip was a hunting knife with a staghorn handle. 'Bonnie has a tomahawk we could take along,' she said.

'It's my brother's old Boy Scout hand-axe. But we probably shouldn't take it with us. I mean, we don't want to look like we've come to do battle.'

'I agree,' Bert said. 'I think we should just play it very cool.'

'Maybe you should do the talking,' Rick suggested. 'You were good with them this morning.'

'Okay.'

'And no mouthing off,' Bonnie told Andrea.

'You think I'm stupid?'

'You flipped them off, didn't you?'

'That was different. They were ten miles away.' She scrunched up her face and said, 'Uh-oh. You don't suppose that's why they came down? Maybe I pissed them off and they came down to pound the shit out of me.'

Her tone was half joking, but Rick could see that the possibility had her worried.

He'd read, last month, of a motorist being killed because he gave the finger to the driver of a pickup truck that cut him off. The pickup stopped, blocking the road. The driver got out, pulled the man from the car, and beat him to death with a tire iron.

'I'm sure your gesture didn't help the situation,' Bonnie said.

'I doubt if that's why they're here,' Bert said, and Rick nodded in agreement.

'Good. Glad of that. So all they want to do is fuck our butts off.'

'Hilarious,' Bonnie muttered.

'Come on,' Bert said. 'Let's get it over with.'

She led the way. Rick followed. His leg muscles felt soft and shaky.

Everything, he realized, felt soft and shaky, as if his skin was filled with jelly.

'Oh, and incidentally,' Bert murmured, over her shoulder, 'I came across cougar tracks when I went for a pee back there.' She glanced at the girls' faces and saw that she had all of their attention. 'Just thought you ought to know.'

'Should we whistle a happy tune?' Andrea asked.

'Should we shut up?' Bonnie suggested.

'Everybody wearing clean panties?'

Rick heard a soft whack.

'Hey!'

'Just cut it out,' said Bonnie. 'There's nothing funny going on here.'

'Why don't you lighten up.' Andrea sounded hurt. 'Just because we're walking toward our imminent defilement and demise, you don't have to be so fucking *tense* about it.'

Rick looked back. 'We'll be okay,' he said.

Andrea made a grim smile. 'Encouragement from the male. You ever hear the one about the Lone Ranger and Tonto? They're surrounded by an Injun war party, they're out of ammo. The Lone Ranger turns to Tonto and says, "Looks like we're gonna buy the ranch." And Tonto, he says, "What you mean *we*, white man?"'

We're not out of ammo, Rick thought. He wanted to lift his shirt-tail and let her see the revolver, but he'd promised Bert to keep the gun secret from the girls.

It would ease their minds, knowing.

But Bert was right. If Andrea knew about the gun, she might become very brave and make matters worse.

'We'll be all right,' he said.

'Yeah? You got an Uzi or something?'

'No, but I'm good with my dukes.'

She smiled. 'That's consoling.'

'Is this banter absolutely necessary?' Bert asked.

Rick faced forward again. 'Just trying to keep up the morale of the troops.'

Her eyes flashed. She looked shaky. Rick realized, suddenly, that he no longer felt loose and shivery inside. 'The banter helps,' he said. 'Why don't I take over the lead.'

Bert nodded. She stepped aside. Though the late afternoon was mild and they had been walking in the shade, she was wet. Honey-colored curls were stuck to her forehead. Her face and neck looked slick. The sides of her pale blue shirt were dark. Rick saw that she had buttoned it all the way up. He stopped in front of her.

'Are you okay?' he asked.

A corner of her mouth twitched. 'Maybe we should turn back,' she said. 'The more I think about it . . .'

'Why don't I go on ahead,' Rick suggested. 'You and the girls could wait here. There's no need for all of us to confront those creeps.'

'I'm not going to let you do it alone,' Bert said.

'Besides,' Bonnie added, 'we don't even know for sure where they are. Or the wildlife, and I'm talking cats, here, for that matter.'

'Yeah,' Andrea said. 'What if you go on your own, and the guys, or the cats, jump the rest of us?'

'The bastards are probably up near those rocks,' Rick said, pointing. He deliberately didn't mention cats. They hadn't actually *seen* a cougar anyway, so in his opinion, The Thugateers posed a more immediate danger.

The rocks suddenly seemed very close. There it was again. Whoever, *whatever* it was, ducked out of the way, behind another rock. It wasn't one of the teens. Too thin, too wiry. Too spindly. What the hell was it? Good thing he'd got the gun.

For godsake, what *is* it about this place?

One thing's for sure. *Little House on the Prairie* it ain't.

Too right . . .

Best not alarm the girls till I know the score about our mystery stalker.

'We'd better all stick together,' Andrea said. 'It'll be four against three. Even if some of us are of the female variety, it doesn't mean we're helpless.'

'And we've got our knives,' Bonnie added.

'We'll stay together,' Bert said.

Rick kept going. She moved on behind him. He felt her hand rub lightly for a moment between his shoulder blades. Then it was gone.

He walked along the shoreline path, closer and closer to the rocks where the boys had been crouching to watch Bonnie and Andrea. He saw no heads among the rocks.

They would've seen us coming by now, he thought. They probably took to the trees. We may not find them at all.

He passed the rocks, and looked back at the place where they'd been.

Gone.

Bert touched his shoulder. He snapped his head to the left.

Jase was sitting on a log beside the fire ring of a campsite not far from shore. He wore jeans and no shirt. He was staring at them. A cigarette hung from a corner of his mouth.

Luke was stretched out on a sleeping bag in a patch of sunlight. His hands were folded under his head. He wore sunglasses and jockey shorts. His skin looked almost as white as his underwear, except for a cluster of zits in the center of his chest.

Wally, sitting cross-legged in the shade, was stripping the wrapper off a Mars bar. He still wore his cut-off jeans and camouflage shirt.

'Hi there,' Jase said as Rick entered the clearing. Bert moved up beside him, and he heard the footsteps of the girls to the rear.

Wally looked up from his candy bar. A smile spread across his broad face. Luke propped himself up with straight arms and crossed his outstretched legs at the ankles.

'Thought you people would be on the other side of the pass by now,' Jase said.

'We thought you would, too,' Bert told him.

'Nope. When we got to this place, we decided to flake out.'

'Wally was whining about his feet,' Luke said.

Wally, chewing on his candy bar, nodded agreement.

'So you didn't go up the mountain at all?' Bert asked.

'Nope. Been here since about noon.'

'Funny. We walked right by this place a couple of hours ago and you weren't here.'

'Don't know how that happened.'

'Must've been while we were gathering firewood,' Luke said.

Rick glanced at the pile of kindling and branches near the fireplace. He hadn't noticed it when he and Bert had looked at the campsite earlier. But he was certain that the boys' packs hadn't been here either.

They're lying, he thought. Of course they are. They'd been the ones with the binoculars high up on the trail, and they'd come back down because of the women.

'Are you going to introduce us to your friends?' Jase asked.

'Tweedle-dee and Tweedle-dum,' Andrea said.

Luke grinned.

'The friendly type,' Jase said, and mashed his cigarette under his boot.

'I don't like being spied on,' Andrea said.

'Shut up, would you?' Bonnie muttered.

'Has somebody been spying on you?' Jase asked.

'Sounds like she means us,' Luke said. 'Do you mean us?'

'Who do you think I mean, anus-face?'

'Woooo.'

Bert whirled around and glared at Andrea. 'Would you *please* stop it?'

'You people must have us mixed up with someone else,' Jase said, all innocence. 'We haven't been spying on anyone. We've just been hanging out, relaxing. Isn't that right, Wally?'

Wally swallowed and nodded. His face was bright red.

'Isn't that right, Luke?'

'We have simply been minding our own business. Frankly, I find myself disgruntled. Not only are we being unjustly accused, but my face has been maligned by this vicious wench.'

'I think *you're* the one getting spied on,' Wally blurted.

'Indeed. I believe they came here for the sole purpose of ogling me in my dainties.'

'Nothing there to ogle,' Andrea said.

Wally whooped. Jase's thin lips turned up. Bonnie squeezed Andrea's shoulder, making her grimace for a moment before she knocked the hand away.

With a thumb, Luke hooked out his waistband and peered down the front. 'Oh yeah,' he said, 'something there all right. Want to see?'

'That's about enough,' Rick said.

The elastic snapped down. Luke grinned at him.

'I don't know what you guys think you're up to, but I'd suggest you pack up your stuff and get out of here,' Rick said.

Jase narrowed his eyes. 'Hey, man, it's a free country. You don't like us here, *you* move on.'

'And have you follow us there, too?'

'We haven't followed you anywhere. We were here first. You don't like it, tough.'

'We're not leaving,' Bert told him. 'We're staying exactly where we are – and I'm sure you know where that is. We saw you looking at the girls from those rocks by the shore. Now here's the thing. Stay away. Don't come anywhere near our camp, or else.'

'Oooo, I'm trembling,' Luke said. 'I'm so scared I just don't know *what* to do.'

Jase sneered. 'I don't know what your problem is. You come in here like gangbusters, calling us names, telling us to get out of here, threatening us. Where do you get off, huh? We didn't do shit to you. Sure, we took a look when those two were swimming. Why not? It's a public lake. They want to go swimming, we got every right to watch. So we watched, so what? I tell you, the view wasn't all that terrific. As for staying away from your camp, you can bet on it. Give me one good reason why we'd *want* to go near your camp.'

'They probably think we want to molest them,' Luke said.

'Wishful thinking,' Jase said.

Wally, staring at the ground, chuckled.

'Just stay away,' Bert said. 'We don't want any trouble.'

'You stay away from us. We're not interested. You gals get the hots, you'll just have to settle for him.' He looked at Rick. 'I'm sure he'd be glad to . . .'

'Shut your face,' Rick snapped.

He felt a tug on his arm. 'Come on,' Bert said. 'Let's get out of here.'

'Yeah,' Jase said. 'Take him away before he loses his temper and hurts me.'

Rick stepped backward as Bert pulled him. Bonnie turned away from the boys. Andrea, still facing them, slipped her knife out of its sheath and pointed it at Jase. 'I'm gonna be watching for you shit-heads,' she said, then turned around.

They walked toward the shoreline path.

The boys began taunting them from a distance.

'Oooooo,' from Luke.

'Now they're threatening us with weapons,' Jase said. 'We oughta get the cops on them.'

'What cops?' Wally asked.

'That's right, there ain't no cops out here.'

'Oh, dear!' Luke blurted. 'Who, oh who, shall save us from this tribe of paranoid Amazons? Are we damned? Is this all she wrote? And me without a will!'

'Hey,' Wally said, 'you should've shown them your dick.'

'Wally's getting brave,' Rick muttered.

'They wouldn't have known what it was,' Luke said. 'Anyway, I didn't want to turn on that fag who's with them.'

Rick looked over his shoulder. The trees were in his way.

'What a bunch of crotch lice,' Andrea said.

'Keep your voice down,' Bonnie told her.

'They can't hear me.'

'How many dykes does it take to screw a fag?' Wally's voice. Yelling.

'I don't know, how many?' Luke.

'*Three*, you dork! Two to hold him down and one to hold him up!'

'The guy's a wit,' Rick said.

Bert, walking beside him on the path, suddenly stopped and turned around. She glared toward the trees concealing the boys' camp. Suddenly, she shouted, '*I gave you my mosquito repellent, you fat tub of lard!*'

Rick looked at her, amazed.

'Well, I did,' she said. A corner of her mouth turned up. Rick patted her rump.

They heard nothing more from the boys as they hiked back to camp.

Chapter Seventeen

'Is something the matter?' Jerry asked.

What could possibly be the matter? Gillian thought. i've just spent last night and today in the house of a rapist, a psycho, a homicidal maniac.

She shrugged her shoulders.

'You seem a little distant.'

She forced a smile and waved across the patio table at him. 'I'm all right here. No more than, oh, four feet away.'

'Didn't like the dinner?' he asked.

'It was awful. That's why I gobbled it down like a sow.'

'Are you saying it was swill?'

Gillian laughed softly.

In spite of his little joke, Jerry still looked concerned. 'Is it something I did?'

'No. For heaven's sake. You've been great.'

'If you're still upset about this afternoon . . .'

'It's not that. So I lost my pants in your pool? Big deal, huh? Yeah. Cripes.' She picked up her mai-tai and drank the last of it. 'It's Fredrick Holden.'

'Who?'

Gillian realized that she had slipped. Maybe it's Freudian, she thought. Maybe I want to tell him the truth, the whole truth. And what would he think of me then? The girl's a lunatic who gets her jollies playing Goldilocks.

'Uncle Fredrick,' she said. 'I've found some things that have me worried.'

'That's right, you mentioned this afternoon about his gruesome taste in books.'

'It's more than just books. I had some time to kill before coming over and thought I'd take a look at one of his video tapes. I put one in his VCR. It was supposed to be *The Howling*. That's what the case said. It turned out to be some kind of sicko sado-masochistic shit called *Torture Slave*. I just watched a minute of it. The thing was vile. I mean, I've seen a few porno movies in my time. But this was different. This was like something they don't carry at the corner video shop. I did some snooping, and he's got a whole bunch of movies like that. They're all hidden inside cases for stuff like *Star Wars* and *E.T.*'

'How well do you know your Uncle Fredrick?' Jerry asked. He sounded worried.

'Not very well,' Gillian said, surprised and glad that he hadn't made any jokes about wishing she had brought the tape along with her.

'Has he ever tried anything with you?'

She shook her head.

'It seems pretty odd that he would ask you to house-sit for him. He must've known that you might look at some of his videos. They weren't hidden? They were right out in plain sight?'

'On the shelves in his den.'

'Apparently, he didn't care if you looked at them. Maybe he *wanted* you to look at them.'

'Why would he want that?'

'I'd hate to speculate. I mean, he's your uncle.'

Sure he is, Gillian thought.

'How long is he supposed to be away on this trip of his?'

'He told me he'd come back Thursday,' Gillian said.

Jerry frowned at her. 'I think it might be a good idea for you to get out of there. I think you should leave right away, go back to your own apartment and stay away from the guy.'

'Trying to get rid of me?' Gillian asked.

'I'm serious. If those films are as bad as you say, he isn't just a normal horny guy who enjoys skin flicks. And the fact that he left them out for you to see . . . I don't like it. I don't think you should stay in his house. He might be planning to come back early, and . . . and I don't think you should be there when he does.'

And Jerry doesn't even know about the scrapbook, she thought. Just the movies are enough to make him fear for my safety. Tell him about the scrapbook . . .

And he'd probably want to call the police.

And it would all come out that I'm a criminal. No thanks.

'As a matter of fact,' she said, 'I already made up my mind to leave. I'm all packed up and ready to go. Hell, I'd be gone now except I had to collect on your bribe of dinner.'

Gillian stood up, lifting her plate and glass off the table. 'Come on, let's take the dishes in.'

He loaded his hands and followed her into the kitchen. Three trips later, the patio table was clear. Gillian opened his dishwasher.

'No way,' Jerry said. 'These can wait. Would you care for an after-dinner drink?'

'Trying to get me sloshed?'

Jerry stepped up behind her. He put his hands on her shoulders. The feel of them seemed to radiate down her body. The force of her reaction surprised Gillian. Is this the first time he's touched me? she wondered.

If you don't count towing me to poolside after my crash.

'How about coffee?' he asked.

'I was just kidding about you trying to get me drunk.'

'I know. I'd rather have coffee myself. I'd hate to spend the rest of our evening in a drunken stupor.'

'Me too.'

He gave her shoulders a gentle squeeze, then stepped away and began to prepare a pot of coffee.

Gillian turned around. She leaned back against the counter. Its edge pressed her an inch above the abrasions. She wasn't in pain there, just a little tender. She watched Jerry.

He had dressed nicely for the dinner. He wore a neatly pressed, short-sleeved plaid shirt that was very much like the blouse that Gillian had decided to wear. His slacks were white, the same as Gillian's shorts. He wore topsiders, she wore sandals.

'Do you realize we match?' she asked.

He smiled. 'I noticed.' He dumped scoops of coffee into the filter.

It felt good to be with him.

She wished she could tell him her secret.

Maybe someday, she thought.

Don't count your chickens . . .

'There's a pen and notepad by the phone,' Jerry said. 'In case you want to give me your phone number.' He glanced over his shoulder at her. 'I don't even know your last name. I looked you up under Holden, but you weren't there.'

'He's my mother's brother,' she said.

Jerry's tried to find me in the telephone book. He wants my number. He doesn't want to lose me after I leave tonight.

God. All right!

'I'm O'Neill,' she told him.

'Gillian O'Neill. Nice.'

She stepped over to the telephone. On the pad there, she wrote her name, address and telephone number.

You're really giving it away, she thought. *You broke the fuck in next door.* He'll be able to tell the cops exactly where to find you.

It won't come to that. Probably.

So what if there's a risk?

While standing by the phone, she copied his number off the sticker. She tore it from the bottom of the paper and tucked it into the pocket of her blouse.

Soon, the coffee was done. They took their mugs outside and sat at the table by the pool.

It was dusk. Darkness was not far away.

'I love this time of the evening,' Gillian said. 'It's so peaceful.'

'Yeah.' Jerry sipped his coffee. 'We used to go out after supper for some bounce-or-fly on the street in front of the house.'

'I did that. Didn't get up to bat very often, though. I wasn't much of a catch.'

'I bet you were a good catch. I have the feeling you were something of a tomboy.'

'Oh, hell yes.' She drank some more coffee. It was hot and good. 'I could knock a ball a mile. I just couldn't lay my mitt on it.'

'Do you still like to play ball?'

'You being a wiseguy?'

Jerry smiled and they lapsed into silence. It was getting darker now.

'And now? I mean, what do you do now?' he asked.

Here it comes. Story time again, folks.

'Do? In my spare time? Well, I don't play bounce-or-fly, that's for sure!'

Jerry raised his eyebrows. Did he detect a challenge in her tone? If so, he wasn't sure he wanted to pursue the matter of her spare-time activities anymore. They had something good going here, and he didn't want to mess up.

She winked, threw him a quizzical smile and said, 'I scribble.'

'Scribble?'

'Sure. I scribble. Anything that comes to mind, really. Anything and everything. I have this wild, untamable imagination, and when I get bored with life, I just, well . . . scribble . . .'

'Okay. So you scribble. Do you often get bored?'

'Yep. Pretty often.'

'You bored now?'

'Nope.'

'Good. I would hate to think . . .'

'Jerry. Stop it. I'm having a great time. You're the perfect host,' she laughed. 'And I couldn't be less bored. Honestly. So please, let's drop it.'

Jerry laughed. 'As a matter of fact, I was thinking we might head over to a park sometime. I could pitch, you could hit.'

'Like after dinner some night? That'd be neat. Of course, if you're into reliving childhood games, there never was anything as good as hide-and-seek. The hiding part, that's what I liked. Forget being "it". I loved to run off and duck into places that were small and dark where they'd never find you. It was always a little scary if you found a good place. I remember how my heart used to pound. Like I was afraid I'd get grabbed by something while I was waiting.'

'It was always such a let-down,' Jerry said, 'when they gave up looking.'

'Right. It's not that you wanted to be found, but you didn't want to be abandoned.'

'Remember what a drag it was when you'd hear your parents calling your name? You knew it was time to go in.'

'That's one of the great things about being an adult. Nobody to stop your fun.' Gillian's heart started pounding hard. 'Speaking of fun,' she said through a tightness that had suddenly squeezed her throat.

Jerry raised his eyebrows and waited.

'Why don't we go swimming?'

He beamed. 'Hell, yes. What about your injury, though?'

'I'm just skinned a little. The water will feel good.'

'Great. But wasn't your bikini wrecked?'

'I'll go in in my skivvies.'

'Skivvies?'

'My bra and panties. If you will.' She shrugged and smiled. She took a sip of coffee. She had trouble swallowing it. 'That sound all right to you?'

'This is the same Gillian O'Neill who was here this afternoon and didn't want to be seen in a bikini?'

'Not exactly,' she said. 'This is a Gillian who's gotten to know you better.'

'And who's had a few mai-tais.'

'I'm perfectly sober. Somewhat sober. Besides, it's dark now. Of course, if *you're* too bashful . . .'

'I'll go in and get the towels,' he said. He took a final drink of coffee, then pushed his chair away from the table, got up, and went into the house.

Gillian was relieved that he'd left. She suspected that he'd gone for the towels as a ploy to let her undress in privacy. Decent of him. She had thought she would have to strip in front of him, and had rather looked forward to it, but this made it easier.

She stood up. With trembling hands, she unbuttoned her blouse and took it off. She folded it and placed it on the seat of her chair. Then she stepped out of her sandals. She lowered her shorts, stepped out of them, and dropped them onto her blouse.

The warm breeze roamed her body. She felt naked. Looking down at herself, she supposed that the black bra and panties were no more revealing than her bikini had been. Though the bra had lace cups, the darkness of the night prevented much from showing.

Still, she thought. This isn't a bikini, this is undies.

Jerry might have been right about the mai-tais.

Too late to back down now.

Who *wants* to back down? she asked herself.

She felt daring. It reminded her of the way she used to get when she broke into houses. The feverish thrill of the break-ins had diminished over the past couple of years, so that recently it had been little more than a faint stir of excitement. Not like this. This was intense. Her heart was slamming. Her mouth was dry. Her nipples ached under the soft touch of the bra. Her panties were clinging in front.

She looked at the lighted kitchen door. No sign of Jerry.

Reaching back with one hand, she peeled off her bandage. She set it down on her shorts.

Then she stepped to the edge of the pool and dove in. The cold of the water was a harsh shock for an instant. Then it felt fine. It felt better than fine, caressing her everywhere as she glided along below the surface. When her fingertips touched the tiles at the far side, she came up.

She swam toward the shallow end. Finding the bottom with her feet, she stood up. The water covered her to the neck.

Jerry opened the sliding door and stepped out, holding towels in his arms. 'You're already in,' he said. 'I missed the show.'

'Tough toenails,' Gillian said. Then she gritted her teeth to stop the tremor in her jaw.

Jerry dropped the towels onto the table. 'So you just get to stay in there and watch me?' he asked.

'That's the picture.'

Shaking his head, he sat down on a chair and took off his shoes and socks. Then he stood and removed his shirt.

'Maybe you could turn on the patio lights,' Gillian suggested.

'Yucka yucka,' he said. He unbuckled his belt, opened the waist button of his trousers, and slid the zipper down.

'We could use some stripper music,' Gillian said.

He pulled his trousers down.

Gillian thought he was wearing boxer shorts, but a white cord hung over the elastic waistband.

'That's a swimming suit!' she blurted. 'Cheat! Cheat!'

Jerry shrugged. 'No reason we should *both* embarrass ourselves.'

'Creep! Heel! Scab!'

Laughing, he said, 'Okay, okay,' and pulled down the trunks. He was wearing something white and scanty.

'Is that a swimming suit, too?' Gillian asked.

'Nope. I swear.'

'Better not be. We had a deal.'

'How do I know *you* don't have a suit on?'

'Just have to take my word for it.'

Turning away, he walked toward the house. He stopped at a switch plate on the wall. His arm went up. The water surrounding Gillian was suddenly illuminated by lights below the surface.

She looked down at herself. Her breasts and bra were distinct in the shimmering light, the lower areas of her body slightly blurred.

'How's that?' Jerry called, his hand still on the switch. 'Or would you prefer it dark?'

'This is nice,' she said.

He walked toward the pool. He stopped at its edge and rubbed his hands together. 'How's the water?' he asked.

'It won't kill you.'

Balancing on one foot, he crouched a bit and dipped his toes in. The light from the pool fluttered on him. He looked lean and strong. His brief shorts hugged his hips. His penis, bulging against the thin fabric, looked as if it might thrust its way up through the waistband.

He seemed very nonchalant as he took his foot out of the water and rubbed his hands together again. Doesn't he realize? Gillian wondered. Of course he does. And he knows I'm watching. He must want me to see, want me to know he's turned on.

He took a deep breath, then leaped from the side in a low powerful dive that took him far out over the water before he knifed in with barely a splash. He was a pale streak below the surface for a moment. Then he came up at the wall and gripped its edge. 'Not bad,' he said, 'after the first shock.'

Gillian nodded. She didn't trust her voice. It would probably come out shaking.

Jerry stayed where he was, hanging onto the edge of the pool several yards away.

Gillian stayed where she was, too.

This is silly, she thought. Say something. Do something.

'Let's see one of those fancy dives,' Jerry said.

'Oh, sure thing.' She was right. Her voice shook when she spoke. 'You just want me to lose my pants again.'

'Never crossed my mind.' Jerry pushed himself away from the wall. He kicked and stroked his way slowly backward, but he headed straight for the other side instead of approaching Gillian.

Don't just stand here like a jerk, she told herself.

Leaning forward, she left her feet. She did the breast stroke toward the deep end, keeping her face out of the water and gazing at Jerry as she glided closer to him. He had stopped short of the wall. Treading water, he watched her go by.

'That isn't your bikini,' he said.

'That's right.' Under the diving board, she turned around to face him. She kicked hard, reached high, and caught an edge of the board with one hand. Pulling herself up, she clutched the other side of the board. She hung there, out of the water to her waist. The air felt chilly on her wet skin.

Jerry stared at her.

She let go with one hand. Dangling under the board, she pawed her side with a floppy hand, stuck her chin out, and grunted like an ape.

Jerry didn't crack a smile.

'You're not amused?' Gillian asked.

'Me Tarzan,' he said, and lunged at her.

Gillian yelped. She clutched the board with her other hand, pulled herself up and raised her legs. She kicked water at Jerry. He grabbed one of her ankles. 'Don't you da—!' He tugged. She lost her hold. Dropping rump-first, she took a deep breath.

She kept her eyes open. At first, she saw only white froth. Then Jerry was above her. His eyes were open, too. His mouth was shut, but curled up at the corners in a mischievous grin.

He was above her, not touching her, just gazing down and grinning. He waved. Then he twisted around and began swimming away, still under the surface.

Gillian went after him.

She gained on him.

She grabbed his foot. A pull sent her rushing forward over the backs of his legs. She hooked the fingers of her other hand under the band of his shorts, but let go as he rolled and looked up at her.

His impish grin was gone.

He reached up to her. His hands stroked the sides of her head, slid down along her neck and caressed her shoulders. Gillian ran her hands lightly down his forearms.

Letting go of him, she swam forward. She felt his touch all the way down her body as she glided over him. The she twisted around and stood and gulped air.

Jerry came up.

They faced each other.

The water was as high as Gillian's neck.

Jerry moved into her arms. They held each other. They were both gasping, and didn't kiss.

'Tarzan,' she said. She looked into his eyes. His wet lashes made tiny points.

'Jane?' he asked.

'Gillian and Jerry,' she whispered.

She hugged him tightly. He was warm and smooth and hard.

Chapter Eighteen

We just need to get through tonight, Rick thought as he lay in his sleeping bag, staring up at the slanting walls of the tent.

After dinner, Bert had taken out her map. She had studied it with her flashlight while they sat around the campfire, and found a route that would lead them around the foot of the mountain, avoiding the trail up to Dead Mule Pass. 'We can wait and make sure the creeps are on their way up to the pass. Then we'll take this trail, and it'll be the last we ever see of them.'

'Unless they come back down again when they realize what we're doing,' Andrea said.

Bonnie got up from the log where she'd been sitting, and crouched behind Bert to look at the new route. 'I don't know,' she said. 'That would take us right to the edge of the wilderness area. Look at that road. The trail runs almost over to it.'

'Afraid we'll get hit by cars?' Andrea asked.

'It's just a crummy little dirt road,' Bert said. 'Not like we'll be back in civilization.'

'I guess this is better than having to cope with those jerks.'

'Who are probably gonna jump us before long.'

'For godsake, Andrea.'

'She has a point,' Rick said. 'It's all well and good to make plans for tomorrow, but the main thing is getting through tonight.'

'They could be watching us right now,' Andrea said, gazing into the darkness beyond the campfire. 'Just waiting for the right moment to make their move.'

'What are we going to do?' Bonnie asked. 'We've got to turn in sooner or later.'

'We'll just have to post guards,' Rick said. 'Can you two hang in for a couple of hours?'

'Sure,' Bonnie said.

Andrea nodded.

'Stay by the fire and keep watch while Bert and I get some sleep. Then we'll relieve you, stand watch for a couple of hours, and get you up for another turn.'

'Funzies,' Andrea muttered.

'Whatever you do,' Bert said, 'stay together.'

'Right,' Rick agreed. 'Nobody should go off alone for any reason.'

'Not even to pee,' Bert said. 'If you have to do that, stay close to camp. Better yet, don't even leave the clearing.'

'And let out a shout if anything starts to happen.'

Rick had considered giving the revolver to them before he and Bert turned in. He decided not to. That way, he would still have the final control over everyone's safety. Though the tent flaps were down, they weren't zippered shut and neither was the mosquito netting. He was fully dressed except for shoes. He could be out of the tent, gun in hand, at the first sound of trouble.

He wished he could sleep. Bert had dropped off almost at once. At first, he had been able to hear the hushed voices of the girls. Though their words were masked by distance and the rushing sound of the wind, at least the talking had assured him that everything was okay. During the past half hour or so, however, he hadn't heard them at all.

He heard the wind. He heard the crackle and pop of the campfire. Sometimes there was a soft crunch like a footstep near the tent, which could have been a pine cone or limb hitting the ground; could have been almost anything – including a footstep.

Mr Shadow Man?

The girls are fine, he told himself. They just ran out of things to talk about.

They'll come along pretty soon to wake us up for our turn.

Rick pulled his arm out of the sleeping bag and checked his wristwatch. Ten forty-five. Their turn at standing guard wasn't supposed to start until eleven-thirty. He returned his arm to the warmth of the bag.

Maybe the girls fell asleep, he thought. Sure. Bonnie's sitting on a log, Andrea on a rock. They might drowse a little, but they aren't going to conk out.

What if the cougar shows up? Nosing around for a late-night snack . . .

Why don't you just crawl out of your bag and take a quick look?

What if they're not there?

He pictured them sitting close to the fire while Jase, Luke and Wally crept up behind them. Arms hooked the girls across the throats and jerked them backward off their seats. Choked, unable to shout for help, they were dragged away from the camp. Taken far off into the trees.

They're right outside the tent, Rick told himself quickly before he could start imagining more. Nothing's happened. It's all in your mind.

He slipped the revolver out of the boot near his head and sat up. The fluttering light of the fire was faintly visible through the translucent tent flaps.

He squirmed out of his sleeping bag, picked up his rolled parka, and crawled to the front of the tent. There, he parted the flaps a bit and peered out through the gap.

Bonnie and Andrea were sitting by the fire, Andrea leaning forward to add a stick to the blaze.

I *knew* it was all in my mind, he thought.

You didn't know any such thing.

Rick put on his parka. The warmth felt good. He slipped into his jogging shoes and tied their laces. He put the revolver inside his coat and clamped it against his side. Then he crawled out.

Bonnie saw him coming and looked at her watch. 'You're early,' she said.

'Couldn't sleep, anyway. How's it going?'

'No problem,' Bonnie said.

Andrea grimaced. 'No problem if you don't count freezing your ass numb.'

'Stick it in the fire,' Rick suggested.

'Then she complains about the rivets in her jeans burning holes in her butt,' Bonnie said, smiling.

'You can't win,' Andrea said.

'Well, I'll take over the watch. You two can go ahead and sack out. That should thaw you out,' he told Andrea.

'What about Bert?' she asked.

'I'll let her sleep for a while.' He sat down on a flat rock, leaned forward, and held his hands out over the fire. 'No point in both of us suffering.'

'I'm not sure there's a point to any of this,' Bonnie said. 'They haven't tried anything yet. Maybe we've just blown this whole thing out of proportion. You know? I mean, who's going to look the other way if he's seen a couple of gals in bikinis. And, when you think about it, that's really all they did, isn't it?'

'They didn't come all the way down the mountain,' Andrea said, 'just for a closer look.'

'They claimed they were never up there.'

'They lied.'

'It's very possible they won't try anything,' Rick said, trying to sound as reasonable as Bonnie. 'But we should be prepared in case they do. All it'll cost us is a little discomfort. I think that's preferable to letting our guard down and hoping for the best.'

Andrea nodded her agreement. 'I don't want to wake up and find a strange cock in my—'

'Cut it out,' Bonnie said.

'That's the first thing I'd do.'

Bonnie shot her a sour look and Rick grinned. 'Anyway, I'll keep watch. So you won't have to worry about that.'

'Are you just going to let Bert sleep?' Andrea asked.

'Might as well.'

'I'll stay for a while then.'

'What about your frozen ass?' Bonnie asked.

'I think somebody should stay out with Rick, don't you? If he's alone, he can't cover his back.'

'Whatever you want,' Bonnie said. 'I'm turning in. And if you're asking, I'd advise you to do the same, Andrea.'

'Yeah, sure. See you soon, Bonnie.'

After Bonnie was inside her tent, Andrea got up from her rock. She turned her back to the fire and bent over. Her jeans were tight and faded, their rear pockets frayed. There was a butterfly patch over her left buttock. 'Pardon the view,' she said, looking over her shoulder at Rick.

'View's not bad.'

She rubbed her seat with both hands. Then she stood up straight and turned around. 'It's true about the rivets, you know. They heat up really fast. I've probably got little red burn spots on my butt.' She sat down again and pushed her hands into the pockets of her puffy down vest.

'Don't your arms get cold?' Rick asked. They were covered only by the sleeves of her plaid shirt.

'They're all right. How long have you and Bert been going together?'

'A few months.'

'Live together?'

'Not yet.'

'Oh yeah? Who's the holdout?'

'She's not ready to give up her independence.'

'Where've I heard that before?' Andrea smiled. She looked beautiful, her eyes shining, her face burnished in the trembling glow of the firelight, glossy curls hanging across her forehead from under the edge of her stocking cap. 'How come you let her talk you into this torture-fest they call backpacking?'

'She had her heart set on it. I didn't want to disappoint her.'

'That's about the way I got into this. Bonnie got the goddamn call of the wild, and talked me into coming along. Too bad we all didn't run into each other a lot earlier. Those two sourdoughs could've kept each other company and left us out of it.'

Rick smiled. 'Those are the breaks.'

'What would you like to be doing right now, if you weren't stuck out here in the armpit of the universe?'

'Ideally. Maybe sitting at home with a drink, watching a good movie on the VCR.'

'Yeah. All right. What kind of movies do you like?'

'All kinds. Thrillers, mostly.'

'I knew a guy who lived off campus and had a VCR. All he ever played on it were sex movies. The idea was, I was supposed to get turned on and go crazy.'

'Did it work?'

She smiled. 'Maybe. How about Bert? Does she like to watch that kind of stuff?'

'She'd rather do it than watch.'

'Well, lucky you. Does she see . . . other guys?'

'Not that I'm aware of.'

'What about you?'

'I'm not into guys.'

'You know what I mean.'

Rick's heart quickened. Good Christ, he thought. Don't jump to conclusions, maybe she's just curious. 'I haven't,' he said. 'It . . . hasn't come up.'

'It has now,' Andrea said.

'She might wake up.' His voice came out hoarse.

'That's a chance we'd have to take. We could go off into the trees.'

'What about our three friends? Not to mention maybe mountain lions on the prowl?'

Still smiling, Andrea stood and brushed off the seat of her jeans. 'I can see you're not ready for this. But it's gonna be a long night. If you change your mind, you'll know where to find me.' She nodded toward her tent.

'Bonnie's in there.'

'She won't tell. In fact, I'm sure she'd be happy to keep watch later on. We could use the tent.'

'I don't know.'

'Think about it,' she said. Then she turned away. She strolled across the camp, bent down, and crawled into her tent.

For a long time, Rick sat motionless.

He stared at Andrea's tent.

Then he got up. He went to his pack and took out the bottle. When he returned to the fire, he sat on the rock where Andrea had been. That way, her tent was behind him so he wouldn't have to look at it.

He opened his parka, took out the revolver, and rested it on his lap. Then he unscrewed the cap of his bottle and drank. The bourbon heated a path down his throat, spread warmth through his stomach.

You're going to stop thinking about Andrea, he told himself.

He thought about how she had looked sitting across from him in the firelight. He remembered the way she had rubbed the seat of her jeans and he could almost feel her buttocks through the warm denim. He had half expected her to show him the marks that she suspected the hot rivets had put on her rump. If the rivets felt so hot, were they pressing her bare skin? Wasn't she wearing panties? He wondered if she had taken off her jeans before getting into her sleeping bag. Maybe she had taken off everything, and was lying awake, naked in the snug warmth, waiting for him.

If you change your mind, you'll know where to find me.

I'm not going to change my mind. Not the right place. Not the right time. There's Bert. And you never know when those three scum-bags might come sneaking out of the trees.

Rick looked quickly over his shoulder. He scanned the darkness behind him. Then his gaze lingered on Andrea's tent.

When their time for watch comes up, he thought, she'll probably stay inside, expecting me. How am I going to handle that?

Maybe I won't tell them when it's time. Maybe I'll just stay here all night.

He turned again to the fire. He took another drink and looked toward the dark bushes. A rustle. Then the crack of breaking twigs. His head snapped forward, eyes riveted to the bushes. His breath came in shallow gulps.

Christ. My nerves are shot.

Another swig.

And another rustle. More of a flurry this time.

Birds?

599

Not in the dark.

The Thugateers? Jase, Luke – but not Wally, the scrote'd be asleep. Who then?

Rick held still for a while.

No more rustles.

Silence.

Thank God.

Then, '*Drink is the devil's curse! 'Tis Satan's brew to be sure. It poisoneth the soul!*

'*Repent, sinner, and mend thy ways afore it's too late . . .'*

The words hissed loudly in Rick's left ear.

It was *that* close.

He twisted away and rolled off the rock. Hit the ground and lay there. Gasping for breath. Panting with fear. Choking on the pall of fetid breath that still warmed his cheek. It was wet with spittle. Uhhh . . . He rolled over, heaving and grunting with disgust. Slashing at his face with both hands.

'God almighty!'

Outlined in the darkness, a man dressed in animal skins stood astride Rick's body, his bony arms akimbo on his hips. Atop his head was the head of a coyote, flaps of gray fur hanging and winging about his shoulders. The coyote's mouth hung open, showing teeth and a lolling tongue. There were dark holes where its eyes had been.

The weird headgear swung back and forth as its owner shook with rage. Rage? Rick couldn't distinguish. Laughter? Yeah. The bastard was laughing. High-pitched squeals of glee.

A sweaty, hormonal *animal* odor swept up Rick's nostrils as the creature side-stepped away from his body and skipped backward.

'What . . . *who* in hell are you?' demanded Rick. The goddamn bastard was right about the devil's brew. I *am* seeing things – I gotta be!

'Angus is the name. Dearly beloved son of the Right Rev. John Brown McTavish! I was brought to this wilderness fifty years ago to preach the good Lord's word. Aye. Praise be to the Lord. *A*-men!'

With a manic cackle the creature lifted a scrawny arm above his head, crooked the other at his hip, did a quick jig and then vanished, cackling, into the night.

The bottle was three-quarters empty. Rick held it toward the fire and shook it, watching the amber fluid swirl.

So that's what it was. Stalking us. A bastard preacher-man gone ape. My God . . . The fuckin' cotton-pickin' lunatic . . . Aawgghh . . .

Better cut it out or I won't have any left for tomorrow night.

He stood up. The revolver slid off his lap and dropped, its muzzle pounding his left foot. He winced at the sudden hurt, then bent over and picked up the weapon. He carried it in one hand, the bottle in the other. Bending over his pack, he put away the bottle.

He stood up straight. He breathed deeply. The chill night air smelled of pine. Just like a Christmas tree lot. He was a kid, and he'd gone with Dad and Julie to the Lopez Ranch to pick out a tree. They wandered through a maze of spruce and pine. Their breath made white plumes. Julie wore a down vest. Her jeans had a butterfly patch on the seat. Her jeans were cut off so high that the bottoms of her rear pockets hung out. Odd that she would wear such pants on a night like this. Odd, but nice.

Julie slipped in sideways between two trees, and vanished. Rick stayed with his father. Together, they inspected a silver spruce to see if it had any bare spots. It looked good. 'Go find your mother,' Dad said. 'We'd better get her approval.'

Rick squeezed his way through the trees, smelling their rich scent, feeling their limbs run like soft, cool brushes against his body. He came out the other side.

And almost tripped over Julie's leg. She was sprawled on the ground of an aisle between the rows of Christmas trees, naked except for a single knee sock. Bert lay nearby, the handle of a knife standing upright in the center of her chest. Reeling, Rick staggered sideways. His bare foot (why was he naked?) came down on Bonnie's belly, slipped into a gash and sank deep into her warm guts. With a gasp, he pulled his foot free and stumbled to the other side of her body before falling. He landed on his hands and knees between Andrea's spread legs.

Jase and Luke were on each side of him, holding Andrea by the ankles. Wally was sitting on her face.

'Go to it,' Jase urged him.

'You killed her! You killed them all!'

'You did,' Luke said.

'All your fault,' Wally said, and bounced on Andrea's face, his blubber shaking.

'No!' But Rick looked down at himself. His body was slick with blood, his penis erect.

'What are you waiting for?' Jase asked. 'Go to it, pal.'

'Don't worry about Bert,' Luke said. 'She'll never know.' He chuckled.

NO!

Rick was on his knees, doubled over, his forehead pressed against the cool damp mat of the forest floor. He pushed himself up. The revolver was clamped between his thighs. He wrapped his hand around its grips, and stood up. His legs had pins and needles, and he was barely able to keep himself up.

The campfire had burnt down to a heap of glowing embers. He looked at Bert's tent, then at the girls' tent. Then he scanned the dark trees surrounding the camp.

He wondered how long he'd been out of it.

Must've been a long time, or his legs wouldn't have fallen asleep like that.

What if Jase and Luke and Wally had come while he was . . . was what?

What the hell was all that, anyway? he wondered.

An hallucination? A nightmare? A premonition?

And Angus, the mad preacher. A fantasy? Or the real thing?

His heart started thudding hard. He licked his dry lips.

He walked to the remains of the fire, crouched there and tossed sticks onto the embers. White smoke rose off the sticks like thick steam. The wind shredded the smoke and cast it away.

With a sudden *whup*, flames erupted.

Firelight shimmered on the front of the girls' tent.

Rick stood up, trembling. He switched the revolver to his left hand and wiped his right hand dry on the leg of his pants. He fingered the handle of the knife sheathed at his hip.

He glanced at Bert's tent and half hoped to see the flaps bulge and Bert crawl out, ready to join him on the watch – and in time to stop him.

He turned toward the other tent.

Were they both asleep in there? Or was Andrea still awake, waiting for him?

He pictured the way they had looked on the ground in the Christmas tree lot, all three of them, and Julie – naked and dead. *Go for it*, Jase whispered.

Taking the revolver into his right hand again, Rick stepped around the fire and walked away from its heat.

Chapter Nineteen

Monday, June 23

Jerry had said, 'Why don't you stay here tonight? We'll get your stuff out of your uncle's place and bring it over.'

'Right now?' Gillian had asked.

'Maybe not *right* now.'

They were both naked in bed. He was lying on his side, propped up on an elbow, looking at her body in the candlelight while his other hand rested open on her hip, fingertips moving ever so slightly in the curls of her pubic hair. Gillian was on her back, hands folded beneath her head. She felt worn out and wonderful.

'In a little while,' Jerry said.

'I might not be able to walk,' she told him.

He laughed softly.

'I'm serious. You ruined me. I might need a wheelchair.'

Gillian wished, now, that she had taken him up on the offer. She didn't want to leave her suitcase in Fredrick Holden's house overnight, and now Jerry was asleep.

But she had been lying there, peaceful and weary, his fingers toying with her hair, feeling too good, too full, too ruined to move – even the short distance towards his side of the bed so she could get away from the cool, wet place on the sheet.

We *should* go over now, she had thought. Get it over with. Then I'll never have to set foot in that maniac's house again.

She had been about to tell Jerry, but his hand moved. His fingertips slid and her breath snagged.

'Are you really ruined?' he whispered.

She took a hand out from under her head. She touched him. Then she rolled toward him, smiling, shaking her head, nudging him onto his back. Straddling him, she held his shoulders and eased herself slowly down. His warm thickness spread her, slid in deeper and deeper, filled her. She sighed and shut her eyes. She felt his hands close gently over her breasts.

All thoughts of going next door for her suitcase were gone.

When the thoughts came back, she was lying on top of Jerry. Her cheek was against his shoulder. She felt spittle at the corner of her mouth. Lifting her head, she wiped her mouth and saw a shiny area glimmering in the candlelight where she had drooled on his shoulder in her sleep. She rubbed it off gently with the heel of her hand. He didn't wake up.

He'll probably wake up when I climb off, she thought.

His arms had been around Gillian just before she'd fallen asleep, but now they were out to the sides, as if they had simply dropped onto the mattress when he'd conked out.

His legs were still straight together between her legs.

His penis had been inside her, and she could feel that it was still inside her, but not very far.

Pushing at the mattress with her hands and knees, she carefully raised herself.

She felt a pulling sensation.

Permanently stuck, Gillian thought, and smiled.

Though it still took a slight pull that stung Gillian and must've hurt Jerry as well, she freed herself without waking him.

Maybe I *should* wake him up, she thought. He said he'd go over with me.

Working her way slowly backward, she stopped when his penis was just below her face.

I could wake him up in a way he wouldn't mind at all, she thought.

Just let him sleep. I can take care of this myself.

She kept backing up until her knees found the end of the bed. Then she climbed off.

Only stubs were left of the candles on the dresser and on the nightstands to either side of the bed. Gillian tiptoed from candle to candle, and puffed out each flame.

She entered the lighted hallway and followed it to the kitchen. A clock on the kitchen wall showed 2:38.

Lord, Gillian thought. How did it get so late?

She slid open the back door. The pool still shimmered pale blue in the darkness.

How did it get so late, indeed?

We must've been in the pool more than an hour after the Tarzan Jane business.

Gillian walked to the far side of the pool. Squatting there, she picked up her bra and panties, Jerry's briefs. They were still wet.

She remembered how the garments had hit the concrete deck with sodden splats when they were tossed from the pool. And the feel of Jerry when she first embraced him naked in the water. And the sudden urgency, and how he had entered her and she had wrapped her legs around him and he had walked her to a corner of the shallow end and she had stretched out her arms and hung onto the edges of the pool until it ended fast with a quaking inside that made her cry out.

The memory of it left her a little breathless, a little aroused.

She stood up with the undergarments in her hands. Wringing them out, she walked to the pool corner where he had taken her, where he had held her for so long afterward and where she had finally said, 'Now what'll we do for fun?' Jerry suggested playing Marco Polo, a water version of hide-and-seek.

So they had played that game for a while, taking turns as the blind searcher, as the quarry. The hiding reminded Gillian of how it had been when she was a kid, but this time she looked forward to being found. The kisses. The touching. Which grew more intense as the game progressed until finally they climbed from the pool, rubbed each other with towels as they shivered in night air that had seemed terribly cold, and went inside to the bedroom.

The air now seemed warm. It's because you're not soaking wet, Gillian thought.

She went to the table. She draped the undergarments on the back of Jerry's chair.

Her bandage was still on top of her piled clothes. She had nearly forgotten about the scrapes. The worst of the two had caused her a few pains during the night when Jerry touched it by accident or when it rubbed too hard against the sheet, but those had been only minor irritations, whispers in the noisy crowd of competing sensations.

She fingered the bad scrape. It felt dry, a little stiff, as if all that time in the water had leached out the wound's moisture. So she left the bandage off. She stepped into her white shorts, fastened them at her waist, and put her blouse on. Buttoning it with one hand, she took the bandage into the kitchen and tossed it in the waste container.

She went to the bedroom. In the faint light from the hallway, she could see Jerry stretched out on the bed. He looked as if he hadn't moved a muscle.

I could just leave the suitcase, she thought. We could go over in the morning. Jerry had said he would take a floating holiday – no pun intended.

I don't want it hanging over my head, she decided. We'll have better things to do when we wake up.

She walked back down the hall, moved carefully through the dark living room, and opened Jerry's front door. She unlocked it so she could get back inside. Then she stepped out and quickly pulled it shut.

The grass was dewy under her bare feet as she crossed the lawn. She stayed close to the front of Jerry's house. Fredrick's driveway was empty.

What did you expect? Gillian asked herself. Did you think he'd come home while you were at Jerry's?

It was a possibility. She knew that she would've heard his car pull into the driveway if he'd returned while she was in the pool. But Jerry's bedroom was on the other side of the house. From there, she couldn't have heard it. And she'd hardly been listening for it. And she'd been asleep part of the time.

But the car wasn't there.

Fredrick Holden was still on his trip – maybe on one of his killing sprees.

Which will come to a quick stop, Gillian thought, once I've sent his scrapbook and a little anonymous note to the police.

She stepped onto his driveway. Its pavement felt warmer than the grass.

She glanced quickly up and down the block. Most of the houses were dark except for a few porch lights. She saw no one, and no cars moved on the street.

She came to the walkway that led to the front door. Its painted surface would be slick under wet bare feet, so she moved carefully even though the dew on her feet had mostly been blotted off while she crossed the driveway.

That would be just the thing, she thought. Take a slide and bust your keester.

No more than one crash and burn per day, please.

She climbed the stairs to the stoop.

She realized that she was gritting her teeth and trembling. The night was warm and she wasn't even wet. So knock off the shakes, she told herself. What are you, scared or something? What's to be scared of? Oh, nothing much.

Shit, no.

She gripped the door handle. Her thumb depressed the leaf-shaped metal tab and she heard the latch draw back. But she didn't open the door.

She licked her lips.

Do it, she told herself. Get your damned suitcase and get the hell out of here. Grab it, you'll be back in Jerry's house in about fifteen seconds, maybe eight if you put on the old spring.

She took a deep breath.

Maybe I should wait for Jerry, she thought.

Damn it, the suitcase is right at the door. All I have to do is reach in. Maybe one step into the house, that's all. Then I'm home free.

She swung open the door.

The house was dark. It was supposed to be. Fredrick's timer was set to shut off the lamp at eleven.

Her suitcase was a dim shape on the floor, just far enough inside so the opening door wouldn't knock against it.

Exactly where she'd left it.

No sweat.

Glad I didn't wake Jerry up for this.

She stepped over the threshold, took one more step, bent forward and reached for the suitcase handle.

A pale hand shot past the edge of the door, snatched Gillian's wrist, and swung her stumbling forward into the dark. The suitcase tripped her. She knocked it over and fell across it.

The hand on her wrist was gone.

The front door thudded shut.

She scurried forward, knees on the suitcase, then on the carpet. She started to push herself up, but someone landed on her back, smashing her down flat. Her breath blasted out. She turned her head in time to prevent the front of her face from pounding the floor, and pain flashed through her cheekbone and jaw. Then something – a fist? – struck the other side of her face.

She wondered vaguely what was happening. Somebody's been waiting behind the door?

Not . . .

She couldn't think of the name. The owner. Not him. Not him! A burglar? She'd left the door unlocked.

Another punch smashed the side of her face.

The weight left her body. Fingers dug into her armpits and she was lifted. Her knees rested on the floor for a moment. Then she was hoisted higher, jerked backward against a body, swung around and pulled, heels dragging along the carpet. Out of the living room. Into the hall. Through a doorway.

The hands thrust her away and let go. She flapped her arms, grabbing at the darkness for a moment before she hit the floor flat on her back. A dim figure leaped past her sprawled body.

She squinted when light stabbed her eyes.

Through a tingling in her ears, she heard a man's voice. 'Oh, you're a beauty, a real first-rate beauty.'

She raised her head. A man was standing near her feet, smiling down at her. He looked younger than thirty. He looked clean-cut with his short brown hair, white knit shirt and blue slacks. There was glee in his smile and eyes.

It's him, Gillian thought. Oh Jesus.

'I'm glad you dropped in,' he said. 'I've been waiting for you. Knew you'd be back.'

He unbuckled his belt and slid it out of the loops of his slacks. He doubled it.

'Does anybody know you're here?'

Gillian shook her head. She raised her knees.

'Answer me.'

'No,' she gasped. 'Nobody knows.'

'Where were you tonight?'

'No place.'

'Not what I wanted to hear,' he said, and rushed forward, swinging the belt.

Gillian flung up her arms. The belt snapped against her, lashed her arms and belly and legs as the man danced around her, bending and whipping. She rolled over and covered her head. The belt smacked her back and buttocks. She shivered with the stinging pain. She heard herself whimpering, making sharp sucking sounds each time the belt hit her.

He's not going to stop, she thought. He's . . . enjoying himself.

When he pranced past her head, she reached out and grabbed his ankles. She tugged, but he stayed up and lashed her harder than before, the belt whistling and slapping her sides and rump. Lurching forward, she tried to bite his ankle. He tore himself free and leaped backward in time to avoid her teeth.

'Ooee! A fighter! I'm gonna have fun with you.'

Dropping to his knees in front of Gillian, he grabbed her hair. She yelped and felt as if her scalp were being ripped as she was jerked up.

They were both on their knees, facing each other.

His fists were tight against the sides of her head, clenching her hair.

His face was blurry through Gillian's tears, but she saw that he was still smiling. He had slobber on his chin.

His hands shot down. They snatched the neck of her blouse and yanked. The front flew open and he peeled the blouse off her shoulders, tugging it halfway down so it pinned her arms at her sides.

He stared at her breasts. His eyes were so wide they seemed lidless.

'Where were you tonight?' he asked.

'I . . . went . . . for a walk.'

'Bad lie.' He pinched her nipples and twisted them. As pain streaked through her, she realized vaguely that he had let go, and then she saw a fist floating up from his side. It seemed to be coming at her very slowly and she thought that she should have no trouble at all ducking it, and then it crashed into her face.

The telephone was ringing. Gillian felt a rush of terror.

I won't answer it, she thought. If I don't pick it up, Mom and Dad will be all right. Just ignore it. It'll stop.

It didn't stop.

She sat up in bed.

The handset was in its cradle. Blood streamed from both ends. Puddles of blood were spreading over the top of the nightstand.

'No!' she cried out. 'Stop!'

The phone kept ringing. The blood began to dribble off the nightstand's edges.

Then the handset leaped from the cradle and flew at her. It sprayed her face with blood. It wrapped the cord around her neck. She started to choke. She pulled at the cord, but it tangled her hands, bound them.

The mouthpiece pressed against her mouth, spouting blood down her throat as the cord strangled her.

Then the receiver mashed her ear. 'Your turn,' whispered the voice of the phone. 'Your turn now.'

Gillian jerked awake.

But the nightmare didn't stop. She *was* being choked. Her hands *were* bound. She struggled in the darkness, trying not to panic. The cord at her throat kept tightening. But when she straightened her arms, it loosened. She sucked air into her burning lungs.

A surge of motion tipped Gillian.

Something was vibrating under her. She could hear an engine sound and the hiss of wheels spinning on a road.

I'm in a car.

Her eyes saw only black. She blinked them to make sure they were open.

On a car floor. The back seat floor? she wondered. But no light. None at all. And no driveshaft bump under my side.

Gillian's legs were bent. She began to straighten them, very slowly in case the movement should tighten the rope across her throat. Though she could feel that her ankles were tied, there didn't seem to be any line connecting them to her neck. She unbent her knees a little more. A wire snagged one of her feet.

A tail light wire? A brake light wire? One or the other.

Gillian knew where she was.

In the trunk of Fredrick Holden's car.

Her heart started slamming, pumping pain into her head, making her battered face burn.

Oooh, I'm gonna have fun with you.

Chapter Twenty

Rick wished, once again, that he had brought the bottle with him. He was shivering. His neck was stiff, and the rigid muscles seemed to go right up into the back of his skull, squeezing pain into his head. The bourbon might have helped. On the other hand, he would have polished it off a long time ago, probably during the first hour of his vigil, and he would've ended up totally plastered; it might've even been enough to knock him out.

I'd be no good to anyone, he thought, zonked out of my gourd.

Yeah. But what good is this, anyway?

This is doing a lot of good, he told himself. It's the one sure way to keep those bastards from sneaking out of the woods and jumping us. And it got me away from Andrea, away from temptation.

Rick was seated on the ground with his back against a tree trunk, the revolver resting on his lap.

He thought about his visit from the preacher-man.

Jeez, what a performance!

The bastard was mad as a coot but most probably harmless. Christ, he'd been out in the wilderness for fifty years or more. Enough to turn anybody crazy . . .

Through a gap in the bushes ahead, he could see Jase, Luke and Wally in their sleeping bags. If the boys had a tent, they'd decided not to use it. They'd sacked out around the fire.

The fire had still been flickering when Rick arrived. Later, nothing remained except a red glow, though sometimes a flame had climbed out of the rubble like a fatally wounded survivor, quivered in the darkness for a little while, and died. Even the glow had faded out, finally. For the past hour or so, the fire had been dark and smokeless.

Rick needed no firelight. He could see the shapes on the ground better without it. The night was cloudless and pale. Where direct moonlight made it through the trees (and a patch of it fell on his left knee), Rick thought it was almost bright enough to read by. It layered everything it touched with a milky hue. And it touched the sleeping figures of Jase, Luke and Wally. They were mottled with patches of dingy white. And totally black everywhere else, as if they didn't exist at all except where the moon found them.

All three had seemed to be asleep when Rick arrived, and they hadn't moved since, except to alter their positions slightly. One of the bags would bulge when a body curled up or rolled under its surface, would jut when a knee pushed it up.

From the size of the mound, Rick knew which bag held Wally. Jase and Luke were in the other two, but he didn't know which was which. Even when the fire had been going, he hadn't been able to tell them apart. One wore a hooded sweatshirt, the other a dark stocking cap, and their faces had been turned away or half buried in their sleeping bags.

Though he couldn't tell which body was Jase, which Luke, all three of the creeps were accounted for. They were right here, asleep, and they wouldn't be sneaking over to the other camp as long as Rick kept watch.

The watch, he had realized long ago, was probably unnecessary.

Several times, he'd almost convinced himself to quit and return to camp.

But maybe, just maybe, their plan was to get up in the dim hours before dawn and attack when they could be certain to catch everyone fast asleep.

They'd overpower us before we knew what was happening.

You don't have to quit, Rick told himself now. You could just hurry over to the camp and take some aspirin (and grab the bottle?) and come back.

This headache's going to kill me if I don't do something about it.

Rick lifted the revolver off his lap. Slowly, he drew in his legs. He got his feet beneath him, pushed himself away from the tree trunk, and started to rise.

A sleeping bag flipped open.

Rick dropped to a squat.

Peering through the gap in the bushes, he saw moonlit bits and pieces of a person sitting up. It was the kid in the hooded sweatshirt. He couldn't make out whether it was Jase or Luke.

His heart hammered, pounding spikes of pain into his head.

Thank God I didn't leave, he thought. This is it. This is when they make their move.

The kid pulled his legs out of the bag. He seemed to be wearing gray sweatpants. He twisted around, picked up a pair of boots that had been left near his head, and started to put them on.

Though Rick heard only the wind, something must've disturbed Wally's sleep. Maybe the other kid had spoken, or maybe it was just the sound of his movements. The big mound shifted and Wally raised his head.

There were voices too soft to understand.

Wally started getting out of his bag.

'DON'T MOVE!' Rick shouted.

Both heads snapped toward him and the person in the third sleeping bag sat up fast, the bag still around his shoulders. Rick lunged forward through the bushes, arm stretched out, revolver jerking from side to side as he aimed from target to target.

Wally squealed and threw his arms around his head.

'Holy fuckin' shit!' Jase's voice, sharp with alarm. He was the one in the sweatsuit.

Luke sat motionless, all but his head enclosed in the bag.

Rick halted about two yards from Wally. He stood with his feet apart, knees slightly bent. He clutched the wrist of his gunhand.

'Christ, don't shoot!' Wally bellowed.

'Just nobody move. Nobody move a muscle.'

'What the fuck are you doing?' Jase blurted. 'You nuts? What is this?'

In a calm voice, Luke said, 'I believe this is what is known as a pre-emptive strike.'

'What the fuck are you talking about, Burgher?'

'This poor deluded son of a bitch believes that we have designs on his harem.'

'Aw jeez,' Wally said. 'Aw jeez, I knew we were gonna get it. We shouldn'ta looked at 'em. Jeez.'

'We didn't do nothing, mister,' Jase said. 'I don't know what your trouble is. So we looked at them. What's the big deal?'

'It wouldn't have stopped with looking,' Rick said. 'And you know it.'

'See a shrink, pal.'

'Stop it, Jase,' Wally whined. 'He's gotta *gun!*'

'So what're you gonna do, mister, shoot us?' There was bluster in Jase's voice, and there was fear.

'All depends,' Rick said.

'If we wanted to violate your ladies,' Luke said, 'why haven't we done it? You'll note that we were peacefully sleeping until a few moments ago when you barged in.'

'Your two friends were already up.'

'I was gonna take a fuckin' *leak*,' Jase said.

'Me too. I just woke up 'cause Jase was messing around, and I had to go.'

'Don't give me that shit,' Rick said. 'I know what you were going to do.'

'You're nuts, man.' Jase wrapped his arms around his chest. 'It's *cold.* Who'd want to slip it to those babes when it's this cold? You've gotta be kidding.'

'I wouldn't rape a person even if it was hot out,' Wally said in a small voice. 'You'd go to prison. And besides, I just wouldn't do it.'

'On top of which,' Luke added, 'I left my condoms at home. I most certainly wouldn't jeopardize my health by using a bare tool on strangers.'

'Yeah,' Wally said. 'Me too. God, you could get AIDS or something. You could die.'

616

'That's right,' Jase said. 'Whatever those babes got, we don't want it. They're all yours. So go on back and ream 'em out.'

Rick aimed the revolver at him. 'Shut up,' he said.

'You aren't gonna shoot.'

'Don't *say* that!' Wally blurted.

'I think you'd better leave now,' Luke said.

'If you're not,' Jase said, 'I'm gonna have a smoke.'

'You've broken the law,' Luke went on while Jase got to his knees, turned away and crawled over his ground cloth toward his pack. 'You've come into our camp and threatened us with a gun. I think, if we were to tell a ranger about this incident . . .'

'Don't *say* that!' Wally shook his head. 'We aren't gonna tell, mister. Honest. We'll keep our mouths shut.'

Jase, hunched over his pack, looked over his shoulder. 'That's for sure,' he said. 'We talk to the cops, it'll probably be *us* that gets jammed up. Who're they gonna believe, you or us?'

'Right,' Wally said. 'We won't tell. No way.'

Jase poked a cigarette into his mouth. He stood up, turning his back to Rick. 'So what're you gonna do? Gun us down? Shoot our dicks off . . .?'

'*Jase!* Don't *say* that!'

What *am* I going to do with them? Rick wondered. Have them tie each other up? That'd be stupid. They could work themselves free in a while, no matter how well they might be tied. Then they'd be more dangerous than ever. Maybe just make them pack up and hike out of here. I could stay with them partway up the trail. But what's to keep them from turning around and coming back? Maybe just knowing that I've got a gun. Wally, for sure, wouldn't dare come back. But the others might. Maybe I should just keep them covered until morning. When Bert and the girls wake up and find out I'm gone, they'll come looking. They'll come armed. Then there'll be four of us, and . . .

Jase whirled around. His arm flew up. Something in his hand flashed in the moonlight, and he threw it. A knife shot at Rick, flipping end over end.

He started to duck.

Pain crashed through his head. His vision exploded with lights. He staggered and fell. His back hit the ground.

Someone was on him, sitting on his chest, wrenching the gun from his hand. 'Okay fucker.' Jase's voice. A harsh whisper. Rick's vision cleared and he saw Jase raise the revolver, ready to whip it across his face.

Wally grabbed Jase's wrist. 'Hey, don't. We got him.'

'Let go my hand.'

Wally released it.

Jase stood up, straddling Rick. He was gasping for breath. He aimed the revolver at Rick's face and thumbed back the hammer.

'No!' Wally cried out.

'Jesus!' Luke yelled.

'He's got it coming,' Jase said, and fired.

The explosion slammed Rick's ears. The bullet kicked a spray of forest scrap against his cheek.

'Come on out,' Jase called.

Rick was on a rock near the campfire, sitting where they had placed him only a few minutes ago. Luke had already started the fire. It blazed brightly now, and Rick felt its warmth on his face.

Wally was standing on one side of him, Jase on the other.

Jase raised the gun overhead. 'Come on,' he called again. 'We can hear you gals sneaking around out there. We've had enough fun 'n games, so stop fucking around.'

'Get out of here!' Rick yelled.

'You shut up,' Jase told him.

'I'm coming in.' Bert's voice.

'Don't!'

A shape slipped out from behind a tree beyond the clearing. It moved forward, footsteps quietly crunching on the forest floor. It was Bert. She came into the firelight and stopped on the other side of Wally's empty sleeping bag.

She wore the pale blue warm-up suit and wool socks she had slept in. She wore no shoes. A knife in her right hand hung at her side.

'Call in the other two,' Jase said.

'There's no need for them.'

Luke tossed more twigs onto the fire, then rose from his crouch and faced her. 'Bert, right?' he asked.

She nodded.

'Bert, we've got the gun. That means we're in control. We can do *whatever* we want. So when Jase tells you to call in the other girls, the prudent move on your part is to follow instructions.'

'They haven't done anything to you,' she said. Her voice was low and steady.

So damn brave, Rick thought. He could see the fear in her eyes, but she wasn't giving in. She had walked right into their camp and now she was standing up to them. He wished he could go to her and put his arms around her. He wished he could make all of this stop.

I had my chance. I blew it.

Now Bert will be the one to pay.

'Call the girls in,' Jase told her again.

'No way. Let's go, Rick.'

Wally clamped a hand on his shoulder.

'Nobody goes anywhere,' Jase said.

Bert scraped her lower lip across the edges of her teeth. 'What do you want?'

'Three fuckin' guesses.'

'We want to discuss the situation,' Luke said, 'with everyone present. We don't enjoy the idea of having those two jungle warriors creeping around out there.'

'You just want to "discuss the situation",' Bert said. 'Sure thing. Have your discussion with me.' The knife came up from her side. She held it in front of her belly, blade straight out. 'Who wants first try?'

Jase didn't say a word. He left Rick's side and stepped around the fire.

'Run!' Rick cried.

She spread her feet slightly. The knife in her fist circled as Jase approached her.

'Jeez,' Wally said.

'I wouldn't,' Luke warned.

Jase stopped in front of Bert. 'You're a dope,' Jase told her. 'But you've got balls.' He reversed the revolver. Holding it by the barrel, he offered it to her.

Looking perplexed, Bert took the gun from him.

'Your fuckin' boyfriend here paid us a visit with this thing. He shouldn't be allowed to play with guns. Now how about you call off your troops, take this dork out of our face, and go back to your own camp so we can get some fuckin' sleep around here?'

Bert nodded.

Wally let go of Rick's arm. Rick stood up, stepped around the camp-fire, and followed Bert out of the clearing. They reached the shore-line path.

Bert suddenly hurled the revolver.

'No!'

It was too late. The handgun tumbled against the pale moonlit sky and dropped with a heavy splash into the lake.

She turned to Rick. 'We're better off without it,' she said. 'I'll buy you a new one when we get home.'

'It's all right,' he muttered, and took her into his arms. He held her gently against him. She was warm. He felt her fingers stroking his hair.

'I was so scared when I heard that shot,' she said.

'I didn't fire it. They took it away from me.'

'That's when you got the lump on your forehead?'

'Jase threw a knife. Just the handle got me, I guess. But they took the gun from me.'

'Well, I love you anyway.'

He kissed her, and they were still kissing when sounds of footfalls approached. They eased apart. Bonnie and Andrea came out of the trees.

Bonnie had a hatchet in her hand. Andrea had a knife. Apparently, neither girl had wasted time getting dressed. Bonnie was in her socks and a pale body stocking that clung to her like skin and made her look naked. Andrea wore her down vest and skimpy dark panties. She was barefoot.

They were in a sour mood. Cross, as if they'd had an argument that had almost, but not quite, simmered down. They were still fired up. The atmosphere around them bristled with tension and they looked just about ready to use their weapons on anybody who said a wrong word.

Rick glanced from one to the other and realized that Andrea had indeed expected him to join her. She'd lain in her sleeping bag, naked or just in her panties, and waited for him.

Bonnie had known this, and had probably kicked up about it.

Flattering. But he'd managed to stay away. And he was glad. He had Bert. Bert was all he ever really wanted, better than he deserved. He'd been stupid even to consider . . .

'They just let you go?' Andrea asked.

'We were watching,' Bonnie said. 'But we couldn't hear what was going on.'

'They never meant us any harm,' Bert explained.

'What were you doing there?' Andrea asked Rick. 'My Christ, we heard a shot and . . .'

'Let's get back to camp,' Rick said. 'I'll explain everything.'

'Yeah, let's,' Andrea said. 'I'm colder than the left tit of an Arctic witch.' She turned away. She started to run ahead of them, and Rick didn't bother watching.

He took hold of Bert's hand. 'There's something,' he said, 'that needs to be told.'

Rick built the campfire to a high blaze while the others were in their tents. They came out one at a time after dressing for the early morning chill, and sat down around the fire.

Bert sat on the log beside Rick. She put an arm around his back.

'First,' Rick said, 'I want to thank all of you for rushing to my rescue. It took a lot of guts, and . . . I really appreciate it. The thing is, apparently no rescue was necessary. There never was any danger from Jase or Luke or Wally. That was all in our heads. In *my* head.'

'They did spy on the girls,' Bert reminded him.

'But like they said, who wouldn't? You take any normal guy, and he's not going to turn the other way if he has a chance to look at some attractive females – especially if they're not wearing much. It wasn't any crime.'

'They came all the way down the mountain,' Andrea said.

'They denied that,' Bonnie reminded her.

'If they did come down,' Rick said, 'we don't know for sure that it had anything to do with us. But I thought they planned to rape and . . . when I collapsed on the trail, I was having some kind of dream or vision that they'd killed all three of you. And I had another dream like that tonight while I was on watch. I was afraid it might be a premonition or something, a warning – so I could stop them sneaking in here.'

'You start telling us you're psychic,' Andrea said, 'I'm gonna shit right here and now.'

'I've never been psychic.'

'Thank God. 'Cause if those were premonitions . . .'

'He said they weren't,' Bonnie told her.

'No, all he said was that he'd never been psychic. That doesn't mean you can discount the possibility that those visions of his—'

'Andrea also believes in extra-terrestrial life forms, ghosts, astrology and Ouija boards.' Bonnie shook her head and grinned. 'Not to mention Tarot cards – and don't believe her when she says she isn't psychic. She is.' She looked meaningfully at Andrea.

'Remember the time you said that dummy Marion Dahl was gonna be off sick and wouldn't be in class the next day and she was? Sick, I mean.'

'I keep an open mind, that's all. I don't disbelieve shit just 'cause people tell me it's supernatural nonsense.'

'I don't think there was anything supernatural about the tricks my imagination was playing,' Rick said.

'I sure the hell hope not,' Andrea said.

'I mean, it's pretty obvious at this point that Jase and the others never meant us any harm.'

'You were worried all along,' Bert said, 'about making this trip. Even before we ran into those three guys, you were a nervous wreck. Then, when they showed up, it all seemed to focus on them. You were convinced they were trouble long before you ever had those – hallucinations, or whatever.'

'Yeah. I guess I expected history to repeat itself.' He saw confusion in Bert's eyes. 'I didn't tell you everything,' he said, 'about what happened on that other camping trip.' He looked at Andrea and Bonnie. 'The last time I went camping was when I was fourteen. I've already told Bert about it. How I broke my leg and my father left me to go for help. What I didn't tell her before was that my stepmother was with us. Julie. She stayed with me. And a couple of guys came into the camp. They knocked me out. They raped and killed Julie. They did it while I was unconscious. When I came to, the two guys were gone. Julie was naked on the ground and she was dead.'

'Jesus,' Bert muttered. 'I wish you'd told me.'

'I've never told anyone.'

Bert shook her head. Her eyes glimmered wet in the firelight. Her hand moved up Rick's back and curled around the nape of his neck. 'It must've been so awful for you. I'm so sorry.'

'Anyway, that's why I brought the gun along. I got Julie killed, but I wasn't going to let it happen to you. Then when we met you two,' he said, glancing at Andrea and Bonnie, 'it was all part of the same thing.'

'You couldn't save Julie,' Andrea said, 'so it's like you wanted to save all of us – to make up for it.'

'Something like that, I guess.'

'Heavy,' Andrea said.

'If I'd known what happened before,' Bert said, 'I never would've talked you into this.'

'You were so eager. I didn't want to spoil it for you. Besides, I had no idea I'd suddenly turn into a total paranoid. That other was a long time ago. I figured I'd be able to handle being in the mountains again. But when we got here, it all came back fresh as if the years in between just folded up. Then Jase and his pals walked into the camp. That's what the others did, just walked into camp and the next thing I knew Julie was dead. The way I saw it, it was all starting over again. But this time I was ready and I had a gun and nobody was going to get hurt except the guys.'

623

'And I threw away the gun,' Bert muttered.

'You *what*?' Andrea blurted.

'I threw it in the lake.'

'Holy limping Jesus.'

'It's all right,' Rick said. 'We're better off without it. I could've . . . I came pretty close to shooting those guys tonight. And they were innocent.'

'Innocent, my ass.'

'They're creeps,' Bert said, 'but they're not rapists or killers.'

'That remains to be seen,' Andrea said.

'They had my gun,' Rick told her. 'They could've done whatever they wanted. All they did was hand it over to Bert.'

'We really misjudged those guys,' Bonnie said.

'*I* sure did,' Rick said, 'and I think the rest of you caught it from me. It was contagious. I was so obsessed with this thing.'

'For good reason,' Bert told him.

'If I'd just . . . really thought about it rationally. I mean, the odds against something like that happening twice . . . It almost *couldn't* happen again with odds like that.'

'You hear about the guy who got caught trying to take a bomb with him on an airline flight?' Andrea asked. 'They said to him, "Are you nuts? You could've killed yourself and everyone else on the flight." He told them it didn't have a detonator, so they said, "Then what's the bomb for?" He said it was a safety precaution. He said, "You ever hear of *two* bombs on a plane?"'

Nobody laughed.

'Cute,' Bonnie muttered.

'The odds.'

'We get it,' Bonnie said.

Bert rubbed the back of Rick's neck. 'Are you about ready to turn in?' she asked.

'Yeah.'

'Does this mean we're not going to stand watch any more?' Andrea asked.

'What's the point,' Bonnie said.

'I guess I'll stay up for a while, then. Make sure nobody sneaks up on us and . . .' She stopped herself. She shrugged. 'I'm not very tired anyway.'

'Suit yourself,' Bonnie told her. 'But there's really no point.'

'Maybe not. But it can't hurt to be careful. Rick did have those visions.'

'Just the daydreams of a disordered mind,' he said, smiling a bit.

'Besides,' Bert said, 'the odds.'

'Yeah, the odds. Did you know it's a common misconception that lightning doesn't strike the same place twice? It does hit the same place twice. Frequently.'

'On that cheerful note,' Bert said, 'goodnight.' Rick told the girls goodnight, and followed her into the tent.

As they lay close together in the darkness, Rick said, 'Yeah. 'Nother thing. I met Angus, our friendly neighborhood preacher-man, earlier. Says he's lived out here fifty years. Caught me drinking the "devil's brew" and told me to repent of my wicked ways, or else. He's out of his gourd. A real freak.'

'Angus?'

'Yes. The bastard that's been following us around – never mentioned him before. All I'd seen was his shadow. Thought it was part of my general paranoia. But he sure scared the shit outa me tonight. Jumping out like that. Turns out he's just your average harmless maniac. I guess.'

He started to tell Bert the whole story but she rolled over and put a finger to his lips.

'Tell me about Angus tomorrow,' she said.

Chapter Twenty-one

Gillian had thought it wouldn't last long. Half an hour, maybe. Just long enough for Holden to take her up into the hills, probably somewhere along Mulholland, where he'd find a secluded area and open the trunk and do what he had in mind.

This can't be happening.

It's happened to a lot of others. It happens all the time. This time, it's my turn. I'll be dead. After he's done with me. It's impossible.

Gillian knew it was possible.

Not inevitable, though, she told herself. *It's not over yet. It doesn't have to turn out that way. Maybe he'll get a flat, or the cops will stop him, or . . .*

The wires at her feet.

She explored them with the toes of her right foot – the foot on the bottom. There seemed to be a central cable stretched along the front of the trunk. Small clusters of wires ran off it. These, she thought, must be attached to the car's right rear lights.

Cops will stop a car with dead lights.

Though her feet were bound together tightly at the ankles, she was able to spread them open as if they were hinged at the heels. She clamped the main cable between them. She pulled at it, trying to work the wiring loose without a struggle that might make the rope across her throat go tight.

You'll never break the connection this way, she realized.

Stop screwing around, this is your life!

She ripped at the cable. Newspapers whispered and crackled beneath

626

her as she slid. Her knees pounded the front of the trunk. The rope dug into her throat. She jammed her hands down to give herself slack, bent forward slightly, felt the rope rub between her legs and buttocks, felt the pressure ease across her throat, and kicked back with both feet. The cable gave. It didn't flop loose, but Gillian was certain that some of the small wires running off to the lights must've popped free. She pictured the car moving along the road, the lights dead on its right rear side.

Now if we just get pulled over, she thought.

They didn't get pulled over.

And Holden didn't stop in a secluded place in the Hollywood Hills to finish with her.

They would've been there by now.

Hours had seemed to go by after Gillian's struggle with the wiring.

Lying on her side had become unbearable after a while, so she had experimented with moving and found to her surprise that she could lie on her back. By angling herself across the trunk, she was actually able to stretch her legs out. The rope at her throat seemed more like a nuisance than a threat. She had figured out that it would not choke her so long as she kept her back straight and her arms stretched down. But the rope made it impossible for her to reach the knots and work on them. That's what it's for, she knew.

In bits and pieces over the hours, during short periods of time when she could focus her mind, Gillian had assembled the puzzle of what Holden must've done after she lost consciousness in his house.

First, he stripped her naked. Probably fooled with her. He would, wouldn't he? Yeah. Maybe even fucked her, though she had no way of knowing, not after the condition Jerry had left her in. When he finished messing with her, he tied her up. Oh, he must've got some extra jollies from that, running the rope down from her hands, centering it so it went right into her, turning her over and pulling it up so tight she could actually feel it against her anus, then looping it around her throat so it would choke her if she struggled. Her arms must've been bent just a little while he did all that; otherwise, she would've been strangled by now. He probably left some slack on purpose, not wanting to have her die in the trunk and miss the fun. Then he bound her ankles together.

Somehow, he got her to his car. His car hadn't been in the driveway when Gillian went to his house. Maybe he'd put it into the garage. If that's where it was, he'd simply carried her out the back door to the garage, opened up the trunk, and dropped her in. Maybe took out the spare tire first to make more room, and spread newspapers on the floor of the trunk before putting her in. Newspapers that could be removed later, and burned to destroy any evidence that might be left behind: blood, semen, hairs, the kind of stuff cops vacuum out of a suspect's trunk and put under a microscope and use in court. Holden had read a lot of books. He knew about such things.

What had he done with her suitcase and clothes? Probably brought them along. He wouldn't be stupid enough to leave them in his house. When they got where they were going, he would burn them or bury them or just leave them by her body. Took his scrapbook out of the suitcase, of course. He'd probably searched her suitcase while she was at Jerry's. Must've been a shocker to find the scrapbook and realize she knew his secret. If he'd had any ideas about letting her live, that had put a stop to them. He'd probably had no such ideas, though. How could he pass up a chance like this – to have a victim walk right into his house? Like getting a surprise gift. Which he couldn't wait to unwrap and try out.

Only try out, though. His own house was no place for really having fun. Not for a careful man like Holden, who traveled out of state to find his victims, who never even killed them in their own homes or apartments but took them out to wild areas where their bodies wouldn't be found for days or weeks, or at all.

So where's he taking me? Gillian wondered.

Someplace far away, she thought, or we'd be there by now.

She wondered if it was still night. After sunrise, it wouldn't matter so much about the dead lights. Maybe she had nailed a brake light, but what good would that do?

Where *is* he taking me?

From the smooth, steady ride and the engine sounds, she guessed that they were on a freeway – had been on a freeway most of the time.

We're going very far away, she thought, and then felt herself slip away again.

She woke up gasping with fear and bathed in sweat.

Sweat?

The air in the trunk felt warm. She couldn't remember it being warm before. She could remember shivering sometimes and wishing she had clothes on, or at least a sheet to cover herself. The warmth meant sunlight.

It's daytime.

She wondered what time they had left Holden's house. Maybe three or three-thirty in the morning? There was no way to be sure, since she'd been unconscious, but he'd probably been quick to get on the road. The sun would start heating things up by seven or eight. If it was much later than that, the trunk would probably be a lot hotter.

So we've been on the road about four hours, maybe longer.

If he headed south, we're well into Mexico by now. East, we're in Arizona.

'Crucify me on a cactus,' she heard herself mumble. 'Ha ha.' No joke. She could see herself on one of those saguaros that stood in the desert like mutant men with upraised arms. She felt nails in her palms, the spines piercing her back and buttocks and legs. The sun seared her bare skin. She heard her skin sizzling like bacon on a skillet. Squinting through the glare of the noon sun, she saw Holden smile and drop to his hands and knees and crawl toward her. Bones littered his way – glaring white skulls, ribcages, parts of a dozen bodies or twenty. The bones clinked and clattered as Holden scuttled through them. Some dissolved into white powder that puffed, and he was crawling through a cloud of bone dust. When he emerged from the cloud, he was no longer Fredrick Holden. He was a tarantula, fat and furry and half a foot across. And scurrying toward Gillian's feet. Gasping, she tried to move her feet away from it. Skeleton fingers held her feet to the hot desert ground. She couldn't move. The spider climbed onto her bare left foot, walked up the skeleton hand at her ankle as if the finger bones were the rungs of a ladder. It moved up her shin. It sat for a moment on her knee as if resting. Then it began crawling up Gillian's thigh, and she screamed.

The scream snatched her away from the horrors in the desert. She was in the trunk again, panting. When she opened her eyes, they both burned as if someone had flung saltwater into her face. She realized it was sweat.

The trunk was very hot. The black air felt like a heavy blanket pressing down on her, suffocating her.

I won't suffocate, she told herself. This trunk isn't airtight. I'll just cook.

I must've been out a while, she thought.

She was drenched. Even lying motionless, she could feel runnels sliding down her body, tickling her. The newspapers felt sodden under her back. She rolled onto her right side. Sweat must have been clinging to her skin in tiny beads like raindrops, standing in pools in the hollows of her throat and navel. It cascaded off her when she rolled. She heard it spill onto the newspapers.

The change of position helped. Much of the paper peeled off her back with the turn. A sheet of it still adhered to her buttocks, but there was nothing she could do. She lay there motionless, her eyes shut tight to keep the sweat from stinging them. The trickles continued. Her legs, pressed together, felt as if they were lathered with hot butter. Only her mouth was dry. Her tongue touched dry flakes along her lips.

The floor of the trunk suddenly tipped beneath her. She flinched and choked herself on the rope and quickly bent her knees, rumpling the papers but stopping her forward roll.

The car's going uphill, she thought. Up a steep hill.

It had moved up and down many times before, rocking her slightly, but never anything like this.

He's taking me into the mountains, she thought.

Chapter Twenty-two

Rick jerked awake as something smacked the wall of his tent. He lifted his head. The blue tent was murky inside with daylight. He thought a pine cone must've fallen. But then the tent was struck twice more, and other objects, missing, thumped the ground outside.

Bert moved, rubbing him, and he looked down at her. 'What's going on?' she whispered.

'They're throwing stuff.'

The sleeping bag's zipper was on the other side of Bert. He couldn't get to it without crawling over her, so he started to squirm out the top. Bert rolled away from him. He heard the zipper slide with a sound like ripping fabric.

'So long, Rick the Prick!' Jason's voice. It came from a distance. 'So long, cunts!'

Rick was half out of the bag, sitting up, his hand on the knife propped upright inside his hiking boot. Bert had slid out the open side. She was on her elbows. At the sound of Jase's voice, she stopped trying to get out.

'It *hasn't* been nice knowing you!' Luke called.

'FUCK YOU AND THE HORSES YOU RODE IN ON!' That one came from Andrea. From nearby. Her tent?

Bert shook her head.

There was distant, derisive laughter from the boys.

Rick sat motionless, waiting. Bert didn't move either. She was still stretched out, lying half across her empty sleeping bag, propped up on her elbows, naked to the knees. Her feet were still inside

631

Rick's bag. Her breasts rose and fell as she breathed.

'I guess they're gone,' Rick finally said.

'Good riddance to bad rubbish.' Smiling, she lay back and folded her hands behind her head. One of her feet stroked the side of Rick's leg. 'I hope that's the last of them.'

'We'll take that other trail.'

'And make sure, first, they're really going up to Dead Mule Pass.' Bert took her legs out of Rick's bag and stretched them out on top of it. 'It's hot in here. Must be late.'

He flipped the sleeping bag off his hot legs. The air felt good on them. 'When Jase handed the gun to you, it changed everything. That . . . I think that pretty much shattered my obsession with Julie and the rest of it.'

'God, if I'd known what you went through. I feel like such a jerk for forcing you into this trip.'

'It was probably good for me. I *know* you've been good for me.'

'We don't have to go on, though. If we turn around, we could be back at the car this afternoon. Would you rather do that?'

'I don't know. I think I'll be all right now. And I'd hate to cheat you out of the rest . . .'

'I wouldn't mind. This hasn't exactly gone the way I'd hoped, anyway.'

Rick nodded. 'Bet you didn't expect it to be this exciting.'

'Or this crowded.'

'Well, now that Jase and his pals are gone . . .'

'That only leaves Andrea and Bonnie.'

'Maybe we ought to split up with them.' That, Rick knew, was what Bert wanted. Strangely, the idea of leaving the girls behind didn't disturb him. He felt no disappointment. Andrea was a temptation and she had offered herself to him. If she were gone, he could stop struggling against the urge to take her up on it. And he could be alone with Bert.

'They're nice and everything,' Bert said. 'Andrea's kind of a kick.'

'She's sure got a mouth,' Rick added.

'But it's like having guests. Even if you like their company, they're in the way.'

Rick suddenly had a thought that made his heart quicken. 'How about this?' he asked. 'We'll have a leisurely breakfast, tell the girls to go on without us, and then we'll get all our stuff together. And we'll hike around the end of the lake to our stream.'

'You mean, stay there?' Her voice was eager, her eyes bright.

'All day. And we'll pitch our tent down by the inlet and spend the night. Does that sound okay?'

'It sounds perfect. Too good to be true.'

'But true,' Rick said.

Chapter Twenty-three

The ride became a torture as the heat in the trunk grew worse and the car climbed and dropped and made sharp turns, sliding Gillian over the newspapers, trying to throw her forward and back, the rope squeezing her throat each time she flinched at the sudden movements.

It can't go on much longer, she thought.

We're in the mountains. We'll stop soon and he'll let me out.

Let me out. No! God, what am I going to do!

The car slowed abruptly, throwing Gillian onto her back. Her knees flew up. Her left knee bumped the lid of the trunk before she could straighten her legs.

She felt the car make a sharp turn. Then it began moving forward. It was no longer on pavement. On a dirt road? The floor of the trunk shuddered under her back, shaking her, sometimes bouncing her roughly.

It won't be long now.

I'm sorry, Jerry, she thought. I shouldn't have left without you. But then he might've gotten you, too, so maybe it's better this way.

Knowing that she would never see Jerry again, Gillian felt a twist of sorrow and loss.

It's not over yet, she told herself.

Then the car stopped and the engine went silent.

Gillian felt a change inside herself as if a switch had been thrown. She no longer felt the stifling heat, or the pains of her bound and battered body, the awful fear. Her heartbeat thundered. She shivered. She felt *cold*. Even her mind felt cold. And sharp.

He's gonna have to work for it.

The trunk lid swung up. Daylight poured down on Gillian, blinding her. Cool air lapped her burning wet body. The air smelled of pine and damp earth. Squinting, she peered out. The opening was about three feet high. Beyond it, she saw the green of trees and a few pale patches of sky. Fredrick Holden wasn't there.

He must've used a trunk release on his dashboard.

Gillian heard the soft sound of a breeze whispering through the woods. There were birds singing, chirping, squawking. She even heard the flutter of wings. The whiny buzz of a mosquito.

Where is he?

She heard a footstep. It made a quiet crunching sound on the ground. Then there were more footsteps.

He's coming!

He stood over the trunk and stared down at her.

Didn't do anything, just stared as if entranced by the look of Gillian stretched out in his trunk, naked and gleaming with sweat, tied up and helpless.

His eyes seemed to bulge. His mouth hung open. Gillian could see his chest move as he breathed rapidly. He closed his mouth, licked his lips and swallowed. Then he rubbed a forearm across his mouth.

'All mine,' he muttered as if to himself. 'Allll mine.'

He bent over the trunk. His hands swirled over Gillian's slick skin as if he were fingerpainting.

Go ahead. Enjoy the hell out of this. I'll get my turn.

The hands slid on her shoulders, circled and kneaded her breasts, swarmed over her belly and down her thighs, slipped between her thighs and slithered there, delving around the rope. Then they roamed up her body again and lingered on her breasts as if he couldn't get enough of the slippery way they felt, especially when he squeezed them.

'Untie me,' Gillian said. Her voice came out in a dry, raspy whisper. 'I'll do wonderful things to you.'

He slapped her face hard.

Then he rubbed his hands on his shirt. They left dark stains on the pale fabric. His right hand dropped out of sight below the edge of the trunk. It came back with a knife.

It was a huge knife with a long, broad blade. A bowie knife?

Leaning over the trunk, he cut through the rope around Gillian's ankles. The edge of the blade scraped lightly along the side of her calf and kept moving higher. Goosebumps crawled over her skin. She tried not to shiver. She couldn't help it. She wanted to clamp her legs together, but that would push the blade into her thigh.

He's gonna ram it right up into me.

No, he won't, she thought. He can't have blood in his trunk. Even the newspapers wouldn't hold it all. He's smart enough to know that.

The knife turned. The point lightly traced its way up the hollow where her leg joined her groin, followed it to her hip.

The knife rose above her. Holden kept it in his hand while he wiped his mouth again with his forearm. Then it came down slowly and Gillian thought he was going to free her hands. The blade pressed, instead, against her pubic mound. She saw his arm make a sawing motion, but she felt no pain. He's cutting the rope, she realized. That's all.

That's all?

She felt the rope part. Her hands were still bound together, but now she would be able to raise them without choking herself.

And my feet are loose, she thought.

He'd take me easily in a fight, but I can make a run for it.

Holden pressed the blade to her throat. With his other hand, he reached behind her neck. He grabbed the rope and yanked it. Gillian felt as if she were being scorched by the streaking rope, but then it was out from under her.

Holden clutched the end of it with his left hand. 'Up,' he said, and tugged it like a leash. Gillian sat up. Sweat streamed down her body, dripped off her chin and breasts. Sodden newspapers clung to her back.

With his rope hand, Holden peeled the papers off. 'Out,' he said. His command was followed by another tug. Gillian winced.

Bracing herself with forearms on the edge of the trunk, she turned and got to her knees. She had papers on her rump. They stayed stuck to her while she swung a leg out of the trunk. Her knee found the bumper. It slipped off when she put her weight on it. She squirmed on the edge. The rope at her throat was yanked, and she tumbled out, rolling. The bumper hit her side. She bounced off it and slammed the ground . . . and reached up and caught the rope and jerked it. Holden yelped. His arm snapped forward. The end of the rope flew from his hand.

Gillian flipped over. She rammed the fists of her tied hands against the ground and thrust herself up, and was almost to her feet when Holden's kick caught her hip and sent her hurling sideways. She crashed against the rear of the car. It knocked her away. She fell and rolled and tried to keep rolling but Holden pinned her down with a shoe on her belly.

He stared down at her. He was breathing hard. He rubbed his lips again with his forearm.

Then he stomped.

Pain blasted through Gillian.

Wheezing and dazed, she was only vaguely aware of Holden picking up the rope, of how he pulled it and how she crawled, and how he picked her up and braced her against a tree trunk. By the time her mind cleared, it was too late.

Holden no longer held the rope. She couldn't see where it was, but she felt it around her neck, against her right ear, against the side of her head. Its other end, she knew, must be tied to a branch above her.

She tried to grab for it.

Something stopped her.

She looked down. She was wearing a black leather belt. It was cinched tight around her waist. Her bound hands were lashed to it with rope – probably some of the rope that Holden had cut off her feet.

When did he do that? she wondered.

I must've been out for a while.

She looked around. The car was a few yards away, its trunk and driver's door still open. But she didn't see Holden anywhere.

Soon, she heard him tramping through the woods.

He came into the clearing. His arms were loaded with twigs and sticks. He gazed at Gillian and walked toward her.

Jesus, he's gonna burn me at the stake like a witch!

But he dropped the bundle a safe distance away from her. He cleared an area surrounding it. He gathered up all the newspapers from the trunk of his car and stuffed them into the heap of wood. He found the paper that had come out of the trunk on Gillian's rump. The breeze had tossed it into a bush, where it waited for him, snagged.

He touched a match to the pile.

I knew he'd do this, Gillian thought.

The papers had been spread in the trunk like papers at the bottom of a bird cage – to catch her debris so the cops would have nothing to find if they ever searched. Now, the papers were being burnt.

He won't be putting me back in the trunk.

I'll be left here.

Panic blew through Gillian like a frigid wind.

'You can't *do* this!' she cried out. 'Please!'

'Shut up or I'll cut your tongue out.'

She snapped her mouth shut. She sucked air through her nostrils. The air was acrid with smoke.

Holden walked slowly to the car. He opened a rear door and pulled out Gillian's suitcase. He carried it to the fire, set it flat on the ground, and opened it.

On top were the white shorts and plaid blouse she had worn to Jerry's. Holden held the blouse over the fire until flames started crawling up its tails. Then he dropped it into the blaze. He picked up her shorts and tossed them onto the flames. As the white fabric curled and blackened, he looked over at Gillian. 'What were you doing in my house?' he asked.

'You told me not to talk.'

'I changed my mind. Talk. What were you doing there?'

'I just break into houses,' Gillian said. 'I stay in them when people are away.'

'What for?'

'It's exciting.'

He laughed. '*Real* exciting, this time. You must be crazy or something.'

'Look who's talking.'

'You think I'm crazy?' He looked amused by the idea. 'I'm not crazy. I just do what any guy'd do if he had the guts.'

'Bullshit.'

'Yeah, you'd be surprised.' He lifted out her tank-top and gym shorts and tossed them into the fire. 'Isn't a man alive doesn't take one look at a piece like you and want to rip her clothes off and fuck her brains out. They just don't have the guts or they'd do it. Me, I do it.'

'Then you kill them,' Gillian said.

'Dead girls tell no tales. How long you think I'd last if I let them live?'

'You enjoy killing people – and hurting them?'

He grinned and threw her skirt into the fire. 'Just part of the game. Have to break some eggs if you're gonna make an omelet.'

'You could get any woman you want. You don't have to do it this way. You're handsome and rich.'

'Rich, huh? You're a little snoop, aren't you?' He tossed her heels into the fire.

My sandals are still at Jerry's, Gillian thought. So are my panties and bra. All that he'll find of me when he wakes up.

'You know what they say,' Holden told her. 'Money can't buy happiness.'

'It'll buy a lot of women.'

'Whores. Riddled with disease. Who wants that? I'm real particular who I touch.' He took a plastic bag out of the suitcase, opened it, and pulled out Gillian's bikini. The bag shrank on the fire and burst into flames. 'What'd you do, use my hot tub?'

Gillian nodded. She couldn't let him know that she'd been in Jerry's pool.

'Wore a bikini in the hot tub. That's a laugh. You're a very modest young lady.'

'That's me,' she muttered.

Holden dangled the bikini top over the flames. Steam rose off its damp fabric. He dropped it, then rubbed the pants on his face. 'Mmmm, delicious.'

'You're a pig.'

'Oink oink,' he said, and laughed. The pants fluttered down into the blaze. He took her camera out of the suitcase and held it toward her. 'What's this for?'

'Dental floss.'

'You babes are such a riot. If you aren't screaming and weeping and pleading, you turn into wise-asses. There oughta be a bounty on you.' He opened the back of the camera and removed the film cartridge. 'You got pictures of my place in here?'

'Develop them and find out for yourself.'

'You're a real prize, you know that? Where do you get off, breaking into a man's private domain and taking fucking *snapshots*?'

'Where do you get off, killing people?'

'Right between my legs, hon.' He dropped the film into the fire. 'Seriously, you took pictures of my place?'

'I take pictures of all the places I stay. I have albums full of them.'

'No kidding. And you think *I'm* crazy.'

'Yeah, a madman.'

'Mad is right. But not crazy. If I was crazy, you think I could've done thirty-two babes without ever even getting *questioned* by the cops, much less busted? You think a crazy man would do that?'

'If he's smart.'

Black, greasy smoke curled off the film.

'At least you're right about that,' Holden said. 'I *am* smart. Take you, for instance. They find your body out here, *if* they find it, they aren't gonna know who the fuck you are, much less where you came from. I mean, they won't even think of *looking* in the goddamn San Fernando Valley. Hon, we're more than three hundred miles away. If they do find you, they'll think you're from San Francisco or Sacramento or some damn place. We're so far away you won't even turn up in the LA papers.'

'That'll make it tough to keep your scrapbook current,' Gillian muttered.

He laughed. 'Oh, I'll manage. There's this news-stand in Hollywood, carries papers from everywhere. What were you gonna do, give my scrapbook to the cops?'

'If you're so smart, you shouldn't have kept it around.'

'Shit, it's not evidence. It sure would've made them look at me, though, wouldn't it? I'm lucky I got back when I did.'

'Who'd you kill this time out?'

'Oh, a real sweetie. Linda Ryan.' He had lifted a handful of socks and panties out of Gillian's suitcase, but he held onto them and stared past the fire. 'A real beauty. Sixteen years old. Spotted her leaving a 7-Eleven and followed her home. That was what, Thursday? Friday night, her folks left her alone. She was a fighter, too. Like you.' He turned his head and smiled at Gillian. 'But she cried and pleaded at the end. You will, too.'

He tossed the clothes into the fire, then gazed at Gillian for a long time. He rubbed his forearm across his mouth. 'I'm gonna have real fun with you.'

He got off his knees, picked up the suitcase, and dumped the rest of its contents into the fire. For a few seconds, the flames were covered by clothing and her leather toilet kit and handbag. Then they broke through, crackling and blazing high.

He kicked the camera into the fire.

He turned the suitcase in his hand, inspecting it, apparently un-decided about its fate. Then he carried it to his car, leaving his knife on the ground by the fire. Gillian quickly jerked up her knees. The rope stopped her, squeezed her throat. She swung, keeping her neck muscles tensed. Blood seemed trapped inside her head. She felt as if her face were swelling up, as if her eyes might pop from their sockets. Shooting her legs down, Gillian stood up straight and gasped for breath. She looked toward the car. Her vision was dark as if clouds had covered the sun.

Holden was swinging her suitcase into the backseat.

He came back to the fire, apparently unaware of Gillian's attempt.

Squatting, he picked up the enormous knife. He poked the fire with it, shoving some unburnt rags into the leaping flames. Then he used the blade to separate some fiery brands from the main pile. They formed a smaller pyre at his feet. He eased the broad blade into the midst of the flames and rested the handle on the ground.

He left it there.

Oh, Jesus.

Standing up, he faced Gillian.

'Hey,' she gasped. 'Come on.'

Grinning, he pulled off his shirt. His torso was lean and tanned and muscular. He tossed his shirt to the ground.

He wore no belt. His belt was strapped around Gillian's waist.

He unbuttoned his slacks and lowered the zipper and his rigid penis sprang out and someone not very far away yelled, '*Pick it up, man. What's the matter, you got lead in your ass?*'

The livid color drained out of Holden's face. He tucked his penis in. He zipped his pants and buttoned them and whirled around. He grabbed his knife out of the small fire. He snatched up his shirt.

The shirt fluttered, clamped in his teeth, as he ran at Gillian.

He swung the heavy blade. It thunked the branch above her head. The rope dropped in front of her like a dead snake. Holden grabbed it, then let it go. His shoulder rammed Gillian's belly. She folded over him.

He ran with her.

His shoulder pounded her guts, keeping her breathless and unable to yell for help.

Her face was against his bare back.

She saw the brown wooden grips of a revolver above the waistband of his slacks.

She reached for it with her bound hands.

And almost got it.

Please!

Holden flung her into the trunk of his car and slammed the lid shut.

Chapter Twenty-four

'Let's take a breather,' Bert said, and sat down on a rock shelf beside the trail.

Rick sat down beside her. When he leaned back, the sloping rock took the weight of the pack off his shoulders.

'Whatever happened to your cigars?' Bert asked.

'Want one?'

'Maybe a puff of yours.'

Rick slipped free of the straps. He stood up, turned around, and opened a side pocket of his pack. The pocket was partly open where he'd kept his revolver. He found matches and the pack of cigars. Sitting down, he unwrapped a cigar and lit it. He took a few puffs, savoring the sweet aroma of the smoke.

Then he passed it to Bert.

She poked it into her mouth and wiggled her eyebrows.

'Hooray for Captain Spalding,' Rick said.

She blew smoke in his face and handed the cigar back.

'Funny,' he said. 'You don't look worn out, weary, exhausted and pooped.'

'I've picked up some of your tricks.'

'Isn't necessary, though. I don't want to run into the girls any more than you do.'

'It's been nice without them.'

'It was even nicer by the stream,' he said.

'Yeah. Can't win. I feel like we're getting dumped on right and left.' She leaned back. The rear brim of her Aussie hat bumped her pack.

The hat slid down her face. She caught it, held it on her thigh, tilted her face into the sunlight and closed her eyes. 'It would've been so wonderful.'

'It *was* for a while.'

'Yeah,' she muttered. 'Before a bunch of assorted goons put in their appearance.'

That morning, after dressing, they had left the tent. The girls weren't up yet. And they still weren't up when they returned from the stream where they'd washed and brushed their teeth. Back in camp, they built up the fire, made coffee and a fine breakfast of scrambled eggs with chunks whittled off the bacon bar. As they finished eating, Bonnie came out of her tent.

'Andrea's zonked,' she said. 'Didn't get much sleep last night.'

Rick felt himself blush. I didn't do anything, he told himself. He wondered if Bonnie had still been awake when Andrea returned to the tent after making her offer. Had Andrea told her about it?

'Just woke up long enough to say goodbye to our friends?' Bert asked.

'That's about it. I'll get her up, though. We don't want to keep you waiting.'

'That's all right,' Rick said.

'We're going to head over to a place we found on the other side of the lake,' Bert explained, 'and spend the day there.'

'I thought we were going to take the trail that bypasses the mountain.'

'We'll be staying behind,' Bert said.

Bonnie nodded. Rick thought he caught a brief look of relief on her face. 'Well,' she said, 'I guess we'll go on. Andrea might not be too happy about it, but . . . you two didn't come out here to have us in your hair.'

'We've enjoyed traveling with you,' Bert said.

'Yeah,' Rick said.

'It's certainly been an adventure,' Bonnie said.

'Sorry about that,' Rick told her.

'Well, I think if you hadn't been with us, those guys really might've started trouble. So thanks.'

They were folding their tent and Bonnie was sipping coffee by the fire when Andrea appeared. She got to her feet in front of her tent and stretched in the sunlight. She wore her faded blue shorts and her gray T-shirt. 'You guys look like you're about ready to hit the trail,' she said.

'They're not going with us,' Bonnie told her.

Frowning, she walked over to them. 'What's the deal?' she asked.

'Bert and I are planning to camp at a place we found on the other side of the lake,' Rick said.

Andrea looked hurt. 'What's the problem?'

'No problem,' Bert assured her. 'The guys are out of the way, and . . .'

'I thought we'd all stick together. I mean, we're even *parked* in the same place.'

'Well,' Rick said, 'we want to have some time to ourselves.'

She stared at him.

In the moment that their eyes met, Rick felt as if she were asking if he really wanted to leave her, was this Bert's idea, did he *have* to go, did he understand what he would be missing?

'So, it's *adios*, huh?' she asked.

'Not for a while,' Bert said.

Andrea returned to the fire. She sat there with Bonnie, sipping coffee and talking quietly while Rick and Bert finished packing.

Shouldering their packs, they went to the girls. 'Guess we'll be on our way,' Bert said.

Bonnie stood up and shook hands with her, then with Rick. 'It's been nice traveling with you.'

'Same here,' Rick said.

Andrea stood up. 'We don't even know each other's full names,' she said. 'I'm Andrea Winston, this is Bonnie Jones.'

'I'm Bert Lindsey,' she said, and shook hands.

Andrea offered her hand to Rick. He held it briefly as he introduced himself. 'Richard Wainwright.'

'If either of you ever get down to LA,' Bert said, 'make sure to look us up. We could get together for dinner or something.'

'We're in the San Fernando valley,' Rick said.

'And you're in the phone book?'

'Yep.'

'Well,' Andrea said, 'who knows? Maybe we'll see each other again some time.'

Rick followed Bert to the lakeside trail. There, he looked back and waved. Andrea had a strange look on her face. A knowing smile.

My Christ, Rick thought, she's going to show up at my door. Maybe next week, maybe next month.

His heart raced with the prospect.

Maybe she'll forget my name, he told himself.

She won't.

I'll just treat her as a friend, and . . .

What if it's over with Bert by then? What if we've broken up?

What if we break up and Andrea *doesn't* come along?

Her name is Winston. I can always find her through the university at Santa Cruz.

Why am I thinking this nonsense? Everything's great with Bert.

But you never know.

Bert, ahead of him, looked to the left. Rick saw that they were passing the clearing where Jase, Luke and Wally had camped.

Won't ever see *them* again, he thought.

'We forgot to give our names to The Three Thugateers,' he said.

Bert smiled back at him. 'What an oversight! How will they ever manage to look us up?'

When she faced away again, Rick looked over at the lake. He pictured himself diving for his revolver. Probably wouldn't find it, anyway, he told himself. And Bert wouldn't be too pleased if he tried. He kept walking.

Soon, they rounded the end of the lake and climbed to the top of the rock slope overlooking the stream. 'Do you feel like a dip?' Bert asked.

'Do I look like one?'

She laughed. They crossed the stream, hopping from rock to rock, then made their way down to the clearing by the inlet. There, they put down their packs. 'This time,' Bert said, 'we'll have towels.'

'And let's take a sleeping bag with us,' Rick suggested. 'That was hard on my elbows and knees yesterday.'

They found their towels and placed them on top of Rick's sleeping bag roll. Sitting on a rock, Bert took off her boots and socks. She stood up and stepped out of her shorts and panties. She left her shirt on, and Rick stayed in his jockey shorts.

On the way up to the stream, Rick stayed behind her. He watched her long bare legs. He watched the way her shirt-tail swayed and fluttered, giving him glimpses of her shadowed rump. The stolen glances, he realized, were somehow even more enticing than when she was naked.

Just don't fall and break your leg, he thought. We don't have the revolver anymore.

He pictured Julie on the ground. He felt a rush of fear.

Isn't it ever going to end?

Not while we're in the mountains.

This'll be great, he told himself. Yesterday over here was great. Nothing to worry about. The guys are gone.

They reached the side of the stream at a place where the water tumbled down off a ledge and formed a pool. Rick turned around slowly, scanning the area.

'Checking for voyeurs?' Bert asked, smiling.

'We're really out in the open.'

'That's what's nice about it. Didn't bother you yesterday.'

He turned toward the lake. Only patches of blue were visible through the trees. The tops of nearby trees blocked his view of the trail leading up to Dead Mule Pass. The same trees, he supposed, would prevent anyone on the trail from seeing them, even with binoculars.

'Don't worry about it,' Bert said.

'What, me worry?' Rick spread out the sleeping bag. Bert dropped the towels onto it.

He stood up and went to Bert and kissed her. Her arms went around him.

647

The feel of Bert soothed his fears, melted his cold tightness.

He stroked her back, slid his hands down and under the draping tails of her shirt. He caressed the smooth mounds of her buttocks. He ran his hands up her back. As he curled them over her shoulders, Bert stretched the front of his elastic waistband and dragged his shorts down around his thighs. He felt her cool, gliding fingers.

Moaning, he lowered his hands. He squeezed her rump, but it slid out of his hands as she crouched. She pulled the shorts down to his ankles and he stepped out of them. He felt a gentle kiss. Her tongue lapped the underside of his shaft. Then her lips opened and slid down him. She was wet and tight and she sucked.

Then she was rising. Rick felt air on his wet penis. He opened her shirt and spread it wide before she squeezed herself against him and her slick mouth joined his lips.

Soon, she eased back a little. She gazed at Rick as he slipped the shirt off her shoulders. She reached back and shook the sleeves down her arms. The movements made her breasts shake slightly. Rick caressed them. He bent down and licked a jutting nipple. He pressed it between his lips. He opened wide and filled his mouth with her breast, tongue swirling over the springy nub. He felt her trembling fingers in his hair. He moved to the other breast and took it in, and as he sucked he put a hand between her legs. She spread her legs to make room for it. He slipped fingers into her. She squirmed and clenched his hair.

She pulled his hair gently and he let his head go back, the breast sliding out of his mouth. His fingers kept stroking. Bert's hips kept moving in a slow, languid way as she rubbed herself on his hand. Her mouth hung open. Her eyes had a vague look for long seconds, then seemed to focus on Rick's eyes. She moved his hand away as she lowered herself. He felt the light touch of her fingers on his penis, guiding him. She sank lower, taking him in, sheathing him. He went to his knees. Then he was all the way in, buried in her hugging warmth. She wrapped her arms around him and thrust her tongue into his mouth.

His knees hurt, but he didn't care. Bert was tight against him. They were locked together in a hard embrace. They were joined by his penis and her tongue. They had made love many times before, but somehow this time was different. He felt the difference. He didn't think about it, but he knew it was there. She wasn't his girlfriend or his lover. They were two parts of the same person and he felt a surge of joy that didn't overwhelm his passion but fired it instead.

Bert gasped into his mouth. Her tongue pushed in more deeply. He pulled at it and clenched her buttocks. She was motionless against him, but inside she clutched and squeezed him and seemed to be sucking him up. He fought to control himself.

She started to whimper. And then she shuddered against him and Rick gave up trying to hold back. He quaked, his penis far up into the center of her, suddenly jerking and pulsing, pumping out his semen, throbbing hard until he was drained.

When it was done, they stayed together, panting for air. Bert rested her chin on his shoulder. Her hair tickled his cheek. Her hands lay on his back, almost heavy, as if she were too spent to lift them. Spent or not, she kept certain muscles contracted to hold him inside her. He caressed her buttocks.

Later, she placed her open hands on the sides of his face and looked him in the eyes. 'Could we stay like this forever?' she whispered.

'Maybe.'

'Might be hard on the knees.'

'What knees?'

She laughed, her nipples moving against his chest. Then she kissed him lightly on the mouth. Her vagina tightened, giving him a friendly farewell squeeze that brought a fresh stir of arousal so that he was growing hard again as she slid off him.

Bert duck-walked backward and sat on the sleeping bag. Her knees were red. She brushed them off. The grit left her skin pitted. Rick stood up. One of his knees popped when he straightened it. He bent over and rubbed them.

'We've got matching knees,' Bert said.

'Should've used the sleeping bag. That's what it's here for.'

'Any port in a storm,' Bert said.

Rick limped and sat down beside her. He put an arm around her back.

'When are we going to take that dip?' she asked.

'I think I'd rather rest for a while before I brave the freezing waters.'

'Then rest,' she said. She turned him and guided him. He lay down on the sleeping bag, head on Bert's lap. Her legs were stretched out. She was leaning back, braced up on her arms. She smiled down at him. 'Close your eyes.'

'Are you kidding?' He turned his head and kissed the hot skin below her navel.

Bert stroked his hair.

His gaze roamed up the sleek bare slope of her body, studying her flat belly and the curves of her ribs, lingering on the smooth undersides of her breasts, on the twin rumpled disks of darker skin with jutting posts of flesh in the center of each. He looked up the valley between her breasts, at the hollow of her throat, at the soft sweep of her collar bones, her shoulders, her slender neck. Her face. She was smiling down at him.

'This may be as good as it gets,' he said.

'Oh, I don't know. As good as it gets was maybe ten minutes ago.'

'Think so?' Rick asked.

She shook her head. 'Not really. It's all part of the same thing, isn't it.'

His heart suddenly quickened. 'I love you, Bert.'

Her smile died. 'I love you, too,' she whispered.

She pressed her lips together. Her eyes shimmered . . .

'FOULNESS! STENCH!'

Bert gasped and flinched rigid at the sudden shouts. Rick lurched up. Prancing on a rock slab beside the stream no more than twenty feet above them was Angus, waving a large wooden club overhead.

'FILTH OF SATAN!'

Bert twisted away from the stranger. She flung an arm across her breasts, glanced up at Rick with shocked eyes, and looked back over her shoulder at the wild man.

'Angus . . .'

Rick sprang to his feet, his heart slamming. He had an urge to laugh – or scream, he didn't know which. His old buddy, the King of the

Wild Frontier. Savior of souls. Christ. What a time to show up. The bastard. That coyote's head, with its mouth hanging open and those teeth an' all – no wonder he'd given Bert such a fright.

Rick didn't believe this was happening to them.

This is mad!

Angus hopped up and down like a crazy thing, shaking his stick, the coyote head bouncing but not falling off.

'MAGGOTS! GET THEE GONE!'

'Get out of here, you damn lunatic!' Rick yelled.

'ANGUS MOUNTAIN KING! GET! NAKED INTERLOPERS! VERMIN! TURDS!'

Angus ducked and skipped aside as a rock shot by, barely missing his head.

Rick looked at Bert. She was on her knees, reaching for another rock. She grabbed one and reared up.

'WHORE!'

'Crazy old fart!' she shouted, and hurled the rock at him. It struck his bare knee, just below the hem of his animal-skin robe.

He scurried backward.

Rick crouched. He picked up some of the chips of rock and joined Bert in throwing them at Angus.

The old man retreated up the slope, shaking his stick and shouting over his shoulder, 'SICKNESS! DEFILERS! PUKE AND PISS!'

A rock thrown by Bert skimmed the top of his head. His coyote hat flew off. Suddenly, he looked a sorrowful sight; his straggly gray beard shook and trembled as he mumbled more profanities. He dropped to his hands and knees, grabbed the hat by its snout, scurried up and ran. Soon, he disappeared among the trees near a bend in the stream.

Rick and Bert faced each other. Her face was ashen, her eyes wide. 'That, I presume, was Angus the Mountain King. You never did get around to telling me the whole story last night . . .'

'Yeah, sorry. I should have prepared you for that. I told you, he's a maniac, a freak. But, on the whole, probably harmless. Probably gets off on watching folks doin' what comes naturally . . .'

651

Bert was not convinced. She was still pale and Rick could see she was shaking.

'Let's get out of here.' She hurried into her shirt. She tried to fasten the buttons while Rick put on his shorts. Her hands trembled too much so she gave up.

They rushed down to the clearing. In minutes, they were dressed and packed.

On the shoreline trail, they hiked fast and looked back often. They reached yesterday's campsite. The girls had already packed up and gone.

Bert stopped by the dead remains of the fire. She was breathing hard. Her shirt was still open. She lifted its front, baring her midriff, and knotted the ends together. 'Should we head for the car?'

'If you want to.'

'Don't *you?*'

'It was awfully nice before the Wild Man of the Mountains dropped by.'

'What *is* he? What really makes him tick? He's out of it, sure. And gets his kicks spying on other people. Yuck. What a sicko.'

'He's a hermit, I guess. Mad as a hatter.'

'Don't mention hats. My God.' She took a deep breath and shook her head.

'I *suppose* he was probably harmless.'

'A High Sierra shopping cart man,' Bert muttered.

'I wonder if he would've bothered us again.'

'What, you want to go back and find out?'

'I hate to leave that place.'

Bert looked into his eyes. 'It wasn't the place, it was us.'

'That's true. But the place was special, too.'

'He ruined it.'

'Maybe we can find somewhere else.'

Bert raised her eyebrows. 'Does that mean you don't want to leave?'

'I guess that's what it means. We ought to be able to find another nice, private place.'

'That one didn't turn out to be so private.'

'It was for a while.'

'What have we got here, a convert?'

'Apparently. Why don't we take the trail you picked out yesterday?'

'The one the girls are taking?'

'We'll walk slowly.'

'They can't be very far ahead of us,' Bert said. 'We weren't gone all that long.'

'If we run into them, we do. But we won't stay with them. I want to find a place where we can be alone.'

'Pick up where we left off?' Bert asked.

'Before the rude interruption.'

'Fine with me.'

Rick twisted the burning stub of his cigar against the rock by his hip. Then he rolled the remains between his thumb and forefinger, crumbling the cigar to flakes of brown leaf that drifted down onto the trail.

He looked at Bert. She was beside him, leaning back against her pack, her legs stretched down to the trail. Her hat with its one side turned up rested on her thigh, held there by the weight of her curled hand on its brim. Her belly was the color of dry sand. It had light, downy hair that was almost too fine to see. Her shirt was tied below the swell of her breasts. Her mouth was open slightly. Specks of sweat glistened above her lip and below her closed eyes. The hair across her forehead shone golden in the sunlight and moved as the soft breeze blew through it.

Maybe she was simply resting. Maybe she was asleep.

Rick decided not to disturb her.

There was no reason to hurry.

He felt perfectly content. So far, it had been one helluva trip, he reflected, and in some strange way he was sorry that it was all over. Back in civilization he wondered if they'd still feel the same way about each other. The same way as they did now.

Wide open spaces – and a touch of danger – did funny things to people. Heightened their senses. Made them think things they wouldn't normally think – or feel. What if . . . well, suppose Bert didn't feel the same about him when she hit the real world again.

What if . . .?

He hoped not. He sincerely hoped not.

Meanwhile, he was quite content. He wouldn't mind sitting here all day, he thought. Just looking at her . . .

Chapter Twenty-five

It was late when they woke next day. Ten-thirty. No nymphets invaded their space. No teen thugs. No Angus. They were alone. Just as they'd planned from the first, a vacation together, away from it all. Rick lay back and thought how different things would've turned out if only it had stayed that way.

No Andrea to disturb his dreams. No Bonnie to give him the snake-eye. Yeah, so they could *still* have met up with The Three Thugateers. And Angus, the Wild Man of the Mountains. In an ideal world, he supposed he and Bert could have handled all four of those dudes. Could've and would've, most likely.

With some help from my trusty equalizer . . .

Rick frowned. Not for the first time did he bitterly regret Bert having tossed his gun into the lake. Oh well, at least we have our knives – and I suppose in an emergency we can hurl a nifty rock or two.

Bonnie's hatchet would've been useful . . .

Bert's eyes were closed, but she was smiling.

'You thinking what I'm thinking, honey?'

'Mmm . . . maybe. Just depends. What *are* you thinking?'

'That I could murder a coffee. And a long lazy swim.'

'Oh great!' Rick said. 'And bring the wrath of that goddamn Angus down on our heads again!'

Bert faced him and leaned up on an elbow. She was naked, happy and smiling. The forefinger of her free hand traced slow circles on his chest.

'Hey. Ricky baby. Think positive. That's all over now. This is us, remember? We're on vacation and having a great time. Come on lazybones, let's go. Race you to the coffee pot!'

She swung back the flap of her bag and stretched luxuriously. She could afford to – as of right now she had him all to herself. Rick watched her smooth tanned back and the way her arms twisted provocatively above her head as she stretched. He reached out to touch her skin, then gave a sigh of resignation and let his hand drop. Plenty of time for that later.

Sins of the flesh!

Whoa boy, for a moment there you sounded like our lunatic preacher . . .

'Go on, get the coffee going, woman, and let a man get dressed in peace!'

They were alone now. Together. He savored the thought like a kid with a special Christmas toy. He had this all-over warm feeling because he knew they both cherished the *joy* of being together – the *tenderness* of it.

Nothing else mattered.

They'd been through hell and come through the other side okay. From here on in it's vacation time, folks.

Enjoy!

They heated up and drank what was left of last night's coffee. It tasted gritty, bitter. Like something from the bottom of a lion's cage, but hey, what the heck? Right now it was nectar from the gods.

'Let's just mosey around awhile before we set off back on the trail,' Bert said. 'Let's live a little; enjoy ourselves. Might as well, since we're here.'

'Suppose we meet up with Angus?'

'Then we'll turn right around and get back on the trail again. Whatever. C'mon, Rick. We can't keep saying *what if?* We're two responsible people. Innocent people, doing what hundreds of other responsible, innocent people do every year. Hit the trail and enjoy this great big beautiful country of ours!'

He held up his hands and said, 'Okay, okay. Let's do it.'

*

It was hot on top of the ridge. The blinding sun scorched their heads, despite the hats they wore. Rick checked his wristwatch. Two forty-five, near enough. They'd been on the back-of-beyond trail an hour and a quarter. Before that, they'd lingered over coffee, eaten beans and a couple of oaty breakfast bars. Then they'd spent some time in the stream. He sure could use that cool stream water right now. He imagined himself naked, scooping it up in cupped hands. All sparkling and cold. Sluicing down over his head, his shoulders, chest, and trickling all the way to his feet.

'You thinking what I'm thinking?' Bert asked.

'Probably. It's goddamn hot up here.' He swatted away a bunch of mosquitoes swarming around his head. They parted, and came back for more. Persistent little bastards. Sizing him up for grub. He splatted one on his arm. It squelched red. *His* blood, he guessed. Or maybe Bert's. Or . . .

Bert pointed to a finger of pale gray smoke curling skyward. It came from a cabin, halfway down the other side of the ridge. 'Who'd live in a place like that? Kinda isolated don't you think?'

They stared at the cabin. It was a dilapidated place, sprawling in an untidy heap, part hidden amidst the tall dark pines. It looked like a good place not to visit.

So who suggested it might be an adventure to take a closer look? Rick couldn't remember. Whatever. At the time, it seemed okay to investigate and discover who needed isolation so desperately as to put up sticks out here in the wilderness.

On the way down Rick decided that it was a bad idea, breaking in on somebody's solitude like this. But Bert insisted. 'It's an adventure, Rick. We *are* on vacation after all, aren't we?' The way she looked at him, all innocent and eager, almost made Rick change his mind. Trying hard to convince himself, he reasoned that, time-wise, a slight detour wouldn't make a major difference. And they didn't exactly have a deadline to meet . . .

They descended at a slow jog, their packs bumping on their backs, propelling them forward.

'Did anybody mention climbing back up the mountain with these packs on our backs?' Rick muttered, under his breath.

The cabin was old; fifty, sixty years old, Rick reckoned. And it was in bad repair. The filthy rag stretched across the front window looked as if it'd hung there since the year dot. A broken-down rocker with a greasy plaid cushion propped up on its seat stood on the rotting porch.

The bad feeling Rick had had before suddenly got worse. He climbed the wooden steps and looked at Bert, poking around, pushing open the cabin door which was already ajar. The door had a small window in it. Its glass was stained with grime. A round hole had been rubbed in the dirt.

A peephole.

Bert's curiosity got the better of her; she was about to step inside.

'Bert . . .' he began.

A manic whoop cut through the stillness, then tapered off into a coy giggle. The giggle ended in a humorless titter.

Angus.

Who else?

Appearing from the far end of the cabin, making his way slowly along the porch toward them. Head cocked like a wary animal.

Angus with a gun this time. An old hunting rifle held loosely but, Rick saw, with the practiced ease of an expert. It hung cocked in the crook of his arm.

King of the Wild Frontier or Preacher-Man. *Which is he today?* Rick wondered. *Whatever, the guy means business . . .*

Bert, taken off guard, backed up against the doorframe. Her face had paled. A look of defiance had the twist of fear that was already teasing her gut.

'Hi Angus,' she managed, cheerfully. 'Care to give two weary travelers a drink of water?'

The coyote skins, even in this heat, shook around the preacher's shoulders. His bony chest was naked. Roughly stitched skin trousers covered his bowed legs. He let out a bark that Bert took to be laughter. She blanched again, hearing the triumphant ring to it.

'Yeah,' Rick bluffed. 'We were just passing by and thought you might offer us a drink – then we'll be on our way . . . On the other hand, no worries about the drink. We'll just be on our way. Bert?'

'Why yes,' she chirped. 'We'll be on our way. Er . . . have a nice day, Angus!'

Suddenly they were looking down the barrel of the preacher's gun. His face was screwed up alongside.

Easy does it . . . Rick's eyes signaled the message to Bert.

Catching his drift, she nodded imperceptibly.

The gun jerked toward the cabin door.

'Get on it, get on in there, my fine, young travelin' friends.'

Angus at his most amiable. Most wily.

A bullet clicked home.

Angus at his most persuasive, most *lethal*, Rick decided.

They turned and trouped in through the doorway.

First thing they noticed was the stench. Rotten food, human smells and something else; gamey, putrid. Couldn't make out what it was. Angus jostled them to a deal table. It was stained with coffee, food and God knew what else. The surface was cluttered and cracked with age.

Sweeping aside the dirty crocks, stale food and other debris, Angus made one end clear. He jerked the gun again.

They slid out of their packs and sat down.

Taking the rickety spindle-back chairs either side of the table, Bert had her back to the door. Rick faced her. Angus took his place at the head of the table, to the right of Bert, and eased himself into a wooden armchair. The rifle rested across his bony knees.

A moment's silence. Then Angus snatched off his hat and tossed it to one side. It landed in a mangy heap on the cabin floor. His head was bare, but for a few long gray hairs crawling through patches of thick, yellow scales. Grinning, he made his scraggly beard wiggle at them, and tapped the table-top with a bony forefinger. Bert stared in disgust at the finger's long, grimy nail, noting that all of his nails were black – and curved, like the talons of a giant bird of prey.

'Put 'em down, right here!' he ordered. 'That's it. You heard me right first time. Them huntin' knives you got tucked away in there.'

They didn't want to do it, but right at this moment there wasn't a hope in hell of playing it any other way. Angus held the aces. And the gun.

Slowly, they unfastened their belts and placed the sheathed weapons, and the looped belts, side by side at the center of the table. Angus leaned over, raked them in and dropped them into his lap.

Rick and Bert remained poker-faced. Wouldn't do to let the bastard see that taking their knives was any major deal.

'Well, now,' Angus smiled craftily, looking from one to the other. 'Ain't this fine an' dandy. Just the three of us. Sitting here like old friends.' He settled back into the curve of his chair and smiled some more.

Way too big for a skinny runt like him, Bert thought. It's built for a bigger man . . . She glanced around the one-room cabin. Seated on her side of the table, she didn't have to move her head to do it.

A tousled bed with grimy, greasy covers stood in the top right corner. The filthy ticking pillow skewed sideways, half on, half off the mattress. Bert's eyes followed the pillow downward. To a huddle of dark canvas stashed beneath the bed. A loop or a strap had strayed from the pile. It lay curled like a snake on the worn wood floor.

A breath of fear flicked at her throat.

Over the brass-knobbed headrail hung a framed picture of Christ on the cross. Bert figured it probably served as a reminder to Angus to keep up the Lord's good works. She pictured him jumping out at them yesterday. Screaming insults and vile words.

No chance he'd forget, she reckoned.

To the right, sunlight filtered through a dirty rag-draped window. In the corner stood a large store cupboard. Its dark veneer had been polished at some stage of its life, but not anymore. She looked at the dull, wormy wood and reckoned it must be at least a hundred years old. An heirloom.

Like the dresser, with its heavy, carved shelves towering above the good-sized set of storage drawers. The whole thing filled most of the cabin's facing wall. Religious bric-à-brac and faded sepia photographs in brass frames littered the shelves and top surface of the drawers.

Bert's eyes lingered on a picture of a small, gentle-looking woman standing by the side of a seated, autocratic man. Both were laced up to the chin in Victorian-style dress.

In particular, she studied a photograph of a young girl with mournful eyes. She wore a crocheted shawl and stood with one arm across the shoulders of a small, pixie-faced boy with blond curls.

Family photos.

Was Angus that small boy?

An old Indian blanket thrown roughly over a wooden rail came next. Bert reckoned it could hide another door. Or a secret store of weapons, maybe. Her mind worked overtime. *If Angus got caught off guard, Rick could tackle him. I could rush the blanket, grab a gun or something, and we could shoot our way out . . .*

Yeah. Pigs might fly.

Her eyes slid around to the left, taking in the plastered walls scarred at intervals by brown floral wallpaper. A section of the left-hand wall, the far side of one of the cabin's three windows, boasted a rogue's gallery of faded heads.

Clerics of long ago. Much of a muchness: dog collars, round wide-brimmed hats and pursed, pained expressions. Different images of two men, it appeared. One, the elder, had a full bushy beard and mean eyes. The other had the same mean eyes, but was younger and clean shaven.

Father and son.

To her left, by the remaining window, stood a brownstone sink. Next to it, a lit stove made tiny spitting, crackling noises. It exuded a malodorous stink. The ash can beneath the stove was catching gobs and spills of grease. The falling grease made dark holes in the mounds of fine gray ash.

'You interested in my pictures, whore? Them there's my daddy an' my granddaddy. Both good men of the cloth. Preachin' the Lord's word all of their lives . . .

'Yessir . . . they wus good men, my daddy and my granddaddy. Men a mother could be proud of. Ridding the world as they did, of SCUM LIKE YOU!'

'You bastard . . .' Rick caught Bert's warning look and snapped his mouth shut.

'No offence. No offence . . .' Angus said, with a lewd smirk at Bert. 'Gotta keep on doin' the Lord's work.'

He carries on like this, I'll kill him, thought Rick.

Interpreting his thoughts, Bert gave a small frown, and shook her head.

Angus was gone. Oblivious to the mental dialogue of his captives, he nursed his rifle lovingly against his chest, his bony fingers caressing the hard steel. He began rocking to and fro. The knife belts in his lap shifted and chittered. The sound roused him from his reverie and he continued his story.

'My daddy and his daddy afore him were strong Scottish Presbyterian. Ministers of the cloth, both. Back in Perthshire, Scotland, my granddaddy ministered to his flock of good folk . . . and kept them free from sin. *A*-men.

'Jist as the good Lord woulda wished.

'When he died, my daddy took over. But, in a wee while, that same flock turned on my daddy, so they did . . .'

His attention wandered again. Mumbling to himself, he looked up and stared for a long time at a brass crucifix hanging over the door.

Rick coughed. 'And then what, Angus?' He looked at his wrist-watch. 'Whoa. So late? We really must be moving on. What d'you say, Bert?'

Relieved that Rick had broken the tension, Bert said, 'Yes, sure thing. We better get going. Mustn't keep the girls waiting, must we, Rick? Promised we'd be back before dark.'

In a flash, Angus was on his feet. The knives fell to the floor with a clattering *thunk*. He gripped his gun and shoved it at them with both hands.

'SIT DOWN, FILTH! I haven't finished yet. You ain't goin' nowhere till I've had my say!'

They all sat down. Angus gave them another crafty smile and resumed his story.

'First off, you can't fool me. Them girls broke camp a while back.

They on their way to somewhere else by now. That means you're on your lonesome. Two lost sheep who've gone astray!' He giggled at his own words, then fell silent, his loose, wet lips pulsating gently beneath his beard. Testing the effect of the pun on his audience.

He leered slyly at Bert.

'See, now, where wus I? Yep. Then my daddy heard that there was a need for God's ministers over here in the United States of America. So we came over in a sailing ship. My daddy, my mammy and Maire and me. We traveled across the seas to this great country and finally dropped anchor, so to speak, in the Tehachapis.

'My daddy preached an' he preached till he was blue in the face. He loved his flock, oh my, how he loved them people. Mammy would cry and say that there was no need for him to love and care for them so much. 'Specially the young 'uns. She was there, she said – he didn't need no more love . . .

'And then he got to lovin' Maire. The Lord's wishes, he swore. An' my daddy, he allus carried out the good Lord's wishes. Praise be to the Lord. *A*-men.'

If I keep him talking, looking my way, Rick thought, *Bert could break out before he gets a chance to use his gun. I could overpower him. And we could be on our way.*

As if.

'Anyways. One night, them good church folk held a meetin' and a whole contingent of them marched over to our house and told my daddy to get out. They said he wus evil. Not fit to be a man of the cloth, they said.

'Daddy told them to go away and he closed the door, right in their faces. Went straight in to Maire's room and loved her some more. I could hear her pleadin' an' cryin'. She wus saying, *Daddy please don't. Don't Daddy, you're hurtin' me* . . .

'When Mammy went in, she found my sister Maire dead in her bed. A seizure, so my mammy said. She ran out into the night a-screaming for help and Daddy got his gun, the one that's setting on my knee this very minute, and shot her dead.

'My daddy and me gathered up a few family treasures, took to the hills, 'n built us this mighty fine cabin, so we did. My daddy told me we were poor wanderers, a-travelin' the wilderness with only wild things for company. Jist like the Lord Jesus Christ, he said. Only we stayed more 'n forty days an' forty nights. We stuck it out for much longer. All of my daddy's natural born life, turned out . . .

'An' I been here since my daddy passed on. Lookin' after God's creatures and spreadin' the word. This 'ere mountain country is my *home*. It gets a bit lonesome sometimes and I don't have much truck with outsiders . . . but, it's my home . . .'

'That's it.' Rick stood up. So did Bert. Grabbing their packs, they started for the door.

A gunshot whined and hit the roof.

'No you don't. Filthy swine! Foul defilers! I'm not yet done with ye. REPENT AND BE SAVED!'

He marched them through the door, out onto the stoop and round to the back of the cabin.

Chapter Twenty-six

Bert's heart sank when she saw where they were headed.

Toward a cage-like pen made from tough, pine staves about twelve feet high and bound together by stout twine.

Angus danced around them, herding, prodding, maneuvering them together with his rifle. The cage door was open.

'Ready and waiting,' Bert muttered.

An almighty crack descended on Rick's head and a gasp shot from his lips. He groaned, folded and went down on all fours.

What the . . .?

All in a day's work for Angus. Suddenly, he was business-like; prodding Rick with the rifle butt, kicking and pushing him into the cage.

Fuck.

Rick slid along the dirt floor, lurched to his knees and tried to stand. His legs gave and he crashed, face down, into the mat of foul-smelling straw.

Angus darted behind Bert and poked her sharply in the back. She stalled. Another vicious poke sent her sprawling onto the floor of the cage. Angus cackled to himself as he quickly secured the cage door with a strong plait of twine.

'Rest awhile my travelin' friends!' he simpered. 'Rest and repent ye of your sins. Praise the Lord!'

'Shit, shit, shit,' wailed Bert. She stood with her hands rattling the staves in angry frustration.

Rick got to his feet. 'Okay,' he panted. 'He's got us for now. But we'll get out. No sweat.' He wasn't sure how, but they'd make it. If it was the last thing he . . .

This is too ridiculous for words. We're two intelligent, professional people. Doing nobody any harm. All we ever wanted was to be left alone . . .

This can't be happening to us. It can't. I won't let it . . ,

Rick bashed the palings with a clenched fist. All the way down one side of the cage, the staves shook in unison. A blinding pain shot through his skull. And his fist. The pain in his head was bad, but now his fist . . .

He cursed. They both needed his two hands to be in working order. Trust him to go and get a loused-up fist . . .

The crack on his head from the rifle butt had raised a fair-sized lump. He groaned and pictured a bottle of Jim Beam, standing on the bar, back in his apartment. A glass, half filled with sparkling rocks, was ready and waiting. The amber fluid glinted seductively, beckoning to him . . .

Rick closed his eyes against the screeching pain in his head. Oh, for anything, but *anything* vaguely alcoholic, preferably straight from the bottle. And aspirin. Got some in my pack.

Angus, would you mind fetching me some water and aspirin? The aspirin's in my pack, by the way.

Christ, give me strength.

When that fuckin' turd leaves us alone, we'll find a way out of his goddamn cage.

'Rick,' Bert said quietly. 'Look at this.' She pointed to a heap of canvas humps in the corner of the cage.

'Backpacks. Old backpacks, Rick.' She looked at him and the same thought passed between them.

'Huh. Kids who never got around to repenting . . .' Rick said.

'Looks that way.'

'Probably butchered and got eaten for breakfast.'

Rick's watch told him it was six o'clock already. 'We rest up till dark. Okay?' he whispered. 'Meanwhile, we'll figure out a way to escape.'

Bert was near to tears. 'Oh, sure, Rick. What d'you suggest? Please Angus, let us outa here 'cos we want to go home now?'

Rick hadn't got an answer. Yet. They couldn't climb over the staves. Too high, too pointed and far too dangerous. They couldn't try to shake the staves loose from their moorings either. Angus might be watching.

When it got dark, they'd find a way.

They sat together, their backs leaning against the palings. They felt *defeated.*

Bert huffed loudly. 'I'm so hot and sticky. Can't take my shirt off; our friendly fuckin' neighborhood creep'd probably get off on it.'

'Rest while we can, Bert, that's about all we *can* do.'

As the shadows lengthened around the cage, they fell silent and dozed a little.

A low, throaty snarl brought Rick to his senses.

He lay stretched out on the floor. Eyes closed.

Christ. His head hurt.

What in the name of Jesus happened to us these last few hours?

He remembered this morning, so long ago now, sitting and staring at Bert, thinking that he could do that all day.

Hell, I shoulda just done it. Stayed there. All day.

Bert?

Where *is* Bert . . .

Rick's hand shot to his head. It felt like it had been kicked around a baseball pitch, non-stop. He groaned and let his hand drop to his side. Easier that way. Just lying there.

Eyes open now.

Staring at the night sky . . .

Another low snarl. More like a warning growl, Rick thought. It was deep, throaty and seemed like it was sending him a message.

Coming to getcha, white man . . .

Okay. Here I am . . .

He watched the clusters of stars above.

Constellations.

Asteroids.

Planets.

They were all up there, in the yawning blackness.

He moved his head – first to one side, then the other.

The lump on it throbbed like crazy. He lifted his left hand to feel it.

Ouch . . . maybe I should have a brain scan . . .

A gut-wrenching stench brought him to. A den of *lions*?

He sat up.

Flashes of pain shot fresh stars into the hurt already there. He groped his eyes with a hand and saw more bright lights.

Fuck stars. I got big, blinding asteroids.

Rocking to and fro, he remembered where he was. And why.

Small, stifled sobs caught his attention. They broke off, snagging in their owner's throat. Sobs and wails of frustration.

Louder this time.

'Bert?'

'Rick . . .' she sniffed. 'Thank God you're awake. You passed out.'

'Yeah. My head's killing me.'

'Rick, I've not heard Angus for a while. But I've heard his play-mates . . .'

A low warning snarl was joined by another. And another. And another in a higher key. Then a sharp yelp as if its owner had received a hefty swipe.

'Yeah. Cougars, Rick. They're here and they're close . . .'

Rick staggered to his feet and moved forward, hands held before him. God, it was dark.

And that fuckin' *smell* . . .

His outstretched arms touched palings. Placed about four inches apart. He fingered the twine holding them together at intervals, and tugged at the staves.

God, I need a drink. My mouth's like the bottom of a lion's cage.

Nice choice of words, Rick. Go to the top of the class.

The staves had been hammered in firmly. Too firmly. There was no moving them. No tools to loosen them with either. Rick's heart sank.

'Wooden bars all around and goddamn mountain lions waiting for our skins,' he muttered.

'If we could just loosen the staves, perhaps I could slip through . . .' Bert muttered, testing each one to see if she could work it free.

A blinding light slashed through the darkness. As they covered their eyes against it, the preacher's high-pitched giggle rang out.

'Welcome to "Braeside" chapel of rest for all ye who are heavy laden. You're very welcome indeed to lay down your weary bones and tarry here for a wee while.'

The r's were strongly pronounced – a bizarre parody of a Scottish accent. A pious greeting you might expect from a preacher's wife.

Angus stood outlined in the yellow glow from the doorway. A gnome-like figure, hopping from one foot to the other in excitement. He held a lighted candle in one hand.

'So that's what was hiding behind the blanket,' Bert muttered. 'Not weapons. Not stove-wood. Another door.'

Another peephole.

Angus was wearing his coyote hat again. It swung about his shoulders as he giggled. Over his free arm he nursed the old rifle. He still hopped from one leg to the other like a maniac.

He scuttled forward, the flickering flame lighting up the dog snout from underneath. His straggly beard was in serious danger of going up in smoke.

Angus glared at his prisoners. His eyes, gleaming through the holes in the coyote head, darted gimlet sparks in their direction. His beard moved up and down as he cackled and jibbered an endless stream of profanities.

'Rick,' Bert whispered. 'What is this screwball gonna do with us?'

Angus hurried past their cage. 'Here, kitty, kitty, kitty . . .' he called softly into the darkness.

A volley of mild growls and snarls came back.

The preacher turned to look at Bert over his shoulder. 'Does that answer your question, *whore*?' he simpered, with sneering emphasis on the last word. 'My kitties haven't had a good meal in quite a wee while. Not since the last godless sinners passed this way. Hee, hee . . .'

'He's crazy.'

'Bert, hold on. Don't say anything to spook the guy.'

Bert's eyes flashed with impatience. 'What d'ya think I'm nuts or something?'

Rick grinned and kept his eyes on Angus.

Yeah. The guy *was* crazy. But crazy like a fox, and Rick knew he had to be just as clever. Get into his mindset and play him along at his own game.

'He's got our knives, so we can't get physical,' he whispered. 'Maybe if we talked him into opening the gate to this place, we could rush him.'

Right on cue, Angus set the lighted candle down on the grass. Then, like a magician performing his best trick, he fumbled at the waist of his trousers and with a flourish, produced two knives. Still in their sheaths. He held them by their belts, one in each hand, and jiggled them in the candlelight.

'You'll not be needing these little beauties. Filth! Defilers!' he taunted, throwing the belts down onto the grass.

'Okay, Rick. Do your stuff. Start talking,' Bert muttered.

The cougars milled around in the background. Getting restless. Snuffling, giving sharp little whines.

Peering through the darkness, Rick and Bert could see them pacing around in their compound – another 'cage' of strong, supple staves bound together by twine – about five yards from their own. The cats' noses pointed skyward. Sniffing out the human scent. Slinking around their pen, one after the other, their powerful tails swinging low and threatening.

The cats were hungry – and impatient. Most of all, hungry.

'He's out of his gourd,' Rick hissed back. 'You can't reason with a madman. We'll just have to play it by ear. There's got to be a chance to break out, somehow.'

He hoped to God there would be. They'd have to make a desperate move soon or they'd wind up dead, for sure. Sweat streamed from his armpits. If it weren't so damned hot.

And still.

Like the unbearable calm you get before a storm.

The moon was a smooth round disk, hanging high in the soft night sky. Rick watched it and wondered if they'd be around to look at it tomorrow night. He grunted in disgust. Because of that stupid, damn-fool idea of theirs, they were here, imprisoned in the preacher's stinking back yard.

In this clammy, stench-ridden hell-hole.

'Rick, look at this.' Bert pointed to the ground. A shard of glass, picked out by the moon, glimmered gently in the dark soil.

Rick screened her body with his. Bert bent to pick up the glass. She retrieved it quickly and stood up.

'Probably left by the last weary travelers,' she mouthed.

Wonder what happened to them?

Don't ask . . .

Pressing the piece of glass to her lips, she breathed a silent 'thank you' to the last occupants of the cage.

Angus had his back to them, facing the cats, mumbling and whining exaggerated words of endearment. He'd left the candle burning by their cage. He seemed in a world of his own, but his rifle was still cocked and resting on his left arm.

King of the Wild Frontier.

Behind him in the cage, Rick was gripping staves, shaking them back and forth. Looking up now and again to make sure Angus was still talking to the animals.

He was.

No joy with the staves, though.

Firm as rocks.

Bert followed suit and suddenly hit paydirt. One of the staves jiggled about in her hand. They exchanged triumphant glances. Bert bent down to see if she could work another one loose.

Yes.

She began working on the twine with the glass shard.

Rick was having a hard time with his staves. He'd only worked his way through six by the time Angus quit his conversation with the cats.

Shit.

'Not much longer now kitties. Come sun-up, you'll have the biggest breakfast you've eaten in a long, long time. You all, and me both — we'll have us a mighty toothsome meal!'

Still working on the twine, Bert watched him from behind the bars. From where she was standing, Mr Preacher-Man looked like he was in serious need of some sleep. He may be a lunatic, but he was old and frail. Should be tucked up in his flea-ridden rags by now.

Sweet dreams, turd bastard . . .

She worked on the twine some more.

Yes!

It had come free in her hand. A quick wrench and she'd cleared the stave from its moorings. Adjusting her balance, she held it poised like a spear; threw back her arm and zoomed it through the air, straight at Angus.

His rifle fell to the ground.

'Ha!' he shrieked, clutching his hat and side-stepping out of the way. 'BITCH! WHORE! FILTH! You'll rue the day you did that . . .'

He tailed off as Bert bent down and slid her body easily through the eight-inch gap. With a yell, she bent and grabbed the stave again and thrust it deep into his bare shoulder. Blood spurted and spilled down the fur skins.

Looks like a wounded animal, Bert thought.

But instead of going down, he plucked out the stave, threw it to the ground and kicked it aside, blood still pouring from the gash. He came for her, slowly but surely, his arms spread wide. She caught the evil glint in his sunken eyes. He reminded her of a snake mesmerizing a rabbit.

And for a moment she *was* mesmerized.

Rick saw what was happening.

Zombie-like, Angus moved forward. Through the gaping holes, his eyes were mean and menacing . . .

Feverishly, his bony fingers worked at the front flap of the skin trousers. They fell loose and he shook them down, stepped out of them and kicked them out of the way. His skinny body glistened with blood and sweat. The hole in his shoulder still pumped blood.

His horny erection jerked in anticipation.

*

Rick found a stave that moved in his grasp. He wrenched it around until it came free. He'd already cut through the twine with the glass shard.

The space between the two poles was too narrow for his body. He pushed. Tried to force his way through but couldn't quite make it.

Shit!

Bert screamed 'Rick!' as Angus knocked her to the ground.

He leapt on top of her, his filthy dog furs swinging over her body. The fur got in his way, so he grabbed his hat by the snout and flung it to the ground. Rick caught sight of the preacher's pate, gleaming in the moonlight and ludicrously sprouting long gray hairs from its scaly patches.

Blood still ran freely from Angus's shoulder. It flowed down through Bert's blue chambray shirt and onto her chest. Her arms were sprayed and spattered with blood as she struggled to free herself.

With rising hysteria, Bert felt the man's strength. He was thin, old, but wiry and *incredibly* strong. Tearing open her shorts, he dragged them, and her panties, down her flailing legs. Then, like some greedy, parasitic vine, he coiled his own corded, bony ones around her. She struggled violently against his vice-like grip and, still under him, managed to force her knees up against his bony chest.

She screamed again. 'Rick, I can't fight him – he's so strong! *Get him off me! Pleeease!*'

Her voice rose hysterically. Through it all, she could hear the cougars mewling and whining with excitement.

The second stave broke free from its moorings. Rick tossed it away and forced himself through the gap. He'd made it! Rushing forward he flung himself at the slobbering, quaking figure jerking up and down on top of Bert. It was shoving, panting, making small whimpering noises.

Rick fought back vomit as he landed on top of them.

God, the bastard's doing it. He's raping her.

Rick wrenched the jibbering preacher away from Bert and threw him off her.

Angus's back hit the ground hard. He grunted and whimpered with the shock of it. Eyes, wide-open, bulged out of his head, and his slack, slobbering mouth worked behind the blood-flecked beard. Rick stared down at the emaciated body. Still writhing in some kind of ecstasy, glistening with the exertion. The wormy penis was a thin, sharp spike, refusing to lie down. A long stream of semen slimed from it to Bert's bare leg.

'Aaarrgg!'

Released, Bert rolled away from the conflict, tears of revulsion streaming down her cheeks.

The crud tried to fuck me . . .

But he didn't make it in.

Nearly did, though.

God. How did we get into this fucking nightmare? Why aren't we in some expensive hotel in Maui? Why are we here in this . . . this stinking hell-hole?

The preacher's breath came shouting out in snarls and pants as Rick slashed him across the face with the back of his damaged hand. White hot pain seared Rick's knuckles. But he couldn't stop. Again and again he brought his fist back and forth across the bony skull.

Blood, his and the preacher's both, clotted the filthy beard and spattered the ground around them.

Slowly, Bert stood up, dragged up her panties and fastened her shorts. Then squirmed as she saw the semen on her legs. Plunging her hand into her shorts pocket, she found a wad of tissue and rubbed vigorously at the mess. First one leg and then the other.

Satisfied she was as clean as she could get, she tossed the soiled paper and turned her attention to Rick.

'He's gone, Rick. You're only hurting yourself more. Let's go. Jesus, Rick, just let's go.'

She saw tears of rage and revulsion falling down Rick's face. He looked up at her. 'Christ, Bert. We didn't *need* this. The sicko tried to fuck you, Bert. I mean, how did this thing HAPPEN?'

Nursing his shattered hand, he rose to his feet. She wrapped an arm around his waist and they turned to go.

Rick staggered and fell from a terrific blow from behind. Bert nearly went with him.

Regaining her balance, she whipped around and came face to face with a cougar. White muzzle, dark mask, pale golden eyes. Up so close she saw the spittle drooling from its teeth and felt the heat of its rancid breath.

Jesus. A big one. Granddaddy of them all.

A group of maybe four tawny bodies milled around the compound. The roughly made barred gate had swung open. The cats saw it and filed through at a trot.

Coming their way.

Rick stayed on his knees. No choice, the cat's front paws were holding him down. He felt its steaming hot breath in the nape of his neck.

A wet, fleshy tongue investigated his ear.

Bert's heart sank faster and she felt sweat ooze from her armpits. *Oh my God*, she panicked. *What shall I do? I should know, but I can't think straight . . .*

Then, like watching an old movie, a childhood memory reeled through her mind. She saw four lions sitting upright on big round drums in a circus ring. A fat ringmaster in red coat and white breeches faced one of the lions. He held a whip which he kept flicking at the beast. The lion pawed the air, trying to grab the whip . . . The other lions grumbled, became restless. Angry roars broke out. She remembered her ten-year-old self thinking what a goddamn stupid thing to do . . .

IDIOT. This is *not* a traveling circus.

This is for real. Out of the corner of her eye she saw the hungry way the cat was nuzzling Rick's neck. Do it, girl.

Do it.

She did it.

Bending quickly, she grabbed the bloodied stave from the ground. Momentarily distracted, the cat growled and lunged for her. But she had the stave now, held like a spear, above her head. She leapt out of the cat's reach and did a little war dance, to keep it distracted.

She gained its full attention.

The cat reached her easily in a single bound.

As it roared and swiped at her, she thrust the stave deep into its gaping maw. The cat fell back, shaking its head, gurgling blood. Sprays of it spurted from its mouth. Drenching her hair, face, body and legs. As it shook its head, more red spurted on to her – and all over Rick.

The cat pawed the ground, withdrawing from them, padding backward, uttering strangled, whimpering noises. Still shaking its head, trying to free the stave.

Its paws worked at the wood but the stave didn't budge. With a final roar, the cat twisted over and lay panting on its side. The stave had gone through the throat and was poking out the other side.

'Come on!' Bert shouted.

Momentarily, the other cats had retreated, watching, lynx-eyed, from a distance. But they were really excited now. Creeping forward, they sniffed and butted the head of the fallen cat – then, one by one, smelling fear in the air, their noses lifted. Their interest in Rick and Bert was swift, sudden.

They closed in for the kill . . .

Bert gripped Rick's arm.

'The knives, Bert,' Rick panted. 'They're around here someplace.'

'Oh, leave them, Rick.' Frowning, she looked around in the darkness. By some miracle there they were, close to her feet, belt buckles glinting in the moonlight. Where Angus had thrown them.

She bent down, hooked them up and grabbed Rick's good hand. Why she snapped her head around at that moment, she couldn't say. But she did, and saw a head, half buried in the dark clumps of grass. It was a woman's head with tousled brown hair and an eaten face. Most of the face was gone, but one eye remained. Wide open. It stared at Bert.

Swaying with shock, Bert clung tightly onto Rick's hand. They both legged it through the cabin door and slammed it shut behind them.

For a moment, they leant back against the door, acutely aware of the roaring cats on the other side. The door shook as heavy paws pounded and tore at the wood.

Kicking the Indian blanket out of his way, Rick made a grab for one of the wooden chairs and stashed it against the quaking door.

Angus!

Bert reached up for a quick peek through the small window in the door. It was misted with grime but she could still see the preacher.

Alive. Only just.

He was on his back, his bare, spindly legs curling against his chest. His arms were up, vainly shielding his head.

Come sun-up, you'll have the biggest breakfast you've eaten in a long time . . .

A strong-looking cat, a young male, was taking powerful swipes at him, rocking his body back and forth, moving him around like a rag doll. The other cats were spiteful, restless; prowling around impatiently, swiping at each other. A couple pushed their noses in, but instinct kept them from going for the kill. The big male would take his share first.

The cat nosed around the man's upturned butt and sniffed its way through the slowly cycling legs. Then gave all of its attention to the soft genitals . . .

The preacher's puny erection had died long since.

Piercing screams told them when the cougar made its first strike. The big male dealt with the innards, shaking its head like a cat with a rat, until the bunch of steaming gut stretched like elastic and broke free from its moorings.

Another shake and the cat dragged the bloodied entrails outside of the body, gathering the hot, dripping mess into his powerful maw. It nosed upward, a jaw-full of the dripping trophy glistening yellow in the dawn light.

Gobs of dark blood dripped from the prize, down the cougar's chops and made slimy trails on the grass. The cat lay down, took the kill between its paws and started to eat.

Curls of warm mist rose up from around the feast.

In seconds, Angus was covered in a roiling mound of tawny bodies, each hungry cat fighting for its share of the kill.

Don't hurt me, Daddy, please don't hurt me . . .

Too late. Deed's already done . . .

The cats squabbled among themselves, each fighting to tear off its own share of the preacher. One, its nose bloodied from the kill, carried a dark skinny arm between its jaws. It moved away from the others and settled down to devour its trophy.

'Oh, God . . .' breathed Bert. 'The guy was horrible – sick and mad. But he didn't deserve to die like this . . .'

Rick wanted to vomit, but the carnage happening before them was like a magnet. He couldn't tear his eyes away.

'Show's over, Rick,' Bert said. 'Let's go before I barf all over the place.'

'Yeah, you're right. Let's get outa here,' he agreed.

They hurried through the cabin, fastening their belts as they went and adjusting their hunting knives. They found their packs where they'd dropped them earlier and thrust their arms through the straps.

It was sun-up by the time they hit the trail again and they didn't stop until they'd reached the fork in the path. They were exhausted, breathless, but at least they were alive. They had their packs – and their knives.

'I just wish I hadn't seen that eaten head, Rick. That coulda been us, y'know? Thank God *we're* still around to tell the tale,' Bert said.

'You can say that again.' Rick's injured hand was painful and he wondered how long it'd be before they hit the stream again. He could use some cold water to ease the pain and the swelling.

'. . . could use a beer, too,' he muttered.

'And me.'

'Yeah, one for the road and how 'bout a nice juicy burger on the side.' He gave a faint grin.

'Christ. Have a heart,' Bert grimaced. 'On the other hand, maybe don't have a heart. Too soon to talk offal after the slaughter-fest down at Chez Angus, don't you think?'

Gratefully, they looked deep into each other's eyes and Rick felt a sudden surge of joy. It sure was good to be alive.

'C'mon,' he said. 'Let's put some miles between us and this crazy place.'

Chapter Twenty-seven

After parting company with Rick and Bert, the girls fell quiet. Trudging on in silence, they already felt lonesome. The goddamn *emptiness* of this whole terrain was getting to them so much, it was scary.

Andrea spoke first. 'I don't know that we did the right thing, Bonnie. Maybe we should have insisted we all stay together.'

'What are you, nuts or something? They practically told us to go our own ways. Or weren't you listening to those people?'

'Sure, I know that. But I could've persuaded Rick. Y'know?'

'Yeah. I bet,' Bonnie sneered. 'You made a fool of yourself back there with Rick. You know that, Andrea, don't you?'

'You mean you were jealous of the way he came on to me?'

'Jealous? You *threw* yourself at him. Practically handed yourself to him on a plate. I'm surprised Bert didn't kick up about that. I admire her. She's got a lotta patience, that woman!'

'Oh yeah? Then how come if he loved her so much he invited himself to my tent? Answer me that, why don'cha?'

'Let's not go over that particular scenario anymore, Andrea. *Purrlease!* You're so hung up on yourself I'm surprised you don't have an orgasm every time you look in the mirror!'

Andrea plumped herself down on a smooth slab of rock. She edged out of her pack and swung it to the ground.

Holy Moses. Was she *pooped*!

And what's more, she didn't like the way the conversation was headed. She could do without all this shit about her and Rick.

With a sigh, she flipped off her ballcap and wiped her brow with the back of her hand.

'Bonnie Jones. If you don't stop handing me insults like this, I ain't goin' nowhere with you. It's too darn hot to argue and I don't know why we're traveling by ourselves, anyway. We coulda gone on ahead of the others – or trailed behind. We needn't have gone *with* them . . .'

Andrea was almost whining now. She mopped her brow again.

Then lifted the hem of her gray T-shirt, bent her head down and wiped all of her face with it. It didn't help much; sweat was still rolling down her cheeks.

Bonnie tried to reason with her. 'Okay, okay. But you heard them say they'd rather travel alone. Rick specifically said they wanted some time to themselves.

'And if it helps, I don't know why we had to come out here into the boonies, anyway. Come to think about it, it was a dumb thing to do. But we *did* discuss it, Andrea, before we set out. When we had taco and fries and cola at Pepe's Pitstop, the day you took your social history books back to the library and they were overdue. Remember? We talked it over and agreed that a week's vacation by ourselves, *alone* in the Sierras, would clinch it.'

Andrea sniffed at the front of her T-shirt.

God, it stinks. After this is all over, I'm gonna toss this thing in the trash, no kidding.

She screwed up her eyes and peered at Bonnie, standing before her, hands on hips, with her back to the sun.

'Clinch what?' she asked suspiciously.

'Whether we could make it together, dummy. Christ, Andrea. Don't make me spell it out.'

Bonnie huffed in frustration and edged her way out of her backpack. Pushing out her chest, she bent at the knees and lowered the bulky pack to the ground. She collapsed on the smooth rock shelf beside Andrea, stretched out her sturdy legs and examined the toes of her boots . . .

Okay. Let's take it slowly. From the top.

With a small sigh of resignation she began, 'Look, Andrea, you know how I feel about you. I just hoped that . . . you know . . . a little time spent together and you'd begin to feel the same about me, too.'

Bonnie warmed to her subject.

'I mean, you seemed to get off on me, at the first. Now you go all girly and start making out with the first goddamn available male you see.'

Andrea sounded repentant. 'Sorry, Bonnie. I've been a grade-A idiot, I know. But I can't help myself. Maybe . . . well, the thing is, maybe I'm not cut out to be a dyke, after all.'

She traced circles on her smooth, tanned knee. Bonnie watched her do it and thought how much she'd like to take her in her arms.

I mean, make the sparks fly.

Float her boat until she screams for more.

Hell. She was no fucking expert at dykedom herself.

What experience had she had? She only knew that from age fifteen-ish she'd been significantly different from the other girls in class.

Always awkward around guys, she'd never actually dated one – not that she'd ever been asked. Wouldn't have gone with one even if she had.

Neither was she in awe of guys. Not like the other bimbos, describing in ecstatic terms how they'd been to the movies/the game/the beach with this fantastic guy etc., etc. . . .

Instead, she'd always aimed to come out top. The guys didn't like that. At college she'd always had to be *better* than they were. Better at everything, sport, science, cultural studies – all of that . . .

And then there was that, well . . . call it an exploratory fling, if you like, with Deena Alvarez, her cultural studies tutor.

Dark, sensuous Deena.

She of the sensational body, full, voluptuous breasts and nipples like dark, ripe berries.

Okay. She'd been too wary; scared that she wouldn't make the grade. And in the end she'd come away feeling totally exasperated with herself. Embarrassed. Pissed off. In a nutshell, she was just too damned inexperienced. The demanding Deena had eventually gotten impatient with her – she, and her fumbling, inadequate responses. Within a week Bonnie had been out on her ear with a bunch of insecurities as high as the Empire State.

And Deena moved on to that *total* dork; the dumbest of all dumb broads, Caroll Helliman.

Bonnie flushed at the memory of that particular put-down. Yeah. That really had been a swinging blow to her pride and dignity. She knew she was better at most things, including sex, than that slut Caroll, who acted no better than cheap trailer trash, with her minis up to her ass and those fancy low-cut blouses of hers. Plus a gnat-size brain that got no further than the color of her lipstick. Jeez, Deena musta been *desperate*.

Caroll's folks were loaded, though. They were in real estate. Had a hunk of their own the size of Disneyland. But, no matter how many sackloads of dough they had, Bonnie decided, it'd never buy 'class' for their sleaze of a daughter.

What the hell. She'd bounced back from that and had had a smoldering affair with raven-haired Lindy Carson, nubile daughter of one of the night porters at UCSC.

That went sour when she caught the lovely Lindy naked and cavorting in the shower with half of the college baseball team. From then on in, it had been 'no way, Jose' for Bonnie. Sex was off the menu.

Romance was for the birds, so to speak.

Then along came Andrea. Fragile, elegant, graceful Andrea, with her upturned nose, glossy blonde hair and slender legs that went on forever. Yeah, Bonnie decided. Andrea was the one for her, all right.

Now, here on vacation in the Sierras, the question had to be asked. *Was* she the one?

I'll work on her some more. She doesn't play ball, I'll find somebody else who will, thought Bonnie, knowing that if Andrea didn't come across now, she might as well chuck it in.

Plenty of others out there.

May well be, but there's only one Andrea.

It's make or break time.

'Bonnie . . .' Andrea twisted her hands, looking slightly embarrassed.

'What is it? You can't stand the sight of me? You wanna phone home and ask your mom if it's okay to be a dyke? What's the problem, Andrea? Spit it out.'

Andrea spat it out. Slowly and with feeling.

'You know how I get these hunches sometimes . . . like *premonitions?*'

Jesus Christ, that's all we need . . . Three teenage fuckin' hoods.
Now we get a message from beyond.

'You have mentioned them before. Go on.'

'Well . . .' Andrea twirled a strand of sweat-damp hair round her finger.

She was obviously ill at ease. Bonnie prepared herself for some bad news.

'What would you say if I said don't let's go back by way of Dead Mule Pass?'

Andrea picked at the hem of her T-shirt, uncomfortable, knowing that Bonnie was staring at her, open-mouthed.

'I just get this feeling, Bonnie,' she went on quietly. 'It's a really strong feeling that we should take another route.'

Andrea slipped off the rock and faced Bonnie. Then, reaching out, she caressed Bonnie's shoulder. The touch was gentle and timid, like the flutter of a small bird. With mounting impatience, Bonnie shrugged it off.

'Please,' Andrea said in a small voice. She knew she would cry in a minute if Bonnie didn't say something nice to her.

Like, *It's okay. You're with me. I'll look after you.* Or, *Don't mind me, I didn't mean what I said about you and Rick.*

Instead she got a gesture of bored resignation from Bonnie and, 'Er . . . okay. If that's what you want.'

Bonnie slid off the rock and hunkered down to open her pack.

Pulling out a well-thumbed map of the Sierra Nevada mountains, she spread it on the rock before them and began to trace out another route.

'There isn't another recognized route to Mulligan Lake,' she announced eventually. 'We could go up this ridge, here, and then drop down, by-passing Dead Mule Pass. But it's out of the way; we're not likely to meet many other backpackers along there. You get into trouble on the Mulligan Lake Route, and you'd see other hikers and maybe a ranger on patrol to help out.

'Sorry, but the way I see it, Andrea, the main route is the only way to go.'

'Damn.'

'But we're not likely to hit a problem, are we? I mean, the terrible trio have gone their own way by now.'

'*Please*, Bonnie.'

'Hey. Somebody's gotta act responsible around here. We can't go wandering off down some lonesome ol' trail nobody uses. Nobody except those with no business on the official route, that is. Talk sense!'

'Okay.' Andrea lifted her chin defiantly. 'Don't say I didn't warn you.'

She swung up her pack, shrugged her arms into the straps and adjusted her load. Bonnie followed suit. She glanced sideways at Andrea's self-righteous expression.

'Okay. Okay,' she said, with a dramatic sigh. 'We'll do it the hard way. Main route to Mulligan Lake, it isn't. Trail of the lonesome pine, it is.'

Bonnie stomped on ahead. She wasn't happy about choosing the ridge route. They had their knives, and could throw a mean rock if trouble broke out. And she still had her brother's hatchet . . . But what if one of them broke a leg or fell into a crevasse – anything could happen.

And probably would, she thought, gloomily.

One of them had to stay behind, they could get chomped by a goddamn cougar.

'You're not happy with this, are you, Bonnie?'

Andrea was striding out, abreast of Bonnie now. She took a peek at Bonnie's set face.

'The hell I'm not happy with it. But, my mystic munchkin, if you've got a funny feeling about reaching Mulligan Lake by the tried and tested, we'll go the ridge route. No problem. The map says it's the quickest route anyway, so that's one consolation.'

They were climbing now; a cluster of pines up ahead told them that the trail – *what trail?* – began right here. They kept on trucking. This way, they'd soon get through and back to their vehicle in no time.

Not worth hassling about.

Who needs the main route, anyway?

They pressed on up the rough grass track. Then, 'Bonnie, are you hearing what I'm hearing?'

Bonnie stopped and listened.

'Yeah. Guys' voices,' she replied.

'What d'you reckon? Men or boys?'

'Haven't the foggiest. Whatever they are, they sure sound as if they're whooping it up.'

Andrea stopped, hand on hip, and listened some more. The whoops got louder. Men. A group of men, *gotta be backpackers* were headed their way. *But they sound more like hooligans than your average hiker*, she thought.

More shouts. Bursts of coarse laughter rang out through the trees ahead. The voices:

'Hey, Wilbur. I fancy a bit o' skirt! How 'bout you?'

'You'll be lucky 'round these parts! Don't see no skirt hereabouts. Can you see anything that vaguely looks like a skirt, from where you're standing, Bud?'

'Not from where he's standin', he can't. He's busy takin' a leak!'

'Aw, leave it out, Wilbur. Go get yourself another beer.'

Loud guffaws echoed through the dark trees.

*

Bonnie and Andrea tensed as they heard footfalls coming toward them on their left, through the forest undergrowth. The footfalls got closer, but they still couldn't see the guys.

Then, 'Shoulda brought that Nicole along. She'd oblige us, all three. Yessirree. An' then ask for more!'

They heard whoops of laughter, lewd, suggestive. Then it simmered down to muffled, low-key banter.

Andrea and Bonnie couldn't quite hear what was being said.

The next gust of laughter seemed a helluva lot nearer to where they were standing. Holding their breath, they looked at each other, wondering what to do.

''Nother can of beer, Wilbur?'

'Sure, Dean, chuck it across . . .'

The slap of a hand catching a beer.

'They're shit-faced . . .' Bonnie whispered. 'But it sounds like maybe they're settling down. Taking a goddamn rest. And we've got to walk along the path, right past them – there's no other way!'

'So what? We just ignore them. Pretend we haven't seen them and just, well, just walk on by . . .'

'Oh yeah. Great. Andrea, haven't you learnt your lesson yet? We got rid of The Three Thugateers, now we meet up with a second bunch, with bells on this time. We had enough hassle with the first lot. Now we got these wiseguys who look as if they mean business. Serious business. And sounds like they're gagging for it, too. And you say *walk on by*? The $64,000 question is, sweet-cakes, will they *let* us "walk on by"? You bet your sweet life they won't!'

Bonnie fumed under her breath. She snatched off her straw hat and fanned her flushed cheeks with it. Andrea could be a real *dork*, sometimes.

'Hey! What have we here? Guys, come on over. Think we just found ourselves a coupla playmates!'

The speaker appeared to the left of them. Right out of nowhere. *Must've been walking through the trees, caught sight of us and then side-stepped out onto the path.*

More like they knew we were here and were coming to get us the whole time. How could they? We haven't even reached them yet.

The guy leered at the two girls. He was drunk and it showed. His chunky red face creased into an idiot smile as he sized them up. He waved a can of beer in his left hand. A hunting rifle hung loosely in the other. He wore a red check shirt gaping open, one side tucked into blue jean pants. The other side hung down his thigh.

Thick, black hair covered his barrel chest.

'Shit-faced', Bonnie muttered to herself.

A hootnanny hillbilly, straight out of *Deliverance*.

The guy's unsteady legs were thrust into tan cowboy boots.

He'd appeared on the path, suddenly, out of the patch of pines. The girls gasped as they saw how near to them he really was. About five yards away and weaving in their direction all the time.

Answering shouts and a couple of disbelieving grunts came from the goon's buddies.

'You're shitting us, right?'

'Get your backsides on over here and find out!'

One shouted back that he'd be along when he'd had a pee.

Bonnie grabbed Andrea's arm.

'Okay, let's run for it!'

'You bet . . .'

Mashing their hats well down onto their heads, they turned tail and ran back past the pines and onward down the grass track. Their packs pounded their backs like lumpy lead weights.

Dead Mule Pass, here we come!

'Hey, come on back here, now . . . We won't hurt you none. Jest want to be friendly like. Come on back, y'hear?'

The thick voice taunted them over the rapidly growing distance. Then, in a sing-song voice that sounded loud and close, 'Don't know what you're missin'!'

He was on them.

Right behind and closing in.

Must be one of those gun-happy, big cat killers with nothing better to do, Bonnie thought in disgust. Probably a whole bunch of them back there. Trackin' down mountain lions, drinkin' themselves shit-faced first, to get their courage up.

The girls stumbled over the rough grass, regained their footing and picked up speed again.

But the guy was still close enough for them to hear him grunting for breath as he chugged along.

Must be fit. I'll give him that, Bonnie marveled. Must've flown down that track . . .

A gunshot cracked overhead.

Then, 'Christ Jesus! Aawwgg . . .'

Bonnie paused and looked back.

Their tormentor lay sprawled headlong on the track.

She saw him wave a fist in their direction, his red, swollen face mouthing obscenities.

She hurried along after Andrea.

The girls got away while the going was good. They reached the rock they'd been sitting on earlier and took the trail to Dead Mule Pass. Andrea seemed to have forgotten her objection to this particular route. They pounded along for a while, then slowed up slightly, figuring they'd cleared enough distance between themselves and the guys on the ridge to make a clean getaway.

Even so, they decided it was better not to linger.

They strode steadily down the track for some twenty minutes before Andrea spoke. She was almost breathless and her words huffed from her lips in short bursts.

'That was a narrow miss . . . Couldn't take any more hassle from rampant males. Had enough of them to last me a lifetime . . . Men are such chauvinistic PIGS. Thinking that every woman is fair game. AND, that no problem at all, women are just standing around WAITING for them to get into their knickers . . . God, they're such SHIT-heads!'

Bonnie slowed down to catch breath. She smiled philosophically.

'Yeah. Carried on past those guys and we'd have been dead meat for sure.'

'Bonnie . . .'

'What is it?'

Silence.

Bonnie waited for her to say her piece.

'I'm sorry. *I'm sorry,*' Andrea muttered, shame-faced. 'I never get things right, do I?'

'Go on! You're not doing too badly. You're a bit of a girl, is all.' Bonnie humped her pack more comfortably on her back and turned to smile at Andrea.

Relieved that their earlier tension seemed to have gone, Andrea responded eagerly. A nice warm feeling passed between them.

Thirty minutes farther down the trail they called a halt.

They were parched and badly needed a reviving sip of water – cold would have been nice, but they were more than ready to settle for warm. Twisting out of their packs, they dumped them onto the grass and flung themselves down alongside.

Eventually, their breathing became easier, more measured. Lying there together, in silence, they relaxed. The herby fragrance of the warm grass beneath them felt good. Through half-closed eyes they watched the cloudless sky overhead and listened to the distant stream, tumbling and gurgling through the rocks.

The sound reminded them that they hadn't taken that drink yet. Hadn't had one since they broke camp this morning. Struggling to a sitting position, they unfastened their packs and brought out their water bottles. Taking long, leisurely swigs, their tension drifted away and they felt, for the first time in hours – days, it seemed – that danger was now way behind them. Andrea yawned and they both stretched out again on the warm, rough grass. It smelled sweet and clean.

'Sure you don't mind coming along this route, after all? In spite of your premonition?' Bonnie asked, chewing on a stalk of grass. 'No option, y'know. With those creeps blocking our path.'

'I probably got it wrong way round in the first place,' Andrea replied cheerfully. 'My premonition could've been warning me against taking the lonesome pine route, not this one. Could've misinterpreted the message. In which case, looks like everything's turned out okay!'

'And what about Rick? Still lusting after him?'

'Goddamn it, Bonnie. Gimme a break. I'm sorry I made a fool of myself, believe me. But Rick's history. He's no different than the rest . . . Really.'

She found Bonnie's hand and gave it a squeeze.

'Could be,' Bonnie murmured, hardly daring to believe the way things were going. 'Anyway, don't you dare say sorry again . . .'

Leaning up on her right elbow, Andrea turned to face her. Looking deep into Bonnie's eyes, she leaned over a little and kissed her gently on the lips.

Then on her cheeks, her forehead, and, as Bonnie closed her eyes, Andrea touched her lids, gently, with her lips. Then her mouth again. She was more demanding this time.

With a faint gasp of delight, Bonnie twisted quickly and came on top of her. Then, shifting her weight off Andrea, she leaned away and lifted up the soft gray T-shirt. She sighed when she saw Andrea's small, perfectly formed breasts. They were smooth shiny mounds, the color of milky coffee. Her nipples, exposed to the warm, balmy air, grew hard and pert as she looked at them.

Bonnie drew away from Andrea and lay, head resting on one arm, looking at her.

No need for words.

They were together now. That's all that mattered. Wasn't this what their vacation had been about? Finding each other?

They'd found each other all right.

Now, all they wanted was to get away from this place . . . return to Santa Cruz and get on with their lives. Together.

Bonnie felt the joy grow inside her; it blossomed until she could contain it no longer. Their eyes met, lingered and finally drew apart.

*

Andrea gave Bonnie a long, slow smile, their hands reached out and, for some time, they lay there. Content to be together. Staring at the hot sky. At a wisp of cloud, which had appeared, it seemed, from nowhere. Andrea watched it move across the broad sweep of blue.

'Bonnie?'

'Uh-huh?'

'Y'know Rick?' Andrea felt awkward about bringing Rick into the equation. Especially just after she and Bonnie had made love for the first time. But she had to get it out of her system, once and for all. She moved her head so she could see Bonnie's face. Bonnie was suddenly quite still. She kept on staring skyward.

'Well, I didn't *want* him and all that stuff. I want you to know that, Bonnie. I was testing *myself*. Wondering how it would be – y'know? Seeing if I could go through with it. I'm glad he didn't take me up on it now. Because I know it was *you* that I really wanted, Bonnie. It was you all the time. Only, I was too scared to admit it . . .'

'You're a dummy. Y'know that, Andrea Winston?'

'You think so?'

'I sure do. You're such a *girl*; and I love you for it.' With studied nonchalance, Bonnie still gazed skyward. Andrea grinned, leaned up on an elbow and kissed her full on the mouth. It felt good. She did it again. They both laughed. Bonnie rolled over, quickly, grabbed her by the shoulders and held her down. And kissed her. And for a while they were lost in each other.

Drawn to the heat, a bunch of mosquitoes danced around their faces. Bonnie swore, rolled over and swatted them out of her hair, off her face and arms. Andrea, already sitting up, slapped busily at her legs. Strange how they hadn't noticed the little bastards before . . .

They gave up swatting and, laughing at themselves, fell back onto the soft grass. Their lips still curving with their own secret smiles, they remained in silence for a while longer. Neither wanted to break the spell; their amazing, magical bond that had changed everything for them both.

They grinned and toasted themselves with the last of their water.

Chinking the sun-warmed bottles together, they drained the final dregs.

They sat in silence for a while longer. Then Bonnie looked at her wristwatch. Almost an hour had passed since they'd made love. She said to Andrea, 'You okay to carry on? I vote we get moving. Been out here in the wilds, livin' next to nature, for too long. Kinda gets to you after a while!'

Andrea blushed and smiled. 'You're the boss,' she said.

Feeling hot, happy, and emotionally replete, Bonnie and Andrea both felt a twist of sadness at leaving this, *their* special spot in the wilderness. They fastened up their packs, shrugged into the straps, adjusted themselves and, hand in hand, continued along the trail toward Mulligan Lake.

Chapter Twenty-eight

The car stopped again.

There was a quiet sound of the latch releasing. The trunk lid started to lift open. Gillian, on her back with the belt and rope clamped in her teeth, bolted up. She grabbed the edge of the trunk, flung a leg over it, and rolled. She dropped. She heard the car door shut. Her side rammed the bumper. She heard rushing foot-falls as she hit the ground. Flipping over, she thrust herself up and ran.

Holden raced at her from behind. His breath came out in snarls. Gillian hissed in pain as something raked her right calf. She kicked the leg forward as fast as she could and heard the rustly sound of a body smashing onto the pine needles that matted the forest floor. Holden gasped out a quick 'Awg!'

A glance back. He was skidding on his belly. He must've made a dive for her.

The thought flashed through Gillian's mind that she should whirl around and try to overpower him while he was down. She tore the belt and rope from her teeth and pictured herself beating him with them, but she kept on running, knowing it would've been foolish to fight him. This way, at least, she was sure to gain the few moments it would take him to get back onto his feet.

She dashed through the pines. Springy limbs smacked her body and bent away. Others scratched. She leaped over rocks, over barriers of fallen trees. Rocks and twigs and pine cones punished her feet. But all the pain seemed to belong to someone else. She was free. Though

Holden was pounding through the woods behind her, she still had her lead, she still had her chance.

I'll make it.

He won't get me again!

He'd had her but someone had come along and he'd rushed her into the trunk but with hands still tied to the belt. Untying herself had been easy. She'd been given her chance.

Gillian lunged between two trees. The branches tried to hold her back, shoving at her face and chest, but she plowed through. And found herself in a flat, sunlit clearing.

She picked up speed. She tucked her head down and darted her long legs out fast and far. The belt and rope in her right hand flew as she pumped her arms. They lashed her face and shoulder and breast, they whipped her thigh and groin. They scorched her. She wanted to throw them down. But she might need them later. She couldn't waste time balling them up to stop their flailing. So she ran as hard as she could, bearing the pain, hoping the snapping belt and rope would stay away from her eyes.

The sound of Holden's crashing feet went silent. 'Stop or I'll shoot!' he shouted.

Gillian sprinted across the clearing. She heard her harsh breathing, the soft crushing noise of her footfalls, the sharp smack of the belt striking her bare skin, the softer *whup* of the rope's lash.

She listened for a gunshot.

She could almost feel a slug crashing into her back. Right between the shoulder blades.

He doesn't want to kill me, she thought. That'd spoil his fun.

He'll try to go for the legs.

The sound of the gun reached her ears, filled her head. It was a quick metallic clack.

Silencer?

She heard the sound again and realized it was the hammer dropping.

The hammer snapped down fast, again and again. Gillian didn't try to count the quick hard clacks, but they went on and on.

She glanced back.

Holden stood in a shooter's stance at the edge of the clearing, far behind her. The front of his pale knit shirt had a dark patch of blood on one side a few inches above his waist. He brought the revolver up close to his face and scowled at it.

That was all Gillian saw before she swung her head forward again. *Empty gun,* she thought. *What luck!*

Then she thought, *My good Christ, I'm the one who unloaded it!*

It was the revolver she'd found yesterday in his desk. Had to be. She remembered the cartridges tumbling into her palm, how she had dropped them into her shirt pocket and the heavy feel of them against her breast. Then she had put the revolver back into the drawer where it belonged – where Holden must've grabbed it before driving her from his home.

I saved my life.

The thought astonished her.

Not only had she rendered the revolver harmless, but it had caused Holden to stop while he took aim and snapped the hammer down on all the empty chambers. Now he was far behind her.

You're not out of it yet, she warned herself. Don't let it go to your head. You've had a couple of reprieves, that's all. You're in the middle of nowhere and he's not going to give up.

She came to the edge of the clearing, dodged a tree, and dashed into the shadows.

Hide? she wondered.

Not yet. But maybe soon. Duck behind some rocks or something. He might see you do it. Then he'd have you.

If you're going to do it, you'd better do it now.

Hide. If you get away with it, you can backtrack to the car. Maybe he left the keys.

Fat chance.

Maybe he did.

If the keys are gone, disable the car. Stay on the dirt road; you'll get to a real road. Flag down a car . . .

I'm naked.

Big fucking deal.

Maybe I can find something in his car to put on.

Gillian heard him racing through the woods. A long way off. She looked back and couldn't see him.

Do it! she thought. *Hide!*

Still running as fast as she could, she swung her head from side to side. The tree trunks looked too skinny to hide behind. There were no clumps of bushes in sight. The few rocks jutting out of the forest floor seemed too small.

Climb?

He'll see me.

People don't look up. That'd been a big point in some novel she'd read years ago. The thought had intrigued her at the time, and she'd never forgotten it. People look down and around, but they rarely look up.

Get above Holden, maybe he'll run right by.

Off to the right, not far ahead, stood a pine that was much bigger than most of the others. Its lower branches drooped to within a yard of the ground. Its upper trunk was completely hidden by the surrounding green of its bushy limbs.

Gillian raced toward it. As she ran, she shoved the belt between her teeth. She balled up the rope and pitched it to her right. It uncoiled in midair, sailed down, and dropped over a sapling about twenty feet away. She wished it had gone farther, but that was good enough. It might throw Holden off her trail.

If he sees it.

She dashed the rest of the way to the tree, dropped to her knees and scurried beneath the umbrella of its foliage. She crawled to the trunk. She stood up. The lowest branch was as high as her shoulders. She wrapped herself around the trunk and began to shin up it. The belt was in her way. A few times, it got caught between her chest and the trunk, and tugged at her jaw. But she kept her grip on the belt, freed it when it snagged, and kept on climbing.

She heard the distant crunch of Holden's footfalls.

They were coming closer and closer.

She got a knee onto the lowest branch. Reaching up, she clutched a limb. She carefully straightened herself. She raised her left leg, squirmed against the trunk, found a foothold on the other side of the trunk, and thrust herself higher.

Holden sounded very close now. His shoes were thudding on the forest floor. She heard him gasping for breath.

Peering around the trunk, she saw patches of light through the tree's curtain of foliage. But she couldn't see Holden.

If I can't see him, he can't see me.

She wanted to climb higher.

The branches above her feet looked thick, but not as thick as those she had stepped onto before. If she put her weight on one and it bent even a little bit, a whole section of green on the outside of the tree might shake and give her away.

So she stood motionless, left foot braced on the branch, arms and legs hugging the trunk. Hearing Holden's approach, she pressed herself more tightly against the trunk. She wished she could sink into it and disappear.

The sounds of the rushing footsteps stopped.

Near the place where the rope had landed?

He knows he's lost me, Gillian thought. He doesn't see me anywhere ahead, doesn't hear me running. He's starting to suspect I've tried to hide on him. He's trying to figure out where.

Her heart thudded wildly. Calm down, she told herself. Pretend we're playing hide-and-seek.

Pretend, hell!

Strange. She'd spoken so fondly of playing hide-and-seek to Jerry. Just yesterday.

And here I am now, playing it for keeps.

She wondered if she had ever tried hiding in trees. And then she remembered that she had – many times. She remembered standing on branches high up, clinging as the tree swayed in the wind, staring down as the kid who was 'it' searched the yard and never looked up. The thrill had been like a giggle trapped in her throat.

Had she ever been found when she was hiding in a tree? She didn't think so. They found her when she hid in bushes, under stairs, in window wells, but not when she climbed trees.

Maybe that's the real reason she had decided to climb this one.

The forgotten trick of a kid game.

It worked then, she told herself. It'll work now.

It better.

What's he doing?

For the past minute – maybe longer – Gillian hadn't heard a single footstep. He'd been panting for air when he arrived, but that had stopped very quickly.

If he left, she thought, I would've heard him. He must just be standing there, looking around, listening, waiting. Maybe he thinks I'll decide the coast is clear and come out of hiding.

Maybe he did leave.

That's what he wants me to think.

I'll stay here all day. All night. Whatever it takes.

Footsteps rushed toward her tree.

Gillian's heart lurched. She jerked her face back from the trunk and looked down.

Holden scurried under the hanging limbs, stood and gazed up at her.

Her breath blasted out as if she'd been punched in the stomach.

Holden's knife was lashed to the end of a stick – tied there with the rope she had thrown to lead him astray.

The stick was six feet long.

Before Gillian could move, he jabbed upward with the makeshift spear. Its point sank into her right buttock. Yelping, she reached down for the knife. It pulled out of her and slashed at her hand, but missed.

She tugged the belt from her teeth and twisted herself away from the trunk. She pivoted, her right leg swinging backward through the air, foot kicking at the shaft of Holden's knife-spear, then finding its way onto the same branch as her left foot.

The maneuver had turned Gillian around. She no longer had her back to Holden. She hugged the trunk with her left arm. Her right arm swung, whipping at the knife with the buckle-end of the belt.

The knife circled on the end of its stick. The lashing belt did little to keep it away. It slashed and thrust. Sometimes it got her. It poked the side of a calf. It nicked a hip. It sliced a thigh. It cut a half-inch slit across the top of her pubic mound.

Gillian knew he was toying with her. If he wanted, he could hack her to pieces or bury the blade in her. Instead, he tortured her with shallow stabs and slices.

He stared up at her with wide, eager eyes. His lips were a straight line. His tongue slid out between them as he made a hard sweeping slash at Gillian's belly. The blade missed her by no more than an inch. As it passed, she struck it with her belt. The end of the belt wrapped the wooden shaft and she tugged. Holden tugged at the same instant. The belt jerked from her hand. Holden's lips curled into a smile. He shook his spear. The belt slid down its shaft and dropped to the ground.

Gillian unhooked her arm from the tree trunk. As she side-stepped carefully, Holden jabbed the blade at her face. She flinched and nearly lost her balance. Her right arm waved. Her left hand grabbed an overhead branch. The knife point stung her left armpit, then scraped along the underside of her breast. The blade moved up between her breasts and turned, its edge pressing into her right breast.

She darted her right arm in, grabbed the shaft just below the knife handle, thrust it away from her body and leaped.

Leaped forward, diving, clutching the spear with her other hand as she flew.

Flew over Holden's head.

Insane, she thought. Like diving into an empty pool.

She kept her grip on the spear as she crashed headfirst through a tangle of limbs that beat against her falling body. A branch pounded her hip, throwing her over. Then her back struck the ground.

She raised her head. Her skin was a maze of welts, scratches, and bleeding cuts. They itched and burned. But she couldn't worry about that now.

The dive had carried her through the wall of foliage surrounding the pine. The spear was still in her hands. It had snapped in the fall, leaving only a few inches of shaft jutting out below the knife's handle.

But she had the knife!

Gazing between her feet, she saw Holden scuttling through the shadows under the tree.

She gasped, rolled over, pushed herself up and whirled around to face him.

He held the rest of the spear – a long crooked pole. The break had left it with a point. He walked toward Gillian, both hands on the pole, shaking it at her. 'Gonna shove it up your ass,' he whispered. 'Gonna make you a scarecrow.'

I've got the knife, she thought. But his words sent ice through her bones. He seemed so sure.

He lunged forward, driving the pole toward her belly. Gillian slashed at it. The heavy blade knocked it aside. She threw herself at Holden, swinging the knife in a backhand stroke. He hurled himself out of its path and the blade cut only air. She glimpsed a blur of streaking pole and cried out as a blast of pain shot up her arm. Stunned, she saw the knife fly from her hand.

Holden turned, watching the knife, and started to go after it while it was still falling.

Gillian whirled around and ran.

It's over, she thought.

Christ, I had the knife.

She sprinted.

It's over, but I won't make it easy for him.

Her arm throbbed. Her wounds burned. She felt blood and sweat sliding down her skin. Branches whipped her. Her feet snagged on something and she fell and skidded and scurried up again and kept on running.

In the distance ahead, the forest shadows were broken by brightness.

Another clearing? she wondered.

Maybe a lake!

If it's a lake up there, I'll dive in and swim. Maybe Holden can't swim!

She glanced back.

Holden was racing after her, no more than twenty feet away. He had the pole down at his side, clutched in his left hand. His right hand held the knife.

Gillian dashed out of the trees.

Clear open space ahead.

Rocky ground for a few more yards.

But no lake.

A valley.

Gillian tried to stop.

GOD, NO! was her final thought before she stumbled off the edge.

Chapter Twenty-nine

This is it, Gillian thought as she plummeted.

Her feet hit rock. Her knees shot up, one striking her chin like a pitched hardball.

She was lying on the beach. She could hear the nearby surf. Her skin was sizzling.

I'm going to have a doozy of a sunburn, she thought.

I'd better roll over.

She couldn't move. The sun seemed to be pressing down on her, holding her motionless.

If I don't roll over . . .

A kid ran by, kicking up sand. Grains of it flew into Gillian's open mouth. She started to choke.

Coughing, she raised her head and pushed herself up on her elbows. The sight of her naked, battered body destroyed the dream. She coughed and spat. Blood sprayed her chest. So did bits of something – not sand, though. Chips of broken teeth? Her vision darkened and swam. She twisted quickly onto her side and vomited.

When she was done, she squirmed away from the mess. She rolled onto her back and her right leg slipped into emptiness. With a gasp of alarm, she jerked it up and crossed it over her other leg. Her pounding heart sent waves of pain through her head. She patted the ground and felt an edge of rock no more than two inches from her side.

Carefully, she sat up. She looked around, forcing her head to turn on her tight neck.

She was sitting on a shelf of rock that jutted out no more than five or six feet from the sheer face of the mountain. It was less than four feet wide. The center was depressed slightly, and as sandy as a beach.

She started to look down, felt a swell of panic, and scooted cautiously until her back pressed the solid wall of rock. There, she gripped the edge beside her right hip. She took deep breaths. She shut her eyes, but snapped them open, fearful of falling. Too close to the edge. She eased herself closer to the middle.

What am I doing here?

She tried to think back. Her brain pulsed and burned with the headache. Her memory seemed scattered.

She remembered a fall – from a diving board. At Jerry's swimming pool. But that was a long time ago.

At least I remembered it, she thought. A place to start.

The board had torn off her bikini pants. Jerry gave her a robe to wear. She wore it next door, to the place she was staying. That was a house she'd broken into. She must've been on one of her adventures, her intrusions.

She'd gone back to the house. She remembered opening the drier to put the robe in, and . . .

The scrapbook.

Fredrick Holden.

She suddenly remembered. She skipped her mind over the nightmare that started with her capture, touching on bits and pieces of her ordeal, and found the part she needed to remember.

The last seconds.

Holden had been chasing her through the woods. She'd rushed right up to the edge of a cliff, tried to stop, teetered for a moment, then fallen. She'd expected her body to be dashed apart on the rocks far below.

By some miracle, she was still alive.

By the miracle of landing on this, she thought, looking at the small shelf surrounding her.

She couldn't remember landing. She must've been knocked sense-less by . . .

Holden!

Wincing, she twisted her head and looked up the mountain.

Holden was nowhere in sight.

The wall looming above her was nearly vertical. She couldn't see the top.

From what Gillian could see, however, she guessed that her perch must be well below the edge.

She realized she would have a better view if she crawled out to the end of the shelf and turned her back to the open space.

No way.

Instead, she raised her knees. Her right knee was stiff and swollen, and hurt when she bent it. But she kept it bent along with her left, to hold her feet away from the edge when she scooted forward. With her back a few inches from the wall, she looked over each shoulder and scanned the area above her.

She still couldn't see Holden.

Still couldn't see the top.

But she saw that the rock face was slightly concave. Though the angle was so slight that the mountainside didn't appear to overhang her, there was enough tilt to prevent Holden from climbing down to her.

Unless he had a good long rope.

There was no mountain climbing rope in the trunk of his car, that she knew. And she would bet he didn't have one in the front, either.

Only one way he'll get down here, she thought. The same way I did.

He's a fucking lunatic, but he's not suicidal. *Nobody* would jump off up there on the chance of landing the way I did. Not even me. I would've let him catch me before I would've jumped. Maybe.

If he tries it, he'll miss.

If he lands here, I'll kick him off.

He won't try it. Not a chance. He cares a hell of a lot for his own hide. Here's a bastard who goes *out of state* to do his killings, who drove me hundreds of miles just so my body wouldn't turn up near his neighborhood. He's a bastard who loves himself and wants to live so he can go on torturing and murdering. No way is he going to jump off a goddamn cliff.

But he can't let me live. No way is he going to drive away and leave me breathing.

Gillian slid backward until she was safely against the wall again.

Maybe he thinks I'm dead, she told herself.

He must have gone to the edge of the cliff and looked down. If he did that, he saw me. I was out cold for a while. Was he still looking when I woke up and tossed my cookies?

Maybe, maybe not. Maybe he *does* think I'm dead.

I must've *looked* dead. Gillian straightened out her legs, moaning at the pain in her knee. Yeah, she thought, I look messed up pretty good.

Her skin was shiny with sweat, glowing from the sun, streaked and smeared with blood and dirt, cross-hatched with fresh welts, scratched and scraped, split in six or eight places from knife wounds that looked raw but no longer bled. There were swollen patches of red, a deeper hue than the sun had caused, that would turn into bruises. There were even purple-gray marks left over from the beating at his house like an undercoating of old hurts. Gillian touched her face. She felt dry, puffy lips, a knot on the point of her chin, a left cheek that seemed like twice its normal size. She could actually see a slope of cheek below her eye.

She ran her tongue gently along the broken edges of her teeth.

And started to weep.

Cut it out, she told herself. I'm alive.

My dentist is gonna love me.

Couple months, I'll look good as new.

If I'm still alive. If I make it out of here.

Holden, he's not gonna leave till he's sure I'm dead.

Maybe he does think I'm dead, she told herself again.

A guy like him, how come he didn't drop some rocks on me? When he saw me down here, he could've bombed me till he crushed my head. How come he didn't?

Maybe he fell.

The thought struck her like a promise of life. She wiped the tears from her eyes.

What if Holden came running out of the trees, full tilt, the same way I did? What if he couldn't stop in time, either, and went right over the edge?

She whispered, 'Jesus,' through her broken lips.

Then she crawled forward on her hands and knees. When she neared the edge, a falling sensation forced her to lie down flat. She squirmed a few more inches forward, then peered down over the rim.

A short distance below her perch, other rocks protruded from the mountain wall. None were large enough to break a fall. The slope was still nearly vertical for fifty or sixty feet. If Holden went off the cliff, he would've dropped that distance, then crashed onto the boulders that were heaped at the foot of the wall.

Gillian didn't see his body.

Doesn't prove anything, she told herself. The body might've gone down in between the rocks.

Some were the size of refrigerators, others the size of cars. They were all tilted and tipped every which way, with big shadowy gaps between their edges. A body could fall into one of those crevices, Gillian thought, and never be found.

She felt a trickle of joy.

But over the years she had lived like a thief in sixty-six houses and she had never been caught until this time. Luck, she knew, had been a factor in that. But the main factor was her mind. She'd gotten away with her intrusions because she was smart. She didn't let herself run on luck, hoping for the best. She studied the possibilities, foresaw the dangers, took precautions, and was always creative and quick enough to keep herself safe.

So now, in spite of her thrill at the thought that Holden lay broken and lifeless among the rocks below, she warned herself not to count on it.

You don't see his goddamn body. Therefore, he isn't dead.

If he isn't dead, what's he doing?

For some dumb *crazy* kind of reason – *why, at a time like this?* – she was back in the white stucco house on Silverston. The deco place. If ever she made it back to LA in one piece, *which, let's face it, doesn't seem too likely*, the memory of the hot tub she'd taken that day would live on in her mind forever.

What happened afterwards, though, in number 1309, almost put paid to her illustrious career. Of intrusions, house-sittings, that is.

Finito. Full stop.

She wished that it had. Then she wouldn't be here now, halfway up this bastard mountain, bare-ass naked and a murdering psycho after her hide.

Back to the house that time forgot . . .

She'd lain there, soaking up the sheer luxury of that tub, breathing in lilac perfume, like she was in some mystical Garden of Allah.

Then the bathroom door blew ajar. That's right, a puff of wind opened the door.

She remembered thinking, *Holy shit . . .*

And sitting up with a start, arms wrapped around her breasts, shivering in the cold draught. Faint, familiar music wafted through the door. So faint, it was hardly there at all.

Then, the weirdest thing. She'd had this powerful urge to get up out of the tub, wrap herself in one of those thick white towels hanging over the towel rail and walk out the door.

Leaving a trail of wet footprints behind her, she padded across the marble landing. No ideas as to where her feet were taking her. In a kind of dream, she let them have their lead. They took her to a white door which had the name A-L-I-C-E printed on it in silver letters. ALICE?

Alice who?

Looking at those letters made her feel like she'd stumbled across somebody's private place. Somebody's *very* private place.

A special place.

The old familiar buzz tugged at the pit of her stomach. It melded into an ache, setting her mons alight with longing.

'Here goes,' she breathed. She'd invaded a lot of private space in her time. One more wouldn't hurt.

Her breath came out in huffs, quick and shallow. Not knowing what she would find behind the door, she opened it, slowly, and peeped into a tiny room that was straight from the past.

Chintzy flowered drapes, a doll's cradle, a rocking chair.

And a big, brown teddy bear sitting in the far corner. The bear wore several bald patches and stared across at her with beady eyes. She imagined it saying, *Who are you? You're an intruder. You don't belong here.*

Her eyes turned to the small single bed. Not much more than a cot, really. Floral drapes were drawn around it. Not knowing why, she knew that she *must* open them. It was as if she'd come to this house specifically to discover what lay behind the drapes.

Stepping forward, she did just that. Slowly. Drawing back the fabric with tentative fingers. A gasp broke from her lips. Wide-eyed, she stared at a small wizened figure, prostrate on the bed. It was no more than four feet ten at the most.

Little Bo Peep in a long floral dress, matching poke bonnet and a shepherd's crook by her side. Little Bo Peep with a drunken monkey face and bright rouge spots high on her cheeks. And ludicrously red, cupid bow lips.

The large blue eyes, ringed with thick mascara'd lashes – *false, they had to be, they were so long and curly* – gazed curiously into Gillian's face.

She gasped, clamping a hand over her mouth. She felt the warm towel swish down her legs and fall around her ankles.

My GOD!

This is it. Curtains. I've been caught out. No more intrusions for this baby. Hello, real world – LAPD, here I come . . .

'*I'm sorry . . .*' she began. Then clamped her lips together, hard. Something was up. The blue eyes weren't moving.

Slowly, carefully, Gillian reached out and lifted Little Bo Peep's thin, blueveined hand. The bony fingers sparkled with clusters of gold and diamond rings. The hand was ice cold. Stiff. Gillian let it fall back onto the white lace bed sheets.

*

She exhaled slowly, gratefully. A huge feeling of relief built up inside her. The initial shock over, she looked down at the figure on the bed and felt a brief surge of pity.

No more sheep for this Little Bo Peep, she murmured to herself.

Gillian got out of there. Fast. Checking first, making sure she'd left no trace of her presence behind. Nothing that could involve her with Bo Peep's death. She touched her Minolta, briefly, and grimaced. Yuk. No. No photographs for her files this time.

Anyway. Cases like these, you can't be too sure. Film could get lost, or stolen. Unless the finder was either a weirdo or somebody seriously interested in nursery rhymes, the film could easily end up in the wrong hands.

For a full three months after that, intrusions were out. Gillian had to admit, though, there were days back there when she'd been sorely tempted. She'd resisted, but it hadn't been easy. When she'd felt like giving in, she had only to remember that strange shrunken figure lying dead in its cot.

Yeah. The memory of that house on Silverston still haunted her like some terrible dream.

Would've made a spooky movie, though.

One day, she reckoned, she was gonna meet up with real trouble. Find herself doing time, no sweat. So she quit. No more house-sitting, she promised herself. That last time at Creepy Hollow had scared the shit clean out of her.

Then the old urge, that all-consuming desire, *need*, came flooding back. As inviting, as seductive as ever.

Yeah, Mr Fat'n'sassy Shrink. I'm hooked on other people's private places. I coulda told you that . . . 'n saved myself a whole heap o' money in the process.

If she'd been into visiting shrinks, that is.

Which she wasn't.

She rolled onto her shoulder and looked around. The sheer face of the mountain continued for some distance, maybe a few hundred yards. Then it dissolved like a more gradual slope.

A slope that Holden could descend.

He could go down that way, Gillian thought, approach from below, and get to me by climbing up.

She didn't see him, but the area along the base of the slope was heavily wooded. Holden could be down there, out of sight, making his way through the trees along the edge of the valley.

She spotted a trail among the trees. On the far side of the trail was a stream. It rushed along, shining in the afternoon sunlight. In places, it was white with froth. Gillian could hear the distant sound of it tumbling through the rocks.

She rolled flat again. The trail and stream followed the side of the gulley. Directly below her, the trees opened up. That was good. If Holden descended all the way to the bottom and came through the woods, he'd be in plain sight for a while before reaching the heaped boulders.

Turning her head, Gillian scanned the area to her left. The trail and stream were visible for only a short distance before the clearing. They vanished around the foot of a bluff that was nearly as high as Gillian's perch. She looked back. A glance at the mountainside was enough to convince her that Holden wouldn't try to descend on that side. It was steep, and it stayed steep.

So now we know, she thought, which way he'll come.

If he comes.

If he's not dead in the rocks down there.

I've got two choices, she thought. I can either stay here or climb down.

I'll have to climb down sooner or later.

But he'd have a hard time getting to me here. He can't sneak up on me.

Gillian wiped sweat out of her eyes, looked around, and saw plenty of good-sized rocks within reach.

I can bash his brains in before he ever gets near me.

But he's too smart to make himself a target. As long as I'm here, I'm trapped and he knows where I am. What if he waits for night? What if I fall asleep or pass out, and he makes it up here while I'm zonked?

I can't last forever up here.

She felt the sun beating down on her, broiling her back. She felt sweat sliding down her skin. Her tongue was a dry slab.

She hadn't taken a drink since last night. She'd spent hours sweating inside the trunk of Holden's car.

If I wait too long, she thought, I won't be *able* to climb down.

She found herself staring at the stream. She listened to it rushing over the rocks. She could almost taste it.

Through the trees to the left of the clearing, she saw it cascading, white as snow. Straight in front of her, it formed a clear, glinting pool. She pictured herself sliding into the chill water, sucking it into her mouth.

If I start down now, she thought, I'll be there in half an hour. Maybe less.

If Holden doesn't get me.

If he shows up, I'll stone him. Plenty of ammunition.

Gillian squirmed backward away from the edge, then got to her hands and knees. The movement made her head pound. A wave of dizziness washed by. It left her frightened.

If that happens while I'm trying to climb down . . .

Get going.

She sat down, then scooted herself toward the right-hand side of the shelf. Her feet went out over the edge. Her calves scraped. Then her feet dropped out of sight and the pain reminded her to be careful of her right knee.

What if it's too weak to hold me up?

She kept inching forward. Her legs dangled. She clutched the edge of the shelf with both hands and leaned out.

Her toes were nearly touching the next rock down.

She lay backward and rolled over. Then she squirmed on her belly, easing herself off the ledge until her feet found the rock. Carefully, she pushed herself away from the shelf.

She stood on the foothold, still holding the upper ledge with both hands.

So far, she thought, not bad.

She looked down at her destination. The sparkling pool of the stream.

And she saw Holden pass between two trees as he walked along the trail far below. For moments, he was hidden by the woods. Then he appeared against the edge of the clearing. He still carried the broken stick in one hand, his knife in the other. He turned and gazed up at the slope.

His head suddenly snapped to the side.

He shoved the knife blade down a rear pocket of his pants.

Gillian looked to the left.

'Oh my Christ,' she muttered.

Just this side of the place where the trail vanished behind the outcropping were two women with backpacks. The one in the lead raised a hand in greeting. Holden waved to her.

He walked toward the women.

'RUN!' Gillian shouted. 'GET OUT OF HERE!'

Neither hiker turned a head.

Gillian yelled and yelled as the gap narrowed between the two women and Holden.

It's the damn stream! she thought.

They were so close to it, the noise of the rushing water was masking her shouts.

She let go of the ledge. Balancing on the rock, she squatted, then she sat down and straddled it. She clawed the slope behind her and pulled loose a chip of stone. She hurled it at the women. It flew out in a high arch, dropped beyond the clustered boulders below, and vanished in undergrowth at the edge of the clearing.

The second hiker glanced toward the place where the stone had landed. But she kept walking. She stopped beside her friend, took off her ballcap, and rubbed a forearm across her brow.

They both faced Holden. He was no more than three feet in front of them. From the gestures, Gillian guessed that they were talking. Holden pointed to the trail behind him. He shrugged. Then his stick whipped through the air. It struck the stout woman across the side of the head. Her straw hat flew off. Her legs folded. Her knees hit the ground and she dropped forward flat on her face.

Gillian heard herself shriek, 'NO!'

The other woman spun around and ran up the trail. She flung off her pack. Holden leaped over it. He grabbed the knife out of his rear pocket as he chased her.

She was fast, but Holden gained on her. Reaching out, he grabbed the back of her gray T-shirt. The fabric stretched, tenting out behind her. Then she staggered and danced sideways as if being swung on the end of a rope. Her feet tangled. She went down, tumbling and rolling. Holden pounced on her.

Chapter Thirty

'We could stop anywhere along here,' Rick said.

'I'd rather find a place,' Bert said, 'where the stream isn't so close to the trail. We'd have people hiking right by our camp.'

Rick smiled. 'Yeah, this trail is Grand Central Station around here.'

They hadn't seen anyone except Angus the lunatic since leaving the girls. But Rick agreed with Bert. If they kept going, they might find a good secluded area.

'Why don't we just give it another hour?' Bert suggested. 'It'd be nice to get settled while we have some of the afternoon ahead of us.'

'How far's Mulligan Lake?'

'More like two hours.'

'Andrea and Bonnie'll probably be there,' Rick said.

'Well, we won't go that far.' She looked at him, a corner of her mouth curling up. 'Unless you want to.'

'I just want to get someplace where we'll have plenty of privacy.'

'Me too.'

They walked side by side around a bend in the trail that took them past a stone corner. Rick reached below Bert's pack and squeezed her rump. 'What have you got in mind?' he asked.

She looked at him and raised an eyebrow. 'A little of this, a little of that.' Her face turned forward again and she stopped abruptly.

Rick halted beside her.

On the trail at their feet lay a red backpack.

'What the hell?' Rick muttered. 'Looks like one of . . .'

She grabbed his arm so hard that pain streaked through it. She was gazing past him, to the right.

Rick turned his head.

He thought, *It's another hallucination, has to be, but how can* Bert *be seeing it?*

He stared.

The trail where he stood with Bert was slightly higher than the clearing ahead, and gave him a perfect view.

Can't be real. Impossible.

It was worse than his daydreams, his visions, worse than anything he had ever imagined. Julie's death seemed *pristine* compared to this.

One of the bodies was a naked man. He lay on his back near the sprawled remains of a girl. Rick refused to look straight at the girl, to see what had been done to her. He gazed at the man. The man looked as if he were *made* of blood, as if his skin had been peeled off.

Rick let his eyes dart past the third body, a twisted, faceless thing.

Strewn about the bodies was clothing: a pair of cut-off jeans with one leg split open; a yellow blouse; a torn rag of panties; faded blue gym shorts; a gray T-shirt sliced down the front, rumpled in such a way that the letters UC showed. Some of the clothes were sprinkled red as if they had been sprayed from a distance, and Rick realized vaguely that the girls must've already been naked when the blood began to fly.

The girls.

Andrea and Bonnie.

He couldn't look at their bodies, but the clothes were enough.

The other clothes belonged to the man: shoes placed neatly together with socks tucked inside, folded trousers, a knit shirt on the ground near the pants.

Who is he? Rick wondered.

Did *he* do this? Why's he dead?

Bert, standing at Rick's side, bent over and heaved. She had her knife clutched in her right hand. It was pressed to the side of her leg, and the blade jerked as spasms shook her body.

Already has her knife out, Rick thought. Got through the shock and saw the danger. Why didn't I?

If I only had the gun!

Rick drew his own knife from the scabbard on his belt. Then he squirmed out of his shoulder straps. His pack dropped to the trail behind him. He scanned the clearing, the base of the slope a distance to the right, the trees beyond the clearing, the stream to the left and the wooded area on its other side. Saw no one. Imagined Jase and Luke and Wally charging at them from the rear. Whirled around. No one. He raised his eyes. No one scurrying down the rocks.

'RICK!'

He began to turn and everything seemed to be in slow motion. He saw Bert's pack falling toward the trail behind her legs. Her arm began to move upward, pointing with the knife. He finished his turn. The man of blood was sitting up. His eyes were open. He had a red erection.

Rick grabbed Bert's shirt and pulled. She twisted slowly toward him, her shirt coming off her shoulder, her right breast exposed, the knotted fabric across her chest slipping apart. 'RUN!' he yelled in her face. His voice seemed far away and echoing. He saw her head shake slowly from side to side, her hair swaying out below the edges of her hat. 'GO!' he yelled again, and then he released her shirt and started toward the man.

The man, somehow already up, wasn't coming at them. Instead, he ran away. His back wasn't red. It had a deep tan except for his white, flexing buttocks. He only ran a few steps. His arms reached out. He grabbed a long stick slanting up out of one of the bodies (a broad-boned body . . . Bonnie?). He tugged it out with both hands. It made a sucking sound. He pivoted, swinging it like a baseball bat. Rick, almost upon him, flung up his arms to protect his head. His wrist exploded with pain. But the knife stayed in his numb hand. The man leaped out of his way. Rick couldn't stop. His forward foot came down on a thigh of the corpse. The body turned under his weight. An outstretched arm flopped up as if reaching for him. He tried to miss it as he stumbled, but the toe of his boot smashed the forearm down and he thought, *I'm sorry*, as he staggered past the body, trying to stay up.

Something crashed against the back of his head. He slammed the ground and skidded.

He lifted his face out of the grass.

Was I out? What if it's all over, and Bert . . .?

He looked over his shoulder.

Bert was on her feet, face to face with the man, trying to wrestle the shaft out of his hands. Her knife was clenched in her teeth. She was being twisted and shaken like a doll, no match for the killer.

Rick started to get up.

The pole was snatched from Bert's grip. She reached for the knife between her teeth. Before she could grab it, the man drove an end of the pole into her belly. Her mouth made a wide O. She stumbled backward, folding, and her rump pounded the ground.

The man left Bert sitting there, turned away, and squatted by the head of the other corpse.

Andrea?

She'd been scalped.

She had a knife in her mouth. But not crossways, pirate fashion, like Bert. The broad handle stuck straight up from her lips. The man clutched it and pulled. Andrea's raw head lifted as the blade slid out.

A huge blade.

The man's eyes, bulging white in his red mask, fixed on Rick.

Rick was almost on him.

The man jerked the knife the rest of the way out, ripping through a cheek. The blade swept past Rick's belly. He felt a hot sting as it nicked his side. As he lunged at the crouching man, he slashed downward. His knife skidded on the man's forehead, sliced the left eyeball, cut through a nostril, tore a diagonal gash through his lips and chin, swept down and split the back of Rick's own left hand.

Even as the knife cut his hand, his charging body smashed the man backward. Onto Andrea's face. Rick, hunched low and off balance, hurled himself over her ravaged body, hit the ground on the other side, and rolled.

He got to his hands and knees. He looked.

The man was scuttling toward him, shrieking, blood spouting from

717

his face. Bert swept by. Flying? She was four feet off the ground, stretched out straight, open shirt flapping behind her like the cape of a super-heroine from a strange, erotic comic book, knife in her right hand. Her bare chest hit the man's back with a slapping sound. He was smashed flat. Bert's arms were out past his side. She threw an elbow high and tried to bring her arm down to stab him, but he thrust himself up, twisting and throwing her off.

He got to his knees, swung around and rammed the knife down. It missed Bert. She was rolling. He went after her on his knees.

Rick scurried toward him and drove his knife down. It sank deep into the man's calf. He yanked it out. His left hand grabbed the man's hip and pulled. His fingers slipped off the slick skin. Snarling, he threw himself forward. His chest pushed against the man's buttocks. He raised the knife high, ready to plunge it into the middle of the back, when an elbow crashed against the side of his head.

The blow dazed him, sent him sprawling.

He lay on his back. The few clouds in the pale blue sky were slowly spinning. His ears rang.

'RICK!' Bert's voice, high and terrified through the ringing.

He lifted his head, turned it.

The ground tilted and tipped, much like the clouds.

Bert was on her back, writhing under the man. He was sitting across her hips, leaning down over her, pinning her wrists to the ground. Blood from his gashed face splashed Bert, rained down on her cheeks and lips, trickled down her chin.

The man's knife stood up straight, its blade embedded in the ground a few inches above her shoulder.

Rick rolled over. As he struggled to raise himself, the man's right hand flew up, releasing Bert's wrist. She wasn't quick enough to block the punch. It crashed against her cheek. Her head snapped to the side. Her body went limp.

The man jerked his knife out of the ground.

He scooted backward, his blood spilling a trail onto her chest and belly and shorts. Then he was sitting on her knees. He slipped the broad blade down the front of her shorts and ripped. The edge came

718

up through her waistband, severed her belt, slit open the tan fabric down her left thigh and parted the small cuff.

Rick forced himself up to his knees while he watched.

What is this man!

Face torn from forehead to chin, eye split open, a bone-deep stab wound in his left calf – and he's *stripping* her!!

He clawed Bert's pants open like a flap, baring her left leg, her groin. He tugged at the other side so hard that her breasts shook. The shorts slid out from under her and down to her knees.

Rick's knife flew end over end.

Jase threw a knife at me, he remembered.

Hit me handle-first.

This one better do the job.

It flashed past the back of the man's head, missing by more than an inch.

The man didn't even seem to notice.

He was working Bert's pants farther down her legs.

'NO!' Rick yelled.

He turned toward Rick, stared at him with one eye, and spat blood. His red penis was standing rigid and thick.

Rick shoved himself up, took a wobbly step forward, and fell.

The man turned again to Bert. He got his knees between her legs. With the dull edge of his knife, he shoved her left leg aside.

Rick crawled toward him.

He had no weapon and the man had the knife. He didn't care.

'I'LL KILL YOU!' he yelled.

The man ignored him.

Then there was someone else.

For a moment, Rick thought it was one of the girls. It *was* a girl and she was naked and torn and bloody, but not mutilated like Andrea or Bonnie, not a butchered carcass, not dead.

She ducked as she ran, and swept Rick's knife off the ground where it had landed after his throw.

She ran straight toward the man.

His head turned.

She leaped, twisting herself in midair, coming down behind him, between Bert's spread feet. She grabbed the man's hair. Her right knee buckled. She dropped to her rump and threw herself backward, still clutching the man's hair.

He flopped on top of her, head between her breasts.

For an instant, two knives waved above his squirming body.

The knife in the girl's hand flashed down and ripped across his throat.

Blood erupted.

The man flapped his arms, his knife slashing through the red curtain rising from his neck. He kicked his feet high.

Rick thought vaguely that he hoped the bastard wouldn't kick Bert in the face.

The shower of blood diminished, then stopped, as if a faucet had been turned off.

The man lay sprawled motionless on top of Bert and the stranger.

Nobody moved.

Chapter Thirty-one

Thursday, June 26

'Police today received a package containing a scrapbook allegedly belonging to Fredrick James Holden, who was slain Monday during a killing spree that left two hikers dead in the Sierra wilderness.

'The scrapbook, which contained newspaper clippings related to disappearances and killings of an undisclosed number of young women in several different states, was accompanied by an anonymous note which read, "I found this in Holden's house. He murdered these people."

'This latest revelation only deepens the puzzle of Fredrick James Holden, the orphan who was taken into the home of his aunt at the age of four and inherited her wealth twelve years later when she was raped and viciously murdered in her bed, along with the celebrated fashion designer Harriet Woodall. In light of the recent developments, authorities now speculate that the double homicide may have been the work of the same man responsible for Monday's killing rampage.

'The scrapbook received today by the police opens the possibility that Fredrick James Holden may have been involved in a nationwide string of sex slayings. But *was* the scrapbook the property of this man? And who mailed it to the authorities? How much might this person know about the trail of killings revealed in the pages of the scrapbook? With more on this story, we take you live to Henry Gonzalez.'

'Thank you, Laura. I'm coming to you live from the Encino home of Dr Richard Wainwright, the prominent ophthalmologist who, along with his fiancée Bert Lindsey, was assaulted by Fredrick James Holden shortly after Monday's double-homicide.

'Dr Wainwright, is it your opinion that Holden's scrapbook was sent to the police by the woman who called herself Mary Smith?'

'I have no idea. It wouldn't surprise me, though.'

'Miss Lindsey?'

'We've talked about it. We both think she may have sent it. She had something to hide, we're sure of that.'

'Could you tell us more about her?'

'She was eighteen or twenty, blonde, very attractive . . .'

'She was very beaten up. She'd been cut with a knife, and sustained a lot of superficial injuries while she was escaping from the bas— killer.'

'We bathed in the stream after . . . after he was dead. All of us were bloody. Then we patched up some of her wounds with my first aid kit.'

'She didn't say much.'

'None of us did. I think we were all in a state of shock.'

'She did tell us that her name was Mary Smith, and she'd been abducted the night before. Holden brought her out to the mountains in the trunk of his car. She said he'd intended to kill her "like the others".'

'That's one reason we think she might be the one who sent the scrapbook. She seemed to have knowledge of other murders.'

'Also the fact that she skipped out on us.'

'Wearing my clothes. Not that I resent that. Hell, she saved us. She came out of nowhere like some kind of crazed, avenging angel and slit the throat of that animal.'

'But you say, Dr Wainwright, that she skipped out.'

'We took Holden's car. It was on a dirt road about an hour's hike away. She drove until we found my car, which was on a different road about ten miles off. Bert and I took my car, and she followed us. She was supposed to follow us till we found a police or sheriff's station, but she took off.'

'She was right behind us one minute. Then she was gone.'

'You feel, then, that she had some reason to avoid a confrontation with the authorities?'

'Looks that way.'

'But she sent the scrapbook, I'd bet on it.'

'Do you have anything you'd like to say to Mary Smith if she should be watching this broadcast?'

'You bet. Mary Smith, whoever you are, we love you.'

'We're not interested in revealing your identity to anyone. But we'd like to thank you – in person, if that's possible. I'm in the phone book, Richard Wainwright.'

'This is Henry Gonzalez for Eyewitness News. Back to you, Laura.'

Gillian pressed the remote button, and the television screen went blank. Leaning back against the bedrest, she sighed.

'They seem like nice people,' Jerry said.

'They are.'

He took hold of her hand. 'There's that old Chinese proverb . . . I think it's supposed to be Chinese.'

'That you're responsible for people after you save their lives?'

'That's it.'

'That's bullshit.'

Jerry laughed softly.

'She said they love me.'

'Yeah.'

'That's really nice.'

'I don't think there's any reason to worry that they'll tell on you.'

'No.'

'Even if they did, it's not that big a deal. There'd be publicity, though. And the cops would want to talk to you.'

The hell they would. Like, how's that again? How many times did you say, Miss O'Neill – er, Miss Smith? You broke into sixty-six homes?

'But you'd be a hero. You already are. Mary Smith is.'

Fuck Mary Smith. And Gillian O'Neill. Time I got myself a new alibi. How about Trisha Scott? Mmmm . . . Okay. Try this for size:

Following the outstanding success of Gone Midnight, *a sequel to this record-breaking blockbuster movie is now in the pipeline. As we speak, award-winning screenwriter, Trisha Scott, is completing yet another great script.*

Our mole at Sierra Studios tells us filming is due to start early next year . . .

'Sure. A hero. And I'd probably get prosecuted for violating Holden's civil rights.'

'Maybe you'd better stay anonymous. But like I said, they won't tell. How about having them over?'

'Like a dinner party?'

'A swim and a barbecue.'

'That might be nice. But let's wait a while till it all calms down. And I'd like a chance to heal before anyone sees me in a bikini.'

'Yeah,' Jerry said. 'Don't want to put them off their food.'

Gillian slapped his thigh.

'You look fine,' he told her.

'Sure. Like I went through a garbage disposal.'

And she suddenly pictured the carcasses of the two young women, the way they had looked when she stood above them after crawling out from under Holden. Then she was on her mountainside perch, staring down, and they were still alive and she heard their screams over the rush of the stream as Holden worked on them.

Gillian felt herself shrivel inside, tight and cold. Goosebumps rose on her skin.

'Jerry?'

'Uh-huh?'

'Jerry. D'you love me?'

'Do bees like honey? Does night follow day? Did Rhett love Scarlett?'

'Funneee. I mean it, pal. I need to know if you *really* love me. Y'know? *Really* care.'

'As in, follow you to the ends of the earth?'

'You got it.'

'Where's this leading, Gill? And why so serious, at this hour?'

'Because, dummy, I am about to spill a whole mess o' beans. Like tell you a story, the like of which you've probably never heard before. And all of it is true. It's about me. So. I need to trust you. I need to know that you love me enough to say, hey, what the heck. It's you I love, not your goddamn life history.'

Jerry leaned up on an elbow and looked at her. Tears were coursing down her cut and bruised cheeks.

'My God, Gillian. What's wrong?'

Okay. She'd had a rough time. A terrible time, what with Fredrick Holden an' all; and he her uncle, too. But he had an overwhelming feeling that there was something else. That something much bigger was on her mind.

'If you love me and we stay together, I want you to *know* me. The *real* Gillian O'Neill. No matter how many alibis I have, what I do for a living, what position I sleep in at nights, what brand of coffee I drink . . . I just need to come clean, Jerry. And after you've heard what I have to say, I want you to be honest. Tell me you love me and that my secrets'll be safe with you. Or, tell me you don't want to know, and I'll just clam up and go to sleep.'

She looked so miserable that he took her in his arms and shushed her, just like a baby. Love, compassion and concern for her welled up inside him. He'd never felt like this about anyone before, in all of his life.

'There, now, my love. No need to worry about a thing. I do love you – believe me, I do. Just the way you are. No frills. No hidden agendas. Just you. If you're about to tell me that you're an award-winning scriptwriter, don't bother. I already know. Anything else, I don't need to be told.'

Turning to him, she whispered, 'Hold me some more.'

He did.

They lay on their sides, wrapped in each other's arms. Jerry held her gently.

'How come you know I write screenplays?'

'You told me. You said you "scribbled". Remember? Well, I watched this film a while back. About this diehard female mercenary caught up in some kind of Greek political plot. Good swimmer, too. Swam in mountain lakes, hid out in caves and all that stuff. Come to think of it, just the damn fool sort of thing you'd probably get up to. Caught the name of the screenwriter, too. Matched yours.'

'A regular Perry Mason. You shoulda told me.' She smiled and gave a small yelp.

'What is it . . .?'

'My cut lip just opened up again.'

Jerry held her closer and she snuggled into the curve of his body. He felt warm and smooth. Soon, the gripping chill inside her melted and a wonderful relief flooded her being.

One day, she promised herself, one day, I guess I'll tell him the full story. Not yet, though: not tonight.

Gillian tightened her arms around him. She pressed herself hard against him, and the feel of his body on her bruised and wounded skin was as soothing as a kiss.